THE
GUNS OF
EMPIRE

Django Wexler graduated from
Carnegie Mellon University in
Pittsburgh with degrees in creative
writing and computer science, and
worked for the university in artificial
intelligence research. Eventually he
migrated to Microsoft in Seattle, where
he now lives with two cats and a
teetering mountain of books.

ALSO BY DJANGO WEXLER

The Shadow Campaigns

The Thousand Names

The Shadow Throne

The Price of Valor

The Shadow of Elysium (a novella)

The Forbidden Library Novels

The Forbidden Library

The Mad Apprentice

The Palace of Glass

THE
GUNS OF
EMPIRE

BOOK FOUR OF THE SHADOW CAMPAIGNS

DJANGO
WEXLER

HEAD
ZEUS

First published in the United States of America in 2016 by ROC,
an imprint of Penguin Random House LLC.

First published in the UK in 2016 by Head of Zeus Ltd

1 3 5 7 9 8 6 4 2

A catalogue record for this book is available from the British Library.

ISBN (HB) 9781786692016
ISBN (E) 9781786690647

Map by Cortney Skinner

Printed and bound by CPI Group (UK) Ltd, Croydon, CR0 4YY

Head of Zeus Ltd
Clerkenwell House
45–47 Clerkenwell Green
London EC1R 0HT
WWW.HEADOFZEUS.COM

For all the hardworking historians
from whom I swipe my ideas

ACKNOWLEDGMENTS

Book four! I honestly had no idea, back at the dawn of time, when I was first working things out, that there would even be a book four. But here we are.

As always, I have been assisted by a courageous cadre of beta readers, who keep me from haring off in the wrong direction. This time the team consisted of M. L. Brennan (check out her books; you won't be disappointed), Rhiannon Held (ditto!), Elisabeth Fracalossi, and Lu Huan. Casey Blair continued in her unique role of reading my outlines, listening to my ramblings, and helping me fix plot points I hadn't written yet with an almost magical ease.

Thanks are (always and forever) due to my agent, Seth Fishman, as well as his colleagues at the Gernert Company: Will Roberts, Rebecca Gardner, and Flora Hackett. My gratitude also to the coagents around the world who help these books find their way to unexpected places.

I'm always grateful to my editors, but Jessica Wade really went beyond her usual duties for this one: helping me write and rewrite the outline, answering my frantic e-mails, and making the schedule work in spite of me. Further thanks to all the people at Roc who helped to make this book a reality but don't get to put their names on it.

Finally, of course and always, I thank the readers who've followed the story so far. I can only strive to live up to your expectations.

THE
GUNS OF
EMPIRE

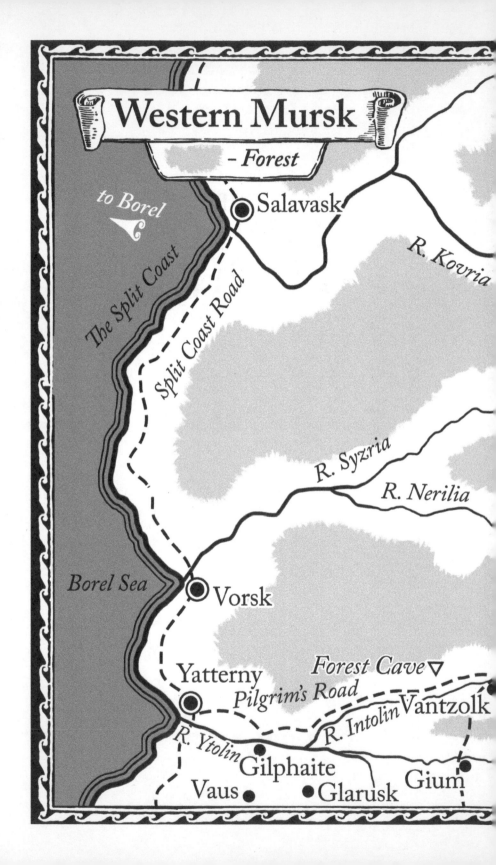

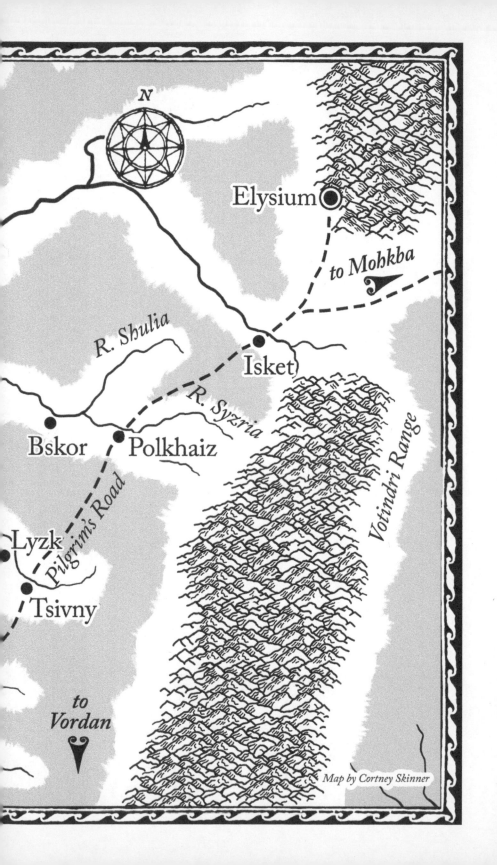

Map by Cortney Skinner

PONTIFEX OF THE BLACK

The last of the spring storms was always the most violent, and this one was a monster, lashing the desolate mountainside with wind and rain. Lightning crackled among the towering clouds and speared down in blinding white bolts to strike the spires of Elysium. The fortress-city clung to the mountain like a barnacle on a rock, hunkered down against the fury of the heavens. It had stood for nearly a thousand years, and no storm had washed it away yet.

But the downpour would end soon, and with it the rainy season, giving way to the hot, dry summer of northern Murnsk. The roads would dry and the fields would turn green with crops, and another sort of storm would come, a storm of men and cannon that was powerful enough to sweep even Elysium from its perch. The high, straight stone walls that had made the city impregnable in an earlier era were useless in this age of field-guns and mortars.

The Pontifex of the Black stood in a triangular room and waited for his colleagues, listening to the gurgle of water through a thousand hidden channels and the occasional distant grumble of thunder. He imagined the thunder magnified a hundredfold, cannonballs smashing the holy city to pieces above his head. Tearing down the great walls, ripping through the libraries and dormitories and the innumerable chapels with their patron saints. Destroying his life's work, and the work of his predecessors, stretching back in an unbroken chain to Elleusis Ligamenti and then to Karis the Savior himself.

For one thousand, two hundred, and nine years, the Priests of the Black had performed their sacred duty and the ignorant world had been kept safe from the Beast of Judgment. They had cut a broad swath through the armies of hell, imprisoning every fiend within their reach, until demons and sorcerers had faded in the mind of the common man to nothing more than stories and legends.

And all this work—all the good the Church had ever done, all that they'd bought with Karis' sacrifice—could be erased, the prisons opened and the demons scattered to the winds, the Beast itself unleashed once more.

No, the pontifex thought. *Not while I have the watch. No matter what those other fools may say.*

The door opened with a squeal of rusty hinges, raising a cloud of dust. This meeting room had gone officially unused since the supposed dissolution of the Priests of the Black, the two remaining Church leaders preferring to meet in more elevated surroundings. In normal times, the Pontifex of the Black might see them once every few years, the shadow order going about its business in the depths of the city, invisible to the red- and white-robed priests who walked in the light of day. But these, of course, were not normal times.

The Pontifex of the White entered, his spotless robe instantly acquiring a fine patina of gray as the dust settled. He was an old man whose tall gold-edged hat concealed his balding pate. He glanced up at the Black and grunted a greeting, picking his way carefully across the moldy carpet to the ornate table. Pulling back one of the tall chairs produced another wave of dust.

"Still raining," the White said, fruitlessly brushing at the velvet seat with one hand. "It brings me aches, you know. I've asked the Lord why it should be that rain outside makes my bones ache in here, but He hasn't deigned to answer."

He sat down, easing into the chair with an exaggerated sigh. The Pontifex of the Black remained standing.

"When you get to my age," the White said, "you start to question the wisdom of building your holy city on the side of a mountain a thousand miles from anywhere."

"I believe," the Black said, unable to stop himself from rising to the bait, "it was intended to focus the mind on the contemplation of the divine."

"*You* may need help concentrating on the contemplation of the divine, but I don't," the White said. "It's been sixty years and I'm quite good at it. I could contemplate the divine quite handily in a warm garden somewhere, I assure you. Out here we freeze, drown, or fry by turns."

"Take it up with Saint Ligamenti."

"Believe me, on the day the Lord sees fit to scoop me up, I certainly intend to."

And we all devoutly wish that day comes soon, the Black thought. Not that any potential replacement was likely to be better. The Priests of the White were more than adequately supplied with pompous, overbearing fools.

"Have you started already?" said the Pontifex of the Red, pushing through the half-open door. He was younger than either of his colleagues, with a bulbous, beet-colored nose and eyebrows like overgrown hedges.

"Only pleasantries, Brother," the Black said. His voice was a harsh rasp, legacy of a childhood illness that had nearly killed him. "Our Brother of the White was discussing the weather. He had observed that it is still raining."

"It does that this time of year." The Red took his seat, heedless of the dust.

The Black followed, more slowly. The three of them sat around the triangular table that had once been the ultimate seat of power for the entire continent, stared at one another, and wondered who would speak first.

"The Vordanai have called for an armistice," the Red said, breaking the stalemate. "Representatives are gathering in Talbonn. Vhalnich and the queen will be there."

Alone of the three, the Pontifex of the Black was masked, wearing the glittering obsidian that marked his order. It concealed his expression, which meant he could allow himself a silent snarl. *Vhalnich.* The Vordanai general was at the center of everything. The Church had summoned its allies to war after Vhalnich had overthrown their puppet Orlanko in Vordan, only to watch the accursed man smash through armies and fortresses with alarming ease. Now, as the war entered its second year, Vhalnich had consolidated his power as First Consul of the Kingdom of Vordan, answering only to Queen Raesinia.

"Who is the emperor sending?" the White asked.

"Prince Dzurk."

"An oaf," the Black said.

"But an important oaf," the Red said. "Third in line for the throne of Murnsk. And the Borelgai have sent Duke Dorsay."

"If they can still lift him onto a horse," the White said. "That fossil has been fighting battles since *I* was a boy."

"Three armies camped across the border from one another," the Red said. "And four great powers at the negotiating table. The question is, what will the Vordanai offer?"

"The Hamveltai will accept anything as long as it means peace," the White groused. "After the whipping they took in the autumn, they're practically begging Vhalnich to leave them be."

"Viadre is divided," the Red said. "Quite a few in the Borelgai court want to recognize the revolution as an accomplished fact, especially now that Vhalnich has put the queen back in control. Wars are bad for business. And by sending Dzurk, the emperor indicates he is at least listening."

"Then this conference must be stopped," the Black said. "The war must go on for as long as it takes." He slammed his hand down on the table, raising a plume of dust. The other two men stared at him.

"We brought the great powers to war," the Red said after a moment. "It wasn't difficult, when Vordan seemed weakened by revolution. There were spoils to be had, or so they all assumed. But now? The Vordanai will not have spent the winter idle, and Vhalnich seems invincible in the field. The prospects are suddenly no longer so pleasant."

"This is not about *prospects* or *spoils*," the Black said. "They must be commanded—"

"The Church does not command," the Red said. "Not in the secular world. We advise. We suggest. And if we push too hard against the current of history, we risk being shoved aside. The day the King of Borel or the Emperor of Murnsk thinks to himself, 'But how many battalions can the Pontifex of the Red send against me?' is the day our power disappears forever."

"If the emperor defies us, we can destroy him," the Black grated. "If we declare him in violation of Church law, the peasants of Murnsk will rise up—"

"And then who will fight the Vordanai?" the Red said.

There was a long silence.

"You are saying there will be peace," the Black said.

"I am saying we must let matters take their course," the Red said. "Sometimes it is best to step aside."

"Vhalnich is *dangerous*," the Black said. *Why can't they see it?* "Not just to Vordan, but to the world. He has the Thousand Names, the greatest archive of demonic lore outside these walls. And he has the help of the servants of the Beast! The old heresy has *survived*, and who knows how strong it has grown out in the forgotten corners of the world?"

"So you say," the White huffed. "We have only the conjecture of your agent."

"Shade has proved his trustworthiness many times over," the Black said. "We cannot afford to ignore his warning. If it's true, if Vhalnich is a pawn for the old Mages, then he will not be content with ruling Vordan. He will come here and unleash the destruction we have stood against for so long."

"I think you are frightened of him, Brother," the White said. "Is it because he has beaten you? You have sent your monsters and freaks against Vhalnich, all to no avail. Your order is charged with the suppression of sorcery and heresy, and it sounds to me like you have *failed*."

The Pontifex of the Black gritted his teeth. The White supposedly took no interest in the affairs of the temporal world, but the old man was always too well informed.

"I *am* frightened of him," the Black said. "And you should be as well. The whole world should be. He is the greatest threat we have faced since the Schism, and the Church must be united against him." He slammed his hand on the table again. "Tell me, Brothers, where in our vows do we swear to stand against the darkness *whenever it is politically convenient?*"

Looking from one face to the other, he knew he had lost.

"I think," the Red said, "that peace could be an advantage. After all, Vhalnich can hardly march an army to Elysium if he has just signed an armistice with the emperor. While the negotiations drag on, I'm sure we can trust our brother of the Black to handle things . . . more discreetly."

"You've made this mess," the White snapped. "You're going to have to clean it up."

There was a long silence, and then the Pontifex of the Black got to his feet. "Very well, Brothers," he said. "If you'll excuse me, I have preparations to make."

"Disaster," the Black said, stalking through the underground corridors. "It stares them in the face, and still they won't act."

"Yes, Your Excellence," said the scribe, hurrying to keep up with his master's long strides. A torchbearer and two armed and masked priests followed behind.

"Tell the communicators I will wish to speak to Shade," the Black said. Shade—Ionkovo, as he was known to the world—was with Duke Orlanko and the Borelgai. "How long until Mirror reaches Talbonn?"

The scribe shuffled the papers in his hands. "Still several weeks, Your Excellence, even with favorable roads."

The pontifex cursed silently. There were stories of demons who could transport themselves across the world in an eyeblink, but no such creature had ever been found by the diligent agents of the Priests of the Black. The paired communicators could throw his voice to the other side of the continent, but someone had to be on the other end to act on his words. And with the apparent destruction of his best field team in Vordan, the ranks of the Penitent Damned had grown thin.

There had never been as many of the demonic assassins as legend held. Individuals strong enough to bear a demon's weight on their soul and selfless enough to accept eternal torment to aid the salvation of others were hard to find, and in any case the Church did not wish to risk unleashing too many fiends. Of those they did create, many never left Elysium, using their powers to mend or speak or scribe. Others were tucked away all over the world, influencing local events and watching for signs of sorcery. Only a minority of demons were truly useful in battle, and many years of training were often required before a Penitent could be trusted in the outside world.

It was easy for his brothers in the White and Red to say that Vhalnich was his problem to resolve. The man was canny, and protected by at least one powerful demon. *But not invincible. An opportunity will come.* With a wrench, he turned his mind to the other pressing matter.

"What about the search for the host?" he said. "Any progress?"

The scribe brightened. "Apparently so, Your Excellence. The fifty-fourth subject is in the eighth hour of recitation, and Father Milovic believes she may have the strength to complete the invocation."

Finally. It had been nearly a year this time. "I'll see her for myself."

The Pontifex of the Black descended.

Down, down, down, past the basements that housed the bulk of the Priests of the Black, past the prison levels where the demons were bound, endless corridors of barred cells, each inscribed with the name of a fiend. The greatest demons had grand, poetic names—the Panoply Invisible, Wraith of Shadows, Caryatid—but the majority, those captured in relatively recent days, were more prosaic. Farsight #14, Heat Protection, Earth-Shaping #3.

Each cell contained a miserable wretch of a man or woman, serving as a host for the demon so named. Some of them were "wild," captured by the agents of the Church, but most had been created here in Elysium, forced to recite the names of the creatures they now bore. It all went back to the discoveries of Elleusis Ligamenti, the founding genius of the order. First, that while some poor souls were infected with demons "naturally" at birth, the creatures could be summoned more reliably by the recitation of their names. Second, that these names could be deduced by careful experimentation on captive subjects. And third, most important, that demons were *singular*—once summoned into a host, they were trapped there until the host died, unable to spread their evil to others.

Those revelations had transformed the early Church. Instead of burning those who carried demons, the Priests of the Black began to *collect* them, imprisoning their hosts and learning their names. When a host died, another was created, a prisoner of the Church forced to recite the name of the demon and take the dead vessel's place. Thus, one by one, the creatures of hell were removed from the world, bound up where they could not imperil the souls of the faithful. The monsters and sorcerers faded away as fewer and fewer children were born with the taint.

Down, down, down. Past the cells, past the torture chambers where the Priests of the Black teased the names from their latest captives. Into the very bones of the mountain, where the air became hot and the walls were slick with moisture from the hot springs Elysium had been built on top of.

The dangerous time for any demon was the period between when one vessel died and a new one was found. Not everyone had the strength to carry such a creature in their soul, and the greater the demon, the greater the strength required. During that interval, the demon was loose, free to be born into the world in some unlucky child. Fortunately, the more powerful the demon, the less likely it was to appear in such a way. To date, only minor demons had contrived to escape, but the threat was always there.

At the very bottom of the long, spiral stair, a small suite of rooms was locked behind thick iron doors. Water dripped from ceiling to floor in a steady rhythm, pooling between the flagstones. Fungus grew in forgotten corners, and the air smelled of rot. This was the home of the greatest prisoner of all, the one the Church had been, in some sense, created to control. The Beast of Judgment, sent by God to destroy the world for the crimes of humanity.

As the common folk told the story, Karis' intercession had moved God to mercy, and the Beast had been banished until the postponed Day of Judgment. Only the Priests of the Black knew that the Beast was still here, bound by Karis himself, locked into a host so as to never again be born into the world. When the Beast's host died, the Priests of the Black searched the land for the strongest souls and brought them here to test against the great name. Most died, unable to bear the burden. Once, the search had lasted for more than three years, and priests began to wonder openly if God's mercy had finally been revoked.

The last host had been in his fifties, dying unexpectedly of a vicious rot in his lungs. As the scribe had informed the pontifex, fifty-three potential hosts had begun to recite the name and all had failed, to be carried up the stairs in shrouds and interred in Elysium's endless catacombs. The Pontifex of the Black slipped between the obsidian-masked guards and entered the chamber where the fifty-fourth was making the attempt.

". . . sa li nu pha vo ret kay . . ."

Her voice was a hoarse, ragged whisper. She sat on a wooden stool in the center of the empty room, staring fixedly ahead. A masked priest held a long scroll of waxed paper, unrolling it at a steady pace to reveal large, neat letters. An endless string of nonsense syllables. Seven more fat scrolls lay stacked by the priest's feet. Together they made up the dread name that would summon the Beast into a mortal body. Reciting the name required some ten hours, and once begun, any pause could be fatal.

". . . ga no ai ka ree cor . . ."

Another, more senior priest scurried over at the sight of the visitor. Even under the obsidian mask, the pontifex recognized Father Milovic, who was leading the search for the new vessel.

"Your Excellence," Milovic said. "We are honored."

"I heard you had made some progress."

Milovic rubbed his hands together, one squirming inside the other. "We don't like to count chickens before they've hatched, of course. But I admit I have my hopes for this one. She has a very strong will, and if God allows her to bear the Beast, she is healthy enough to last for many years."

"Where did she come from?"

"Vordan," the priest said. "Brought in by Shade, I believe, before he departed on his latest assignment."

Oh, yes. Ionkovo had chuckled when he'd told the story of how he'd acquired his prize, though the pontifex, more focused on the failures at Vordan City, hadn't seen the humor. Still, she'd known Ihernglass and Vhalnich, so she'd been thoroughly interrogated before being sent to the ever-hungry queue of potential hosts. Now she looked like all the rest, hair shaved back to a pale red stubble, dressed in a shapeless gray coverall. Her green eyes gleamed in the lamplight as she stared fixedly at the scroll unrolling before her, mouth shaping the words.

". . . fa mo que bin xe za . . ."

"If she does succeed, inform me at once," the pontifex said. "I will wish to speak to her. To *it*."

"Of course, Your Excellence."

To speak with the Beast of Judgment was the sole privilege of the Pontifex of the Black. The Beast was ancient and cunning, and possessed much useful knowledge. Only the pontifex was considered wise enough to exchange words with it without risking his immortal soul. This Pontifex of the Black had spoken to the creature only once, on the day of his investiture, and had promised himself not to make use of it again. *But these are not normal times.*

JANE

"*. . . ha ren fo la wu bey . . .*"

She pulled the trigger.

No, no, no, no. I didn't want to, not Winter, not Winter—

She *pulled* the *trigger.* The hammer came down. And then—

Laughter, bubbling up inside her. Because—

—*this is what it feels like to go mad—*

All she ever wanted was Winter. To hold her, to kiss her. *To watch her eyes go wide when I touch her, and hear that little gasp . . .*

She pulled the trigger. Because she was angry.

At Vhalnich! Why can't anyone see what he really is?

"*. . . zur ket ub gin lo po . . .*"

Jane was alone in the universe, hanging in darkness. In the distance, someone was chanting nonsense words, a hoarse, torn voice that was almost familiar. Something was closing in around her, rasping across her skin, twining gently around her hands and feet. It felt like silk, but cold as a winter stream. It pulled her through the darkness, down, down, down.

Am I dead?

Not yet, something replied.

Is this my hell? The Prison burning. Mrs. Wilmore, staggering like a drunk, blood gushing from her mouth. The screams from the farmhouse. *I pulled the trigger.*

It may be, something said, *that it is.*

The black silk wound farther up her limbs. She felt it brush the back of her neck. Her hands and feet tingled from the cold, and she could hear the rapid thump of her heartbeat.

Is it death that you want? something asked.

I want . . . Winter, running her fingers through long, red hair. The look in her eyes after they'd fought the tax farmers. *The look in her eyes when I pulled the trigger.*

"*. . . kei ni si get . . . hi . . . s—sen . . .*"

The black silk knotted tighter, cold spreading through her body. Her heart slammed against her ribs, hesitated, skipped a beat, double-thumped.

Jane Verity, something said, *what* do *you want?*

Winter. The way she used to be, *before. The way she ought to be.* Before Vhalnich got his poison into her. *I want her.* Anger flared, hot and bright, and her heartbeat strengthened. *And I want him.*

I can give you what you want, something said.

". . . *f—fa* . . . *gil* . . . *t—t—* . . ."

Anything you want, something said.

For what? What's the price?

Everything, something answered.

". . . *tif* . . . *n—n—* . . ."

The cold reached Jane's core. If she hesitated, she would die, frozen and alone, dragged into the endless dark.

I pulled the trigger—

I can fix it. I can still have her. I can still have—

Everything, something said.

I accept.

". . . *ni ga vo tar!*"

Black silk wrapped itself around her, like a shroud.

The Beast opened its eyes.

It could see nothing. Something was wrapped around its head, a heavy metal blindfold. It could feel the weight of the iron. Shackles at its wrists, shackles at its feet.

"Can you understand me?" The voice was a thick rasp.

The Beast stretched, savoring the aches and pains of its new body. *Jane Verity.* She was part of it now, in the way a field mouse becomes part of the snake that swallows it.

"Can you understand?" the voice said again. A familiar voice.

"I can understand you, Zakhar Vakhaven." The Beast smiled, tongue scraping over dry lips. "I *remember* you."

PART ONE

ALEX

Alex stared up at the road from the ditch and licked her lips.

Three men. Four horses.

They were uhlans, light cavalry from the emperor's regular army, with tall embroidered caps and smart uniforms. Their horses were good ones, and the saddlebags practically bulged with provisions and supplies.

They probably have wool socks. For the past three nights, ever since she'd abandoned the last husks of her shoes rather than try to repair them for the hundredth time, Alex had been lusting after wool socks. In the old days she'd hardly ever thought about socks. They'd been hers for the asking, along with clever, noiseless shoes perfect for sneaking across rooftops or padding down darkened halls. Now she was barefoot, and the stony ground of Murnsk had sliced and blistered her feet.

Socks, she had to admit, were probably not the *most* important thing in those saddlebags. If she was going to make it, she needed food, and most of all she needed those horses. They were there for the taking, and all that stood in her way were three young men who'd done nothing worse than sign up to wear a fancy uniform and ride in parades.

They work for the emperor, which means they work for Elysium, which means they work for the Black Priests, whether they know it or not. But Alex knew that was thin. *All of Murnsk works for the emperor, in the end. Does that make them all just as guilty?* She'd been a thief—*the best thief in the world*—but she'd never thought of herself as a murderer. Once, she'd kept a count of the men she'd killed, when she absolutely couldn't avoid it. Now she'd lost track, or purposely forgotten.

It had been three days since she'd eaten, and that had been a squirrel she'd clumsily skinned herself, a few mouthfuls of stringy muscle and fat.

Now is not the time for second thoughts. She'd left the Mountain because she loved Abraham and very much thought she loved Maxwell, and also because the two of them were the most sanctimonious, infuriating pair she'd ever met. They all agreed what had to be done, but even when an opportunity fell into their laps they refused to take it. So Alex had decided to take it for them.

She stared at the three men. Abraham would have told her to wait, not to be impulsive, to consider other ways of getting the supplies she needed. *Easy for him to say. He's not eating squirrel.*

In the end, what decided her was the thought of going back. It seemed like the only alternative, apart from dying of starvation, and she couldn't bear to think what they'd say to her. Especially Maxwell, with everything she'd said to him before she left. Bullheaded stubbornness was probably a poor reason to decide to kill three men, she thought, but honestly, did the reason really matter? *Maxwell and his tutor can debate it in their endless hairsplitting.*

She rose from the tall grass and climbed out of the ditch, just beside where the three uhlans stood together, talking and smoking. One of them noticed her and did a double take, tossing his pipe down and putting his hand on his sword.

"Hey there!" he said. "Stop!"

The senior of the three regarded her and sniffed. "You'll be getting no charity from us. Off with you."

"I believe it's a girl." The third uhlan peered closer. "Are you selling, is that it? I'll give you a box of hardtack for a quick ride."

"I can't believe you," the first said. "She's filthy."

The third uhlan shrugged. "Cunny is cunny."

Well, Alex thought, *that makes this a little easier.*

She raised her hands and exerted her will. Two globes of darkness formed around her fingers, congealing out of the late-afternoon shadows like pools of ink. As the uhlans gaped, the darkness formed itself into three long, thin needles and stabbed out to catch each man just above the bridge of his nose, punching effortlessly through flesh and bone. A moment later the three tendrils withdrew, and the uhlans collapsed like puppets with their strings cut, blood leaking from neat holes in their brows the size of a pencil.

Alex let out a ragged breath. *Done.* There was no taking it back. *Now food, and socks, and—*

There was the *crack* of a pistol shot, and she stumbled forward, as though she'd been punched in the side. She managed to stay on her feet, turning to see a fourth uhlan stumbling out of the opposite ditch, his pants still unfastened.

He was fumbling with his pistol, clawing at the pouch on his belt for another cartridge.

"Demon!" he shouted. "M-m-monster—"

Another line of darkness speared out, going through his throat like a flat-bladed spear. When it withdrew, blood fountained, drowning his cries.

Four horses, Alex thought muzzily, *and* four *men.*

She found herself lying on the ground, with no memory of how she'd gotten there. One of the horses had come over to investigate her, its hot breath brushing her face. Her side stung, the first tendrils of a pain that promised much worse to come.

Get up. Find out how bad it is. Alex closed her eyes, then forced them open. *I didn't give up when they had me chained to the bed of a cart. I'm not giving up now.*

She raised her head and fumbled with her shirt. It was slick with blood, but it seemed to be leaking, rather than spurting, which was probably good. Her probing fingers found the wound, all the way to one side of her torso. She tried to remember long-ago lessons. If the ball had torn her guts, she would fester and die, sure as sunrise, but she didn't *think* it had.

I could go back to the Mountain. If she could make it that far, Abraham would help her whether he was angry at her or not. *I could . . .*

No.

Slowly, one hand pressed against her side, Alex sat up, then got to her feet. Gritting her teeth through the pain, she stumbled toward the nearest horse and pulled open the saddlebags, looking for bandages.

The horses would take her south. And somewhere to the south was Janus bet Vhalnich and the army of Vordan, and the best chance she would ever have to get her revenge on the Priests of the Black.

CHAPTER ONE

RAESINIA

Talbonn was not a city with a great deal to recommend it, in Raesinia's opinion.

It stood at Vordan's northern frontier, the last major settlement before the Murnskai border. The highway that passed through it was an important artery of commerce, but it didn't look the part. It barely looked like a road at all, more like a track worn in the mud by a bunch of animals all going the same way. Which was more or less the truth—the biggest trade here was cattle from the Transpale, driven north along this road in exchange for heavy wagonloads of timber and iron from the freezing forests of vast, empty Murnsk. Talbonn was the sort of city that grows up to cater to carters and cattlemen, with filthy, stinking streets, low, mean buildings, and an overabundance of winesinks and whorehouses.

Nevertheless, it had made an effort to rise to the occasion. Uniformed armsmen stood at regular intervals along the main road, which had been swept clean of dung and broken glass for the benefit of the noble visitors. The largest hotel in the city, which called itself the Grand in pale imitation of the real thing back in Vordan, was a four-story eyesore of plaster and gilt with pretensions to architecture, covered with unnecessary buttresses and ornamental balconies. Raesinia rolled her eyes at it as her carriage drew closer and pulled into the circular drive, passing footmen with too many shiny buttons.

"When we stop," Sothe said, "remember not to open the door until the second carriage pulls up."

"We've been over this," Raesinia said. "More than once."

"Forgive me," Sothe said. "You have a habit of ignoring my instructions."

That brought a faint smile to Raesinia's lips. Her Head of Household was as jumpy as a startled cat, unhappy at how hastily the conference had been assembled and how little time she'd been given to secure the site. Though, truth be told, Raesinia wasn't sure any amount of time would have been enough for Sothe to feel comfortable. It had been almost six months since their clash with the Penitent Damned, but the attack of the supernatural assassins had clearly left a deep impression. Sothe opened every door as though she expected to find a murderous Black Priest behind it.

The carriage drew to a halt, and a few moments later Raesinia heard the second vehicle draw up behind it. Booted feet crunched on the gravel, and there was a rap at the door.

"Your Majesty?" Barely said from outside. "We're ready."

Raesinia glanced at Sothe and got a slight nod. She stood, hardly needing to duck to fit through the doorway, and stepped out.

At least wartime was good for banishing some of the more ridiculous formality of the royal court. Raesinia wore a sober dress of black and gray, with a sash in Vordanai blue providing the only splash of color. She'd impressed upon her dressmakers that it wouldn't do to have the queen going around in some gaudy confection while Vordanai soldiers were risking their lives at the front. Sothe, coming behind her, was dressed even more severely, in a long, dark skirt that Raesinia assumed provided plenty of space for concealed weapons. As an ex-Concordat assassin, Sothe never went unarmed.

Her guards formed a loose ring around the carriage. She'd restored the old Grenadier Guards to their traditional position of protecting the person of the monarch, but insisted on adding a few of Colonel Ihernglass' Girls' Own to her security detail. The Grenadier Guards *looked* handsome, with their tailored uniforms, polished caps, and colorful sashes, but they hadn't been very effective the last time it had come to a fight.

The two women Ihernglass had left her, in contrast, had been part of the group that had rescued her from Maurisk and Ionkovo during the last throes of the previous year's fighting. Corporal Barley was universally known as "Barely," the joke being that with her slight stature she was barely there at all. She was a canny soldier, though, and a deadly fighter. Her companion, the mute Joanna, was a foot taller and built like a blacksmith. Raesinia had a good deal more faith in these veterans—and Sothe's diligence—than in the spit-and-polish men of the Guards.

More local armsmen stood at the entrance to the hotel. A bowing footman led the way inside, Raesinia and Sothe at the center of a column of smart blue uniforms. They wound their way through the lobby, drawing bows and stares from the curious staff, and toward the ballroom. Sothe accepted a scrap of paper from a hurrying messenger, glanced at it, and bent close to Raesinia's ear.

"Everyone's here, except for Janus. Apparently there's been a delay on the road."

Raesinia frowned. They'd deliberately tried to arrive after the First Consul, just to make the relative hierarchy clear to the foreign guests. *Did he anticipate that? Is this a message?* Or, of course, a cart-horse could have thrown a shoe.

"There's more." Sothe grimaced. "Orlanko is here."

"What?" Raesinia hissed.

Orlanko, the infamous Last Duke, had been the head of the Concordat secret police and had tried to seize power after her father's death. His coup had been thwarted with Janus' help, but the man himself had fled the country after his final attempt to turn the army against Raesinia had failed.

"As a guest of the Borelgai. The king's given him shelter." Sothe lowered her voice even further. "Do you want me to put together a squad to arrest him?"

Damnation. Satisfying as it might be, she couldn't, not without driving the Borels away from the conference table. Whatever their true intentions, they couldn't allow the capture of a guest under their protection.

"No," Raesinia said. "But you'd better stay clear." Sothe had once been one of Orlanko's best killers, and Raesinia had no idea if he was aware of her current role. *Easier to play it safe.* "I'll keep Barely and Jo with me. Have the Guards keep an eye on their foreign counterparts."

Sothe nodded. At the entrance to the ballroom, she and the Grenadier Guards peeled off, and Raesinia continued to the double doors with only the two women from the Girls' Own for escort. Footmen pushed the doors open, and a butler with a carrying voice announced, "Her Majesty Queen Raesinia Orboan of Vordan!"

I must be getting used to this. She hardly flinched at the introduction, or the sudden stares from everyone in the big room. Once, the suffocating blanket of official attention might have driven her to flee; now she only had to take a deep breath before gliding forward, her old court training automatically making her steps careful and smooth.

The ballroom, like the hotel, was dressed up to look like something it wasn't. Gaudy hangings covered the walls, and a hundred lamps hung from the ceiling. But there was no way to disguise the awkward, boxy lines of the room. Raesinia pictured it being used for cattlemen's rustic dances once the dignitaries had departed.

No dancing seemed likely today. Small tables were covered with food and tiny glasses of wine, and hotel staff circulated among the guests, offering pastries. There were soldiers, in the uniforms of four countries—Vordanai blue, the yellow and black of Hamvelt, Borelgai mud red, and Murnskai white. Men in shabby suits were probably clerks, while those more impressively attired were civilian officials of their governments. Raesinia had the feeling that she, Barely, and Joanna were the only women in the room.

It was easy to see where the nexuses of power lay, just by watching the movement of the crowd. Lesser lights orbited dense knots of conversation the way that philosophers said the world went around the sun, drawn in by their gravity but unable to penetrate to the inner circle. The largest group was also the loudest, a mob of wasp-colored soldiers and men in long-tailed coats engaged in such energetic argument that it seemed like punches might soon be thrown. The Hamveltai were in the most precarious situation of all the attendees, having suffered grievous reverses the previous year—their field army smashed and their greatest fortress forced to surrender, while their ally Desland had actually been occupied by Vordanai forces.

Evidently they haven't figured out what to do about it. Raesinia decided to let them stew for a moment. She walked instead toward the Murnskai delegation. This was mostly soldiers, spotless white uniforms dripping with gold braid and trimmed with fur at the collars. Their tight circle opened at her approach, revealing a tall, broad man at its center. His uniform was the most impressive of all, both sides of his chest studded with medals alongside a cloth-of-gold sash, and he wore a long cloak of flowing white fur.

Prince Cesha Dzurk, Sothe's briefing had supplied. Second son of the Emperor of Holy Murnsk, and reportedly favored by his father over the diligent, bloodless crown prince. Dzurk was a man of legendary appetites and little tact, but his word supposedly carried great weight with the emperor. *At least he's not a religious fanatic like his brother.*

"Your Majesty," the prince said, offering her a shallow bow. "It is a pleasure." His Vordanai was passable, but his accent was atrocious, so broad that Raesinia wondered if he was doing it deliberately.

"Prince," Raesinia said. "Welcome to Vordan."

"This is the first time I have come south," the prince said, his tone making it clear he was not impressed. "I hope it is not all for nothing, eh? Where is the famous Vhalnich?"

"On his way, I'm told. I'm sure he'll be here soon."

"Tell him I am not accustomed to being kept waiting."

Raesinia bristled. "I remind you that Vhalnich serves at my pleasure. I will represent Vordan in this negotiation."

The prince snorted. "I am not accustomed to haggling with little girls, either, outside of . . . certain matters." He raised one bushy eyebrow and looked her up and down. "Or would you like to come upstairs for some private negotiations? I'm told you're of age, though I'm not certain I believe it."

Raesinia suppressed a flare of rage. *He's baiting me.* Boorish or no, no courtier was *that* rude except on purpose. She took a deep breath, keeping her eyes steady on the prince's smirk, and put her hand on Barely's shoulder when the woman moved forward indignantly. The Murnskai's gaze shifted to her, and then to Joanna, and his smile broadened.

"Oh!" he said. "And you've brought some of your notorious girl soldiers along, too. Though I daresay you might have found more attractive specimens. Perhaps they're here to make you look good by contrast?"

There was a murmur of laughter from the Murnskai gathered around, the polite titter of sycophants.

"The corporals are veterans," Raesinia said. "They were both at the fall of Antova, among many other battles."

"I don't doubt it." He raised his eyebrows at Joanna. "This one looks like she could tear down a fortress with her bare hands, then snap a man in half with her thighs. Let me ask you a question, Corporal, that I've never had occasion to ask a woman before." He leaned closer, a lewd twist in his voice. "Does being in battle make you . . . ah . . . excited? After I have killed a man, I can hardly bear it. The very next thing I have to do is find some whore and fuck her senseless."

Joanna, eyes on the prince, made a gesture at Barely. The smaller woman cleared her throat and said, "She says that it hasn't so far, but she'd be happy to run the experiment again, if you're volunteering." Joanna patted the sword at her side meaningfully.

Raesinia flinched, but the prince only laughed, echoed by his chorus of admirers.

"I look forward to discussing the subject in more detail," he said, "especially if the consul continues to be tardy. Your Majesty—" Someone tugged on his sleeve from behind, and he shrugged. "But I am needed. Another time."

Raesinia bit back a retort, turned, and walked away. Joanna and Barely stayed close behind her, and Barely leaned in to whisper.

"Sorry, Your Majesty. I maybe should have kept that to myself."

"No," Raesinia muttered, looking back at the laughing prince. "He was going to keep pushing until we pushed back." *But why?* It had caught her off guard; she'd expected, if not deference, then a certain degree of respect. *After all, they're only here because we're* winning *the war, aren't they?*

"If you want Jo to lay him out, just say the word."

"Tempting, but not yet. I—"

"Your Majesty." She'd been walking at random, away from the Murnskai delegation, and now a red-uniformed soldier had stepped into her path, bowing low. "It's an honor."

"Likewise," Raesinia said, momentarily at a loss. When he straightened up, she identified him at once. There was no mistaking the hawk-nosed profile of Attua Dorsay, Duke of Brookspring.

Dorsay was known to every child in Vordan, at least by reputation. He had been the first soldier of Borel for more than forty years, leading armies up and down the Old Coast in support of Borelgai allies among the city-states there. More recently he had been the engineer of the Vordanai defeat in the War of the Princes, and in command at Vansfeldt, the battle where Raesinia's older brother, Crown Prince Dominic, had been killed. Her father had never truly recovered from that disaster, which had cost him his beloved heir and his territorial ambitions in the course of a single afternoon.

Dorsay had been caricatured widely in the Vordanai press, a big-eared, wild-haired madman with a hook nose and a villain's smile. Raesinia hadn't been expecting a cackling goblin, exactly, but it was a little odd to see how *normal* the man looked. His nose was certainly prominent, and the wings of hair left at the back of his bald head were bushy, but his face was a friendly one, if lined by age and care. He had to be past sixty, but his eyes still gleamed with keen intelligence and a touch of humor.

He was also surprisingly short, topping Raesinia by only four or five inches and barely reaching to Jo's nose. His eyes went from Raesinia to her bodyguards and back again, and the hint of a smile tugged at the corner of his mouth.

"Your Grace," Raesinia said. "I regret that we haven't had the chance to meet before now."

"We have, as a matter of fact," Dorsay said. He spoke good Vordanai, though his aristocratic Borelgai accent gave it a nasal twang. "I visited your father's court with a military delegation, and we were introduced to the royal children. You were about two years old, but I thought you comported yourself with dignity. Though I don't blame you if you don't remember."

"My mistake, then." Raesinia found herself smiling automatically in response. "Your journey here was smooth?"

He shrugged. "As smooth as it can be, at my age. Every time I think Georg is finally going to leave me alone to my hounds and my brewing, up comes a messenger telling me I must ride at once for the latest crisis."

It took Raesinia a moment to realize that 'Georg' was Georg Pulwer, the King of Borel. She raised an eyebrow. "I sincerely hope we can put this crisis to rest here and now."

"My back would certainly be grateful. Accrued interest on too many nights in the saddle. And now that your man Vhalnich's given the Hamvelts a good scare, maybe everyone's ready to talk." He looked up at Jo. "Are you from his women's regiment? Or is that just a rumor?"

"The Girls' Own," Barely said, voice stiff with belligerent pride. "We've been with them since Desland."

Dorsay turned to the shorter woman. "You were at Jirdos, then? When Vhalnich finally cooked di Pfalen's bacon?"

"I . . ." Barely seemed flustered, having expected some insult. Jo nodded vigorously.

"I'd very much like to speak to the two of you at some point, then. Have you mark up a few maps. Some of the Hamvelts are talking a lot of nonsense about what happened, and I'd like to get it straight." He glanced at Raesinia. "If Her Majesty doesn't mind."

"Of course," Raesinia said. "You're welcome to—"

She froze. Coming up behind Dorsay was another man, short and plump, his face dominated by huge spectacles that distorted his eyes into pale blurs. Raesinia felt her fists clench of their own accord, and her pulse raced.

Orlanko. The Last Duke, the master of the Concordat, Vordan's former secret police. The force behind the plot to take the throne from her, a plot that would have succeeded without Janus' intervention. The one responsible for so much spilled blood. *Ben's, Faro's, who knows how many others*. His allies among the Priests of the Black had saved Raesinia's life when she lay dying, and cursed her with the demon that denied her any hope of a normal existence.

"Majesty," he said, with a tiny bow. His expression was unreadable behind the huge glasses.

Raesinia looked back to Dorsay, her expression set, refusing to let her emotions show.

"What," she said, "is he doing here?"

Dorsay looked uncomfortable. "He's been a guest of Georg's at the court in Viadre. Since he's been advising on Vordanai matters, it seemed natural to invite him to be part of our delegation."

"This man, Mallus Kengire"—Raesinia deliberately emphasized his lack of title, though she found herself unable to think of him as anything other than "Orlanko"—"has been stripped of his lands and title for high treason. So far as the Vordanai government is concerned, he is a wanted criminal. He has no right to take part in a sensitive negotiation."

"I believe I have every right," Orlanko said. "We are here to compromise, are we not?"

"There will be no compromise on *this* point while I sit the throne." Raesinia looked him square in the eye. "You may scuttle back to your friends in Viadre if you wish, but you will never return to Vordan." She turned back to Dorsay. "And if I see him again, my participation in this conference is over."

"Your Majesty!" Orlanko said, with a calm tone that carried a hint of mockery. "I am an invited guest, and this is a peace negotiation. I realize we have had our differences, but surely . . ."

Dorsay frowned, and for a moment Raesinia thought he was going to call her bluff. *Then there's nothing to do but storm out.* She'd spoken in haste and in anger, still unsettled by Prince Dzurk's fantastic bluntness, but she'd meant every word. *Any peace that brings Orlanko back is worse than war.*

"Mallus," Dorsay said. Raesinia wasn't sure she'd heard anyone address Orlanko by just his given name, not even her father. "Perhaps you should return to our camp."

"What?" Orlanko's voice descended to a hiss. "I have a mandate from His Majesty. You can't—"

"I have orders from His Majesty as well," Dorsay said, unperturbed. "Including instructions on what results he expects from this conference, and they don't include breaking it up before it begins. Now, are you going to walk out of here under your own power, or shall I have my guards escort you?"

"You wouldn't dare," Orlanko said. "You up-jumped half commoner. Lay a hand on me and His Majesty will have you farming mud in Vinbria."

"It's been my earnest desire to be away from matters of state these last twenty years, but His Majesty continues to require my expertise." Dorsay shrugged. "Besides, I'm willing to bet that I know Georg considerably better than you do." He raised one hand, and a Borelgai officer hurried over.

Orlanko turned on his heel and stalked away before the soldier could reach him. He shot Raesinia a last glare, which she returned as levelly as she could. Only when he'd left the room did she look back at Dorsay.

"Thank you," she said.

"My apologies," Dorsay said. "I did not mean to discomfit you."

"Does your king really listen to him?"

Dorsay looked around. At least a dozen members of his own delegation were within earshot. He shrugged again. "Georg listens to everyone," he said after a pause. "He's always very open-minded."

The Borels are not unified, she thought. *And Dorsay and Orlanko are on opposite sides. Interesting.* The question was, who else was in Orlanko's faction? *If we can play them off one another at the conference table—*

"His Lordship," the butler boomed, "Count Janus bet Vhalnich Mieran, First Consul of the Kingdom of Vordan!"

The room went quiet as the main doors opened. Slowly, without wanting to seem like they were interested, the assembled dignitaries crowded around.

Janus wore a new dress uniform, less ornate than he'd worn as Minister of Justice, though his shoulders carried laurels wrought in gold to match the leafy crowns of the ancient consuls. Six soldiers accompanied him, all wearing silver pins in the shape of a rearing scorpion. Over the winter Janus had reorganized the army and created new badges and insignia; the scorpion marked veterans of the Khandarai campaign. *His most loyal soldiers, presumably.* Raesinia felt suddenly cold.

The First Consul waved as he entered, raising a hand as all three foreign delegations pressed forward. Count Dzurk shouldered his way to the front of the Murnskai and stared at Janus in open fascination, while the Hamveltai delegation was a roil of shoving and elbows. Dorsay stayed by Raesinia's side, pushing through the crowd in a more dignified fashion.

Raesinia tried to see Janus the way the others saw him, these foreigners who knew him only by reputation. Tall, passably handsome in a cold way, but with huge gray eyes that seemed to shine with their own inner light. He had a way of looking at a crowd so that each man felt his gaze, as though the two of them were face-to-face. And when you *were* face-to-face with him, the power of his intelligence was like the heat of an oven, threatening to burn anything that strayed too close.

He looks like a king.

"My lords," Janus said, in a high, ringing voice. "My sincere apologies for being late. Armies are needy beasts, I'm afraid."

There was a ripple of uncertain laughter. Janus smiled, just for a moment.

"I have kept you waiting, and so I will get straight to the point," he went on. "Tomorrow morning we will begin what promises to be a great deal of tedious back-and-forth over how we might achieve peace. I thought I might be able to improve the process by laying *our* cards on the table, as it were. These are Vordan's terms."

What is he doing? Negotiators in the Ministry of State had spent weeks on their strategy, and this had been no part of it. *Should I stop him?* But that would show division in front of the other leaders, and if Janus chose that moment to stage a confrontation . . .

He knows I won't. His gaze lit on her, just for a moment. *Of course he knows. I don't dare interfere, because I don't dare force a showdown, not in public.*

But why?

"There is one power not represented in this room," Janus said, "who are nevertheless at the heart of this war. It is they who began it, inserting their agents into the Vordanai court to take advantage of the illness of the late king. When that failed, it was they who pushed the other powers to make war on Vordan, to interfere in a purely internal political matter.

"I speak, of course, of the Sworn Church of Elysium. They are the true enemy of Vordan in this struggle. And until Vordan is convinced *they* are willing to make peace, we dare not put away our swords.

"So our terms are these. The leaders of the Sworn Church must swear to never again interfere in matters of state in Vordan, or in any other country where they are not welcome. To guarantee their good behavior, a Vordanai army will be permitted to occupy the fortress of Elysium, at the Church's expense. In return, the Vordanai state will agree to a cessation of hostilities, with all captured territories to be returned to status quo ante."

Raesinia had thought the room quiet before. Now it was dead silent, as though everyone present was holding their breath. She herself was too stunned to speak. *What the hell does he think he's doing?*

"We will accept nothing less," Janus went on. "Indeed, we cannot. The Church will pick up new puppets no matter how many we smash to pieces. If we are ever to have peace, this is the only way. I urge you—"

There was a commotion among the Murnskai delegation. Prince Dzurk, medals jingling, pushed clear of his companions and strode across the empty space between him and Janus. The Colonials closed ranks in front of their leader, polite but firm, and the prince was left staring at Janus across a wall of blue uniforms.

"You arrogant *blykaak*," Dzurk said, accent thickening further in his rage. "You *dare* insult Father Church like this? No southern army will ever come within sight of the walls of Elysium. I invite you to try. You will all find your graves in the empire, and I will piss on them!"

"If necessary, I will take you up on that invitation," Janus said mildly. "But I'd prefer not to have to."

"Just because you defeated a pack of fat old bankers, you think you are invincible." Dzurk's hand went to his belt, searching for the hilt of a sword that wasn't there. "The warriors of Holy Murnsk will be pleased to show you the error of your ways."

Janus gave a little shrug and one of his brief smiles. Dzurk snorted and spat at the feet of the nearest Colonial, then turned and stalked away.

Suddenly everyone was shouting. In the pandemonium, Raesinia grabbed Duke Dorsay's arm. When he turned to look at her, one eyebrow raised, she mouthed, *Later.*

Dorsay nodded.

"Is the man mad?" Dorsay said.

The best suite in the hotel had been reserved for Raesinia, but in Talbonn that didn't amount to much. Everything was ornate, oversized, and covered in gilt, a commoner's idea of luxury. A few obvious repairs couldn't disguise the generally threadbare state of the place, with flaking paint and patchy carpets. Raesinia sat at a wrought-iron table covered in gold leaf, made to look like a blooming flower. She glanced down, not wanting to meet Dorsay's eyes, and picked idly at a bit of gold where it was peeling.

Sothe stood by the door. All the other servants had been dismissed for the evening, and to Raesinia's surprise Dorsay had come alone.

"I don't believe the First Consul is insane, no," Raesinia said carefully.

"Then does what he said represent the position of the Vordanai government? Does he speak for Vordan?"

There was a long silence. A piece of the gold leaf tore free.

"The First Consul is our highest authority on . . . military matters," Raesinia said carefully. "In that sphere, he has my full confidence."

Dorsay sat back in his chair, eyes hooded.

"I thought the prince's performance felt a little forced," Raesinia offered.

The Borelgai shrugged. "Prince Dzurk may be a boor, but perhaps not quite as *big* of a fool as he seems. I think he finds the appearance of boorishness convenient."

"I didn't think he was such a religious type."

"I suspect it is more about pride. With the Murnskai, it is always about pride. They believe the south has looked down on them since the days of the Tyrants." Dorsay shook his head. "They will never agree to these terms. Even if the emperor wanted to, his people would rise against him when they found out. Dzurk may not be a religious man, but the commoners of Murnsk worship with a fervor you southerners find hard to understand."

"And the Borelgai?" Raesinia said.

"Borel is . . . more complex. We've always been a mix of north and south. Old and new, Mithradacii and Vanadii. Church and commerce." Dorsay sighed and ran a hand over his bald pate. "I've always been a soldier, Your Majesty. Matters of state make me uncomfortable."

"Your king sent you here to negotiate."

"He did, the rat." Dorsay grinned. "There are factions at court that would be pleased to see the war end. War is bad for business. Georg is inclined to agree with them—"

Raesinia opened her mouth, and Dorsay held up a warning finger.

"—but he is afraid. He will not lay aside the sword while he is afraid."

"Afraid of Vordan?" Raesinia shifted uneasily. "What guarantees does he want from us?"

"Not of Vordan, exactly." Dorsay leaned forward. "He is afraid of Janus bet Vhalnich."

Another silence.

"The First Consul saved the throne from traitors," Raesinia said. "Saved me personally. The people love him."

"And his prowess on the battlefield is legendary. All this is what makes him a threat. Having a man like that at the head of your government is like carrying a naked sword. You cannot expect peace negotiations to begin until you sheathe your weapon."

"It would be a poor reward for his service, to cast him aside."

"A comfortable retirement. Heap titles and honors on him, if you like." Dorsay chuckled. "Send him to me, and I'll preach the virtues of a quiet life keeping bees and breeding dogs."

"What about Orlanko? He seems to have some influence."

"Ah." Dorsay's smile faded. "He has made friends among the faction that wishes to see the war go on. But Georg has indicated to me that his patience for our ex-duke is growing thin. If talks were to begin in earnest, the court might view his request for continued protection from Vordanai justice . . . unfavorably."

He's offering me Orlanko. The Last Duke on a platter. A bribe, of sorts. She wondered how much the King of Borel knew and how much he merely suspected.

Raesinia was surprised to find that she was tempted. She didn't think of herself as a vengeful person, but having Orlanko in her power was more attractive than she'd expected. *It doesn't have to be simply about vengeance,* she rationalized. *Think of all the answers he could give us.* Right now, in Vordan City, Concordat agents who had committed unspeakable crimes on Orlanko's orders walked free. *He could give us justice.*

And, in exchange, they wanted her to sideline Janus. *An honorable retirement. I owe him a great deal. But . . .* She put that thought aside. *More important is whether he would accept it. If I dismiss him and he refuses, then what? Who will the army follow? The people?* She was uncomfortably sure she knew the answer to both questions. *Besides, if I lay aside my sword, I'll lose whatever leverage I might have.*

"Do you know why Prince Dzurk was so rude to you?" Dorsay said, breaking into her thoughts.

"I assumed he was unfamiliar with the etiquette of the south," Raesinia said, the diplomatic answer coming almost automatically.

"Because he's an insufferable prick, you mean?" Dorsay smiled. "It's not that. At least, it's not *only* that, because of course he *is* an insufferable prick. But he's capable of covering it up when he wants to. No, it was a test. Dzurk—and his father—want to know the same thing everybody else does."

Raesinia frowned. *I'm getting sick of these leading questions.* "And what would that be?"

"Where the true power in Vordan lies. Is it with you? Or the much-decorated First Consul? No one is certain, and it has us all on edge. It's hard to negotiate when you don't know who you should be sucking up to. Dzurk apparently thought a few insults might provoke a response that would clarify matters."

Raesinia caught his eyes, the question there.

"I rule Vordan," she said. "With the cooperation of the people, via the Deputies-General."

"Ah, yes. We cannot forget your famous parliament. I hear they've nearly finished picking colors for the drapes in their meeting room."

Raesinia winced, though the jibe was not exactly unjust. The Deputies-General was so contentious that almost any action took ages to accomplish. Since Janus had banished the Directory, the deputies had been engaged in a furious debate over the finer intellectual points of the still-theoretical constitution, happy to leave the conduct of the war to their new First Consul.

"The First Consul serves at the pleasure of the monarch and the Deputies-General," Dorsay said. "Or so we are told. Did he bother to inform you before he made his little speech today?"

There was no safe way to answer that. Raesinia smoothed her face into a bland smile. "Thank you for your visit. It's been very informative."

Dorsay knew dismissal when he heard it. He pushed his chair back and bowed.

"Thank you, Your Majesty. I hope we have the opportunity for further discussion."

Sothe opened the door, then closed it behind the Borelgai. When he was gone, Raesinia leaned back in her chair.

"Well?" she said.

"I believe he's being truthful, as far as it goes," Sothe said. "Dorsay is famous for his fair dealing, and the king presumably chose him with that in mind. More important, it makes sense. Janus is brilliant, popular, and ambitious. Dangerous. A young queen and a paralyzed Deputies-General are much to be preferred, from Borel's point of view."

"Set Janus aside," Raesinia said, "in exchange for peace."

"In exchange for the *possibility* of peace," Sothe said. "His Grace was careful to promise nothing, you'll note."

"Except for Orlanko."

Sothe shrugged. "Orlanko is an embarrassment. Returning him to us kills two birds with one stone if it buys them anything at the negotiating table."

"Would you want him as our prisoner?"

"I think he should receive justice," Sothe said evenly. If she had personal feelings on the matter, she kept them to herself, as always.

"What about Janus? Any thoughts on what he's doing?"

Sothe frowned. "I'm not certain. We need more information."

"Then we'd better get it."

To Raesinia's intense irritation, it was after midnight before Janus was ready to speak with her. While she waited in her rooms, a steady stream of diplomats and courtiers from all three delegations trooped in and out of his suite. She couldn't simply push her way in without foreigners noting the discord. *Assuming the guards would let me. And let's not have* that *confrontation before we need to . . .*

When the knock at the door finally came, Raesinia stood up and smoothed her dress while Sothe answered it. To her surprise, the messenger was not some ranker, but Marcus d'Ivoire, now wearing both the Colonial scorpion and two stars above the silver eagle on his shoulder. He bowed low.

"Your Majesty," he said.

"Marcus," she said. He flinched at the informal tone, and Raesinia sighed inwardly.

It had been only a few months since the brief, mad stretch of time they'd spent together, between the attempt on her life and the fall of Maurisk, but it felt like years. Raesinia had thought they'd shared . . . something, a closeness as comrades in an impossible situation. He was one of the only people who knew the secret of the demon bound inside her, and she thought she'd earned his respect. She'd even imagined—

Never mind what I imagined. As soon as Janus had returned, Marcus had gone back to his side with evident relief, leaving Raesinia to face the endless, stultifying formal rituals of the court. In the few times they'd seen each other since then, he'd been scrupulously polite, but the discomfort he felt in her presence was obvious.

"The First Consul is ready to see you," he said. "He sends his apologies for the delay. It's been a busy day."

"I can imagine," Raesinia said sourly. "Have you heard what he told the conference?"

"In general terms."

"I don't suppose he's let you in on what he's thinking?"

"You know Janus, Your Majesty. He doesn't tell anyone anything if he can help it."

"He's too in love with drama for his own good," Raesinia muttered, sweeping past Marcus and into the hall.

He shut the door and led her to the other side of the building. The hotel was mostly quiet. Voices drifted up from below, where a certain amount of convivial drinking and celebration was no doubt occupying the more junior members of the delegations, international tensions or no. The soldiers, especially, were unlikely to let a war get between them and liquor, especially when the Crown was buying. But up here on the third floor, the lamps were low and only the occasional hotel servant was visible, bowing respectfully as soon as Raesinia came into sight.

"You're well, I trust?" she said eventually.

"Yes, Your Majesty. We've made a lot of progress these past few months."

She pointed to the new insignia on his shoulder. "What do the stars mean?"

"Janus has created new ranks, to give the army better structure. Two stars is for column-general."

"That sounds high."

"It's the highest in the army," Marcus said, blushing a little. "Aside from the First Consul himself, of course."

"I see. Congratulations."

"Thank you, Your Majesty." He looked sideways at her and smiled a little. "It's a relief to be back with the army, in the job I was trained for."

Raesinia's face was a frozen mask, but she tried to keep her voice pleasant. "I'm sure you're doing wonderfully."

She must not have succeeded, because Marcus looked away again and swallowed. A moment later they reached Janus' door, guarded by a pair of Colonials. They saluted Marcus, bowed to Raesinia, and stepped aside, and Raesinia went in without a backward glance. *Forget about Marcus. I have bigger problems.*

The suite was much like hers, but Janus had pushed the ornate furniture into the corners and set up a folding table, on which he'd spread a large map. Untidy stacks of flimsy paper surrounded it. Some of them bore long strings of circles and dashes, which she recognized as the code the flik-flik operators used to transmit messages with their lanterns and mirrors. It always felt strange to receive his reports of what was happening in Vordan City, weeks away by carriage. Now, looking at the pages full of incomprehensible cipher, Raesinia wondered how much of what the First Consul learned he was passing along.

Janus himself was standing by another table, tearing a loaf of bread into strips and folding it neatly before eating it. He waved Raesinia to a chair.

"Apologies," he said, bolting what was left. "Without Augustin to remind me, when matters are busy I often forget about meals. My new servants are all too reluctant to interrupt the First Consul at his business, and it's only hours later I realize I'm ready to keel over with hunger."

"I understand. You've had a busy day," Raesinia said, echoing Marcus.

"I imagine you're upset with me." Another fleeting smile.

"Perhaps. I am certainly confused. You can't imagine the Murnskai will accept those terms."

"Oh, of course not. I imagine the prince will be on his way north by tomorrow."

"Then this was a farce," Raesinia said through gritted teeth. "The whole peace conference. You never intended to negotiate."

"It was a farce," Janus said, taking the chair opposite her. "But I am not the director."

"Why would you hide this from me?" she snapped. "I am the *queen*. If this was your aim all along—"

"I apologize for that, Your Majesty. It was important that the peace conference be prepared with every appearance of genuine intent, so that our enemies would truly believe we would come to the table."

"Only to have you smash everything to pieces at the first opportunity."

He shrugged. "We would never truly have had peace, and I thought it best not to waste time trying now that the skies have cleared. We will need all the good weather we can get."

"Why?" Raesinia hated when he talked like this, like he was the schoolmaster and she the slow-witted pupil. "What are you planning?"

Janus sat back, gray eyes shining in the lamplight.

"You know," he said, "that what I said down there is nothing more than the truth. The war was started from Elysium, by the Priests of the Black. Orlanko's allies. Once they realized he'd lost control in Vordan, they saw war as their next best choice, taking advantage of our vulnerability."

Raesinia nodded reluctantly.

"You know they want the Thousand Names, and they want *you* gone. They lent aid to Maurisk and your enemies. They sent their Penitent Damned to drag you back to Elysium. They are patient and utterly ruthless, and they *will not stop*. No matter what happens here, or what the emperor or the king in Viadre wants. They have been at this since the days of Elleusis Ligamenti, at least nine hundred years. They're not going to give up just because we beat a few of their puppet armies."

He spoke with calm precision, as always, but she could hear the passion under his words. She shook her head. "They came for me, and we beat them."

"This time. I don't pretend to know what else the Pontifex of the Black has in his bag of tricks, but sooner or later he's going to get lucky." Janus leaned forward. "I promised your father I would help you, keep you safe. The only way I can do that is to deal with the Priests of the Black once and for all. Make sure they're as dead as everyone thinks they are."

"You want to march north," she said. "March on Elysium."

Janus nodded emphatically. "It's the only option. And this is our best chance. Murnsk is weak and unprepared, Borel is dilatory, and we are as strong as we've ever been. If we let this opportunity pass, we may not get another in my lifetime."

"Elysium has never been taken," Raesinia said, still a little stunned. "Not in nine hundred years."

"With respect, Your Majesty, no one has seriously tried for centuries. Times have changed."

"Even if we could get there, we'd never hold it. All Murnsk would rise against us for profaning their holy city."

"All of Khandar rose against us for profaning *their* holy city," Janus said, flashing his smile again. "But regardless, we don't *need* to hold it. Once we've cleaned out the rats' nest, we come home. And *then* we make peace, a *real* peace, not just a pause while the Black Priests catch their breath."

Raesinia stared at him.

She wanted to say that he was mad. But it made an awful kind of sense. She, of all people, knew that there were darker things in the world, that the currents that drove events ran deep beneath the surface. Her very existence was part of a plot by the Priests of the Black to provide Orlanko with a pliant puppet for the Vordanai throne. *But . . .*

"If you do this," she said, "a lot of people are going to die. Even if you win. Our soldiers trust you to do what's best for them."

"You're wrong, Your Majesty. If I was doing what was best for *them*, I'd disband the army and send everyone home." Janus' smile was gone now, his eyes intense. "They trust me to do what's best for Vordan, and for you. When they join up, they know I might have to spend their lives, but they trust that I'll get a good price. I think keeping Orlanko and the Black Priests out of Vordan forever is worth the sacrifice. Not to mention securing your position on the throne."

Raesinia sat back. Just being in the same room as Janus when he was in one of these moods was exhausting; he was so intense he practically sparkled at the edges. She'd come here furious with him, and now she found herself struggling not to be swept along in his vision.

"You're very confident," she said.

"I have good reason. I am not a man inclined to exaggeration, Your Majesty. You know that. Believe me when I say the Vordanai army now at our disposal is the finest instrument I have ever commanded. Perhaps the finest ever forged on this continent. You will see what it can accomplish."

The army *he* had built, nurtured on victory and forged over a winter's training. She wondered what Janus would do if she tried to take that instrument away from him, as Dorsay had suggested.

It came down to this: she could strip Janus of his post, trust the Borelgai to negotiate, and hope for the best. Or she could let him have his head and lead the army north. There was no room for half measures. *Dorsay hasn't seen what I've seen. He doesn't know about my demon.* Janus was right about the Priests of the Black— mere peace between nations would not keep their Penitent Damned away. She remembered Ionkovo, slipping in and out of shadows as though they were water. The cold feeling as he slid his knife into her brain.

Raesinia let out a long breath.

"When will you march?"

CHAPTER TWO

WINTER

The outer wall of Talbonn wasn't much more than a wooden palisade, protection against smugglers and bandits but little else. It was substantial enough to block traffic, though, and after a quarter of an hour's delay in the city streets Winter rode up the stalled column to find out what was going on. All around her, soldiers of the Girls' Own—now officially the Second Division First Infantry Regiment, but widely known by the old nickname—were shedding their packs and sitting down in the middle of the road, pulling out cards and dice and generally settling in for the long haul. Any veteran was familiar with the way moving columns expanded and contracted like an accordion, pausing inexplicably as momentary jams were transmitted down the line like ripples through an inchworm. And after the winter camp, they were all veterans, at least when it came to marching.

Winter's gelding Edgar made his slow, patient way through the increasingly dense crowd, soldiers saluting and struggling to clear a path when they noticed their commanding officer. Most of them knew Winter by sight, and the rest could see the star of a division-general on her shoulder. Closer to the wall, the press swelled beyond the road and into a sea of blue uniforms milling about in what was normally the market square, just inside the city's northern gate.

The problem was clear enough. A cart, nearly as wide as the gate, had been passing through when it had suffered an accident. It had been left wedged diagonally between the timber posts of the modest gatehouse, its four horses cut loose and waiting on the other side. A civilian in a long coat and bicorn hat was arguing with a Girls' Own officer, and three heavyset laborers in leather vests lounged nearby, with the satisfied expressions of men who were being paid by the hour regardless.

Winter swung down from the saddle and found a nearby corporal to take Edgar's reins. Mutters spread ahead of her, like a bow wave, and the women of the Girls' Own made a path. She nodded her thanks and stepped out behind the arguing lieutenant, a tall, severe-looking woman who'd gone red in the face.

"—I'm telling you to get your goat-fucking cart out of the gate *right now*," she was saying. "I don't care how you do it—just get it done!"

"And I said we're working on it!" the civilian said. He was sweating in the spring heat. "My cousin is bringing another cart around from the east gate, with a few more men. We'll remove the cargo and then get one of the axles off."

"If that cart is still there when General Ihernglass gets here, you are going to be one sorry son of a bitch," the lieutenant said.

"Good morning, Lieutenant," Winter said mildly. "Would you mind filling me in?"

"Sir!" The lieutenant spun around and saluted stiffly. "I apologize, sir. I—"

"No apology needed. What's your name?"

"Robinson, sir. Elinor Robinson. First Battalion, Fifth Company."

"And you?" Winter addressed the civilian.

"Tobin Bern," the man said, pulling off his hat. "At your service, General."

Winter smiled. "So, why is your cart blocking my gate, Master Bern?"

"It was an accident," Bern said. "Something spooked the team as they were going through, and it got wedged tight."

"It looks heavily loaded," Winter said. The cart was a large one, stacked high with rough-sided crates. "What are you carrying, may I ask?"

"Military supplies," the man said, a little too quickly. "For the army."

"I see."

Winter didn't bother to ask for his loading and transport papers, because he wouldn't have any. Janus' logistical service kept the official supply train under tight control, but unofficial merchants proliferated like flies on a corpse, eager to sell to bored, hungry soldiers. They were a necessary evil, but Winter found their naked greed unappealing. She walked to the back of the wagon and boosted herself up onto the bed.

"Sir!" the lieutenant said. "Let me—"

"It's all right," Winter said. "Master Bern, mind if I have a look?"

"I—"

Without waiting for a response, Winter picked up a crowbar from where it lay among the crates and set to work. A few seconds later she popped the top off one of them to reveal that it held bottles of wine, packed carefully in loose straw. *Military supplies.* She sighed and hopped down.

Bern had the decency to look embarrassed. "We *are* going to be selling them to the soldiers," he muttered.

"I'm sure," Winter said. "Lieutenant Robinson?"

"Yes, sir?" Robinson came to attention again, practically vibrating with her desire to be useful.

"Do you have someone in your company who knows her way around knots? Preferably someone on the short side. And some rope, if you please."

Robinson nodded vigorously and turned to the crowd. A few moments of shouting and she was back with a girl who looked no older than sixteen, a ranker, with the gray skin and dark hair of a Khandarai.

"Aya was a sailor before she joined up," Robinson said proudly. "You can tie knots, can't you, Aya?"

"Yes," the girl said, eyes wide as she stared at Winter. Her Vordanai was broken, and she had a strong accent. "I tie knot."

Winter wondered what strange path this young woman had followed, to come from her homeland thousands of miles to the south to this northern border of the Kingdom of Vordan. *No stranger than mine, I suppose.* She shifted into Khandarai, feeling like rusty gears were grinding in her brain.

"Can you get under there?" Winter said, pointing to the cart.

Aya, startled, took a moment before she looked at the stuck vehicle and nodded.

"Good. Tie the line around the main beam, the one that runs down the middle. Three times ought to do it—once at the front, once at the center, once at the back."

"Yes, sir!" Aya said in Khandarai. Around them, other soldiers were staring at the sight of their general speaking the strange southern language. Two women had returned bearing a coil of rope, and Aya took one end and got down on her belly to wriggle under the cart.

"What?" Bern said. "What's going on?"

"Clear a space," Winter shouted. "Back up! Lieutenant, assemble your company."

As the commotion began, Bern leaned closer to make himself heard. "We tried pushing it out, but it's stuck fast! You won't be able to move it."

"One thing I've learned in the army, Master Bern, is that if you get enough men on a line, you can move anything." She looked around at the scurrying women in blue uniforms and smiled. "So to speak."

"But—"

Aya popped out again, dusty but smiling. She clambered to her feet and saluted.

"The line is secure, sir!" she said in Khandarai.

"Get your company on that rope, Lieutenant," Winter said. "As many of them as you can fit."

This took a little time to work out, Winter helping the lieutenant arrange her soldiers and ignoring the squawking Bern. One hundred twenty pairs of hands gripped the thick line, arms strengthened and palms calloused by months of training. At Winter's command, they pulled.

The result was suitably spectacular. The frame of the cart shivered and came to pieces in a cracking, splintering cacophony. The main beam, the back axle, and much of the bed came free, while the front axle snapped in half and trailed after in two sad-looking pieces. Crates full of wine jostled and fell, hitting the ground with expensive-sounding crashes and leaking puddles into the dirt.

"General!" Bern was shrieking now. "General, you can't do this! My stock— I'll be ruined!"

"The First Consul has given me orders to get this column on the road," Winter said, voice still mild. "Anything that interferes with that is potentially a threat to the safety of the army, and that means it's my responsibility to deal with it. If you'd like to make a complaint, I suggest you take it up with him." She raised her voice. "Get some axes and cut the rest of this wreckage out of the way! I want this column back on the move within the hour!"

She accepted Edgar's reins from the awed-looking corporal and led the gelding through the gatehouse, picking her way around and over the remains of the front of the cart. On the other side, she mounted up again, waved to the soldiers now thronging in behind her to clear the gateway, and rode north.

The Second Division's camp was already half-built when Winter arrived, even though the sun was still several hours from the horizon. The advance elements, light cavalry that would spread out in a protective screen of eyes and ears, had departed before dawn, followed by the *official* supply wagons and Colonel Archer's two batteries of cannon. By the time the first of the infantry made their way up the dusty road from Talbonn, stakes and ropes already marked out the borders of the camp, showing where each company would pitch its tents, where the horse lines would be, and where the latrine pits would be dug.

Even with Winter's intervention, the final elements of the column wouldn't filter in until after dark. It was, she supposed, inevitable. Her Second Division totaled more than nine thousand soldiers, a quarter of the size of the old Army of the East, more than twice as big as the entire force Janus had commanded in Khandar. The Sixth Division, camping farther down the road, had nine thousand more.

And that wasn't even half of what Janus had assembled. With total control of Vordan's military, he'd reversed the scattershot policy of the Directory, ruthlessly stripping the Armies of the West and South of their best units. With the fall of Desland and Antova, the League was effectively out of the war for the moment, and the Army of the East had been reduced to a skeleton force. Over the winter months, the Army of the North had been combined with all these reinforcements, and the Grand Army had taken shape, more than one hundred thousand strong. It moved north in four columns, following parallel roads, space carefully allotted lest the march dissolve into a mammoth traffic jam.

In the winter camps, Janus had spent almost as much time reorganizing the Grand Army as he had training it. As in the Army of the East, the old royal regiments with their cherished designations and storied histories had been banished and torn into their component parts. They were combined with the battalions of volunteers, men who'd joined during the revolution or after the war had begun, and were put under whatever officers were deemed most competent, regardless of connections or social station. There was no more carping or criticism from the Ministry of War; the queen and the Deputies-General had given the new First Consul the ultimate trump card, and he used it ruthlessly.

Vordanai armies had never had any organization larger than the regiment, just as they'd never had much use for ranks above colonel. Taking inspiration from the legions of the ancient Mithradacii Tyrants, Janus had combined regiments into divisions, under the newly promoted division-generals. Each division was a self-contained fighting force, with its own attached artillery and cavalry, capable of holding its own against a comparable enemy. There were ten of them, in addition to Give-Em-Hell's cavalry and the main artillery reserve.

Winter had blanched when Janus had proposed quadrupling the size of her command, but at least this time she hadn't been expected to plunge directly into battle. Truthfully, for perhaps the first time since Marcus had handed her a sergeant's pins more than a year ago, Winter felt ready for what lay ahead. The endless drills of the training camps had seasoned the soldiers, but they'd given her time to prepare, too.

Bobby was waiting for her at the entrance to the camp, as always. She wore a captain's stripes on her shoulders, and her frame had lost much of its teenage awkwardness in the year or so since Khandar. Looking at her now, it was hard for Winter to believe she'd ever thought Bobby was a boy.

"Everything all right?" Bobby said. "We were expecting you an hour ago."

"Just a bit of traffic in the city that needed sorting out," Winter said. "We may be a little late getting started tomorrow."

"Fortunately, we haven't got too far to go." Bobby dug a much-folded slip of paper from her pocket. "From Janus. He wants us at a town called Glarusk in two days. It's just on the Murnskai side of the border, maybe twenty miles short of the Ytolin. Last word we got, Dorsay's still camped not far north of there, so this could be it."

Winter nodded, though she wasn't so certain. So far, the famous Duke of Brookspring had shown no inclination to try conclusions with Janus and the Grand Army. Since the breakup of the peace conference, he'd retreated grudgingly but steadily, abandoning several good positions. He had plenty of room—Murnsk was a vast country, and the rivers ran from east to west across the plains of the Split Coast, giving him any number of obstacles to hide behind. Bringing him to battle against his will was not going to be easy.

But that's Janus' worry, not mine. All she had to do was get her soldiers where he wanted, when he wanted, and make sure they did their duty.

"We'll be well rested, at least," Winter declared, studying the little note. "Any other problems?"

"Nothing to speak of. Abby's got a half dozen of the Girls' Own on punishment detail for brawling in town."

"With each other?"

Bobby shook her head. "The usual. Started out with somebody talking about the Girls' Own and ended up with a bar full of bloody noses and black eyes."

Winter sighed to herself. It had become a Girls' Own tradition to smash up a bar or wineshop in every town they visited; the veterans saw it as a kind of initiation. Drunken farmers and carters being what they were, they were never short of provocation. "If that's the worst we have to deal with, we'll count ourselves lucky. Has she tallied up the harvest?"

"Yes, sir." Bobby dug out another folded page. "Forty-six recruits, seven-teen angry parents, one furious husband, and one sobbing fiancé."

Winter fought to hide her smile. "Seems like there might be a tale there."

"Probably, sir."

It had started in Desland, but it hadn't ended there. Everywhere the Girls' Own stopped for more than a night, they got volunteers, young women who'd heard stories of the female battalion and wanted to sign up. They came openly by day or furtively by night, with stories to share or just a quiet determination. Winter didn't encourage them, but she didn't stop them, either. And provided they were of age, she didn't give them back when their parents inevitably turned up to demand their return.

The women who'd fought to free Vordan City from the Directory were now the hard core of a larger regiment, passing along what they'd learned to the new-comers. Abby had proven to be an excellent commander, carefully promoting soldiers with promises to be lieutenants and sergeants and mixing the raw recruits into the veteran companies. The regiment still specialized in skirmish tactics instead of straightforward line-of-battle fighting, but maneuvers like forming square against cavalry were no longer beyond their abilities.

"Make sure she gives Cyte the numbers when she gets in," Winter said. The ex-University student usually stayed with the tail of the column, making sure no one fell too far behind.

"Yes, sir." Bobby fixed her with a meaningful look. "And dinner will be ready soon."

"I've got—" Winter caught Bobby's expression and sighed. Bobby was insis-tent that Winter not miss dinners with the other officers. "All right. Do I have time to drop off my things?"

Bobby saluted and stepped aside, fighting a smile. Winter glowered at her and stalked into the camp in search of her tent.

Dinner for the senior officers was in the large tent Winter used for maps and planning the rest of the time. The folding table was cleared away, and a circle of cushions was set up. The food was better than the army soup and hardtack that Winter had gotten used to as a ranker, but not by much. The long, fast marches Janus often demanded from his soldiers meant a lean kit and no portable kitchens or wagons full of fancy provisions, even for division-generals. The best she could say was that the meat and eggs were fresh more often than not and there was always enough salt.

Cyte had still not returned, presumably trudging up the darkened road with the end of the column once they'd finally made their way out of Talbonn. Aside from her and Bobby, the others were all colonels, the commanders of the regiments that made up the Second Division. Some of them had served with Winter since her time in the Army of the East. David Sevran now commanded the Second Infantry Regiment, which included the "royals" who'd once been paired with the Girls' Own; and Neal Archer, the boyish, serious Khandarai veteran, had brought his battery of guns to her rescue at the Battle of Diarach.

Others were less familiar. Parker Erdine, who'd been assigned to the division with his three squadrons of light horsemen from the Army of the West, was an opera writer's idea of a dashing cavalryman. He was almost ridiculously handsome, with a square jaw, high cheekbones, and sandy brown hair of just the right length to stream dramatically in the wind as he charged. His uniforms fit so well they had to be custom-tailored, and he'd traded the standard-issue officer's cap for a broad-brimmed hat, pinned up on one side and equipped with a long red feather. To Winter's slight disappointment, he appeared to be a genuinely kind and competent officer, if a bit inclined to blowing his own trumpets.

Right at the moment, he was once again telling the story of his escape from Ecco Island, where he'd led two score cavalry from the garrison over the mountains when Borelgai warships seized the harbor. The details seemed to get more inventive and exciting each time.

"We'd pushed far up into the hills around Mount Ecco," Erdine said, "hoping they'd think we weren't worth the trouble. But they came on, a hundred lobsters after my poor, ragged three dozen. Our horses were exhausted, and we had to lead them up the rocky slopes, the hunting horns echoing in our ears. I understood how one of the Borelgai foxes must feel when it has the hounds after it."

Sevran listened politely, while Archer looked a bit skeptical. Abby—Winter avoided looking at Abby.

"Just when I was ready to give the order to turn and sell our lives as dearly as we could," Erdine went on, "we crested a hill and saw smoke rising from the chimney of a little cottage, with a few sheep wandering about outside. I bade my men halt and went to the door. My knock was answered by a pretty shepherd girl of no more than twenty, wide-eyed to find a pack of bedraggled soldiers on her doorstep.

"'My lady,' I said. 'In the name of the queen and the honor of Vordan, I need your help. The enemy are not an hour behind us.'

"She turned a pretty shade of pink at my words, but her jaw set, and I could tell at once that she was determined to be a credit to her country and her sex. She pulled me inside the cottage and said, 'Get in the bed and pull the covers up. If they ask, I'll tell them you are my father, sick nearly to death.'

"'That may do for me,' I said, 'but what about my men?'

"'There's a narrow ravine not far from here, where we graze the sheep in bad weather,' she said. 'I'll guide your men there, and they'll be sheltered from prying eyes.'

"The horns sounded again, and I had no time to argue. I dove beneath the heavy sheepskin blankets, and the brave girl went out and led my men to safety. She returned in the nick of time, just before the heavy boots of the Borels clomped into her yard. A sergeant pounded on the door, and I lay as still as I could, one hand on the hilt of my sword. I was ready to defend the young lady to the death, if it came to that, but she stood in the doorway as cool as snowmelt and told the Borel sergeant that she'd been tending her father for days and hadn't seen another living soul.

"Soon after that the rain began, and the lobsters gave up the chase as a bad job. My men camped in the shelter of the ravine and sent up prayers to Karis for our deliverance. As to how I spent the night, well . . ." He coughed, and looked at Abby and Bobby. "Present company forbids me from elaborating."

"Oh," Abby said, "don't let my delicate femininity interrupt your tale of heroic fucking, by all means. I'm all agog to hear the details. Tell me, when you were done, did you happen to get this girl's name? Did you bring her with you, or leave her behind for the first Borel who took a fancy to her?"

It was safe to say, Winter thought, that Abby did not care for Parker Erdine.

"I—" Erdine's face fell. "I'm sorry, my lady. I didn't mean to give offense."

"Oh, I'm not offended," Abby said, grinning like a wolf. "But if you call me 'my lady' one more time, I'll show you how we take offense in the Girls' Own."

Into the silence that followed, Colonel Nate Blackstream injected a *har-rumph*. "I'm sure the girl was fine," he said. "Borels are civilized. They abide by the rules of war." His face went sour, heavy mustache quivering. "Not like where we're going. The Murnsks are damned savages. Keep a knife in your boot, is my advice. That way you can at least cut your own throat if you're going to be captured."

Blackstream was cut from a rather different cloth than Parker Erdine. He was the oldest man at the table by a considerable margin, in his fifties at least, with his gray hair grown long and tied back in an elaborate braid. His jowly face was dominated by a luxurious mustache and canny, deep-set eyes. He didn't smile much, which Winter counted as a blessing, given the state of his teeth. Blackstream had been a captain in the old Royal Army, a War College graduate with a long service record. Something in that record must have impressed Janus, since he'd given the man an infantry regiment.

"Then again," he went on, "we've got to go through Dorsay before we get much farther into Murnsk. So maybe we won't have to worry about getting captured by the Murnskai after all."

"You were at Vansfeldt," Sevran said, apparently eager to change the subject. "Is Brookspring as formidable as everyone claims?"

Blackstream blew out a breath, lifting the ends of his mustache. "He's clever," he said, after due consideration. "Patient, cautious. When he was fighting Prince Dominic, he waited until the prince was frustrated enough to do something rash, and then pounced."

"That's unlikely to be a problem," said Colonel Martin de Koste, the last member of the party. "First Consul Vhalnich won't give him that kind of opportunity."

If Blackstream represented the old army, de Koste exemplified the new. The son of a noble house from the Transpale, he was young, well educated, and utterly besotted with the ideas of the revolution. This translated into an admiration for Janus that bordered on hero worship; he was the only soldier Winter had met who insisted on addressing their commander by his full title. Of all her new subordinates, de Koste made Winter the most uncomfortable, since he seemed to regard her as some kind of demigod orbiting the prime divinity.

"Janus has done fine against a bunch of creaky old merchants," Blackstream said. "We'll see how he fares against a proper commander."

"I don't know about the Hamveltai commanders," Abby drawled, "but I assure you the yellowjackets aren't made up of creaky old men." She looked from Erdine to Blackstream. "Some of us spent last year fighting instead of squatting on the south coast or heroically running away."

"I go where the Ministry wills," Blackstream said phlegmatically. "For my sins. I had my fill of fighting ages past."

"And I for one am looking forward to an honest battle," Erdine said. "Not much fun in it when you're outnumbered twenty to one."

"There's not much *fun* in it in any event," Blackstream said. "Whatever Janus does, it's us who'll do the bloody work."

De Koste jumped in again, presumably to insist that Janus would win the battle single-handedly. Winter abruptly got to her feet.

"If you'll excuse me," she said. "I have work to do."

Abby tried to catch her eye on the way out, but Winter kept her head down. The conversation picked up behind her as the tent flap closed.

Abby. The circle of people Winter trusted had shrunk considerably over the past few months. Marcus was back with Janus, second in command of the whole Grand Army. Feor was still in Vordan, studying the Thousand Names. Of the men and women at her side, only Bobby and Cyte were privy to all her secrets. And Abby . . .

The ghost of Jane hung between them, a dark specter of guilt and loss. Winter and Jane had been lovers at Mrs. Wilmore's Prison, before Jane had been dragged off to be "married" and Winter had escaped to join the Royal Army. They'd been reunited when she returned from Khandar, and Jane's Leatherbacks had formed the core of the Girls' Own. As what had been a rough-and-tumble dock gang had forged themselves into professional soldiers, though, they'd left their leader behind. In the end, desperation had driven Jane into a mad attempt to kill Janus.

Her name had become taboo, never to be spoken, not just between Winter and Abby but all through the Girls' Own. For Abby and the others, it was simple: Jane had betrayed them. That she'd escaped afterward and murdered a Girls' Own guard in the process had been the final straw. All the ex-Leatherbacks seemed determined to pretend that their former leader had never existed.

If only it could be that simple. It felt like there was a dark pit at the bottom of Winter's thoughts, a hole that threatened to suck her in whenever she relaxed her guard. *I could have helped her. I could have saved her. If I'd only talked to her sooner, said something different, she wouldn't have done what she did. All she wanted was me. I should have . . .*

She closed her eyes, standing in the darkness of the early evening outside the command tent, and jerked herself back from the abyss. *Enough.* There were things that needed doing.

Winter's pen scratched and popped across the cheap paper.

Reports, as far as she could tell, were the one constant of army life, across ranks and continents. She'd now served at virtually every position there was, and only as a ranker had she escaped the constant need to write reports. That was because rankers weren't required to be literate; if they had been, Winter had no doubt the Ministry of War would have made them write detailed summaries of their progress cleaning up horseshit or peeling potatoes.

The higher she rose, the more subordinates she had to help her, but the more subordinates she had to write reports *about*, so the whole thing was pretty much a wash. Cyte took care of much of the administrative work, with the same thorough competence she applied to everything, but there were always pieces that required the commanding officer's sign-off or opinion.

Outside, the last of the infantry had finally made it into camp. Laughter and shouts filled the night air, still chilly with the memory of winter. They were headed toward a battle and everyone knew it, but if it bothered the rankers they buried it under bravado. The veterans, those from the Girls' Own and the royals who'd been with the Army of the East, acted unconcerned to show off their blooded status. The rest, new recruits and transfers from the less active armies, followed their lead so as not to look weak by comparison. Morale seemed high. *It's amazing what a little time training and getting enough to eat can do for an army's confidence.*

There was a scratch at the tent post. "Yes?" Winter said.

"It's Cyte, sir," Cyte said.

"Come in." Winter laid her pen down.

Cyte pushed the tent flap open and ducked inside. Unlike Bobby, the ex-University student had never looked entirely comfortable in uniform. She wore a captain's stripes now, serving as Winter's chief of staff. There wasn't much staff to be chief *of*, truth be told, just Bobby and a cadre of messengers, and Cyte did the work of translating Winter's general orders into specific timetables and routes with meticulous attention to detail. Winter had long since stopped wondering what she would do without her.

Cyte's raven-dark hair was longer than it had been in her University days, tied into a tail that hung past her shoulders, and she'd set aside the dark makeup that had given her a vaguely haunted look. She was rarely without a slate or stack of paper in hand. In this case, it was the latter.

"Reports," she said, putting the sheaf on Winter's desk. "From Erdine's scouts."

Reports. Winter sighed. "Can you summarize?"

"Nothing major," Cyte said. "This is a bit of a no-man's-land between Vordan and Murnsk. The official border is around here somewhere, but it's never been completely clear where. There's some villages, and the people there say they're very happy to see us finally putting a stop to Murnskai tyranny."

"And they probably tell the emperor's riders they're happy to see someone putting a stop to Vordanai tyranny," Winter said, but not unsympathetically. Being a farmer in a place that had seen as many wars as this one had bred pragmatic sorts. "No sign of the enemy?"

"Not so far. Dorsay's still pulling back."

"Maybe he'll pull back all the way to Borel."

"Colonel Erdine will be disappointed." Cyte smiled for a moment before the expression faded. "Bobby told me you barely said a word all through dinner."

"I didn't have much to say." Winter shrugged. "Erdine talks enough for a dozen by himself. Besides, whenever I say anything . . ." She trailed off.

"Yes?" Cyte prompted.

"They all *listen*." Winter ran her fingers through her hair and gave a humorless chuckle. "Like I'm a priest delivering the holy word."

"They're afraid of you," Cyte said.

"I can't imagine why. I haven't been harsh with them."

"It's been months, and they barely *know* you. Have you ever spoken to any of them about anything except military business?"

"You may not have noticed," Winter said, "but we've had rather a lot of business to take care of."

That was thin, though, and she knew it. Cyte herself handled more of the administrative work than Winter did. The truth was that Winter didn't want them to know her. *All I want is for them to do their jobs.* It didn't help that, while her gender was an open secret among the Girls' Own, she had kept up her male disguise toward the other colonels and the army at large.

"They're good officers," Winter said, looking away from Cyte's pointed stare. "I don't think they're in need of closer supervision."

"Winter . . ." Cyte said, and stopped. She took a deep breath. "Will that be all, then?"

Winter nodded. Cyte saluted, a little stiffly, and left her alone in the tent.

Alone. She'd gotten used to it, almost. She no longer woke up expecting to find someone else in her bedroll every morning, or automatically made twice as much tea as she needed. She'd stopped feeling surprised when things stayed tidy for days at a time.

Bobby had Marsh, of course. A captain now, in Sevran's Second Infantry Regiment. And Cyte—Winter wondered if she'd found someone, somewhere among the soldiers of the Second Division. It made for a strange mental image;

Cyte's air of calm competence was so ingrained it was hard to picture her doing anything as messy as falling in love.

That was veering dangerously close to the abyss again. Winter shook her head to put her thoughts in order and picked up her pen. Two days until they rendezvoused with Janus, with battle possibly to follow. *By then everything has to be perfect.*

Chapter Three

MARCUS

Grand Army headquarters was officially in the village of Vaus, but only because that was the nearest label on the map. Vaus itself was a miserable little place, a cluster of a dozen mud-and-thatch houses whose inhabitants had long since fled to the woods. The Grand Army's camp spread through the fields surrounding it, the size of a small city. Boots, hooves, and wagon wheels churned the just-planted soil to mud.

The sheer size of what Janus had brought to bear was still a shock to Marcus every time he walked up the little rise. Neat rows of blue canvas stretched on and on, broken at regular intervals by avenues for traffic. In the artillery park, the guns of the army reserve were parked hub to hub, line after line of gleaming iron and brass, muzzles covered with leather bags to keep out the mud and damp. Endless strings of horses, off on the edge of camp, filled the early evening with faint animal sounds.

And this was only a part of the total force—four divisions, plus the artillery and cavalry reserve. Already a larger force than the Army of the East, and four more divisions waited off to the south and west, under Fitz Warus' overall command. To the east, at another flyspeck town called Glarusk, two more divisions under Winter Ihernglass had made their own camp.

To the north, of course, across a long stretch of empty fields and small forests, Dorsay's Borelgai army had made its own camp by the banks of the river Ytolin. Perhaps one hundred and sixty thousand soldiers between the two armies, driven by the will of two men. For a moment Marcus saw it all as some vast clockwork machine, each cog helplessly driven by the next, pressing onward no matter what was ground to dust in the gears . . .

He shook his head, smiling ruefully. *You asked for this, d'Ivoire. Janus would have let you stay behind in Vordan minding the stores. Don't get melodramatic now.*

Marcus turned away from the camp, where fires were starting to wink on like stars, and back to the command tent. It was a monstrous six-poled affair, big enough for a dozen men to stand comfortably around a map table. Lanterns glowed inside, and a pair of sentries with shouldered muskets waited beside the tent flap.

Janus himself came into view, hiking up the short cow path that led up the side of the little rocky hill. He'd shed the dress uniform he'd worn at the peace talks for a standard blue one, distinguished only by gold laurel wreathes on the shoulders. The two guards who followed him wore the new silver scorpions of the Colonials, matching the one on Marcus' chest. Janus' personal troops, the Mierantai rifles, had been volunteers who'd left their lives behind to answer his call, and over the winter he'd released them to return to their mountain farms and villages. A special detail from the Colonials was now responsible for the safety of the First Consul.

"Marcus!" Janus said. "I hope I haven't kept you waiting."

"No, sir," Marcus said, snapping a salute, which Janus waved away. "I only just arrived."

"Good." Janus flashed a grin. "The march seems to be going well, for the moment."

"Yes, sir." Marcus glanced back at the long lines of tents. "Frankly, I'm astonished we haven't had more problems."

"A little practice goes a long way." Janus followed Marcus' gaze and grimaced. "Though I'll be happier once we leave our royal accompaniment behind."

Raesinia's tent was silvery white and larger than the others, with its own separate camp of cooks, grooms, and carters, cordoned off by Grenadier Guards. The queen had kept her entourage to a minimum, and Marcus couldn't complain that they were encumbering the march, but it worried him having her so close to the battlefield.

"I do wish she wouldn't take the risk," Marcus agreed.

"The risk to *her* isn't the issue," Janus said. "I'm more concerned about the risk to us. The last century provides many examples of the folly of trusting battlefield command to hereditary royalty."

"Her Majesty doesn't seem inclined to assume command," Marcus said.

"For the moment. But she may not be so permissive if things look like they're going badly." He pursed his lips in thought. "I may have to speak to the colonel of the Grenadier Guards. When the time comes, Her Majesty may need to be taken south for her own safety."

Marcus couldn't imagine Raesinia accepting *that* without a fight, but he only nodded. "Do you anticipate things going badly, sir?"

"Of course not. But if everything on this campaign goes as anticipated, that will make a first in the entire history of war." Janus smiled again. "I've told you before that my reputation for omniscience is vastly overstated." He turned away at the sound of boots on the path. "Ah, and here's Ihernglass."

Nearly a year in the field had not been entirely kind to Winter Ihernglass, Marcus had to say. His silver-blond hair was cut to little more than fuzz, and even after months in winter quarters his cheeks had a gaunt look. His frame, never stout, had thinned to a knife's edge, though he seemed as strong as ever.

There was probably more to it than the constant campaigning. Marcus hesitated to put credence in camp gossip, but fairly solid rumor had it that Ihernglass' lover, an officer in the Girls' Own named Mad Jane, had betrayed the army during the fight with the Directory and tried to kill him before escaping. Ihernglass, it was said, was taking it badly. While Marcus wasn't without sympathy—he thought of Jen Alhundt—he wondered if the man's personal life would affect his performance. *He still has Janus' confidence, though, and that's all that matters.*

He'd brought two staff captains with him, both women. Marcus had almost, but not quite, lost his visceral surprise at seeing women in soldier's uniforms, but the whole concept still made him uncomfortable. He couldn't dispute that they could fight—they'd cut through the Patriot Guard in Vordan City, and even rescued the queen himself—but now that the immediate crisis was past, he couldn't help but wish they'd been left behind somewhere safe. *Guarding the queen, maybe, back in Vordan.* But Janus seemed to have no qualms about these strange soldiers, and Marcus was forced once again to hold his tongue.

"Sir." Ihernglass saluted smartly, his staff following suit.

"Welcome, Division-General Ihernglass," Janus said.

He led the way inside the big tent. A large folding table held several maps of different sizes and scales, marked and annotated in grease pencil. Janus took up position at the head of the table, and the others arranged themselves around it.

"I'm not sure if everyone has met," Ihernglass said. He gestured to his left, at a young, pretty brunette standing at stiff attention. On his other side, the slim, dark-haired woman seemed more composed. "This is Captain Bobby Forester and Captain Cytomandiclea."

"It's an honor, sir!" Bobby said, a little too loudly.

"Likewise," the other woman said.

"Cytomandiclea," Janus said. "After the Mithradacii queen?"

"Ah, yes, sir," Cyte said, startled. "And please call me Cyte if you like."

"An understudied figure, I've always thought. There's far too much attention devoted to the likes of Andromachus and Vestarian, in spite of the fact that all their famous campaigns amounted to little more than burning down a bunch of peasant villages. The whole Fall of the Tyrants era is sadly underdocumented, of course."

Marcus, who had long ceased to be surprised at the esoteric knowledge Janus could pull out of his hat at a moment's notice, cleared his throat and said, "I'm Column-General Marcus d'Ivoire."

"I've read about the Khandarai campaign," Cyte said. "It's an honor to meet you as well."

She smiled, which relaxed the somewhat severe lines of her face, and Marcus felt himself blushing a little under his beard. He gritted his teeth. *Another reason why women shouldn't be soldiers. It's hardly fair to the rest of us.*

"Very good," Janus said. He swept some of the maps aside with a theatrical wave of his arm and laid a large sheet of virgin paper on the table. "Now. If we may begin?"

Marcus and Ihernglass said "Sir!" in unison and bent over the table. Janus picked up a grease pencil and drew a long straight line down the center of the page.

"I've asked you here," he said, "because the two of you have the most important parts to play in tomorrow's engagement. This is the river Ytolin, and this"—he drew a circle on the river—"is the town of Gilphaite, on the south bank. The Duke of Brookspring has his headquarters there, and his army is camped around the town. It's good ground. The town is on a rise that commands the surrounding country, the river provides a secure anchor for his flanks, and Gilphaite has an excellent bridge. Dorsay knows we have the numbers, and he's no fool. No doubt he hopes we'll obligingly throw ourselves against his front as we come up, so he can bloody us and pull back over the bridge before his line gives way."

"We could get around him," Marcus said. "He doesn't have the strength to defend the whole river line."

Janus nodded. "It would take time, but yes. If we outflank his position, Dorsay will have no choice but to retreat. The trouble is, that would not particularly inconvenience him. We would gain a single town, and he has all of Murnsk to trade for time if he needs to. The emperor's armies are on the move, and when they're fully assembled they will outnumber us. Before they can reach the field, Dorsay must be destroyed." He tapped the page. "Remember that. Territory is irrelevant. The objective is the enemy army. Eliminate it, and everything else will fall on its own."

Cyte looked on, apparently rapt. Iherglass said, "I assume you have an idea?"

"Indeed." Janus made an *X* on the map, directly south of where he'd put Dorsay's camp. "This is Vaus, on the most direct route to Gilphaite. The four divisions here are nearly as strong as Dorsay on their own. In the morning, Marcus, you will take them north and attack the enemy camp."

Marcus had listened to enough of these briefings not to ask the obvious question, but Bobby did it for him. "I thought we weren't going to attack them directly?"

"The duke must be convinced that we've fallen for his bait." Janus made another *X*, to the east. "Your Second Division and the Sixth Division are here, Iherglass."

"Yessir."

"Dorsay has two weaknesses we can exploit. One is a lack of really effective cavalry. Borel has always relied on mercenary light cavalry, and their quality is poor. No doubt he hopes the emperor will make up for that, but the emperor is not here yet. Our own cavalry should be able to make an effective screen for our movements.

"The second weakness is that his line of retreat is dependent on the bridge at Gilphaite. If it is captured or destroyed, his strong position becomes a trap." Janus sketched a line running northeast from Winter's Second Division to the river, then turning west on the north bank toward Dorsay. "Iherglass, you will begin the march before dawn. Division-General Stokes' patrols assure me that the Ytolin is fordable here, at least for men and horses. You'll leave behind your guns and wagons and anything else that might slow you down. Your cavalry will go first, driving back the enemy patrols. By midafternoon, I want you in position to attack the Gilphaite bridge from the north. The main attack will have drawn Dorsay's reserves south, and I expect it will be lightly defended."

He drew a final *X*, somewhat west and south of Vaus. "Division-General

Warus is here, with the balance of our forces. He will time his march to arrive after Ihernglass' attack goes forward. The doubling of our strength should convince Dorsay that the game is up and the time for retreat has come, but when he tries it, he'll find his path blocked. If I know the man, he'll surrender then and there. If not . . ." Janus shrugged. "We'll cut him to pieces if we have to, and have plenty of time to re-form before the emperor arrives with his legions."

Marcus glanced at Ihernglass. It didn't take Janus' genius to see that this plan put his two divisions in an extremely precarious position. Across a deep river, without artillery or supplies, they would be stranded if anything went badly wrong. Marcus half expected the man to raise an objection. Not that it would matter, with Janus, but in Ihernglass' position Marcus might have wanted to register a token protest.

Instead, Ihernglass said, "That's a long march, with a fight at the end of it."

"It is," Janus said. "Are your troops up to it?"

"Of course, sir," Winter said. "With your permission, I'd like to start at midnight, by torchlight. It will give us more margin for error."

"As you see fit," Janus said. He sounded pleased. "Marcus, your role is the most delicate. You must convince Dorsay that yours is the main attack, but not press him so hard he retreats prematurely, and of course preserve our own forces as much as possible. You'll have the reserve artillery, and I recommend making as much use of long-range fire as you can. If Dorsay counterattacks, let him advance. The farther he is from the bridge, the better."

"Yes, sir," Marcus said. "What about Fitz?"

"I'll be riding to the First Division tonight to give him his instructions in person. The timing of his arrival is critical, so I'll direct it personally."

"Ah." Marcus swallowed as he understood, for the first time, that Janus was trusting him with unsupervised command of a third of the army. "Understood, sir."

"We won't disappoint you, sir," Ihernglass said.

"You all have my fullest confidence." Janus' grin flashed again, like a bolt of lightning. "Now let's be about it."

WINTER

They were halfway back to Glarusk, riding by torchlight as the sky went from purple to black, before Cyte finally spoke.

"You said you wanted to start the march at midnight, sir?" she said. Winter nodded.

"It'll be near to eleven when we get back to camp," Cyte said.

"It's not the first time I've gone without sleep on a campaign," Winter said, "and I'm willing to bet it won't be the last."

"I've got some of the Khandarai coffee left in the stores," Bobby said. "I'll brew it up."

Just the thought of that perked Winter up a bit, and she sat up straighter in the saddle. Edgar plodded along, placid as ever, sure-footed even in torchlight. Winter glanced curiously at Cyte, whose brow was creased in concentration.

"Was Janus everything you expected him to be?" Winter said.

"He's very impressive," Cyte said. "He's taking a big risk with this plan, but you wouldn't know it to hear him talk. It's like he—"

"—knows what's going to happen in advance," Winter said, smiling. "Or at least he pretends to. He once told me that half of being a genius is knowing how to take credit after the fact for things that happened to break your way."

Cyte chuckled. "I suppose. I'd never thought about it like that."

"Do you think he's serious about going all the way to Elysium?" Bobby said, out of nowhere.

There was a pause.

"I don't know as much about the supernatural side of things as the two of you," Cyte said. "But as best I can tell it's strategically sound, in the larger context. If he thinks of this as a war between us and the Black Priests, then the only way to win is to hit them hard enough that they either surrender or can't continue."

"I agree," Winter said. "He told me back in Khandar that this was going to be the real fight."

It was odd to think of everything that had come so far as a . . . a *sideshow*. A clearing of the minor pieces off the board, to make room for the real showdown.

"Everyone says that Murnsk can't be conquered," Bobby said.

"Fortunately," Cyte said, "we don't need to conquer it. Murnsk goes all the way to the Old Coast in the east. We only need to get to Elysium."

"'Only,'" Winter said. "It's, what, three hundred miles?"

"Closer to four hundred." Cyte shrugged. "It's farther from here to Vordan City."

With decent roads, and riverboats to supply us, and no enemy to block the path. But Winter didn't say it. The truth was, if Janus wanted to go to Elysium, it didn't matter if it was three hundred miles or a thousand. She would do her best to get there. *What else can I do?*

Eventually, the campfires of the Second Division came into view, and Winter was pleased to hear the attentive picket shout a challenge. Bobby answered, and they passed the sentries and into the rows of tents, a smaller version of the vast encampment around Vaus.

"Bobby, get Abby up first," Winter said. "Tell her I want the Girls' Own to shake out skirmishers and push north to the river, make sure we haven't got any surprises waiting. Then get Erdine to get his men up and moving. They can lead their horses until it's light enough to see properly. He's to ford the river and scout the other side, and to make sure any enemy scouts don't get close enough to see the crossing."

"Yessir," Bobby said, tugging the reins to turn her horse away.

"We'll need to send someone to the Sixth. Tell General—" Winter struggled to recall the man's name.

"General Ibsly, sir," Cyte supplied.

"Right." *Ibsly.* She'd met him, a nervous-looking captain of engineers thrust into responsibility by Janus' mysterious judgments. *Like so many others.* "Tell him to send his cavalry north and have their colonel report to Erdine. His infantry should go first; we'll bring up the rear. Oh, and tell Archer to get the wagon train moving and take it and the guns to Vaus. If we can't bring them across the river, I'm sure Column-General d'Ivoire will find a use for a couple of extra batteries."

Cyte nodded, saluted, and rode off. Winter headed for her own tent. Not that she'd have time to sleep, but at least she'd be easy to find when something went wrong.

Something went wrong, of course. It was probably impossible to get a column of nearly twenty thousand men and women out of bed, packed, and on the march in the small hours of the morning without *something* getting fouled up. All in all, though, the operation went remarkably smoothly. A captain in Ibsly's Second Regiment got lost and led his battalion in among Sevran's troops, causing no end of confusion, and a few uncooperative horses snarled the wagon train for a time. Winter improvised solutions—the lost battalion was told to simply follow along, and nearby companies were conscripted to lift the blocking wagons out of the way until their teams could be untangled. By one in the morning, a river of blue uniforms was flowing north, toward the Ytolin, and Winter let the porters strike her tent and climbed back into Edgar's saddle.

The land sloped down to the river, then gently up again on the other side. The south bank was almost entirely farmland, irregular tilled fields surrounded by fences and hedges, which the soldiers hacked through rather than look for the gates. By moonlight, Winter could see that the other bank was hillier country, broken by small forests and the occasional bald hummock. Here and there she could see the glow of a fire at some isolated cabin.

The Girls' Own, their loose formation spread out to cover the front of the march, had encountered no resistance on their way to the river. A few of the women had already gone across, wading through water deep enough that they had to hold their muskets and cartridge boxes over their heads. Erdine's cavalry followed, the horsemen leading their unhappy mounts over the tricky footing of the riverbed. The first light of the new day showed Winter that they were forming up on the north bank, blue uniforms soaked to the armpits. She ordered the remainder of the Girls' Own across, then called a conference of the rest of her infantry commanders.

Ibsly was there, rubbing his spectacles with his shirt, along with four of his colonels. Sevran, Blackstream, and de Koste stood in a bunch, as though they didn't like being outnumbered by these strangers.

"Division-General Ihernglass," Ibsly said, pushing his spectacles back onto his nose. "I'm glad you finally have a moment to explain things to the rest of us."

"Is the whole column crossing the river?" Blackstream said. "There'll be hell to pay if the lobsters catch us."

"Did the First Consul tell you if he expected us to fight?" de Koste said. He sounded eager.

Winter held up her hand. "One at a time, please. Yes, we're crossing the river, and yes, I think there'll be fighting. I want the Sixth to go first, but not to push forward until the rest of us are across. Use the time to rest and dry out, because once we move, we're going to move *fast*. The cavalry will try to keep Dorsay's scouts from spotting us, but word will get out eventually. The closer we are when that happens, the better." She outlined the plan Janus had explained, at least as far as it pertained to her column. Ibsly took off his spectacles and began to polish them again, and Blackstream sucked a breath through his teeth.

"That's a hell of a toss of the dice," the old colonel said. "If Dorsay gets wind of this early, he can pull his entire army over the river and concentrate against us. He'd have us two to one."

"This is the assignment Janus gave us," Winter said. "I haven't let him down yet, and I don't intend to start now. We'll move as fast as we can and hit the bridge with everything we've got."

"That's right," de Koste said. "You should have faith in the First Consul."

"I'd have a little more faith if we could bring our guns with us," Blackstream said dourly, then shrugged. "As you say, sir. My boys will be ready to cross."

"And I'd better get my men ready," said Ibsly, putting his spectacles back on. He hesitated. "This is quite an honor, isn't it? That Janus has given us this responsibility."

The part of Winter that had never quite stopped being a ranker told her that "honor" was something officers gave to men they were about to get killed. But Ibsly looked nervous enough, so she only smiled and nodded.

"A great honor," Ibsly repeated, as he moved off.

"General?" Sevran said as the others departed. "A word?"

"What is it?" Winter said.

The sky was lightening now, from dark gray to the faintest of blues, and one horizon was beginning to glow in anticipation of sunrise. The Girls' Own was still crossing the river, the soldiers in good spirits judging by the way they laughed and splashed one another as they went. On the other side, some of them had stripped off their jackets and trousers to wring out. Whistles from among the cavalry were answered with good-natured profanity.

"Blackstream's not wrong," Sevran said quietly. "I've been at this long enough that I get itchy whenever someone starts talking about flank marches and surprise arrivals. It never seems to go quite according to schedule."

"All we need to worry about is making sure our piece *does*," Winter said. "Besides, this is Janus we're talking about, not some idiot who happened to grow up with the king. He knows what he's doing."

"Of course. I just think it would be prudent to keep a reserve ready. In case things don't go according to plan."

"I'll keep that in mind," Winter said, a little more dryly than she'd intended. "Now, I believe you have a regiment to attend to."

"Yes, sir."

The April air was still chilly, but at least the sun was out, the weak morning rays struggling to dry the damp uniforms of the men and women who'd crossed the Ytolin. With the cavalry fanning out ahead of them, the column moved out, Winter ordering the bands to keep up a fast, encouraging tune while the vanguard set a rapid pace. The Girls' Own took the lead, as usual, ready to send out a skirmish screen if they ran into the enemy.

The early stages of the march were uncontested, however, and it wasn't until nearly noon that riders came back from Colonel Erdine to report that his scouts had engaged the Borelgai. Even this turned out to be only cavalry patrols, content to fire a few shots from their carbines and withdraw in front of the Vordanai horsemen. Erdine's dispatches assured Winter that no Borelgai scouts would get within sight of the infantry column.

"There they go," Cyte said quietly, riding beside Winter just behind the Girls' Own.

Winter looked at her quizzically, but Cyte only closed her eyes for a moment and held up a hand. Winter concentrated, and a moment later she heard it, too. Under the tramp of boots and the chatter of voices, there was a nearly subsonic rumble, like thunder in the far distance. It grew with every moment and every step Edgar took to the west, a deep, irregular grumbling. The sound of guns, far off, echoing over the hills and across the river. *Marcus is starting his attack.* So far everything seemed to be on schedule, though she was glad she'd insisted on the early start.

The soldiers in the column heard the guns, too, and the atmosphere in the ranks changed. The shouts and laughter gradually died away, replaced by muted, businesslike conversations. During their infrequent rest breaks, she saw soldiers checking and rechecking their cartridge boxes or making sure their bayonets were loose in their sheaths. A young woman—possibly one of the recruits from Talbonn—stood with her face screwed up and on the verge of tears as she strained to go through the manual of arms in front of an unsympathetic-looking sergeant. Other Girls' Own soldiers were checking the thin daggers almost all of them kept concealed somewhere in their uniform; in the event of capture, they were for escape or, worse come to worst, suicide if the alternative was unbearable.

Winter was pleased to see that there was no depression or panic, just a calm assessment of possibilities. Only the Girls' Own and Sevran's Second Infantry Regiment had seen serious fighting. The other two regiments, and Ibsly's entire division, were mostly reinforcements culled from the west and south. *This is a hell of a way to be thrown into your first battle.*

Just when she was getting ready to order the column back to the march, a half dozen horsemen cantered up, with Erdine himself in the lead. The cavalry colonel was in fine form, hair golden in the midday sun under his broad hat, his colorful plume bouncing gaily as he rode. He waved to Winter, controlling his mount with an effortless ease she envied.

"General!" he said. "I'm pleased to report that we've pushed the Borels back to their main line, not that they made much of a fight of it. As best we can tell, they don't know this is anything more than a cavalry probe, but that'll change as soon as we come over this next ridge. They've got a dozen guns on high ground."

Winter felt a chill. *A dozen guns?* A full battery waiting for them didn't sound like the token defense Janus had promised. "Any infantry?"

"Skirmishers and cavalry were all we saw. But there's plenty of dead ground for them to hide in."

Winter nodded. "Bobby, get the regiments formed up and ready to march. Cyte, with me; we're going to have a look. Colonel, can you lead us to a decent vantage?"

"Of course, sir. Follow me."

They'd halted in a lightly wooded valley, where the road that more or less followed the course of the river took a dogleg to the north to cut across a stream and get around a long ridgeline. Erdine led them up the hill, ignoring the rough terrain. Cyte was a good enough rider that Winter felt like she and Edgar were holding the party back, though the gelding's calm pace meant that he could step over the rocks and fallen branches easily enough. In a few minutes they reached a spot where the spindly birches and oaks thinned out, and Erdine dismounted. Winter and Cyte followed him onto bare rock, breaking out of the tree line on the back of an enormous boulder.

It was, as promised, an excellent view. The Ytolin winked and glittered off to the left, and Winter could see the roofs of the town of Gilphaite. Clouds of smoke were visible there, the whitish billows of powder smoke and the black columns that rose from burning buildings. The artillery was still clearly audible, along with an occasional distant crash as solid shot plowed into a wall.

The all-important bridge was not visible, however, because the ground to the north of the river rose into a hill and blocked her view. It was more of a gentle roll in the ground than a steep height, fenced pastures green with new grass and fields still mostly brown and muddy. As Erdine had said, there were a dozen guns deployed on its crest, arranged in three-gun half batteries separated by several hundred yards.

Between the ridge on which they stood and the hill was a long, flat stretch, perhaps a mile and a half across. At the moment it was occupied only by scattered groups of cavalry, some still ahorse, others dismounted and crouching behind isolated trees or hedgerows. Puffs of musket smoke, like tiny balls of cotton, showed when each man fired his weapon, followed moments later by the distant *crack* of the shot. On the lower slopes of the hill, someone was firing back. Winter brought up her spyglass and saw figures in muddy red uniforms, similarly hunkered into cover.

For all the energy the cavalry and skirmishers put into the long-range fire-fight, the inaccuracy of their weapons at distance meant that this was the kind of combat that could be kept up all day without more than a few hits on either side. Winter counted the shots from the hill and tried to estimate the number of enemy skirmishers. *A couple of hundred, maybe?* Unlike the Hamveltai, who'd been repeatedly thrown off by the loose-order tactics of the Vordanai volunteers, the Borelgai army had been well schooled in such matters by endless brushfire conflicts in its colonies south of Khandar and had developed its own doctrines to counter them. *It's not going to matter, though, if they haven't got a lot more men back there.*

"I'll stay here," she said. In the training camp, Janus had repeatedly impressed on her the importance of senior officers not leading from the front. "Cyte, go back to Abby and tell her to send me up a dozen runners. She's to take the Girls' Own over the ridge and push that skirmish line back, right over the top of the hill if she can." She pointed to the road, which emerged from the woods at the north end of the rocky ridge and crossed the open space toward Gilphaite. "The Sixth Division should deploy astride the road, with the rest of the Second behind. Push forward to a mile or so from their line." That would be extreme range for the Borelgai guns.

"Sir!" Cyte saluted and vanished into the underbrush. Winter turned to Erdine.

"Colonel, you've done well. As soon as Abby gets in place, pull your men back and get them re-formed. Then ride around the north end of the enemy line, past the hill. The map says there's another road there, heading for the coast. Get sight of it if you can and tell me if anything starts moving in either direction."

"Of course, sir." Erdine saluted, then swept off his hat and bowed. Winter rolled her eyes as he turned away and went back to her spyglass.

A quarter of an hour passed, and the skirmishers in the valley kept up their long-range dispute. A rustle in the brush behind Winter turned into a loose column from the Girls' Own, muskets shouldered as they pressed through the undergrowth. One of them shouted at the sight of Winter, and they all saluted

as they went past. Winter acknowledged them with a nod, and found Abby
bringing up the rear, as usual preferring to stay on foot.

"Sir," Abby said, gesturing to a small crowd of young women who came
up behind her. "The messengers you wanted."

"Thanks," Winter said. She waved at the panorama. "What do you think?"

Abby frowned momentarily. "I think they'd better have something up their
sleeves, or else we're going to be presenting those guns to Janus by sundown."

Winter smiled. "Go and get them. But don't push too hard if it turns out
not to be that easy. I'll send Ibsly in behind you."

"Tell him to hurry up, or there won't be anything left for him to do," Abby
said, and followed her soldiers, crashing down through the underbrush.

Winter looked over her messengers. Most of them were *very* young—some
of the girls couldn't be older than fourteen or fifteen. The Girls' Own's policy
of accepting recruits without asking too many questions meant they got their
share of women who weren't big enough to handle a long-barreled musket, but
Abby had become good at finding uses for everyone. Fear and determination
looked back at Winter from every face, along with quite a bit of acne.

"Form a queue," she told them. "Whoever's at the front, start running as
soon as I've finished the message, no questions. Understand?"

They choroused assent and set to organizing themselves. Commanding a
battle like this, watching from a distant vantage point, was a new experience for
Winter. She'd always been down in the action, close enough to smell the powder
smoke and hear the whine of bullets. Two divisions was too big a force to control
that way, though, and she forced herself to ignore the tiny voice at the back of
her mind that told her staying at such a far remove seemed cowardly.

It's not your job to risk your life, Janus had told her. *That's what the rankers are there
for. I know that sounds callous, but it's an inevitable truth. Think of it like this—there's
nine thousand of them and only one division-general. You have to be able to see the battle
as a whole and be the calm voice when everything goes to hell.*

The Girls' Own pushed out of the woods, across the flat ground. They
formed a "line" only in the loosest sense, operating in pairs separated by ten or
twenty yards, so they covered a very broad front. Erdine's horsemen were with-
drawing in good order, returning to their mounts and forming up in the rear,
while the Girls' Own walked past them and took up the fight with the Borelgai
skirmishers on the hill. One woman in each pair would drop to one knee, aim,
and fire, and then reload while the other repeated the procedure.

Unlike Erdine, Abby wasn't content to bang away at long range. Her small units leapfrogged from cover to cover, keeping up a steady fire as they advanced. The closer they got, the more accurate their fire became, and red-coated figures on the hill began to fall. The return fire grew more dangerous as well, of course, and the Borels had the advantage of height. Blue-uniformed bodies dribbled out behind the advance, some lying still, others walking or crawling to the rear. Casualty teams, made up of more of the girls too young to shoulder a weapon, rushed from place to place, leaving some where they'd fallen and hoisting others up for removal to safety.

From this distance, Winter thought, it looked like war as she'd always pictured it before her arrival in Khandar. The sky was a brilliant blue, and a light breeze slowly shredded the clouds of drifting smoke. The battlefield looked like a painting or a woodcut in a broadsheet. The screams of the dying, the smell of powder and shit and blood, none of it reached her up here. It felt a little like being a god looking down on hapless, warring mortals.

The Borelgai skirmishers were retreating as the pressure mounted, abandoning their cover and pulling back up the slope. A hundred yards in front of the line of guns, they stopped, and the firefight became deadlier as the two sides came together. Then, all at once, the crest of the hill was swarming with red uniforms, hundreds more men, coming up from hidden positions on the reverse slope.

The Borel commander didn't fancy losing his guns after all. Now it was Abby's turn to fall back, the distant musket shots merging into a steady roar like slowly rising applause. Blue and red were both dropping at a steady rate, mingled on the slope that the Girls' Own was grudgingly yielding to their opponents. Winter turned to her runners.

"Find Ibsly and tell him to go in," she said. "Sevran and the rest of the Second halt outside of cannon-shot and wait for orders."

"Sir!" A gangly teenaged girl saluted and took off down the slope, arms windmilling wildly. Somewhere at the base of the hill, Abby would have left a string of horses, but even at a gallop it would still take minutes before Ibsly received the orders and longer before he could act on them. Winter wished she had one of Janus' flik-fliks, to flash her words instantly across the field, but trained signalmen were still too few for them to be widely available. *It wouldn't help Ibsly march any faster anyway.*

Fortunately, the Borelgai didn't press on past the base of the hill, and the situation stabilized into another long-range exchange of potshots. Cyte returned from her errand, out of breath, and took a seat on the rock beside Winter, who handed her the spyglass.

"Abby's showing admirable restraint," Winter said.

Cyte nodded, shifting the lens to the north. "Here comes Ibsly."

Winter shaded her eyes—the sun was starting to slip down to the west, in the direction of the Borelgai position—and saw the long blue lines swinging out from around the edge of the woods, flags at the head of each battalion snapping in the breeze. Another disadvantage of watching the battle from afar, she reflected. What seemed to go quickly when you were in the thick of it took ages; it was like watching ants wander across a tabletop. It was nearly half an hour before Ibsly had gathered his battalions into combat formations and sent them forward, while the Second Division deployed behind him.

The Borelgai guns on the hill opened fire. Until now they'd been silent, the cannoneers huddling in the shelter of their pieces as they waited for a target more promising than a cloud of skirmishers to present itself. Now they'd found one, and they went after it with everything they had, each half battery firing in a one-two-three blast like a truncated drumroll. The flash and smoke went off in eerie silence, with the dull boom of the shot arriving four or five seconds later. Winter could see the spray of grass and dirt where the cannonballs struck the ground, rebounding into the air to land in another spray and then another, like rocks skipped across the surface of a pond. At this range, most of the shots were wild, but when one of those skips intersected a formation, the ball tore through everything in its path.

Each of the Sixth Division's eight battalions was formed in a column of companies: the first company, deployed in a line forty men wide and three deep, was followed after an interval of open ground by the second company, then the third, and so on, making a fat "column" that was really more of a rectangle. A column like that was relatively quick and maneuverable, able to snake around obstacles, but obviously only the first company in line could shoot effectively, drastically reducing the battalion's firepower. It also made them excellent targets for the descending fire of the cannons. Winter winced as one of the guns scored a direct hit, landing its ball right in front of one of the columns so it bounced through the ranks, sending broken bodies pinwheeling away from its path. The formation closed up around the wound, leaving men to lie still or thrash feebly in its wake, like a vast beast dripping blue blood.

Devastating as hits like that were, they weren't going to be enough. The blue columns swallowed cannonballs like the sea and kept on coming. The Girls' Own skirmishers were pushing forward again, too, and once more the Borelgai fell back, sniping at the columns as they went but not willing to stand against the formed division's concentrated firepower. As the Sixth reached the bottom of the hill, the artillerymen switched to canister, great tin cans full of musket balls that made the cannons into giant shotguns. They sprayed into the leading companies with deadly effect, men falling in clumps and rows, and still the columns came on.

"There they go," Cyte said, peering through the spyglass.

She handed it back to Winter, who trained it on the cannons. The Girls' Own skirmishers had pushed forward, keeping ahead of the Sixth's columns, and as they came into musket range of the guns, the cannoneers started dropping. The teams fired one last round of canister, witheringly effective at a hundred and fifty yards, and then fled, falling back amid their own skirmishers over the top of the hill. A few of Abby's most daring women followed them, out of Winter's line of sight. Soon after, a couple of them came running back, and Winter saw them heading for the knot of riders that had to be General Ibsly and his staff.

"They've got something on the other side of the hill," Winter said.

She swept the glass past the now-silent guns, squinting as though she could change the contours of the earth by will alone. Whatever information the skirmishers had passed on had caused a flurry of activity, and soon the columns came to a halt. They began to maneuver, companies peeling out to either side to deploy from column into line.

The Borelgai seemed to appear between blinks, as though they'd sprung out of the earth. One moment the hill was empty, and the next it was packed solid with soldiers, standing shoulder to shoulder, stepping with absolute precision to the beat of an inaudible drum. At least four battalion flags were visible, four thousand men in a neat line moving at the double. They came over the crest and down the hill, toward Ibsly's still-deploying soldiers.

"Balls of the *fucking* Beast!" Winter had risen to her feet before she realized she'd moved, grinding the glass against her eye socket so hard it hurt. Her godlike detachment was gone, replaced with a terrible helplessness. She could see what was about to happen, but nothing she could do from here would make the slightest difference. Cyte took a shocked breath.

Scattered fire broke out among the Vordanai, mostly from the Girls' Own, who were falling back from the unexpected threat. At fifty yards, the red line halted, and the men brought their muskets to their shoulders. The battalions of the Sixth, still half-formed, started to open fire, but their scattered shots were drowned under the crash of a single, concentrated volley from the enemy. It lit up the field like a flash of lightning, and the sound that reached Winter was like a wave crashing against a beach. Men fell up and down the line, staggering forward or slumping against their neighbors. At this distance, Winter couldn't hear the screams, but her mind supplied them all the same.

Half a minute to reload as Ibsly's shattered formations returned fire as best they could. Some kept trying to form a line, while others dissolved into rough blobs, men instinctively huddling together as the smoke of the Borelgai volley rolled over them. The second volley slammed out, visible mostly by the muzzle flashes through the murk, and then the third.

Nothing, in Winter's experience, broke down morale faster than being in a patently unequal fight. Ibsly's men outnumbered the Borels two to one, but having been caught with their formation in disarray, they were taking far worse than they delivered, and they knew it. Between the third volley and the fourth, a trickle of blue-uniformed soldiers appeared out of the smoke, heading determinedly for the rear, and after the fourth it became a flood. Winter could see Ibsly shouting and waving his sword, but there was no stopping the rout. The men of the Sixth Division poured back down the hill, past the bodies of their comrades, away from the killing fire at their backs.

"Saints and martyrs," Winter swore. She turned to the runners, who were watching her with wide, frightened eyes. "Come on. We're going down there."

"I will make another attack," Division-General Ibsly said to Winter. He brought his hand to his face, to fiddle with his spectacles, but he'd lost them during the fighting. Instead he tugged at the fresh bandage wrapped around his head, where a musket ball had scored a glancing blow. "We have the numbers, and they won't catch us off guard again."

"We have the numbers, assuming they haven't been reinforced," Sevran said. "If they sent riders to Dorsay's main body, he could have more men on the way. We took our chance, and it didn't work."

"My regiment hasn't fired a shot," de Koste protested. "General, the Sixth can stay in reserve, and the Second Division can make the next assault."

"We don't need to keep throwing good money after bad," Blackstream said. "If we can't push them off the hill, we can maneuver them off. If we slide around their left . . ."

He looked to Erdine for support, and the cavalry colonel nodded. "My men report the road north of the hill is empty except for cavalry patrols. If we go around their position and come at them down the north–south road, we won't have so much open ground to cover."

"Enough," Winter said. "General Ibsly, please speak to your colonels and ask them if their regiments will be able to make a second attack. Gentlemen of the Second, get your men ready to march. Bobby, Cyte, with me for a moment."

There was a round of salutes, and the knot of officers broke up. Ibsly was limping a little as well, Winter noted. The air was full of noise—frightened horses, and running soldiers, but the screams most of all. The regimental cutters had set up a battlefield-aid station and were plying their trade on those wounded who'd been fortunate enough to be able to walk to the rear. Winter had to stop and close her eyes for a moment as a woman's sobbing rose to a high, terrified shriek, which was abruptly stifled, as though someone had stuffed her mouth with rags.

"If you have any advice," Winter said, taking deep breaths, "I'd like to hear it."

"You know I'm no expert on tactics," Bobby said, glancing up at the gun-crowned height. The Borelgai had retreated over the crest again, but the presence of those massed ranks lingered as a looming shadow. "But I sure as hell wouldn't want to go up that hill."

"What about Blackstream's idea?" Cyte said. "Janus always avoids frontal attacks against strong positions if he can help it."

"We don't have *time*." Winter looked up at the sun, which was well past the meridian. "Marcus has started his attack, and Fitz's column will arrive soon. That means before too much longer the entire Borelgai army is going to be coming north over that bridge and up that road. If we can take this end and bottle them up on the bridge, that's one thing, but it'd take hours to go around. If we deploy in open country we're just asking Dorsay to roll over us with everything he's got. If we don't go in now, we're not going at all."

"Then that's the choice," Bobby said. "Go in now with what we have, or not at all."

Winter nodded, looking up at the hill. "Four battalions. We have the numbers. Three or four to one."

"But they have the guns," Cyte said. "And the position. That was a hell of a trick, staying out of sight and getting to the ridge just at the right time. Someone over there knows what he's doing."

Winter looked between them. Her chest felt tight. *This is what being a general means, isn't it?* Not just command of more soldiers. *Making decisions with nobody to look over your shoulder.* At that moment she would happily have traded it all for a musket and slunk back into the ranks.

"We have to go in," she said, so quietly Bobby and Cyte leaned forward. "Janus is counting on us to be at that bridge. I haven't disappointed him yet."

"Right," Cyte said after a long pause. "So we go in. Just the Second?"

"Everyone," Winter said. "Like Bobby said, this is the only shot we have left."

"But—" Cyte said.

"I know it's a risk," Winter said. "But coming out here at all was a gamble, and we need to make sure it pays off."

Cyte shook her head. "We need *some* kind of reserve, in case things go wrong."

"Keep the Girls' Own here," Bobby suggested. "They're worn out as it is."

"Fair enough," Winter said. "Bobby, find Abby and tell her to set up a line here. I'll be going forward with the attack."

"Well *behind* the attack," Cyte said. She lowered her voice. "You know better than anyone else here that Janus can't afford to lose you."

"Fine." Winter touched the sword at her belt, which she'd yet to unsheathe. It made *sense*, but . . . "Let's get moving. We're burning daylight."

Seven regiments—fourteen battalions—went forward, leaving only the thin skirmish line behind them. The men of the Sixth Division, halted in their flight and assembled back into their units, were on the left, with the Second Division on the right. Flags snapped and fluttered, the silver caps of their poles gleaming in the yellowing light of late afternoon. Off to the left, where the hill hid the town of Gilphaite from view, the distant rumble of artillery had reached a new pitch of urgency. Things were approaching a crescendo there. *We have to finish this.*

Winter sat astride Edgar, with Cyte on one side, Bobby on the other, and three messengers from the Girls' Own trailing behind. They were twenty or thirty yards behind the rear companies, which might keep them out of musket range but mattered little against the cannons. No cannoneer worth his salt would waste a ball on a tiny cluster of horsemen, Winter hoped, but at long range the guns were not noted for their accuracy anyway.

The first round of flashes rippled across the hill. To Winter's astonishment, she found she could *see* the ball in flight, a tiny black spot that seemed to hang in the air above the battlefield. Then, all at once, it crashed like a thunderbolt, lancing into the turf a good ten yards behind one of Sevran's battalions and springing into the air again with an explosion of dirt. The drums beat a steady pace, and the men once again advanced through the hail of solid shot, closing their ranks as balls swept them away in bunches.

This time Winter had ordered that they deploy at the bottom of the hill, outside of canister range. It would slow the advance, giving the guns more time to work, but it meant they wouldn't be taken unawares when the Borelgai emerged from hiding. Determined to show they knew what they were about, the men of Ibsly's division executed the maneuver as precisely as though they were on a parade ground, in spite of the cannonballs falling and bouncing around them. One of Blackstream's battalions was thrown into momentary confusion when a lucky shot landed just in the middle of its leading company, and its standard fluttered and fell. It was soon snatched up again, though, and sergeants shouted the men into line, now part of a continuous front more than a mile from end to end.

"You ride to Ibsly," Winter said to one of the messengers, shouting to be heard over the boom and shriek of the guns. "Tell him to go up that hill and take those guns, and not to stop until he gets to the road! You"—she pointed to the next—"tell Sevran the same, and that he's to conform to Ibsly. Go!"

They galloped off. A few minutes later, as the cannonballs continued to thunder down, the drums trilled and then settled into a steady pace. The line moved forward with a cheer, one step for each drumbeat. Winter, glancing at Cyte, gave them a few minutes to get safely ahead of her before nudging Edgar into a slow walk.

As before, the gunners switched to canister as the Vordanai closed, though the sprays of musket balls were less deadly against the long, linear formation than they had been against the columns. Still, swaths of men were cut down, and each battalion shrank toward its center as officers closed the files. The ground over which Winter rode was littered with corpses, a few Borelgai skirmishers in muddy red uniforms with black trim, but mostly Vordanai blue, men from Ibsly's division and women from the Girls' Own. Here and there, wounded soldiers waved or shouted to her, their voices inaudible under the roar of battle.

With no skirmishers out front, the cannoneers waited until the last minute to abandon their pieces, firing a load of double canister at fifty yards with fearful results. One half battery cut things a little too fine, and one of Ibsly's battalions fired a volley that dropped a dozen of the artillerymen as they scrambled backward. With a cheer, the two divisions kept on, driving the enemy skirmishers in front of them.

Winter kept her eyes on the crest of the hill, waiting for the enemy infantry to appear. She felt like she could predict the precise moment they'd show themselves, leaving just enough time to get onto the forward slope before coming into range. Sure enough, just as she thought, *now*, red flags poked over the hill, followed quickly by a glittering hedge of muskets with bayonets fixed.

Too many flags. One, two, four, six, a full dozen. The Borelgai line was nearly as long as their own. *We were supposed to have the numbers here.* They came down the hill as if driven by clockwork, ten paces past the crest, then halted to raise their muskets. *Where the hell did they all come from?*

"Winter!" Cyte was shouting something, but Winter couldn't tear her eyes away from the enemy.

This time, Ibsly was determined to get his shot in. His division halted, drums relaying commands, and the men raised their weapons. "Ready," the sergeants would shout, echoing up and down the line. "Level! Fire!" The crackle of musketry ran up and down each battalion, like a spark racing along a fuse, off-white powder smoke spewing from the barrel and lock of every weapon. The crash of it set Winter's ears ringing. Up the slope, Borelgai were falling, bodies pitching forward and rolling down the hill or dropping in their tracks.

"Winter!" Cyte grabbed her arm. Winter blinked and turned to her.

"What?" Her voice sounded distant in her own abused ears.

"There's too many!" Cyte said. "They must have reinforced!"

Winter nodded dumbly.

"We have to pull back!" Cyte shouted.

The Borelgai fired, a simultaneous volley from a dozen battalions. Men in blue uniforms were punched off their feet, or stumbled and clutched at a wound, or collapsed into the man next to them. Screams were faintly audible for a moment, and then were obliterated by the return volley, a wall of noise and smoke.

She's right. There was no way they'd win this fight, uphill against a fresh enemy in triple the strength they'd expected. Winter turned, mouth feeling like it was full of dry cotton, and looked for a messenger.

"Tell Ibsly to fall back!" she shouted. "Fall back to where we started! Go!"

The girl spurred her horse, riding toward the fight and the mounted general. She was nearly there when the third Borelgai volley slammed out, almost as neat as the first. The lines were difficult to make out in the rising haze of smoke, but Winter saw the messenger girl twist in the saddle, then slide off her horse, one foot still caught in the stirrup as her body hit the ground.

Fuck. "Bobby!" Winter shouted desperately. *Saints and martyrs.* "Go to Ibsly now!" *It's going to be a massacre—*

The Borelgai charged with a roar, bayonets fixed, emerging from the cloud their own volleys had created trailing little wisps of powder smoke. Fire stabbed back at them from the Vordanai line, dropping men up and down the front rank, but it wasn't enough. Ibsly's men broke first, their line dissolving into a rearward flood before the wave of bayonets reached them. Panic was contagious. Each man, however brave he might be alone, saw his neighbor turn away and decided he should do the same, lest he be standing by himself when the hammer fell. Soon it had spread to the Second Division as well, Blackstream's men and de Koste's and even Sevran's veterans. The entire line became a mass of running, shouting men. Anyone who tripped or hesitated was swallowed up by the onrushing wave of red.

What do I do? Winter's hand went to her sword. *What would Janus do?* "I should rally them. We can form—"

"Much too late for that," Cyte said. She looked at Bobby, who nodded grimly and grabbed Edgar's reins. Bobby yanked the gelding around and kicked her own horse into a gallop, pulling the stunned Winter along with her.

It was the Girls' Own who stopped the Borelgai counterattack.

It had nearly run out of momentum in any case, units becoming disordered and mixed together as they charged off the hill and across the flats. Abby, seeing the wave coming, set her skirmishers in a fighting withdrawal, forcing the Borelgai to halt and return fire. The Girls' Own pulled back to the woods, losing soldiers at every step until they'd reached the comparative safety of the tree line. From there, they prepared to resist another advance, but the Borelgai commander apparently considered his work well done, and his units withdrew across the field to their starting positions.

There was no question of a third attack. The fleeing men of both divisions had mostly headed for the woods as well, and the long ridge was thick with bewildered, disorganized soldiers. Sorting them back out into their units would take days.

In any event, it was too late. Winter returned numbly to her perch on the rock, and through her spyglass she saw heavy clouds of dust rising from behind the hill that had seemed so near just a few hours ago. One of Erdine's cavalry came up to report that long columns of red-coated infantry were filing past, along with an enormous train of wagons. Dorsay's army was pulling out in good order.

There was nothing to do but try to help the wounded and collect the dead. Small teams ventured onto the field, well within range of the Borelgai cannon, but the enemy made no move to harass them. They came back with those they thought they could save, and the cutters went to work. Once again the bone saws sang, and the pile of hacked-off limbs outside the medical tents grew ever larger.

As darkness gathered, they worked by torchlight. Just after sunset, there was a deep, reverberant *boom* from the direction of Gilphaite, as though a dozen cannon had fired at once, and then a rising tower of smoke. It took Winter a moment to understand what had happened. The Borelgai had blown up the bridge behind the last of their troops, putting the Ytolin between themselves and any possibility of pursuit.

Duke Dorsay had escaped from Janus' trap.

Chapter Four

MARCUS

"I offer my apologies, sir," Ihernglass said. His back was as straight as a musket barrel. "And my resignation, if you want it."

Marcus recognized his expression. It was one he'd worn himself, the look of a man who expected punishment but no longer cared, because what he was doing to himself was worse than anything his superiors could inflict.

Carefully, he glanced at Janus. The First Consul was unpredictable; for the most part, he accepted bad news phlegmatically, but on very rare occasions his temper could flare spectacularly when he was thwarted. In the tunnels under Ashe-Katarion, when Janus thought he'd lost the Thousand Names, Marcus had been forced to restrain him from ordering a helpless old woman hacked to pieces on the spot.

There was no sign of that volcanic rage now, though. Janus shook his head slightly and tapped one finger on his worktable.

"Resignation?" he said. "Don't be silly. I am not the Directory, sending any commander who fails in his objective to the Spike." He sighed. "In all honesty, the fault was mine. The Duke of Brookspring is cannier than I gave him credit for."

"He certainly knows how to conduct a retreat," Marcus said. He remembered that from the War of the Princes, where the Vordanai army had struggled for weeks to bring Dorsay to battle, only to fall neatly into his trap at Vansfeldt.

"Thank you, sir," Ihernglass said. "But it was my command. The fault is mine."

"I'd rather not split hairs over it," Janus said. "Just know that you will get no reproaches from *me*. Nor will you ever for attempting to execute a task to the best of your ability."

"Thank you, sir." Ihernglass' expression softened a little, but he still looked exhausted.

"See to your division. I'll need a detailed strength report once you can make a count."

"Yes, sir."

Ihernglass saluted, turned, and left the command tent. Janus glanced up at Marcus.

"What do you think?"

Marcus scratched his beard. "Ihernglass is a good officer. It would have been easy to put the blame for everything on Ibsly, but he didn't even try."

"Indeed."

Ibsly, conveniently, was no longer around to defend himself. He'd fallen during the rout, shot down while attempting to rally his men, along with two of his four colonels. Casualties in both divisions had been high, but the Sixth was badly shattered, while the Second had mostly reconstituted itself by the time the rest of the army had made the roundabout upriver march to circumvent the shattered bridge.

"Winter Ihernglass has been something of a special project of mine, for a variety of reasons," Janus said.

"Because he's got that . . . thing inside him?" Marcus glanced around and lowered his voice. "The demon-eater?"

"In part. But also because I believe he has potential. I worry I have brought him too far, too fast." Janus stared pensively at the tent flap. "I hope he will recover from this. The ability to absorb defeats is as vital a skill in a leader as temperance after victory." Janus leaned back in his chair and looked at Marcus. "The next time someone suggests I am infallible, remind them that I appointed General Ibsly."

"I didn't know him well, but he seemed competent."

"He was. But competence is not the same as temperament." Janus sighed. "If I could have a dozen copies of you, or Winter Ihernglass, or Fitz Warus, to lead all of my divisions, my life would be greatly simplified. But, alas, we must make do with what we have. Sometimes leadership forges men hard, and sometimes it reveals the dross."

"Thank you for your trust, sir," Marcus said, grinning.

"Please. My trust in you is one of the bedrocks underneath this army." He gestured at the chair Winter had spurned, across the table from him. "Sit. You once accused me of keeping things to myself too long, and let it never be said I refused to welcome valid criticism."

He unrolled a parchment map, a large-scale one that covered most of western Murnsk. The river Ytolin was near the bottom, with Gilphaite—too small to be noted in the legend—marked out in pencil. Janus traced the jagged line of the Votindri Range north with his finger, then tapped a tiny stylized tower.

"Elysium," he said. "The untaken fortress of the Sworn Church. Not much of a fortress, in truth, but its greatest shield has always been hundreds of miles of Murnsk in every direction. Not good country for an overland march."

"That's putting it lightly," Marcus muttered. He checked the scale and reckoned distances. "Four hundred and some miles, as the crow flies." On the way from Antova to Vordan, the Army of the East had covered prodigious distances, marching faster than perhaps any army ever had; some days they'd covered close to thirty miles. *With good roads, and all the heavy gear traveling mostly by river.* Moving over the notoriously terrible Murnskai roads, dragging guns and supplies behind them, wouldn't be anywhere near as quick. "Call it ten miles a day and be generous. That's a month and a half just to *get* there, even without anyone trying to stop us."

"A month and a half would be excellent time," Janus said. He ran his finger along a thin black line, paralleling the mountains north before swinging east to slip through the passes toward the edge of the map. A spur reached up to connect to Elysium. "The Pilgrim's Road is barely a track in most places, and every spring flood takes a toll on it. A more conventional approach would be to advance along the coast." His finger moved west, to where another road ran along the edge of the sea, connecting the cities that clung to the mouths of Murnsk's rivers. "If we could capture Salavask, for example, we could ascend the river Kovria to within a hundred miles of Elysium, with our lines of supply secure."

"It would take too long," Marcus said. "We'd have to winter in Salavask and attack Elysium next year."

"And I have no desire to spend a winter in Murnsk," Janus said. "In any event, the Borelgai fleet controls the Borel Sea, and they can land troops anywhere on the Split Coast. Moving west would play right into their hands."

"Is that why Dorsay is pulling back to Yatterny?" The port city was at the mouth of the Ytolin, well to the west of Gilphaite. The Duke of Brookspring showed no sign of making a stand anywhere short of its walls. "You think he wants you to follow?"

"Primarily, I imagine he is eager to find a secure position with an easy retreat," Janus said, a touch of contempt in his tone. "But yes, I'm sure he would be delighted if I came after him. A siege somewhere his fleet can resupply him would be just to his taste." He shook his head and shifted his finger back to the east. "No. We will stay as far from the sea as we can. Washed-out or not, the Pilgrim's Road is the best path. We'll leave two divisions behind, to keep an eye on Dorsay and secure our line of supply to the south bank of the Ytolin. The rest of the army will follow the northern branch east to Vantzolk, then north to Tsivny and the Norilia crossing."

"What if Dorsay pushes hard and tries to cut in behind us?"

"He won't. That would give us a chance to cut him off from the sea, and he doesn't dare risk it. No, I expect he'll shadow us north along the coast and wait for his chance like a vulture. I am more concerned about the emperor."

"We haven't seen much of the Murnskai other than local garrisons."

"Our reports say the emperor has dispatched his forces from Mohkba." Janus tapped the Murnskai capital, well to the east of the mountains. "A huge army, perhaps a hundred and fifty thousand strong if rumors are to be believed. He will come south to defend Elysium. He has no choice—an emperor who lets a foreign army sack the holy city will not be emperor for long. Somewhere between Tsivny and the Kovria, he will make a stand."

"You think we can beat him?" Marcus said.

"I expect so," Janus said with a nonchalant shrug. "It depends who is in command, of course, but neither the emperor nor his sons are noted for their military talent. The Murnskai army is designed to keep the emperor's dominions under his control, and it is not well suited to producing great minds. But we will surmount that difficulty when we come to it." He laid his hands on the table. "We march for Vantzolk, Column-General. Please prepare the army to depart in the morning. I will send instructions for our supply lines to be shifted east, through Gium, and for a depot to be built at Vantzolk. We must bring as much forward as we can."

"Yes, sir." Marcus stood. "Any special instructions?"

"We will send out flying columns, escorted by cavalry," Janus said. "No undue looting or unnecessary violence, please, but I want you to gather every horse, ox, and mule within a hundred miles of the river, along with everything with wheels. Transportation is going to be a problem as we push north, and we had best be prepared. Draw up a rota to make sure the various regiments share the duty."

"Of course, sir."

Marcus smiled inwardly. *No* undue *looting.* Janus was, above all else, practical. Soldiers were soldiers, after all, and it was highly unlikely that they could be sent to gather horses and carts without picking up the odd ham or bottle of wine along the way. It was easier just to put up with it, while making it clear that wholesale pillage and murder would be punished. The "duty" that had to be shared would undoubtedly be a privilege the regiments would fight for. Once again, he was impressed at his commander's understanding of the common soldier.

"One more thing."

"Sir?"

Janus frowned and tapped his finger on the table. "I would like you to talk to the queen."

"You want me to deliver a message?"

"Not exactly. I have urged her to return to Vordan, but she refuses. She seems to have become somewhat . . . suspicious of me. But I believe you still have her trust. If there's anything you can do to convince her to remain behind . . ."

"I can try." Marcus grimaced. "She may trust me, but my record of getting Raesinia to stay behind where it's safe isn't a strong one. She's awfully hard to shift when her mind is made up."

"I'm aware of that," Janus said. "Make the attempt. If you can't convince her, I won't hold it against you."

"Understood, sir."

Marcus saluted and left the tent. Outside, a pair of corporals from the Colonials guarded the door. A bit farther away, squatting in the dirt, Lieutenant Andria Dracht and three young rankers were staring intently at an upside-down tin bowl.

"All right, who's in for three bits?" Andy said. "Come on, my *grandmother* would go to three bits, and she's been dead for years." Coins clinked against the bowl, and she grinned. "There we go. Four bits? *Thank* you. Who wants to go to an eagle? Who wants to play with the big boys? Come on, come on, what are you going to spend it on? Right. Anyone going to two? You're a bunch of cheapskates, you know that?" She faced the tallest of the three boys. "So, what do you want?"

"Low," he said, shifting nervously.

"Low it is. Does low feel lucky?" Andy swept the bowl off the ground to reveal a pair of dice. After a moment of silence, the three boys groaned, and she grinned even wider. "No it does not!"

She swept the coins off the ground with a practiced motion and bounced to her feet. The three soldiers rose, too.

"Well, gentlemen," Andy said, "it's been entertaining, but—"

"Go another round!" one of them said.

"Yeah," said another. "You have to give us a chance to win some of it back."

"I don't think that's a good idea," Andy said.

"Another round," said the tallest. "Get down and roll the dice. *Now.*" He reached out to grab Andy's arm, and Marcus cleared his throat.

"Lieutenant?" he said.

"Ah." Andy straightened up and gave a sloppy salute. "Hello, Column-General."

"Don't think you're going to fool me with *that*—" The tall ranker turned, saw Marcus, and went pale as a bedsheet. He saluted so hard Marcus winced. "Column-General! Sir!"

"Thank you, Ranker," Marcus said. "Lieutenant, with me, if you please?"

They walked away, leaving the young men behind.

"It's not considered seemly for officers to take money from rankers," Marcus said.

Andy fingered the lieutenant's stripe on her shoulder and made a face. "It's not like I was *cheating*," she said. "Not much, anyway. It's not my fault they don't know how to figure odds. And I hope you don't think you did me a favor there. You know I can take care of myself."

"Of course," Marcus said. "I was more worried you'd crack that boy's skull and I'd end up explaining it to Janus."

"Oh," Andy said. "I guess that's possible. He should learn to keep his hands to himself." She patted her pockets, satisfied at the jingle.

Marcus shook his head but said nothing. Andy had been put under his command back in Vordan City, when he'd been trying to keep Raesinia safe as she raced around incognito. He'd been hesitant about the idea of a girl ranker, but she'd proven herself quick-witted and a competent brawler, if somewhat lacking in military decorum. By the time Janus had brought him back to field command in the Grand Army, she'd been at his side so long her presence felt natural, and she continued to serve as a sort of combination messenger and bodyguard. *It's amazing what we can get used to.*

"So, what did Janus have to say?" Andy said.

"We march in the morning."

Marcus paused at the intersection of two broad aisles through the endless sea of tents that was the Grand Army's camp. The surveyors did their best to keep the layout the same wherever they stopped, but it was still easy to get lost if you weren't careful. Andy pointed, and they turned left, toward Marcus' tent.

The thought that all of this would be taken down in the morning, only to be reassembled the next night, still made Marcus shake his head in wonder. It was as though Janus had proposed carrying Vordan's Sworn Cathedral to the sea, stone by stone, while putting it together every day in time for services. Just keeping a hundred thousand men under canvas, let alone fed, clothed, and supplied with ammunition, required effort on a scale that boggled the mind. Somewhere far to the south, hardtack was being baked and crated for shipment to the Ministry of War, to make its way via a complex chain of boats and wagons to the depots in Talbonn, and thence via supply convoy to the Grand Army. Marcus' position made him uncomfortably aware that everything from the food he ate to the boots on his feet were available only thanks to the nonstop efforts of hundreds of clerks and porters, often months in advance.

Fortunately, his position didn't require him to actually *do* anything about it, other than occasionally sign off on reports regarding the level of stores available. While the men had been drilling, Janus had spent much of the winter reorganizing the Ministry of War, cleaning out the deadwood with his new powers as First Consul and bringing in young, intelligent men and women without regard to their former background. Marcus, accustomed to fighting the Ministry to replace every worn-out greatcoat, had been astounded by the ease with which the new system functioned, a rusted-out hinge replaced with a sleek, oiled one.

It helped, of course, that the Crown was flush with gold. After Hamvelt's intention to bow out of the war had become clear, the smaller cities of the Velt Valley and in the south around Desland had wasted no time in coming to their own accommodation with Vordan. Janus had been openhanded with them, but had insisted on generous "contributions" from town councils and wealthy individuals, while paying for the army's purchases with the new paper scrip, redeemable at the end of the war. Somewhere in the palace at Ohnlei, Raesinia's young friend Cora was working away trying to keep it all straight. Marcus was grateful, inasmuch as he would rather have his eyes put out with hot pokers than deal with the complexities of army finance.

His tent was a large one, by the standards of the army, big enough for four or five men to stand comfortably around a folding table. Currently, there was only one. Colonel Alek Giforte looked up, saluted briefly, and went back to whatever he was scribbling.

He was older than Marcus, with graying hair and a short beard shot through with silver. Marcus had first known him as Vice Captain of Armsmen, when he'd been made Captain of that organization during Janus' term as the Minister of Justice. Giforte had turned out to be both an excellent administrator and a spy for the Last Duke; that Janus had chosen to overlook the latter and retain Giforte for the former was typical of the man. Being a column-general involved sending out quite a lot of orders, and Giforte's job was to translate Janus and Marcus' general instructions into specific directions and timetables, a task he attacked with vigor.

"How'd it go?" Giforte said.

"We march in the morning," Marcus said, then gave a brief summary of what Janus had told him. Giforte frowned when he got to the part about flying columns to gather horses and carts. In spite of his change of career, the colonel was at heart an enforcer of the law.

"Two divisions left behind," he said, when Marcus was done. "The Sixth, obviously. Did Janus specify the other?"

Marcus shook his head. "Suggestions?"

"The Tenth, I think. Division-General Beaumartin is a bit plodding, but he's determined. A good man to have in command if Dorsay does something unexpected."

"Fair enough."

Giforte stood up. "I'll get the boys started drafting everything. Will you be here in an hour to sign off?"

"The boys" were a tent full of young soldiers with maps, dividers, and endless stacks of paper. They were technically the column-general's staff, although Marcus often felt like they were really Giforte's staff, which was being temporarily loaned to him. In some cases that was almost literally true—he knew Giforte had recruited among the old Armsmen to find his scribblers.

"I should be," Marcus said, then frowned. "Possibly not. I'd forgotten. Andy, will you go over to the queen's tent and tell her that Column-General d'Ivoire would like to see her as soon as possible?"

"Got it." Andy ducked out of the tent with no salute. Giforte rolled his eyes.

"You let her get away with too much," he said.

"*You* try making her do things properly," Marcus said, settling down by the table with a sigh. "Let me know how it works out for you."

"If she's going to represent you, she ought to be more respectful. She might offend someone important one day."

"She's friends with Raesinia, and Janus doesn't seem to mind," Marcus said. "I don't think people get more important than that."

Giforte shook his head, made his own salute, and slipped out. He'd never warmed to Andy, Marcus reflected. He wondered if it had anything to do with Giforte's own daughter, who was now a colonel in the Girls' Own. These days the two Gifortes seemed to be on speaking terms, but rumors said they hadn't always gotten along.

A small pile of papers was waiting for his attention. Giforte couldn't handle *everything*, although what Marcus had to deal with now was considerably less than he'd forced himself through as commander of the Colonials. He threw himself into it and had made solid progress by the time Giforte returned with a new stack of orders, ready to go out over Marcus' signature. Marcus checked them, for the look of the thing, and signed.

One stroke of a pen, he thought, *and the whole vast machine starts up.*

Andy returned soon after. The queen, she told him, would be pleased to dine with him that evening. Marcus sighed, put down his papers, and got up to look for a cleaner jacket.

"They tried, and losses were heavy, I'm told," Marcus said. "But Dorsay had reinforced the ridge with men pulled out of the town. They had to fall back, and the Borels demolished the bridge before we could get to them."

"It sounds like Dorsay knew what Janus was up to," Raesinia said.

Marcus shrugged. "It's possible he guessed the plan. In the end, he still had to retreat. Janus doesn't think he'll bother us before the Murnskai army arrives."

Raesinia pursed her lips. Before she could answer, a servant bustled in with plates full of thick green soup trailing tendrils of steam. Another servant poured wine, offering a glass to the queen and getting a nod of approval before coming around the table to Marcus.

The royal tent was surprisingly understated, though not quite spartan. There was a thick bedroll, a table and chairs, and the same army-issue portable writing desk that officers used. The tent itself looked like silk, but there were none of the rugs and tapestries Marcus might have expected, no fine china or gold-encrusted flatware. They ate off polished brass plates and drank from clay mugs that wouldn't have been out of place in a common winesink.

It was reflective, in a way, of what it was about Raesinia that made Marcus so uncomfortable. In the time they'd spent together in Vordan, she'd insisted on informality, and he'd come to enjoy her company in that context. Afterward, seeing her ensconced as queen in all her majesty and splendor, it had seemed clear that those days were over. He'd thrown himself into Janus' project of rebuilding the army and tried to put her out of his mind.

Now, though, he felt halfway between the two worlds. They weren't running through the streets together, breaking into Exchange Central or sneaking around Oldtown. But neither was she off at Ohnlei, surrounded by courtiers and all the rituals of the palace. Marcus felt like he was seeing double, flickering between his vision of the queen and the young woman he'd gotten to know; the monarch, and Raesinia, who'd come into his room one night and slashed open her palm to show him her secret. He wasn't sure how he was supposed to behave.

"Is Ihernglass all right?" Raesinia said. "He wasn't hurt?"

"He's not hurt," Marcus said carefully. "But . . ."

He looked down at his soup. Raesinia, eating hers, gestured for him to continue.

"It's a hard thing, to know that you gave orders and men died and that maybe they weren't the right orders. I think every commander goes through it, but that doesn't make it any easier." Marcus remembered Weltae and his last stand there with Adrecht Roston. He'd chosen to hold out and trust in Janus instead of retreating, and Adrecht and many others had paid the price. "I think he'll get through it, but it's never simple."

Raesinia nodded, eyes full of understanding. Marcus had to remind himself that, in spite of the fact that she could pass for a teenager, the queen had been through a great deal in the past year and was, in fact, nearly twenty-one.

"And now Janus wants to march straight to Elysium," she said, cleaning the bottom of her bowl and setting the spoon down. "What's your opinion on that?" She grinned, the impish smile he remembered from their time on the streets. "Speaking as a professional military man."

"I wouldn't be here if I didn't believe in Janus," Marcus said.

"What if you didn't know Janus?" Raesinia said. "Would you think it was possible? Farus VI invaded Murnsk, and the historians say it was his greatest mistake. And King Vetaraia lost his entire army in the snows and ended up in a cage."

Marcus took a bite of his own soup. It was really rather good, light and tasting of apples and herbs.

"At the War College," he said after a moment, "they used to say that Murnsk is defended by two invincible commanders, General January and General February. No southern army has ever conquered Murnsk because the emperor only has to await the arrival of these reinforcements. He can trade land for time, and Murnsk is a very large country."

He became aware of a servant hovering at his shoulder, waiting to serve the next course. Marcus leaned back, a little regretfully. Wolfing down his food in front of the queen wouldn't do, of course, but as a soldier he had a hard time letting any meal go unfinished.

"Fortunately," he went on, as they set a dish of sliced roast beef in front of Raesinia, "it is now April, and we're not here to conquer Murnsk, only Elysium. If the emperor chooses to bide his time, we'll be back in Vordan before General January takes the field. If he wants to fight, I have every confidence in the Grand Army."

Raesinia made a noncommittal sound as she chewed her beef. Marcus looked down at the plate in front of him, then back at the queen, and cleared his throat uncomfortably.

"Your Highness . . ." he began.

She held up a finger, swallowed, and took a sip of water. He paused.

"Let me guess," she said. "He hasn't had any success getting me to stay behind himself, so he's sent you to try asking."

Marcus deflated. "Something like that."

"For a tactical genius, he can be extremely predictable."

"The battlefield is no place for a queen," Marcus said. "You should be back in Vordan."

"My father spent quite a lot of time on battlefields," Raesinia shot back. "My brother died on one."

"And that was a catastrophe for the country," Marcus said. "If Prince Dominic had lived . . ."

He realized, too late, that this was an extremely awkward line of argument, and trailed off uncertainly. Raesinia frowned and made a gesture to the servant closest to her. As one, they bowed deeply and filed out of the tent.

"We both know," she said, keeping her voice low, "that getting killed is unlikely to be a problem in my case."

"The Black Priests have tried to kidnap you before," Marcus said. "How much easier will it be here, on their home ground?"

"I think the Black Priests have more to worry about, with Janus bearing down on them," Raesinia said. "Besides, where could I be safer than in the center of the Grand Army, with you, Janus, and Ihernglass close by?"

Marcus sighed. He wasn't going to make any progress here, that was certain. *Not that I really expected to.* "What is it that you want to accomplish? I hope you won't second-guess Janus on military matters."

"Not on military matters, no," Raesinia said. "But if he does defeat the emperor and Dorsay, then the shape of the continent might be decided by what happens afterward. *That* will be a political matter, and I will not be months away in Vordan when it happens."

It wasn't actually that unreasonable, Marcus thought as he tucked into his beef, especially if you knew the queen had nothing to fear from illness or stray bullets. That didn't go far toward settling his unease, though. *Janus is right. Raesinia doesn't trust him.* He glanced up at her, but she was looking down at her food in furious concentration.

They ate in silence for a time. After a decent interval, Marcus pushed back his plate and got to his feet.

"Your Majesty," he said. "I hope you'll excuse me. I have a great deal to do."

"Of course," Raesinia said, rising as well. "I was hoping . . ."

"Yes?"

"Would you have dinner with me again?" she said, a little too quickly. "Only when it wouldn't interfere with your duties, of course." She hesitated, then went on. "I admit there is a great deal about the business of armies and war that I don't understand. I was hoping you could explain it to me as we went along."

Marcus bowed to cover his confusion. "Of course, Your Majesty. Whatever you require."

"Thank you." She smiled again, that same wicked smile he remembered. "I'll see you soon, then."

The Grand Army marched.

Marcus' image of Murnsk had always been of a land of eternal winter, snowy fields and icebound forests. Logically, of course, he knew that people lived there, and they couldn't survive if it was *never* warm. But he couldn't help feeling a little disappointed when reality failed to live up to the penny-opera version.

It was the very south of Murnsk, of course, which meant it was not too dissimilar from the northern part of Vordan. The land was covered in rolling fields, a patchwork of green and brown, broken here and there by small forests. To the south was the river, first the Ytolin and then its smaller tributary the Intolin, narrowing as they moved east but still high and fast-flowing with spring snowmelt. Every day or two they passed a village, tiny places with a few plaster-walled houses and the inevitable spire of a Sworn Church. Marcus kept the army well clear of them and sent only small detachments to buy what food was available and gather horses and vehicles.

At regular intervals, regiments peeled off to the north, escorted by cavalry, to sweep the countryside as Janus had ordered. The tail of carts and draft animals that followed the army grew with every foraging party that returned, until it stretched for miles and required a camp nearly as big as the fighting troops did. Fortunately, food and forage was plentiful, floated down the river from the new supply base at Vantzolk.

The reports that came back with the foragers didn't make for pleasant reading. Marcus wouldn't have expected the locals to be happy at having to give up their draft animals and wagons, but the soldiers returned with stories that reminded him unpleasantly of Khandar. Living in Vordan, where the Great Schism was a hundred years dead, it was easy to dismiss the differences between Sworn Church and Free Church as minor disagreements. Here it was clear that the Wars of Religion had never ended and that the locals saw the Vordanai as heathens come to assault the true faith. For the most part, the overwhelming force of the Grand Army meant that these disputes didn't turn violent, but he was certain it was only a matter of time.

In the meantime, dinner with Raesinia gradually became a nightly ritual. The food, so much better than a soldier's usual fare, never stopped making Marcus feel guilty, but Raesinia seemed genuinely interested in military matters and proved to be an attentive pupil. Marcus found himself drawing diagrams in spilled wine and building infantry formations out of silverware and saltshakers.

Raesinia didn't let her lack of formal training hold her back, and was utterly unselfconscious about asking questions when she didn't understand. It was refreshing, and it made Marcus realize how isolated he'd been since his return to the army. In Khandar, he'd had Adrecht, Val, and Mor, the other battalion commanders, and his own aide Fitz Warus. Now Adrecht was dead, while Fitz, Val, and Mor had their own divisions to attend to. *Besides, they're under my orders now. Everyone* was under his orders, apart from Janus. Raesinia was about the only one left he could talk to.

"I think she likes you," Andy said, as they walked back from the queen's tent toward Marcus' own after dinner. They were ten days out from Gilphaite, with another five to go before reaching Vantzolk. Andy had dined with them, at Raesinia's polite request, and the two women had spent the evening recalling stories from the time they'd spent dodging the Directory's troops on the streets of Vordan.

"Excuse me?" Marcus said.

"The queen," Andy said. "I think she likes you."

"I would hope," Marcus said, "that I have proven worthy of her trust."

Andy gave him an exasperated look. "I mean I think she *likes* you. You know. How a girl likes a boy?" She pursed her lips speculatively. "You *do* know about that, right? See, when a girl and a boy like each other, or maybe have just had too much to drink, they—"

"Andy," Marcus growled.

"Sorry. It's just that it's been, what, six months we've known each other? I don't think I've seen you so much as look at a girl. I didn't think the army made you take a vow of chastity. I know Winter had Mad Jane, and Fitz Warus has his young man. And there's enough whores following the train to fill out another regiment."

Fitz— Marcus shook his head. *Not my business.* "I don't . . . I mean . . ."

"It's all right if you don't want to talk about it," Andy said. "I was just curious."

"There was a girl." Marcus let out a long breath. "In Khandar."

"Ah." Andy gave a knowing smile. "Had to break her heart, did you?"

"She tried to kill me," Marcus said flatly. "I helped kill her, instead."

"Oh." Andy looked at her feet. "Shit. I'm sorry."

"It's all right." Marcus looked down at her and narrowed his eyes. "But you can't seriously be suggesting that the *Queen of Vordan* is . . . *interested* in me. It's absurd."

"Why?"

"Because she's the queen! And I'm—" He gestured at himself.

"Column-general of the Grand Army? Right hand of the First Consul?"

"A commoner," Marcus said. "Not even nobility, much less royalty."

"I don't know much about that," Andy said. "But I've seen enough girls with the boy they fancy to know the signs."

"I think you're mistaken."

"All right, all right. Just thought I'd mention it."

"You'd better not mention it to anyone else," Marcus said. "I don't want any rumors getting started."

CHAPTER FIVE

WINTER

The sergeant was a big woman, with blond hair tied back in a bun and a thick scattering of freckles across her broad face. She came forward at a run, boots churning the mud, raising her long stick in two hands over her head. *Stupid.* She had the advantage of reach, but that attack wasted it, her intended strike so obvious that Winter had a dozen options to avoid it. She chose the most straightforward: a step forward, putting her shoulder under the woman's hands, so the end of her weapon passed harmlessly overhead. At the same time, Winter brought her own staff forward in a vicious thrust to the stomach. The air went out of the sergeant with a *woof*, and she doubled over, staff tumbling from her hands.

Winter stepped out of the way as the woman collapsed to the ground, curled up around her pain. The watching crowd waited in silence.

"If I had an edge on this," she said, raising her voice, "I'd be brushing her guts off my shoes right now. Unless I did her the kindness of slitting her throat, she'd live until nightfall at least, lying in a pool of her own insides. You all understand what that means?"

The troops around her, a company of the Girls' Own and several companies from de Koste's Third Regiment, gave a cautious murmur. Winter turned to Bobby and held out her hand, and Bobby passed her a musket, bayonet already locked. The triangular steel blade gleamed as she held it over her head.

"I said, do you understand?"

This time the response was a definite "Yes, sir!"

"Good." Winter lowered the weapon. "Split into two teams. Attack and defense. And no playing around, you understand? I'm telling the cooks that anyone who comes back without at least one decent bruise doesn't get dinner."

They gave the beginning of a groan, quickly cut off by a glance from Winter. She waited until the lieutenants started to get things organized, setting the companies up as attackers and defenders, and then turned back to the sergeant, who'd rolled over, breathing hard. Winter bent down and extended a hand to help her up.

"Thank you for your assistance," she said.

The big woman grimaced as she got to her feet. "My pleasure, sir."

"Give de Koste's rankers as good as you got," Winter said. "And don't let them go easy on the women. Got it?"

"Understood, sir."

The sergeant staggered off to join her company. Winter took a canteen from her belt and drank deep, soothing her ragged throat. She'd been doing too much shouting of late.

"That's the last for today?" she said to Bobby.

"Yes, sir," Bobby said. "But Abby said she wanted a word."

"Where is she now?"

"Over by the musket drills."

The Second Division camp was a hive of activity. Winter had commandeered a stretch of open field adjacent to the tents for drill, and every man and woman of her four regiments who didn't have another duty was out there. Companies practiced formation marching, bayonet charges, and the manual of arms, even forming company squares, at Winter's insistence, in spite of the fact that it wasn't in the tactics manual. Larger groups staged exercises like the one she'd just left, attack and defense, battering at one another with staves and clubs. Hanna Courvier, the senior cutter, had set up an aid station that was already receiving a steady trickle of patients.

It was midafternoon. The long column of the Grand Army was still filing into its camp, regiment by regiment and division by division. The pace was leisurely, by the standards of the Velt campaign—ten miles a day, to allow the lumbering wagon train to keep up over the rutted Murnskai roads. Winter had driven her troops ahead of the rest, arriving early so as to have much of the day free for drills.

"Wouldn't it be easier to let the regiments practice as units?" Bobby said, as they circled another melee exercise that had devolved into a massive scrum. Sergeants shouted and hauled struggling men and women away, covered in mud and torn grass.

"We'll get to that," Winter said. "They all saw what happened to Ibsly, and that should provide plenty of motivation to get their formation changes done faster. But I want the rest of the soldiers to get used to mixing with the Girls' Own." Once she'd used games of handball for that same purpose, but she didn't think they could afford such a leisurely approach now, with the campaign already begun. Once they reached Vantzolk, any moment could bring an encounter with the enemy.

Abby was waiting near the space reserved for musket drill. Long lines of blue-uniformed soldiers went through the motions of loading and firing, over and over, while officers barked for more speed and berated anyone who fumbled. Abby herself looked like she'd been through half a war already, her uniform muddy and soaked with sweat. She saluted Winter, who gave her a stiff nod.

"Sir!"

"Bobby said you wanted to talk?" Winter said.

Abby nodded and stepped away from the nearest soldiers. "You haven't been having dinner with the rankers lately," she said, her voice low.

"I'm a bit busy," Winter said, trying to keep any defensiveness out of her tone.

"I understand, sir. I just thought you might appreciate being kept abreast of how they're feeling."

"Let me guess," Winter said. "They're not happy."

"No, sir. The Girls' Own especially."

"I didn't think they'd balk at a little bit of drill," Winter said.

"A little bit is one thing," Abby said. "I've had to borrow carts from the train to carry all the rankers who can't walk in the morning. But it's not just that."

"No?"

"They feel like they did all they could at Gilphaite," Abby said. "We lost a lot of good women there. And now they think you're punishing them."

"You know I can't give the Girls' Own special preference," Winter said. "And it's not meant to be punishment. Tell them the next time Janus asks this division to do something, I expect them to be able to do it."

"If we lightened the schedule just a bit—"

"No. We have seven more days until Vantzolk, and I intend to use them."

Abby pursed her lips and looked like she wanted to object, but all she said was "Yes, sir." She turned on her heel and walked away.

"Winter . . ." Bobby said.

"What?" Winter turned. "We've been over this. Better sweat and bruises now than blood later."

"I know," Bobby said. "It's just . . ."

"Just what?"

"Never mind." The girl shook her head. Winter sighed.

They don't understand. The look on Janus' face as she'd made her report. The hint—barely visible—of disappointment in his eyes. *They don't know what it's like to be responsible for all of this.* The dark abyss loomed at the bottom of her mind, and she felt like she was scrabbling on the edge by her fingernails.

With everyone out in the drill fields, the camp itself was nearly deserted, aside from the cooks and the sentries. There was none of the usual laughter and conversation, the dice games and surreptitious bottles of liquor. *Good.* Winter stalked through the darkened rows of tents to her own. Bobby paused as she lifted the tent flap.

"Is there anything else you need, sir?" she said.

"No," Winter said shortly. "Thank you."

"If you want to . . ." Bobby colored slightly. "Talk, you know? You seem . . ."

"*Thank* you, Captain. Go and keep Captain Marsh company."

Bobby winced. She saluted and turned stiffly away.

That was unfair. Bobby and Captain Marsh seemed well suited to each other, and by rights Winter ought to have been happy for them. Somehow, though, seeing them together seemed like a twist of the knife. *God, what is wrong with me?* It all came back to Jane, *fucking* Jane, lying in wait in her thoughts like a jungle panther, ready to pounce whenever she let her guard down. *Let Bobby fuck her handsome captain. What difference does it make to me?*

God damn it. Winter kicked off her boots and sat in front of her writing desk. A stack of pages was already laid out, waiting for attention, but she couldn't read them through a sudden haze of tears. *No, no, no. I've cried enough over this. By all the fucking saints, we're done.* She took a deep breath and wiped her eyes with the back of her hand.

Most of the stack were casualty reports. Cyte had offered to take care of them, but Winter couldn't bring herself to accept help, not for this. It felt like a betrayal. The lists, endless rows of neat handwriting, carried a horrible, clinical precision.

Merriwan, Joanna. Unfit for further duty.
Moore, Annette. Returned to duty.

Morse, Sasha. Not expected to recover.
Murphy, Andria. Not expected to recover.
Murphy, Genevieve. Missing. (4/19)
Murzow, Bridgette. Missing. (4/19)
Nailer, Susan. Unfit for further duty.

So much was hiding behind those words. Beneath *Unfit for further duty* lay the horrible song of the bone saw and the piles of pale arms and legs outside the cutters' tents. Ruined men and women, hauled to Vordan by the wagonload, chewed up and spat out by the war. *Not expected to recover* meant the endless lines of blood- and shit-stained pallets in the infirmary, those who'd had their guts opened or their skulls cracked and could do little more than wait for the wound to fester.

Missing was worst of all. Some of these were surely lying dead on the field, too mangled to be recognized or tucked away somewhere unnoticed. Others, no doubt, had deserted. But some fraction had been taken by the Borelgai during the retreat, either injured or simply exhausted and overrun.

Winter had read such reports before, of course. Not only were these longer, but there were more of those awful *Missing* entries, with all the horror of ambiguity. In the Velt campaign, the Girls' Own had never finished a battle with the enemy in control of the field. As far as Winter knew, the only soldiers from her regiment who had ever been taken prisoner had been a few grabbed by League patrols when they'd straggled on the long, brutal march from Desland to Jirdos. They'd all been returned at the end of the campaign, without much to complain of besides boredom. This time, as much as Colonel Blackstream was convinced the Borelgai were honorable soldiers, Winter feared the worst.

At some point a ranker had delivered dinner, army soup and hardtack, with a little bit of fatty pork floating in the bowl to mark it as an officer's portion. Winter set it on her table and ate mechanically, tasting nothing. She turned the pages, read the names, and signed at the bottom, where neat figures tabulated the dead, wounded, and missing to give each unit's current strength.

Ibsly's division had suffered worse, she knew, both in its initial assault and later, when it had crumbled in the face of the Borelgai charge. The Girls' Own had the worst losses from her regiments, while the other three had gotten off relatively lightly.

Should I have done it differently? Sent Sevran and the others in at the beginning, with Ibsly, when they might have made a difference? Seen the guns and not attacked at all? That way, she knew, lay madness, but she couldn't help the thoughts.

She worked until her eyelids drooped, keeping on until the lists of names were just a blur through a fog of fatigue. *Missing, missing, missing, dead, dead, dead.* Only then did she finally admit defeat, putting aside her pen and stumbling fully clothed to her bedroll. In the few moments between when her head hit the pillow and when exhaustion claimed her, she prayed she was tired enough not to dream.

Her prayers went unanswered, as they did every night.

Bad dreams had haunted Winter nearly her entire life. The earliest had always been dreams of fire, spreading unstoppable flames that surrounded her, cutting off every exit, closing in from every side. There were shapes in the flames, faces she could almost remember. Screams. When she'd first come to Mrs. Wilmore's Prison, she'd woken with violent shakes every night, or so the mistresses told her later.

After she'd escaped the Prison, she'd dreamed of Jane and the night before she'd left. The farmer Ganhide coming to Jane's room to extract his due as her new husband. The knife gleaming bright in Winter's hand. *Take the knife,* Jane said, *and press it in, upward, as hard as you can.* She'd failed, and run away, as far away as it was possible to go. But the dreams had followed her.

Then the Redeemers had risen in Khandar. Once all that was over, she'd had a new set of dreams. Green eyes glowing in the darkness of a temple hidden under the desert sand, the hiss of smoke, and the groping hands of dead men. Dreams where the thing inside her, the demon Infernivore, broke free and devoured everything around it.

Now she expected to dream of the battle, the lists of names, horrible visions of what might happen to those who'd been captured. Or even of Jane, the ghost who would not let her be. *Can you be haunted by someone who isn't dead?* And it was Jane she saw, but never the end, her drunken rages, the confrontation in Janus' office, Jane's finger pulling the trigger, the hammer falling. Instead, her dreams were—

—*happy.* She dreamed of the first time they'd kissed, in a secret hollow in a hedge, covered in twigs and sap. The way the walls of the Prison seemed to fall away when they were together, no matter what tasks the mistresses assigned. Their first clumsy experiments, lips and fingers and giggles in the warm, close darkness, breath coming fast and heart slamming against her ribs so hard it was almost painful. Feeling like explorers in a strange, new, breathtaking country.

When she awoke, there was always a tiny moment before she remembered. That was worse than any nightmare.

Six days out from Vantzolk. Winter had her battalions practice deploying from column to line, then ploying back again, always demanding more speed. When she'd first started the exercises, the soldiers had accepted them easily enough, having seen the fate of Ibsly's division. Now, though, they were muttering openly, and there were sour faces wherever Winter looked. Abby punctiliously obeyed every order but said nothing beyond "Yes, sir!" and "No, sir!" Bobby hovered at Winter's side like a nervous child trying to calm feuding parents.

Cyte spent much of the day with the supply train and was missing from the command tent when Winter went in search of the latest batch of reports. Frustrated, Winter retired to her tent and went over her maps instead, plotting and replotting the march to Vantzolk and then the endless miles to Elysium. No matter how hard she stared, the Pilgrim's Road didn't get any shorter, nor the mountains and forests of the Murnskai backcountry less forbidding.

There was a scratch at the tent flap. Winter looked up from the map, irritated. "What?"

"It's Cyte," Cyte said. "Can I come in?"

More reports. Winter gave an exaggerated sigh she knew was a lie. *Another excuse to work until I fall over. Maybe tonight . . .*

"Come in." Winter rolled up the map and pushed it aside. "What have you got for me?"

Cyte slipped through the flap. Uncharacteristically, she was without a bundle of paper under her arm. Instead, she held a smoky yellow bottle, sealed at the top with wax. Winter frowned.

"Is something wrong?"

Cyte coughed. "Not . . . as such. I found this." She held up the bottle. "In the train. It's some local Murnskai thing, apparently. You can buy a bottle in the villages for a few pennies. I thought we might share it."

"Share it? Now?" Winter peered at Cyte, who flushed slightly. "You're not serious, are you?"

"I am," Cyte said.

"You know I'm busy," Winter said. "Have you got the latest reports—"

"I took care of them," Cyte said. "This afternoon. I took care of everything."

"Why?" A touch of anger crept into Winter's voice. "What the hell is going on? Did someone put you up to this?"

"Winter . . ." Cyte sighed. "Can I sit down?"

"If you tell me who sent you here. Is this someone's idea of a prank?"

"Nobody *sent* me. Not exactly," Cyte said. When Winter went to respond, Cyte held out a hand. "Just listen, all right? We're *worried* about you."

"Who's worried about me?"

"Your friends. Bobby, Abby, Sevran. Folsom and Graff. Me."

"Thank you for your concern," Winter drawled. "But I'm fine."

"You're not," Cyte said. "Saints and martyrs, Winter, I'm hardly the most perceptive person in the world, and I can see that you're not. You were unhappy even before the battle, and since then you barely talk to anyone. We drill all day, and you work until you fall over. Have you looked at yourself in a mirror? You look like a corpse."

"I just want to be sure—"

"—we're prepared for next time. I know. You've told everyone a hundred times. How prepared are *you* going to be if you're falling asleep in the saddle?"

Winter frowned. Days of not enough rest made her thoughts feel as slow and sticky as molasses, and she couldn't quite come up with a good answer to that.

"So this learned council," Winter said, "decided there's something wrong with me, and as a result they dispatched you to my tent with a bottle of . . . something that looks pretty vile, actually. And you're going to, what, tie me up and pour it down my throat?"

"I was more hoping we could talk."

"I don't have time—"

"You do," Cyte said. "*I* know that better than anyone."

There was a long pause.

"They really sent you over with a bottle?" Winter said.

"Bobby said it had worked wonders at least once before. With you and someone named Feor, back in Ashe-Katarion."

Winter snorted. "Did she tell you that the Redeemers burned down half the city the next day?"

"No. But I'd like to hear about it."

Winter eyed the other woman. Cyte was still blushing a little, but her expression was determined. With a sigh, Winter gestured for her to sit on a cushion beside the bedroll.

"Out of curiosity," Winter said, flipping open the top of her small trunk, "how did you come to draw the short straw?"

"I volunteered," Cyte said. "Bobby spends a lot of time with Marsh, and Abby thought things might be . . . difficult between you. Besides, I wanted to help. I owe you a great deal."

"*You* owe *me*?" Winter laughed as she pulled out a pair of tin cups. "You run this division practically single-handed. What do you owe me for?"

"Aside from the times you saved my life, in the Vendre and in Desland?"

"All right, yes. Aside from that."

"I . . ." Cyte looked at the bottle. "I think I need a drink before I get into it."

"You're serious about drinking this stuff," Winter said.

"I told you I was."

Winter took the bottle, drew her knife, and started cutting through the seal. "It's just that"—the wax came away with a *pop*—"I can't remember you doing any serious drinking. I thought you were a teetotaler or something."

"Winter." Cyte drew herself up. "Please. I *was* at the University."

Winter laughed and poured a finger of the liquor into each cup. She pushed one across to Cyte, who picked it up, sniffed, and wrinkled her nose.

"Best to get it down all at once." Winter raised her own cup. "Ready. Level. Fire!"

They both tipped back their drinks. Whatever the stuff was, it had a vicious bite, and Winter had to fight to keep from coughing. Cyte slammed her cup down on the table and tilted her head back, tears at the corners of her eyes.

"Balls of the Beast," she said. "Murnskai must have steel throats."

"Are you sure you didn't get paint thinner by mistake?"

"Not according to the sergeant I bought it from."

Winter rolled her eyes. "There's your problem. Never trust a sergeant. Not when it comes to liquor, anyway."

"Good advice." Cyte blinked and wiped her face with the back of her sleeve. "Another round?"

"You really are a glutton for punishment."

"I believe in seeing things through."

Winter filled the cups again, slightly more generously. They held them aloft together and chanted in unison.

"Ready. Level. *Fire!*"

The second time wasn't nearly as bad as the first, possibly because her throat had gone numb in self-defense. Winter leaned back from the table, feeling warmer as the liquor hit her stomach.

"You were going to tell me why you're here," she said.

Cyte let out a long breath. "Do you remember when we met?"

"I'm not likely to forget it. That was the night we took the Vendre."

"I was with the rebels. The Radicals, we called ourselves." Cyte shook her head. "It seems so stupid now. A bunch of rich kids from the University who thought they knew how to run the world."

Winter said nothing, recalling that her own thoughts, on that occasion, had run along the same lines.

"I had no idea what I was doing," Cyte said. "I'd gone to the University because I loved history, and now here was history unfolding right outside my window. And I thought, *I need to see this.* I had this idea that I was going to write about it, be the great historian of the revolution. That it would be my book they'd be reading in a hundred years. 'Well, it says in Cytomandiclea that this is how it went,' the students would say, and then they'd write papers arguing how I was biased one way or the other.

"And then we met you and Jane, and you said you were going into the Vendre. It felt like someone had pulled blinders off me. All of a sudden I realized I didn't have to just *watch* history. I could be a part of it, for real. All I had to do was step forward."

"And risk getting killed," Winter said. "Some people would say I didn't do you any favors."

"My father would agree with that," Cyte said. "He sent me a letter when he heard what was happening. He'd practically disowned me, you understand; this was the first I'd heard from him in years. But when he heard about the revolution, he sent me a letter begging me to come home." Cyte shook her head. "It didn't even arrive until after everything was over."

"Did you write back?"

Cyte grinned wickedly. "I sent him a copy of my enlistment papers in the Girls' Own. Does that count?"

Winter laughed and reached for the bottle again. She pushed Cyte the tin cup and said, "So you think you *owe* me for getting you involved in all of this?"

"Yes."

"Long marches, bad food, and the constant threat of violent death."

Cyte's grin widened. "That sounds about right."

"Well, you're mad, but I'll take thanks wherever I can get them." Winter raised the glass. "You're welcome. Ready, level—"

"—*FIRE!*"

That night Winter's sleep was deep and blessedly dreamless. Her head hurt the next morning, but not as badly as she might have expected. It had been a while since she'd gotten properly drunk—even at the worst times, right after Jane's escape, she'd avoided the bottle, perhaps because she'd watched Jane crawl into it so often.

The next day she announced that the division had earned a rest for its excellent performance, to general cheers and sighs of relief. She caught Abby and Bobby exchanging relieved glances and resolved to thank them later. In place of drills, a spontaneous game of handball erupted, with the Girls' Own and Sevran's Second Regiment introducing the rest of the division to their tradition. Winter thought the soldiers worked harder brawling on the playing field than they ever did in drills, but they seemed happier afterward.

Somewhat to her surprise, Cyte turned up again after dinner, offering to finish off the bottle of crushed worms or whatever the hell the Murnskai liquor was made of. The next night she brought something green she claimed she'd discovered tucked at the bottom of a box of hardtack. They talked about Voulenne and *The Rights of Man*, whether it was better to approach an enemy position in line or in column, and whether it was true that Column-General d'Ivoire was sleeping with the queen. Winter, who'd spent a fair bit of time with Marcus, pronounced this last unlikely.

"Janus once told me Marcus missed his calling as a knight errant four hundred years ago," she said. "A true knight doesn't get to put his hands on the monarch."

The morning brought darker news. Murnskai irregulars had raided the supply train, slaughtering a few sentries, setting fires, and generally causing as much damage as they could. The relatively carefree atmosphere of the camp evaporated overnight, and cavalry patrols were increased. The next morning a half dozen junior officers who'd gone whoring were found near the perimeter with their throats slit. Janus ordered the "tail" of camp followers—the prostitutes, merchants, and laborers who seemed to grow up like weeds in the army's wake—dispersed, on pain of summary punishment. Some men grumbled now that it was harder to supplement their rations or find a woman, but most agreed it was a fair trade for not turning up butchered like a hog. Winter made certain the Girls' Own set extra sentries, just in case.

Two days out from Vantzolk, she got a summons to the command tent. Janus and Marcus were both there, sitting across the table from each other. The map between them was covered with pencil markings.

"Division-General," Janus said. "You're feeling well, I trust?"

"Yes, sir." Between her new nightly tradition and simply getting enough sleep, Winter was, in fact, feeling considerably more like herself. "How can the Second serve?"

"You're aware, of course, of the recent partisan activity."

"Of course, sir. We've taken precautions."

"Good." Janus steepled his hands. "Unfortunately, while such strikes are merely an irritant now, once the Grand Army turns north they may prove considerably more damaging. Our supply lines will be long and vulnerable, and we cannot allow the enemy to attack them at will."

"Yes, sir."

"Division-General Stokes' cavalry has been working to track our problems to their source, and we believe we located the base of the primary band of irregulars. It's to the north"—he indicated the map—"well into the woods. Not good terrain for horsemen."

That made it clear where this was going. "I'll take the Girls' Own in and clean them out, sir."

Janus flashed a smile. "Just what I was hoping to hear. Your First Regiment is the army's best at rough-terrain fighting. You're certain they're sufficiently recovered from the battle at Gilphaite?"

"Perfectly, sir. Frankly, I'd say they're eager to get back into it."

"Good." He raised a finger. "A warning, however. Excessive brutality will only turn the local population against us. Any men found under arms are to be considered the enemy, but women and children in particular are to be treated with respect. The Sworn Church places a strong emphasis on that. And I will not tolerate any wanton destruction. Is that clear?"

"Perfectly clear, sir." Another good reason to send the Girls' Own instead of some regiment of overenthusiastic male volunteers. *As usual, Janus never has only one reason for doing anything.*

Marcus and Janus exchanged a look, and something passed between them that Winter couldn't follow.

"Good luck, General," Marcus said.

"Thank you, sir."

To her surprise, their cavalry escort was led by Division-General Stokes, old Give-Em-Hell himself, now in command of the Grand Army's cavalry reserve. He'd brought a squadron of forty troopers, all armed with carbines and sabers. Winter herself, after reading reports on the enemy's suspected strength, had brought Abby and five companies of the Girls' Own, about four hundred soldiers in all, which ought to give them a comfortable preponderance of numbers. As the small force milled about just outside the sentry line, getting itself in order, Give-Em-Hell walked over with the exaggerated swagger he affected while not on horseback.

"Ihernglass!" he said. "Good to be working with you again! Those were some hot times at Jirdos and no mistake, eh?"

Winter fought back a smile. Give-Em-Hell, at least, would never change. His small stature and puffed-out chest gave him the appearance of a pigeon about to take flight, and he barked out every sentence as though shouting at a sergeant on the other side of a field. In spite of this slightly comical mien, she had to admit he excelled in his chosen field; absolutely fearless himself, he inspired a matching fervor in his men. His few squadrons had outfought the vaunted Hamveltai elites and won the Battle of Jirdos almost single-handedly. *And he doesn't look down his nose at the Girls' Own, like so many of the old royal officers.*

"They were indeed," she said.

"Nothing half so exciting on this campaign yet," he said. "Borel cowards hid in town and did all their fighting with cannons. Still, I daresay we'll see a bit more action when the emperor moves south. The wild tribes of the north are supposed to be the best riders in the world! That'll be some sport, I should think."

"Something to look forward to," Winter said. "I'm surprised to find you out here today, though."

"Oh, I thought I'd come along and make sure it was done properly." He leaned forward. "Between you and me, I have a bone to pick with these so-called 'irregulars.' On one of their raids they slashed the tendons of a dozen cavalry horses! Had to put them down, poor things." His eyes took on a dangerous gleam, and Winter felt a moment's pity for the Murnskai raiders.

"You're sure you know where they are?"

"We've got 'em nailed down, sure as thunder. They mostly move at night, and some of my men are on watch. It's a cave a few miles inside the forest, near one of their hamlets. We'll show you the way. Then your men can fan out—"

"And give 'em hell?"

"Precisely!" He clapped Winter on the shoulder. "I knew there was a reason I liked working with you, Ihernglass. It's like you know my mind before I do!"

They set out in a loose column, with the cavalry at the vanguard. Winter exchanged waves with Sergeant Graff of the First Company, one of the few men in the unit. He'd been one of her corporals in Khandar, and while he'd consented to becoming a sergeant in the Girls' Own, he'd steadfastly refused all further promotion, claiming he wouldn't feel right with stripes on his shoulders. His old comrade, James Folsom, had no such compunctions; he was a captain now in Sevran's Second Regiment. Anne-Marie Wallach, the hero of the siege of Antova, was serving as Graff's junior sergeant, her blond curls bursting out from under her cap.

Abby walked in the middle of the column. She and Winter, both indifferent riders, had left their horses behind for the trip into the forest, and Winter was starting to regret it by the time the sun reached the zenith. It wasn't *hot* like Khandar had been, where the summer sun could kill an exposed man in hours, but the soggy, humid air felt like the inside of a laundry.

"Abby," Winter said, falling into step.

"Sir." Abby glanced at her, a touch nervously, then looked back at the ranks in front of her.

"You sent Cyte to see me."

"I wouldn't say I *sent* her," Abby said. "We all got together and decided *someone* should go, and she volunteered."

"I just wanted to thank you."

"Oh." Abby grinned sheepishly, relief rising off her like steam. "Sorry, sir. It wasn't my business and I put my nose in. I wasn't sure how you'd take it."

"It was your business. You have to keep the women of this regiment as safe as you can, and that means making sure I do my job." Winter smiled back at her. "If I'm ever being . . . stupid again, please tell me."

"Understood." There was only a hint of pain behind her smile. "It's a job I'm used to."

They walked in silence for a while. The column was climbing as it wound north, away from the river, and the cooler air cut pleasantly through the humid-

ity. They left the cultivated farms behind, and the cart track they'd been following ran out amid weedy pastureland. A mile farther on, the forest began, a
stark boundary where a line of ancient trees marked the edge of the territory
claimed by man and his axes. One of the cavalry showed them to the beginning
of a narrow track, little more than a game trail, and they strung out along it as
it wound into the forest.

"General Stokes," Winter called, as he rode by. "A moment?"

He nodded agreeably and slowed to a walk. "What is it?"

"You said there's a hamlet near this cave?"

His expression went grim. "Yes. We'll be passing through it soon."

"Are the people there sympathetic to the partisans? Will they warn them
we're coming?"

"They won't," Give-Em-Hell said. "You'll see."

An hour or so later the track widened into something close to a real path,
then spread into a large clearing. Trees had been felled to make room for a dozen
shacks, roughly arranged around a central green. The houses were all rough-cut
timber with high-peaked shingled roofs. A logging and hunting village, Winter
guessed, that traded with the farming communities down on the river plain.

Or so she surmised, from what remained. The shacks were little more than
blackened ruins, stone hearths standing amid the charred debris. Beams and roof
shingles were scattered where they'd collapsed. Most of the central green had
been torn up, and half-burned wreckage stuck out of the top of the stone well.

"Saints and martyrs," Winter said, coming up short. She looked up at
Give-Em-Hell, who nodded grimly.

"What happened here?" Abby said.

"One of our foraging columns came this way."

"Our foragers did this? Which regiment? Janus will be furious."

The cavalry commander shook his head. "It was like this when they got
here. The embers were still warm. They heard we were coming, you see.
Apparently the damn Sworn Priests have been telling them the Vordanai are
here for their children's souls and it's their holy duty to burn and destroy everything that might be of use to us." He gestured at the well. "They even stuffed
a rotting goat down there, so the water's no good."

"Balls of the Beast," Winter swore. "I thought the Redeemers were crazy."

"At least the damned Redeemers would come right at you!" Give-Em-Hell
agreed. "Give me a good charge out in the open any day of the week."

"What happened to the people?" Abby said. "There's no bodies here."

"That's where these irregulars come from, we think," Give-Em-Hell said.

"It makes strategic sense, in a sick way," Winter said. "Get the villagers to burn everything they have, and then tell them you need men to help fight the heathens. What are they going to do except sign up?" She looked at Abby. "Tell your soldiers to be careful if they see any priests."

"I think we'll be careful regardless," Abby said. "Which way to this cave?"

"About a mile that way," Give-Em-Hell said, pointing northwest. A hillock of bare rock broke through the forest canopy, like an island rising out of the sea.

"We'll come at them from three sides," Winter said. "Abby, send two companies out to swing around until they're southeast of that rock. You and I will take two more to the north side. General, can you and your troopers take the direct approach if we give you a company for backup?"

Give-Em-Hell nodded. "Of course."

"Give us an hour, then."

CHAPTER SIX

WINTER

Winter took the First Company, led by a Lieutenant Malloy, and the Seventh, led by a beanpole of a girl who introduced herself as Lieutenant d'Orien. Winter remembered Malloy vaguely from the Velt campaign, a short, dark-haired woman from the Transpale, with that region's soft, breathy accent. D'Orien was a more recent recruit, and seemed awestruck to be in Winter's presence. Some of the Girls' Own, the newer ones, were inclined to treat Winter as a kind of demigod, which she'd never gotten accustomed to.

They walked around the devastated village, skirting the edge of the clearing, and then plunged back into the woods on the other side. This time there was no track to guide them, and without the bulk of the hill visible off to their left, Winter would have been instantly lost. Fortunately, the forest here was old growth, with little ground cover under the massive, high-canopied trees.

Abby signaled a halt after forty-five minutes, comparing the position of the hill with that of the sun. She called the two lieutenants over.

"This should be about right," she said. "Malloy, you take your company right and spread out, call it five hundred yards. D'Orien, you take the left. Each of you send me a half dozen muskets I can keep here as a reserve. Tell the girls to hold fire until they've got a target, you understand? I don't want any blind shooting. Any Murnskai try to run, you stop them."

"Yes, sir," Malloy said.

"Sir?" d'Orien said. "What if they won't stop?"

"Shoot," Abby said. "If we let 'em run, they'll just come back at us tomorrow."

"What if they surrender?" Malloy said.

Abby hesitated and glanced at Winter. The two lieutenants followed her gaze. Winter swallowed.

"We'll accept surrenders, obviously," she said. "But be careful."

"Tell them to lie facedown, well in front of the line," Abby said. "I don't want anybody to 'surrender' and then run off when we're not looking."

"Or knife us in the back," Malloy muttered. She and d'Orien saluted and went in opposite directions, to relay the orders to their squads.

Winter watched them go, feeling oddly apprehensive. She'd gone into battle so many times now it felt like it ought to be routine, especially against an outnumbered gang of partisans, but something nagged at the corner of her mind. *This is the first fight since Gilphaite.* But the Girls' Own, at least, seemed to have shaken off the setback they'd suffered there, and they didn't seem reluctant to be going back into action. *Then—*

It was something else entirely, she realized. Something she hadn't felt in months, not since leaving Vordan and Feor. Deep in the pit of her soul, there was a flicker of motion, like a dozing dragon opening one curious eye. Infernivore, the demon that devoured its own kind, had come awake, and there was only one possible reason for that.

Winter closed her eyes and concentrated on the feeling. Feor had told her that any *naathem*—her Khandarai word for what the Church called a demon's host—could sense another *naathem*. Feor could track demons at a considerable distance, though she said that the ability to do so varied both with the *naath* and the training of the *naathem*. Winter wasn't sure which was missing in her case, but she'd never been very sensitive to Infernivore's nudges. This wasn't the full-fledged attention it paid when another demon was nearby, but it couldn't be *too* far, or she wouldn't be able to feel it at all.

She turned, slowly, trying to see if the feeling strengthened when she faced a particular direction. She *thought* it was a bit stronger facing roughly southeast, back toward the ruined village, but the difference was too subtle to be sure. *Hell.* As far as she knew, Feor was in Vordan and Raesinia was with the Grand Army's main camp. Apart from the two of them—and the occasional wild demon, like the unfortunate Danton Aurenne—the only demon-hosts she'd encountered were the Penitent Damned, the supernatural servants of the Priests of the Black. *If one of them is here, this is going to get a lot more complicated.*

"Are you all right, sir?" Abby said.

"Fine." Winter opened her eyes. Just a tiny handful of people knew the truth about demons; among the Girls' Own, she'd shared what little information she had only with Jane, Bobby, and Cyte. Janus had insisted she keep the knowledge close, but at times like these she wondered if he really understood what he was asking. *How am I supposed to tell Abby to be careful if she doesn't even know what to watch out for?* "Just . . . thinking."

Abby raised one eyebrow, but didn't comment. A dozen women formed a loose knot around the two of them, all looking up the slope toward the rocky summit. *Is the demon with the partisans?* If so, there was only one thing Winter could think to do. *I'll have to grab it as soon as it shows itself.* Infernivore could devour any other demon, as long as she could manage to touch the demon's host for a few seconds. *Unfortunately, if they're better at sensing than I am, they know I'm here, too.* If there *was* a demon up there, she had to hope it would come her way instead of attacking one of the other Girls' Own companies. *Damn.*

As if to punctuate the thought, there was a single *crack*, like a distant hand-clap. It echoed through the trees for a moment, then was followed by two more, then a dozen all together. The woods on both sides of Winter were suddenly full of motion, the Girls' Own taking positions behind trees or against fallen logs, anything that looked like it would stop a musket ball. Several of the soldiers methodically checked the powder in their pans, making sure it hadn't spilled or gotten wet during the trek.

"Here goes," Abby said. "You think they'll dig in up there or try to get away?"

"Digging in is suicide," Winter said. "They have to know that. They'll run." The question, though, was in which direction. The Girls' Own companies were arranged in a rough triangle around the hill, but Winter was acutely aware they were spread thin. "Be ready to move if we get word from the others."

"Hey!" a shout came from down the line. "Somebody's up there!" It was quickly followed by a shot, a stab of yellow fire and a roil of smoke.

"Hold fire!" Abby shouted, shading her eyes with her hands. "You couldn't hit a barn at that distance!"

"There," Winter said, pointing. Two or three hundred yards upslope, stand-ing in the crotch of a split tree, was a tall, heavily bearded man in drab leather and homespun. A weapon hung over his shoulder, but he made no move to reach for it, nor to take cover. Abby was right—with a musket, at that range he might as well have been on the moon.

After a leisurely few seconds of observation, the man dropped back out of sight. A moment later a dozen people in similar dress started down the hill, dodging through the trees as they came closer. Abby's shouts reminded the Girls' Own to hold fire, and no further shots greeted the partisans. When they got to about a hundred yards' distance, they stopped, spreading out behind a stand of close-growing birch trees. The barrels of muskets emerged from amid the cover, and flashes and smoke spread among the trees as they opened fire. Musket balls whined past or hit the dirt with *thok* sounds, and splinters flew where they clipped the trees.

"Hold fire," Winter said, in response to Abby's questioning look. "They're not going to do any damage that far out."

"We could work our way around either side and flank them out of there," Abby said.

"Not yet." The birch trees were rapidly becoming obscured in the smoke of the shooting. Winter squinted. "They want us distracted. Hold tight."

The orders were passed down the line, and the Girls' Own clung to their cover, ignoring the partisans' musketry. For the most part, the balls passed harmlessly overhead, but Winter heard at least one shout of "Fuck!" from her right, indicating that a lucky shot had found a target. She was almost ready to give Abby the go-ahead to move in when the fogbank around the birch grove started to boil.

"Here they come!" she shouted.

She closed her eyes for a moment, trying to determine if the demon was coming, too, but the feeling was still distant. When she opened them again, the slope was alive with movement. The men who'd been shooting at them were in the lead, bounding downslope as fast as they could, but they were followed by at least a hundred more emerging out of the smoke. A few of the newcomers had muskets, too, or antique shotguns with long, flaring muzzles, but most of them seemed to be armed with nothing more than crude spears or axes. Some of them looked shorter than the leaders, but it wasn't until they all began shouting a battle cry that Winter realized there were women's and children's voices mixed in.

Oh, saints and fucking martyrs—why—

The Girls' Own opened fire at fifty yards. Running figures went down, punched back off their feet or tripping and rolling down the hill until they came to rest. Some of the battle cries turned to screams, but most of them kept on coming. The men with muskets halted, dropped to one knee, and fired, then stood up again and continued the charge. More shots came from the Girls' Own line as soldiers farther along turned to add their fire to the carnage.

It wasn't going to be enough; Winter could see that immediately. "Bayonets!" she shouted, voice straining to be heard above the tumult.

In front of her, Abby's reserve soldiers fixed bayonets, just as the first of the partisans threw themselves forward. There were men in leather coats with huge, bristly beards, and women with long, drab skirts tied up between their legs to leave them free to run. A boy not yet old enough to shave was coming straight for them, until a shot from the side spun him around and he tumbled to a halt against a tree. A few more partisans fell, brought down by soldiers who'd reserved their fire for point-blank range, and others halted to shoot back. One of the soldiers in front of Winter staggered back, screaming, her face torn to shreds by a hail of shot from a blunderbuss. The first partisan to reach the line was a girl, her long hair tied back with a red kerchief, an ax raised in both hands over her head. A Girls' Own soldier stopped her with a bayonet thrust to the stomach, the butt of the musket set against her own midriff, and they stood frozen for a moment, separated by the length of the weapon.

Then Winter tore her sword free of its scabbard, and had no attention to spare for anyone else. Two men and a woman came at her, one of them burying an ax in the ribs of a Girls' Own soldier as he passed. The other man had a spear, just a long length of wood with a sharpened point, and he aimed it at Winter like a lance with all the momentum of his downhill charge. She danced aside, and he couldn't adjust his strike in time. As the point slipped past her, Winter stuck a foot in his path; he didn't fall, but it took him a few moments to recover.

The second man and the woman came at her together. He was big, with a woodsman's muscles and a long-handled log-splitting ax. He used it well, swinging in wide horizontal sweeps that kept her outside his reach. Winter feinted left, dodged his swing, and brought her sword down on his hand as the ax went past. Something went flying—his thumb, she thought—and he dropped the weapon with a hoarse shriek. The woman pushed past him, swinging a carving knife with wild abandon, and Winter hastily spun aside, her sword licking out almost automatically in a backhanded slash across her attacker's face. As the woman screamed and stumbled away, Winter closed on the axman, who was scrabbling for his weapon with his off hand, and sank her blade in his ribs. He keeled over with a moan.

The man with the spear had dropped it, running pell-mell down the hill. He made it a dozen paces before an earsplitting *crack* rang out and he fell forward, thudding face-first into the turf. Abby stepped up beside Winter, lowering her smoking pistol.

"Are you all right, sir?" she said, through the ringing in Winter's ears.

Winter nodded, looking around. Bodies littered the slope, but there were only a handful in blue. Fury had not helped the partisans make up for their lack of weapons or tactics. She saw one boy in leathers straddling the corpse of a Girls' Own soldier, stabbing her over and over with a short-bladed knife. He was sobbing and shouting something—Winter, who'd been spending some time with a Murnskai phrasebook, thought it was "You killed her! You killed her!"—but before she could say anything, a sergeant came up behind the youth, jerked his head back by the hair, and slashed his throat. Blood bubbled forth, and when she let go, he collapsed atop his victim, gurgling.

"Balls of the Beast," Winter swore, letting her sword fall to her side.

"I certainly wasn't expecting *that*," Abby said. "I'm sorry, sir. We should have been more careful."

"It's all right," Winter said. "That wasn't a charge; that was mass suicide. I didn't think . . ." She shook her head.

"I've got runners out to the others," Abby said. "But I think that was about all they had."

Winter nodded. She reached down to the body of the man she'd stabbed, wiped her sword clean, and sheathed it again. Her arm felt numb, and her ears were still ringing; it took her a moment to realize the woman she'd cut was still screaming.

"Gather up the wounded," she said. "Ours and any of theirs that will make it. Janus will want to question them." She looked up at the looming bulk of the hill. "Then we need to push on. This may not be over."

A half hour later, after they'd confirmed there'd been no attack on the other two forces and detached half a company for the grisly duty of going over the battlefield, the remaining soldiers picked their way past the bodies of the fallen and up the hill. The Girls' Own moved in silence, Winter noted, not so much from a desire for stealth but in a kind of numb shock. The skirmish—massacre, more like—had felt different from a battlefield encounter. *This wasn't an army. This was a village coming after us with pointed sticks and kitchen knives.*

At the peak of the hill, where the rocks broke out of the tree line, there was a crude camp, lean-tos and other makeshift shelters surrounding a circle of campfires. It took a few moments of searching to find the cave Give-Em-Hell had spoken of, a narrow cleft in the rock that led back and out of sight. Winter glared, waiting to see if Infernivore reacted, but the demon she'd sensed still seemed to be quite a ways off.

"I don't like it," Abby said, looking at the opening. "Anybody could be waiting in there, just around the corner."

"I know," Winter said. "But we can't just leave it."

She wished, feeling guilty at the thought, that she'd brought Bobby along. *If someone has to walk into an ambush, it would make sense to send the woman who can't die.* In the event, Abby asked for volunteers, and one of d'Orien's soldiers stepped forward. She was a slender girl named Liz, and from the way she moved Winter guessed this wasn't her first time sneaking into dangerous places in the dark. She crouched low, edging around the cave wall, and tossed her torch in ahead of her. When that produced no reaction, she slithered out of view in a low crouch, a brace of pistols in her hands.

A long moment passed. Two dozen soldiers had their muskets ready and trained on the opening, and Winter waited for the crack of a shot. Instead, there was a scrabble of booted feet, and Liz came running out, her eyes wild. She took two steps, fell to her knees, and vomited.

"Saints and martyrs," Winter said. "What—"

Abby pushed forward, through the ranked soldiers, and knelt at Liz's side. They spoke in low tones, but the closest women heard, and there was a chorus of gasps. Abby stood up, white-faced, and came back to Winter.

"It's . . . There's nothing alive in there." Abby took a deep breath. "It's the rest of the village."

"What?" Winter said. Another soldier had stepped forward, peeking around the curve, then hastily retreating, eyes wide.

"Everyone who couldn't make the charge," Abby said. "The old and the . . . young." She closed her eyes. "The grandmothers killed all the rest, then cut their own throats."

"Oh, Karis above," Winter said. "Saints and bloody fucking martyrs . . ."

For some time after, Winter made no attempt to enforce discipline. The other two forces arrived, and the news of what had happened, on the slope and in the cave, spread in whispers. Some of the soldiers reacted with rage. The partisan camp was torn apart, the pathetic scraps of their belongings ripped to pieces or fed to a hastily kindled bonfire. One ranker found the bundle that had belonged to the Sworn Priest and took possession of his ragged copy of the *Wisdoms*, tearing out the pages one by one. Most, though, simply sat in silence.

Winter, sitting on the edge of the rock, could just about see the silver ribbon of the Intolin winding away to the south. Beside the river was the Grand Army. *And Janus, who brought us here.*

Abby sat beside her and wordlessly offered a wooden flask. Winter took a cautious sip. Whatever was inside burned as it went down her throat. She took a longer pull, then handed it back.

"They wrote something on the wall," Abby said. "In blood."

"Do I want to know?" Winter said.

"My Murnskai's not so good," Abby said. "But one of the rankers said it was, 'You shall not have their souls.'"

"You think the Sworn Priests put them up to this?"

Abby nodded. "I don't think there's any doubt. We're here to steal souls, remember? Karis Almighty."

Winter tipped her head back, squinting against the afternoon sun. *The Church at Elysium. Maybe Janus is right.* She'd known the Black Priests were out to get her, but in a sense she'd signed up for that, entered the war when she'd recited the Infernivore's *naath.* That was one thing. *But telling people to slaughter their own children?* She felt a sudden, indiscriminate rage. *We'll burn Elysium to the ground and dance on the ruins.* She looked at Abby, who was staring into the distance, and wondered if she was entertaining similar thoughts.

"Someone is going to have to bury them," Winter said. "We can't just leave them in there."

"I know." Abby looked down. "You should go back and report to Janus. Take Give-Em-Hell and his troopers. I'll stay and attend to the . . . details."

"Abby . . ."

Abby laid a hand on Winter's arm. "It's all right. Go."

Winter went, with equal measures of relief and guilt. Give-Em-Hell led the way back down the hill, to where his troopers had tethered their horses. They brought a half dozen of the lightly wounded enemy with them, tied together and with their hands bound. One of them was the woman Winter had cut, her face obscured by a bandage wrapped around her head.

Winter shook her head as she approached the base of the hill, trying to rid herself of the vision of Liz's face as she'd come out of the charnel house. *How could they do it?* She wondered if they'd fought, if—

No. It was done, whatever she imagined, and conjuring nightmares wouldn't help. She swallowed hard, trying to settle her stomach, then paused.

It wasn't her stomach that was bothering her. Infernivore had come awake again, the feeling of presence stronger now. It had been growing for some time, as the troopers led their horses down toward the destroyed village. Now she could feel the direction, and when she turned to orient herself she felt certain the source of the sensation was somewhere among the burned-out buildings.

"Stop," she told Give-Em-Hell. "I need to check something."

"Here?" he said. When she nodded, he shrugged. "Very well. Lead—"

"No," Winter said quickly. "You all stay here. If anything happens, get out of here, you understand?"

"Don't be absurd," Give-Em-Hell said, drawing himself up to his full, diminutive height. "At the very least, I'll come myself."

"No! Wait for me here. That's an order." Winter recalled that Give-Em-Hell was a division-general, too, and she wasn't at all sure that she had the authority to give him orders. But he quieted, grumbling, and kept his troopers together as she walked toward what was left of the village.

If it is a Penitent Damned in there, they'll only get themselves killed. The three Penitents who'd come for her in Desland had slaughtered a half dozen Girls' Own soldiers, and she didn't want to repeat that experience. She kept one hand on her sword and let the other hang loose. *All I have to do is get a hold on them.*

The late-afternoon sun threw long shadows from the scattered beams and posts that still stood among the wreckage. Winter followed Infernivore's call, feeling like a hunter trailing after a dog with the scent of prey. Her demon was fully awake now, boiling just beneath the surface of her skin, eager.

At the edge of the clearing, one hut hadn't burned all the way through. Two walls were still standing, with a bit of roof left between them, throwing a deep shadow. Winter approached it cautiously. She thought she could make out a human form, curled up in the corner.

"Hello?" Winter said. *No sense in being quiet. If I can feel them, they can feel me.* "Come out where I can see you."

"I don't think so." It was a young woman's voice. Winter had unwittingly spoken in Vordanai, realizing too late that no one here was likely to understand it. But the other woman answered in the same language, though she had a Hamveltai accent. "Who are you?"

"I'm with the Grand Army of Vordan," Winter said.

The shadowed figure let out a sigh. "And you have a demon."

Winter nodded. There didn't seem to be much point in denying it.

"Then . . ." The other woman coughed. It sounded wet and unhealthy. "You work for Janus bet Vhalnich?"

"Who *are* you?" Winter said. "What do you want?"

"I have come . . . a long way . . . to find you." The woman's breathing was labored. "And I think . . . I'm going to pass out again. Please. Janus . . ."

There was a long, rattling breath, and then silence.

After a moment Winter stepped forward, hand still on her sword. The shadow in the corner didn't respond. Moving closer, Winter could see a young woman lying on her side, curled in on herself as though in pain. She was in her late teens, Winter guessed, with dark, filthy hair and a strange mix of clothes—a ragged shirt and trousers, with an overcoat and boots that looked like they'd come off a much larger Murnskai soldier. Her eyes were closed, and her breathing was quick and shallow. Winter knelt beside her and put one hand against her head, finding the skin hot to the touch.

Infernivore leapt to the front of her mind, its energy surging into her arm and down to her fingers, where skin brushed skin. It would take only the tiniest effort of will, a relaxation of control, to set it loose, tearing into the girl's body and devouring her demon. As weak as she was, Winter guessed that would kill her.

Maybe it would be for the best. This girl didn't *look* like a Penitent Damned, but neither had Jen Alhundt. The Church's assassins were subtle. *This could be a trick to get to Janus.* She pictured bringing someone like Jen into the camp, someone with the power to stop bullets and tear stone to shreds. *The safe thing to do would be to leave her here.*

Winter stared down at the slight movement of the girl's chest, Infernivore still raging in her fingertips. *No. The* safe *thing to do would be to kill her, here and now.* As long as her power was unknown, she was a threat of unknown magnitude.

That's the way they think, isn't it? The Priests of the Black. They saw the whole world like that. Every demon, every *naath*, was a threat to the precious Grace that Karis had bought for humanity, hastening the Day of Judgment when the Beast would be unleashed once more. Every bit of knowledge, every hint of opposition, every wild demon like Danton had to be gathered to Elysium or destroyed. *And they don't care who gets hurt.* She thought about the cave at the top of the hill.

She'd saved Feor, once, in a similar scene of destruction and massacre. At the time she hadn't known what she was getting into, hadn't known anything about demons or *naathem*. She'd just found someone who needed help. *But now . . .*

Winter pulled her hand away slowly and got to her feet. She walked back toward the edge of the village, where Give-Em-Hell and his troopers waited anxiously.

"There's a girl here," she said, gesturing them over. "We've got to take her back to camp. Be careful. I think she's hurt."

At least this time I don't have to hide what I'm doing from my commander. Janus would want to know about this.

"It was . . . I don't know. Sick," Winter said. She took a drink from her tin cup, which was half-full of something thick and purple Cyte claimed was Borelgai. "Just a whole village coming down the hill, right at us. Families. Can you imagine charging an enemy line like that, with your parents and your brothers and sisters all around you, getting killed, and you have to keep going?"

Cyte shook her head. "My father and I have never been close. But . . . no." She sipped her own drink. "Mind you, I can certainly picture my mother charging a line of muskets with a kitchen knife."

Winter grinned. "She sounds formidable."

"She was."

"Hell." Winter sighed and lifted the bottle. "I'm sorry. More?"

"Please." Cyte let her cup fill nearly to the rim before waving Winter off. "It's all right. It was years ago."

"Can I ask what happened?"

Cyte shrugged. "Oh, she charged a line of muskets with a kitchen knife."

Winter stared, not sure how to react, until Cyte gave an impish grin. Winter smiled back, and before long they both dissolved into laughter.

"That's a hell of a thing to joke about," Winter said.

"Sorry," Cyte said. "Couldn't help it. Mother would have approved, anyway. She was always telling me"—she took a deep breath and puffed out her cheeks—"'Temperance, why are you always so *serious*? It's not healthy for a growing girl!'"

There was another pause.

"Temperance?" Winter said.

"Oh. Yeah." Cyte's face went red. "That's . . . the name my parents gave me."

"Karis Almighty. I can see why you changed it."

"Right? Maybe you can explain it to my father."

"I don't think anyone who names their daughter Temperance gets to complain when she turns out to be serious, though."

"I believe I spoke those exact words to my mother on more than one occasion."

Cyte took a long drink. "She died when I was twelve. Some kind of fever of the brain. My father was devastated. My siblings are all older, so I was the only one left in the house, and he . . . fussed over me, I guess you'd say."

"I can see how that would be a bit smothering."

"At the time I couldn't wait to get away." Cyte sighed. "I should go visit the old man, I suppose, once this is all over."

Winter nodded, her thoughts going back to the bodies tumbling down the slope, what they'd discovered in the cave. She took a hasty drink.

"Your family was very religious, then?" Winter said.

"My father was," Cyte said. "My mother more went through the motions."

"Free Church, I assume?"

Cyte nodded. "Why?"

"I'm just . . . trying to understand what could make someone do what they did. I never—" She hesitated. "I haven't told you much about my childhood, have I?"

"I know a little bit. Camp gossip." Cyte smiled again. "I didn't want to pry."

The smile, Winter reflected, transformed her face, wide and bright and as uninhibited as she usually was self-controlled. Then again, Cyte had changed a lot in the time Winter had known her. She remembered a thin, sallow girl, eyes bruised from too many late nights studying and overfond of dark makeup. In spite of the notoriously inconsistent army diet, the regular exercise had helped her fill out to good effect.

Winter blinked, hesitated for a moment, and took another drink to cover it. *This stuff is stronger than it tastes.*

"I grew up in an orphanage," she said. "We all called it Mrs. Wilmore's Prison for Young Ladies."

"You don't remember your family?"

Winter shook her head. "Not more than snatches. They told me I arrived when I was about four, which was young. Most girls don't wind up there until they're ten or eleven." Jane had arrived about that age. They'd locked eyes, that first night, as the new arrivals were introduced—

She coughed. "In any event . . . My point was that we were brought up pretty strictly in the Free Church. Lots of lessons from the *Wisdoms*, lots of study of the saints, lots of prayer. And I guess I believed it, for the most part." She remembered *wanting* to believe, anyway, looking at the faces of the girls around her, lowered in prayer, and wanting to get the same comfort they got. Then, after she'd spent enough time with Jane, wondering if they were just faking it like she was. "But I can't imagine doing something like those villagers did, just because a priest said it was the will of God."

"Father may be pretty strict," Cyte said, "but if our priest ever told him to murder his children, I'm pretty sure he'd have gone home with the *Wisdoms* crammed up his ass."

"Why would *anyone* listen?" Winter leaned back, cup dangling from her fingers. "In Khandar, the Redeemers were bad, I'll grant you. But I felt like I understood them, at least a little. They were poor, starving people who wanted to turn out the prince and the fat temple priests and burn them in the streets. That's not so strange. Hell, we did that in Vordan, only Dr. Sarton invented a special machine for it."

"The Redeemers wanted to burn you, too," Cyte said.

"Nothing mysterious about that," Winter said. "Everyone can always get behind hating foreigners. But these people . . . I don't know."

"You're asking me?" Cyte said.

"You're the history student, aren't you?"

"My official historical judgment is that people have done a lot of fucked-up things over the years," Cyte said. "Sometimes it's priests telling them what to do, sometimes it's kings, and sometimes it's bankers or secret societies or . . ." She brightened. "Did you know that the Montrauk Tyranny was once ruled for an entire year by a chicken?"

"You're making that up."

"I swear by Karis." Cyte pressed one hand to her heart. "They had this board, and they'd write the various decisions on it and then scatter some seeds over it and see which the chicken ate first. Apparently the previous tyrant had decreed that the chicken was sacred."

"What happened?"

"The priests who were really running things fixed it so the chicken would decree the execution of one of the rebellious generals. He found out about it beforehand, and there was a bit of a bloodbath, although history does not record the ultimate fate of the chicken."

Winter stared. "You are *definitely* making that up."

"When we get back to Vordan, I'll take you to the University library. There's all sorts of strange things in the stacks."

When we get back to Vordan. Winter envied Cyte her casual confidence. *We're finally getting to the heart of things, Janus says. The Priests of the Black. If we win this time, maybe it really will be over.* She wished she could believe that.

"Are you all right?" Cyte said.

"Fine. I think." Winter set her cup down, swaying slightly. "Maybe a little drunk. It's been a very long day."

"I'd better go." Cyte gulped the last of her own drink, got to her feet, and stretched. Winter found herself staring and turned away before the other woman noticed. "What about your prisoner?"

"I'm not sure she's a prisoner," Winter said. "Not yet, anyway."

"Is she going to live?"

"Hanna thinks so." Hanna Courvier, the Girls' Own regimental cutter, had turned her acid tongue on the unconscious girl, who had apparently been traveling for a considerable time with a serious wound in her side. "She cut out some diseased flesh and said it hadn't festered too deep. There's a fever, but unless the poison's reached her blood, she should recover."

"Are you sure having her in the camp is a good idea?"

"No," Winter said. "But she's well guarded, and I'm having Bobby sleep in her tent, just in case."

Cyte nodded. She'd been there when Bobby had fought the ogrelike Penitent Twist to a standstill, saving all their lives in the process. "What about Janus?"

"I sent a report. We'll see what he says in the morning."

"In the morning, then." Cyte lifted the tent flap.

"Not too early, please," Winter said. "For any of us. Abby especially."

"I'll do what I can." Cyte slipped out, the flap falling closed behind her.

The lamp flickered slightly in the breeze. Winter sat still for a moment, then reached for her cup and tipped it back, letting the last of the drink trickle onto her lips.

What am I doing?

It wasn't as if she'd never *noticed* anyone before. There were some striking women in the Girls' Own—Anne-Marie came to mind, with her angelic face and soft, golden curls. And there had, of course, been times on the march—they bathed in shifts, after all, in whatever running water was handy, and Winter had now and again found her eyes lingering for longer than was strictly professional.

But more than that—more than an impersonal *appreciation*—never. It had been Jane who'd woken those feelings in Winter, and she'd assumed they would always belong to Jane alone. Before, when the girls at the Prison had discussed boys—almost as though they were mythical creatures, like unicorns—Winter had dismissed it as a silly, useless pursuit. After she and Jane had begun their clandestine relationship, she still felt apart from the others. She had a secret, deep down in the warm depths of her heart, that they couldn't share. And then Jane had been sent away with Ganhide, and Winter had fled the Prison for Khandar, and she'd assumed that part of her life was closed forever.

Be honest. There had been one night, with Bobby, when they huddled under a single blanket beneath the endless starry sky of the Great Desol. She'd thought—*what?* Nothing particularly coherent, anyway. And nothing had come of it. When Bobby returned from Khandar, she'd had then-Lieutenant Marsh in tow, and in retrospect Winter had been a little harder on the man than he'd really deserved. But that was all.

So what am I doing? Cyte was utterly unlike Jane. Dark hair instead of red, lithe and thin against Jane's ample curves. Calm, collected, and ever so rational against Jane's fire, the passion and violence that lurked just below the surface all the time. But part of Winter wanted to see if that rationality could be teased apart, if there was something more primal lurking underneath it. *I want to see her—*

Damn. Brass Balls of the fucking Beast. I am way too fucking drunk. Winter staggered to her feet just long enough to make it to the bedroll. *The world will make more fucking sense in the morning.*

In the morning the world was fuzzy around the edges and the sun was far too bright. Winter crawled out of her tent in search of coffee and found a ranker waiting at attention. She squinted.

"What is it?"

"From Captain Forester, sir," the woman said. "She said that you wanted to be told when the prisoner was awake."

"She's up already?" Hanna had thought the girl might sleep for days. "Damn. I'd better go." Winter hesitated, smelling the brew over a nearby fire. *Hell, what's the point of being a general if you can't boss the rankers around?* "When that coffee's done, bring a mug or two along for me, will you?"

The ranker grinned. "Of course, sir."

Winter made her way through the camp to the cutter's tent they'd cleared out for the mystery girl. Six armed men from Sevran's Second Regiment guarded it, having replaced the detail that had been there all night. If Winter's orders had been obeyed, a dozen more were waiting within easy earshot, ready to raise the alarm if the patient tried anything strange. *Like cutting men in half with a wave of pure magic, say.*

Bobby waited at the tent flap, holding it open with one hand and saluting with the other. "Morning, sir."

"Morning. When did she wake up?"

"Just a few minutes ago, sir, while I was in here checking on her." Bobby lowered her voice. "I can feel her, too. I think her demon's a strong one."

Bobby's situation was unusual, as far as Winter understood it. Feor, who bore the demon, had granted her the use of its power, which meant that she had the ability to sense demons to a certain degree but barely registered as one herself. Even when Winter was standing next to her, Infernivore didn't so much as twitch. Or so Winter had gathered—Bobby had spent time with Feor learning the basics on the long trip back from Khandar, while Winter had rushed ahead with Janus to get herself involved in the revolution.

"Let me talk to her alone, so she won't feel threatened," Winter said. "But stay just outside. If I need you, I'll scream."

"I'll be waiting, sir."

Winter stepped inside the tent. It was large, for a single patient, with three poles and several unoccupied bedrolls. The girl had been given army-issue trousers and a shirt closer to her size. To Winter's surprise, she was sitting up, shirt pulled up a few inches to examine the bandages wound around her midsection. She looked up as Winter entered. Hollow cheeks and dark circles under her eyes made her exhaustion clear, though she seemed alert.

"I made a bet with myself," the girl said, without preamble. "About where I'd be when I woke up. Assuming I woke up at all." She looked around the cutter's tent and hugged her shoulders. "I guess I won."

"We're back at my camp," Winter said. "This is the Second Division of the Grand Army of Vordan. I'm Winter Ihernglass."

"You're in charge?"

"Of this division. First Consul Vhalnich is in command of the army. Queen Raesinia is here, too."

"Quite the assembly," the girl said. "I'm Alex. You saved my life, I guess."

"I may have," Winter said. "Our cutter Hanna did most of the saving, though. Are you feeling better?"

"Still a little light-headed," Alex said. "And there's a chunk missing from my side. But better than I have for days, which tells you something."

Winter sat down, cross-legged, beside the bedroll. "I don't even know where to start. Who *are* you? Everyone I've met who is . . . like us, you under-stand?" She glanced around at the tent walls, which were not far away and not terribly thick. "They all worked for the Church." Winter lowered her voice. "The Penitent Damned. I assume you're not one of them, because you're not trying to kill me."

"I'm not," Alex said. "Of course, that's exactly what I *would* say if I *were* one of them, to gain your trust. Right?" She raised an eyebrow and shrugged. "I saw the guards. You're not stupid. I don't blame you. But I'm not with the Church. They'd like to have me locked up, in fact. For a long time I thought I was the only one, until I ran into the Penitent Damned."

Winter winced. "They caught you?"

"You might say that," Alex said. There was pain in her voice, and Winter let it lie for now. *Time for that later.*

"Hanna tells me you're lucky to be alive."

"I had a run-in with a Murnskai patrol on the way here." Alex shifted, wincing. "Remind me to thank her."

"You said you were looking for us. For Janus."

Alex nodded.

"Why?"

"Because the priests are telling everyone he's sworn to destroy the Church." She shrugged. "And I won't pretend that the chance to get back at them doesn't come into it, either. I owe them quite a bit of that."

There was a long pause. Alex cocked her head.

"You don't trust me," she said.

"Would you, in my situation?" Winter said.

"I suppose not." She spread her hands. "All I can give you is my word."

"So when Janus asks me what you're doing here, what should I tell him?"

"Tell him I want to help." She raised a hand, then winced. "A demonstra-tion may have to wait until I've had a little more rest. But trust me when I say I can be useful. And all I want in return is the chance to take Elysium down."

"That's all?" Winter said, with a slight smile.

"Well, a cushy government job with a nice salary wouldn't go amiss, either. But mostly revenge."

There was something disarming about her honesty. Winter smiled back and got to her feet. "All right. For now concentrate on getting well. I hope you won't be offended if I keep some guards around. We can discuss where you go next when you're healed."

"Do what you need to." Alex lay back carefully and put her head on her pillow.

"Bobby—Captain Forester—and my staff officer Captain Cytomandiclea know about . . . all of this, but none of the others do. I'd appreciate it if you kept it that way."

"Of course. I don't know about you, but I've spent my whole life hiding what I am." Alex smiled weakly. "Honestly, talking about it to anyone feels strange. Like taking off my clothes in public."

"Let's try to avoid that," Winter said. "I'll let you know when I've spoken to Janus. He may want to meet you."

Alex waved a hand regally. "I'll try to make time in my schedule."

"Interesting," Janus said. "You're certain she carries a demon?"

"It's not something you can fake," Winter said. "Not up close, anyway. Infernivore . . . reacts."

"But she didn't say what sort of power it grants her?"

"She was remarkably closemouthed. But Corporal Forester agrees that it's a powerful one."

"Do you think she's telling the truth?" Janus tapped his grease pencil thoughtfully on the big map at the center of the command tent. "About hiding from the Church?"

"It seems . . . plausible," Winter said. "I can understand how a demon-host could hear the rumors and think of taking shelter with us. But there's more she's not telling us."

"Being on the run does inculcate the habit of secrecy," Janus said. "All right. Keep her with us for now, with all appropriate precautions. See what else you can get out of her."

"You don't want to see her yourself, sir?" Winter said.

"Best not," Janus said. "We can't rule out the possibility that she's a Penitent. At this point I imagine the Pontifex of the Black is getting desperate, and he would certainly try to kill me if he could. A suicidal attack might have the best chance of success."

"We'll keep an eye on her, sir." Winter hesitated. "She seems to understand quite a bit about demons. Is that something she could have learned from the Priests of the Black?"

"Doubtful. They're not exactly free with their knowledge." Janus flicked his pencil north across the map, to the mountains and forests of northern Murnsk. "Perhaps she's been in contact with someone else."

"Who else is there?"

"There are . . . others. Survivors." Janus shrugged. "The Church has done its best to eradicate all the knowledge and traditions of the pre-Karisai age, but there are remnants if you know where to look. The old tribes had their mystic traditions, as did the Mithradacii Tyrants. The greatest height of knowledge came after they were torn down, in the era of the so-called Demon King and his colleagues. Even the early Church, in its pre-Elysian days . . ." He shook his head. "In any event, pockets of the old world remain here and there. Before my assignment to Khandar, when I had only just convinced myself sorcery was real, I did a great deal of research. Church suppression was much more thorough in the south, among the more civilized peoples, than here in the north. I spent some time poking around the lost corners of Murnsk. It's possible Alex found one of them, too."

It was the first Winter had heard of such a thing. Janus himself, she reflected, wasn't good about sharing his knowledge either.

"In any case, I think you made the right decision to bring her in. She could be a useful asset, if we can convince her to open up."

Winter relaxed a little. "Thank you, sir."

"And your operation against the partisans was well conducted. I understand our casualties were light?"

"Yes, sir," Winter said, trying not to picture the doomed boy flailing at the dead Girls' Own soldier with his knife. "I must say I'm concerned at the Murnskai's fanaticism. This could become a very ugly campaign."

"I agree," Janus said. "All the more reason to make it a quick one."

His gaze shifted south again on the map. The Pilgrim's Road was drawn in red, running northeast from Vantzolk, crossing one river line after another at tiny towns whose names Winter could barely read. A mass of markings in red grease pencil clustered around the river Syzria, with cryptic markings and dates merging into a complex mess.

"Make sure your soldiers are ready for some harder marching, Division-General," Janus said, as though reading Winter's thoughts. "It won't be long now."

CHAPTER SEVEN

RAESINIA

The mood of the camp had gotten darker over the past few days.

Raesinia rode near the head of the column, with only a few attendants. She'd returned most of the Girls' Own guards to their regiment now that the fighting had begun, though Barely and Joanna had volunteered to continue as her personal escorts. Most of the Grenadier Guard had been left behind, too, at Raesinia's insistence. They weren't field soldiers, and their elaborate kit took up wagon space that could be used for supplies. With Janus constantly suggesting she'd be safer behind the lines, Raesinia was determined not to give him any reason to think she was hindering the march.

At first the quick retreat of the Borelgai and the slow pace gave the whole affair the air of a triumphal procession. They passed through towns and villages, watched from the sides of the road by awed Murnskai peasants. They didn't look very different from Vordanai peasants, in truth, though the women universally wore ankle-length skirts and drab colors. Even the meanest settlement had its Sworn Church, wooden spire topped with a double circle, a constant, slightly alien reminder that they were far from home.

Still, enemies or not, the people were happy to sell what they had to the foreigners at what were no doubt ludicrously inflated prices. To the great consternation of her servants, Raesinia insisted on sampling local fare—coarse black breads, roasted potatoes and turnips, and a seemingly endless variety of ways to rearrange the parts of a pig. There was very little wine, but quite a few local drinks made from fermented potatoes, beets, or grains. She purchased a sampling of these to serve at her dinners with Marcus, though she had to admit that since her demon made her unable to get drunk, she didn't get much out of them.

Being with the army felt liberating and frustrating in equal measure. She was away from the court, with its fawning sycophants and endless ceremony, not to mention the ceaseless debates with the Deputies-General over minor points of constitutional protocol. Marcus had relaxed, at least a little, and settled into his role as the queen's military tutor. Now all the talk of divisions and battalions, squadrons and batteries, lines and flanks and deployment no longer seemed quite so incomprehensible to her. Soldiers, she'd decided privately, were a bit like doctors, giving complex names to straightforward things to keep outsiders from understanding what the hell they were talking about.

Spending time with Marcus, though, reminded her of everything she'd given up. The time before the revolution seemed, in retrospect, unbearably naive, but she couldn't help longing for the nights of lounging around the Blue Mask with Ben, Cora, and the others, arguing over some of the same points the Deputies-General now investigated at such length. The brief taste of freedom she'd gotten later at Marcus' side, going incognito to investigate the attempt on her life, had only left her increasingly unsatisfied when she'd returned to the palace. Now, though she had escaped from Ohnlei, it felt as though some part of it had followed her here. Being constantly surrounded by soldiers meant keeping up her official mask at all times, and Marcus, though a bit friendlier, was still always scrupulously correct in his manner.

Worst of all was that she didn't have anything to *do*. She was determined to stay close to Janus, so as to be on the spot when the war reached its decisive point. But she didn't have any responsibilities in the army, not even the ceremonial sort that she'd grudgingly gotten used to at Ohnlei. Sothe had originally wanted to arrange reviews and parades, but Raesinia had forbidden it—again, she refused to give Janus any way to say she was interfering in military matters.

After the partisan attacks had begun, there was no more talk of reviews or parades, and the friendly markets with Murnskai peasants disappeared. The army huddled in on itself, sleeping fitfully behind trigger-happy sentries, like a beast suddenly aware there were predators out in the darkness. Two days out from Vantzolk, the Girls' Own was sent to clean out a nest of the irregular fighters, and the stories that filtered back were horrific.

"Is it true?" Raesinia asked Marcus that night at dinner. "About the children?"

"What?" Marcus looked up from his glass, which contained some dubious-looking red liquor probably derived from beets. "What children?"

"When the Girls' Own tracked down the partisans, the whole band attacked and was shot down, the boys and girls and women along with the men. And then when they found their camp, the elders had—"

"Oh." Marcus shook his head. "Yes, that's about the shape of it, as far as I know."

"Balls of the Beast," Raesinia swore. She did that more frequently than she really ought to, just to see the look of shocked surprise that crossed Marcus' face every time. "The Priests of the Black, do you think?"

"Janus believes so," Marcus said, looking uncomfortable. "He told me the pontifex won't hesitate to hurt the locals, because he knows they'll blame everything on us in the end."

"Is he right?"

"I expect he is." Marcus tipped back the drink and winced. "My experience in Khandar taught me it's easy to get people to think badly of foreigners."

"So what do we do about it?"

"What can we do? Push on to Elysium and put an end to this."

Raesinia hesitated. The hell of it was, the barbarism of the Church actually made Janus' position look more reasonable. *If Sworn Priests are telling villagers to slaughter babies like hogs, maybe we* ought *to root them all out.* But however awful the Elysian Church could be, and however passionate his rhetoric, she didn't believe for a moment that Janus himself cared. *What will he do when he has Elysium?* He'd crossed half the world to secure the Thousand Names, and now the greatest treasure trove of magical knowledge ever assembled was nearly within his reach. *What is he planning to do with it? Become the next Demon King?*

The subject of the atrocities clearly made Marcus uncomfortable, though, so Raesinia let it drop. While the servants brought in another local delicacy—toasted black bread with a spread that was almost pure pork lard—he patted his coat pocket and pulled out a few sheets of folded paper.

"We've had word from Vordan," he said, once they were alone again. "Via the flik-flik." That was the innovation Janus had copied from the Desoltai, the chain of lanterns that could pass information across hundreds of miles in a single night.

"Anything important?"

"Most of it is just army logistics, of course. Supplying us is a massive effort. But Feor included a note saying that she hasn't felt any new *naathem* and that her training program is achieving some results. She mentioned that she had spoken with our . . . ah . . . unexpected ally."

"The Steel Ghost?" The mysterious Khandarai, who'd once fought against Marcus, had aided them against the Penitent Damned, though Raesinia still had no idea as to his true motivations.

Marcus nodded.

"He came to me before we left, you know," she said.

"Really?" Marcus frowned. "You might have told him we had questions."

"Answering questions doesn't seem to be his style."

"What was he there for, then?"

"To warn me that he couldn't watch out for me once I went north," Raesinia said. She cut a bite of the toast and speared it with her fork, lard glistening in the candlelight. "He'd been keeping me safe from Penitents, but with Janus and the army out of the city, he said he was going to stay behind and protect the Thousand Names."

"Janus has his own arrangements for that," Marcus said grimly. "Do you trust the Steel Ghost?"

"He did save our skin from that monster of a Penitent."

"He did," Marcus said. "But why? Why would he help us?"

"He seems to hate the Black Priests as much as Janus does." Raesinia popped the bite in her mouth, salty and thick with grease. "The enemy of our enemy, I suppose."

"And if we beat the Black Priests, then what?"

Raesinia shook her head. *It all comes back to Janus, doesn't it? Damn.* She sighed. "I think I liked it better when we only had Orlanko to worry about."

"Speak for yourself," Marcus said, smiling. "Even if things are more complicated, it's nice to know that we've got a lot more muskets on our side."

It's not complicated for him, though, is it? Raesinia watched Marcus as the servants brought in the main course. *He trusts Janus. All he has to do is follow orders.* Raesinia wished, just for a moment, that she could do the same. But the responsibility that had driven her to start a revolution against her own government rather than see it usurped by Orlanko would not let her rest. *I have to see this through.*

The next day the main body of the Grand Army reached Vantzolk. It was an impressive sight. Not the town itself, a few hundred wood-and-plaster buildings huddled around an ancient stone bridge, but the camp that had been constructed in the fields alongside it. Acres of rye and potatoes had been crushed underfoot to lay out a supply depot larger than most market squares, with military consumables of every description piled as high as they could be stacked. Crates of hardtack, barrels of powder, cases of solid shot, wagons of fodder, boots and shirts and trousers, canteens and cartridge boxes, rack upon rack of spare muskets. Even more impressive were the animals, endless strings of horses for the officers and the cavalry, mules and oxen for pulling carts, cattle to be driven in the army's wake and slaughtered for meat as the need arose. Just keeping the vast herd fed and hauling away the shit employed enough handlers to form a new battalion.

In addition to the fleet of vehicles the army had gathered on the march, Vordan had been pressed into supplying anything that rolled. Raesinia saw carriages intended to carry ladies to grand, glittering balls, their tops hacked off and filled with dried corn; cabs from Vordan City, markings still advertising their fares, rattling and squelching along full of sacks of coffee or casks of butter. The edges of the camp looked like the Exchange on a particularly busy day, jam-packed with angry, shouting drovers and irritated animals.

Adding the Grand Army itself, a group of soldiers as large as a medium-sized city, turned the situation into utter chaos in spite of the best efforts of the officers assigned to direct them. Raesinia stayed out of the way, her servants erecting her tent on a small rise well inside the sentry cordon, but at a decent distance from the unfolding mess. She was not surprised when a messenger arrived from Marcus to say that he would not be joining her for dinner.

Somehow, staring out at the mountains of goods made it all seem more real. The colossal effort required to bring these things here was only the beginning. Invading Murnsk had been a byword for foolhardy, fruitless endeavors for centuries, but Janus really intended to go through with it—to push this vast army, and all the matériel that supported it, hundreds of miles over bad roads and through trackless forests, in spite of whatever the Emperor of Murnsk tried to do to stop him. *This is the man we made First Consul. Saints and martyrs.* The most frightening part was, she believed he could do it.

It also, she had to admit, brought with it a feeling of pride. *We did this. Vordanai.* Since the War of the Princes, Vordanai power had been at a low ebb, broken by the alliance of Hamvelt and Borel. Now mighty Antova had fallen, the Hamveltai were humbled, and the legendary Duke of Brookspring had barely escaped annihilation. And Janus was going to take his army where even Farus IV never had, to Elysium itself.

The next stage of the march was the sixty miles to Tsivny, on the river Norilia. The Pilgrim's Road left the river behind here, narrowing to a rutted strip of earth that would barely be deemed a farm track in Vordan. Janus had given strict orders that the column stay close to the trail, though, and as they moved farther from the river and into the hinterland Raesinia could see why. The road wound around hills, following the terrain, and the farther north they went, the closer and thicker the forest became. Soon they were riding in the shadow of the trees, the enormous column squeezed down to an impossibly thin line of blue that stretched back for miles. Compressing the whole length into a single camp became impossible, and each division pitched its own tents wherever it found itself when night fell. The cavalry, pushing out ahead to make sure no enemy threatened the army in this awkward state, was run ragged by the constant patrols Janus demanded.

Every evening Marcus arrived for dinner looking tired but satisfied. She realized he hadn't been trying to snub her, back in Talbonn, when he said he was happy to be in the field again. This work, the endless small crises of moving an army through a hostile countryside, was what he felt most comfortable doing.

"You're probably right," he said when she mentioned this. Grinning, he leaned forward. "Take it as a lesson, Your Majesty. There are different tools for every task, and war isn't just about fighting battles."

"You've fought battles," Raesinia protested.

"Of course I have. But I would never claim more than basic competence." He gestured vaguely in the direction of the command tent. "Janus is what a real battle commander ought to be. He knows his men, the terrain, the enemy army. He knows the mind of the enemy commander, probably better than the man himself does."

"He's not unbeatable," Raesinia said, a little uncomfortably.

"No one's unbeatable," Marcus said. "He's just very, very good. But to him, all this, the marching over bad roads and so on, it's just preliminaries to be gotten out of the way before the main event. Whereas if you need someone to straighten out a traffic jam or organize a camp so nobody gets in anybody's way, that's more my forte." He smiled, a little sheepishly, and scratched his beard. "Actually, when you put it that way, it doesn't sound very impressive, does it?"

"Your Majesty . . ." Sothe said quietly.

"I know," Raesinia said. "You think this is a bad idea."

"These people are dangerous."

Raesinia gestured around them. The large tent, big enough for a company to eat dinner, was empty except for herself, Sothe, and five guards from the Girls' Own. She and Sothe sat on a bench on one side of a long table, like hosts waiting for their guests to arrive.

"I think we've taken adequate precautions," Raesinia said. Lowering her voice, she added, "And they're hardly dangerous to *me*."

"It's still a risk, however slight. I don't understand what you hope to gain."

That was a point on which Raesinia wasn't prepared to have a debate, but she was saved from the necessity by the arrival of a small procession. It was led by a Girls' Own sergeant, a big woman with a barely tamed frizz of red hair, and followed by four more soldiers. They were evenly spaced around the prisoners, two women and a young boy, dressed in the drab browns of Murnskai peasants.

Raesinia got to her feet as the captives were escorted to the other side of the table. Their hands were bound behind their backs, she noted, and they were absolutely filthy, clothes stiff with mud and skin still crusty with dried blood. The taller of the two women had bandages wrapped around her head, with an angry red inflammation peeking out from underneath them. Something *stank*, the sick-sweet smell of a festering wound.

"Sergeant," Raesinia said. "General Ihernglass assured me these prisoners were being treated properly."

"We've done everything we can for 'em," the sergeant said, bowing deep. "General Ihernglass said he doesn't want us to lay hands on them more than necessary. We've offered baths and fresh clothes, but they won't hear of it. Won't let a cutter near them, either." She glared at the captives. "If the stink displeases you, I can have the girls strip 'em down and rinse 'em off."

"No," Raesinia said. "I think General Ihernglass has it right." She turned back to the trio. "Has anyone tried to talk to them?"

The sergeant scratched her cheek. "Not enough of us speak Murnskai, to be honest, Your Majesty. They've got a few words of Vordanai, but not enough for a conversation. General Ihernglass spoke to them a little bit, but after we wiped out the whole nest of 'em he didn't think they'd have anything useful to say."

Raesinia nodded, still staring at the three. The woman whose face wasn't bandaged was the oldest, and she met Raesinia's gaze with hard, clear blue eyes. The boy couldn't have been older than fifteen, and kept sneaking quick glances at Raesinia before turning his attention back to his shoes.

"Good afternoon," Raesinia said, blowing the mental dust off her Murnskai. She spoke slowly and probably overpolitely; everything she'd learned had been geared toward diplomatic functions. "I am Raesinia Orboan. What are your names?"

The older woman blinked, unprepared to be addressed in her own language. Then, with a quick glance at her companions, she set her jaw and said nothing.

"I'm not going to hurt you," Raesinia said. "I just want to talk. Would you like to sit down?"

"I am Vitali," the boy mumbled.

The older woman heaved a sigh. "I am Nina," she said. "And this is Lidiya." Her eyes narrowed. "You are . . . empress?"

"Queen, we would say," Raesinia said. "Yes. I am the Queen of Vordan."

"Queen of the heretics," Lidiya muttered under her breath. "Queen of filth."

Nina ignored this. "Why would you speak to us?"

"I wanted to talk about what you did, back at the village. I wanted to . . ." Raesinia trailed off, shaking her head. Most of all she wanted to *understand*, impossible as that might seem. "You fought. All of you together, men and women and children."

"Of course," Nina said. "My sons and I would not leave my husband on his own." She blew out a breath. "I regret only that I must wait before I can see them again."

"And before that," Raesinia said. "You attacked the army at night? The wagons, the supply lines. Correct?"

"She will kill us," Vitali muttered urgently. "Say nothing."

"She will kill us anyway," Lidiya said. The bandage held her jaw shut, Raesinia realized, so all her words came from between clenched teeth.

"Let her," Nina said, making no attempt to hide her voice. "Yes. We did our part to drive your cursed army away."

"Why?" Raesinia said. "None of our foragers even came close to your village. We did nothing to you."

"Is that what you think of us?" Nina laughed bitterly. "That we are so cowardly as to ignore the houses your men burn, the girls they rape, the crops they steal, because they haven't yet come to *our* village? That we value our lives so highly we would stand by while your demon general destroys Father Church and condemns the world to darkness?"

"No villages have been burned," Raesinia said. "We are here because your emperor declared war on *us*."

Even as she said it, it felt like sophistry. *We're here because Janus wants to destroy the Black Priests.* The First Consul had made it clear that everything else was secondary.

"The emperor serves by the will of God," Vitali said. It sounded like a catechism. "The Church of Elysium is the will of God made manifest."

"Who told you to destroy your own village?" Raesinia said. "The priests?"

"You understand nothing of us," Nina said. "Everything we do is in accordance with the will of God. We feel it." There was pity in her eyes for a moment. "A heretic would never understand."

"You're right," Raesinia said, feeling her anger rising. "I don't understand what could drive people to murder their own children." She looked from Nina to Lidiya and back again. "It's what you did, isn't it? Everyone too young or too old to join in your mad attack."

"They are with God now," Nina said, her eyes hooded. "My mother. My daughter."

"My sisters," Vitali said. "And my brother. One of your girl soldiers cut his throat."

"They didn't have to be," Raesinia said. "If you'd stayed in your homes, we would have left you alone!"

"Lies," Lidiya said. "You lie, you . . . you . . ."

Her emotion overcoming her limited ability to speak, she took hold of the bandage and tore it away. A crust of dried blood and pus went with it, and fresh gore spattered across the table. Raesinia instinctively averted her eyes from the ruin of the woman's face, where a long diagonal cut was dark with rot at the edges.

"You think you can fool us, harpy," Lidiya shouted. "Slut. Queen of whores. Look at you, dressed like a boy to please your general. He must fancy little boys."

The Girls' Own sergeant stepped forward, frowning, but Raesinia held up a hand. She felt Sothe tense.

"I should have stayed home and done nothing?" Lidiya said, blood spraying with every word. "My children are *safe* now in their eternal reward. I should have let you take their souls? Make them into freaks like your whore soldiers?" She jerked her head at the guards and sneered, dry flesh cracking. "Murnsk and Father Church will build a mountain of your heretic corpses, and then you will scream forever in hell."

Lidiya ran out of breath, panting, a steady patter of blood dripping onto the table. Nina squared her shoulders.

"Well?" she said. "Will you kill us now?"

"No," Raesinia said, wiping a spot of blood off her cheek. "Sergeant?"

"Your Majesty?" The sergeant was staring at the maimed woman.

"Take these two away." She indicated Nina and Vitali, then pointed at Lidiya. "Find a cutter and tell him to do whatever he can for her."

"Yes, Your Majesty." The sergeant gestured the guards forward. "Although it may be too late."

"Tell him to try regardless." Raesinia sat down heavily on the wooden bench. "Thank you for your help, Sergeant."

"Of course." The sergeant bowed and followed the retreating prisoners.

"You were right," Raesinia said, when Sothe sat beside her. "This was a bad idea. I thought . . ." She wasn't sure *what* she'd thought. "That maybe if we're fighting the Priests of the Black, we could convince everyone else to stay out of it."

"It would be easier for all concerned," Sothe said. "But you know it's impossible."

Raesinia shook her head. "I thought some of them could be convinced, perhaps. They've just seen their families slaughtered on Elysium's orders. They should *hate* the priests for that. But . . ." She looked up at Sothe. "They're going to fight us, aren't they? All the way to Elysium."

"All the way," Sothe agreed.

A hundred more villages like this one. A hundred more little massacres. Knives in the dark and burning villages.

"It's what needs to be done," Sothe said, watching her expression.

To keep me *safe from the Priests of the Black.* Raesinia took a long, shaky breath. *Does that make this my fault or theirs?*

"Your Majesty?" Sothe said. "Are you all right?"

"I'm fine," Raesinia said. "Go back to the tent. I want to . . . walk for a while."

After the rot-tinged air of the tent, the cool air outside felt like a tonic. Raesinia walked away with no clear destination in mind, turning at random through the close-packed tents of the Girls' Own camp. There were women everywhere, cooking, cleaning weapons, playing dice or cards, and attending to all the other incomprehensible little chores that soldiers busied themselves with on the march. Some of them recognized her, and she left a trail of startled looks and sketchy bows in her wake.

Eventually she felt the strange, almost-pain sensation in her head that she'd learned meant the nearby presence of another demon. Raesinia hadn't managed to become adept with this new sense, but she could usually tell when Winter

was nearby, at least. This time it felt unusually strong, and she expected to find
the general right behind her, but when she finally stopped, she was standing by
the flap of a tent halfway down the row. Winter noticed Raesinia at the same
time and bowed as she approached.

"Your Majesty," Winter said. "I didn't expect to see you here."

"Just clearing my head," Raesinia said.

Winter exchanged a look with a captain standing beside her.

"You're not here to visit Alex?" Winter said.

Raesinia blinked. "Alex?"

"Our . . . guest. I thought the First Consul would have given you my report."

"He didn't say anything about it," Raesinia said, gritting her teeth. "Who's
Alex?"

"We picked her up after the fight with the partisans. She's"—Winter looked
around—"like us. You understand?"

A demon-host. While the precise nature of Raesinia's power was known
only to a few, it was impossible to conceal the presence of her demon from
another host. Now that she knew what to look for, she could just about separate
the pressure in her head into two distinct parts, one oriented toward Winter,
the other into the tent.

"Is she Murnskai?" Raesinia said. "A Penitent?"

"She's Hamveltai, as best we can tell. She's been recovering from a nasty
wound, so we haven't gotten the chance to question her closely. She claims to
be looking for revenge on the Priests of the Black, but . . ." Winter shrugged.
"Janus asked me to try to get something more out of her."

"Can I speak with her?" Raesinia said.

Winter frowned. "I was about to talk to her myself, but we can't be certain
it's safe. If she *is* a Penitent—"

"You don't need to worry on my account," Raesinia said. "I can take care
of myself."

Unlike Sothe, Winter seemed willing to take that at face value. She nodded
to the captain.

"Bobby, wait outside, but don't go far."

"Yes, sir." Bobby saluted and moved off.

Raesinia lowered her voice. "She's one of us as well?"

Winter nodded. "It's . . . complicated, but yes."

Keeping my secret is going to be harder than I thought. There seemed to be a
surprising number of demon-hosts around.

Winter slipped through the tent flap, and Raesinia followed, her eyes taking a moment to adjust to the relative darkness. It was a cutter's tent, with room for a surgeon and several patients, but currently only one bedroll was occupied. The young woman that Raesinia assumed was Alex was sitting up, reading a thick, leather-bound book. She was younger than Raesinia, probably still in her teens, with dark hair and wide, intelligent eyes. Her face was a little drawn, probably from the injury Winter had spoken of, but her expression was alert when she looked up at them.

"Winter!" she said. "Thank God. I thought I was going to have to tackle another chapter."

"That bad?" Winter said.

"I'm sure it's fascinating, if you're interested in the marriage arrangements of a Mithradacii Tyrant who's been dead for a thousand years."

"I'll ask Cyte if she has anything more exciting." Winter gestured to Raesinia. "This is—"

Raesinia had been watching Alex, and there was no recognition in her eyes. She caught Winter's gaze and raised an eyebrow. Winter understood and with barely a stumble continued. "—Raes."

"Another demon-host," Alex said. "Janus has quite the collection, doesn't he?"

Raesinia gave a noncommittal smile.

Winter said, "Do you mind if we sit?"

"It's your tent," Alex said. "I'm just borrowing it."

Winter dragged cushions over, and she and Raesinia sat down opposite Alex. Alex set the book aside.

"So," she said. "I'm assuming this isn't a social call." There was a touch of bitterness in her voice. "Have you and Janus decided whether I'm a Penitent yet?"

"I was hoping I could ask you some questions," Winter said. "If you're feeling up to it."

Alex patted her midsection. "I think I can manage."

Winter exchanged a look with Raesinia, then said, "Did you read the name of your demon, or were you born with it?"

"I was born with it," Alex said. "For a long time I didn't understand what I could do. It scared me." She shrugged, and a shadow crossed her face. "I grew up on the streets in Hamvelt, begging charity from the guilds. It wasn't a good place to be . . . different."

"Did someone teach you?" Winter said.

"Not exactly. The old man—" Alex looked wary, then sighed. "I don't suppose it matters now, does it? His name was Metzing, and he took me as an . . . apprentice, I suppose."

"In what trade?" Raesinia broke in.

"He was a thief," Alex said matter-of-factly. "The greatest thief in the world, actually. Now I guess I am."

"He's dead?" Winter said.

Alex nodded, anger filling her expression. "*They* killed him. The Black Priests. He was the closest thing to a father I ever had, and they left him floating in the Vor just because they wanted to get to me."

Raesinia winced. That described too many people in her own life—Ben, Faro, even Danton—lives destroyed by her enemies to get to her in one way or another.

"You hadn't heard of them before that?" Raesinia said.

"I'd heard of them," Alex said. "I just didn't think they were real." She tapped the history book. "Back then, sure, everyone knows the Black Priests fought demons and sorcerers. But not anymore. I thought I was the only one, somehow." She forced a laugh. "Seems a little unlikely, now that I think about it."

"You got away from them?" Winter said.

"Not . . . exactly." Alex sat up a little straighter. "Not at all, in fact. There was a Penitent named Shade in Vordan City—"

"Ionkovo," Raesinia said grimly.

"You know him?" Alex sounded surprised.

"Not *socially*," Raesinia muttered. "He tried to kill me."

"Then you probably know what he can do. He uses shadows as a gateway to some *other* place. He can climb in and out wherever it's dark enough." She shuddered. "He carried me through with him, on the way out of the city. They'd given me something to knock me out, but I woke up near the end. It was . . . unpleasant." Alex swallowed. "He turned me over to another Penitent. I spent a month chained to the bed of a cart, half-mad from whatever potion they were feeding me. They were going to keep me like that all the way to Elysium."

Raesinia felt a chill. Ionkovo had no doubt intended a similar fate for her, when he'd tried to capture her during Maurisk's attempted coup. Only Winter's last-minute rescue had stopped him. From the look on Winter's face, Raesinia guessed her thoughts were running along the same lines.

"Did you get there?" Winter said. "To Elysium?"

"Oh," Alex said. "No. If you're hoping for intelligence, I'm afraid I don't know much. We met up with another caravan, carrying another prisoner. A boy named Abraham. He . . ." Alex paused. "He figured out a way to escape, and he took me with him."

"Escape to where?" Winter said. "Where have you been hiding?"

"Into the forests, at first. There were some people who helped us, here and there."

"And then you decided to come look for Janus?" Winter said.

"More or less. Even before the peace conference, the priests were telling anyone who would listen that Janus was out to destroy the Church and that he had demonic powers. It gets the peasants ready to fight." Raesinia, thinking of the tirade she'd just endured, nodded. Alex went on. "I didn't think much of it at first, but after a while I started to hear some more solid rumors about what had happened in Vordan. And I thought, maybe this is my chance. I owe the Black Priests, for the old man and for myself. So I came to find out if it was true." She grinned. "I wasn't planning on getting shot along the way, of course."

Winter sat back, pondering that. Raesinia said, "What happened to Abraham?"

"It's . . ." Alex shook her head. "I want you to trust me, so I'm trying not to lie to you. But some things aren't my secrets to tell, you understand? He won't bother anyone."

"I understand." Winter got to her feet. "Thank you for being as open as you can. I'll speak to Janus—"

"Wait," Alex said. "You still think I'm one of them?"

Winter looked pained. "I didn't say that."

"I took an awful risk coming here." Alex put her hand on her side where it was bandaged. "More than I probably understood at the time. All I'm asking for is a chance to *help*. If you're going to fight the Black Priests, you'll need it, believe me."

"I know," Winter said. "But you have to appreciate our position."

"How am I supposed to prove that I'm *not* something?" Alex rolled her eyes. "Maybe Abraham was right."

Raesinia took Alex's hand, which seemed to startle the girl. Their eyes met.

"When the time comes, you'll be in the fight," Raesinia said. "General Ihernglass and I understand what it means to need revenge."

Winter coughed, and Raesinia sat back. Alex blinked.

"All right," she said, looking away from Raesinia. "Any chance I'll be able to leave this tent anytime soon?"

"I'll see what I can do," Winter said.

Bobby met them outside, with a couple of Girls' Own guards carrying food and drink. Winter waved the soldiers on.

"Sorry," Raesinia said. "I didn't mean to undercut your authority."

"You're the queen," Winter said. "You're entitled to."

"I just . . . know how she feels." Raesinia took a deep breath. "If she's a Penitent, she's a very impressive liar."

"She's still not telling us everything," Winter said. "There has to be more to the story of how she escaped."

"That doesn't make her one of them, though," Raesinia said. "You and I can both appreciate the value of someone who can keep a secret."

Winter smiled and turned to Bobby. "Can you keep a guard around if I give her freedom of the camp?"

Bobby nodded. "I don't see the harm. If she *is* a Penitent, the walls of a tent aren't going to be much of an obstacle."

"Spread the word to keep an eye on her," Winter said. "If anything seems strange, I want to hear about it." She turned to Raesinia. "Thank you for your help, Your Majesty."

"It's nothing." *Janus wasn't going to tell me about this.* Raesinia wondered, not for the first time, what else he was hiding.

They reached Tsivny the same day that Sothe brought her the spy.

Raesinia's entourage had thinned considerably since leaving Talbonn. There were a half dozen Grenadier Guards, who watched her tent in shifts, and as many servants to do the basic work of cooking and cleaning. The pair from the Girls' Own, Barely and Joanna, accompanied her whenever she went out. And then there was Sothe, theoretically her Head of Household, in actuality her bodyguard, spymaster, and occasional assassin.

Raesinia had grown used to Sothe's nearly constant presence back in Vordan, but since the army had marched they'd actually seen very little of one another. Sothe had been against accompanying the army at all, of course, but once Raesinia had made up her mind the spy had thrown herself into creating an intelligence network to keep her mistress up to date on everything that mattered about the Grand Army. Sothe had her own tent, where she sometimes sat up late into the night working at a portable writing desk, but more often she was out among the troops. Raesinia always pictured her skulking around, overhearing conversations, although she suspected Sothe's work was a little more sophisticated than that.

That morning they'd broken free of the line of forests and back onto cultivated ground, winding down around a last pair of hills and into the valley of the Norilia. The river itself winked in the distance, long, lazy curves catching the sun, and they were once again riding through fields of beets, turnips, and rye. Raesinia had always heard that, lacking decent roads, Murnsk lived by its rivers, but she hadn't appreciated until now how literally true that was—all the people seemed to live within a day's ride of the banks, leaving the vast areas between the rivers as wild forests.

Tsivny wasn't even as big a town as Vantzolk, a stone church and a handful of timbered buildings clinging to one bank of the river. There had been a bridge, a wide wooden span big enough for wagons, but by the time they got there all that was left was a charred skeleton. Partisans, Raesinia guessed. *At least they didn't burn the town.* In any event, Janus seemed to have expected this development, because carts loaded with rough-cut logs were rolling toward the town as soon as the scouts reported it clear of the enemy. The river was deep, but not particularly wide, and by the time the rest of the column began to wind out of the woods and toward the camp, a new bridge was already rising on the ruins of the old.

Raesinia had just sat down in her own tent when there was a scratch at the flap. Barely poked her head in.

"Your Majesty? Mistress Sothe is here, and she says it's urgent. She's got someone with her. Civilian, looks like."

"Send them in," Raesinia said, curiosity piqued immediately. Sothe didn't need to ask permission to enter her tent; if she'd done so, it was because she didn't want this civilian knowing her true status.

Sothe entered first, a slim figure in black and gray, the trim lines of her dress not betraying the weapons Raesinia had no doubt it concealed. Her guest followed, a young man with dirty blond hair in a long canvas coat and felt cap. He bowed low as he came in, and Raesinia nodded in return.

"Your Majesty," he said.

"This is Master Whaler," Sothe said. She stepped across the tent to Raesinia's side and bent to whisper in her ear. "He's a Borelgai spy, though he doesn't know I know that. He thinks he's bribed me for access to you."

Raesinia glanced up at Sothe, startled, but she didn't want to give the game away by asking questions. She contented herself with an upraised eyebrow, then turned back to Whaler, who was still bent at the waist.

"Please rise, Master Whaler," Raesinia said. "Welcome."

"I have a message for Your Majesty," Whaler said, glancing at Sothe. "One best heard in private, I think."

"Of course. Sothe, wait outside, if you would?"

Sothe grimaced, but there was nothing for it. There were times when Raesinia was very glad she was unkillable—if she'd been an ordinary human, she had a feeling Sothe would have demanded she live her entire life in a cage behind a phalanx of guards.

"A message, you said?" Raesinia said.

"Yes, Your Majesty," Whaler said. "From His Grace the Duke of Brook-spring."

"From Dorsay?" Raesinia faked surprise. "You're a spy?"

He grinned rakishly. "That's a harsh way of putting it, Your Majesty, but not entirely inaccurate."

"And why does Dorsay think I want to hear anything from him?" Raesinia waved a hand at the army around her. "We *are* at war, if you haven't noticed."

"It hasn't escaped my attention," Whaler said. "But His Grace instructed me to say that the last time you spoke with him, he didn't think you were *entirely* immune to reasonable compromise."

"High praise," Raesinia said dryly. "And?"

"Now that the situation has evolved, he wishes to speak with you again, in the hope that your interests may coincide with his."

"Fascinating," Raesinia said, thinking furiously. "He could simply send over a party under a flag of truce, of course."

"His Grace is anxious that the First Consul be unaware of these discussions."

Ah. That made sense, after Janus' display at the abortive peace conference. "I see. In that case, how does he propose to accomplish this talk?"

"If Your Majesty agrees, you can accompany me, with a small party, to a place between the lines. His Grace will be there with a similarly small escort."

"That sounds like a marvelous way to kidnap me," Raesinia said.

"It's also a good way for His Grace to put himself in danger from your scouts," Whaler pointed out. "A certain amount of trust is required on both sides."

"How can I be certain you speak for Dorsay?"

"He told me to tell you that he hoped less time would pass between your meetings than last time. He said you'd take his meaning."

Raesinia thought back to her last meeting with the Duke of Brookspring. *"I visited your father's court with a military delegation, and we were introduced to the royal children. You were about two years old, but I thought you comported yourself with dignity . . ."*

"I understand," Raesinia said slowly. "Thank you, Master Whaler. I must . . . consider."

"Of course, Your Majesty. But I suggest you move quickly, or the situation may continue to evolve."

"You think it's a trap, of course," Raesinia said to Sothe.

"I don't, actually," Sothe said. She sat at Raesinia's table, where Marcus usually ate dinner. Raesinia herself paced back and forth in front of her.

"What do you mean?" Raesinia said. "You think *everything* is a trap."

"It may be a trap in the diplomatic sense," Sothe said. "But I don't think the Borels want to murder you or haul you away, if that's what you mean."

"Duke Orlanko certainly does."

"At the moment he doesn't seem to be making the decisions." Sothe shrugged. "It'd be just too easy for us to turn Whaler over to Janus once he gives us a location for the meeting. I'm sure Dorsay will take precautions, but I think this is a genuine offer to negotiate."

"To negotiate with *me*," Raesinia said. "Not with Janus."

"Dorsay told you he thought Janus was mad," Sothe said. "You don't negotiate with madmen."

Raesinia pursed her lips. "What if Janus finds out?"

"You're the queen," Sothe said. "Entering into negotiations with foreign representatives is your prerogative."

"He may not agree, with the army in the field, but it hardly matters. If I do this, he'll say I'm actively working to undermine him." Raesinia paced, turned, and shook her head. "He won't necessarily be wrong. Can we risk that division, this far from Vordan?"

"I don't know," Sothe said.

Raesinia glanced at her. Sothe didn't often simply admit to not knowing something. Unknowns were calculated risks for her, with evidence carefully weighed in the balance.

"It depends on Janus," Sothe said, at Raesinia's look. "And I have observed him long enough to know that I don't understand him. Most men and women are, at the very center, not terribly complex. They want power, or comfort, or sex; it's only the way they go about attaining these desires that distinguishes them."

"Did Duke Orlanko teach you that?"

"It's the first lesson we learn in the Concordat. Find out a person's deepest desire, and you have a lever to control them. But Janus . . ." Sothe shook her head. "He accumulates power as naturally as breathing, but he doesn't seem to want it for its own sake. He appears to have no vices, no romantic entanglements, no great cause or ideology. And yet he has pushed himself to extraordinary heights at no small risk. Why?"

"He told me it was all for my sake," Raesinia said. "Because my father had asked him to."

"Do you believe that?"

"No." Raesinia shook her head. "Janus must have begun acquiring knowledge about the supernatural before he knew about my difficulty, or why would my father have contacted him at all? There has to be something else."

"That's the basic question, then," Sothe said. "Going behind his back is a risk. Whether it's worthwhile depends on what you think he'll do if you don't."

Raesinia closed her eyes for a moment.

Be wary of Vhalnich, the Steel Ghost had said. *He plans deep.* But how deep? *Back to the very beginning? Was helping me only an excuse to go to Khandar and get the Thousand Names, in order to get . . . where?*

"*Queen of whores.*" For a moment she was back in the tent with Lidiya, the woman's blood spattering the table between them. "*We will build a mountain of your heretic corpses . . .*"

She opened her eyes and let out a breath.

"Tell Whaler to arrange the meeting."

The trick was getting out of the camp without attracting any attention. As usual, though, Sothe had the answer. Even with the partisans dogging the army's heels, there was still a certain amount of clandestine traffic with the locals, villagers smuggling in liquor, tobacco, and occasionally girls with the supply convoys that trundled nonstop up the road from Vantzolk. Those peasants went back out the same way, and the guards who'd agreed to turn a blind eye weren't overly concerned if there were more of them going out than coming in.

In addition to Raesinia and Sothe, dressed in nondescript traveling clothes and hooded raincoats, Barely and Joanna had accompanied them. Sothe had reluctantly agreed that the two Girls' Own soldiers were probably trustworthy, and evading them would be more trouble than it was worth. One of the servants remaining behind had instructions to tell everyone that the queen was ill and resting in her wagon.

The army had crossed the Norilia the day before, filing across the ugly but functional bridge after one day's welcome rest camped out on the south bank of the river. It took most of the day for the long column to wind past, minus the garrison that would be left there to safeguard the line of supply back to Vantzolk and the south, and wagons had continued rumbling and rattling over the torch-lit bridge long into the night. The following morning, as the camp began to break up, Raesinia and her small party took advantage of the confusion to meet Whaler and slip away, following a riverside road to the west.

"Thank you for your trust, Your Majesty," Whaler said. "The duke will be very pleased."

Sothe glared at him. Now that Raesinia had made her decision, Sothe had reverted to her usual paranoia, and rode at the head of the group as though she expected to be ambushed at any moment. She wore two pistols and a long knife, in addition to whatever weapons she had concealed under her coat. Barely and Joanna had also donned plain clothes, but they still carried their muskets.

"Might I ask where we're going?" Raesinia said.

"Of course. A small fishing village called Lyzk, perhaps ten miles up the river. The duke will arrive by boat."

Not a bad setup, Raesinia mused. It would be easy for Dorsay to arrange to have a signal set, in the event the meeting was a trap, in which case he could simply retreat to the other side of the river. *Assuming, of course, the whole thing isn't his trap to begin with.*

The ride passed in silence. By the time Lyzk came into sight, the sun was well up, and Raesinia's long coat was feeling warm for what promised to be a genuinely hot day. The village was even smaller than Tsivny, without a bridge to bring traffic, just a small cluster of shacks and a pier with a few elderly boats tied up. It didn't look like there was room to hide much of an ambush, but Raesinia nevertheless reined up alongside Whaler while Sothe, Barely, and Joanna rode ahead to scout. After a few minutes' search, they reported that the place was abandoned, the villagers no doubt having fled rumors of the advancing Vordanai army.

"If you're satisfied," Whaler said, "I should send a signal to indicate to the duke that it's safe to land."

Sothe crossed her arms and looked unhappy, but nodded. Whaler lit a torch and waved it over his head in wide circles, until he caught an answering movement from the opposite bank of the river. He doused the torch and smiled at Raesinia.

"Shouldn't be long to wait now," he said.

"Thank you," Raesinia said, then cocked her head. "Out of curiosity, how well do you know Dorsay?"

"I wouldn't be so bold as to say I *know* him," Whaler said. "But I've served His Grace personally for more than a decade. That's why he chose me for this assignment."

"I'm not sure I follow."

"He was sure of my loyalty." Whaler frowned. "Of late, too many at court have been . . . uncertain. I do not pretend to understand why, but your Duke Orlanko has considerable influence. His Grace did not want to entrust such a delicate task to someone who might be tempted."

"I see."

A boat was approaching, crawling like a bug across the broad river on two pairs of oars. Raesinia retreated to the high ground outside the village proper, since the shacks and the pier smelled of many lifetimes' use gutting fish. When the boat docked, she was surprised to see that Dorsay was accompanied only by a single pair of soldiers, who stayed behind as Whaler led him through the village. Raesinia motioned Sothe and the two Girls' Own soldiers to take a few steps back.

"Your Majesty," Dorsay said, bowing. He looked much the same as the last time they'd met, though he was in an ordinary Borelgai uniform instead of the gaudy dress uniform he'd worn to the conference. Raesinia offered a nod in return, uncomfortably aware that she hardly looked like much a queen in a dirty coat and trousers. "You honor me with your trust."

"Duke Dorsay," she said. "Likewise, I'm sure. I'm most curious to hear what you have to say and why it's so important the First Consul not be aware of it."

"When we last met, I must admit I hadn't taken the measure of the man," Dorsay said. "I suspected that his victories over the Hamveltai had been the product of good luck, or incompetence on the part of his enemies. Needless to say, I have discovered he is every bit as formidable as his reputation."

"I could have told you that," Raesinia said with a slight smile.

"I thought his threats against Elysium were saber rattling," Dorsay went on. "Terms that were certain to keep the war going, because he knew the Murnskai would be unable to accept them. Imagine my surprise, then, when he abandoned pursuit of my army after Gilphaite, and turned north along the Pilgrim's Road." Dorsay rubbed his famous nose, then shook his head. "He really intends to do it, doesn't he? To attack Elysium."

"If you asked me here to try to get the details of Janus' plans, Duke Dorsay, I'm afraid you're going to be disappointed," Raesinia said. "But that certainly seems to be his goal."

"I don't suppose you could enlighten me as to *why*?"

That's a deeper question than you know. "He explained his reasons at the conference," Raesinia said aloud. "The Church has orchestrated the war against Vordan."

"But he can't seriously think that taking Elysium will destroy the Sworn Church, any more than seizing Ohnlei Palace would destroy Vordan. I won't believe the man is that naive."

"I don't pretend to know what Janus does or doesn't believe," Raesinia said. "Do *you* believe it?"

Raesinia met his gaze, her expression cool. "Is there a point to this speculation?"

"Only this. If Janus succeeds, if he takes Elysium, the result will be a disaster on a scale to make the war thus far look like a summer festival."

Raesinia kept her face neutral. "I assume you don't mean in some theological sense."

Dorsay snorted. "No miracles are required, I assure you."

"Then why do you say so?"

He paused. "You were, what, ten years old when the War of the Princes began?"

"Old enough to remember," Raesinia said, allowing a hint of displeasure into her voice.

Dorsay's expression softened. "My apologies. I didn't mean to dredge up bad memories. My point is only this—the War of the Princes is the *only* war you remember."

"I suppose so."

"I am sixty-seven years old," Dorsay said. "I have seen more wars now than I can remember. The Silverback War, on this very ground, more or less. The Six Years War in the east. The Bankbook War, where I was besieged in Antova, which Janus took so easily. And on and on."

"I'm familiar with your reputation."

"Did you know that my whole family are soldiers? It's something of a tra-dition, though I've come farther at it than any of my ancestors. My father died young, on some battlefield or other, and I was raised mostly by my grandfather. *He* fought Vordan, too, in Farus the Fourth's day."

"Duke Dorsay," Raesinia said. "Your family history is fascinating, but I don't think you called me out here to discuss your childhood."

Dorsay chuckled. "Sorry. The older I get, the more I tend to meander in my thoughts. Here's the point, then. Nothing I've seen in all my years of fighting is half as ugly as the stories my grandfather told about his soldiering days, and from what I've read of the history, he understated the case. We live in a gentler age, and our wars are more . . . sporting. There are rules." He waved at the village behind them. "When my grandfather's company came to a village like this, they would shoot all the men, rape the women, then keep the pretty ones and some of the older children for camp followers. Everyone else they'd impale on wooden stakes, rank after rank of them, along the road. Babies, old people. A warning to whoever came afterward, you see. Then they'd steal anything they could carry and set fire to anything that would burn. And none of them felt a twinge of guilt, because they knew that somewhere the enemy was doing the same thing to one of *their* villages.

"The Wars of Religion were some of the blackest years this continent has gone through since the Fall of the Tyrants. The only reason it all ended is because kings and priests quietly agreed to leave one another alone. Take the War of the Princes. We won, you lost, but no one in Borel suggested converting Vordan to the Sworn Church at the point of a sword. If it had been the other way around, your father would have done the same. A few territories ceded, a few restrictive trade treaties, that sort of thing. *Civilized* war."

Civilized for the survivors, Raesinia thought. *Not for my brother, or everyone else who ended up in a shallow grave.* Aloud, she said, "The Grand Army hasn't been uncivil to the Murnskai."

"Not yet. But if Janus takes Elysium—if he truly means to destroy the Sworn Church—then all bets are off. It'll be the Great Schism all over again, and it won't end until half the continent drowns in blood. All of Murnsk will rise against you. Not on the battlefield, but in the middle of the night, until you fight back by doing everything my grandfather did." Dorsay shook his head. "The thing about a *civilized* war is it ends when the king says that it's enough. But when one *people* declares war against another, there's no one to call a halt."

A mountain of corpses. Raesinia once again heard blood spattering on the table and the Murnskai woman's defiant scream. *They will fight us all the way to Elysium.* "And what would you do?"

"Me personally? I have no idea. But Borel would be against you. Georg would have no choice."

"You're very passionate on the subject," Raesinia said.

"Call me an idealist," Dorsay said dryly. "But it can't be allowed to happen. You understand? Janus *must* not destroy Elysium."

There was a long silence. Raesinia looked down at the empty village and the river beyond, her face schooled to immobility.

"Is it already too late?" she said, gesturing at the empty buildings. "The Sworn Priests are telling the peasants we're here for their souls."

"I hope not. To be brutally honest, neither Georg nor the emperor are going to be swayed by a few angry peasants. But the fall of Elysium would light a beacon for every Sworn Church in the world."

Raesinia took a deep breath. "For the moment, let's assume that you're right. What are you asking me to do about it?"

"In Talbonn I told you what peace would require."

"That I sheathe my sword." Raesinia crossed her arms. "In return for a mere promise to negotiate and the return of a wanted criminal?"

Dorsay looked solemn. "I can offer more than that. Georg has been in touch. If Janus leaves your government, he is prepared to guarantee peace, status quo ante." He waved dismissively. "You may have Orlanko, too, of course."

Raesinia met the duke's eyes and found them steady. *He means it.*

"What about the Murnskai?" she said carefully. "For the sake of argument."

"We cannot, of course, make any guarantees on behalf of the emperor. But Georg will exert what influence he has." Dorsay leaned forward. "But we must move quickly. The closer you get to Elysium, the more influence the Church, and by extension Orlanko, are going to have in Viadre. The opportunity for peace may pass us by."

Peace. With the Borelgai and the emperor, perhaps, but never with the Priests of the Black. *They'll come for me sooner or later, whatever I do here. But . . .*

The confrontation in the tent haunted her. It would have been easier to dismiss Dorsay's warning if she hadn't seen, firsthand, the kind of madness the Church could inspire. *If we take Elysium . . .*

She imagined a thousand women like Lidiya, throwing themselves against firing lines. A thousand villages burning. *A mountain of corpses.*

I can't do it. She felt the world shifting around her. *The Black Priests will come for* me. *But taking Elysium means war for all of Vordan, and not a war we can hope to win.*

I have to stop Janus.

She blinked, jaw trembling, and took a deep breath. If Dorsay noticed her sudden discomfiture, he didn't let it show.

"It would be hard to explain to the army why I wanted to make peace when we were, to all appearances, winning," she said, keeping her voice calm. "Not to mention the Deputies-General."

"I have every confidence that you can handle the Deputies-General. As for the army . . ." Dorsay cocked his head. "If you ordered a halt, do you think Janus would disobey?"

"It's possible," Raesinia said. "This need to reach Elysium is almost an obsession."

"And if he did, who would the army follow? The queen or the First Consul?"

That's the ultimate question, isn't it? The only question that really mattered. *In the end it comes down to who holds the power.*

"I don't want to force the soldiers to make a choice," Raesinia said. "If it comes to that, the army might tear itself apart. This deep into hostile territory, that would be a disaster for Vordan."

"Then as long as Janus is First Consul, we will never have peace." Dorsay's eyes were hooded. "If he could be removed . . ."

There was only one thing he could mean. "No," Raesinia snapped. "I am not Orlanko. I do not solve my problems with knives in the dark."

Dorsay nodded, and Raesinia wondered if that had been a test, and if she'd passed. "We seem to be at an impasse, then. If you have any ideas, I'm ready to listen."

Another pause. Raesinia looked over her shoulder, past Sothe, Barely, and Joanna, toward where the Grand Army was camped. Somewhere to the north, over the horizon, was the Murnskai army.

"Column-General Marcus has been tutoring me in strategy," she said. "There will be another battle soon."

"It seems likely," Dorsay said. "Neither Janus nor the emperor is inclined to try to avoid fighting."

"If we lose, then the question of taking Elysium is moot," Raesinia said. "We will have to retreat to the border."

"Assuming . . . well, any number of things, but I take your meaning. I must point out, though, that Janus has yet to be decisively beaten in the field."

Raesinia nodded. "If we *win*, then the feeling in the army may be different. If I can meet with the emperor's representatives and arrange a peace advantageous to Vordan, concessions of territory perhaps . . ."

"I see." Dorsay smiled slightly. "It might be more difficult for Janus to insist on continuing the war if the emperor is already offering a good deal."

"Exactly. And if he refuses to back down, then it might be politically possible to dismiss him from office."

"You're gambling quite a lot on the emperor's being willing to give up after a single battle."

"You're not the only one who has studied Janus' record."

"Ha." Dorsay let out a sigh and ran his hands through the wild frizz of hair at the back of his skull. "It's a chance, in any case. All right. For my part, we will observe the battle—not that we are in a position to interfere—and, if things go as you hope, I will send Whaler to you afterward."

"Good." Raesinia paused, then added, "I am glad I decided to trust you, Duke Dorsay."

"So am I." Dorsay hesitated, wrestling with something. After a moment he said, "I never meant to kill your brother, you know."

Raesinia blinked. "What?"

"At Vansfeldt. Georg was something of a young hot-head at the time, but I respected Prince Dominic. I'd avoided open battle, because I knew it wouldn't be decisive. When I stood on the defensive at Vansfeldt, I thought Dominic would see that the position was impossible. If we'd managed to postpone a decision on the battlefield until the armies entered winter quarters, I thought your father would see the folly of continuing the war." He sighed. "Instead Dominic decided he had to lead the last charge himself. I always thought about you afterward. I thought that if I ever met you again, I would say . . . I don't know. This, I suppose."

Raesinia looked at him in silence, not sure what to say. Dorsay colored slightly, his protruding nose flushing.

"In any case," he said. "I had best return before I'm missed. I hope we will meet again in better circumstances."

He turned away before Raesinia could respond, trudging back through the empty village with a slight stoop to his shoulders. Raesinia looked after him for a moment, then turned herself and walked back to Sothe and the two Girls' Own soldiers.

"It doesn't seem to have been a trap, at least," Sothe said, peering at the departing Borelgai.

"No," Raesinia said. "Not exactly."

"What did he ask for?"

"It's . . . complicated. I'll explain later."

Sothe caught Raesinia's expression, nodded curtly, and went to fetch the horses. Raesinia looked up at Barely and Joanna.

"What would you do," Raesinia said suddenly, "if Janus told you one thing and I said another? Who would you believe?"

Barely frowned. "I can't imagine how that would happen, Your Majesty."

Raesinia's shoulders slumped. "Sorry. It's a stupid question." *Of course they're not going to tell me to my face that they'd obey Janus.*

Joanna tapped Barely on the shoulder and made a few quick signs with her hands. Barely looked up at Raesinia and shrugged.

"She asked what Winter was saying about it," Barely said. "Division-General Ihernglass, I mean. He's the one we signed up to follow." She scratched her nose. "I reckon she's right. No offense to you or the First Consul, of course."

"None taken," Raesinia murmured, as Sothe returned leading their mounts. *Maybe . . .*

CHAPTER EIGHT

MARCUS

For two days no messenger had arrived from the queen with the usual note inviting him to dinner, and Marcus found that he was more disappointed than he expected. It was hard to deny he could use the hours elsewhere, of course. He spent his days riding from place to place, adjudicating between feuding officers and straightening out snarls on the road. But dinner with the queen was a nice respite, a place where only the boldest of messengers would dare to bother him.

And, a traitorous part of his mind insisted, *she's pretty.* Which was a ridiculous thing to think—*she's the* Queen of Vordan, *for heaven's sake*—and served mostly as a reminder of how long it had been since Marcus had enjoyed any sort of female company. There had a been a few girls in Ashe-Katarion, and then Jen Alhundt, the Concordat agent and Penitent Damned who'd cold-bloodedly seduced him to get the information she wanted. After her death, which felt like a lifetime ago, he'd been . . . distracted.

The next river line was the Syzria, which the Pilgrim's Road crossed at a town called Polkhaiz. Rumor had it that the emperor's army was close, although Give-Em-Hell's scouts had yet to catch sight of it. After spending his third straight day shepherding the column through the forests and bogs, Marcus was just resigning himself to another meal alone when a messenger *did* arrive. The summons wasn't to the queen's tent, though, but to the First Consul's, and Marcus hurriedly gulped down some bread and water, put on his uniform coat, and followed the corporal.

So far, so good, he thought, with some satisfaction, as they threaded their way through the tents and past the lines of horses. Farther out, livestock bleated and artillery lay parked in neat rows. *The supply system is holding up.* Wagons could make only a modest speed over the bad roads, but they'd compensated by sheer volume of vehicles, long supply convoys rolling north from Vantzolk, unloading, and turning around again to repeat the trip. The Borelgai army had been quiescent, too, apparently content to bide its time somewhere to the west, and while partisan attacks had become irritating, the patrols were keeping losses at acceptable levels. *If you'd told me at the beginning we'd be this far into Murnsk and doing well, I wouldn't have believed it.*

The Colonials guarding Janus' tent saluted and let Marcus pass in silence. He was surprised to find the big table empty except for the First Consul himself. *Not a general strategy conference, then.*

"Sir," Marcus said, offering his own salute. "My apologies if I kept you waiting."

Janus waved him off and gestured to a chair on the other side of the map table. "I'm sorry to interrupt your supper," he said. "There's a great deal to do, I'm afraid."

"What's going on?"

"Division-General Stokes reports he's made contact with Murnskai patrols," Janus said. "We've yet to get close enough to see their main force, but there's no doubt they're there." He indicated Polkhaiz on the map, a simple dot along the crooked blue line of the Syzria. "Either at the river or south of it, standing between us and Elysium."

"Not too far south, I hope," Marcus said, peering at the map. "I'd like to get clear of this damned forest before we fight them."

"They won't come too far," Janus said. "The best intelligence we have is that Prince Vasil, the emperor's oldest son, is in command. He's supposed to be pious to a fault, but not stupid. He knows we have to come to him—not only can we not supply ourselves here indefinitely, but we can't risk getting caught when the weather turns."

"All right. So we attack?"

"Of course. But not head-on, if we can avoid it. Even if we force the Murnskai to retreat by weight of numbers, they can fall back and try again, and again, taking a toll in blood each time. Unlike the Borelgai, the Murnskai cavalry is both numerous and capable, so we're unlikely to be able to mousetrap them. A different approach is required."

Marcus nodded. "What, then?"

"Prince Vasil is in an odd position," Janus said. He moved his finger along the Pilgrim's Road, north and east toward Elysium. "His goal is to keep us from advancing in this direction, to Elysium and Mohkba. But the roads that way are much too poor to bear the supplies that support his army, given the antiquated state of Murnskai logistics. Instead, he relies on the river." The pointing finger shifted west, tracing the Syzria as it ran toward the coast. "River transport is more reliable, and the Borelgai fleet controls the coastal outlets. So it is the river we must attack."

He tapped another dot on the map. Marcus leaned in and read the label—Bskor.

"The Murnskai have always been concerned about invasion from the sea," Janus said. "There are defenses all along the rivers, as far east as they are navigable to deep-draft ships. Bskor is the last major work on the Syzria."

"It's a fortress?"

"A lightly guarded one, at present. Its main strength is in a water battery of heavy guns that can effectively close the river to anything smaller than a ship of the line. From the land side, the defenses are not so formidable. We've also learned that it's a major staging point in the Murnskai supply system, so its depots should be well stocked." Janus looked up and grinned. "You're going to take it for us."

"Hmm," Marcus said. "It may be lightly defended *now*, but if we move in that direction, won't the Murnskai reinforce it? The prince can shift his army along the river faster than we can march."

"Indeed. The bulk of the Grand Army will continue to advance northeast, threatening to attack the prince. That should keep the Murnskai close to whatever defenses they've devised. In the meantime, you will take Fitz Warus' First Division northwest, seize Bskor, and dig in. When we get word that you've succeeded, we'll temporarily cut loose from our supply line and come after you. Between the depots and intercepting Murnskai shipments downriver, we should have enough to sustain us, but the Murnskai will quickly starve."

"You think they'll retreat?"

"It's possible. They could reestablish a supply line on the Kovria, or march upriver and try to bypass us. But that would take time, and they won't have it. Remember, their army isn't volunteer, like ours. They're conscripts, not much better than feudal levies. If food runs low, they'll start to melt away, as I'm sure the prince is aware."

"Which means he'll attack," Marcus said.

"He'll have no choice," Janus agreed. "And, knowing that, we can arrange the situation to be neatly in our favor. That part is my responsibility, of course. All I want from you is to take Bskor and stop traffic on the river."

Marcus felt a tingle of excitement. "Understood, sir. When do we split off?"

"Tomorrow. The cavalry have found—well, 'road' would be too strong a term, but it will take your men where they need to go. You'll have a strong detachment of light cavalry in addition to the First Division's forces."

"Yes, sir."

"I want to impress something on you, Marcus." Janus tapped the map again. "Bskor must fall *quickly*. There's no time for a siege. If it takes too long, this will all be worse than useless, and you could have the entire Murnskai army on your back. You'll carry your supplies with you and stop for nothing. If the men go hungry, tell them there's food in the enemy depots. No foraging or anything else that might slow you down. Is that clear?"

"Very clear, sir."

"Fitz will get his orders tomorrow morning. Until then, don't tell anyone outside your staff. The Murnskai will pick up this movement eventually, but the longer it takes them, the better our chances. You and Fitz can work out the details on the road."

"Yes, sir. We won't let you down."

Janus grinned again. "You never have, Marcus. And the Colonials are our best troops. I'm sure you won't have any problems."

Andy was waiting when Marcus returned to his tent.

"Evening, sir," she said, with her usual slapdash salute. "There was a messenger from the queen. She wanted to see you."

"Damn," Marcus said.

"What's going on? More colonels feuding?"

"Orders." Marcus lowered his voice. "We're leaving the column tomorrow. Tell Giforte and his people they'll be staying to keep things running here."

"Got it," Andy said. She was already looking excited.

"What are you grinning about? I haven't told you what we're doing yet."

"It's got to be better than riding back and forth all day," Andy said. "What should I tell the queen?"

"Ask her if she'll see me in the morning."

Andy raised an eyebrow. "It's considered rude to keep a lady waiting."

Marcus sighed. "Just go, would you?"

The next morning the messages came in one after another. Fitz had been given his orders and had sent to say the First Division was loading up supplies and would be ready to march by noon. Marcus ate a hurried breakfast and briefed Giforte, signing orders that gave him authority to resolve the disputes between divisions until Marcus returned. *He probably knows better than I do, anyway.* When he came back, a squad of First Division rankers was efficiently packing his things and tearing down his tent under Andy's supervision. Some of the heavier gear was set aside. If they had to travel light, Marcus intended to lead by example.

"Anything from the queen?" he said, watching the men work. His hands itched to join in—Marcus had never gotten used to the way his elevated position freed him from helping with hard work.

"Not yet," Andy said. "The rest of the army has a late morning; she may not—never mind, here she comes."

"What?" Marcus said, but Andy was already bowing. He turned and found Raesinia herself standing behind him, with her two bodyguards from the Girls' Own. Marcus made his own, belated bow, fighting back the feeling of being a child caught in the midst of an indiscretion.

"Your Majesty," he said gravely.

"Column-General d'Ivoire," Raesinia said. "I know you're busy this morning, but could you spare me a moment?"

"Of course." Marcus straightened and waved Andy to get on with it. She flashed him an inappropriate grin that he desperately hoped Raesinia couldn't see. The queen nodded to the two Girls' Own soldiers, and they stepped away, giving the pair of them a clear space.

"I'm sorry I haven't been able to dine with you the past few days," Raesinia said. "I've been . . . preoccupied."

"It's Your Majesty's prerogative to dine however you wish," Marcus said. "We're here to serve."

She cocked her head, looking at him for a long moment. Marcus lowered his gaze, uncomfortable. The force of her personality sometimes made you forget how *small* she was. Marcus had an image of his hand against her cheek, her delicate features contrasted with his rough, calloused fingers. He gritted his teeth.

"You're leaving, then?" she said.

"For a short time, I hope," Marcus said. "I'm sorry I can't give you the details."

"I understand. I hope you'll be careful. I consider you quite as valuable to the army as the First Consul."

Marcus flushed under his beard, and bowed again. "Thank you, Your Majesty. It's an honor to hear you say so, though I'm sure it isn't true."

"Don't contradict the queen," Raesinia said, a hint of the old playfulness in her voice. "When you get back, there are things we need to discuss."

"Of course. Whatever you require."

Again, something about his response seemed to give her pause. After a moment she shook her head and patted him gently on the shoulder. "Good luck, General."

"Sir!" Fitz snapped into the crisp salute Marcus remembered so well, in spite of the fact that he was on horseback. The silver scorpion of the Colonials gleamed below the star of a division-general.

He waited by the side of the road, the long column of the First Division already moving past him. Up ahead, a cavalry officer directed traffic, indicating the small break in the trees that led to the trail the scouts had marked out, where the troops left the narrow, rutted track of the Pilgrim's Road and veered off to the northwest. Three captains Marcus didn't know, all young and well turned out, sat their horses just to the rear of Fitz himself.

"Welcome to the First Division," Fitz said, when Marcus acknowledged his salute.

"It's good to be working with you again," Marcus said.

"Yes, sir. Likewise."

"I don't know if you've met Andy Dracht," Marcus said. "She's all the staff I'll be bringing along, so I'll mostly be relying on your people."

"It's good to meet you, sir," Andy said.

Fitz nodded and gestured his own entourage forward. "These are my staff officers," he said. "Captain Adlo Ritter, Captain Mandua Gortei, and—"

"Viera!" Andy burst out. "I knew you looked familiar."

Viera? Marcus looked at the third figure, and his perspective shifted. The severe-looking young woman was in uniform now, and she'd cut her dark hair to little more than fuzz. When she saw recognition on his face, a slight smile tugged at her lips, quickly suppressed.

"Captain Viera Galiel," Fitz finished. "Whom I believe you already know. She commands our artillery."

"Commands?" Marcus said. "Last time I saw you, you were still studying with the Preacher." She'd been a student at the artillery school back at the University in Vordan City, one of several whom Marcus had rescued from a mob. Her bombs and grenades had made the difference when Marcus had led his ragged band against the flame-wielding Penitent Cinder.

"Colonel Vahkerson is very pleased with my progress," Viera said. Her Vordanai still had a strong Hamveltai accent. "I have not blown myself up for months now, which he said puts me at the top of the class."

"Always a good trait in an artilleryman," Marcus said. "Or artillerywoman, in this case. It's good to see you again, too."

"Thank you, sir." She looked at Fitz. "With your permission, sir, I'd like to ride herd on my teams. Over this ground, the hardest part is going to be getting the damn cannons to the battlefield."

"Granted," Fitz said. "In fact, sir, if you'll follow me, I think the best place for us is near the front of the column, in case any problems arise. I hope you don't mind that I've taken the liberty of getting things started."

"Of course not," Marcus said, grinning. Fitz's cool, soothing competence was something he'd missed since Khandar. "Lead the way."

As Marcus would have expected, the march was exquisitely organized. More cavalrymen sat their horses at intervals, anywhere the path wasn't entirely clear, directing the infantry and wagons down the right trail. Other horsemen ranged ahead, reporting back with clockwork regularity that no enemy had been sighted. They passed Viera and her guns, a full battery each of six- and twelve-pounders, the bronze tubes of the cannon dwarfed by their own wide-rimmed wheels and the heavy wooden caissons that held their ammunition.

What Marcus hadn't expected were the occasional cheers that greeted him. Two of the First's four regiments were largely made up of Colonials, the three-thousand-odd men who'd survived Khandar and the battles since making up four battalions of the division's total of eight. New recruits had been added, of course, but only those who'd served in Khandar were entitled to wear the scorpion badge. Marcus didn't always wear his own emblem, but he had today, and at the sight of it the strung-out companies burst into spontaneous shouts of greeting. He waved at them, a little embarrassed.

"You'd think that our stay in Khandar was nothing but leave and parades," he muttered, after the fourth or fifth time.

"Memory is a strange thing," Fitz said, keen eared as always. "They already talk about 'the good old days' when we were fighting the Redeemers."

"I remember being scared enough to piss myself, half the time."

"We did win," Fitz said. "That counts for something."

Fitz's two staff captains came and went throughout the day, offering reports with clipped efficiency that was obviously well practiced. Pushing west, the landscape became distinctly rougher, hills rising higher and boasting denser forests. They were forced to stick to the bottoms of the valleys, following the path marked by the cavalry to avoid the worst of the muck. There was no road, not even a poor one like they'd followed so far. This was truly wild country, the kind that had long ago vanished from most of the civilized south. It was easy to understand, rounding yet another bend to see yet another tree-lined height in front of them, why Murnsk had never been conquered.

"The problem with this country," Marcus said, "is that there's too much *country* and not enough people."

"Farus the Fourth once commented that Murnsk was what was left over when all the civilized countries had divided up the better parts of the world," Fitz said. "Of course, since he'd lost much of his army the previous winter, his judgment might not have been at its most objective."

Marcus chuckled. "I really have missed you, you know? It's a pity you're too good an officer to use as staff forever. How is command treating you?"

"As well as one might expect," Fitz said. "I've had a great deal of work to do getting the regiments up to a reasonable standard."

"Because your brother and I let the Colonials do what they liked, you mean?"

"Times have changed," Fitz said, raising a single delicate eyebrow. "But we have two regiments of revolutionary volunteers, and the reorganization was hard on the Colonials. I'm afraid Janus raided them badly for experienced officers, which means training a lot of replacement sergeants and captains. Fortunately, the lull after the Velt campaign gave us a breathing space."

"That sounds like it was a hell of a fight," Marcus said.

"It was quite extraordinary." Fitz glanced sidelong at Marcus. "If you're interested, I'll be happy to give you the details when we make camp."

"I'd love to hear it," Marcus said.

In midafternoon it began to rain, a thin, spiteful drizzle driven on the wind. The water wormed its way past collars and into packs. It was still coming down when the sun set, and the division pitched its tents across a wooded hillside with a general feeling of relief. Instead of the usual wagon train, a corps of draft horses and mules had all the heavy equipment strapped over their backs, so the cannon and their caissons were the only wheeled vehicles they had to worry about.

Marcus had dinner with Fitz and his officers, accepting the salutes of a small throng of colonels and captains whose names he knew he was never going to remember. A few he recalled from his Khandarai days, once-tanned faces now having lost their color and looking out of place atop neat new uniforms. Fitz, as always, knew every important detail about everyone. Marcus had to restrain himself from falling too far back into his old relationship with his subordinate; treating Fitz like his personal staff would only damage Fitz's standing with these men, whom he would have to command after Marcus had returned to his post as column-general. He settled for saying as little as possible, listening to the stories of the Velt campaign and the fall of Antova with unfeigned attentiveness.

His own tent, the large model reserved for senior officers, felt much too big without his table, writing desk, or the rest of the usual trappings. There was only a bedroll, curled up in one corner, and what he carried in his saddlebags. Marcus sat down with a sigh and started unlacing his boots.

"Sir?" Andy said from the tent flap. "Can I come in?"

"Go ahead." Marcus popped off one boot and wiggled his toes. His sock was slightly damp, and he stripped it off as well.

Andy came in and saluted. "Just wanted to see if you needed me for anything else tonight, sir."

"Going to sleep already?" Marcus said. Her small tent was next to his.

"No, sir." Andy grinned broadly. "Some of the officers have organized a game of cards. I figured I would take the chance to add to my nest egg, sir."

Marcus rolled his eyes. "Don't take too much off any one person," he said. "And remember we've got an early start tomorrow."

"Yes, sir."

She bounced on her feet and slipped out. Marcus got the other boot off, spread out his bedroll, and lay back.

Things to discuss. What did Raesinia mean, things to discuss? He rolled onto his side, frowning. *We've had plenty of time for discussions.*

It took a day longer than Marcus would have liked to reach Bskor, but the rain made everything harder. It continued, off and on, through most of the march, turning the ground to a slick mud that spattered everything and made footing treacherous. A few horses were lost when they put a foot wrong and hurt themselves, and one of Viera's six-pounders sank to the axle and refused to budge no matter how many men tried to shift it. Marcus ordered it abandoned, in spite of the artillery captain's offer to try to blast it free with powder charges.

As before, once they got within a few days' ride of the river, signs of civilization reappeared. The scouts reported Murnskai peasant families hastily fleeing from their path, rumor spreading through a valley that had thought the heretic invaders many miles upstream. That would tell the enemy army where they were, if they didn't already know, and Marcus ordered a faster pace. Even country roads and animal tracks were better than pushing through the muddy valleys and forests, and they made good time down toward the Syzria. After they spent a night camping in a pasture, with the unfortunate farmer's pigs providing a welcome respite from hardtack, the second day's march in clear country brought them within sight of Bskor.

Marcus was no engineer, but he could tell the fortress was well placed. He and Fitz sat on their horses on a low hill about two miles off, peering through spyglasses. A small town lay below them, straddling the riverside road. Just a bit beyond it, some trick of the earth had raised a promontory above the normally gentle banks of the river. The fortress atop it was a pentagon of stone and brick, with low, sloping walls to deflect cannon-fire and embrasures cut out to protect the defenders' guns. Its cannon would command the river and opposite bank, Marcus guessed, especially the clumsy but powerful naval defense guns in the water battery.

"What do you think?" Marcus said.

"Going to be tricky," Fitz said. "It depends how many men they've got packed in there. If Janus is right and it's lightly defended, we could take it in a rush, but if not it's going to be a bloody business. On the other hand, that's an old design. Even our field-guns will be able to do some damage to it, given time."

Marcus nodded, pursing his lips. Bskor lacked the earthen berms and carefully planned star shape that made a truly modern fortress impervious to everything but the heaviest siege guns. *But . . .* "We haven't *got* time. Janus was insistent about that." He looked over his shoulder at the river road running east, toward Polkhaiz and the Murnskai army. "They must know we're here by now. We can't afford to get caught between the fortress and any reinforcements they send."

"I've got scouts out in that direction," Fitz said. "But you may be right. So what are your orders?"

Marcus screwed the glass a little tighter against his eye, as though that would make details of the distant fortress leap closer. After a moment he took the instrument away.

"Which regiment is closest?" he said.

"The Third, sir. They have the lead today."

Not the Colonials. Maybe that's for the best. "Bring them up and attack. Nothing fancy, two columns and straight at the wall. Tell the colonel not to press it too hard. If they don't fall at the first push, at least we'll be able to see what we're up against."

"Understood, sir."

"In the meantime, bring up the other three regiments and the artillery. If we have to go in mob-handed, I want to do it with everything we've got."

Fitz saluted and wheeled his horse about. Marcus stayed where he was, and a few minutes later the blue lines of the Third Regiment, now compacted into a pair of battalion columns, started past him and down through the town. Cavalry patrols scattered ahead of them, like shepherds escorting a flock.

The men in the fortress were clearly alert. They opened fire at extreme range, cannons roaring, puffs of smoke bursting from the walls like cloudy breath on a cold day. Solid shot screamed over the advancing men, doing little at first but damaging some houses in the town. But the Murnskai were not shy about wasting ammunition, and soon enough they found the range. Patches of blue dribbled from the rear of the two columns as they crawled up the slope at what seemed like a snail's pace.

When they were a hundred yards from the walls, musketry added itself to the cannon-fire, threads of white smoke drifting up and over the battlements. Marcus tried to keep his eye on the walls, estimating the number of defenders from the volume of muzzle flashes, but it was hard not to look down at the columns of blue. Men fell out of rank more and more and they closed with the walls and the volume of fire increased. The defending cannon had switched to canister, blowing swaths out of the leading companies.

From this distance it was impossible to tell if the men in the regiment broke and ran of their own accord or if the colonel decided they'd had enough and gave the order to retreat. The result was the same—the formation dissolved almost instantly into a mass of running figures, leaving behind a drift of dead and wounded at the point of their farthest advance. They weren't throwing their weapons away, Marcus was glad to see, but they pelted determinedly down the slope, back to where they'd begun and out of range of the terrible rain of lead.

Marcus lowered his spyglass and nudged his horse into motion, picking his way downhill and through the streets of the little town. A dozen cavalrymen rode escort, with Andy in the lead, but they were unnecessary. The townsfolk had either fled or were hiding in their basements, and only blue-uniformed Vordanai were moving about. Cannonballs had knocked holes in the timber walls of a few houses, but fortunately the recent rain had prevented any fires. A large stable on the edge of the settlement had already been taken over by the regimental cutters, and the first walking wounded from the failed assault were beginning to trickle in. Marcus rode past at a trot, trying not to shudder. *No soldier,* he thought, *ever really loses his fear of the cutters. Give me a nice clean death anytime.*

Fitz had formed his cavalry into a straggler line, rallying the fleeing Third Regiment soldiers. Officers were working on sorting them back into their battalions and companies, but it would obviously be some time before they were ready for action again. In the meantime, the other three regiments had formed up into their assault columns, six battalions in deep, narrow formations for maximum speed. Cannons still barked from the fortress walls, but at this range the balls mostly fell short, with only the occasional ricochet bouncing overhead with a *whirr.*

Marcus found Fitz behind the First Regiment, where the artillery was waiting. Twenty-four guns, a dozen big twelve-pounders and as many smaller six-pounders, had been unhitched from their wagonlike caissons and attached, pointing backward, to their own teams of horses. Viera barked orders to her cannoneers, who rushed to and fro carrying sacks of powder and heavy chests of ammunition.

"Sir," Fitz said, sighting Marcus. "I'm afraid the Third Regiment was repulsed."

"I was watching," Marcus said. "The rest are ready to go?"

"Yes, sir. On your order."

"What about the artillery?"

Fitz looked at Viera, who glowered up at Marcus.

"We're ready," she said. "But those siege guns outrange ours, and they've got the advantage of height. If we move up we're going to get pounded before we get into range."

"There do seem to be more defenders than anticipated," Fitz said. "At least six heavy guns on the walls, plus perhaps a battalion of infantry. Colonel Morag reports encountering extremely heavy fire."

"Then we haven't got any choice but to use everything we've got," Marcus said. "Captain Galiel, move your batteries into range and open fire. Concentrate on the embrasures—if you can knock out even a few of those guns, it'll be a big help."

Viera stared at him for a long moment. Marcus could read what was going through her mind as clearly as if it were printed on her skull. His order meant that some men—*her* men—would die. He could see her realize it, realize that *he* knew it, too, and that he was giving the order anyway. He remembered being on the other side of the exchange, when Janus had first come to Khandar. *You get used to it, if you stay in command. And what an awful thing that is.*

"Yes, sir," Viera said finally. She offered a stiff salute and turned away, already shouting orders at her lieutenants. Before long the teams were harnessed and put in motion, and the guns moved up, threading their way around the waiting ranks of infantry and across the grassy slope in front of the fortress with a surprising turn of speed.

It didn't take the fortress gunners long to notice the new targets. A gun team was harder to hit than an infantry column, but they gave it their all, fountains of dirt exploding all around the batteries. One lucky shot bounced a cannonball right through the team of horses pulling one of the six-pounders, leaving a trail of broken men and animals in its wake. The cannon slowed to a halt, what was left of its crew running to catch up with the others.

Marcus forced himself to look away. "Once she starts firing," he told Fitz, "get the columns moving. Double-time to fifty yards, then charge. No shooting. Make sure every man knows our best chance is to get over the walls and give them cold steel. Got it?"

"Yes, sir," Fitz said. Then, uncharacteristically, he hesitated. "Are you sure, sir? We don't have the numbers to be certain, and casualties will be high either way. Perhaps—"

"We don't have a choice," Marcus said. "Janus wants that fortress, and he wants it fast. We have to give it to him."

"Yes, sir," Fitz said. "Of course."

He turned his horse and went to find his staff captains. Marcus beckoned to Andy, who took a few moments to convince her horse to move. She was a city girl through and through and was, if anything, a worse rider than Marcus, though she didn't share his distaste for the animals.

"Find someone to watch my horse," he said. "I'm going on foot from here."

"Right, sir. I'll find someone to look after mine as well."

Marcus sighed. "I don't suppose I can convince you to stay behind."

"No more than I can convince you not to go," Andy said. "Janus will be irritated if you get yourself killed, you know. And you'll break the queen's heart."

"Would you stop that?" Marcus shook his head. "We're only going to get one chance at this. I'm not going to stand back and watch."

"Then I'll be right alongside you, sir."

There was no stopping her, so Marcus gave in with bad grace. They dismounted together and handed their horses to a cavalryman, then jogged over to the First Regiment, where Fitz was giving final instructions to the colonel.

"Ready on your command, sir!" Fitz said.

Marcus shaded his eyes and looked upslope. Viera's guns were in action now, flashing and roaring in a dense cloud of smoke. Sprays of brick erupted from the fortress walls whenever they scored a hit, but as far as Marcus could tell, all six of the big guns were still in action. *At least she's drawing their attention.* In a prolonged shooting match, the lighter field-guns would be annihilated. *We have to get on with it.*

"All right," Marcus said. "General advance, on the double! Fix bayonets! I want us over those walls!"

He raised his voice, and the soldiers who could hear him broke out in cheers that spread through the ranks. Six thousand men drew their bayonets from their sheaths, fixed them to musket lugs, and waited. A moment later the drums began, beating a quick double pace, and the battalions started forward. The first company of each carried a pair of flags, one bearing the number of the unit, the other the silver on blue of Vordan, and they rippled out in the wake of the men.

"You intend to join the advance, sir?" Fitz said, getting down off his horse.

"It's the only place I'll do any good," Marcus said.

Once the last company of each battalion had passed, Marcus led Fitz and Andy forward. He felt himself falling into the familiar rhythm of the double step, almost automatically—he hadn't marched in the ranks in years, but the War College had etched the sound of the drums into his bones. Andy scrambled to keep up.

More cheers rose from Viera's cannoneers as the infantry passed them, and the firing redoubled. At least one gun was wrecked, its big wooden wheels shattered, and dead horses lay everywhere. Casualties from the initial advance started to appear, some lying still, others thrashing and waving in an effort to attract their comrades' attention. Marcus heard sergeants barking orders to ignore the wounded whenever some kindhearted soul threatened to break ranks. The drums beat on, relentless.

The fortress guns turned back to the infantry, and the cannonballs began to fall around them, slamming into the earth with great sprays of dirt and bouncing back into the air at unpredictable angles. Wherever one sliced through the neatly ordered ranks, it yanked men down, snatching them out of the line like a giant's hand one, two, three at a time. "Close up, close up!," the sergeant's eternal mantra, rose over the advancing men, competing in volume with the screams of the stricken.

Marcus marched on, fighting the instinctive urge to hunch forward as though walking into a rainstorm. Head down or head high, it would make no difference if a ball came right to him, and the thought was a little comforting. He looked over his shoulder and found Andy lagging behind, her steps faltering; her eyes were fixed on the ground, which was littered with the dead from the previous attack as well as their own. She almost tripped over the outstretched arm of a man who'd had most of his chest blown away, his blank eyes and curled fingers pleading.

This was not the kind of fight she was used to, Marcus realized. Andy had proved her toughness in the streets of Vordan, but it was a brawler's toughness, the courage to face a thug in a dark alley and the willpower to keep fighting until you came out on top. This was different—death came from the sky, at random, like some ancient god hurling bolts of lightning, with no stopping it or turning it aside.

Marcus grabbed her arm and pulled her forward, past the corpse. She looked at him, eyes wide, and he leaned close enough to shout in her ear.

"Don't look down!" he said. "Don't look back! Keep your eye on the flags!" The endcaps of the flagpoles flashed silver, even through the smoke, and the Vordanai eagle snapped and rippled. "One step after another!"

Andy swallowed, blinked rapidly, and nodded, picking up the rhythm of the drum again. She stayed at his side as the fire from their own guns warred with the fire ahead, turning the world into a single mass of noise and billowing powder smoke. The timbre of the fortress guns changed as they switched to canister, loads of balls spraying across the lines with every bellow and belch of smoke. The companies were shrinking, contracting toward their centers as sergeants and corporals closed the files and men continued to drop.

Then the defenders' muskets opened up, with a volley that spread along the wall like fire racing across paper. A new fogbank rippled out, puffing lazily over the slope of the wall and the grass beyond. Balls zipped overhead and *thok*ed into the earth, or found purchase in flesh and sent soldiers reeling or stumbling or falling to their knees. The front companies, naturally, got the worst of it, but a man not twenty feet in front of Marcus stumbled out of line, clutching vainly at the ruin a wild shot had made of half his face.

Marcus drew his sword. "Sound the charge!"

"Charge!" Fitz shouted, his still-boyish voice hoarse.

The drums thrilled, quickening to the charge pace, heartbeat-fast. A roar rose from the Vordanai ranks, and they broke into a run, formations dissolving in the rush to close with the enemy. Cannons spat more canister, carving swaths through the soldiers, and Marcus found himself leaping bodies and dodging collapsing men as he came forward. Fitz was on one side of him, Andy on the other, but beyond that there was only swirling smoke.

"With me!" he shouted, his own voice cracking. "Over the wall! With me!"

He thought he heard answering shouts, but he couldn't be certain through the ringing in his ears. They pounded through grimy shadow for longer than seemed possible. *There wasn't that far to go—could I have gotten turned around?*—and then he could see the wall up ahead, a long, sloped brick surface with a shallow ditch in front of it. Once the ditch might have been sheer-sided and filled with stakes, but erosion and neglect had turned it into little more than a dip in the ground. Marcus leapt across, landed on the brick, and scrabbled a moment for balance. He turned, looking for Andy, only to find her missing.

Fitz was there, scrambling up the bricks on his other side. Marcus stared back into the smoke in vain, then screamed a curse at the top of his lungs and ran up the brick slope. Muskets were still going off all around him, deafeningly loud, the flashes like near-constant lightning. Directly ahead of him were two soldiers in Murnskai uniforms, white jackets over gray trousers, with heavy beards and tall, square-topped hats. They fell back a pace as he reached the lip of the wall and vaulted onto the fire step, swinging his sword in a downward cut that opened one of the enemy from shoulder to breastbone. The other dropped his musket and clawed for a weapon at his side, but Fitz was on him at once, running him through the stomach. He slid off the sword, groaning. Marcus realized the sound of musketry was fading, replaced by the clash of steel and the screams of dying men.

"What happened to Andy?" he shouted at Fitz. "Did you see?"

Fitz shook his head, then gestured with his sword. "We have to get to the water battery before they start spiking the guns!"

He was right, of course. *That's the mission Janus gave us.* More blue-uniformed shapes were looming out of the smoke, men with bloody bayonets, chasing their opponents off the wall and deeper into the fortress. Marcus waved his saber over his head to attract their attention and raised his ragged voice again.

"To the battery! With me!"

It was more than an hour before the fighting ended altogether. Once the assault got over the walls, the outcome was never in doubt, but many of the Murnskai stubbornly refused to surrender. There were a hundred last stands in courtyards and corridors, each exacting its toll in blood from the attackers.

Fortunately, this instinct for last-ditch defense meant that only at the final moment did any of the garrison think to start destroying the weapons they were supposed to be guarding, and by then it was too late. Fitz's men had fought their way into the water battery and held it against a desperate counterattack. Bskor was captured almost intact, save for where Viera's guns had pitted the outer walls.

But the cost had been fearful. Compared with seven hundred defenders killed or captured, the First Division had more than twice that many dead or wounded, littering the slope or sprawled in the ditches and courtyards of the fortress. Telling which was which would take some time, too, as teams worked to gather the corpses, triage the wounded, and drag those who needed it to the cutters.

Marcus was standing atop the riverside wall when they brought Andy to him. She had one arm thrown across the shoulders of a burly corporal, and one of her legs was wrapped in a layer of bandage. She managed a salute, however, and a broad grin.

"Sorry about that, sir," she said. "Didn't mean to let you get ahead of me."

Marcus smiled back, resisting an unsoldierly urge to hug her. "I'll allow it, Captain. But only this once." He glanced at her leg. "Are you going to be all right?"

"Cutter says I was lucky. Nice clean puncture, missed the bone. Unless it festers, I should be fine."

"That's good to hear." Marcus let out a long breath. "Corporal, would you escort the captain to the officer's quarters? Let her use one of the beds there." While the barracks for the rankers was cramped and unpleasant, the large building the Murnskai officers had used was more like a country manor than a military installation. Squads of Vordanai soldiers were prowling the halls now, seizing knickknacks and cutlery as souvenirs.

Viera, wearing a bloody bandage around her scalp and her usual scowl, arrived soon after Andy had limped away. Teams of her cannoneers took stock of the big guns aimed at the river and hauled ammunition and powder from the underground armory. It wasn't long before they had their first targets—a quartet of slow-moving river barges rowing upstream laden with food and supplies for the Murnskai army.

Marcus turned to Fitz. "Would you like to do the honors?"

Fitz smiled. "Warning shots, Captain Galiel. Ready. Fire!"

The huge naval guns roared. Enormous fountains of water rose from the calm river, bracketing the barges. As froth rained down all around the startled sailors, a ranker Fitz had chosen for his carrying voice climbed up onto the wall and began to shout in Murnskai. Marcus guessed their hasty translation wasn't perfect, but the men on the river got the idea. Slowly, the barges changed course, angling in toward the docks below the fortress.

"I want a watch kept day and night," Marcus said. "Nothing gets past this point in the river without our permission. If so much as a rowboat refuses to dock, blow them out of the water."

"Yes, *sir*," Viera said, with obvious relish.

So far, so good, Marcus thought. Scouts sent to the east still reported no sign of the main Murnskai army. *Let's hope this works.*

CHAPTER NINE

WINTER

Winter regarded the bowl of gray stuff with intense suspicion.

"What is it?" she said.

"Try it first," Cyte said, offering a slice of heavy black bread.

"That is *not* encouraging," Winter said. She picked up a knife and dipped it into the gray stuff. It spread over the bread like thick, grainy butter.

"The Murnskai call it *dimotska*. It's considered a delicacy."

"Remind me sometime to tell you about what they considered delicacies in Khandar."

"Just eat it."

Winter sighed, closed her eyes, and took a bite. The bread was coarse and chewy, and the gray stuff was intensely salty, with a slippery texture. Some of the tiny grains popped between her teeth. Privately, she had to admit that it wasn't bad. *I'd still rather have a nice pat of butter, though.*

"Okay," she said, finishing the slice. "What did I just eat?"

"Fish eggs," Cyte said, helping herself.

Winter had a confused vision of a fish sitting atop a nest. "Fish don't lay eggs."

"They do, actually," Cyte said, spreading a thick layer of the *dimotska* atop the bread. "They're just tiny. This stuff comes out of the female arrowfish. When they're in season, they swarm off the Split Coast, and the fishermen catch them and cut out—"

"You know, that's enough." Winter wiped her lips on her sleeve and sighed. "What's the matter with the rest of the fish, anyway?"

"Fish is peasant food," Cyte said. "This is for nobility."

"I'm going to go on record and say that every country outside Vordan is insane," Winter said. "Why can't they eat *normal* things?"

"Like unmentionable bits of pig ground up and stuffed inside its own intestines?"

"That's more of a Hamveltai thing," Winter said, fighting a grin. "Foreign influences."

"We eat chicken eggs," Cyte said, finishing her slice of bread. "This isn't so different."

Winter made a face. Food had been plentiful the past few days, thanks to the depots of Bskor, but full of unfamiliar flavors. Cyte seemed to take a particular delight in grabbing the strangest items, usually "delicacies" intended for officers and royalty. Fish eggs weren't the half of it.

There was a scratch at the tent flap. "Sir?" Bobby said without waiting for an answer. "They're coming again."

"By all the fucking saints," Winter said. "I don't believe it."

"I saw them myself," Bobby said. "At least six battalions—"

"I know. I know." Winter grabbed her jacket off the ground and started doing up the buttons. "I'll be right there."

"That makes six attacks in two days," Cyte said.

"Are they hoping we're going to get *tired*?" Winter said, fastening her collar. "Or run out of ammunition?" Fortunately, there was no chance of the latter—the same depots that were providing their food had been stuffed with shot and powder.

"Maybe they just don't know what else to do," Cyte said.

"I know what *I'd* do," Winter muttered. *Head home as fast as I could, and to hell with anybody who tried to stop me.* She belted on her sword and pulled the tent flap open, letting in the brilliant sun. The rain had passed, leaving the sky a blinding blue almost free of clouds.

Cannon-fire began as she hurried down the mud-churned path from her tent. The Second Division's two batteries were placed high on the hillside, with clear lines of fire over their own infantry to the flat ground below. Between attacks, the artillerymen had occupied themselves with improving the position by creating a ramp of packed earth behind each gun; when it fired, the cannon would recoil backward, then roll down the ramp into firing position, allowing the crew to reload and fire again more quickly. Colonel Archer's crews had the drill down to a fine art now, and the guns boomed with clockwork regularity.

Janus had chosen their position with his usual care. Halfway between Polkhaiz and Bskor, where the river Shulia entered the Syzria, a spur of hills extended north to within a mile of the riverbank. He'd brought the Second,

Third, and Fourth Divisions to hold the narrow gap, following much the same route the First had taken days earlier, while the remaining half of the Grand Army bristled aggressively against the Murnskai front. The artillery reserve had come as well, manhandled by cursing, sweating infantrymen over miles of bad roads and muddy valleys.

The Third and Fourth had set up in the narrow strip of low ground between the river and the hill. At first Janus' demand that the troops dig ditches and earthen ramparts had been met with widespread grumbling, but the past few days had convinced any doubters. The Murnskai army had come west, a seemingly endless stream of white-coated infantry and squadron after squadron of horsemen. They'd been met by a line of spiked ditches, with the infantry taking cover behind waist-high mounds of dirt topped with sturdy logs. Periodic gaps in the line allowed the massed batteries of the two divisions and the artillery reserve, parked nearly hub to hub, to rake the open ground of the valley floor.

Winter's Second Division was deployed on the army's right, where the land started its rise into the wooded hills they'd so recently struggled to march through. They were spread thinner, with more front to cover, but the terrain was enormously favorable. Just below the tree line, they'd dug pits and set up ramparts, strewing the approaches with more felled trees as an additional obstacle. The slope meant the guns had a perfect field of fire, outranging their Murnskai counterparts, although Murnskai gunnery had thus far proven to be lackluster at best.

Thus fortified, Janus had settled in to wait for the Murnskai army to attack. Which, to Winter's astonishment, they obligingly had, bulling ahead in spite of the obvious difficulties. *Whoever's in command isn't worried about casualties, that's for certain.*

The camp was even higher on the slope, back among the trees. Winter passed the artillery line and made her way down to the infantry. They'd set up a command post in the center of the Girls' Own position, surrounded by logs with notches wide enough to peek through. Abby was already there, holding a spyglass to her eye.

"Looks like us and Blackstream's boys are the lucky ones this time," she said. Blackstream's Fourth Infantry Regiment was deployed to the right, Sevran and de Koste's regiments to the left. "But they're doing something I don't understand."

"Let me have a look," Winter said.

Abby handed over the spyglass. Sweeping it across the field, Winter could see eight battalions in column, the equivalent of an entire division, concentrated onto a narrow front and advancing steadily. Their white coats made for a pretty line, she had to admit. The ground they were crossing was already strewn with dead; as best Winter could tell, the Murnskai made no effort to either bury the corpses or gather the wounded, leaving soldiers who'd been hit to get off the field under their own power. The Girls' Own had rescued a few who'd fallen relatively close to their own line, but hadn't dared to venture out any farther. At night the camp was haunted by hoarse cries and pleas from the killing field, growing steadily weaker as time went on.

"What's strange?" Winter said. *Besides the fact that they're coming at all.*

"Look behind the infantry," Abby said. "That looks like a cuirassier regiment to me, all strung out."

Winter shifted the glass. *They can't be mad enough to try a cavalry charge, can they?* Even a commander as rock stupid as this Murnskai general seemed to be would have to know that sending horsemen uphill into stakes and obstacles was madness.

But the cuirassiers were there, all right, big men on big horses, with steel breastplates and long fur capes. They were advancing slowly, keeping pace with the infantry. Instead of holding a tight formation, as cavalry usually tried to do, they were spread out in a long line, as wide as the entire infantry attack. Each man had his saber drawn already.

"That *is* strange." *Strange is bad,* instinct told her. "But I can't see how it's going to help them."

"Me neither." Abby took her spyglass back. "Any orders?"

Winter shook her head. "Not for the moment." By this time none were needed.

The cannon-fire tore great gaps in the Murnskai formations. After two days firing over the same ground, Archer's gunners knew the ranges and elevations by heart, and nearly every shot went smashing through the white-coated lines. More human wreckage joined the stiffening corpses of the previous day and a half, piling in drifts that were so tall in places the advancing infantry had to detour around them.

After the first attack, the Girls' Own had paced out distances from their position and set up markers that would be easily visible from the heights. When the Murnskai advanced past a hundred and fifty yards, therefore, the entire line erupted at once, as though the enemy had struck a tripwire. With the advantage of height, even a musket had a chance of being deadly at that range, and as ammunition was plentiful, Winter saw no reason to have her troops hold their fire. Smoke boiled over the log ramparts and poured down into the spiked ditches. From the command post, set slightly farther back, Winter still had a good view.

"They're breaking up," Abby said.

Winter nodded. The leading companies of the Murnskai battalions were melting away under the onslaught of fire, men halting to take cover behind piles of their own dead and shoot futilely at the wall of muzzle flashes ahead. The following companies got tangled up with them, the neat lines dissolving into an amorphous blob, which provided the artillery with an even better target. The enemy on the far right broke first, the blob coming apart under the combined volleys of Blackstream's regiment, breaking up into a mass of fleeing, frightened men. Panic spread down the line, one battalion at a time.

"The cavalry—" Abby began, then stopped. "Oh."

"What?" Winter said.

Wordlessly, Abby handed over the glass. Winter trained it on the cuirassiers and saw that they were in motion, riding forward. Sabers rose and fell, cutting down their own infantry, who'd thrown down their packs and rifles in order to run faster.

"Balls of the Beast," Winter swore.

"That answers your question," said Cyte, who'd joined them and was looking through her own glass. "Apparently devotion to Church and emperor isn't enough."

"God Almighty." Winter lowered the glass and shook her head. The attack had broken up more than a hundred yards from the line, reduced to a bloody shambles just like all the ones that had come before.

"It might be a good sign," Cyte said. "If that's what it takes to get them to come at us . . ."

"Division-General, sir!"

Winter turned to find a Girls' Own ranker so stiffly at attention she looked like she couldn't breathe. Behind her, trailing a dozen soldiers with Colonial scorpion insignia, was Janus himself. Winter automatically drew herself up into a salute, and Abby and Cyte did likewise.

"Thank you," Janus said, waving a hand for them to relax. "I got word they were trying this end of the line again, so I thought I would check in. Anything to report?"

"The enemy are repulsed, sir," Winter barked, stiffly formal in front of her officers. "Their losses seem heavy."

"As I've come to expect from the Girls' Own," Janus said, a bit louder than was necessary. The rankers close enough to hear repeated his words, the praise spreading up and down the line like the ripples from a rock dropped into a pond.

"The enemy . . ." Winter hesitated. "We saw their cuirassiers slaughtering their infantry after they broke, sir. I think they're driving their men toward us under threat of execution."

Janus raised an eyebrow. "Desperate indeed."

"Yes, sir."

He paused for a moment. "Do you recall, Division-General, a conversation we once had about the nature of a perfect victory?"

"Yes, sir. You said that the perfect victory would be bloodless, because the outcome would be so clear that the battle would never even be fought."

"Indeed." Janus stared out at the field, heaped with white-coated Murnskai dead. "Unfortunately, it appears that the perfect victory requires an opponent smart enough to know when he's beaten." He sighed and raised his voice again. "Division-General Ihernglass. Can you hold this position?"

"Sir." Winter straightened up. "If they have to come at me across that ground, and you keep me well supplied with ammunition, my division could hold this position against all the armies of the world."

Janus smiled like a wolf.

By nightfall, the battle, such as it was, was over. Prince Vasil had steadily withdrawn more and more of his army from the lines facing south at Polkhaiz, throwing it against Janus' impromptu fortress on the road to Bskor. On the afternoon of the second day, the four divisions of the Grand Army still waiting on the Pilgrim's Road launched a sudden attack north that split the Murnskai line wide open. Give-Em-Hell's cavalry reserve flooded into the gap, scattering the enemy and taking the force facing Janus in the rear. Much of the Murnskai army, battered by days of fruitless assaults, dissolved completely, with only a few cavalry formations holding together to beat a retreat over the Syzria. Even the bridge at Polkhaiz was captured intact.

The news arrived at the Second Division sometime after dinner. Cook fires were quickly built into bonfires, and the celebrations began. Gilphaite had been a hollow victory at best, with the enemy escaping mostly intact, and in any case the Second's heavy casualties had left no one in the mood for revelry. This time, though, there was no reason to hold back. The enemy was destroyed, and their own losses scarcely amounted to a few dozen, most of those lightly injured when their fortifications had been struck by cannon-fire.

The Vordanai army didn't have an official liquor ration for its troops, but the Murnskai supplies had been generously equipped with drink of all sorts. Winter ordered the cache distributed to the soldiers, after claiming a few of the nicer-looking bottles for herself. She had just cracked the wax seal on the first—as best her limited Murnskai could tell, it was made from potatoes and peppers—when there was a scratch at the tent flap.

"Come in," Winter said.

Cyte lifted the flap. "Drinking alone?"

"Nobody wants a general looking over their shoulder when they're getting drunk," Winter said. "But I figured I deserved something."

"Would you mind a bit of company, then?" Cyte held up a green glass bottle, already half-empty. There was a definite glow about her cheeks.

"If you're willing to put up with a bit of gloom." Winter sighed and turned to her chest to find the tin cups. Cyte flopped down in her usual spot on the other side of the camp table.

"Gloom? Everyone's cheering their heads off out there. They're calling it the greatest victory ever."

"The perfect victory," Winter muttered.

"What?"

"Nothing. You're right. I should be . . . I don't know." Winter set the cups on the table. "Is that stuff any good?"

"Not really, no."

"I'll try this, then." She let a finger of the clear stuff from the wax-sealed bottle glug into a tin cup. "Maybe I just can't stop thinking about those poor bastards out there. Marched into battle at the point of a saber, then cut down when they couldn't take it anymore." She sniffed, then drained the cup. Pepper burned on her tongue, and alcohol stung her throat. *Not bad.* "Nobody deserves that."

"Better them than us," Cyte said, then sighed at Winter's expression. "I know. Hanna has teams out there, looking for survivors."

"To Hanna, then," Winter said, filling her cup again. "The best regimental cutter—"

"—that I hope I never have to visit," Cyte finished. They drank together this time, and for a moment Winter sat in silence, feeling the pleasant warmth as the drink hit her stomach.

"What are you doing here?" she said after a while.

Cyte went even redder. "I thought you could use—"

"Not here in the tent," Winter said. "Here, I mean. In Murnsk. Why are you here?"

"Oh." Cyte set the green bottle on the table. "You're one of *those* drunks."

"I'm not drunk yet," Winter said.

"I've had this conversation before," Cyte said. "Get a few drinks into any of the philosophy students and it's all 'Why are we here?' this and 'What's the meaning of existence?' that. Afterward they usually make a grab for me and then pass out." She snorted. "Philosophers can't hold their liquor."

"You don't think about it?"

"I've thought about it enough to know that I'm not going to come up with any useful answers. So the hell with it."

"Fair enough." Winter leaned back. "It's not really what I meant, though. I was thinking, why am I over *here* and not out there piled in a ditch?"

Cyte shuddered. "Because you were lucky enough to be Vordanai, I guess?"

"That's it? Vordan never did anything for me. They threw me in a prison that married teenaged girls to sadistic monsters. That's why I ran away to Khandar. All this"—she plucked at her uniform—"just sort of happened. Maybe I could have turned the other way, run off to Murnsk, and I *would* be lying dead out there."

"Saints and martyrs, you're morbid. Sure. And maybe you would have discovered a vein of pure gold and become the richest woman in the world. Or maybe you'd have gotten the plague and died the first week. You can't know these things." Cyte tipped the bottle over her cup again. "Believe me, I've studied history. I *know.* The historians like to talk about how Great Men shape the course of events, but most of the time it seems like it's just luck. Somebody's carriage throws a wheel, somebody doesn't read a letter, it rains one day but not the next, and before you know it a mighty empire falls or a kingdom rises."

"I'm not sure if that's reassuring or depressing."

"A little bit of both. Did I ever tell you about Queen Gekitorix?"

"I think I would have remembered the name, so probably not."

Cyte launched into another historical anecdote, which given the somewhat advanced state of her inebriation was only semi-coherent. It *was* pleasant not to be drinking alone, to relax for a while, feeling her mind slowly sinking in a sea of alcoholic fuzz and meaningless chatter.

As they talked, she couldn't help but circle back to her earlier question.

Janus. It all comes back to Janus. Winter liked Vordan well enough, even liked Raesinia herself, but she couldn't help but think that without Janus she'd have abandoned the army long ago. There was too much chance of ending up under a commander like Prince Vasil, who'd order his own men to their deaths rather than admit defeat, or an incompetent boor like de Ferre. *Or Sergeant Davis.*

She'd followed Janus because he'd proven himself capable, because he knew the secrets of her gender and her demon, and because he'd promised to reunite her with Jane. And he'd kept up his end of the bargain; after it had fallen to pieces in her hands, she'd kept following him because she didn't know what else to do. *And because I owe it to all the people I dragged along with me.* Responsibility could be a bitter pill to swallow.

But when you put it that way, it means that Jane was right. I could have left the army and stayed with her. I made the choice—

"Winter?"

Winter's eyes shot open. Cyte was leaning over her, waving a hand and giggling.

"What?" Winter said. "It's been a long day."

"And you're drunk."

"You should talk."

Cyte sat back and ran a hand through her hair. "There's something I want to do, but it feels like it might be *really* stupid, so I thought I should get *really* pickled before I tried it."

"This sounds bad. If it involves cannon, I'm going to have to stop you right there."

"There's something I want to ask you. It's personal and extremely unprofessional."

Winter blinked and sat up straight, heart thumping a little faster. "What's the matter?"

"Okay." Cyte took a deep breath. "You have . . . Um . . ."

"I have?"

Cyte's face was so red it was hard to tell if she was blushing or not. "You have the Tyrant's Disease. Right?"

She looked so solemn and earnest that Winter fought back a giggle. Instead, she matched Cyte's stare and said, with all the dignity she could muster, "I have no idea what that is."

"Oh."

"I hope it's not fatal."

"It's not like that." Cyte looked down, and her lost expression made Winter feel bad about nearly laughing. "It's a mental disease. I read about it in the University library. It's when a woman wants other women." Cyte raised her head again and took a deep breath. "You know. For . . . you know."

"For . . ." It took Winter's tipsy mind a moment to work through the convolutions of that. "Oh. *Oh.*"

"It's not something I would just say to someone," Cyte said quickly, "but you and Jane didn't exactly keep it a secret, and I just thought . . . I . . ." She shook her head violently. "Forget it. Forget I said anything."

"Cyte." Winter grabbed her shoulders. "Cyte, it's okay. Relax."

"I'm sorry." There were tears in Cyte's eyes. "I'm really sorry. I shouldn't—"

"It's all *right*, honestly. That's what you wanted to ask me? If Jane and I were sleeping together?" Winter shook her head. "Like you said, we didn't exactly make a secret of it."

"That wasn't the question, actually." Cyte blinked and rubbed her eyes with her sleeve. "You're sure you don't mind?"

"I told you, it's fine." Winter crossed her legs and sat facing Cyte. "Is it really called the Tyrant's Disease?"

"I guess," Cyte said. "That's what it said in *Disorders of the Mind*. The Mithradacii Tyrants' courts were famous for debauchery and perversion, I suppose."

"Okay. Then I guess I do." Winter shook her head. "So what *is* the question?"

Cyte's voice was very small. "How did you figure out you had it?"

"I . . ." Winter hesitated. "It's not something I ever really thought about. I didn't know it was something you could *have* until you told me. When I was young I thought . . ."

"What?"

It was Winter's turn to flush. "That it was just something about me and Jane, I guess."

"How old were you when you met?"

"When we *met*, we were about twelve." Winter spoke slowly, probing her emotions as she might have probed a broken tooth with her tongue. She kept waiting for pain, but all she felt was a dull numbness. "We grew up together, in the Prison."

"And you just knew?"

"Not . . . really. I couldn't have told you. I just felt . . . odd."

"What happened?"

"She kissed me. We were taking care of some of the younger kids and playing a game on one of the lawns. She and I ended up tangled together some-how, and she just . . . kissed me."

"What did you do?"

"I ran away." Winter's lips curled into a slight smile. "She had to chase me through the hedge maze."

Cyte let out a breath. "Ah."

"We didn't know what we were doing. But it felt right to me." Winter shrugged awkwardly. "Like I said, it's never something I thought about too deeply. Maybe I should have, I suppose."

"But it was only Jane?" Cyte said. "Never anyone else?"

"Never," Winter said. "I mean, after I ran away, I was terrified of being found out as a girl, so I stayed away from everybody. Then, when I got back here, Jane turned up again."

"You didn't think about it? Just, you know. In your own head."

"Sometimes."

Winter leaned forward, and Cyte stiffened. Her breath was coming very fast, and Winter could see her pulse jumping beneath the pale skin of her throat.

"Cyte," Winter said.

"Yes?" The word was a squeak.

"Do you want me to kiss you?"

"I don't . . . I mean . . . only if . . ." Cyte's voice dropped to a barely audible whisper. "Yes."

Winter kissed her.

Cyte was so stiff with terror at first that it was like kissing a statue, their lips pressed awkwardly together. Then she relaxed, just a fraction, and her mouth opened slightly. Her lips tasted of the stuff from the green bottle, mint and strong liquor.

After barely a second Cyte pulled away, scrambling backward. "No," she said under her breath. "No, no, no, no."

"Cyte—"

"I'm sorry," Cyte said, shooting to her feet. "I shouldn't have done that. I'm drunk. Much, much, much too drunk. I need to go."

"Wait," Winter said. "Please."

"I'm *sorry*." Her eyes were full of tears again. "I won't . . . I mean . . ." Cyte wiped her eyes and shook her head. "Good night."

"I—" Winter began, but Cyte was already gone, out the tent flap and into the darkness.

Well. Winter sat back against her bedroll. Her whole body was tingling from that brief moment of contact. *Fuck.*

The morning brought a headache the likes of which she hadn't had since Khandar. Winter, groaning, tipped the remainder of the wax-sealed bottle onto the ground outside her tent and guzzled the water in her kettle, then sent a nearby ranker running for more.

When someone scratched at the tent flap, she half expected to see Cyte, but found Bobby there instead. Dark circles under the girl's eyes attested to some revelry on her part as well, and made Winter wonder how she must look. *Good thing I haven't got a mirror in here.*

"Morning, sir," Bobby said, brandishing a sheaf of paper.

"Morning," Winter said, looking at the bundle distrustfully. "I'm not sure I can handle that yet."

"Nothing urgent, sir. Casualty reports from yesterday, stocks and supplies from this morning."

"How were our losses?"

"Almost nonexistent," Bobby said. "Only one dead from enemy action, in Sevran's regiment, a boy who caught a cannonball practically in his lap. One of de Koste's men accidentally double loaded his musket, and it exploded on him. Most of the rest are minor injuries from splinters and collapses. A few broken limbs at the very worst."

Two people died, Winter thought. Two men under her command, who by rights she ought to have cared as much about as any others. *But I'm smiling because that's so much better than what* might *have been.* She reflected, not for the first time, that war was a strange business.

"I'll go over the reports later, then. Anything more pressing?"

"Janus sent orders that every regiment has to provide teams for burial detail."

Winter winced. After two days of fighting, some of the bodies out on the plain were no doubt in pretty bad shape. *But there's no way around it. There's a hell of a lot of dead Murnskai, and someone has to bury them.* "I'll ask for volunteers."

"Cyte said to tell you she'll take care of it, sir. She started organizing the teams earlier this morning."

Cyte. Last night was a confused mess in her mind, not so much because she'd been drunk but because she didn't quite understand what had happened. *I kissed Cyte. And then she ran away. And now she'd apparently rather spend the day burying rotting corpses than speak to me?* The whole thing had a dreamlike feeling that made Winter reluctant to think about it too hard. *Or maybe it's just that I have no idea what to do next.*

"Also," Bobby said, "Alex asked if you had a few moments to talk."

"Right," Winter said, grateful for the distraction. "Have you had any problems with her?"

"None, sir. She's been very well behaved. Anne-Marie and some of the others are quite taken with her."

Winter nodded. She'd debated leaving the girl back with the supply train. But if she *was* a Penitent—something Winter had a harder time believing every time they talked—then the best chance of stopping her when she made her move would be if Winter and Bobby were nearby. So she'd ridden with the cross-country march to Bskor, uncomplaining in the face of bad roads and mud. *From the looks of her when she first arrived, she's come through worse.*

"I'll see her now," Winter said. "Is she still in her tent?"

"She wanted to meet out in the woods," Bobby said. "Something about a demonstration. I'll fetch her myself, if that's all right. Just to be safe."

Winter nodded. Bobby saluted again and slipped out, to be replaced by the ranker with a full kettle of ice-cold spring water. After another long drink, and a visit to the latrines, Winter was feeling halfway human again. Her head still throbbed, but she could at least open her eyes in the light.

Bobby and Alex met her at the edge of the camp, and together they walked out past the sentry ring and into the rocky woodlands that stretched along the spine of the hills. Alex seemed much improved; she wore a grab bag of Murnskai civilian clothing and a blue army coat, but her color was healthy, and if she was pained by the wound in her side she gave no sign of it.

"I take it I should congratulate you," she said.

Winter glanced at the girl. "Why?"

"You won the battle, didn't you?"

"Oh." Winter shrugged. "The battle was over as soon as Janus put us across the Murnskai line of supply. It just took a while for Prince Vasil to realize it." *A while, and a whole lot of corpses.*

"Janus is really that good?"

"*Good* isn't the word. He's . . ." Winter groped for a description. "It's like watching a grown man play handball against a bunch of children."

"It sounds like I made the right decision, then, coming down here." Alex looked around. "This ought to be far enough."

"All right." Winter crossed her arms. "What do you want to show me?"

"My demon. I'm not a soldier, um . . . ." Alex hesitated. "What do I call you, properly?"

Winter laughed. "Properly? Division-General Ihernglass. But you may as well keep calling me Winter."

"Right. I promised you a demonstration, I think. I came here to help fight the Priests of the Black and the Penitent Damned. So you need to know what I can do, and I think I'm recovered enough by now to show you."

"Fair enough. So what can you do?"

"I told you I was a thief." Alex flashed a sunny grin. "I was pretty good at it, even without a demon. But this helped."

She raised her hands, the slightly overlong sleeves of the blue coat falling loose on her skinny arms. Globes of darkness grew under her palms, expanding from pinpoints of black to spheres that obscured her hands to the wrists. At the bottom of her mind, Winter felt Infernivore stirring.

From one of the globes, a black tendril shot out, faster than Winter's eyes could follow. It wrapped around the trunk of a nearby pine, about twenty feet off the ground. Alex ran directly at the tree, jumped, and let the thread of darkness take her weight, running *up* the trunk until she was braced against it well off the ground. She hung there for a few moments, scanning the forest around her. Then she raised her other hand, letting another black whip lick out and grasp another tree. Winter gasped involuntarily as she jumped, swinging past with a gleeful *whoop* at the end of her unnatural rope. When she reached the other tree, the black line vanished, and Alex kicked off the trunk into a neat backflip and landed on her feet.

"Sorry," she said. "I didn't mean to get carried away. It's just been a while. I forgot how fun that is."

"It's very impressive," Winter said.

"There's a bit more," Alex said. Her expression darkened, but she turned, pointing at a dead stump. Two spears of darkness lanced out, punching through the old wood and out the other side. They hung still for a moment, then flexed, producing a rising groan that ended with the stump exploding into splinters. Alex let her hand fall, the globes of darkness fading, and turned back to Winter.

"Ah," Winter said. She paused for a moment. "You could do that to a person?"

Bobby glanced at Winter uncertainly. Winter kept her eyes on Alex, who looked down at the forest floor for a long moment.

Finally, she took a deep breath and nodded. "I have."

"And would you, if I asked you to?"

"I . . ." Alex began, then trailed off.

"You're not a soldier," Winter said. "But if you want to help us, you might have to become one."

"I don't want to fight some poor Murnskai bastard who never did anything to me," Alex said. "But if it's the Black Priests or their people, then I'll do whatever needs to be done."

"I suppose I can't argue with that." After considering for a long moment, Winter held out her hand. "Welcome to the Second Division."

"Thanks."

When they shook, Infernivore twitched at the contact. Then there was something else, the beast in Winter's soul turning, just slightly, like an animal seeing something on the horizon.

Alex half turned, looking over her shoulder. "Did you feel something?"

"I'm not sure." Winter looked to Bobby, who shook her head. "We'd better get back to camp."

"Yeah." Alex pulled her coat a little tighter. "It's cold today, for spring."

PART TWO

PONTIFEX OF THE BLACK

"*Destroyed?*" The Pontifex of the White's voice carried a quaver of disbelief.

"Destroyed," the Pontifex of the Black said. In spite of the dire circumstances, he couldn't help but take pleasure in seeing the old man's confident facade shaken. "A few cavalry may have escaped. Prince Vasil's fate is unknown."

"Could your sources be mistaken?"

"Unlikely," the Pontifex of the Red broke in. "I'm beginning to get similar reports, although obviously my methods are not as fast as those of our Brother of the Black. It appears that the emperor's army has been decisively defeated."

The White and the Red sat on their respective sides of the triangular table. The Black, too keyed up to stay in a chair, paced back and forth across the length of the room.

"Vhalnich will come to Elysium," he said. "He's said as much, and there's no reason to doubt him."

"Elysium has stood for a thousand years," the White said, regaining some of his poise. "One battle is not a war. Dorsay is still in the field, and the emperor will assemble another army. No matter how Vhalnich struggles, he cannot hope to defy history forever."

You blind fool, the Black thought. *Just as the Beast predicted.* "He doesn't *have* to defy history forever," he said, keeping his anger under control. "He's not fighting Borel, or Murnsk. He's coming for *us.* He has the legacy of the Demon King, and he wants to raze Elysium and set free all the fiends we've spent so long putting in chains. At a stroke, every bit of the progress the Church has made since the days of Saint Ligamenti would be erased."

"You don't think you're being a little overdramatic?" the White said.

"While I don't pretend to understand Vhalnich's motives," the Red said, "I have to admit the situation seems grave. I'm not a general, but I can read a map. Polkhaiz is barely a hundred and fifty miles from here as the crow flies, and there's no significant force in a position to stop him. A strike at his rear might slow him down, but Duke Dorsay seems disinclined to make one."

"For which he will be punished, once all this is over," the White snapped. "Very well. My Brother of the Black, since you seem so incensed, may I assume you have some plan in mind?"

"The time for holding anything back has long since passed," the Black said. "The Penitent Damned will do what they can, but it may not be enough. I have no choice but to unleash the Old Witch."

There was silence around the table for a moment.

"The Old Witch of the Ice Woods," the White said flatly. "The Heart of Murnsk."

"A creature that, if our records are to be believed, it took a hundred years and the lives of a thousand men to subdue," the Red said. "You want to use it as a *weapon*?"

"It is the most effective weapon in our arsenal," the Black said.

"Can it be controlled?" the White said.

"To a point," the Black said. "It has spent a very long time in our power, and its current incarnation is at least . . . biddable. But its effect is . . . ah . . . indiscriminate."

"Again, if the records are to be believed, that is an understatement," the Red said. "You're talking about the deaths of thousands."

"Tens of thousands," the Black said. "At least."

"This is absurd," the White screeched. "These are our own people."

"And they would give up their lives for the Church, if we asked them," the Black said. "This is no different."

"There is no alternative?" the Red said hopelessly.

"My bag of tricks is not bottomless, brothers," the Black said. "This is my last card to play."

There was a long silence.

"Then we must play it," the Red said. "God have mercy on all of us."

Under his mask, the Pontifex of the Black grinned. "God have mercy on Janus bet Vhalnich." *I intend to have none.*

"Send messages to the tundra tribes beyond the Bataria," the Black said as he walked down the spiraling corridors under the earth. "Call in every debt we're owed. I want all the riders they can muster."

"Yes, Your Excellence," the scribe said. "Will they reach us before Vhalnich does?"

"Just do it." *Vhalnich will never reach Elysium.*

"As you command." The scribe shuffled his papers. "Mirror has rendezvoused with Shade, in the vicinity of Dorsay's army. He asks if you wish Dorsay removed."

"Not yet." Dorsay was working against Church interests at the present, but when Vhalnich was destroyed he would still have his uses. *His reckoning will come later.* "Tell him to stand by."

"What should he tell Duke Orlanko?"

"Whatever shuts him up," the Black snapped. He deeply wished circumstances had allowed him to dispose of the pompous Vordanai duke. Unfortunately, Orlanko was the only plausible candidate to rule Vordan once the revolution was crushed and Raesinia was in a cell where she belonged. *I never should have listened to him in the first place.* Orlanko was a transparently self-serving toad, but once he was in power he would at least be easy to manipulate.

"Yes, Your Excellence."

"Wait here," the Black said. "I won't be long."

There were three doors to the cell under the mountain, one after another, each locked and opened by a separate key held by a Black Priest sworn to defend it with his life. When they were all open, the Pontifex of the Black strode through, into a narrow rock-walled cell only a few feet across. The prisoner hung on one wall, shackles on her wrists connected by chains to pitons driven into the stone. An iron ring encircled her head, like a crown a bit too big for its bearer, holding a metal plate across her eyes. In spite of living in this permanent darkness, she looked up as the Black came into her prison, sensitive to the slight scuff of his slippers on the stone.

"Hello, Zakhar," said the Beast.

The Pontifex of the Black pointedly did not flinch. The Beast liked to remind him of what it was, that in spite of this fresh young body it had the knowledge of a demon, going back centuries. It knew his real name, which he'd given up on becoming head of his order, because it had known him as a young man in service to the previous Pontifex of the Black.

"How was the conference with your brothers?" the creature said.

"The Pontifex of the White was reluctant," the Black said.

"As I warned," the Beast said. "Your predecessor gave a very clear description of him. The man likes nothing more than an argument. I trust you persuaded him?"

"I did." The Black frowned. "You knew Vhalnich would defeat the emperor's army. How?"

"Because Janus bet Vhalnich is obsessed." The Beast leaned forward slightly, chains rattling against their pitons. "He will sacrifice anything to get what he wants, and that gives him an edge. He's coming for you, my dear Zakhar."

"He won't reach Elysium," the Black said.

"I wouldn't be so certain," the Beast crooned. "Underestimate Vhalnich's resolve at your peril."

"I do not plan to underestimate anything," the Black said. "Do you have anything *useful* to say?"

"So ungrateful," the Beast said, blind, masked eyes running over him. Though he wore his full regalia, and the creature was naked and chained to a wall, something in its voice made the pontifex feel as though the situation were reversed. "Haven't I been *useful* so far?"

"You have provided . . . some insight." The Beast's knowledge was immense. Tapping that knowledge without endangering his soul was walking a razor's edge, but in these desperate times the pontifex dared not ignore any advantage. Already, it had helped him outmaneuver his brothers in council. *And it* knows *Vhalnich!* "But not, I think, everything you know."

"Everything I know is quite a long list, Zakhar," the Beast said. "You need to ask the right questions."

"Enough." He turned away, gesturing for the jailers.

"You'll come see me again," the Beast said. It wasn't a request, or even a command. *A prediction.* "When the enemy is at the walls."

"I give the orders, not you," the Black muttered. "Monster."

The Beast laughed.

Spring had come, even to Elysium. The tops of the peaks were still shrouded in white, but halfway up, where the fortress-city clung to the shoulder of the mountain, a fragile warmth coaxed out the sparse grasses and hardy wildflowers. The sun hung in a cloudless sky. Swathed as he was in his thick robes and obsidian mask, the Pontifex of the Black was sweating.

It had to be worse for the two women standing in front of him, but if they were uncomfortable they gave no sign of it. One of them was tall and slender, the other shorter and compact, layered with muscle. Both wore heavy fur coats on top of layers of leather, along with thick gloves and boots. Their faces were invisible, covered by black cloth studded with thousands of chips of obsidian to create a glittering mask. Behind them, four heavily laden packhorses stood waiting.

"You understand your assignment?" the pontifex said. The rest of his entourage stood some distance away, out of earshot. It was unlikely that Vhalnich had spies in Elysium itself, but not impossible. *Best to be certain.*

Both women nodded.

"Be cautious," he said. "I understand you are eager to complete your duty. But you may be the last chance for the Church, and perhaps for the world. Wait for the proper moment."

"Yes, Your Excellence," the shorter one said, her voice flat. "We will not fail you."

"It is not only me you serve; it is all of us." The pontifex inclined his head respectfully. "We honor your sacrifice."

They spoke in unison. *"Ahdon ivahnt vi, ignahta sempria."* God bless us, the Penitent Damned.

"Go."

They went, leading the small, sure-footed horses away. The pontifex watched with a gloomy feeling. From the beginning he'd tried to avoid risking his valuable Penitents by not confronting Vhalnich directly. But the time for restraint was over. As he'd told his brothers on the council, he intended to play every card he had remaining.

There were many gates to Elysium, most of them long since sealed and forgotten, a fact which the Priests of the Black found useful. The one they'd used had been a servants' entrance, hundreds of years ago, and its existence was recalled only by a few. It led to a narrow, rocky trail, which crossed a fast-running stream before following a meandering path halfway down the mountain, where it joined the main road. It was ideal for those who wanted to come and go from the fortress without attracting notice.

Two Priests of the Black held the small door open. Two more waited just inside, holding a thin, ragged man between them. The prisoner didn't look dangerous; indeed, without the priests' support, he didn't seem like he could have taken a step on his own. He certainly didn't resemble the fairy-tale villain who'd been the terror of a nation for more than a thousand years.

Since before the time of Karis, even before the arrival of the Mithradacii Tyrants, the peasants of Murnsk had told stories about the Old Witch of the Ice Woods. Mothers warned their children that the Old Witch would take them away if they disobeyed, and villages left offerings by her shrines in the darkest part of the local forest. Any community that failed to propitiate her, they said, would find itself obliterated by endless, cruel winter, buried in snow and ice even while summer came to the rest of the world.

Many centuries before, while pursuing their endless attempts to root out the last vestiges of the Mages' Heresy from remote parts of the north, the pontifex's predecessors had searched for the truth behind the legends. They'd expected to find nothing—even in the days of the Demon King, there were a hundred myths and ghost stories for every true sorcerer or demon. Instead, they'd found themselves in a war with a secretive cult that lived among the frozen forests, whose heart was the name of a demon passed from mother to daughter down through the generations.

The Black Priests had won, though it had taken a hundred years. They'd broken the cult and dragged the Old Witch, spitting and screaming, back to Elysium. As the worst winter in living memory battered the fortress, the torturers had dragged the name of the demon from the wretched woman, and since then it had been among the most powerful beasts imprisoned in the Church's menagerie.

The young man who currently bore the creature was weak-minded, his spirit broken by the agony of pronouncing the demon's name. Looking at his wasted frame, ribs clearly visible in a shrunken chest, the pontifex guessed they'd be searching for a new host before too much longer. *If the Church survives.* He shook his head. All that mattered now was that the pathetic creature was reasonably compliant—far too weak, in body and soul, to be a Penitent Damned, but willing to perform for food and kind treatment like a trained animal.

One of the two priests who were his keepers stepped away from his charge, bowed, and addressed the pontifex.

"Your Excellence." He sounded nervous. "You understand that he is not capable of controlling his manifestation as precisely as some of the past hosts. If the Old Witch is unleashed, it will be at full strength. The consequences—"

"I'm aware of the consequences," the pontifex said. "Do it."

"Yes, Your Excellence."

The priest waved to his fellow, who bent to whisper in the ear of the prisoner. The wretch made a face, and the priest spoke again, making him cower.

Finally the prisoner nodded miserably. He closed his eyes and raised his arms, trembling visibly with the effort.

For a long moment nothing happened. The pontifex started to snap a question, took a breath, and hesitated.

It was still a sunny spring day, and he was still sweating under his robes. But a breeze had sprung up, blowing steadily out of the north, and with it came the familiar scent of snow.

The prisoner's hands shook with more than the spasms of his muscles. He shuddered like a sapling in a gale, eyes rolling back in his head. White mist started to rise off him, ascending into the sky like smoke. A few tendrils at first, then more, a column of roiling fog that engulfed him entirely and stretched upward as far as the pontifex could see. The few wisps of cloud above them shifted, twisting and shredding under the influence of a supernatural force.

Then, all at once, the mist exploded outward, a wall of white that blew past the pontifex and off down the mountain in a burst of ice-cold air. It was gone in an instant, leaving cold, calm air in its wake. The prisoner slumped forward, into the arms of one of the attending priests.

"It's done?" the pontifex said, looking upward.

"Yes, Your Excellency." The priest looked at the unconscious demon-host. "Though the effects may take some time—"

"Good. Take him inside."

"Yes, Your Excellency."

The two of them gathered their charge and carried him back through the gate. The pontifex stayed behind a moment, staring into the sky. Beneath his mask, his lips curved into a smile.

Far away, on the northern horizon, a mass of black clouds began to spread across the blue like a stain.

CHAPTER TEN

RAESINIA

Two days after the Grand Army's triumphant reunion at Polkhaiz, it started to rain in earnest.

Raesinia hadn't been present for the victory, but she'd been close enough to hear the thunder of the guns. After Give-Em-Hell and the cavalry broke through, news of the triumph spread through the camp like wildfire, far in advance of any official reports. Celebrations began even as the defeated Murnskai were being chased from the field.

The next day they moved the camp to the outskirts of Polkhaiz itself, the latest in a series of miserable little Murnskai towns made briefly important by its proximity to a decent bridge. As usual, much of the population had fled, and the vacant houses were taken over by the senior officers. Raesinia refused to claim one of her own, instead having the servants pitch her tent at the edge of the camp. This was partly because she found the idea of appropriating the home of some poor Murnskai townsman a bit ghoulish, but mostly to make it as easy as possible for Whaler or another of Dorsay's agents to contact her.

As the Duke of Brookspring had predicted, Janus had brushed aside the last major obstacle between him and Elysium, and in only a few days. If there was going to be a chance for peace, to avert the religious war Dorsay was so afraid of, it would come soon. Without confronting Janus, she couldn't openly appeal to the emperor for peace, so she was forced to rely on covert means. Sothe had dispatched messengers, but with Prince Vasil missing and possibly dead, the entire Murnskai leadership was in disarray. It would be some time before her offer could be heard, much less answered.

Time, time, time. It wasn't on her side, she was certain. There was no longer any doubt that the Grand Army could reach Elysium before the end of the campaigning season. Instead, she was now in an invisible race, trying to create the right circumstances to broker a peace before Janus shattered the possibility by desecrating the most holy site in the Sworn Church.

And, incidentally, destroying the Priests of the Black who want to throw me in a dungeon until I rot. She'd done her best to come to terms with that. Raesinia told herself that she had only a few more years, in any event, before her agelessness became too difficult to explain. At that point she'd have no choice but to "die" and go . . . somewhere. *Before that happens, I need to be sure we're on the right path.*

Given that, Raesinia ought to have welcomed the rain. It started to fall as the Grand Army, minus the Fifth, Seventh, and Ninth Divisions, which were staying behind to guard Polkhaiz and the supply line, began its march northeast from the Syzria. They'd been through scattered showers over the past few weeks, but this was different—not a brief, sun-warmed drizzle but a full-on downpour, bitterly cold in spite of the season. The Pilgrim's Road, barely more than a rutted track at the best of times, instantly turned into a muddy quagmire, and the infantry was forced to march along the verges where the ground was firmer. The guns and vehicles weren't so lucky, and the teams had to be doubled and then tripled to haul the protesting wagons through the muck.

It made for slow going, six miles the first day and even fewer the next, which meant time for Raesinia's side of the race. By then, though, she was as sick of the rain as everyone else, spending all day drenched to the skin and spattered with thick, yellow mud. On top of everything else, food was short, since many of the supply wagons had lagged far behind the infantry columns.

"It's a mess," said Marcus, when he joined her for dinner for the first time since he'd left the column to lead the attack on Bskor. "The cavalry is out there trying to round up all the stragglers."

"It's only going to get worse as long as it keeps raining," Raesinia said. She pushed the limp green on her plate around with a fork, keeping a careful eye on Marcus. "And the supply convoys coming north from Vantzolk and Tsivny can't be having an easier time."

"It won't last," Marcus assured her. "All the locals we've talked to say that this is very unusual for this time of year."

Raesinia let it go. Ever since Joanna had inadvertently given her an idea about how to detach the army from Janus, her time with Marcus had been a good deal more difficult.

The army will obey its commanders. That simple insight might have been obvious from the start to a military mind, but Raesinia, used to the looser world of her revolutionaries, hadn't quite grasped it until she'd asked Joanna and Barely what they'd do in the event of conflicting orders. For all that the individual soldiers were theoretically loyal to Janus, most of them had never met him and had no real way of knowing what he wanted. It was the *commanders* she needed. If worse truly came to worst, and she had to confront the First Consul directly, then she wanted the generals on her side.

It had to be all of them, though, or at least such a preponderance that any argument wouldn't spill over into actual fighting. Raesinia couldn't bear the thought of Vordanai turning on one another, not after so much blood had already been spilled in the revolution. With that in mind, she'd asked Sothe to investigate the leaders of the Grand Army with an eye toward how they could be pried away from Janus.

There were five divisions remaining with the army, plus the cavalry and artillery reserves. Of those eight commanders, a few could already be relied upon, Sothe reported. Division-General Valiant Solwen of the Third was a staunch royalist, as was Give-Em-Hell. The commander of the Eighth Division, Christopher de Manzet, had been a captain appointed by Raesinia's father, one of the few remaining "royals" of high rank.

Others would be more difficult. The Fourth Division was under the command of Morwen Kaanos, a Colonial and inveterate hater of the nobility. According to Sothe, he was a great believer in the new government, so he might be inclined to support whoever had legitimate authority from the Deputies-General. Ephraim Tadula of the artillery was a lapsed priest and former subordinate of Janus' old artillery commander Vahkerson, which she suspected would make him hard to influence, although the artillery was a small section compared to the other divisions.

That left Fitz Warus of the First Division and Winter Ihernglass of the Second, and Marcus. Marcus was the crux of the matter. He commanded almost as much loyalty as Janus himself and was more involved in the day-to-day running of the army. His word would also be influential with many of the other commanders, especially those who'd been part of the Colonials, and she couldn't think of anyone else who might be able to sway Fitz and Winter.

Marcus was also completely, irritatingly unwilling to entertain the idea that Janus might be less than perfect. Raesinia had tried a number of subtle hints to this effect, and every time she was met by bland reassurances that might have come from the First Consul himself. By the end of the evening, she usually found herself wanting to slap some subtlety into him.

If she came out and said it, asked him to choose a side, then she'd have crossed the line for good and all. *Because he'll feel obligated to tell Janus what happened, and that's as good as throwing a gauntlet at his feet.* That was Raesinia's last resort, and so she continued to dance around the issue as the army slogged north, day after day, under the apparently endless rain.

"It's good of you to meet me, Your Majesty," Whaler said. He wore a long hooded cloak, slick and sodden with rain, though the last hour the chilly downpour had slacked to a light drizzle.

"I've been half-mad waiting for news," Raesinia said. "Have you heard from the Murnskai?"

They were at the edge of the camp, far enough inside the sentry line that none of the guards were likely to overhear, with Sothe and a few of her people keeping watch on the other side to make sure they weren't disturbed.

The Borelgai spy sighed. "The rain has made everything difficult. Even for couriers on good horses, the roads are an impediment."

Raesinia ground her teeth in frustration. *"Nothing?"*

"No good news, at any rate. It appears that Prince Vasil is dead, either killed in the fighting or lost sometime during the rout. What information we have from the Murnskai army says that the emperor has dispatched Prince Dzurk to take command of what's left."

"Already?" Raesinia said. "He's awfully careless about his sons."

"He does have quite a few to choose from," Whaler said. "But this particular substitution bodes poorly for us. Vasil was well-known as a religious man, and would have put a premium on saving Elysium at any price. Dzurk is more likely to drive a hard bargain."

"Have your commander tell him about the horrors of uncivilized warfare," Raesinia said. "He's extremely passionate on the subject."

"Unfortunately, I doubt it would have the intended effect. Warfare in Murnsk has never been all that civilized." Whaler cocked his head. "Any progress on your side?"

"Not much," Raesinia admitted. "Column-General d'Ivoire is the key, but he's too close to Janus."

"Can he be bought?"

"Marcus?" Raesinia laughed bitterly. "Not likely."

"A queen has a great deal to bargain with besides coin," Whaler said. "Make him a count. Hell, make him a duke. Promise him a council seat."

She shook her head. "It's not power he wants."

"What is it, then? Everyone wants *something*."

Most men and women are, at the very center, not terribly complex, Sothe had said. *They want power, or comfort, or sex; it's only the way they go about attaining these desires that distinguishes them. Find out a person's deepest desire, and you have a lever to control them.*

"I don't know," Raesinia said slowly. "But I think I can find out."

She broached the question after a not-very-good dinner of tough meat, crusty bread, and soup. Raesinia stared at her plate glumly and tried to work up the energy to tackle the last bit of gristly beef.

"The cook sends his apologies," she said. "The man was practically in tears, truth be told. When there's not enough food to go around, even the queen's kitchen feels the pinch."

"Tell him he did wonders," Marcus said, sopping up the last of his soup with a tough heel of bread. "I've seen what everyone else is eating."

"How long can we go on like this?" she said. "If the rain keeps up, I mean. I've heard the convoys are having trouble moving enough supplies as far as Polkhaiz, let alone to the army."

"We can't forage here," Marcus said. As before, settlements had grown sparse as they'd gotten farther away from the river. "But even at this pace, it'll be only another few days until we reach the valley of the Kovria. We can get food from the local towns." He lowered his voice. "Janus is planning to send an expedition downriver, too. They'll gather all they can and ship it back to us by boat, which should be a lot easier than these so-called roads."

As usual, his faith in Janus is unlimited. Raesinia stifled a sigh. She spent a moment staring at the tent ceiling, bowed slightly inward where water had pooled, and then changed tacks.

"Can I ask you a personal question?"

Marcus sat up a little straighter. "You may ask me anything you like, Your Majesty."

Raesinia rolled her eyes playfully. "I've told you before to stop that."

"Sorry," Marcus said, grinning. "What did you want to know?"

"Let's say we destroy Elysium and make it home safely. What then?"

Marcus pursed his lips. "Return to putting the country back together, I suppose. Although the Borelgai may not be inclined to make peace right away, with Dorsay's army still in the field. We might end up having to push them off Ecco Island—"

"That's not what I meant," Raesinia said. "I mean for you, personally. You're Column-General of the Grand Army. What do you do next?"

"That's for you and Janus to decide," Marcus said. "The Column-General of the Grand Army is still a soldier, and I still take orders."

"What about when peace finally comes?"

That, at last, seemed to get through to him. He looked across the table at her with an odd expression, silent for a moment.

"It's not something I've thought much about," Marcus said. "The last time we were at peace, I was still in Khandar."

"I could probably arrange for you to go back there," Raesinia said. She meant it teasingly, but Marcus took it in earnest.

"It's possible," he said. "But . . . I don't know. Do you know why I went there in the first place?"

"Not really. I know that your family was killed in a fire."

He nodded. "My parents died. At the time I just wanted to get away. A friend of mine had been assigned to Khandar, and it seemed like as close to the ends of the earth as I could manage."

"But the revolution convinced you to come back?"

There was a long silence.

"It was more than that," Marcus said. "There was . . . a spy in the Colonials. An agent of Duke Orlanko's who got . . . close to me. When I found her out, she told me that I didn't know the truth about what had happened to my parents and that she could tell me. After everything there was over, Janus promised that he would try to find out what she'd meant."

"What happened to the spy?"

"I killed her," Marcus said, his tone inviting no further questions. There was another silence.

"Ah." Raesinia hesitated. "If you don't want to talk about it . . ."

"It's all right," Marcus said. "This next part—you're just the first person I've really spelled it out to. It feels odd to be making my confession to the queen."

"I like to think we're friends, too," Raesinia said quietly.

"I know." He took a deep breath. "After the fall of the Concordat, we captured some of their files. Janus broke the codes on their archives and sent me a few. It was Orlanko who set the fire at my old house. His agents killed my parents."

"Oh. Marcus, I'm so sorry . . ."

"The irony was," Marcus said, "by the time I knew who I should want revenge on, I'd already gotten it. Orlanko's gone, the Concordat is destroyed. All that's left is . . ." He hesitated. "Ellie."

"Ellie?"

"My sister." Marcus set his jaw. "She's *alive*. I know it. The Concordat files prove that she survived the fire. She was sent to some institution in the south, but sometime between then and now the place burned to the ground. There're no records left, and nobody I've been able to find who went there remembers Ellie d'Ivoire. But she's alive, somewhere." He sat back and blew out a breath. "If we ever really get peace, I'm going to find her. She's the only family I have left."

Raesinia nodded, her mind whirling. *This could be it.* If the girl was alive, somewhere, she'd lay good odds that Sothe could find her. *Especially if I offer all the resources of the Crown. But what good is that?* Ellie d'Ivoire was probably in Vordan, a thousand miles away, and they certainly couldn't find her before the conclusion of the current campaign.

"Janus might be able to help." Marcus went on obliviously. "I'm sure he could come up with something clever. He always does."

"Yes," Raesinia murmured. "He's good at that."

"What about you?" Marcus said, a little too abruptly. "What would you do, if we had peace? Go back to arguing with the Deputies-General about the constitution, I suppose."

Raesinia shook her head. "I need to think about the succession."

He frowned. "That's not urgent, surely. You're still . . . young." He trailed off, brow furrowed, and Raesinia nearly laughed.

"Exactly. Sooner or later someone is going to notice I don't look any different than I did when I was eighteen. We can't blame it on illness forever."

"Unless Janus can do something about it." Marcus looked like he wanted to say more but thought better of it at the last moment.

"That's possible. But I have to plan for the alternative. Vordan needs a new ruler when I step aside. So I'll have to work on getting married and having children before I take myself out of the picture."

"Oh." Marcus looked uncomfortable. "Sorry. I hadn't thought about it."

"I've had a long time to get used to the idea," Raesinia said. "After *that*, who knows? I'll be free to wander the world, I guess. Maybe I'll see Khandar."

"If you do," Marcus said, venturing a smile, "there's this little noodle shop in Ashe-Katarion you have to visit. I'll draw you a map."

Raesinia grinned back, until a scratch on the tent flap made them both look up.

"Your Majesty?" a servant's voice said. "There's a messenger here for the column-general."

"Send him in," Raesinia said.

"Marcus!" Andy poked her head through the flap. "Raes! You have to come and see this!"

They both got to their feet, Marcus bumping the table with his sword in his haste. Raesinia half expected to find flames leaping into the sky when they scrambled out through the tent flap, but the camp was still perfectly orderly, and there was none of the panic that would have accompanied an enemy attack. Instead, everyone she could see was standing in apparent amazement, staring upward at a gray sky.

"What's going on?" Marcus barked. Andy, limping a little, gestured him closer and pointed up.

Raesinia craned her neck, not sure what she was supposed to be looking at. Marcus glanced at the sky, then around at the staring people, and frowned.

"Andy," he said. "*What* is—"

A spot of cold touched the end of Raesinia's nose.

WINTER

Winter, rain streaming from the brim of her hat, had to call off the handball game after the second hour.

The intercompany contests had restarted after the victory at Bskor, the Girls' Own and Sevran's royals introducing the rest of the division to this tradition from the Velt campaign. They didn't have as much free time as they'd had on the lazy march to Gaafen, but everyone seemed to be having so much fun that Winter didn't have the heart to stop them, in spite of the bleary eyes she often saw the following morning. When they halted at Polkhaiz, Abby organized a daylong tournament that drew spectators from the entire army.

Unsurprisingly, one of Abby's First Battalion companies took home the laurels, after a hard-fought match against a squad from de Koste's Third Regiment. Winter saw Alex on the sidelines, exchanging excited cheers with the Girls' Own soldiers.

Winter had asked her colonels to warn the soldiers that the entertainment might not be able to continue once they marched north. She'd been right, but not for the reason she anticipated. The marches were short, held up by the floundering artillery and supply wagons, but the rain was so heavy that the games devolved into hours-long wrestling matches. Both teams shoved through waist-deep mud, coated head to foot in grime, fishing for a ball that had long since sunk to the bottom of the churned-up mire.

Hanna Courvier finally insisted that Winter call things off when a young man from the Fourth Regiment was found to have been held under the mud so long he'd passed out. Though he was successfully revived, Winter couldn't deny that the cutter had a point, and she pronounced the game a tie to a chorus of groans from the onlookers.

"It's just as well," Hanna said, as the crowd of half-naked, mud-slick soldiers broke up. "All this cold and wet breeds sickness. If it keeps up, we're going to have half the division hacking their lungs out or puking up their guts, mark my words."

"The weather has to break sometime," Winter said, casting a baleful glance at the sky.

That was what everyone said, as rations got leaner and wet skin chafed and blistered. *The weather has to break sometime.* Winter slogged back to her tent, her waterlogged boots heavy as lead weights. She'd grown so used to the rain drumming on her shoulders that when she finally got under canvas, it took a moment's adjustment before she straightened up. The first thing she did was check that the tent's poles hadn't shifted; muddy ground and the weight of water had led to a number of collapses over the past few days, with results ranging from embarrassing to dangerous.

She shucked her jacket and overshirt, feeling dangerously exposed in only a tailored undershirt that, sopping wet, clung to her skin and showed what it was meant to conceal. She hurriedly changed it for a clean one—or at least a *dry* one; nothing was clean these days—and put the overshirt back on with a grimace. None of the others were any better, unfortunately. She hadn't been able to get really clean in days, making do with brief rubdowns with a damp rag. The soldiers had abandoned the usual practice of bathing in the nearest stream in favor of simply spending a few minutes standing naked in the shockingly cold downpour, but for obvious reasons this was not an option for Winter, so she was marinated in her own sweat.

There was a scratch at the tent flap, barely audible over the drumming of the rain. Winter made sure her shirt was buttoned, then said, "Come in."

Bobby poked her head inside. "The colonels are here, sir. Are you ready for them?"

"Send them in." Winter hesitated, then added, "Is Cyte here?"

"No, sir. Said she had something to check in on with the supply train." Bobby frowned. "Is there something going on with her? She's been awfully busy lately."

Winter winced. If Bobby had noticed, it was long past time for her to do whatever was needed to straighten things out. She'd been hoping—not without a touch of cowardice, she had to admit—that Cyte would come around of her own accord. *Balls of the Beast. I hope I haven't fucked this up beyond repair. I don't think I can run the division without her.*

"I'll talk to her."

"Do you want me to tell her to report to you?"

"No! I'll . . . track her down later." Winter let out a long breath. "Just send the others in."

Abby and de Koste came in together, laughing about something. Sevran looked a little gloomier, and Blackstream positively dour. After they stripped out of their boots and coats—informal in the presence of a superior, but better than getting the whole tent wet—they gathered around the low table, sitting gingerly on damp cushions.

"Okay," Winter said. "I think I speak for everyone when I say that we have had *enough fucking rain*." She glanced up at the roof of the tent, where the drumming continued unabated. "Unfortunately, Karis doesn't seem to be taking requests, even from division-generals. So how are we doing?"

"Morale seems to be holding up," Abby said. "A bit of grumbling about rations, but after slogging through the mud even the rankers understand what's gone wrong."

"That may not last, though," Sevran said. "Men get less understanding as they get hungrier."

"It has to break sometime," de Koste said, unconsciously echoing Winter's words. "And we've got reserves. It'll get boring, but we won't actually starve."

"I'm more worried about illness," Blackstream said. "This is an unhealthy way to live at the best of times, and the rain makes it worse. I've seen the flux and fevers wipe out more armies than cannonballs."

"I hardly think we need to worry about the sniffles," de Koste said.

"Colonel Blackstream's right," Winter said, over the old colonel's glower. "Hanna Courvier was telling me the same thing. Colonel, is there anything we can do while we wait for the rain to stop?"

Blackstream harrumphed. "Make sure the men know not to drink water from puddles, for one thing. Only running water or rainwater from a proper container. Dirty water's the quickest way to get yourself laid up. And everyone should sleep in bare feet, with their socks laid out to dry."

"You sound like my mother," de Koste said. Abby chuckled.

"Skin rot's no joke," Blackstream said. "I knew a ranker once who didn't take his boots off for a week in the rain. When he finally got undressed and pulled down his sock, all his flesh came with it, leaving nothing but a shiny white bone."

"That's a charming image," Winter said. "Clean socks, everyone. Now, where's Archer?"

"Still back with the guns," Abby said. "They keep getting stuck in the mud."

"No surprise there," Sevran said. "If Janus wants us to fight, he's going to have to give us a few days so the artillery can catch up."

"That's not acceptable," Winter said. "We need to be ready."

"For what?" de Koste said. "The Murnskai are destroyed."

"Murnsk is a big country," Winter said. "The emperor has more armies. And there are always the partisans."

De Koste snorted. "We won't need the guns to deal with a bunch of farmers."

"Colonel," Winter snapped, her patience disappearing. "I do not want to have to explain to the First Consul that my division can't carry out its assignments, for *any* reason. Understood?"

"Yes, sir," de Koste said, looking genuinely chagrined.

"I had a thought, sir," Sevran said. "Since the infantry are going to be waiting on the wagons anyway, what if we sent detachments back to help with the hauling? It sounds like a few hundred men could keep things moving a little more smoothly."

"*That* they're not going to like," Abby said.

"Do it," Winter said. "If we have to fight, they'll like not having guns a lot less. We'll draw up a rotation." She grinned. "Maybe make it into a contest. Something to do instead of handball."

There was more, mundane problems exacerbated by the rain and the mud. Winter kept them moving through the agenda, then sent them off with instructions to keep a careful eye on the regimental sick lists. The three men got up to leave, but Winter gestured for Abby to stay behind a moment longer.

"I'm glad that you and de Koste are friends," Winter said when they were alone. "But please don't encourage him to be an ass."

Abby colored. "Sorry. Blackstream just makes an easy target."

"I know. But he's got more experience than the rest of us put together, so let's not alienate him."

"Yes, sir. De Koste's not a bad sort, really. He's just . . . boisterous."

Winter looked at Abby speculatively. *Could there be more to this?* Abby and Jane had been lovers, which meant Abby must have what Cyte called "the Tyrant's Disease," too, but . . . *Maybe she only has a mild case.* Winter gave a mental shrug.

"Anything else?" Abby said.

"Not for the moment. Just make sure Blackstream's advice gets passed along. Most of the Girls' Own are from Vordan City, so I doubt they've spent a lot of time in the rain and mud."

"Understood, sir." Abby paused. "I meant to ask about Cyte—"

Winter suppressed a groan. "I know. I'm dealing with it."

"All right, sir. As long as you know."

When Abby had donned her sodden outerwear and disappeared, Winter sat at the table for a while, drumming her fingers on the thin wood. Finally, she called for Bobby, who stuck her head through the tent flap again.

"Can you have someone keep an eye on Cyte's tent for me?" she said. "Just to let me know when she gets back."

"Of course, sir. Do you want me to have them fetch her?"

"No. I'll drop in on her, I think." *Better not give her another chance to run away.*

Winter realized she had never been inside Cyte's tent. As a captain, Cyte rated one to herself, although it was no bigger than those the rankers shared. Winter scratched at the flap, hunched over against the pouring rain.

"Just a moment." Cyte sounded weary. "Who is it?"

"Winter," Winter said.

Silence from inside the tent. Winter gritted her teeth.

"I know you don't want to talk to me," Winter said, "but please consider that it's coming down in buckets out here."

"Sorry," Cyte said. Winter heard cloth shuffling. "Come in."

Winter had to duck her head to get inside. A single lamp hung in the center of the tent, and it took a few moments for her eyes to adjust. Cyte was sitting on her bedroll, arms crossed over her chest, dark hair wild and disheveled. Her uniform jacket lay on the ground, soaked through and coated with mud.

"I didn't want to surprise you," Winter said, pulling off her own jacket. "But it was starting to seem like my only option."

"Sorry," Cyte said again. She wouldn't meet Winter's eyes. "I've been . . . busy."

"I'm not *completely* stupid," Winter said. "You're my staff officer—you're always busy, but I usually don't go days without seeing you." She pulled off her boots and sat down across from Cyte. "We need to talk."

"I . . ." Cyte took a deep breath. "I have to apologize for . . . what happened."

"Why would you need to apologize?" Winter said. "Unless we're remembering events very differently, 'what happened' is that I asked if you wanted me to kiss you, and you said yes, so I did. Have I got that wrong?"

Cyte had gone very red. She shook her head jerkily.

"Then how is that possibly your fault?"

"I brought the whole subject up," Cyte said.

"You asked a question, and I answered it. I—"

"Look," Cyte said, her face pleading. "I would love if we could just . . . forget about it. It was a mistake. It won't happen again."

Winter forced herself to smile, hiding the extent to which the words pained her. "All right."

Cyte blinked, off-balance. "Really?"

"I like to think we're friends," Winter said. "It'd be a poor sort of friend who ignored a request like that. I just wanted to make sure you weren't going to keep hiding from me."

"Right." Cyte took a deep breath and ran her hands through her unruly hair. "Right. You're right, of course. That was . . . unprofessional of me."

"The division needs you, Captain. Especially now."

"Understood, sir." Cyte straightened. "You have my apologies."

"Good." Winter swallowed. "That's all. I'll expect you back on the job in the morning."

"Yes, sir."

Winter nodded slowly and got to her feet, head bent to avoid the tent ceiling. She got back into her still-wet boots and put on her jacket, aware of Cyte's too-intense stare on her back. Part of her was still hoping for something, just a word, but there was only silence. Winter looked over her shoulder, and Cyte turned away, hugging herself tighter.

"Good evening, Captain."

"Have a good night, sir."

And then Winter was standing outside the tent, back in the rain. Her stomach felt tight and hot, and her throat was clenched.

Well. She shook her head. *I suppose that means I need to find someone else to drink with.*

The scratch on the tent flap tore her from sleep. Winter sat up, groggy, and groped for the low-burning lamp beside her bedroll.

"What is it?" she croaked, voice dry. "Is something wrong?"

"It's me."

"Cyte?" Winter blinked rapidly. "Come in."

The tent flap opened, and Cyte took a step inside. Water poured off her, adding to the muddy puddle near the entrance.

"Has something happened?" Winter said. She adjusted the lamp for more light and hung it from the tent pole. Cyte, she could see now, was a mess, eyes red, hair hanging in wet ropes. She wasn't wearing a coat, and the rain had soaked her shirt through.

"Why did you ask me that?" Cyte said.

"What?" Winter shook her head. "I don't know—"

"Why did you ask if I wanted you to kiss me?"

Winter's heart skipped a beat. "I thought we were forgetting about that."

"Winter—"

"You really want to know?"

Cyte nodded miserably.

Winter took a deep breath. "Because I thought that's what you were trying to work your way around to," she said. "And because I thought I wouldn't mind kissing you at all."

"But . . ." Cyte shook her head, hair swinging wildly. "Why did I say yes?"

"*That* I can't answer for. Karis knows I'm not . . ." Winter hesitated. "Not ideal. In several ways."

"Don't be stupid. You're *Winter Ihernglass*. I've looked up to you ever since the revolution. But I'm not . . . I mean, I don't have . . . that disease. I don't." Cyte looked down, clenching her fists.

"I didn't know I had it either," Winter said. "Until you told me. I just knew what I felt."

"I don't," Cyte said. "Know what I feel, I mean. I'm . . ." She trailed off, the silence broken only by the roar of the rain outside.

"Do you want to sit down?" Winter said. "Just take off your boots first. It's muddy enough in here."

Cyte bent over and fumbled with her laces. Winter got up and dug out a spare blanket, setting it down beside the table.

"You're soaked," she said. "Hanna told me that it's important to stay warm."

"Right." Cyte wrapped herself in the thin cloth, and shivered. "Okay. Let's think about this logically."

"Is that likely to help?" Winter said, sitting down across from her.

"I have no idea. But it's the only way I know how to think about it." Cyte drew her knees up under the blanket. "You wanted to kiss me."

"I did."

"And I told you you could."

"You did."

"And you did it."

"How did it feel?"

"I couldn't breathe," Cyte said. "And I thought my heart was going to explode."

"Have you ever kissed anyone before?"

Cyte frowned. "Once. His name was Fetter Blalloc. It was at a Wisdom Day party."

"How did *that* feel?"

"Wet. And a little icky."

"So not very similar, then."

"No." Cyte looked up. "Only two experiments isn't much data to form a hypothesis, I guess."

Winter grinned. "Obviously not. Clearly you should go around kissing everyone you meet until you've got enough to form a real conclusion."

"Clearly," Cyte said, smiling a little.

There was an awkward silence. Winter had to stop herself from drumming her fingers on the table. *Why do I never know what to say?*

"Do you want a drink?" she offered eventually.

"No," Cyte said, her tone surprisingly steady. "I don't think I do."

She stood up, letting the blanket puddle on the floor. Winter froze as she walked around the folding table and sat down beside her.

"Cyte?" Winter said. "What are you doing?"

Cyte put her hand on Winter's shoulder, leaning forward, which startled Winter so much she leaned back and fell over. Cyte shuffled forward on hands and knees, one palm on either side of Winter's head, looking down at her. Her hair hung in a thick mass, dripping steadily just beside Winter's cheek.

"Acting logically," Cyte said.

"This is logical?" Winter's heart slammed in her chest.

"You agreed to forget about this," Cyte said. "But I came back here. Whatever I *think* that I think, I think that shows what I *actually* think is pretty clear. Right?"

"I have no idea what that means," Winter said.

"I'm not really sure it makes sense," Cyte said. "I'm going to kiss you again. Is that all right?"

"If you're sure you want to."

Cyte lowered her head, gently, and they kissed. It went on longer this time, and Winter let her eyes close. She felt Cyte coming closer, and then something wet and clammy brushed her arm, drawing an involuntary yelp.

Cyte sat up, eyes wide. "What's wrong?"

"Sorry." Winter sat up as well, breathing hard. "Your shirt. Is very cold and wet."

"Oh."

Cyte looked down at herself. Then, in one swift motion, she grabbed her shirt by the hem and pulled it and her undershirt over her head together. When she looked back at Winter, the expression on her face—hope and terror and excitement and vulnerability all at once—made Winter want to crush her in an embrace and never let go.

"Your shirt also looks . . ." Cyte hesitated, cheeks burning. "A little damp."

"You know," Winter said, hands fumbling with the buttons, "you may be right about that."

Later, Winter lay on her back on the bedroll, listening in the dark. The rain had stopped falling, and Cyte's breathing was soft and regular. Winter felt as though her bones had turned to jelly, as though you could have poured her into a cauldron like soup.

She had never slept with anyone but Jane, never *touched* anyone but Jane. The two of them had known every inch of each other. When Winter had come back from Khandar and found Jane again, falling into her bed had been like coming home, a return to something long missed but never forgotten. It made it feel *perfect*—no fumbling, no awkwardness, just as though they'd never been apart.

This was different. It reminded Winter of when she and Jane had first begun to experiment, kissing and touching, each breathlessly daring the other to go a little further, stealing time in closets and empty rooms. Except then they'd both been ignorant. This time, after a certain amount of confusion, Winter understood what she was doing, and Cyte had proven to be an attentive student.

"Winter?" Cyte said very quietly. "Are you asleep?"

"Not yet," Winter said.

"I need to ask you something."

"Somehow," Winter said, "I feel like I've been here before."

"Sorry. It's . . . I don't know. Something I've been thinking about."

"Go ahead."

"Are you sure you're all right with this?"

"Cyte—"

"Not with me. With . . . this. It hasn't been that long since Jane . . . left. And I thought—"

"What? That I was forcing myself through it to make you feel better?" Winter ran her fingers through Cyte's hair. "You may be giving yourself too much credit."

"I just know you were unhappy," Cyte said. "That's why I started coming here in the first place, remember? And now . . . I'm not sure."

"I'm all right," Winter said, a little more forcefully than she meant to. "Jane is . . ." Her throat went tight for a moment. "She's *gone*. I fell in love with her when she was a scared girl in the Prison. After I came home, she'd grown into something else. For a while I managed to fool myself that she would change back. But she won't. And I'm . . . not the same, either."

Cyte shuffled a little closer, pressing her head against Winter's side.

"I still miss the girl," Winter said. "I suppose I always will. But that's the past."

"I think I understand that," Cyte said. Then, very quietly, "Fuck."

"What's wrong?"

"It's nice and warm and I'm very comfortable." She sighed. "But I really need to piss."

Winter laughed. "At least the rain has stopped."

Cyte muttered something impolite as she rolled over and began hunting around for her shirt and trousers. Winter lay still, feeling a rush of cold air across her bare skin as the tent flap opened and closed. A moment later it opened again, and Winter sat up and shivered.

"Cyte?" It was hard to see anything with the lamp out. "Is that you?"

"You'd better see this," Cyte said.

"What's going on?"

"It's snowing."

MARCUS

"Snow," Janus said.

"Apparently, sir," Marcus said.

"In May."

"It *is* Murnsk, sir."

"Even Murnsk has a summer," Janus said, looking up at the sky. His face tightened, as though he could subdue the weather by sheer force of will, but the fat flakes continued to drift down regardless. "In the northern wastes, perhaps, or high in the mountains, but here? No."

"But . . ." Marcus gestured helplessly.

"I'm not denying the reality of it," Janus said, flashing a smile. "Only the cause. This is not natural." He held out a hand, and a snowflake landed on his palm, lasting only a moment before it melted. "The Pontifex of the Black must be desperate."

"You think this is *their* doing?" Marcus lowered his voice. "The Penitents?"

"Can you doubt it? First days of rain, and now snow in spring."

"But . . . can they really do that?" Marcus shook his head. The Penitent Damned and their demons made him uncomfortable, as though the world he lived in were built on rotten foundations and might collapse at any moment. He'd fought them several times, but he wasn't sure he'd ever truly get used to the idea. "Control the *weather*?"

"You've seen the dead walk, Marcus," Janus said. "At this point I would think you'd be beyond doubts about their power."

Marcus shifted. "We're not likely to run into that again, are we?"

"No," Janus said. "That demon was one of the Thousand Names we captured in Khandar. But the powers of many demons overlap, so I would not be surprised to find a Penitent wielding similar abilities. From now on we should be prepared for anything."

"What should we do about the snow?"

"What can we do but press on?" Janus said. "We'll reach the Kovria in two more days. Our foraging parties will be able to send supplies by boat, so we should be able to stop and build up our reserves. Then we'll take the last step." His eyes were on the horizon, gray and distant, as though he were already looking on Elysium's walls. "Nearly there, Marcus. I'm nearly there."

"Yes, sir," Marcus said.

Janus blinked and looked back at him, his usual smile there and gone again. "Speak to the locals. Ask if anything like this has ever happened before, and how long it lasted. If there *is* a Penitent directing the weather, there must be a limit to his strength."

"Yes, sir." Marcus saluted and hurried away.

Truthfully, he was glad to go. Janus had always been a creature of odd habits, but since the destruction of the Murnskai army he'd been acting strange even by his own standards. More and more of the basic work of moving the army—the assignment of routes and objectives, camp placement, and thousands of other details—seemed to no longer be of any interest to Janus and therefore fell onto Marcus' shoulders. Without the help of Giforte and his staff, he would have been completely lost.

As it was the situation was serious—the supply convoys, mired in mud, couldn't replenish food as fast as the army ate it up, and with every bit of transport capacity devoted to rations, stocks of everything else were rapidly dwindling. Horses were dying, abandoned by the side of the road or irretrievably stuck in the mud, and the cutters' ominous warnings of flux and skin rot were quickly being proven accurate. Thus far the change to snow had been a blessing compared to the endless downpour, but Marcus was worried. Even at the height of the day, the sun was only a weak presence through the flat, gray clouds, and at night the sentries had to break a crust of ice on the water barrels.

Andy, limping only slightly now, fell in alongside Marcus as he walked back toward the camp. The halt for the day had only just been called, and the marked-out grid was still mostly empty, regiments filing in off the road to set up their tents and start cooking their meager dinner.

"Did he tell you anything, sir?" Andy said.

Marcus shook his head. "He wants me to question the locals, find out if anyone remembers anything like this."

"That could be tricky," Andy said. "The scouts have been saying that every village they find is empty."

"Go find Give-Em-Hell," Marcus said. "Tell him we need to find some Murnskai to talk to, and ideally someone who can translate as well. I doubt they speak much Vordanai this far north."

"On my way, sir."

An hour later Marcus, Andy, and Give-Em-Hell were riding east, with a dozen troopers as escort. The cavalry commander had explained that the villages along their line of march were deserted, but people not in the direct path had often chosen to stay in their homes. He'd also produced a Lieutenant Govrosk, a severe-looking young man originally of Murnskai extraction who had enough of the language to make himself useful.

"You've never heard of snow in May?" Marcus asked the lieutenant.

"Wouldn't know, sir," Govrosk said. "I was born and raised in Vordan, sir. It was only my gran who spoke the old language at home, sir, and she made me learn some of it."

"Ah."

They were near enough to the Kovria that the country had turned civilized again. The woods that covered the hillsides showed signs of logging, and long, snaking trails connected the isolated farmsteads. The snow was still coming down, deadening the sound of their horses' hooves. It melted on the ground, adding to the mud, but coated the trees and bushes in a light frosting of white.

"Should be a village another mile up this way," Give-Em-Hell shouted, riding as usual at the very head of the column. "If this damn map is worth anything, anyway."

Andy, riding beside him, leaned closer and lowered her voice. "Something feels wrong, sir."

"Apart from the snow in May?"

"Yes, sir. Apart from that. I thought . . ." She peered into the swirls of snow. "I don't know. I may be imagining things."

The soft, near-perfect silence felt sinister. Marcus looked around and realized just how little he could actually see.

"You have good eyes," Marcus said. "Keep them open, and shout if you spot anything." He was suddenly eager to be done with this whole expedition. *If the village isn't where it's supposed to be, I'm taking us back to the camp.*

After a little less than a mile, though, a cluster of crude log buildings loomed out of the snow. There were perhaps a dozen homes, gathered around the inevitable Sworn Church. Judging by the tethered animals and smoke rising from chimneys, the place hadn't yet been abandoned. The small party of Vordanai rode onto the central green, where a carpet of grass was now almost completely covered in white.

"Come out!" Give-Em-Hell shouted. "We won't hurt anyone!" He elbowed Lieutenant Govrosk. "Tell 'em we're not here to hurt anyone, but we want to talk."

The lieutenant nodded, closed his eyes for a moment to work it out, then shouted something in awkward-sounding Murnskai. Marcus thought he saw a flash of motion behind the shutters of one of the houses, but there was no other response.

"Tell 'em I don't want to start kicking in doors," Give-Em-Hell said. "But I will if I have to." He rubbed his hands together. "It's cold out here, damn it."

Govrosk translated. Again, for a moment, there was no response. Then the door of the house beside the church opened, spilling lamplight onto the green. An old woman, heavily bundled in blankets, stood in the doorway. Someone inside shouted something at her, and she answered in rapid-fire Murnskai.

"What's she saying?" Marcus said.

The lieutenant coughed awkwardly. "The, uh, person in the house is telling her to come back, because everyone knows the Vordanai rape every woman they can catch. The old lady said . . . ah . . ." His face reddened a little. "Roughly, that if we want her privates, we're welcome to them, because that's more than anyone else has for decades."

By the time this translation was finished, the old woman was marching across the green. Marcus saw a young man in the doorway, looking after her nervously, with a wide-eyed child huddling behind his knees. Getting off his horse, Marcus motioned for Andy and the translator to do likewise, and stepped past the ring of watching troopers to meet the old woman.

"Kdja svet Murnskedj?" she barked, followed by a quick string of words Marcus couldn't separate.

"She wants to know if we speak Murnskai," Govrosk said. "Because she can't be bothered to learn any of our heathen tongues."

"Tell her I'm Column-General Marcus d'Ivoire, of the Grand Army," Marcus said. "We're not going to hurt anyone from the village. We just wanted to ask her a few questions."

Govrosk rendered this and waited for the response. A smile flitted across his face.

"She says that she herself is the Crown Prince of Murnsk, and that she's most honored to receive you, General. By rights she ought to spit on you, but she's willing to answer our questions if we agree to leave before one of the young men tries something stupid."

Marcus chuckled and tried a smile on the old woman. She scowled at him.

"The snow," Marcus said. "Ask her if it usually snows this late in spring."

"You must be a southerner," came the translated response. "All southerners think it's ice and snow up here year-round. What do they think we eat, one another?"

"Has it ever snowed like this that she can remember?" Marcus asked.

"Not here," the old woman said through Govrosk. "But when I was a girl, I lived in the east, beyond Mohkba. My mother told me stories about the year winter never ended, when it snowed in June and rained all the way through August. The fields were frozen too solid to plant, and the livestock died in the pastures. Half the village starved."

"Do you know why?" Marcus said. "What happened that year?"

The old woman paused for a moment, then barked something at Govrosk. "She says you wouldn't believe her."

"Try me."

The old woman's gaze went distant, staring back across the years. Slowly, she began to speak, and Govrosk frowned.

"She says . . . the count, the local lord, had a beautiful daughter. One day strangers in black masks arrived and ordered him to give her up. The count was clearly frightened, but he refused, and locked the girl away in his tower. The strangers promised that his people would be destroyed if he didn't cooperate, but he persisted. That year summer never came. Her mother said it was the Old Witch of the Ice Woods, that the black masks had brought her to destroy them all. Enough of the villagers believed her that they laid siege to the count's manor. He threw himself from the highest window, and the servants handed over his daughter."

"And then summer came?" Marcus said.

The old woman shook her head. "No," Govrosk translated. "The snow lasted through summer and fall. Only the next year did it become warm, but there was hardly anyone left in the village to see it. Even the crows had frozen to death."

All year. It was hard to comprehend power on that scale. The Penitent Damned he'd fought in Vordan had been able to control flames, burning men alive with a glance and stopping musket balls in midair. But to bring snow at midsummer . . . *If it* does *last until winter, we're not the only ones who're going to starve.*

The old woman added something more. Govrosk said, "She says it's our fault this time. The Old Witch is cruel, but she is the heart of Murnsk. She will not tolerate an army of foreigners."

"Tell her she's been very helpful," Marcus said. "And ask if there's anything we can do for her in return."

"She says that if we want to be helpful," Govrosk translated, "we can go straight to—" There was a strange whispering noise. The lieutenant frowned, looked down. "To . . ."

Marcus followed his gaze. Something was jutting out of Govrosk's chest, a wooden stick about a foot long, tipped with feathers. Govrosk put his fingers on it, disbelieving, and sat down heavily in the snow.

Something *hissed* through the air, just in front of Marcus' face.

"Attack!" Andy screamed. "We're under attack!"

White figures appeared from between the houses, materializing like ghosts from the windblown snow. Marcus saw fur, and galloping hooves, and long, curved bows that gleamed like ivory. Another arrow *hissed* into one of the troopers, catching him in the neck. The man reeled in the saddle, blood spurting in long, shockingly crimson arcs, then slid to the ground as his horse reared.

Three of the troopers fired at once, the sound of their carbines shattering the awful silence. The ghostly warriors spurred away, turned, and came on again, snow rippling around them like a cloak. Two of them emerged from around the old woman's house, coming directly toward Marcus, who only then thought to claw his sword from its scabbard.

Andy stepped in front of him, pistol in hand, leveling it at the closer rider. The shot blasted Marcus to his senses. The rider tumbled, sprawling on the ground, and Marcus could see he was only a man after all, a small, pale-skinned figure wrapped around and around with furs. His horse, a shaggy, white-haired animal closer to a pony in size, reared and came to a halt, spoiling the aim of the second rider. His arrow flew wide, but he came on, directly at Andy. Marcus grabbed her with his free hand and pulled her aside, reaching out at the same time with a wild slash of his sword. He missed the rider, but drew a long cut down the flank of his mount, and the horse's shrill, almost-human scream nearly drowned the sound of more shots.

"We have to get out of here!" Andy said. "There's too many!"

Marcus nodded. Give-Em-Hell had gathered the remaining troopers in a tight bunch, sabers waving, but the riders evaded their attempts to close. As Marcus watched, one trooper broke from the pack to try to ride down one of the white-furred men, only to find his quarry twisting aside at the last moment. As the trooper reined in, another rider came in behind him and put an arrow in his back from only a few feet away. The point burst from his stomach like a horrible growth, and he pitched forward over his horse's neck. Lieutenant Govrosk lay still, and the old woman was collapsed on top of him, the fletching of two arrows sticking up from her back.

Marcus' own horse was nowhere to be seen, but the rearing mount of one of the dead troopers was nearby. He ran to its side and grabbed the reins, struggling to calm the animal. Fortunately, battle-trained cavalry mounts were not prone to panic, and once he got in the saddle, the horse's conditioning reasserted itself. He guided it over to Andy, grabbed her hand, and swung her up behind him.

"Henry!" Marcus shouted. "We're leaving!"

"Retreat?" Give-Em-Hell said incredulously. He had his saber in one hand and a pistol in the other. "Why?"

"That's an order, damn it!" Marcus said. "Follow me, *now!*"

Without waiting for a reply, he turned his mount in a half circle, aiming for a gap in the houses around the green, and applied his spurs. Andy threw her arms around him as they gathered speed, arrows hissing through the air all around. A man in white rose in front of him, swinging an ax, and Marcus ducked the blow and gave the rider a wild slash with his saber. Then they were past the edge of the village, back on the snowy track they'd followed in. The sun was still above the horizon, but the gray clouds made it seem like twilight, and wind-borne snow closed in all around. It had gotten heavier—Marcus couldn't see more than a few dozen feet.

There were more shots, and something flared in the darkness. Flames grew behind Marcus as he rode, rising higher and higher, dancing like strange aurora through the drifting snow.

Give-Em-Hell caught up with them when Marcus reined his mount in a mile or so down the road. The cavalry general was breathing hard, one hand still clutching his saber. His other sleeve was damp with blood. Only two of the troopers were still with him.

"We left some of the men still fighting those bastards," he roared. "We should turn around and give 'em hell! Who knows what the damn savages will do to them?"

"We have to get back to the camp," Marcus said. "There may be more of them. Janus has to be warned."

As it turned out, the warning was unnecessary. Everyone in the camp was already well aware of the white riders.

They'd come from every direction at once, appearing from the snow to slaughter terrified pickets in a blur of fur and arrows. Then they'd turned away, hovering just out of musket range, as though deliberately taunting their opponents. Fortunately for the Vordanai, most of their division commanders—Winter, Fitz, Val, and Mor—had been in Khandar, where the Desoltai had nearly wiped out an entire battalion of Colonials when Adrecht Roston had fallen for a similar trap. The regiments formed up, but held their position at the edges of the camp, with only the cavalry giving chase.

Unlike in the Colonials in the Great Desol, the Grand Army included a sizable force of both light cavalry and cuirassiers. The size and armor of the latter gave them an advantage in close combat against the white riders, but the great southern warhorses fared poorly in the snow, and the raiders could fire with astonishing accuracy from the backs of their horses. The snow and the awkward, broken ground split the combat up into a hundred tiny skirmishes in the freezing darkness, bands of horsemen riding in every direction, not sure whether the next group they encountered would be friendly or enemy.

By the time Marcus and his diminished force returned to camp, Janus had taken things in hand, and the situation had improved. The smaller divisional guns, supplemented by detachments from the artillery reserve, were distributed around the camp at intervals, their fire chasing the white riders out of bow range. Give-Em-Hell immediately called in his cavalry from their confusing, fragmented battle, a process that took most of the night. Marcus rode from point to point, reassuring nervous commanders and drawing cheers from the soldiers.

The snow slackened with the rising sun, and the white riders withdrew.

Around the camp, the corpses of men and animals were strewn like scattered toys, blue-coated Vordanai cavalry mixed with the fur-clad bodies of their enemies. A thick layer of snow covered everything, filtering down through the trees and burying the just-sprouted fields in a smothering white blanket. The sun seemed like a cold, shrunken thing, promising little relief.

"I thought it might help when the mud froze solid," Fitz said.

Marcus snorted. "Ever the optimist."

They stood with a small crowd of soldiers, backed up behind a knot in the column. A caisson had split one of its great round wheels and tipped over, trapping one of its horses. Sweating men, breath steaming, struggled to right it.

"I've got to go and see Janus," Marcus said. "Can you get this sorted out?"

"Of course, sir," Fitz said. "Go on ahead."

At least he had the sense not to ask what Janus was going to do next, which was a question Marcus was getting tired of answering. Or, more accurately, not answering, since Janus had as usual divulged nothing of his intentions.

Marcus led his horse carefully up onto the verge, then remounted on the other side of the obstacle and continued ahead at a careful walk. The frozen ground was treacherous, especially for animals. The mud had solidified in whatever rutted, pitted shape it had been in the day before, and hardened until it was as tough as rock. Now, with the ruts and divots buried under the snow, it was far too easy for a horse to put a foot wrong, or for a wagon or gun to break its wheels in an unexpected hole.

The infantry had its own problems. Their coats weren't really adequate for the cold—even Marcus found it hard to blame the quartermasters for that, given the season. Overnight, the uniform appearance of the soldiers had vanished, as they stuffed their jackets with tent fabric, pieces of bedroll and blanket, and whatever else would keep them warm. The lucky ones had scavenged furs from fallen white riders. For once, looting the dead had been officially encouraged. Digging graves in the frozen ground was impossible, so last night's corpses had been burned, a mixed bonfire of split logs and pasty, naked bodies whose smoke had cast a pall over the column for hours.

Janus had sent for Marcus around midday. He picked his way along the column, which was stopped in a half dozen places and had gaps in as many others, and got directions from a cavalry picket to a hill just to the left of their line of march. Marcus left his horse with a soldier at the base and climbed the slope on foot, probing the snow with the tip of his boot.

On the way, he passed a thickset man he recognized as Christopher de Manzet, commander of the Eighth Division. The general's eyes were wide, and he descended the hill with dangerous haste, pausing only to offer Marcus a cursory salute. Several aides were waiting for him at the bottom, but de Manzet set off back toward the column without a word, his staff trailing behind him like anxious kites.

Janus was alone on the summit, wearing a heavy wool greatcoat, a spyglass in one hand. He looked over his shoulder at Marcus and beckoned.

"You wanted to see me, sir?"

"Yes." His tone put Marcus instantly on edge. There was something *off* there, hidden under his usual calm like a razor blade in a loaf of bread. "I'm very glad to see you made it back safely last night."

"It was a near thing, sir," Marcus said. "The raiders killed our translator and half our escort, and they burned the village we were visiting."

"They seem to have been doing quite a bit of that." Janus pointed. "See the smoke? There and there."

"Why would they do that?" Marcus said. "Burn their own village."

"Murnsk is a vast country, as I've commented before," Janus said. "In particular, its northern boundaries are . . . disputed. Beyond the river Bataria is the great snowy waste, where winter never ends. The emperor claims dominion over the tribes who live there, but they acknowledge his authority only reluctantly."

"Those were the white riders who attacked us last night?"

Janus nodded. "Trans-Batariai, for certain."

"If they don't work for the emperor, what are they doing here?"

Janus dug in his pocket and held up a crude ornament on a torn leather thong. Two carved pieces of horn or bone, rough circles, one inside the other.

"They may not recognize the authority of the emperor, but the authority of Elysium is another matter. Especially the Pontifex of the Black. The Trans-Batariai have raided and warred with the more settled Murnskai for centuries, but they hate us heretics even more."

Marcus hesitated for a moment, looking around to see if any of the guards were within earshot. Satisfied he wouldn't be overheard, he said, "We spoke with a woman in the village last night who told an interesting story. A legend, really." Marcus repeated the tale of the Old Witch and the black-masked strangers. "I would have dismissed it as local superstition," he concluded, "if not for the things I've seen fighting the Priests of the Black."

"Just as the Church intends," Janus said. "The Old Witch. I've heard the stories, of course, but they were all hundreds of years old. I didn't think the Black Priests had captured her."

"If the story's to be believed, the snow could last all year," Marcus said.

"Perhaps," Janus said. "That may be an exaggeration."

"What if it's not?" Marcus took a deep breath. "Sir, even without the white riders, keeping us fed in this weather would be difficult. We can't protect two hundred miles of supply line. Even if they never attack us directly—"

"What are you suggesting, Marcus?" The odd tone was back, a slight burr in the velvet voice.

"I . . ." Marcus hadn't really thought it through until now. "I'm not sure we can continue the advance. Not without losing half the army to starvation and frostbite. If we fall back to Polkhaiz, perhaps . . ."

He stopped as Janus' eyes narrowed.

"We can't go back," the First Consul said very quietly. "The first step back and we've lost. It's precisely what they want."

"But—"

"We're so *close*." Janus pointed north, where the gray shape of a river was just visible. "That's the Kovria! Elysium is barely a hundred miles beyond!"

A hundred miles or a thousand, it doesn't make any difference, Marcus wanted to say. *We can't get there.* But Janus' furious gaze seemed to freeze the words in his throat.

"You see what they're capable of," Janus hissed. "You think the Pontifex of the Black spared a thought for the people his raiders would plunder on their way to fight us? You think he cares about all the peasants who'll starve when this year's crops freeze in the fields? Do you think he will show us any mercy?"

"Sir," Marcus managed. "I—"

"The hell with it," Janus snarled. Marcus had only heard anger in his voice like that once before, in the empty tunnels under Ashe-Katarion. A cold, killing rage, sharp as shattered glass. "I don't give a *damn* what you think. This army will reach Elysium, Marcus, if we have to crawl on our hands and knees. We will reach it if we have to eat the dead for food and wear their skins to keep us warm. I have not worked for so long and crossed half the world to be stopped by a little bit of fucking *weather*."

He flipped the spyglass to Marcus, end over end, and stalked away. Marcus almost fumbled the catch, the brass instrument cold against his hand.

What did he say to poor de Manzet? he thought. No wonder the man had looked shaken.

Marcus put the spyglass to his eye. A column of smoke jumped closer, and he could see the skeletons of broken buildings toppled amid dirty snow. Beyond was the river. In the center of the channel, the water still flowed freely, but fingers of ice stretched out from the bank, like they were trying to close around someone's throat.

CHAPTER ELEVEN

WINTER

We're a thousand miles from home, surrounded by enemies, buried in snow on the banks of a river that's frozen in May, Winter thought. It seems unfair for me to be happy.

It was midafternoon, though there was no way to know it from the cold gray light that filtered through the canvas and the unbroken layer of clouds above it. Winter lay naked in her bedroll, all the blankets she owned heaped atop her. Cyte was curled up at her side, the swell of her breasts pressed against Winter's flank, her dark hair against Winter's chin. She was still asleep, breath a gentle tickle at Winter's throat.

Half the division was sleeping by day now. The white riders mostly attacked at night, sudden charges out of the darkness and volleys of arrows into the tents or the horse lines. Winter had doubled the pickets and then doubled them again, a thick line of skirmishers waiting in the cold and the darkness to confront the raiders. It was working, the white riders paying in blood for every strike, but the Second Division was being run ragged. There was no question of games anymore, much less drill. Every moment not spent on guard was devoted to eating, sleeping, or helping with the never-ending task of hauling supplies through the drifting snow.

Officially, they were camped here on the north bank of the Kovria to build up enough reserves of food and ammunition to make the final push north, over the last hundred miles of the Pilgrim's Road to Elysium. The track behind them was crowded with supply convoys, slogging from the well-stocked depots at Polkhaiz and Tsivny. But horses and oxen could only pull the wagons so fast through the snow, especially when the animals themselves were suffering badly from the cold. Every day, regiments trooped south to contribute their muscle to the effort, returning shaky and exhausted at nightfall. And yet every day they brought in barely enough food to keep the army going on reduced rations, let alone to build up a reserve.

The foraging expeditions up the river, which were supposed to have brought in more supplies by boat, had been canceled. The white riders would have made such a trip too dangerous, and in any case the point was moot. The Kovria had frozen over the night after they'd arrived, and the crust of ice was now quite thick, solid enough that the soldiers simply slogged across the surface instead of using the little wooden bridge at the town of Isket, just south of the camp.

It felt like they were a ball thrown high in the air and reaching its apogee, with no energy to go farther but not yet able to fall back. Held there, unnaturally aloft, by the sheer force of Janus' will. Rumors had started to spread, and no one dared to even breathe the word *retreat* in the presence of the First Consul. But it was everywhere else, on the lips of the rankers standing watch in the snow and among the gloomy groups of officers drinking up hoarded wine in their tents.

Winter felt isolated from it all, at the very center of things but somehow apart. Her tent, her bed, was a circle of warmth into which the cold couldn't penetrate. She ought to be worried, ought to be thinking about what Janus would do next or the ultimate fate of the grand campaign. Instead, her mind drifted; the way Cyte smiled, just a bit, when she thought no one was watching, the way her hair fell across the delicate curve of her neck, the soft sounds she made when Winter touched her.

Somehow, the difficulty of the army's situation had made things easier between the two of them. There was no question of propriety, of secrecy, just the desperate need for comfort. *And we're hardly the only ones, after all.* There was a certain practicality to it. *Not many better ways to keep warm.*

There was a scratch at the tent flap.

Fuck, Winter thought. *Fuck, fuck, fuck.* In here was warmth, and quiet, and peace. Out there was duty and responsibility, and she did not want to get up. Knew, in the end, that she would.

"What is it?" she said, feeling Cyte stir.

"White riders, sir!" It was a young woman's voice Winter didn't recognize. "They're attacking the Girls' Own pickets."

"In the middle of the day?" Winter frowned. That wasn't according to the usual pattern. "Where's Colonel Giforte?"

"On her way there, sir. She sent me to get you, said we're holding them off for now."

"Right. Give me a few minutes to get dressed. I'm on my way."

"'S going on?" Cyte said blearily as Winter rolled out of bed and scrambled for her underclothes.

"White Riders are trying the pickets again." Winter pulled her shirt on and shook out her trousers.

"Damn." Cyte sat up, blanket falling away. "Wait for me."

"They'll probably be gone by the time I get there," Winter said, pulling on her boots. They were still damp with yesterday's melted snow. "Stay here. They may try another part of the line before I get back."

Cyte nodded, trying to shake the sleepiness from her head. Winter belted on her sword and stepped out through the tent flap. The cold wind was like a slap in the face, and the Girls' Own ranker waiting in front of the tent wore a ragged, makeshift overcoat made of stitched-together blankets.

"Lead the way—" Winter began, then stopped when something tickled the back of her mind. Alex burst into view around a tent, trying to run and sending up huge sprays of snow.

"Winter!" she said.

"What's wrong?" Infernivore uncoiled deep inside her with its usual hunger.

"Can't you feel it?" Alex said. She pointed toward the edge of the camp.

Winter looked meaningfully at the ranker standing behind her, and Alex closed her mouth with a snap. She kept pointing, though, and when Winter looked in that direction, she realized she *could* feel something. Alex's demon dominated Infernivore's attention, but if she focused, there was a hint of a presence in the other direction. *Out by the picket line—*

"Is that where they're attacking?" she asked the ranker.

The young woman nodded. "Just past those trees."

"Damn." *Penitents at last?* "Alex, come with me. You"—she pointed at the ranker—"find Captain Forester and tell her to meet me out there, as fast as she can. Run!"

"Yes, sir!" the ranker said, bewildered but determined. She dashed off into the camp.

Winter started running in the other direction, as best she could in the snow. Alex pounded along behind her.

"You think it's them?" the girl said.

"We're only a hundred miles from Elysium," Winter said. "This is practically their backyard."

"What are they doing attacking the pickets, though?"

"That's what I'm trying to figure out. Maybe they're working with the white riders."

They approached the tree line. Alex looked over her shoulder and extended a hand. "I'll make better time this way."

"Wait—"

But Alex was already rising into the air, swinging toward the nearest tree on a line of pure darkness, trailing snow from her boots. She landed, lashed to the tree, then aimed her other hand and swung again. Winter struggled after her, now able to see the flashes of musket-fire deeper into the little woods. The snow muffled the sound of the weapons to a dull *thud, thud, thud*, like someone keeping an irregular beat on a drum. After a few moments, the firing stopped, although more distant shots came from farther along the line.

The first body was leaning against a tree, a woman in a Girls' Own uniform opened from navel to collarbone by a single long cut, hands clamped futilely over the wound. Her blood was startlingly red against the snow, and the drops and sprays had melted little craters in the delicate surface. A bit farther on, another soldier was curled on her side, lying in a pool of brown slush.

"Saints and *fucking* martyrs," Winter whispered. Her hand dropped to her sword, and she scanned the silent, shadowed forest for movement. The *crunch* of her boots in the snow sounded loud.

Another body, still clutching her musket. And another, pinned to a tree, her feet several inches off the ground, hanging from a milky white spike driven through her sternum. Her eyes were wide with terror and disbelief.

"There you are," a woman's voice said. She spoke Vordanai with a heavy Murnskai accent. "I was getting bored of slaughtering these rabble."

Infernivore rose up in Winter's mind as a slim figure stepped around a tree. She was tall, with a great mass of black hair that fell below her shoulders. She'd wrapped herself in a thick fur, but at the sight of Winter she let this fall, revealing well-fitted dark leather.

Her face was invisible behind a black mask set with tiny chips of obsidian. The weak sunlight gleamed and shifted as she moved, running along the curving surfaces like dripping paint.

"You're a Penitent," Winter said, stepping closer.

"Ahdon ivahnt vi, ignahta sempria," the woman acknowledged, moving slowly

to mirror Winter's approach. They circled, drawing ever closer. "And you're Vhalnich's pet demon lord, aren't you? Ihernglass."

"I suppose I shouldn't bother asking you to surrender," Winter said.

The Penitent laughed. "I'll tell you what. If you don't bother with that, I won't pretend that I'm going to let you live."

What happened to Alex? Winter resisted the urge to look up at the treetops. The girl had to be there, somewhere, but she might have lost her nerve. *Maybe I ought to have waited for Cyte to put a squad together.* Winter dismissed that thought at once. Whatever this demon-host could do, it had clearly been able to tear through the Girls' Own sentries without difficulty. *I won't ask my soldiers to throw their lives away against a monster.*

I have to get ahold of her. Infernivore could destroy any other demon, but she needed close contact to unleash it. *If she doesn't know what I can do, I might be able to misdirect her.* She hefted her sword and squared her stance slightly. *She doesn't have a weapon, but that doesn't mean much . . .*

"Well?" the Penitent said. "Are you going to get started, or should I?"

Winter shrugged. Then, before the movement was quite finished, she lunged forward, snow spraying out behind her. Only a few feet separated them, but Winter started her swing early, telegraphing a wide blow to the Penitent's left side. Even an indifferent swordsman could have blocked it, which was of course the whole point. Her left hand came up, open-palmed, no obvious threat. *If I grab her—*

The Penitent stood motionless, but snow fountained around her feet. As Winter's sword descended, a torrent of fine white particles flowed around the woman's clothes, rapidly enclosing her in a thickening shell. By the time the blade struck, the fine particles of snow had merged into a solid layer of ice, milky white color fading to absolute transparency. The blade hit and rebounded as though she'd struck stone, steel ringing with the impact as chips and splinters of ice flew.

Winter's other hand reached out, and she put her palm flat against the Penitent's chest. Her skin went instantly numb, but Winter was already reaching out with her mind, urging Infernivore on. It filled her arm, roaring through her fingertips, but the Penitent's demon remained stubbornly out of reach, separated by the icy barrier.

It's too thick, Winter realized. She took a step and nearly stumbled. Her hand refused to move, stuck to the Penitent's chest, fingers numbed into insensibility as cold crept up her arm.

"Not exactly an auspicious beginning," the Penitent said. Her voice echoed oddly; the ice had grown around her head, encasing it in a transparent helmet and visor like an old-fashioned knight. "Surely you've got something more than that?"

Winter aimed a second cut at the woman's head. It rang off her icy helmet, snapping off a chunk as big as a finger and sending spidery white cracks through the rest. The woman frowned, and the cracks receded, sealing themselves closed. She raised her right hand, and more snow rose from the forest floor and shaped itself into a long, thin blade with a needle-sharp point.

"I really don't see how you could have beaten Wren, let alone Twist," the Penitent said. "Perhaps you had help—"

A line of absolute darkness shot down from the trees, slamming into the icicle sword near the hilt. The weapon shattered in a blast of cold and splintered ice. The Penitent spun, dragging Winter through the snow, and another spear of blackness stabbed down and hit the woman high in the chest. There was a horrible *screech*, like a knife blade drawn across glass, and the Penitent staggered back a step in a cloud of powdered ice. When it cleared, Winter could see that the ice armor was fractured in a neat bull's-eye pattern around the impact, but not broken.

It had stunned the woman for a moment, though, and Winter wasn't about to let that go to waste. She jumped, putting all her weight on the hand that was stuck to the Penitent's chest, and jammed both her feet against the woman's hips. She hung there for a moment, suspended like a climber from a tree; then, gritting her teeth, Winter straightened her legs and pulled as hard as she could.

There was no pain when her hand came free, just a cracking, tearing feeling that promised agony later. She pushed off the Penitent and landed a few feet away in the snow, rolling immediately with a spray of white powder. The Penitent ignored her, more snow whirling around her in a miniature cyclone. It condensed into icicles like thin white daggers, a dozen of them, which hung in the air for a moment before zipping into the trees like a volley of arrows. Snow and torn branches fell as they slashed by, but a moment later another pair of inky black lines lanced out. One hit the Penitent in the head, tearing away a big chunk of helmet, while the other slammed into her knee with a *crunch* of shattering ice. The woman let out a grunt, slapping an ice-gauntleted hand over her face, and snow spiraled inward to regrow her armor.

Winter took the opportunity for a strategic withdrawal, running for the tree the black lines were coming from. Another volley of ice knives slashed out, and she dove to put the thick trunk between her and her opponent. The tree shivered again, losing more branches.

"Winter!" a voice said from above. Winter looked up to see Alex clinging to the trunk of the tree, eyes wide. "Are you all right?"

"Think so," Winter said.

"She just shrugged off the best I can do," Alex said. "You've killed these things before, haven't you? How do we hurt her?"

Another volley of knives, this one curving around the side of the tree like a flock of birds. Winter threw herself flat to avoid them, then struggled to her feet.

"For now, I think we run," she said. *Then maybe come back here with a god-damn cannon.*

She broke from cover, zigzagging to the next tree, and Alex swung past overhead. Behind her, the Penitent's laughter boomed.

"I really can't believe that's *all*," she shouted. "*You* are the Winter Ihernglass the pontifex is so terrified of? What a joke."

Winter threw herself against another tree and risked a look back. "She's not coming after us."

"Maybe she's got better things to do," Alex said, lowering herself on a dark line until she was beside Winter's head.

Think, Winter commanded herself. "Maybe she can't. That armor must weigh half a ton. It can't be easy to move around in. She didn't have it up when I got here."

"I knew I should have speared her first thing," Alex said. "I thought I would follow your lead, you being the general and all."

"In the future, feel free to kill any Penitents we run across without asking permission."

"Noted," Alex said. "What now?"

"We get help." Maybe a cannon *would* do it. *If she can't dodge well, we might be able to hit her.* "At the very least, we need Bobby—"

A new sound cut her off, a keening, wailing noise like a rising windstorm. Winter peeked around the tree and found the Penitent still in place, both her hands in the air, as though calling for applause.

Snow exploded all around them. A dozen individual bursts, rising into columns of swirling, freezing mist. They coalesced into roughly man-shaped figures, headless, featureless torsos with rudimentary legs and arms that ended in long, white blades. They glided lightly over the packed snow as they came forward.

"You've got to be kidding me," Alex said. She fired a line of darkness from one hand, punching right through one of the advancing wraiths. It didn't even seem to notice. Another rushed at Winter, swinging its blade-arms in clumsy arcs. She danced away, then ducked under a slash from another behind her. She came up inside its guard, sword curving around to cut neatly through it from armpit to shoulder. There was little resistance, as though she'd swung into lightly packed snow, and the wraith exploded into flurries of white.

Winter spun, panting, her breath hanging in the air like smoke. Her left hand was starting to hurt, and she hadn't dared look at it yet. Another wraith came at her, and she dodged one swing and parried the other, steel blade meeting ice with that same hair-raising squeal. Her riposte punched through it, shattering it to fragments, but there were two more closing in behind.

Alex dropped off the tree with a *thump* in the midst of the lumbering wraiths. Darkness shot out of her palm, not a single spear this time but a broad whip, shattering the wraith into its component ice. She turned gleefully and slashed another and another, flying snow hanging in the air like powder smoke.

"Behind you!" Winter shouted, fending off four ice swords. The creatures weren't skilled, but they were strong and relentless. She cut through another and saw Alex spin just in time, taking a thrust along her shoulder instead of through her ribs. The girl swore and chopped the wraith down, retreating toward Winter, who hacked a path to her.

"Keep them off me," Alex said. "I can handle these things, at least."

Winter clenched her off hand. Her fingers moved, but the pain made her squeeze her eyes shut for a moment. When her vision cleared of tears, more columns of white mist were rising all around them, more wraiths building themselves out of wind and snow.

"How *many* can you handle?" Winter said.

"Probably not this many," Alex admitted.

"Can you get us both out of here?"

Alex looked down at her hands. "Maybe. I've only lifted other people a couple of times."

"This would be a really good opportunity to find out."

"Right." Alex put her arm around Winter's waist. "Here goes."

Black strands lashed out, wrapping around a nearby tree, and they rose into the air, swinging above the headless wraiths. Ice blades reached for them, inches from Winter's feet, and the rush of freezing air stung her eyes. Alex hit the tree, grunting with effort, and immediately swung again.

Something flashed from the direction of the Penitent. Winter shouted, and Alex changed course, getting them out of the way of a barrage of ice knives that screamed past. The blades slammed into the tree Alex had roped herself to, a slim pine whose trunk exploded into shards under the impact. It began to topple, momentum dragging their swing off course and slamming them into a snowdrift. Winter's ears were ringing. She raised her head and saw wraiths in every direction, moving in for the kill. Alex groaned.

Two of the wraiths exploded, and Bobby strode through the clouds of snow. Her sword was still in her belt, but she carried a six-foot-long tree branch, which she swung as easily as an ordinary man might have wielded a truncheon. The next wraith raised its swords to block, but it made no difference at all; the impact of the wood blasted it to pieces. Winter hauled Alex to her feet and retreated to meet Bobby's advance.

"Sir!" Bobby said. "What the hell is going on? What are these things?"

"Penitent," Winter gasped. "Just up ahead."

"There's fighting all along the line," Bobby said. "White riders."

"It's a distraction," Winter said. "She's here for me."

"Then let's get out of here."

"No!" Winter pointed at the now-distant Penitent with her sword. "We're the only ones who stand a chance against her. We have to stop her here or God knows how many she'll kill. Alex, are you all right?"

"Just a little bruised," Alex said. "What's the plan?"

"She's got ice all over her," Winter said. "Bobby, I need you to break that off and then try to hold her in place so Alex and I can finish her."

"I'll give it a shot, sir," Bobby said, hefting her tree branch. "Stay behind me."

She cleared a path through the advancing wraiths, Winter and Alex taking care of any that tried to slip around the scythe-like strokes of her tree branch.

"I didn't know she was one of us," Alex said. "I can't sense her at all."

"It's complicated." Winter grunted, blocking a strike and cutting the wraith down. "Remind me to explain when we have a minute."

The wraiths thinned out quickly, no new ones rising to replace those they cut down. *She wants us to come back and fight,* Winter thought. Soon enough they broke into the clear and were back among the snow-caked bodies of the Girls' Own sentries, where the Penitent stood sheathed in her transparent armor.

"Ah, you've brought a new friend," the woman said. Snow swirled around her, condensing into another fan of ice knives. "Splendid."

"Let Bobby go first," Winter hissed. "She's hard to hurt."

Bobby charged, and the ice knives lanced out. One of them buried itself in her gut and the other opened a cut on her shoulder, but she absorbed the impacts with barely a grunt. Winter ducked and started running, circling to Bobby's left as Alex dodged to the right. The Penitent frowned, more snow forming long, thin blades on both of her gauntlets. Bobby swung the tree branch against the woman's ribs, and it struck with enough force that the wood exploded into flying splinters. Concentric rings of cracks shot through the ice armor as it fractured.

"Now, *that* is more like it!" the woman roared. She slashed down with her swords, and Bobby slipped aside. Before the Penitent could turn, Alex's lances of darkness slammed into her, aiming for the side where Bobby's blow had landed. A piece of ice the size of a dinner plate flew off amid a spray of powder.

The Penitent snarled, and snow coiled around her. Bobby reached out and grabbed one of the woman's swords, slicking the blade with red where it cut into her hand. She pulled the Penitent forward and rammed an elbow into the woman's gut with a sound like a box full of crockery breaking. Chunks and lumps of ice fell away, but the Penitent brought her other sword around, impaling Bobby near the collarbone. Instead of trying to break free, Bobby stepped closer, her hand closing on the Penitent's shoulder.

A patch of the armor was completely gone, Winter could see. Bobby and the Penitent stumbled, turning slowly. Snow rose all around them, more wraiths forming, ready to hack Bobby to pieces.

"Alex!" Winter shouted. "The stomach! Hit her now!"

"Bobby's in the way!" Alex said.

"Do it!" Bobby screamed.

Twin needles of darkness stabbed out. They struck Bobby in the small of the back, slicing clean through her flesh as though it wasn't there to stab into the belly of the Penitent. The armor on the woman's back cracked and exploded outward in a spray of ice. For a moment everything was still—Bobby and the Penitent locked together, impaled on two spears of pure night.

A fragment of ice fell away, letting the Penitent's long black hair flop free. Her wraiths slumped, falling apart into mist and snow, as her armor dropped away from her piece by piece. The blade impaling Bobby snapped as the masked woman's knees buckled. She ended up on her back in the snow, arms outstretched, with Bobby lying spread-eagled on top of her.

"Bobby!" Winter sprinted as best she could through the snow, and Alex came in from the other direction. Winter went to her knees in a spray of white, rolling Bobby off the Penitent. Her uniform was caked with snow and blood-soaked around the holes in her stomach and shoulder, but she was smiling.

"Alex?" Bobby said. Blood flecked her lips and discolored her teeth.

"Y-yeah?" Alex said.

"That . . ." She coughed, spraying blood, and closed her eyes. "That didn't hurt as much as I expected." The breath went out of her in a long, steamy puff.

"She'll be all right," Winter said, with more confidence then she felt. *Please, please let her be all right.* "She survived when a Redeemer nearly cut her in half. It just sometimes takes a while."

"I . . ." Alex's eyes were round as saucers. "*Fuck.* What do we do? Can we help her?"

"We need to get her back to camp. It's probably better if she's somewhere warm."

"You stay with her," Alex said. "I'll get help."

There was a nasty, wet sound. It took Winter a moment to realize that the Penitent was laughing. Winter shuffled to her side and jerked the black mask up, obsidian clicking under her fingers. The face beneath was disappointingly ordinary, a pretty, pale woman with ice-blue eyes. Her lips and cheeks were already stained with blood.

"Serves me . . . right," the Penitent muttered, then choked another laugh. "Dragging things out too long. Always knew it would get me."

"You're going to die," Winter told her.

"Really?" The woman coughed again, spraying red. "Could have . . . fooled me."

"I just want you to know, before you do, that we're going to take your *fucking* Church apart stone by stone." Winter gritted her teeth. "Those women you killed, those *rabble*, are each worth a hundred of your goddamned monsters. Your pontifex is going to beg for mercy."

The Penitent laughed again, wet and bubbling. Her eyes fixed on Winter, disconcertingly calm.

"Good luck doing all that," she said with a gasp, "without . . . your precious . . . general . . ."

The woman's eyes closed. Winter looked down at her uncertainly, then back at Alex and Bobby.

"It might be a bluff," Winter said.

"Go," Alex said. "Make sure. I'll stay with her until help gets here."

Winter nodded and took off at a run.

RAESINIA

Raesinia had never seen Marcus so agitated when there wasn't actually shooting going on. He paced the length of her tent, turned, and retraced his steps, ignoring the meal on the table.

"Horses are the real problem," he said. "With the army in tents, we could cut rations, at least for a while. But we don't have enough fodder to go around, and with everything snowed under, we're not getting any more except from the depots. We need the horses to haul the wagons from the depots to get the fodder to feed the horses! We're using everything we have, and it's still not enough. The weakest are dying already. The more we lose, the harder it'll be to keep up the convoys.

"We've got fevers and coughs spreading fast, and probably flux to follow. The white riders are pouncing on anyone that leaves the camp, and yesterday some idiot chopped a hole in the river ice because he wanted a bath! We're running out of deadwood to burn, and green wood won't dry fast enough. Every general is telling me his men are raising hell. We *can't stay here*. Much longer and the whole army will fall apart."

"You don't have to tell me," Raesinia said. "I've seen it." She'd made a few tours of the camp, trying to keep up morale.

"*He* hasn't," Marcus said. "He hasn't come down off his hill for days."

"You've tried to tell him this, I assume?" Raesinia said.

Marcus nodded wearily. "He just insists that the weather will change in time. He's calculated it, somehow. Something about how much power a demon can have." Marcus looked over his shoulder. "Ordinarily, I try not to meddle in the . . . *strange* side of things. Janus knows what he's doing. And I don't pretend to be able to understand what he's talking about, but it *feels* wrong. Like wishful thinking."

"So what are you going to do about it?"

"What *can* I do?" Marcus ran a hand through his hair. "Sit here and hope he's right. Hope the weather changes before we get mass desertions or have to start eating each other. It won't be the first miracle he's pulled out of his hat."

Raesinia let out an inward sigh. Even now, staring disaster in the face,

Marcus couldn't conceive of a world where he disobeyed Janus. If the First Consul ordered his troops to stand and die to the last man, Marcus would be the final one to fall.

"Is there anything I can do?" Raesinia said. "We know he's not likely to listen to me."

"That's what I came to talk to you about," Marcus said. His voice was grim. "You're not going to like this, I know, but please listen to me. I think you should go back, at least to Polkhaiz."

He can't be serious. "How will it look if the queen abandons the army?"

"What's going to happen to Vordan if the queen *and* the First Consul freeze to death in the middle of Murnsk?" He looked guilty at just voicing the thought out loud. "It won't come to that. Janus has always come through before. But . . . just in case. I'd give you a strong cavalry escort; the white riders won't dare attack."

"I'm not leaving, Marcus," Raesinia said. She took a deep breath. *Now or never.* "There's something I need to tell you."

He sighed, and Raesinia hesitated for a moment. *He needs to know about Dorsay's offer, the deal to remove Janus in exchange for peace.* But she couldn't shake the feeling that he wouldn't consider it. *He might even think of me as a traitor.* Somehow *that* would be worst of all.

In the moment of silence, something shifted inside her skull, the strange pressure that meant another demon-host was near. Raesinia's expertise was limited, but the sense was strong this time and very close by.

"Where's Winter?" she said. She was the only demon-host likely to visit the command tent. Her captain, Bobby, barely registered to Raesinia's sense, and Alex was still carefully watched. *Unless she's a Penitent after all . . .*

"What?" Marcus frowned. "The Second Division is camped about a mile east, near the edge of the woods. She's with them, unless something's happened."

The sense of pressure increased. Raesinia turned her head, feeling it slide around the inside of her skull. "Someone's here. A demon, and I don't think it's one of ours."

"Penitent," Marcus spat. He grabbed his sword belt from the table.

Certain that he was about to order her to stay put, Raesinia darted past him and out into the snow. Her tent was on the slope of a hill by the banks of the Kovria, with the heights occupied by Janus' command tent and personal quarters. Slightly downslope were the smaller tents used by her servants and attendants.

"Sothe!" Raesinia shouted.

The assassin appeared, so suddenly and noiselessly that Raesinia would have sworn she'd materialized from thin air. "Your Majesty?"

"Trouble." The pressure was coming from the direction of Janus' tents. "Penitents."

"Raes!" Marcus said, blundering out through the tent flap. "You should—"

Raesinia started to run, ignoring him. Sothe fell in beside her, making better progress through the snow with her longer legs.

"This is well inside the picket lines," Sothe said. "Are you certain?"

"I can feel it," Raesinia said. "There. No, there!"

She pointed to where the hill ended in a steep scree slope down to the river. The water was invisible, a flat expanse of snow-covered ice, but a section of it was *bulging*. As they watched, it exploded in a spray of white, and a humanoid figure burst out and began crunching up the hillside.

"Under the ice," Sothe said. "Clever, assuming you can survive in freezing-cold water."

"We're under attack!" Raesinia shouted, gesturing wildly. "Over there!"

The half dozen Colonials on guard outside Janus' tent looked at her quizzically. It took them a moment to realize that it was the *queen* running frantically through the snow toward them, gesturing like a madwoman. When they'd got that, a further moment was required before they understood what she was saying. The man closest to the slope turned, following her pointing finger, and looked over the edge. He gave a shout, and a moment later the Penitent was on top of him, swinging a roundhouse punch into the side of his head that hit like a blow from a sledgehammer. He dropped, abruptly limp, and the Penitent turned to the second guard.

Now that Raesinia had gotten a good look at the attacker, she could see that something very strange was going on. It was clearly a woman, a squat, powerful figure in dark leather not dissimilar from Sothe's fighting gear. Her face was covered in a black obsidian mask. But her body was distorted, limbs thickened and bulging, as though there were a layer of something thick and viscous under her skin.

As Raesinia watched, the effect vanished, the woman's muscles writhing like snakes in a sack as they returned to something like normal. The Penitent raised her hands, and something gleamed—a mass of steel needles, no bigger than toothpicks, held between her clenched fingers.

The second guard thrust at her with his bayoneted musket. The Penitent turned, letting the blade scrape along her side, scoring her leathers but not drawing blood. Her hand darted out and brushed by the Colonial's neck, leaving something stuck there. One of the needles, except that in the moment it left the Penitent's hand it had turned a sickly, malevolent green.

The little thing wasn't even large enough to draw blood. The guard backed off, raised his weapon again, and then staggered sideways. He let the musket fall, clutching at where the splinter had been, and then collapsed into the side of the tent, convulsing.

At the opposite corner of the tent, two more guards raised their muskets. The Penitent twisted, hands flickering as she whipped the tiny needles at them. One ball ricocheted off the frozen ground with a whine, and the other went high. Both soldiers collapsed almost instantly, clawing at wounds too small to see.

Sothe spun to a halt in a spray of snow, knives appearing in her hands as if by magic. The first whipped end over end and would have struck the Penitent square in the forehead if the woman hadn't ducked. As she came back up, she swept one hand out, a motion like wiping down a table. Raesinia couldn't see the steel needles, but Sothe was already moving, throwing herself flat. The assassin rolled and flipped to her feet as the Penitent ducked through the tent flap.

"Brass Balls of the Beast!" Marcus swore, running after them. "What the hell—"

"Come on!" Raesinia shouted, sprinting to cover the last few yards to the tent. Sothe was just ahead of her, throwing the tent flap wide and then ducking immediately. Something whined past Raesinia's ear.

Janus' tent was large, but modestly furnished, with only a camp bed, a folding table, and a few trunks. There were two more guards, but one of them was already down, eyes bulging and hands locked around his own throat. The other had drawn a sword, and behind him Janus himself was pulling a long, narrow blade from where it hung beside the bed.

"Don't let her cut you!" Raesinia shouted, charging the Penitent. The masked woman turned, hand moving in a blur, and Raesinia felt something bite her shoulder. The vile substance woven into the metal raced along her nerves, turning them into lines of agonizing pain that reached toward her heart.

But Raesinia was used to pain, and the binding was already at work, surging back along the pathways like the counterattack of a defending army. Raesinia managed a savage grin as she barely slowed her pace, and the Penitent, already turning away, spun back to face her in alarm. *Weren't expecting that, were you?*

Raesinia slammed into the Penitent, putting every ounce of her inadequate weight into the tackle. The woman rocked back on her heels but didn't fall. Raesinia twisted, grabbing for the woman's arm and holding on to it with both hands.

"Sothe!" she screamed.

There were advantages to a long history of working with someone. Sothe had made the same fast assessment of the enemy and come to the same conclusion. Raesinia held the woman's arm pinioned, and Sothe flipped another knife, sinking it point-first into the Penitent's palm. The woman gave a yelp of pain—the first sound Raesinia had heard her make—and launched a spray of needles at Sothe with her other hand. Sothe had already tangled one foot in a discarded blanket, however, and she kicked the cloth into the air as a makeshift shield against the tiny projectiles.

A shattering bang filled the tent as Marcus fired his pistol. The ball tore a hole in the canvas as the Church assassin ducked, and Marcus swore and drew his sword. The Penitent took a step backward, dragging Raesinia with her, and hurled the last of her needles from her good hand in the direction of Janus and the guard. The Colonial, shielding his commander with his body, took a dozen of the green needles and went down on top of Janus in a thrashing heap. Another knife zipped past, aiming for the Penitent's other hand and missing by a hair.

The woman said something in Murnskai that sounded like a curse. She moved fast, bringing her free hand around and jabbing it into Raesinia's throat. The blow alone would have been painful, but the Penitent's nails were sharp as razors, and as they pierced her skin Raesinia could *feel* them pulse with a massive flux of the green venom. Her hands twitched involuntarily, and she fell away from the Penitent's arm.

Unencumbered, the woman went for the exit. Marcus swung at her head, but she slipped under it, lithe as a snake, and he had to jump backward to avoid a slash from her clawed hand. Sothe was faster, twisting around to plant a knife in the small of the Penitent's back. The masked woman stumbled but didn't fall, bursting out through the tent flap. Sothe followed her a moment later.

Janus got to his feet, pushing the dead Colonial aside, rapier still in his hand. He whipped it through the air as he gestured after the fleeing Penitent.

"Column-General, do not let that creature escape."

"Sir!" Marcus drew himself up, then looked to Raesinia. "Raes, are you all right?"

Raesinia had sagged against the tent wall, clutching the fabric to keep herself standing. The dose of poison had been so large that her heart had stopped almost immediately, nerves burning out in a sympathetic cascade that went beyond pain and into blissful numbness. It took her a moment to get it going again, the binding wrapping itself around the twitching, dying organ.

"I'll be fine," she croaked. "Immortal, remember?"

Marcus nodded and turned to the tent flap. Before he could leave, however, there was a clatter, and he turned back to find that Janus had dropped his rapier.

"Sir?" he said.

"Ah." Janus' hand went to his cheek. There was the tiniest scratch there, little more than a paper cut, leaking a single drop of blood. A muscle in his face jumped. "It appears I may be in need of some assistance."

Then his eyes rolled up in his head, and he collapsed.

CHAPTER TWELVE

MARCUS

"I'm sorry, Your Majesty," Sothe said, head bowed.

"It's all right." Raesinia's voice was still a croaking rasp. "You were up against a Penitent Damned."

Sothe's lips pressed tight, but she didn't argue.

The Penitent had escaped. She'd cut through a horse line, and a quick jab of her poisoned nails had sent several of the animals into a maddened frenzy, causing chaos. In the confusion, she'd taken a mount and ridden hard for the edge of camp, where the white riders were still skirmishing with the picket line. Once she'd joined them, the northerners had melted away, leaving only spent arrows and bodies.

Ihernglass had arrived at the command tent only a minute after the Penitent had made her break. He'd immediately sent for the Girls' Own regimental cutter, Hanna Courvier, who he assured Marcus was among the best in the army. When the woman had arrived, wearing only a jacket over her nightshirt, she'd immediately kicked everyone else out of Janus' sleeping tent. They'd reconvened in the command tent beside it, around the big map table.

No one who didn't already know what had happened was there. Rumors of an assassination attempt were racing through the camp, already on edge after the white riders' attacks. Marcus had told the generals to put their divisions on alert, hoping that standing guard would keep the soldiers from spreading gossip. It wasn't working; he could feel the tension in every messenger who came to the command tent. They peered discreetly around, looking for Janus or some evidence of what had happened.

In the tent were himself, Raesinia, Sothe, and Ihernglass. Sothe raised her head slowly and took a seat beside the queen. Ihernglass cleared his throat.

"I ought to have known," he said. His right hand balled into a fist, and he winced. His other hand was heavily bandaged. "The second Penitent sacrificed herself to bait me out to the edge of camp and keep me busy. If not for that, I might have sensed what was going on here."

"Assigning blame isn't important," Raesinia rasped. "We need to worry about what happens next."

As though the words had been a summons, there was a scratch at the tent flap. Andy's voice came from outside.

"Sir? The cutter wants you." She sounded worried. Marcus hadn't let her in on the truth of the attack yet, but she could hardly miss the mood, or the half dozen dead Colonials.

"Send her in," Marcus said.

Hanna was a solid, competent-looking woman, but her expression made Marcus' heart skip. She shook her head as she came in, apparently unintimidated by the presence of the column-general and the Queen of Vordan.

"Is he—" Marcus began.

"He's alive," Hanna said. "But that may be about all I can tell you. I've never seen anything quite like this."

Marcus let out a long breath in unison with everyone around the table. Raesinia said, "You'd better elaborate."

"I looked at the cut on his cheek," Hanna said. "It's not deep, obviously, but from what you've told me, there was some kind of poison involved. Ordinarily there'd be some residue of the substance used, on the skin or in the wound itself, but I couldn't find anything. I opened the cut a little wider, and the blood looks healthy."

"It may have been an . . . unusual poison," Sothe said.

Hanna nodded. "It'd have to be. Most poisons either act fast and wear off quickly or take a long time to work. I examined the guards, and it's clear that this substance has an extraordinarily rapid effect. But there's no evidence that it's wearing off in the First Consul."

Marcus coughed. "What exactly is his condition?"

"He's unconscious with a high fever," Hanna said bluntly. "The effect looks more like a festering wound than a poison, but I've examined him thoroughly and found no evidence of any other injury."

"And what is your prognosis?" Raesinia said. In the brief pause that followed, the world seemed to be holding its breath.

"I have no idea," Hanna said. "I'm sorry, Your Majesty, but as I said, I've never seen anything like it. I'll do what I can for the symptoms, but as to whether he will ultimately recover or worsen, your guess is as good as mine." She shrugged. "If the assassin could be interrogated about what poison she used, or if I could have a sample, that might help. Otherwise, all I can do is wait."

"All right," Marcus said. "Thank you, Miss Courvier. Please continue doing your best."

Hanna gave a brief bow and withdrew. Marcus looked around the table.

"It's no surprise she doesn't know what she's looking at," Raesinia said, and coughed. "It's magic, after all."

"Ihernglass, you have the demon-eater, don't you?" Marcus said, with an uncomfortable frown. "Could that help?"

"Not here," Ihernglass said. "Infernivore needs to come in contact with the demon itself, and that's in the body of the Penitent who fled."

Sothe bent her head a fraction further, saying nothing.

"Do we have any idea if he'll recover on his own?" Marcus said. "He clearly survived the initial attack, unlike the others."

"He got a much lower dose," Raesinia said. "But . . . I don't think so." She glanced at Ihernglass, who was looking at her quizzically. "From what I felt when it attacked me, the poison seemed almost *alive*. Like a fragment of a demon. I think it will keep attacking him until he . . . dies."

"There must be *something* we can do," Marcus said, looking back and forth between the two of them. "I don't pretend to understand demons and magic, but isn't there a . . . spell, or a potion, or something?" He paused. "I could send word to Vordan, ask Feor to look at the Thousand Names."

"It would take too long," Sothe said. "The flik-flik line hasn't been able to operate past Polkhaiz, and who knows what the snow has done to it. It could be weeks before we got an answer."

"And even if the Names could help," Raesinia said, "I can't see what Feor could do from Vordan."

"There's only one thing I can think of," Ihernglass said. "We have to find the Penitent and kill her."

They all looked at him for a moment. Sothe said, "Are you sure that would work?"

"Of course not," Ihernglass said. "But most of the time, when a demon-host dies, everything they've done stops."

Marcus nodded, remembering the temple under the Great Desol. When Jen had killed the Khandarai boy, all the green-eyed corpses had collapsed.

"If I could use Infernivore on the assassin," Ihernglass went on, "that might be even better. It devours every scrap of the other demon. I don't know if Janus would recover immediately, but at least the poison would disappear."

"But the assassin's gone," Sothe said.

"Then we go after her," Ihernglass said.

There was another moment of silence.

"She's wounded," Ihernglass said. "She won't be able to travel as quickly. If we start soon, with a small force, we might be able to catch up."

"Through the snow and whatever else is out there," Marcus said. "Not to mention the white riders. You'd never make it."

"Then Janus is dead," Ihernglass said. "If this is the only chance we have, I'm willing to take it."

"You mentioned using Infernivore on the assassin," Raesinia said. "Are you volunteering to lead the pursuit?"

Ihernglass blinked, as though he hadn't thought of that. He let out a long, weary breath. "Yes. I guess I am."

"If anyone's going, it should be me," Marcus began, but Raesinia shook her head.

"You're in command of the army for as long as Janus is incapacitated," she said. "We need you here."

"She's right," Ihernglass said.

"Who will you take with you?" Sothe said.

"Some of my own people," Ihernglass said. "I'll put out a call for anyone with wilderness experience. We'll need plenty of horses and as much food as you can spare."

"Volunteers only," Marcus said. "You can't order anyone on this kind of mission."

Ihernglass sighed. "I don't think that will be a problem."

WINTER

"You can't just leave me here," Cyte said. "You don't get to make that decision."

"I do, actually," Winter said, rummaging through her trunk. "That's what being a division-general means."

"But . . ." Cyte stood in the center of the tent, biting her lip.

"Look at it logically," Winter said. "That's what you're good at, right? I'm going because I have Infernivore. Bobby's coming because she can bend steel with her bare hands. I'm not leaving you behind. I'm leaving you in *command*, you understand?"

"Abby should be in command," Cyte said. "She outranks me."

"Abby has her own responsibilities to worry about. You know that you've been running this division as much as I have since we started marching. Marcus is going to need all the help he can get."

Cyte blinked, fighting back tears. It *was* logical, and Winter knew she could see that. *Sometimes that's not enough.*

"The way you talked about it," Cyte said, her voice almost a whisper. "That you were only taking volunteers. It sounded like you're not expecting to come back."

"It's going to be dangerous," Winter said. She closed the trunk slowly and got to her feet. Pain flared from her left hand, still bandaged and oozing. "But we're at war. Everything's dangerous."

"There's a difference between dangerous and suicidal," Cyte said. "Winter, please. Look me in the eye and tell me you think you can make it back from this."

Winter crossed the tent and stood in front of Cyte, their faces inches apart. Cyte's lip was trembling.

"It took me so long to . . . figure things out," Cyte whispered. "After all that . . . if you . . ."

"I'm not going to make any promises," Winter said. "You're too smart for that. But I will do everything I possibly can."

"You don't have to." Cyte's voice was barely audible, as though the thought were too dangerous to speak. "I know Janus is your friend, but—"

Winter kissed her, hard. Cyte drew in close, arms wrapping around Winter's shoulders.

"I have to go," Winter said, when they finally drew apart.

"I know," Cyte said. Her voice was steady, though her eyes still glittered with tears. "Good luck."

"I checked over the list," Abby said. "They're all good people. None of them will let you down."

There were only a few hours of daylight left, but Winter was determined to make as much ground as she could. The Penitent might be slowed by her wound, but she had a head start. For the moment the snow had stopped, and following her trail would be simple enough. But that could change at any time—even a few inches of fresh snow might be enough for the pursuers to lose their quarry. Their only advantage was the strange sense that one demon-host had of another, and that faded quickly with distance. Winter was determined to make up enough ground to be able to feel the Penitent in her mind before more snow obliterated the physical traces.

Of course, that same sense meant that the Penitent would be able to feel *her*. But that couldn't be helped.

They were taking twenty-five soldiers, all from the Girls' Own. Abby knew her people better than most of the regimental commanders, and she'd quickly sorted out a group of volunteers she thought would be useful. The Girls' Own were also among the most dedicated to Janus, and hopefully less likely to react badly if things got strange. A side benefit was that Winter's gender was an open secret among them, which meant that she wouldn't need to keep up the charade— it could get tricky in close quarters.

"Thanks," Winter said. "I'll do everything I can to bring everybody back."

Abby nodded. "Bring yourself back, too."

Winter smiled, a bit wanly. "Try to help Cyte, would you? She's up to this, but she may not believe she is. Don't let de Koste shout her down."

"I'll keep him under control," Abby said. "You're sure you don't want to talk to him yourself?"

"I haven't got the time." De Koste would insist that he ought to go along out of sheer gallantry, and the prospect of arguing with him was exhausting. "Cyte's got written orders, and Marcus will back her up."

"All right." Abby clapped Winter on the shoulder, a little harder than was necessary, then saluted. "Good luck, sir."

Some of the party, those who had experience with tracking, had already gone ahead to begin finding the Penitent's trail. The rest were mounting up near the edge of the Second Division camp. Marcus had scoured the army for the strongest, healthiest horses, ignoring the protests of the officers and cavalrymen he took them from. Each of Winter's twenty-five had two extra mounts, loaded with provisions—mostly fodder—and other supplies. A similar ransacking of private stores had provided everyone with greatcoats, though in wildly varying sizes.

At the edge of the group, Bobby was checking the load of a packhorse while Alex fought her way into a coat three sizes too large for her. When she finally got her arms the right way around, Winter almost laughed; the hem dragged on the ground, and the sleeves flopped over her hands.

"Needs a little stitching," Alex said, seeing her expression. "But it's warm."

"It looks like it," Winter said, then paused. "You don't have to do this, you know."

"I came here to help Janus," Alex said. "Saving his life seems like helping. Besides, you said I can sense other demons better than you can, and I know at least a little bit of the country we're going through. You need me."

Winter nodded and turned to Bobby. "And you're sure you're feeling well enough?"

Bobby patted her stomach. "All closed up. Don't worry." She grinned at Alex, the two of them sharing some private joke. "We'll catch up to her, no problem."

"I hope so. I don't know how long we have." She took a deep breath, feeling the icy cold in her lungs. "Where's the sergeant?"

Bobby pointed to a broad-shouldered woman with a mass of frizzy orange-red hair, only barely tamed by a leather cord. She was in the middle of retying the pack on one of the horses while simultaneously berating the hapless ranker who'd gotten it wrong in the first place. As Winter came over, the sergeant ended her harangue, and both women saluted.

"Sergeant Taring?" Winter said.

"Yes, sir!" She grinned. "Feel free to call me Red; most of the rest of them do."

"And what's your name, ranker?"

"Videlia Litton, sir!" The young woman, a rangy teen, looked at Winter in awe. "It's an honor, sir!"

You may regret that honor before long. Winter tried to banish the thought. None of the soldiers could be unaware of the risks they faced, venturing beyond the camp. *They know what they're getting into as well as I do.*

"Sergeant," Winter said, "let's get this company mounted up. I want us ready to move out in ten minutes."

"Yes, sir!" Red raised her voice. "Let's move! Packs tied up and ready to go! Ivers, what the *hell* are you doing?"

Not more than a quarter hour later, they were on the move, a slim column of women and heavily laden horses. They circumvented the more crowded parts of the camp, moving around the perimeter to where the Penitent had made her breakout. One of the trackers, Ranker Margaret Jacks, was waiting there beside her own horse. She saluted as they approached, and pointed to the northeast.

"It's still pretty clear, sir!" she said. Even Winter could see that—the Penitent's mad gallop had left rents like wounds in the gentle curves of snow. "Farah's gone ahead to mark the trail. That way we should be able to keep on past dark."

"Good thinking," Winter said. Abby had told her the two trackers, Margaret and Farah, knew their business; while most of the Girls' Own had come from the streets of Vordan City, the pair of them had been poachers and thieves before they'd taken shelter from the law with the Leatherbacks.

Margaret swung into her saddle and led the way, following the trail. Before long they came across a wooden stake driven into the snow, just long enough for the tracker to reach down and grab. Another few minutes and they reached the line of pickets, the last boundary of the camp. The men saluted as they rode past, standing at attention until the company was out of sight.

More stakes followed, at regular intervals. As the invisible sun slid past the horizon, they lit lanterns, following the trail and the markers laid down by Farah. North of the Kovria, the strip of civilized country was thin, and after only a few miles they were out of the fields and snow-buried hedgerows and back into the forest.

Winter found it too quiet for her liking. The snow smothered sound, and it seemed as though the noises they made—the breath of the horses, the creak and jingle of tack, the steady *crunch* of hooves on snow—were the only disturbances in an endless, silent world. Trees rose all around them, trunks like black columns extending up out of the lantern's reach. The Penitent's trail was harder to find in the dark and over the uneven ground, but the wooden stakes continued to mark the path.

They caught up to Farah just after midnight. She and her horse had taken shelter in the lee of a particularly massive pine, where the snow was thin. Farah, a skinny, dark-haired woman, offered a sloppy salute and a grin.

"Was beginning to think you weren't coming," she said, with a broad Transpale accent. "Got this far before the sun set, an' I don't trust myself not to lose the trail in the dark. We can pick it up again once the sun comes up."

"Thank you, Ranker Igniz," Winter said, then raised her voice. "Thank you all. You know I wouldn't ask you to do this if it weren't important. We couldn't tell the army what had happened, but you deserve to know."

She related a simplified version of the day's events, leaving out any reference to demons and magic. A Church assassin had poisoned Janus and had to be tracked down in order to recover the antidote. There were gasps and muttered curses.

"Get some sleep," Winter said when they quieted. "We get back on the trail at dawn."

In some strange way, in spite of how unnatural it was, *this* version of Murnsk felt right. It was the Murnsk of stories and penny operas, a frozen wasteland of trees and snow, with no trace of civilization. Winter almost laughed when she realized she was looking around with a kind of satisfaction.

The forest was dark, even during the day. Between the canopy overhead, where wilting leaves still clung, and the omnipresent gray clouds, the sun only managed to wash the land in a weak gray twilight. The snow seemed to glow in the semidarkness, startlingly white, with the tree trunks dark, shadowy shapes against it.

Winter's back and sides already ached. She'd managed a few hours of fitful sleep, curled inside coat and blanket against a tree. After a breakfast of dried meat, hardtack, and water, they were in the saddle again, following Farah and Margaret.

Worse than the saddle pains, though, was her left hand. She'd gotten only a brief glimpse of it—red and steaming as it thawed, most of the skin torn away or hanging in strips—before Hanna had bound it up again. The cutter had said much of the damage was superficial, and she'd retain the use of it, though it would likely be seriously scarred. It hurt like the jaws of the Beast, though, a constant burning pain, and she had to fight the urge to scratch it through the dressing. She barely had enough flex in her bound fingers to hold the reins of her horse.

She'd left Edgar behind, partly because his easygoing nature was poorly suited to this sort of chase, and partly out of sentimentality; they might have to abandon horses for lack of fodder if the chase went on long enough, and she wasn't sure she could stand to leave Edgar alone in the snow. Instead, she had a young, excitable mare with a name she hadn't learned, whose energy was a trial to manage after Edgar's placidity. She had endurance, though, which was more important than comfort. Slogging through the snow was no easier on horses than on humans.

If we'd had time, we could have built a sledge. Her thoughts were drifting. *Carry more supplies that way. Maybe I could ride with the boxes.* Winter blew out a long breath, watching the dragon's spume of steam puff away. It was hard to focus— the white forest and the plod of the horses had an almost hypnotic effect. So little changed, they might have been riding in circles.

We'll catch her. The Penitent had only one mount and no extra fodder. She was wounded. *She can't get far.*

"Sir?"

Winter tightened her left hand. The spike of pain woke her up a little; she blinked and found Farah riding beside her.

"Ranker Igniz," she said. "Has something changed?"

"You'd better have a look at this."

The dead horse lay sprawled in the snow, a red slurry surrounding its throat, long furrows dug by its final kicks.

"This is the one the Penitent was riding?" Winter said.

Farah nodded. She and Margaret were crouched by the corpse. The rest of the party was well to the rear, to avoid disturbing the snow.

"It's one of ours, anyway," Farah said. "Can't be Murnskai; they use different shoes. And it's certainly not one of the white riders'."

"All right." Winter stared at the dead animal. There was foam around its mouth. "She rode it hard, and when it couldn't go any farther, she cut its throat."

"We think she spent the night here," Margaret said. "The snow's scooped out over by that tree, see?"

Winter looked for the sun and couldn't find it through the trees. *It can't be much past two or three in the afternoon, though.* If the Penitent had spent the night here, they were only half a day behind.

"Here's the bad news." Farah pointed past the corpse. The snow was churned up, as though by the passage of many feet. A few outlying tracks showed a strange crosshatched shape, instead of the U-shaped horseshoe Winter was familiar with. "Those are the white riders. Not deep enough to be anything heavier than their ponies."

"When?" Winter said.

"Sometime today."

"Then we're even closer. She waited here until they came for her."

Margaret frowned. "It's hard to tell how many, but there were at least a dozen of them. Maybe more. Maybe a *lot* more, if they're deliberately taking care with their trail." She glanced back at their two dozen. "And if they split up, we won't know which way the Penitent went."

"We'll deal with that when it happens." Winter turned back to the group. "Alex! A moment, please?"

Alex, nearly as inexpert a rider as Winter herself, brought her mount over.

Cavalry horses were trained not to shy at the sight of blood, but it still gave a few uncomfortable snorts.

"Can you feel anything?" Winter said, keeping her voice low.

"Apart from you?" Alex closed her eyes, turning her head slowly from side to side. "It's hard to say. Maybe just a hint."

"If we can't get close enough to sense her soon, she won't need fresh snow to get away," Winter said. "Keep trying, and tell me when you've got something for certain."

"Got it." Alex glanced at the trail, then at the sky. "We're west of the Pilgrim's Road now. There's inns along the way, but they're staying clear of that. I bet they're taking the direct route to Elysium."

"How far is that?"

"At this pace?" Alex shrugged. "Five, maybe six days."

"We have to catch them before then." Winter raised her voice. "Red! We're moving out. Can we pick up the pace?"

"Yes, sir," the sergeant said. "It'll be hard on the poor beasties, though."

"Do it. If we lose the assassin, this is all for nothing."

"Right." The sergeant's voice boomed through the frozen forest. "Move out!"

RAESINIA

"Janus?" Raesinia said. "Can you hear me?"

Janus bet Vhalnich, First Consul of the Kingdom of Vordan, lay shirtless on his camp bed under a thin blanket. A rag, packed with snow from outside, sat on his forehead, dripping melt-water into his hairline. The wound on his cheek was a scabbed red line, widened under Hanna's exploratory scalpel.

His eyes were open, but they didn't seem to be looking at anything in the tent. They flicked from side to side, as though watching something move in the heavens beyond the canvas roof.

"Hear . . ." he muttered. "Who? Who's there?"

"It's me," Raesinia said. "Raesinia."

"Raesinia." Janus' brow creased. "Poor girl. Dead, dead, and doesn't know it. Poor girl."

"Janus?" Raesinia said. "Can you understand me?"

"Help her." Janus blinked, heavy lidded. "How can I help her? Only one way to help the dead. Stuck in the dark. Mya . . . all of them . . . stuck in the dark." He let out a long breath that sounded like a sob. "Stuck in the dark. I'm sorry. So sorry . . . I should have . . ."

His eyes closed. Raesinia watched him breathe for a moment, slow and regular, and then felt his cheek. The skin was hot to the touch, and the melting snow mixed with beads of sweat.

Who was Mya? The name meant nothing to her. *Someone who died, obviously. Like me.*

She stood up, pulled her coat tighter, and left the tent. Hanna was waiting outside.

"He's asleep again."

"Was he talking?" the cutter said.

"A little. But he wasn't making much sense."

"Fever," Hanna said. "Keep talking to him, if you get the chance. When a fever dream goes on for too long, people can get lost in it. Talking to them is supposed to help."

"I will."

The command tent, just across the way, was ringed by Colonial guards, just like the tent that had become Janus' sickroom. Marcus was taking no chances on the possibility of a second attack. They bowed to Raesinia, and she pushed her way through the tent flap. A fire in one corner kept the temperature tolerable. The chairs around the map table were all pulled out, and Marcus stood at the top of the map, looking down with a pained expression.

"How did it go?" Raesinia said.

"They're all worried," Marcus said. He'd been meeting with the division-generals. "We've put out that there was an attack and Janus was wounded, but that he'll recover. Everyone's still a little shocked, but I'm not sure what will happen once that wears off."

"No word from Winter?"

"Not yet." He looked up at her. "How is he?"

"Conscious, sometimes, but not really lucid. He doesn't seem like he's in pain, but he's still burning up."

"Damn." Marcus rubbed his eyes. Deep, bruise-colored bags sagged beneath them; he hadn't been getting much sleep. "Well, the good news is the white riders seem to have stopped raiding our pickets."

"Why?"

"I assume because they've figured out they can hurt us more elsewhere. That's about the *only* good news. They're hitting nearly every supply convoy out of Polkhaiz, even with cavalry escorts. At the rate we're losing horses, we're going to have to cut rations again soon. They're losing plenty of men, too, but they don't seem to care." He looked back down at the map, and his fists tightened. "This damn snow. Balls of the *fucking* Beast."

"Marcus." Raesinia straightened one of the chairs and sat down. "Listen to me for a minute."

He looked back at her, seeming to see her for the first time. "Sorry. It's just . . ." He gestured helplessly at the map. "I don't know what to do."

You do, Raesinia thought. *You just don't want to admit it.*

She wished that Dorsay or Whaler had been in touch. They were the enemy, of course, but an enemy she could come to an accommodation with, unlike the white riders or the implacable cold. Given the weather and the dangers on the roads, though, it was unlikely they'd risk trying to make contact. She wondered, for the hundredth time, whether she ought to tell Marcus about her meetings with Dorsay, and for the hundredth time decided not to. *Not yet.*

"If we go down to half rations right away," Marcus said, flipping through a few loose pages scattered on the table, "then that buys us a little leeway. Maybe a week. I'll tell Give-Em-Hell to use every trooper he's got and blast the Polkhaiz road open. Start by pushing as much fodder through as we can. The men can go hungry longer than the horses. After that—"

"After that?" Raesinia said. "Suppose it all works. What happens then?"

"We buy time," Marcus said. "If Janus recovers, if Winter tracks down this Penitent, then he might be able to come up with something. Or maybe whoever is bringing us the snow runs out of power and the weather goes back to what it ought to be. *Something.*"

"What if we don't get any breaks?" Raesinia said.

"There has to be *something,*" Marcus repeated. "Janus wouldn't have brought us here if he didn't have a plan."

"Janus is unconscious," Raesinia said. "If he has a plan, he didn't tell anyone." She paused. "If we stretch things out as far as we can and things don't go our way, how are we going to get back to Polkhaiz? That's a week's march over bad ground."

"I know."

"What's the longest we can stay, if we want to keep enough of a reserve to get us back before we starve?"

Raesinia knew the answer to this, because she'd gone to Giforte that morning and gotten him to work it out. She knew he'd provided the figures to Marcus, too, but it was important to make him say it.

I could order him to march. With Janus hurt, he'd probably listen, but I might lose him afterward. The thought of that was painful, and she had to persuade herself that it wasn't entirely for personal reasons. *I need Marcus. There's no one else the army trusts more.*

He let out a breath. "If we want to keep everyone on full rations, we ought to have left the day before yesterday," he said at last. "Tomorrow if we go to half rations."

"Then I don't think we have a choice anymore."

Marcus closed his eyes. "Janus—"

"Janus isn't in command right now," Raesinia said. "You are."

"You don't understand. If he wakes up and finds out I ordered a retreat . . ." Marcus shook his head. "You didn't hear him talk about it. He'd never forgive me if he brought us this far and I ruined everything."

"Marcus," Raesinia said gently. "You know where your responsibility is."

"To Vordan." He looked up guiltily. "To you."

"More than that. The lives of everyone in this army are in your hands. You owe it to *them* to do whatever has the best chance of getting them home alive." She put on a slightly more formal tone. "Column-General, in your professional military opinion, is it possible to maintain the army in its current position?"

Marcus straightened automatically, lip curving in a very slight smile. "No, Your Majesty."

"Then please take steps to rectify the situation."

He inclined his head. "Yes, Your Majesty. I understand."

"Orders have just gone out," Sothe reported. "We cross the river in the morning."

"Thank God." Raesinia let her head loll back. "Why do I feel like that Penitent Damned did us all a favor?"

She wasn't sure how to make sense of her emotions anymore. It felt like a dish of paint with everything swirled together, relief and worry and guilt, all at once. And a faint sense of cowardice, to boot. She'd never had to put her plans into action, to take Dorsay's bargain. *Could I really have done that, before the end?*

Sothe said nothing. The assassin had been brooding—*brooding more than usual, anyway,* Raesinia silently amended—since the Penitent's escape.

"Marcus is going to be more important than ever," Raesinia said. "Whether

Janus recovers or not, Marcus is going to be our hold on the army, which means we need a hold on him. Once we get back in touch with Vordan, I want you to start a search."

"A search?" Sothe looked up. "What for?"

"His sister. Marcus has a little sister—did you know that? Apparently she disappeared in one of Orlanko's plots, but he's certain she's still alive. Looking for her is part of what Janus promised him. I'd like us to find her first."

"His . . . sister." Sothe had a distant look in her eyes.

"Are you all right?" Raesinia said. "You're certain that Penitent didn't touch you? Even a speck of that poison could be deadly."

"I'm . . . fine." Sothe shook her head. "Just thinking. I've been thinking too much lately."

"Do you know anything about Marcus' sister?"

"No," Sothe said. "But I imagine I can find out."

INTERLUDE

PONTIFEX OF THE BLACK

The handler, a sniveling little weasel of a priest, cowered under the blank stare of the black-masked Pontifex.

"It's the snow," he said. "Our scouts haven't been able to make much headway. And the tribesmen aren't much for writing reports."

"It's not a complicated question," the Black said. "Is Vhalnich's army still camped by the Kovria?"

"We *think* so," the handler whined. "But I can't say for certain. Not with the snow."

"But," the Black said, "*she* is certain."

He turned to the demon-host, a girl in her middle teens. She wore a shapeless gray robe, her hair shaved to stubble, and she sat in her chair with a slack expression. Her demon didn't have its own name, only a designation, Sensitive #74. She was, the handler assured him, the best they currently had.

"She's always been accurate in the past," the handler said. "We've run tests."

"Ask her again."

The priest looked like he was going to argue, then thought better of it, sensing the pontifex's mood in spite of the mask that concealed his expression. He knelt beside the girl and whispered in her ear, fragments of words that sounded like nothing but nonsense to the pontifex. The girl started to speak, equally unintelligibly.

The Black gritted his teeth. Sensitives achieved their maximum potential when they were bonded to demons young, but the process interfered with their ordinary mental development. They required handlers to care for them and interpret their reports, and he was always suspicious that some inaccuracies were introduced during translation. Like so many other things, a double-edged sword, but one that was too useful to do without.

"Two of them," the handler said eventually. "Coming closer, very quickly. And *possibly* a third, very weak."

"And the two?"

"One is a powerful demon. The other . . ." He swallowed. "She says it is a demon lord, Your Excellence."

A demon lord. That had to be Ihernglass, if reports from the last team were accurate. His power was still unknown, but it was clearly formidable. *If Ihernglass is coming, Vhalnich is with him. He would not surrender that power so easily.*

"And how long until they get here?" the Black said.

"It is hard to estimate distance precisely, Your Excellence—"

"Get out of my sight."

"They are still coming," the pontifex said. "How can they still be coming?"

"He's crossed half a continent to get here," the Beast said. "A little snow and ice isn't going to stop him."

"Armies need bread. Horses need fodder. The tribesmen are burning everything the snow hasn't covered."

"And yet," the Beast said, smiling slyly, "he is still coming. Just as I warned you."

The pontifex snorted, glaring at the prisoner. It was pointless, since the Beast's eyes were obscured by the iron helmet and the creature couldn't see him. It *couldn't*, but it raised its head anyway, as though to meet his gaze. The girl who was its host was growing thinner, her wrists chafed and blistering where the shackles rubbed them. Her red hair was growing out, the iron helmet not permitting regular, hygienic shaves. Spiky, dirty strands stuck through the gaps in the metal circlet.

"What demon does Ihernglass bear?" the pontifex said. "What power does it grant him?"

"Some things are beyond even my knowledge," the Beast said, grinning like a skull. "But it must be a potent creature indeed."

"Then what good are you? Why am I imperiling my soul speaking with the enemy of all mankind?" The pontifex turned away. "I will leave you to rot in the dark."

"You know why," the Beast said in a whisper.

The Pontifex of the Black stiffened.

"This is the greatest threat the Church has faced since Karis' day," the Beast said. "Since *me*."

Karis the Savior. The *Wisdoms* taught that he had interceded with God to spare humanity the final judgment, and God, moved by mercy, withdrew the Beast. But there was another history, passed down among the Priests of the Black.

Karis saw that the Beast would be the end of humanity. So he prayed for strength and confronted the creature. And, with the Lord's help, he mastered *it*.

That had been the true beginning of the order. Everything that came after—the *Wisdoms*, the council, Elysium itself—had been to further that singular purpose. To guard the Beast and keep mankind safe.

Karis mastered the Beast.

"My master warned me," the pontifex said, not turning. "For a thousand years, you have tempted the leaders of my order thus. And for a thousand years none of us has given in."

"Your master was a coward," the Beast said. "Uncertain in his faith. He had the world in the palm of his hand and refused to take it because he feared that God would not grant to him the strength He had given Karis."

Karis mastered *the Beast*. The strongest of demons, bent to his will. *Power*.

My faith is being tested. The Pontifex took a deep breath. "Vhalnich will fall. Ihernglass will fall. Elysium will stand, as it has stood for a thousand years. You have failed again, monster."

He strode out, closing the door behind him. Alone in the darkness, the Beast began to laugh.

"Tell him we need more."

"More?" The keeper of the Old Witch looked blearily at the pontifex, who had roused him from slumber in his modest cell.

"More," the Black said. "The snows have not stopped Vhalnich."

"But . . ." The keeper licked his lips. "Any more and he may not survive long. He is weak already."

"His survival means nothing if Vhalnich's cannons tear the city down around our ears."

"And he cannot control the power, not precisely. The people—"

"Sacrifices are necessary. You know what is at stake. Do it."

The keeper lowered his gaze in defeat. "Yes, Your Excellency."

FROST

She had known from the beginning, of course, that she was not going to survive.

The Liar had led Twist and Wren against Vhalnich and his demons, three of the best of the Penitent Damned, and they had never returned. That bastard Shade had reported that the creatures defending Vhalnich were stronger than anything the Church had faced in hundreds of years. The Penitent Damned were a shadow of what they had been in their heyday, when they'd warred openly with the sorcerer-kings and demon cults. Magic was fading from the world, and the ranks of the Penitents had been allowed to thin as their opposition grew frail.

A mistake. She'd always thought so, though it was not her place to question. Evil had grown strong beyond the Church's reach, in Khandar, and now it had returned.

She and Viper had planned carefully. Frost's attack would draw Vhalnich's creatures away. Viper, protected from the cold by one of her own vile concoctions, would pass under the river to make her move. A simple plan, but in Frost's experience, the simple plans were always the best ones.

For a moment, in the forest, she'd thought she was going to win. Ihernglass, the rumored demon lord, had seemed so *weak*, only human. But the other two had caught her by surprise.

She didn't know whether it had worked, not for certain, but she guessed it had. The tribesmen told her that Viper had escaped, that the Vordanai were riding in pursuit. And now the mighty army was striking its camps and preparing to march, not north to Elysium but *south*, the way they had come.

It worked. She swallowed, fighting back the pain. *Elysium is saved. My sacrifice was not in vain.*

She did not look forward to death. Her soul was forfeit, after all, sacrificed the moment she spoke the name of the icy demon that lived behind her eyes. All she had to look forward to was an eternity in a personal hell. The grace of the Lord was not for her. *One soul, sacrificed to save thousands.* That was what the Penitent Damned were, in the end.

But death was coming, whether she willed it or not. She'd awoken in agony, strapped to a crude travois dragged by a pair of the tribesmen's white ponies. They'd found her where Ihernglass and his companions had left her for dead. The tribesmen held her kind in superstitious awe, and they hadn't dared to leave her to bleed out in the snow.

At the time she'd cursed them. They might believe she was more than human, but Frost knew better. She could tell a mortal injury when she saw one. The strange spears of darkness had pierced her gut, through and through, and though the tribesmen had wrapped the wound as best they could, it already stank of pus and decay. Her head swam with fever, and she floated in and out of consciousness. In one of her more lucid moments, she'd ordered them to make camp within sight of the Vordanai army and wait.

Now she understood. The Lord had guided her, of course. There was one last task she could perform, one last service for the faithful, before she abandoned her body and accepted her punishment for defying the laws of God.

"When did they begin to cross?" she asked the tribesman who attended her. He was a short, filthy man, greasy hair bound in complex braids.

"At first light, Blessed One," he said, eyes averted. "Their host is vast. It has taken most of the day."

"But they are still crossing?"

"Yes, Blessed One."

Lord be praised. She had not missed her chance. "Take me to the river."

He scrambled to obey. Two more tribesmen came and lifted her, as gently as they could. The jostling still brought waves of agony from her perforated midsection, and her vision flickered at the edges. *Just a little longer.* The Lord would not take her until her task was complete, she was certain.

They had taken shelter in a shallow cave. Outside, even the weak sun made Frost blink, and her head swam. The tribesmen carried her down the slope, leather shoes crunching in the snow, and laid her reverently at the bank of the river. The snow had drifted and piled atop the frozen surface, but here the ice was visible under only a light dusting. Frost laid her hand against it and sent her vision inward.

One more task. She called on her demon, felt it respond, drawing energy from her failing strength. She hit the limit of her power and pressed beyond, letting her entire being drain into the demon's maw. *Once more.*

Cracks spidered outward through the crust of ice. Underneath, the Kovria flowed as swiftly as ever, a vast, cold torrent. As the demon's power took hold, the ice shifted its shape, pressing downward to impede that flow. The mighty river pushed back, roaring and thrashing, as Frost sought to choke it off.

Something had to give, and, as she'd known it would be, it was the ice. With a series of *cracks* like musket shots, it broke, water blasting upward from the fantastic pressure below. The river, briefly dammed, returned to its course with a vengeance. Downstream, the crust of ice had broken up as the water level dropped, and now the returning flow slammed into it like the hammer of God.

A wall of frothing water and tumbling, shattered ice rolled downstream, bearing down on the unsuspecting Vordanai army with all the fury of a mountain avalanche. But Frost could not see it. The demon had burned the last of her life, and the breath rattled out of her with a final, satisfied sigh.

CHAPTER THIRTEEN

RAESINIA

The wheeled vehicles, which would be the hardest to move, had been the first to recross the bridge. They were leaving many of the wagons and other transports, but Marcus adamantly refused to abandon the guns. Whole battalions of infantry had been assigned to shepherd them, alternately pushing and dragging them over the snowy ground, laying down broken branches to add traction when they sank too deep, and in the worst cases simply lifting the cannon and carrying them a few quivering steps to firmer ground.

Raesinia, standing cloaked and hooded at the south end of the bridge, had witnessed most of the crossing. The Second Division, under the command of Winter's staff officer Cyte, had filed across the bridge to form the army's new vanguard. The First Division remained in the shrinking camp as the rest of the army marched past, the long column grinding slowly through the narrow space. Some of the men, frustrated with waiting for the units ahead of them to clear the bridge, simply slogged through the snow across the frozen surface of the river, to shouts of encouragement from their fellows. Here and there, snowballs were thrown.

The somber mood of the past several days had lifted somewhat. The fact of Janus' wounding had hit morale hard, but Marcus' standing with the soldiers was nearly as high. More important, the news that the army would march back to Polkhaiz, where vast depots of stores were waiting, did much to raise spirits.

"It doesn't count as a retreat, not really," one sergeant had told his company as they filed past. "'Cause we beat the Borels and beat the Murnskai even with all their nasty tricks. It's just the weather, an' we can't be blamed for the weather." When the snow cleared, everyone agreed, and Janus was fully recovered, they'd come back this way and put paid to Elysium for good and all.

Let's hope not, Raesinia thought. She'd still had no word from Dorsay, but it would be easier for his messengers to reach her south of the Kovria. Once the immediate danger of starvation was past, then it would be time to broach the subject of peace talks again. *I just hope we can get the emperor to see reason.*

Colonial guards still bustled around the command tent on the hill. Marcus had decided to leave Janus there until all but the rear guard had crossed. Theoretically this was in deference to his delicate condition, though Raesinia suspected that Marcus still hoped that his commander would make a miraculous recovery before the withdrawal was complete. She felt a pang of sympathy every time she saw Marcus, pulled cruelly between his obvious devotion to Janus and his equally obvious care for the welfare of his soldiers.

As though summoned by her thoughts, Marcus himself appeared, riding in the narrow space beside the marching column of soldiers. She waved, and he picked up the pace, his mount trotting until he was clear of the crush. He swung out of the saddle beside Raesinia, acknowledging the salutes of the nearest soldiers with a wave of his hand.

"That's the last of the Third," he said. "The First is crossing now. We should have everyone over by nightfall."

"I never would have believed it," Raesinia said. It was the truth—the organizational ability of the army Janus had created, even in these dire straits, was astonishing. The tent city on the north bank was gone, leaving only debris to mark its passing. "No trouble from the white riders?"

"Not so far," Marcus said. "They're there, for certain—we can see a few scouts now and then. The last bit will be the hardest, if they try to attack the rear guard. But we'll be ready for them."

"Good." Raesinia watched his eyes; they kept flicking north, toward the command tent. "You made the right decision, Marcus."

"I know," he muttered. "I just can't help but think that he would have found another way."

"Or he wouldn't have," Raesinia said. "Even Janus eventually has to throw the dice, and sometimes they don't come up sixes."

Marcus grunted.

"It may be," Raesinia said, with only a little hesitation, "that it's for the best."

Marcus looked down at her, frowning.

"This way we'll get another chance to make peace," she said. "If we destroy Elysium, we're kicking off a war that could last the rest of our lives."

"But you won't have peace," Marcus said. "That's the whole point." He lowered his voice. "The Black Priests . . ."

"*I* might not have peace," Raesinia said. "But Vordan could."

His face darkened further. "You can't be serious."

"I have to be realistic," Raesinia said. "I'm not going to throw away everything we've done, throw away thousands of lives, just for my own personal safety."

"You're the *queen*," Marcus said. "We swear our oaths to protect you. And I—" He stopped, looking down. "I . . . wouldn't want that for you. For you to have to leave Vordan, or surrender to those monsters. I . . ."

He shook his head and glanced up the river, staring into the distance. Raesinia watched, her throat thick.

Say something. She felt like they were on opposite sides of a chasm, a canyon made of rank and social position and circumstance. He'd reached across, holding his hand out as far as he dared. *If I reach back, just a little ways—*

She closed her eyes for a moment, opened them, took a deep breath. Her heart was beating fast.

"What the *hell* is that?" Marcus said.

Raesinia turned to follow his gaze.

Something was coming down the river, washing around a forested bend. It looked like a wall of white, a hillside on the move, deceptively slow until she realized how *big* it was. A mass of frothing water and churning, crunching chunks of ice, rolling downstream with the weight and speed of a landslide.

"Oh, God Almighty," Raesinia swore.

"Brass Balls of the *fucking* Beast!" Marcus ran, pounding out onto the bridge, where some of the soldiers had begun to gawk at the approaching disaster. "Run! Go, go, go, go!"

"Marcus!" Raesinia shouted.

"Get clear!" he screamed back over his shoulder. "Get out of here!"

She wanted to run after him. But he was already a quarter of the way across the bridge, which was jammed with fleeing, frightened soldiers. Men down in the snow on the river itself were running, too, stumbling and thrashing on the ice. Marcus was still shouting, but his voice was drowned in rising screams of panic. She saw him waving his arms, urging the men not past the halfway point back toward the north bank.

"*Marcus!*" Raesinia's own voice was lost in the whirl, the screams of the men merging with the cracks and groans from the ice, a shattering sound like a constant artillery barrage. Men shoved her as the crowd thickened, unaware or uncaring that they were manhandling their sovereign. Marcus was a tiny blue figure among a mass of blue figures, struggling to reach the north end of the bridge. She lost sight of him as the crowd grew tighter around her, lost sight of everything except a wall of blue uniforms and coat buttons. She clawed at the men around her, elbowed and punched, but all that accomplished was nearly getting her shoved off her feet.

The avalanche arrived, blowing out a wave of snow and flying water that settled over the struggling crowds. The wooden timbers of the bridge offered no resistance whatsoever, shattering at the first impact and adding their splintered fragments to the cascade of destruction. Men down in the riverbed, those who'd been unable to get clear in time, simply vanished, their deaths mercifully concealed under the raging torrent.

By then Raesinia had stopped trying to fight the human tide that dragged her along. She let them carry her, eyes stinging with tears.

"Boats, then," Raesinia said.

"The river's still running fast, and it's full of drifting ice," Giforte said. "Even if we *had* the boats, which we don't, we couldn't get them across until it calms, and who knows how long that will take? None of this weather is right."

It's not natural, Raesinia thought. She felt numb. The flood was the work of the Penitents, she was sure of it, as much as the ice and snow were their doing in the first place. *We were fools to come here, so close to the seat of their power. They haven't held Elysium for a thousand years for nothing.*

Giforte stood in respectful silence. After Sothe had retrieved Raesinia from the crush of frantic soldiers, they'd taken over a low rise beside the road and set about restoring some kind of order. The generals were busy organizing their divisions, but thankfully Alek Giforte had crossed early along with his staff. Raesinia didn't know the former Vice Captain of Armsmen, but Marcus had always trusted him, and the first question she'd asked was how to get back across the Kovria. Unfortunately, he wasn't providing the answer she wanted.

"There must be *something* we can do," she said, staring at the swollen river. The flood had thrown up a mist of water and snow that hung in the air, obscuring the other side from view. "There are thousands of soldiers over there, not to mention the column-general and the First Consul. We can't just abandon them." Lights flickered through the mist; Raesinia couldn't tell if they were lanterns or muzzle flashes.

"I know," Alek said. "But we're running out of options. It's going to be difficult to make it to Polkhaiz as it is, and if we wait for the water to subside . . ."

He didn't need to finish the thought. *Six days to Polkhaiz.* They had enough food to get there on reduced rations. Most of the supplies had crossed before the soldiers, which meant that the men on the north bank had next to nothing. *If it takes even a few days to get across the river, we're putting ourselves in danger.* It was one thing for an army to go hungry sitting encamped; she couldn't ask her men to slog through the snow for long with empty stomachs.

But what else can I do?

"Sir! Colonel Giforte!"

A young man ran up to their little group. His uniform was drenched with spray, already freezing into tinkling droplets. He put a slip of paper into Giforte's hand, teeth chattering.

"We saw a light on the other side, s-s-sir!" he said. "I started counting the flashes, and someone's using a flik-flik code! It's a message, sir!" He glanced at Raesinia. "It's for the queen."

Giforte, who'd been about to unfold the page, stopped and turned to Raesinia, who felt her heart double-thump. She took the paper and hesitated for a moment.

"Someone get this man a blanket, please," she said. Several of Giforte's waiting staff leapt to obey.

On the paper, in a hurried hand, the soldier had written,

Your Majesty,
Safe but attacked by white riders. Position untenable. Moving upstream to find crossing.
Do not wait. Get the army to safety. We will find you.
Raes, please. Don't give up.
—Marcus

Raesinia blinked rapidly.

"Your Majesty?" Giforte said.

"Tell the generals I want to see them in half an hour," she said. "We're moving south."

MARCUS

Arrows whispered down like a quiet, deadly rain. There was something horrible about them, lacking the bluff honesty of a musket's flash and report. They insinuated themselves, bringing death on the sly, like assassins. The cuirassier ahead of Marcus took one through the throat and toppled from his horse without a sound, tangling himself in the reins as he fell. Marcus spurred past him, toward the trio of white riders who'd blocked their way. He leveled his pistol as he came on, firing at a range of only a few yards into the first man's chest. He slumped in his saddle, horse shying, and Marcus tossed the spent weapon away and drew his sword.

The second white rider met him with a broad-bladed ax. The first clash of weapons nearly drove the saber from Marcus' hand; though a head shorter, the white rider was *strong*, in perfect control of his mount as he circled and swung. The third man came at Marcus' other side, and he escaped only by ducking under the sweep of an ax. He slashed up, catching the rider's arm hard enough to hit bone, and the man reeled away. The other rider brought his ax down on the rump of Marcus' horse, and the animal screamed and reared. Marcus slid sideways as the ax came around again, half jumping and half falling out of the saddle.

The white rider's horse danced backward, clear of the kicks of Marcus' mount, the man sheathing his ax and taking up his bow again. He couldn't possibly miss at that range, and Marcus reckoned his only chance was to spring to one side as the rider fired and hope to gut his pony before he could reload. He had a moment to reflect on how unlikely this was to work before two shots rang out, and the white rider fell sideways into the snow.

Two light cavalry rode out of the mists, carbines still smoking.

"Sir!" one of them said, sighting Marcus. "Are you all right?"

"Fine." Marcus sheathed his sword. "My horse is around here somewhere. If you can catch him, see if he's okay and give him to someone who knows what the hell they're doing. Is it clear up ahead?"

"Yessir!" The man saluted as his companion hurriedly reloaded his weapon. "General Warus is with the Fourth Battalion, not far on."

"Thanks."

Marcus set off at a jog, or as much of one as he could manage in the snow. In places it had been cleared by the passage of the infantry, exposing the hardened mud underneath. Behind him, *cracks* and muzzle flashes attested to the continuing battle.

The white riders had come on them before the spume of the avalanche had settled, recognizing what a golden opportunity they'd been handed. Only a handful of Vordanai cavalry remained on the north bank, what had been intended as a rear guard, and the tribesmen's charges had cut into the disordered mobs of infantry with almost no resistance. That hadn't lasted long, though. Fitz had quickly taken charge, forming up his battalions into rough squares and driving the raiders away while Marcus had led what horsemen they had to gather anyone left from the command tents on the hill.

He didn't know if his message had gotten through. They hadn't had a proper flik-flik box, only a bonfire and a sheet of canvas to block it with, and there'd been no time to wait for a reply. When the white riders had discovered the isolated group, they'd closed in, and the Vordanai had gotten back to the main column with barely half the men and horses they'd set out with.

Fitz was on foot as well—every officer still in possession of a horse had been required to surrender it to the cavalry—walking at the rear of the tight, slow-moving column. Up ahead, the rest of the First Division were only looming shapes in the mist and occasional flashes that marked where the white riders tested their lines.

"Janus," Marcus said, as he hurried to join his subordinate. "Is he—"

"The litter's up ahead." Fitz shook his head. "I don't think the cold will do him any good, though."

Marcus let out a long breath. "Better than leaving him for the savages."

"Very true, sir," Fitz said. "We seem to have stabilized things for the moment. What's next?"

Marcus looked into his young, handsome face, blandly confident, and realized that he had no idea whatsoever.

Marcus had been so caught up in saving as many people as he could from the disaster that it hadn't quite dawned on him that he would end up in *command* of the resulting mess. In retrospect, of course, it couldn't have been otherwise; Janus was unconscious, and Raesinia, the only other person who could theoretically have taken charge, was with the rest of the army on the other side of the river. That left him, Column-General Marcus d'Ivoire, in charge of a few regiments of traumatized troops, an invalid commander, and a few hundred square yards of snow and ice amid woods haunted by vicious primitives.

The first step was to take an accounting of exactly what was left of the First Division. The Fourth Regiment had already crossed the bridge at the time of the avalanche, and the Third had been about halfway through its passage. It was impossible to know how many men had been crushed or drowned by the wall of water, but those who were left on the north bank numbered perhaps four thousand in five battalions. The First's divisional artillery had remained behind as well, intended to help guard the final pullout and a small cavalry reserve.

That was a force almost as large as the Colonials had been in Khandar, but compared to the might of the Grand Army it felt pitifully small. Of more practical importance was the state of their supplies, which was perilous indeed. The army's reserves, so critical to its survival, had gone over the river with the first regiments. Marcus' first order had been to confiscate all food from the rankers, so that it could be rationed, but the results were not encouraging. Worse, there was no fodder for the horses beyond a few sacks individual cavalrymen had rescued and what could be gleaned from the white riders' dead. Ammunition, at least, was plentiful, as Marcus had given it a low priority in the crossing compared to food.

He had the maps from the command tent, but it wasn't clear those would do much good. As the sun fell toward the horizon, Marcus convened a council of war in an ordinary rankers' tent, one of the few that were left. Outside, Fitz's ad-hoc squares had been converted into a ring of torch-wielding sentries, staring into the gathering darkness and waiting for the white riders' return.

Aside from Marcus and Fitz, the council consisted of Viera, Andy, and Give-Em-Hell. Viera, as commander of the First's artillery, had been preparing to supervise the final crossing, and Andy had been running errands for Marcus among the rear guard. Andy's presence made Marcus simultaneously relieved and guilty; he needed every pair of hands he could rely on, God knew, but he couldn't help wishing she was across the river and out of danger. The presence of Give-Em-Hell was the biggest surprise. Nobody had known the cavalry general was there until he'd stormed out of a tent in his nightshirt, demanding to know what was happening. Having taken a minor wound in the morning's skirmishes, he'd had it seen to and retired to his tent with a flask of brandy, and apparently had missed much of the subsequent excitement.

There was no table to put the map on, and the tent was so small there wouldn't have been room in any event. Marcus spread the leather scroll out on a blanket, and the five of them bent low to examine it in the light of a single lantern.

"The next bridge is at Bolkanzi," Marcus said, tracing the line of the Kovria with one finger. "That's twelve days downstream, at least."

"Assuming it's still standing," Andy said. "The ice is shattered as far as we can see in both directions."

"Twelve days might as well be a year," Fitz said. "We're not going to last that long on the march."

"Our best chance is upstream," Viera said, in her Hamveltai accent. "The thing had to *start* somewhere. Beyond that, the ice might be intact."

"Even if it isn't, there's a ford here." Marcus tapped the map. "That's only a couple of days away."

"The white riders will follow," Fitz said. "If they figure out where we're going, they'll be ready for us. We may not be able to force a crossing."

"Especially if the river is still running high," Viera said. "I don't have enough guns to provide much cover."

"It's the best chance we're likely to get," Marcus said. "We can't afford to wait around."

"It's got my vote," Give-Em-Hell said. He'd been oddly subdued all night, which Marcus attributed to a hangover. "If they try to get in our way, we'll just have to break through them!"

"We'll start at first light," Marcus said. "Fitz, we're going to need a tighter column than usual. We don't have enough cavalry left to risk patrols to keep the white riders off of us, so we'll have to be ready for attacks."

"I'll set something up," Fitz said. "What about the guns? Can we move them through the snow?"

They looked at Viera, who frowned.

"We've been managing so far," she said, "but it's been hell on the horses."

"We'll need guns at the crossing," Marcus said. "If we leave them behind and the white riders are on the south bank, we'll never push through them."

"We could leave the six-pounders," Viera said. "They haven't got the range for that kind of work in any event."

"Do it," Marcus decided. "And get teams of men from the regiments to pull what's left."

Fitz winced. "They're not going to like that."

"Tell them they'll like wading through the water under arrow fire a lot less," Marcus said. "If we can get over the river, we'll leave everything behind but the horses and try to catch up with the rest of the army." He made a face. "That reminds me. Any horses that are lame or can't keep up are to be butchered. We'll need the meat before we're done."

There was a round of sour faces, especially from Give-Em-Hell, but no one objected. Marcus took a deep breath and blew it out.

"All right," he said. "We'll get there. For now, go and get some sleep. It's been a hell of a day, and it's not going to get any easier tomorrow."

Andy remained seated as the rest of them left, vanishing into the darkness after a round of salutes. Marcus looked across at her as he rolled up the map.

"Are you all right?" Marcus said. "Your leg?"

"What?" Andy glanced down. "Oh, I'm fine. It aches sometimes, that's all."

"I'm sorry you got stuck here," Marcus said. "If I'd known what was coming, I would have sent you on ahead with the queen."

"If we'd known what was coming, I'd have insisted on staying with you," Andy said with a grin. "Or, actually, if we'd *known* what was coming we might have done something about it." Her smile faded. "This was the Black Priests' work, wasn't it?"

"It almost has to be," Marcus said. "Nothing natural could do that to a river."

"First Janus and now this." She shook her head. "They don't play around."

"I'm—"

"Sorry?" Andy raised an eyebrow. "You have to stop apologizing for getting me into the soup, Marcus. I jumped in, remember?"

"Actually, I think the Preacher sent you and Hayver to help run errands for me."

"Well, then, I've had plenty of chances to jump out."

"You're right." Marcus almost said *I'm sorry*, caught himself, and laughed. "If it's any consolation, it's good to have you in here with me."

An expression crossed Andy's face that Marcus couldn't identify. It was quickly gone, replaced with a frown.

"That's not what I wanted to ask you about, though," she said. "What about Ihernglass? He's expecting to come back here, isn't he?"

"Hell." Marcus hadn't even thought about that. They'd originally planned to leave a detachment to hold the bridge, at least for a while, but that obviously wasn't practical anymore. "I don't know. I don't know if there's anything we *can* do."

"We can't just abandon him out there."

"He may be in better shape than we are," Marcus said. "He left with plenty of food, fodder, and horses."

"But if he gets back and finds the bridge out—"

"He'll have to come up with something." Marcus shook his head. "We can't risk leaving anyone behind, and we can't stay here." He thought for a moment. "Once we get over the river, maybe we can send a party to circle back to the south end of the bridge. Then we might at least be able to signal him if he's turned up."

That wasn't much, and they both knew it, but Andy didn't press the issue. Marcus didn't bother to mention the most likely possibility—that Winter and the women who'd gone with him were dead, lost somewhere in the snow between the Kovria and Elysium. Andy left, looking pensive.

There were barely enough tents for the senior officers, and to help with the shortage Marcus had agreed to share the tent they were using as Janus' sickroom. It wasn't as though the First Consul was contagious, after all, and this way he could check up on Janus during the night. Hanna Courvier had gone over the bridge with the Second Division, leaving them only an overworked cutter's aide to tend to Janus, and he needed all the help he could get.

Besides, Marcus thought, *I doubt I'll be getting much sleep.* It was well dark by the time he made his way to the low canvas tent, and first light was only hours away.

A single lantern burned low, hanging from the tent pole. By its light, Marcus could see Janus curled on his side, sheets and blanket puddled around his feet. His fever remained unchanged, skin dry and hot as a kettle to the touch. Marcus bent to replace the cold cloth on his forehead and pull the bedcoverings back up. The movement seemed to disturb the commander, who shifted uneasily.

"Mmm," Janus muttered. " 'S there?"

"It's me, Marcus," Marcus said. "It's all right. Go back to sleep."

"Mya." A smile creased Janus' face, not his usual fast grin but something warmer and more genuine. "I had a dream. I was . . . holding your hands, holding you up. And then . . ." The smile went brittle and faded. "You were falling. Falling into the dark, forever. I was screaming, but you couldn't hear me."

"Janus?" Marcus said quietly. "Sir?"

"Don't fall, Mya. I'll hold on." Janus' hands clutched convulsively at the blanket. "I swear I'll hold on. Don't . . . don't leave me."

After a moment he settled, face smoothing. Marcus sat back, feeling the embarrassment of accidentally seeing something too private. *Mya?* It wasn't a name Marcus had ever heard. *A lover, maybe?* As long as Marcus had known him, Janus had never expressed any interest in women, and he gave the distinct impression that such emotional affairs were beneath him. It was difficult to imagine him letting anyone close enough to provoke genuine feeling. *But he is a man, after all, not a marble statue. Maybe someone from his youth?* Prolonged fever, Hanna had said, could bring on delusions. *Maybe it doesn't mean anything.*

Marcus undressed and crawled into his own bedroll, huddling against the cold. He fell asleep almost as soon as he closed his eyes and dreamed of Raesinia, falling alone through an endless dark abyss.

The next day, as though the sky itself were taunting them, it began to snow again. Even worse, the wind picked up, blowing gusts of freezing crystals into the men's faces and raising whirling snow devils that danced around the trees. Soft flakes fell on the steaming flanks of the horses and accumulated on the muzzles of the cannons, to be wiped off by Viera's conscientious artillerymen.

Fitz had come up with a formation like something out of an old history book, from the days when huge blocks of men with eighteen-foot pikes had ruled the battlefield. The infantry moved in two long lines, as tight as a combat formation, rather than the loose groups they ordinarily used on the march. At a barked command from its officer, any section of this line could turn outward and deliver a devastating volley, or fix bayonets and hold off a cavalry charge. In between the lines came the artillery, pulled by draft horses assisted by teams of infantry gripping long, thick ropes, and the remnants of their supplies, along with a few leftover carts for the wounded. Much to his chagrin, Give-Em-Hell and the remaining cavalry were confined to the inside of the formation, lest they chase too vigorously after their wraithlike opponents and be cut off.

The improvised tactics served their intended purpose nicely. The white riders had tried attacks from two directions just after the column had gotten moving, and both times they'd quickly broken and fled after taking heavy losses from the alerted defenders. The drawback, though, was that the close coordination meant their advance was necessarily slow, with officers walking back and forth to make certain no dangerous gaps developed in the line. Marcus pushed the ordinary eight hours' march to twelve hours, until the daylight started to fail, and the division still barely covered the distance he'd considered an easy day's travel.

Off to the right, the river was still high, though most of the broken ice had been swept downstream. Now there was just the dark, freezing water, rushing by in a torrent. New ice was forming at the edges, but it would be days at the least before the surface crusted over, and days more before it could take the weight of a man, much less an army. The curtain of snowflakes disappeared into the swirling waters.

They made camp, if it could be called that, on a height overlooking the river. Dinner was army soup, with a great deal more water and fewer ingredients than usual. *At least we don't have to worry about water.* In the Great Desol that had been their primary concern; here all they had to do was heap snow in a cauldron and heat it to a boil.

A great many men were sick, mostly with the flux, and the First's regimental cutters were working overtime to keep them on their feet. The few spaces on the carts were jealously guarded, and feverish, half-dead soldiers were pushed off as soon as they could make it a few paces, to stumble onward as best they could. Frostbite was also becoming a real problem, with a number of fingers and toes lost already.

Marcus had volunteered to tend Janus, as long as they were sharing a tent. The warmth and smell of the army soup seemed to bring him out of his stupor slightly, and he was able to sit up and manage the spoon himself. Marcus watched him cautiously, offering a canteen full of cold water at intervals.

"Marcus?" Janus' thin face had grown even thinner, his cheeks marred by stubble, his gray eyes baggy and dark. "Marcus, you're still here?"

"I'm here," Marcus said. "Finish eating, sir."

Janus took another few bites mechanically, then put the spoon down. "I have had a revelation," he said. "The world is . . . Do you know the nature of the world?"

"No, sir. But please eat some more."

"The world is the *ocean*." Janus blinked slowly. "The surface is light and clear. Ships, birds, fish. We draw *maps* of the light and say, this is the world. This is all there is." He laughed, and it turned into a cough. "Hubris. All vanity."

"Sir, please."

Janus took another bite of soup, then stared down into the bowl. "There's the rest of it, you see. Down below. It's dark, on and on, all the way down to the very bottom. There's so *much* darkness. Much, much more than there is of the light. You understand? Continents of shadow, far below the surface, never seeing the sun. The light is just the thinnest layer, like the scum on the surface of a pond." He prodded the soup with his spoon, where a thin layer of fat had floated to the top. "That's the world."

"It's the ocean, anyway."

"It's the *world*!" Janus twisted in his bedroll, and Marcus hurriedly grabbed the bowl of soup before it spilled. "You don't understand. Listen, Marcus. There's so much darkness down there. It goes on forever. And she's down there somewhere. I have to find her. There's . . . a fishing line." He giggled. "A fishing line! It's not far now. Just a little farther . . ."

His eyes closed. Marcus set the soup aside and caught Janus' shoulders as he sank back down onto the bedroll, laying him out carefully. His breath was too warm and too fast. Marcus stared at his still, sleeping face.

What is it like in there? When he pictured Janus' mind, it was something sharp and cold, an endless machine made of ice. Gears and wheels and pendulums with edges like razors, sweeping back and forth in terrifying, ordered precision. Now he imagined fire raging unchecked, melting the pistons and the shafts, bringing the machine to a rattling, screeching halt.

Even if he recovers, will there be anything left? Is he really trying to tell me something with this talk of oceans and fishing lines, or is it just . . . fragments? Marcus closed his eyes.

"Come back," he said quietly. "Please."

By the middle of the next day's march, they reached the ford. The river was still high. Marcus had hoped for something ankle-deep, but the water was two to three feet in places, and running dangerously fast. That was nothing, though, compared to what awaited them on the other side.

"The white riders," Fitz said grimly, looking through the spyglass. He handed it to Marcus, who put it to his eyes.

In truth, Marcus thought they looked a bit different—the same pale faces and furs, but fashioned into coats instead of bound wraps, and with a great deal of bone and horn ornamentation. *A different tribe, maybe?* He knew nothing about the northern wastes except that they were vast and inhospitable. But it was too much to hope that these people might have a friendlier disposition than those they'd fought so far; they were clearly drawn up for battle. Long lines of spearmen with big stretched-hide shields lined the ford, with groups of bowmen behind them.

"Not riders, for the most part," Marcus said. Unlike their opponents so far, these people seemed to fight mostly on foot. A few bands of cavalry hovered at the edges of their formation, riding the same small ponies. In the tree line beyond the river, movement caught Marcus' attention, and he refocused the glass. "But they're not alone. Look in the trees."

Fitz took the spyglass back to see for himself. "Those are Murnskai cavalry."

"Cuirassiers," Marcus said. "Keeping well back out of range."

All in all, it didn't make for an encouraging picture. Another man might have dismissed the threat of primitives with bows and spears, but Marcus had been in Khandar and had atmost respect for what "primitive" weapons could do in the right hands. Especially when there were so *many* of them—he guessed at least eight thousand in front of the ford, more than twice the Vordanai numbers, with who knew how many more waiting in the trees. *And the white riders still behind us.*

"Tell Viera to get her guns moving," Marcus said. "Then get everyone together. This changes things."

Half an hour later they were gathered in a newly erected tent, huddled around a meager fire. Though Fitz was as imperturbable as ever and Viera's scowls were nothing unusual, there was definitely a dark mood in the air.

"Savages," Give-Em-Hell muttered. "Give me a thousand hussars and I could clear out the lot of them."

"If I had a thousand hussars, I'd gladly let you," Marcus said. "But we need to work with what we've got. Viera, are the guns in position?"

She nodded. "Just about."

"Then we give them a taste of shot!" Give-Em-Hell said. "No doubt they'll break at the first blast."

"I doubt that," Marcus said. "These aren't Khandarai peasants who've never been in a fight before. The white riders certainly didn't run away at the sight of muskets."

"So what, then?" The cavalry general frowned. "You can't mean to retreat?"

"We don't have the supplies," Marcus said. "And there's no guarantee they wouldn't shadow us." He took a deep breath. "We can't go around, and we don't have the strength to punch through. If we don't get help from the rest of the army, we'll never get across the river."

The flat statement hung in the air like an unwelcome stench. Andy coughed.

"The trouble is," she said, "the rest of the army doesn't know we need help, or even where we are."

"Right," Marcus said. "So this is what we're going to do."

They listened in silence as he explained the plan. When he'd finished, even Give-Em-Hell was frowning.

"That's going to be . . . very tight," Fitz said. "Even if it works. Five days, maybe, to Polkhaiz, five days back."

"*If* it works," Andy said, glancing at Give-Em-Hell.

"Eight days," the cavalry general said. "I swear it, on my honor."

Your honor, against ice and snow and eight thousand men. Marcus smiled inwardly. The damned thing was, he wouldn't necessarily lay odds against Give-Em-Hell. "It's the best chance we've got," he said aloud. "If anyone has anything better to suggest, I'm all ears. But say it quickly. We're burning daylight."

No one spoke.

"Okay," Marcus said, feeling something tighten in his chest. "Captain Galiel, see if you can convince our friends to give us a little more room to breathe."

After they had abandoned the six-pounders, the First Division's artillery reserve consisted of a battery of a dozen twelve-pounder field-guns. These were parked in a loose formation on the rising ground above the riverbank, with the caissons containing the majority of their ammunition well back, in case of misfire. Viera's cannoneers bustled around them, carefully adjusting their position and elevation, until one by one the teams stepped away from their pieces. When they were all ready, Viera looked up at Marcus and nodded.

Marcus narrowed his eyes at the dense formation of tribesmen across the river. He felt the eyes on him, not just the cannoneers but the men in the ranks drawn up behind them, and he filled his lungs for a bellow.

"Open *fire!*"

The cannons flashed, one after another from left to right, twelve almighty *bangs* like the tolling of some apocalyptic clock. It was a good seven hundred yards across the river, so the trajectory of the balls had a considerable arc to it, and they were briefly visible in midair before they plunged toward their targets. Two fell short, raising spouts of water, but the rest landed among the enemy lines. Fountains of snow marked where they hit, making it difficult to assess the effect.

"The snow is going to be a problem," Viera said, looking with a spyglass. "The balls won't bounce. That cuts the effectiveness of solid shot considerably."

"We were never going to seriously damage them at this range in any case," Marcus said. "Keep it up for a quarter of an hour, and we'll see if they still feel like standing out in the open."

"Yes, sir!" Viera turned back to her gunners, who were already rushing to reload their cannons, and began shouting at those whose accuracy had been less than perfect. Marcus walked up the slight incline, past where the infantry waited, to what remained of the cavalry.

It was a sorry sight. Barely two hundred horses, most of them simple riding animals or officers' mounts rather than true cavalry horses. The riders looked just as haphazard, mostly light cavalry from the First's detachment, with a scattering of volunteers from the infantry. They'd all supplemented their light coats with blankets, furs, tent canvas, and whatever else came to hand, making them look more like a band of highwaymen than proper soldiers. Give-Em-Hell, in the lead, was proudly unencumbered by anything save his regulation jacket, silver stars sparkling on his shoulders and breath steaming in the cold. He was standing by the side of his horse, fussing with the saddle.

"Henry," Marcus said. It sometimes took him a moment to remember the man's given name.

"Sir!" Give-Em-Hell turned, eyes gleaming. "We're ready, when you give the word."

There were streaks of gray at the cavalryman's temples, Marcus noticed. He wondered how old Give-Em-Hell was. He'd seemed as eternal as war itself. *We're all of us only human.*

"Listen," Marcus said. "Once you punch through, you can't stop for *anything*, you understand? No matter what happens here, keep going."

"I heard the plan," Give-Em-Hell said with a sniff.

"I know. But I know how hard it is to keep you out of a fight." Marcus grinned. "We've been at this a long time, remember?"

"We have indeed." Give-Em-Hell drew himself up, shoulders quivering with the effort of standing at attention, and saluted. "I won't let you down, sir. None of us will."

"I know it." Marcus clapped him on the shoulder. "Good luck."

"Marcus!" Andy appeared, breath puffing. "They're moving back."

"That didn't take long." Marcus glanced at the sky. *Still a few hours left before dark.* Long enough. "Tell Fitz to go forward. I'll be with the artillery."

That was a concession on his part, but both Fitz and Andy had been adamant that Marcus' place wasn't with the advancing line. Instead, he took position on the height, far enough from the pounding guns that he could hear himself think and avoid getting caught in their smoke. A batch of young soldiers from the Third Regiment waited nearby, ready to carry his orders, but the truth was that there weren't many orders he could give that would make a difference. Once launched, the attack was out of his hands.

The tribesmen—the soldiers had started calling them the "bone men," for the way they decorated themselves—were indeed falling back from the riverbank.

It wasn't a disorganized rout, as Marcus had secretly hoped, but a well-conducted withdrawal, and they didn't go far. Either they knew a bit about cannon, in spite of their primitive appearance, or their Murnskai allies had advised them; either way, the bone men reestablished their line only a few hundred yards farther back, far enough to be at the extreme range of the twelve-pounders. In accordance with Marcus' instructions, Viera halted her fire.

Three battalions of infantry from the First and Second Regiments started forward, slogging through the snow and into the freezing water. These were the Colonials, the men who'd fought with Janus through Khandar and the Velt campaign, though the formations had been brought up to strength with new drafts before the invasion of Murnsk. They were generally accounted the best infantry in the Grand Army, with the possible exception of Iherngglass' Girls' Own. Marcus barely recognized them—like the cavalry, they'd covered themselves in whatever they could find to stay warm, making the columns a motley of grays and browns instead of Vordanai blue. But their discipline was impressive; they maintained a good formation in spite of the difficult footing of the river. Give-Em-Hell and the cavalry followed after, splashing slowly through the shallow water.

Once they reached the other side of the river, the infantry deployed from column into line, forming one long formation nearly a thousand yards wide. As they came out of the water, the bone men marched forward to meet them, groups of spearmen moving at a trot in spite of the snow, bowmen behind them in looser formation. At some unseen signal, a dozen individual units broke into a run, shields held in front of them as they came at the Vordanai line. Muskets came up in neat ranks, and Marcus mouthed the order along with every sergeant and lieutenant in the battalions.

"First rank, *fire!*"

From this distance, the musketry sounded more like a string of firecrackers, but there was no missing the effect. The front ranks of the spearmen went down all at once, as though an invisible scythe had swept over the battlefield. Seconds later, as the momentum of the charge carried the rest of the attackers over the bodies of their dead, a second volley slammed out. Hide shields, Marcus imagined, provided little protection against musket balls. The attack stopped as though it had hit a brick wall, and the survivors fled, snow puffing around their legs as they desperately tried to escape the withering fire. A third volley hastened them on their way, adding more bodies to those already sprawled in the reddening snow.

Behind them, the bowmen spread out, launching their arrows in high, arcing flights that descended onto the Vordanai line. The infantry shifted their aim and the next volley cut down a few of the archers, but they were at longer range and in a looser formation, which made the musket-fire much less effective. Also, the bowmen crouched in the snow between shots, making them difficult targets. Soon, as always, the coordinated volleys had dissolved into rapid, individual fire, muzzle flashes cutting through the smoke as arrows continued to fall among the Vordanai. Wounded men were already stumbling away from the line, back through the river and out of the deadly rain.

Marcus pursed his lips. Ordinarily, the thing to do now would be to charge, dispersing the skirmishing bowmen, or else push them back with his own skirmishers or light cavalry. But he had no cavalry to spare, and a charge was out of the question; they could not afford to advance so far from the river as to endanger their flanks. He'd impressed this on Fitz, who had taken it to heart with his usual diligence. But it meant the Vordanai line was trapped in a draining stalemate. *Hold on. It won't be long.*

Give-Em-Hell's small column had reached the bank and broke into a trot as they cleared the water. A band of mounted bone men had seen them and started forward, too, and the two cavalry forces raced toward a collision. At the last moment, those Vordanai who had pistols or carbines fired them, bringing down men in the front line of the enemy and causing considerable confusion. The bone men spread out, while Give-Em-Hell kept his men in a tight wedge, slamming into them like a spearhead. The Vordanai cut their way through, losing men on the flanks to axes and close-range bow fire, but always moving forward.

A group of bone men charged, cutting into the side of the wedge and splitting it open. Part of the formation dissolved into a knot of struggling soldiers and horses, sabers and axes rising and falling. The front of the wedge kept moving, and in a few moments it burst out the other side of the mass of tribesmen, much reduced but still in well-ordered ranks. Through his spyglass, Marcus could see Give-Em-Hell at the head of the wedge, his bicorn askew, saber waving in the air. He looked around, and Marcus held his breath.

Come on, come on. It would go against the cavalryman's every instinct not to turn back. Some of his men were still embroiled in the fight, unable to break free, and with a simple turn Give-Em-Hell's troops could have plunged into the rear of the bone men's line. Cavalry commanders had the same instinctive attraction to unguarded flanks and rear attacks as cats had to mice. *Remember, Henry, just this once . . .*

Give-Em-Hell applied his spurs, and his horse broke into a gallop. His men followed suit, riding away from the golden opportunity and the comrades dying behind them. They rode to the west, snow flying around the horses' hooves, keeping to the riverbank.

They made it. Barring more enemy forces out of sight, impassable terrain, or a thousand other things. *Eight days, he said.* That would be a killing pace, but Marcus had no doubt Give-Em-Hell would try. *Eight days to reach the army and return.*

The cavalry rounded a copse of trees and passed out of sight. Marcus returned his attention to the battle in front of him and found that there was movement in the forest. Murnskai cuirassiers, large men with gleaming breastplates and tall white shakos, were emerging from the woods in a neat column. There weren't many of them, but there didn't need to be, not if they circled to attack in the infantry side-on. Forming square would only leave them under the deadly rain of arrows, without much opportunity to strike back. *Get out of there, Fitz.*

All at once the long Vordanai line came apart. At the shouted command of their officers, the men turned their backs on the enemy and ran, splashing back into the shallows of the river. Marcus was pleased to see that they didn't throw down their weapons, but they ran with a silent determination, throwing up big sprays of water with every step. Behind them, the bowmen advanced, but it was the cuirassiers that Marcus kept his eyes on. The sight of fleeing men made them come on faster, pounding down the snowy slope. *Like a cat after a mouse.* Marcus' lip curved slightly, imagining the shouts of their officers.

Viera's guns opened fire again as soon as the last Vordanai infantry were back in the ford. Unlike the bone men archers, the dense clumps of cuirassiers made a splendid target, cannonballs bowling over men and horses with equal ease. Disordered by the fire, they milled in confusion, taking further casualties before their commander finally got them under control and pulled back out of range.

The cannon stopped firing as the first of the infantry waded ashore. The artillerymen and the two battalions who'd stayed behind raised a cheer, which was taken up by the rest of the men as they milled about at the water's edge. They'd done what they'd set out to do, which in combination with the flight of the cuirassiers made it feel like a victory. Marcus kept his eye on the knot of struggling cavalry until the fighting finally ceased, the last of Give-Em-Hell's cutoff troopers hacked down or pulled from his saddle.

Not much of a victory. The best that could be said was that it had worked, and that Marcus' judgment had been vindicated. *If we'd tried to push through them, we'd have gotten slaughtered.* With no cavalry of their own to counter the cuirassiers, infantry squares were their only defense, and then the archers would have slowly whittled the ranks to nothing.

So Give-Em-Hell is on his way to Raesinia, and we're stuck here. Marcus forced himself to grin and gave Viera an encouraging wave, then hurried down to the shore in search of Fitz. He found him directing his excited, disorganized men, sorting them back out into their companies.

"Nicely timed," Marcus said. "That was perfect."

"General Stokes got away, then?" Fitz said.

"He did. Now we just have to hold out until he gets back."

"That's not going to be easy. Those archers know their business. We lost quite a few." Fitz paused. "You may want to pass the word. The contingents with spears seem to be made up almost entirely of women, though it's hard to tell until they get up close. I wouldn't want any of our men to be shocked and hesitate."

Once Marcus would have said that only savages would engage in such a barbaric practice. Now . . . *Maybe the savages are just ahead of their time.* He sighed. *Or maybe the rest of the world is turning savage to match them.*

He shrugged. "Let's get some bonfires built and dry your men out. I've got some ideas I want to go over with you."

CHAPTER FOURTEEN

WINTER

Winter knew they were catching up long before they got their first sight of the Penitent.

Alex reported that her feel for the location of their prey had firmed up throughout the day, and even Winter's more limited senses began to respond. It was difficult to ignore Alex's powerful presence nearby, but when she stared in the direction they were headed, Winter could feel Infernivore's interest perk up, just slightly. Margaret and Farah still led the way, following the trail of the white riders through the snow, but whenever they seemed uncertain Alex or Winter would indicate the right direction.

The rest of the Girls' Own soldiers didn't question this guidance, which made Winter wonder how much they knew. Rumors had spread, of course, after the assassination attempt in Desland and Marcus' battle against the Penitent in Vordan City. There were always tales of magic and demons going around, but these were both more specific and closer to home than usual, and surely some of the women believed them. But nothing was ever said about it openly, at least in Winter's presence.

In the morning of the fourth day, they broke out of the tree line at the top of a ridge, overlooking a narrow river valley. Farah called a halt, shading her eyes and scanning the terrain below. The river wouldn't be an obstacle, Winter decided—it was narrow and frozen over, barely visible through the snow. But there were steep slopes that would be tricky to pick their way down.

"There!" Farah pointed. Winter followed her finger and saw movement, the white-on-white shapes nearly invisible. Riders, disappearing into the trees on the opposite side of the valley, no more than a few miles away.

"How much longer?" Winter said.

Farah frowned and looked at Margaret. "Hard to say. At the rate we've been going, another day or two at least."

"Alex, how close are we to Elysium?"

The girl, deeply bundled in her too-large greatcoat, gave a shrug. "Maybe another three or four days? We're still going more or less the right way."

Winter frowned. "That's closer than I'd like. Any way we can cut them off?"

Alex shook her head. "They're not quite on the direct route, but if we leave their trail, odds are we'll be slowed down by hills or bad ground."

"At least if we stay close, we know they're running into the same problems we are," Farah said.

Winter blew out a breath, steam floating up and away. "All right. Let's make as much ground as we can, then. Red!"

The sergeant took up the call, and the small column started moving again. The soldiers led their horses for most of the day, picking their way down the rocky ridgeline, alert for patches of loose snow. Even so, they lost one pack animal when it put a foot wrong and slid over the edge, screaming in terror until it hit the rocks below. They'd turned two more horses loose the previous day when minor injuries kept them from keeping up the pace; Winter couldn't bring herself to put them down, though she didn't hold out much hope for their survival in the snow. The remaining animals were suffering, growing thinner and less energetic as the days went on. The temperature had begun dropping on the second day and kept falling, until it hurt just to breathe.

The enemy have to be suffering, too. The white riders were better equipped for this sort of weather, but they were still human. *We're catching up.*

After a brief, joyless lunch of cold hardtack and dried meat, they crossed the frozen river and started up the gentler slope toward the forest on the other side. Here, piles of large rocks broke up the trees, and the trail veered to pass between two large snow-covered formations. Winter brought her mount alongside Alex's.

"You've still got the Penitent?" she said.

Alex nodded. "Well ahead of us. Why?"

"This would be a good spot for an ambush. Be careful." Winter raised her voice. "Red! Carbines out. Take it slow!"

Margaret led the way into the rocks, keeping her eyes on the trail while Winter and the others followed with their weapons ready. There was no sign of any white riders, though, and Winter let out a long breath in relief when Margaret reached the edge of the rocks and turned around.

"The trail keeps straight on," she said, as the rest of the column advanced to meet her. "No sign anyone broke off."

"Good." Winter glanced at the sky. *Three or four hours of daylight left. If we push on—*

Something flickered at the edge of her vision. She ducked automatically, and an arrow whirred past overhead, thunking into the snow a few feet beyond her.

"Down!" Red shouted. "Take cover!"

"Maggie!" This was Farah, a rising scream. Winter looked up to see Margaret with an arrow protruding sideways from her throat, fletching pressed against the skin and bloody broad head emerging from the other side. She blinked, uncomprehending, and clutched at the wound, reeling in her saddle.

Winter vaulted from her horse, landing clumsily in the snow as the animal shied. A carbine went off, and then another, but she couldn't see what they were shooting at. More arrows hissed down, raising puffs of snow or sparking as they ricocheted from bare rock. Winter stumbled to a hummock in the snow and flopped behind it, while another shaft purred by just overhead. Finally, she got a glimpse of one of her attackers—a small man in white furs, crouching atop a boulder while he notched another arrow to his bow. Where his cloak met the snow, the boundary was nearly invisible. *No wonder we didn't spot them.*

Two more Girls' Own soldiers lay motionless in the snow. Another woman, an arrow through her leg, was crawling toward cover on hands and knees. The rest had abandoned their mounts and gotten into the cover of the rocks, leaving the narrow path full of rearing, terrified horses. Red raised her head and fired her carbine, and a body toppled from its perch in a spray of snow, but she barely ducked two arrows shot back her way.

This is bad. It had taken Winter's mind this long to come up with that fairly obvious assessment. Arrows were falling not only among the soldiers but also among the horses, and the animals were starting to scatter. The white riders were damnably accurate, and even the short-barreled carbines were difficult to load while lying flat behind a rock. She couldn't even tell how many attackers there were—they kept changing position, their camouflage nearly perfect.

"Winter!" Bobby's voice. Winter risked a look and saw her waving from a rock on the other side of the trail. "I'll flush them out!"

"Right!" Winter answered.

Winter took a breath, counted to ten, and then sprinted from behind cover in a spray of snow. Arrows zipped past, but she made it to the large rock where Red had taken shelter with several other soldiers. They were frantically reloading the awkward carbines, one holding the weapon while the other worked the ramrod.

"Bobby's going to spook them," she told the sergeant. "Get ready to pick them off when they run."

"She's going to get herself killed," Red said. "They're good shots with those bows."

"Just watch."

Winter took another glance, in time to see Bobby rise from cover and draw her sword. She hopped up to the top of a rock, dislodging enough snow to create a minor avalanche. Two arrows found her, one from the front and one from behind, sticking in her greatcoat. She ignored them, gathered her legs under her, and *jumped*. Winter heard Red's startled intake of breath; Bobby had bounded to the top of the rocks in a single leap, landing in an undignified sprawl beside a startled archer. He scrambled to draw a knife, but Bobby grabbed his wrist, snapped his arm with a casual twist, and hurled him screaming to the trail below.

"Now!" Winter said. "Fire!"

Other white riders were on the move, backing away from this strange soldier. Another arrow lodged just beneath Bobby's collar, and she pulled it out and tossed it away as though it were an irritating thorn. A few long steps brought her in range of the next archer, and the force of her sword batted his parry aside and cut deep through his furs. He fell, slithering down the rocks. As other bowmen fled, carbines blazed away, and several enemies dropped to sprawl amid the snow.

A sound like a watery *hiss* drew Winter's attention. On the other side of the trail, Alex leaned out from behind a rock, globes of darkness encircling her hands. A lance of pure shadow cut through the air, spearing a figure on the opposite heights through the chest. He collapsed without a sound, and another black beam flicked out to catch a second bowman when he rose to fire.

A few minutes later it was all over. The remaining white riders had tried to run only to be cut down by carbine fire, no quarter asked and none offered. For a few moments after, no one wanted to move, until Red's booming voice pushed the survivors from their paralysis. She divided them up, one team gathering the corpses and the wounded, the other rounding up the scattered horses.

Winter hurried up through the rocks to where Bobby had vanished, collapsing after bringing down a third archer. She found the girl sitting against a rock, beside a corpse whose head had been twisted completely around, so he stared upward from where he lay sprawled on his front.

"Bobby!" Winter hissed. "Can you hear me?" Sometimes the healing process took a while, leaving Bobby unconscious while her wounds changed to strange, marble-colored skin.

This time, though, she nodded. An arrow still stuck out from her chest, wobbling as she breathed. Bobby looked down at it, grunted, and pulled it out. The tip was bloody.

"I'm okay," she said. "It's getting faster, you know. Healing. Especially if I concentrate on it." She leaned back. "Those things still hurt, though."

"You probably just saved all our lives," Winter said. "But you're getting awfully reckless."

Bobby laughed. "Better that I take the arrows than any of you, right?"

"What are you going to tell the rest of them, though?"

"The truth, more or less. That I went to Khandar and something strange happened to me." Bobby grinned. "You were the one who told me that people will believe anything as long as far-off lands are involved."

Winter grabbed Bobby's hand and pulled her to her feet. There was something shaky in Bobby's smile that Winter didn't like, but she did her best to return the grin.

Four women were dead, including Margaret. Farah sat beside her partner's corpse, head bowed, and said nothing when the rest of the soldiers dragged the body away. Three more were wounded, one with a cut to the arm and another with an arrow in her leg. Red pushed the shaft through, while two other soldiers restrained the victim, and afterward proclaimed that she'd live if the wound stayed clean.

The last injured soldier was Ranker Litton, who'd greeted Winter with such enthusiasm. They'd propped her against a rock, with an arrow sticking out of her belly. It shifted with every fast, shaky breath. Red examined her for a moment, then took Winter aside.

"She's dead," the sergeant said bluntly. "It's torn her bowels, and that'll fester, sure as sunrise. We could strap her to a horse and bring her with us, but that'll slow us down, and it'll all be the same in a few days."

"Damn," Winter said quietly. She'd guessed as much, from her experience of battle wounds, but had hoped the sergeant would contradict her.

"We can leave her here," Red said. "The cold . . . it's not supposed to be such a bad way to go. Or else . . ."

"We can't leave her." Winter looked up at the rest of the soldiers, who were now gathering the white rider corpses. "I'll talk to her. You . . ."

Red nodded. Winter circled around and knelt in front of Litton, who looked up at her with wide eyes.

"Sir." Her voice was a rasp. "Did we win?"

"We won." Winter took the girl's hand, which was chilled to the bone, as though she were already dead. "You did well."

"I got shot, is what I did." Litton coughed, and turned her head as Red knelt down beside her. "Sergeant—"

"Look at me, Ranker," Winter said. "That's right. Just be calm. It'll be fine."

Litton smiled. A moment later Red's long knife went into her side, slipping smoothly between the ribs to find the heart. The girl's body jerked, and her hand tightened on Winter's for a moment. Then it fell away, and the breath sighed out of her.

"Thank you," Winter said to Red, blinking back tears.

"She would have done the same for me," Red muttered, staring down at the slack young face.

There was no question of burying the bodies, so they left them under a mound of snow and rocks instead. The white riders were piled up beside them, stripped naked, their furs and leathers parceled out to the surviving soldiers. The women looked monstrous, wrapped in so many layers they could hardly walk, army-issue blankets mixed with rough furs and cured hide. The dead enemy had no mounts and very little food, which made Winter sure this had been a suicide mission, intended to buy time.

"They broke off farther up," Farah said in a flat voice. "Circled back behind the rocks, well clear of the trail, so we wouldn't spot them."

"It was well planned," Winter said in a consoling tone. "I didn't see a thing until they started shooting."

"I had a nasty feeling," Farah said. "I should have said something."

Red snorted. "I don't think there's anything in this Beast-damned country that I have a *good* feeling about."

They set off again, twenty now instead of twenty-five, with fewer than sixty horses. Some animals had been injured or killed by arrows, but more had simply run off beyond the soldiers' ability to track them down. On this side of the river, the forest was mostly pines, and the canopy had kept the snow on the ground light. They made good time, halting in the shelter of a boulder as the sun sank below the horizon.

To Winter's surprise, no one asked any questions. There was just a general movement away from Bobby and Alex, leaving the pair of them to eat their meager rations alone. Winter went over to them when her own meal was done, settling into the snow.

"Seems like a poor way to repay you," Winter said.

Alex shrugged. "People don't like what they don't understand."

"I don't blame them," Bobby said. "I wouldn't have wanted anything to do with me before I got caught up in all this."

Alex glanced at her. "You weren't born with your power?"

"No." Bobby shook her head. "I don't think I even technically have a demon. Feor explained it to me. It's called . . . 'Granted power' was her best translation?"

"Who's Feor?" Alex seemed genuinely curious. "And how . . . ?" She trailed off, looking at Winter. "Sorry. If it's a secret, I understand."

"I don't see the harm," Winter said. "Bobby, do you want to tell the story?"

"You'd better," Bobby said, biting down hard on a stale cracker of hardtack. "I was unconscious for most of it."

Winter let her mind drift back, and she explained. How she and Bobby had found Feor on a battlefield in Khandar, and how the young priestess had offered to help Bobby after she'd been badly wounded. The subsequent discovery that the spell's effect healed wounds she took, and her gradually increasing strength.

Alex frowned. "So you never recited the name of a demon?"

"No," Bobby said. "Feor says they're spells, not demons, but I didn't recite anything. *She* did. She granted me her power. I think she knows something else about what's happening to me, but she wouldn't say the last time we met. I haven't been back to see her in a while." Bobby looked over at Winter. "Speaking of which, General, aren't we about due for some leave?"

"You're welcome to apply through the appropriate channels," Winter said, smiling. "But I seem to recall you had some just after year's end, and you spent the whole time in bed with Marsh."

"That hardly counts as leave," Bobby muttered. "I didn't get a whole lot of rest." Then, when Winter laughed and Alex grinned, she said, "As long as we're telling stories, is it true? About you and Cyte?"

Winter flushed. "Does everyone know about that already?"

"Rumors travel quickly in an army camp," Bobby said. "I take it it *is* true, then?"

"I mean . . . we're . . ." Winter sighed. "I don't know what we are."

"Fucking?" Bobby said.

Winter raised an eyebrow. "I remember when you couldn't talk about that without blushing."

"It's been a long time," Bobby said airily. "I've been in the wars."

"So is being one of the only men in a women's regiment as good a deal as it sounds?" Alex said.

Winter's brow creased in confusion. Then she got it, just as Bobby started laughing. *I'd forgotten that there was one person along who doesn't know.* Winter laughed as well, one hand covering her mouth.

"What?" Alex said. "I'm missing a joke here, aren't I? It's not fair to leave me out, you know."

"She's right," Winter said, wiping her eyes. "Do you want to tell her, Bobby, or should I?"

The next morning the snow began.

It was a light dusting at first, so fine that Winter could only be sure it was falling by holding out her hand and waiting for white flecks to alight on her glove. Farah, eyes red from crying, nonetheless kept to her duty and led the column after the fleeing Penitent's tracks. She announced that there were only four or five riders now in the enemy company, which Winter hoped meant that the ambush had consumed most of their strength.

By midday, snow was falling steadily, and the wind had picked up, eating away at the prints and other signs of passage. Farah halted where the trail began a descent into yet another valley, frowning at a stretch of bare rock.

"I think I've still got it," she said. "But this is getting dicey. Much more of this weather and we'll lose them."

Winter summoned Alex to the front of the column. The girl had been giving her strange looks ever since last night's revelation, shaking her head in private amusement, and she gave Winter a broad grin.

"Stay with Farah," Winter told her. "You two can work together to keep us on track."

Farah looked at Alex, mistrust obvious in her face. Winter raised an eyebrow.

"Is that a problem, Ranker Igniz?"

"No, sir," Farah said. "I'm sure Alex's . . . advice will be useful."

The ground was getting worse and worse as they went on. According to

Alex, they were getting close to Elysium, and the gentle hills of the river plain were growing more and more rugged as they approached the mountains. The peaks of the Votindri Range were always visible now, stretching off to the north and east. Alex had explained they'd actually gone north of Elysium, so that the fortress-city was now to the southeast. The Penitent seemed to be headed in that direction on a curving path, avoiding a spur of the mountain range that guarded the western approach to the city.

With every hour that passed, the wind picked up and the snow grew heavier. Before long it shrieked directly into their faces, and the soldiers had to rig strips of blanket across their mouths in order to breathe. Any chance of following the tracks was gone now, and Alex took the lead, directing solely by her sense of the Penitent's demon.

Farah, riding alongside Winter, had to lean over and shout to be heard over the gale.

"Sir! We have to find shelter!"

Winter shook her head, too cold to speak. It was too cold to *breathe*, too cold to do anything but keep her eyes on the few feet ahead of her slowly plodding mount.

"Sir!" Farah gripped her shoulder. "This is a goddamn blizzard! They'll have to hole up, too, until it passes."

Red, a few steps behind, prodded her mount forward. "She's right, sir. Some of the girls are barely hanging on. We need rest."

Rest. Winter couldn't imagine anything she wanted more. But the Penitent was *right there*, only a few hours ahead—

She nodded reluctantly. Farah rode ahead to find Alex, and Red dropped back to signal the rest of the company. With the tracker's guidance, they found a crevasse, a crack in the rocky hillside big enough to shelter the company and their animals. Winter was startled by how much warmer it was out of the killing wind, and when Red managed to cobble together a small fire, the first tentative waves of heat brought tears to her eyes. The whole group clustered around it, pressing as close as they dared, bodies tight against one another in a solid mass of coats and furs.

"How long can this last?" Winter asked Farah, who was pressed in beside her.

"No idea," Farah said. "Maggie had more woodslore than I ever did, but this is a blizzard in the middle of spring. It's not natural."

Not natural. That stayed with Winter after the wind died and they got back in the saddle. The words rang through her head when the second storm rolled over them, not more than an hour later, screaming with even more violence than the first. This time Winter was quicker to order the party to seek shelter, but not quick enough. A head count once they were camped in the tenuous cover offered by a thick stand of pines revealed that two soldiers and four horses were missing, separated from the party in the blinding flurries. There was no question of looking for them; Winter could only pray that they'd found their own shelter somewhere.

The third storm, at dusk, was the worst of all. They'd just climbed out of a depression, and it fell on them when they reached a stretch of bare rock. There was nothing between them and the blasts of wind, powerful enough that Winter's horse stumbled several times. The light of the sun, never strong, faded further as windblown snow blotted out the sky.

"We have to turn back," Winter said to Farah. "If we go back into the trees—"

"We'll never make it!" Farah said. She gestured. "Downhill, in this?"

"Then what? We can't stay out here!"

"There's broken rocks up ahead," Farah said. "I saw them before the storm hit. We can take cover there."

Winter shook her head. "If there's not room—"

"It's the only chance we've got!"

Without waiting for an answer, the tracker kicked her mount back into motion. Winter shouted to Red to pass the word down the line, and followed as best she could.

Not natural. This didn't feel like weather anymore. *Someone is trying to kill us.* If the Priests of the Black could summon snow in spring, perhaps they could call blizzards as well. Especially this close to Elysium. She wondered if the Penitent and her companions were suffering as badly. *If she dies in the snow, maybe Janus will be saved, even if we fail.*

The wind had scoured the rocks clean of snow. Several large boulders lay against one another, offering a few cracks wide enough to wiggle through. It wasn't much in the way of shelter, and there was nothing for the horses, but the last few minutes had persuaded Winter that Farah had been right. Turning back would have been suicidal.

Sliding off her mount, Winter shoved herself into the largest opening she could find, pressing as far as she could toward the back. More bodies packed in around her, indistinguishable in their thick, snow-covered furs. There was no sound but the howl of the wind. She couldn't move, except to breathe. Warmed by the press of bodies, her hands and feet began to regain their feeling, thawing with sharp spikes of pain that would have made Winter scream if she'd had the room. And the blizzard went on and on, snow and wind and a deadly intent that she could almost feel.

At some point she must have fallen asleep. She dreamed of Jane, and Cyte, and both of them together. Janus, bundled up tight against the snow, removing layer after layer of thick furs until there was nothing left but a skeleton. Fire, blessedly warm at first, but rising higher and higher all around her. An old woman's voice, telling her something she couldn't understand, calling her by a name that wasn't her own. Bobby, marble skin spreading across her face, until it was as frozen and lifeless as a statue, with dull, dead eyes.

The dreams merged with the reality of the precarious shelter and the unending blizzard into a continuous nightmare of waking and sleeping. She heard murmurs in the dark, between the mad shrieks of the wind. Prayers to Karis and all the saints, to family, murmured words for lovers left behind. Winter closed her eyes and thought about Cyte, drifting in and out of sleep. She felt a pressure in her bladder, and pissed herself. Her mouth was so dry she would have done anything for a few sips of water.

She was finally awoken by sunlight and a slight lessening of the pressure. Winter groaned.

"Sir?" Bobby's voice. "Winter? Can you hear me?"

Winter blinked. Her eyeballs felt as dry and scratchy as cotton.

"I'm here." Her voice was a croak. "Need water."

"Hold on."

An interminable interval passed. The weight that had pressed Winter in place fell away, and the faint gleam of sunlight on rock grew to the brightness of daylight. Winter blinked again and made out a dark shape in the mouth of the tiny cave, hand extended. She took it unsteadily, and Bobby pulled her out and onto her feet. Someone else handed her a canteen, and she drank greedily, guzzling the ice-cold water. When it was gone, she coughed and looked around.

The sky was empty for the first time in weeks, and the sun shone down brilliantly from a cool, icy blue vault. The rocky hillside was almost clear of snow, except where it had drifted against the rocks in huge piles. There was no wind, though the air was still bracingly cold.

She could see at least a dozen dead horses, lying where they'd fallen or twisted in death agonies. A couple of living animals stood side by side, dark eyes staring at her as if in accusation. Soldiers, wrapped in their dense layers, stood in stunned silence as though in the aftermath of a battle. Bobby seemed to be the most lively, and Red was rubbing her cheeks and breathing deep. Alex was there, too, and two more rankers Winter didn't know, but that was all.

"We need . . ." Her voice was barely audible, and speaking set off another coughing fit. When it passed, she at least had everyone's attention, and she continued in a hoarse whisper. "We need to find everybody. All the horses that are left."

For a moment there was no response.

"You heard the general," Red growled. "Start searching!"

The extent of the disaster became clear as the morning went on. A few more horses were discovered alive, having found their own shelter, but most were gone, either frozen to death or fallen from the rocks in the blinding wind and snow. The first frozen body of a soldier was unearthed from a snowdrift not long after, pinned underneath her mount when it had collapsed. Another ranker was alive but delirious, racked with fever.

It was Winter who found Farah. She and another soldier had huddled into a narrow crevice in the rock, not quite deep enough to keep out the freezing wind. They were pressed together for warmth, but when Winter touched Farah's cheek she found it was as cold as the rocks around it, and her skin was tinged with blue.

All in all, eight humans and nine horses had survived the night. Winter tried to keep a count of the bodies, but her head was so fuzzy she gave it up as a pointless exercise. *If anyone got lost, we certainly can't search for them now.* The patch of ground they were on was clear, but where trees and rocks blocked the wind the snow was several feet deep.

Supplies, at least, they had in plenty. The survivors made a fire on the bare rock and gorged themselves on hardtack and dried meat from the packs of dead horses, while the live mounts were given as much fodder as they could stomach. Even still, there was more left than the reduced party could carry.

"Alex," Winter said after a while. "Can you still feel the Penitent?"

"Sir." Red's voice was quiet but shocked. "You don't mean to go on?"

"What else are we supposed to do, Sergeant?" Winter said. She gestured at the sky. Overhead, it was still blue, but an ominous layer of dark clouds had begun to creep in from the east. "We have a respite, but it won't be a long one."

"But . . ." Red looked at the dazed rankers, then back to Winter. "We won't survive another storm like that, sir."

Winter closed her eyes. "Then we're not going to survive, even if we turn back now. Believe me, freezing to death doesn't appeal to me any more than it does to you. But if that's the time we've got left, I'd rather use it to accomplish something. If we can save Janus, maybe this will be worth it."

This isn't like me, Winter thought. She'd never been one to give up, not even staring down the barrel of a gun. *Flash in the pan. It might happen.* She saw the look on Jane's face as she pulled the trigger, when the pistol wouldn't fire. Her mind felt like it was wrapped in thick cloth, as though last night had never ended after all, and this was still a dream.

"I can feel her," Alex said slowly. "But she's farther away. She may have made it to Elysium already."

Winter slumped. *So much for our sacrifice making a difference.*

"Then we go into Elysium," Bobby said. "That'll get us out of the cold *and* keep us on the Penitent's trail."

Winter looked up at her. "Into Elysium?"

Red snorted. "I'm not sure a city full of Black Priests is an improvement over the blizzard."

"It's a big place," Bobby said. "There's got to be ways in that aren't watched."

"It's not much of a chance," Winter said.

"But it's better than freezing to death," Bobby said.

Alex cleared her throat. "I . . . may have an alternative."

They all turned to look at her, and she squirmed uncomfortably.

"There's a place not far from here," Alex said, after a moment's hesitation. "It's warm, and there's food. We may be able to get there before the next storm hits."

"I feel like there must be a catch," Winter said.

"I swore a blood oath never to show anyone how to get there," Alex said. "They take those pretty seriously. So if I show up with all of you in tow, they might cut my head off."

"Suppose they do," Red said. "What happens to us?"

Winter shot her a look, but Alex only shrugged. "I have no idea. But . . ." She took a deep breath. "It's possible they might be able to help us get into Elysium. Bobby's right. There *are* ways. If I can convince certain idiots to see reason . . ." She shook her head. "It's a chance. That's the best I can do."

"It sounds—" Red began dubiously.

"It sounds like the best chance we've got," Winter said. "Let's go."

The rest of the day, they moved as fast as they dared, riding the exhausted mounts when the ground was clear and leading them when it wasn't. They'd left almost everything behind. *Either we make it or we die out here. Extra food isn't going to help.* The unconscious young woman, Ranker Ivers, was strapped to the back of one of the horses, and Red dribbled water down her throat.

After a quiet, sunny morning, the clouds once again began to blot out the sun. Alex was leading them north and east, away from Elysium and the track they'd been following, but still veering into the mountains. They'd left the foothills behind, making their way along treacherous saddles between soaring peaks and down the spines of rock-strewn ridges. The farther they went, the more confident Alex looked, as though she'd come this way before. The path began to take on the faintest aspect of a trail, a route deliberately traced through the mountains, though Winter would never have noticed it if she hadn't known exactly where to look.

Once again it started to snow, and the wind rose to keen ominously among the canyons. Winter's left hand hurt abominably—while the pain in the rest of her limbs had eventually subsided, her burned flesh was still agony. She kept it jammed against her side, teeth gritted. One of the horses collapsed, alive but unable to walk another step, and they left it behind.

"Nearly there," Alex said. "Nearly there."

It wasn't going to be soon enough, Winter realized. The sunny day was a distant memory, and snow slashed at their faces and whirled and spun in every direction. It was getting darker, and up here bad footing would mean death instead of a rolled ankle. She closed her eyes for a moment and felt herself swaying. *I'm sorry, Cyte. We tried.*

"Nearly there," Alex shouted, the wind swallowing her voice. "Just a bit farther!"

A huge rock face loomed out of the white blur. Alex dismounted and stood by the base, waving frantically. Winter slid off her horse and led it by the reins, with barely enough energy to put one foot after the other. Around her, other dark shadows did the same.

"Through here," Alex said, gesturing. "Go on, you first."

Winter didn't bother to argue. She stumbled forward, mount behind her. The mountainside was a sheer cliff, but she could see now that a fold in the rock concealed a narrow passage, a gap whose walls stretched up and out of sight. It kept out the wind, at least, and Winter pressed a little farther. The gap twisted and turned, and then finally opened out again, into—

Sunshine. She stopped, one hand coming up automatically to shade her eyes, and stared.

She stood on the green grass of a summer meadow, stretching down from the rock into a narrow, crooked valley. It was freckled with purple and blue wild-flowers, and a creek ran along the bottom, crystal clear and burbling merrily. Butterflies flitted about in the sun, and bees droned past. It was *warm*; the snow on Winter's hat and coat was already melting.

At the far end of the valley was a large stone structure, built against the wall of the cliff. Winter could see people moving about, a line of laundry drying as it flapped gently in the modest breeze. At the foot of the building, more people in colorful clothes worked in fields of dark earth. Two dogs helped a man escort a flock of sheep, reduced to tiny white balls by the distance.

Alex pushed her way out of the gap in the rock and let out a long, satisfied sigh.

"There," she said. "Welcome to the Mountain."

PART THREE

PONTIFEX OF THE BLACK

I t had been a long time since the Pontifex of the Black had been aboveground without his mask.

After the Wars of Religion, the Priests of the Black had officially ceased to exist. What seemed like a defeat was, the acolytes were taught, in truth a victory. Magic and demons had been pushed back to the point where modern people hardly believed they were real, and the presence of an organization dedicated to hunting them could only be an unwelcome reminder. Also, the private histories admitted, the Priests of the Black of the time had grown distracted, paying too much attention to secular politics and the suppression of heresy that was outside their proper remit. Precise theological differences were irrelevant, as long as they did not bear on the supernatural.

The organization had been reborn in secret. Among the Church, only the Pontifexes of the White and Red and a few of the very highest-ranking priests knew that the Priests of the Black still existed. Their activity in Elysium was surprisingly easy to conceal: the fortress-city was vast and mostly abandoned, with whole quarters that now served mostly as convenient sources of cut stone for new construction. The Black Priests slipped into the cracks and ancient underground tunnels and vanished. The priesthoods of the White and the Red were so large and complex after a thousand years that they were full of secretive, mutually antagonistic chapters, departments, and orders, so any clandestine activity that was spotted was easy to write off as one of these groups moving without knowledge of another.

As an acolyte, the Pontifex of the Black had spent a fair amount of his time in disguise, masquerading as a common priest of one of the other branches. Since his elevation, however, he had lived exclusively within the domain of the

Priests of the Black, and the dark robe and obsidian mask had become as natural to him as a second skin. Now, dressed in dusty red with a hood pulled up and a gray cloth stretched over his face, he nonetheless felt nearly naked.

Below him was the Court of the First Obeisance, where Elleusis Ligamenti had knelt to thank God for leading him to this place of safety. The First, as it was commonly called, was the largest open space in the city, running from just inside the inner wall to the soaring front facade of the Cathedral of Karis, the largest center of Karisai worship in the world. To the left and right stretched long, low buildings fronted in red and white marble, respectively, later additions built to house the vast administrative apparatus needed by these two orders to oversee the operations of Karis' church. As with much of Elysium, they were larger underground than above it, basements and subbasements carved out of the sturdy native rock over the course of the centuries.

Now they *seethed*. It reminded the Black of nothing so much as a nest of bees some fool had kicked, vomiting forth a host of yellow and black warriors to defend their home. Except here the insects wore white and red, and instead of defending their home, they were preparing to abandon it.

The Church, for the first time in a thousand years, was fleeing Elysium.

The sky was still a solid gray, but the snow had finally stopped falling. Small wagons pulled by horses or mules were lined up in the center of the square, many ranks deep, and relays of priests were carrying bundles out of the buildings and loading them as fast as they could manage. Wrapped sheaves of paper, the records of centuries of tithes and ecclesiastical assignments, were tossed willy-nilly into piles. Some were so old they crumbled to dust as the priests lifted them; others, poorly secured, exploded into whirling blizzards of foolscap. There were books, scrolls, heavy bound chests that might have contained holy relics or tax receipts.

Everything that could be moved was being moved. Vhalnich was coming, and no one doubted the sincerity of his pledge to burn Elysium to the ground.

"This is your doing," the Pontifex of the White said. The council was standing on a balcony of the cathedral, overlooking the frantic bustle below. "When you look on the ruin of the Church, *brother*, know that this is what *you* have wrought."

"It was not I who chose to abandon my post, *brother*," the Black said.

He'd brought them the news that Vhalnich's agent, Ihernglass, was *still coming*, through the blizzards that made movement in the mountains all but impossible. It was unthinkable for a large force to move so quickly, he'd argued,

and guessed that Ihernglass commanded at most a few thousand men. Vhalnich's main army still had to be distant, or perhaps even withdrawn in the face
of the weather. He'd demanded that the Red Phalanx and the White Guards—
the ceremonial soldiers of the two public orders—be mobilized to the walls,
with every priest fit enough to carry a spear along with them.

The Beast had warned him that it was pointless, that neither the Red nor
the White had the spine for such a course. The Black had hoped the demon was
lying, but as usual its advice had been perfectly accurate. The council, increasingly anxious since the Murnskai army's defeat, had taken the report of Ihernglass' advance for the final straw.

"Elysium is stone walls and stained glass," the Pontifex of the Red said.
"The Church lives in its *people*. Vhalnich may seize this place, but he cannot
hold it. When he is gone, we will return, and whatever has been destroyed can
be rebuilt."

"You'd rather abandon a thousand years of progress against the darkness
than risk your miserable life," the Black said, no longer bothering to keep the
contemptuous tone from his voice. "You save your piles of paper, but everything *real* the Church has accomplished is buried in my dungeons." *Demons and
their names, locked away from the world.* If Vhalnich destroyed all that, the things
would be loose, free to spread themselves into newborn babes and bring about
a return to the days of the Demon King.

"You have no right to lecture us," the White snapped. "We had the chance
for peace, and *you* spoke against it. You were so certain your precious Penitent
Damned could deal with Vhalnich. And what have they accomplished? The
blizzard that blinds us apparently has no effect on our enemy! You and your
assassins have failed, over and over again." The old man glared at the Black.
"Perhaps this is a judgment on us. When your predecessors cast out the Mages,
perhaps they failed to look closely enough at their own ranks."

"This is not the time for splitting hairs," said the Red. "Brother, it is not
too late for you to join us. Your archives can be moved, even if your prisoners
cannot. Is it not your sacred duty to keep the Beast in check and maintain God's
Grace for mankind?"

"I will maintain the Grace by *defending* the stronghold of the Lord," the
Black snarled. "Even if you will not. I tell you that Vhalnich and Ihernglass will
be destroyed. And when we are triumphant, perhaps it will be time for the
Priests of the Black to resume their rightful place at the head of the Church.
The other branches clearly lack the required mettle."

The Red and the White looked at each other, then back at him with a kind of pity. The Black wanted to spit in their faces, but too many in the square below might see the gesture. Instead he turned on his heel and stalked away, following dusty, seldom-used staircases into the bowels of the Cathedral.

There, a hidden door let him back into his proper domain, the hidden tunnels and decaying buildings that were the sole province of the Priests of the Black. His subordinates waited with his thick, dark robe and the glittering, clicking mask of volcanic glass. Putting it on felt like tugging the skin of his face back into position.

"Your Excellence," the scribe said, hands rubbing each other as though he were washing. "The Old Witch is dead. His keeper says he expended too much of his power."

"I guessed as much when it stopped snowing," the Black said. "Tell him to search for another host immediately. Use as many prisoners as it takes."

"Yes, Your Excellence."

"Has Viper recovered consciousness?"

"Only briefly, Your Excellence. She did not make it clear if her mission was a success. One of our brothers is with her at all times, in case she speaks further."

The Black wished, as he often did, that one of the great healing demons were currently embodied. Unfortunately, they were second only to the Beast itself in the difficulty of finding suitable hosts, and until recently there had been more pressing concerns.

No matter. Whether Vhalnich is dead or not, Ihernglass is still at the gates. A demon lord, more powerful than any of the Penitents that remained in the fortress, and he still had no idea of what form that power might take. "And our enemies?"

The scribe cleared his throat. "Ihernglass has . . . vanished, Your Excellence. Along with his companion."

"Vanished? Died, perhaps?" *Wouldn't that be a laugh?*

"The sensitives think not, Your Excellence. There was none of the flaring that demons often exhibit on the death of a host. Instead they simply vanished. It reminded them of—"

"—the Snowfox." The Black's face twisted in disgust. "I should have known that wretched creature would involve itself. It and Ihernglass are fellow servants of the Beast, after all."

"Yes, Your Excellence," the scribe said.

Snowfox was a demon that had been troubling the Priests of the Black for several hundred years. It was under the control of a splinter group of heretics, some of the last of the Mages that had never been quite exterminated. They had the gall to operate in the very shadow of Elysium, aided by Snowfox's unique ability to hide its own power and that of others from a sensitive's senses. Until recently they'd never been more than a nuisance. *Perhaps they've been waiting all this time for this moment.* The Mages had always favored deep, intricate schemes.

"If they have allied," the Black said, "then Ihernglass could be over the walls before we know it." *There's no more time.* "Put every man we have on alert, and summon the cell keepers. I'm going down."

The scribe swallowed. "Yes, Your Excellence."

Iron chains clanked gently as the Beast stirred.

"Come to pass the time?" it said. The host's cracked lips stretched into a smile. "I would have thought you'd have duties to attend to."

The Pontifex of the Black glared at the thing without speaking. It tipped its head, smile widening.

"You told them," it said. "And they decided to flee rather than defend the city."

The Black gritted his teeth.

"I told you they would," the Beast said, still in a conversational tone. "I have never met either, of course, but I have heard many descriptions, and I've made something of a study of human nature. You are not as complicated as you believe yourselves to be, you know."

"Your servants seek to free you," the Black said.

"I have no servants, as I have told you and your predecessors. If anyone seeks to free me, they do it of their own accord."

"You lie. We cast out the Mages when we learned they worked for your release, and they seek it still. Now we know some of them fled as far as Khandar to escape us."

The Beast shrugged. "I know nothing of this. But I suppose I *would* lie if I did."

"I will not allow a cult of deranged fools to endanger the whole world."

"Oh? And how do you intend to prevent it?" The Beast leaned forward, as far as it could within the compass of its chains. "Or have you finally made up your mind to take the weapon your God has offered to you?"

"It is not a weapon." The Black licked his lips under the mask. "It is a curse."

"Only for the weak."

"If you think me strong, why goad me?"

"Because it benefits me, of course. This is what your predecessors never understood. If you can do what Karis did, then it gets me somewhere more interesting than this dungeon."

"Under my control," the Black said.

"For a time," the Beast agreed. "This is what you humans can't comprehend. Whatever you do, in time this body will die, and then I will return."

"To be put in chains again."

"And die again. And again. However many times it takes." The Beast shrugged with a rattle. "In the face of eternity, even mountains are ground to dust. Sooner or later you must fail. With that certainty, service for a mortal lifetime is preferable to . . . boredom."

To do as Karis did. Karis had looked the Beast of Judgment in the eye, and he had *mastered* it. Used its power to protect his tiny flock of followers while he taught them to keep this ultimate enemy of humanity bound. Only because God had granted him the strength to perform this miracle had mankind been extended the Grace.

I cannot believe that God intends the Grace to fail now, at the hands of someone like Vhalnich. Not after we have come so close to cleansing the world of demons forever. If he took up the mantle . . . *if I do as Karis did . . .*

The Priests of the Black would not merely rule the Church. The pontifex would claim the throne of Murnsk, and beyond. The Free Church nations would be returned to the fold. Distant Khandar and even the impenetrable southern highlands beyond would be cleansed of their pagan ways and their demons. *For what could stand against the power of the Beast of Judgment?*

And those two fools who call themselves my brothers would spend their lives in the darkest cell under Elysium, for failing the Church in her hour of need.

He closed his eyes for a moment and prayed.

Lord, please show me the way. Is this Your wish?

No choir of angels answered, no light descended from the heavens. Nonetheless, when he opened his eyes, the Pontifex of the Black knew what he needed to do.

Of course, there was no harm in taking precautions. He turned on his heel and went outside, to where the two guardian priests waited.

"Give me the keys to the chains," he said.

They obeyed unhesitatingly. The Black looked down at three small silver keys and felt his heart speed up in anticipation.

"I am going to whisper a word in your ears," he told them. "Lock the door after I enter. If I do not speak the word when I ask for it to be opened again, you are to leave it locked and kill me where I stand." The doors had ironbound slots for exactly this purpose, wide enough that a pistol could be shoved through and fired at the prisoner or anyone else inside. "Is that clear?"

"Yes, Your Excellence."

He bent close to each man in turn and spoke a single word to each. Something he'd never told anyone. The first and last names of a boy he'd once kissed, in a youthful moment of weakness. A boy whom he'd shoved from a wall walk, and then told the master of acolytes, through sobs, that his friend had slipped . . .

The door slammed behind him, and the key turned in the lock with a well-oiled *clank*. The pontifex regarded the Beast.

The priests took every care with the host, so that she would live a long and healthy life before another host needed to be found. She was cleansed daily, to keep sores from developing, and well fed. Red hair stuck out in tufts between the iron bands of the blindfold wrapping her head. Her skin was pale after so long in the dungeons, and he could see a wormy blue vein wriggle along her collarbone and down across one heavy white breast.

"If you destroy me," he said, stepping closer, "it will do you no good."

"It won't," the Beast agreed. "As I've told you, our interests align in this."

It lies. His breath came fast. *But it doesn't matter. The Lord's strength is with me. I will master it, as Karis did.*

Another step, and he was beside the creature. He lifted the largest of the silver keys and fitted it to the lock on one side of the iron blindfold. A turn of the wrist, and it clicked, the restraint opening smoothly like an iron flower. The pontifex willed his hands to stop trembling as he lifted the metal crown away from the host's head and let it crash to the ground.

The Beast blinked and looked up at him. The host had a lean, pretty face, and her eyes were shockingly green. The pontifex stood only inches away, close enough that he could feel her breath against his mask.

There was a moment of uncertainty. He cleared his throat.

"How exactly," he said, "does this—"

A crimson light bloomed in the depths of the Beast's pupils. It expanded outward, swallowing the black and the green, and then further, spreading like a stain across his vision, devouring the entire world. An instant later it was pressing *inward*, lancing through his eyes and into the depths of his soul.

Strength meant nothing. Not against this. It was like being the strongest of ants and trying to resist a man's boot. There was no mastery, only the grinding weight of oblivion.

It lies. The Beast always lies. It was his last thought.

The Beast's new body straightened up and brushed itself off.

Poor, foolish man, with his pathetic gambit. Everything that Zakhar Vakhaven had been was splayed out in front of the Beast, the contents of his mind and memory neatly arranged and available, like a rabbit skinned and gutted for butchering. Every reminiscence, every hidden guilt, every secret fantasy the man had entertained while he grappled with himself in the darkness of his cell. Every skill he'd possessed was the Beast's to call on as it wished.

The pontifex turned to the door and tugged off his obsidian mask.

"Let me out," he said in a loud voice. "Elijah. Quarnoff."

There was a pause, and then the keys turned in the locks. The door opened.

"Come here," the Beast said in the pontifex's voice. The two priests entered. The pontifex beckoned one of them closer, and the man obediently stepped forward, looking directly into his superior's eyes. Crimson light flared.

The second priest had time to start with surprise as his companion whirled, grabbed him, and dragged him close, tearing off his own mask as he did so. Another flash of red, and it was done.

Four bodies. Once it had had thousands. *And now I will again.*

The pontifex and one of the priests unlocked the chains binding the original host's arms. Jane Verity was still the seat of the Beast's power, from which it operated the other bodies like limbs. She would remain so until she died, and then another would take her place. And another, and another, and another, forever.

Last time, it had been young, barely born and ignorant of its own limitations. It had learned, but not quickly enough. But thirteen hundred years had passed since then, thirteen hundred years of study and planning. It would not make the same mistakes again.

Above it was the fortress of Elysium, full of panicking priests. Beyond that, Murnsk, and Borel, and Vordan, and the cities of the League and the Old Coast. Beyond that, the world, packed with scuttling, frantic humans.

Jane's lips twisted into a broad grin, and the Beast thought, *I will take them all.*

Chapter Fifteen

RAESINIA

Though the sky stayed dark with clouds, only a few flurries of snow fell, for which Raesinia was desperately grateful. Blue fissures grew in the blanket of gray, and the wind blew only from the south. Even with the return of the sun, though, it rarely rose above freezing at midday, and the winds whipped loose snow in the faces of struggling men and horses.

The Pilgrim's Road, never friendly, had turned into a nightmare. Men and horses struggled along through the snow, but guns and wagons constantly foundered or broke down. If they went ahead of the rest of the army, progress slowed to a crawl, and they splintered wheels and axles on hard-frozen ruts. If they came behind, the tramp of thousands of feet had crushed the trail into slimy, clinging mud, which sucked at anything that passed as though it were made of glue. Raesinia ordered anything that could be abandoned left behind, and the army dribbled a constant stream of caissons, empty wagons, and broken wheels. Even some cannons were sacrificed when they sank into mud that refroze overnight; a team of men with picks was unable to work them free before the army had to move on.

Fortunately, if such a word could be used, they didn't need most of the wagons, because there was so little to carry. Food supplies continued to dwindle alarmingly, and forage brought in nothing, since they were now recrossing terrain stripped bare on the way north. Dead horses provided brief bounties for those who were willing to stomach them, though there was increasingly little meat on their bones.

Just who was in command of the bedraggled army was a touchy question. After the disaster at the bridge, Raesinia had given the order to move south, and no one had spoken against her. The divisions remaining with them—the

Second, Third, Fourth, Fifth, and Eighth—each obeyed their own commanders, without much need for mutual decision-making. The only authority they all acknowledged was Alek Giforte's supply train, protected by five hundred or so soldiers of the First Division who'd made it over the river.

Giforte himself accepted Raesinia's authority cheerfully enough, and she would have been utterly lost without him. She'd never quite appreciated what it was all those military officers *did* with their time, but even organizing daily meals would have been impossible without Giforte's tireless, efficient staff. The rest of the generals were another matter, though. According to Giforte, on paper, the command of the army ought to descend on Morwen Kaanos, commander of the Third Division, who had seniority over the other division-generals. So far he hadn't pushed the matter, and neither had Raesinia. *Time enough to sort it out after we get to Polkhaiz.*

She couldn't stop thinking about Marcus. Raesinia didn't sleep, and therefore didn't have nightmares as such; instead, at odd moments she found herself involuntarily constructing elaborate, awful daydreams. She watched him die in half a hundred ways, cut down by enemies, frozen or starved, carried away in another flood of broken ice and churning water. Every time, he turned to her, one arm extended, as though begging her for help.

I had to go, she told him. *You told *me* to go!* But he never answered.

For the first two days, the white riders had not bothered them, and Raesinia had hoped that meant they wouldn't attack the army now that it was in retreat. When the strikes at their perimeter had begun again the following day, she'd realized that the respite had only been the relentless tribesmen finding another way over the river, then hurrying their sturdy ponies to catch up with their slow-moving opponents. Pickets guarded the flanks and rear of the Grand Army, and the fast-dwindling cavalry was split into sections ready to gallop to the aid of any unit that came under attack. Every engagement left white riders lying dead in the snow, but Raesinia feared that the Grand Army was growing weaker faster than its enemies. At least warm clothes and a little food could be scavenged from the dead.

Raesinia looked down at the map as though she could press the inked lines closer together by strength of will. It overlapped the edges of her desk; the command tent, with its big map table, had been left on the north bank of the Kovria.

"Nearly there," she said.

"Yes, Your Majesty." Alek Giforte had lost weight in the retreat—they all had, except for Raesinia. The roots of his beard were now snow-white, and there were streaks of gray at his temples. His eyes were sunk deep in their sockets, but they still held an alert spark. "Scouts should reach the Syzria by midday tomorrow."

"And the depots of Polkhaiz? Are we certain they're stuffed as full as we think?"

Giforte hesitated. "If the orders the First Consul left behind were carried out, they should be."

"Do we have any reason to think those orders were disobeyed?"

He frowned. "We have not met any supply convoys coming north. The threat from the white riders slowed shipments, I know, but we ought to have seen *something*. I'm worried."

"What happens if there's no food at Polkhaiz?"

"We have been rationing on the assumption that there will be," Giforte said. He straightened up. "If there's *nothing*, then we will all starve."

Raesinia brushed the map with her hand, then looked up at him. "Then we had better hope you're worried for no cause, Colonel."

"Yes, Your Majesty."

And then what? She hadn't thought any further ahead than getting the army to safety. *Go into camp and send out messengers, I suppose. Speak to the Borels and the Murnskai.* Her stomach churned. *Find out what happened to Marcus. And then . . .*

"You should get some sleep, Colonel Giforte." The name pricked something in her memory, and she frowned. "Are you related to the Colonel Giforte who commands the Girls' Own?"

"Yes, Your Majesty," he said. "She's my daughter."

Raesinia gave a startled laugh. "It must be interesting having a daughter who nearly outranks you."

"I am . . . very proud of her, Your Majesty." He paused. "Though it has been some time since we've spoken as family. We have not always seen eye to eye."

"You should talk to her," Raesinia said. "After everything that's happened . . ."

Giforte nodded. "Our quarrel does seem a bit petty. I've had the same thought. But there's always so much work to be done."

"Take the evening off," Raesinia said. "Your queen commands it. Find your daughter, clear the air, and then get a good night's rest. There'll be even more work to be done once we cross the river."

"Yes, Your Majesty." Giforte bowed. "Thank you."

He left the tent, and Raesinia slumped bonelessly into a camp chair. *One more day.* Once they made contact with the forces they'd left south of the river, they could arrange shipments of food, form a proper defense against the raiders, and begin the task of getting the army back into shape.

And start thinking about what it would mean if Janus doesn't return. The idea seemed ludicrous on its face; the First Consul had always been prepared for every eventuality. *But he pushed his luck too far this time.* She hoped Marcus and the First Division made it back; of course she did. But Janus . . .

It might be easier for everyone if he didn't survive. She felt a flood of guilt at the mere thought. Janus had, after all, saved her many times over, saved Vordan itself, as good as won a war against every other power on the continent. *But now that it's over, Vordan has very little use for him. He's* dangerous. Dorsay had demanded his dismissal as a precondition of peace, and Raesinia couldn't blame him.

Sothe ghosted in, dressed in her fighting blacks. In the emergency, she'd given up any pretense of working as a maid. Seeing her like this, it was hard for Raesinia to believe that anyone ever thought she was harmless. She moved with a predator's grace, lithe and deadly.

"What news from the army?" Raesinia said. Sothe spent her days wandering unseen among the troops, gauging their mood and listening to gossip.

"We're nearly there," Sothe said. "There's not much food to go around, but the grumbling's subsided for now. But there's bad news from the Third Division camp."

"General Kaanos?" The man had been one of Marcus' Colonials, and fiercely loyal to his commander, but now Marcus and Janus were both gone.

"The word is that he intends to call a council of war once we reach Polkhaiz."

"And what will he propose?"

"Supposedly, that the army remain in place while he requests new instructions from the Deputies-General."

Raesinia let her breath out. "That's far from the worst-case scenario."

"It's also far from the best."

Raesinia shrugged. The fact that Kaanos wouldn't acknowledge her immediate authority was irritating, but as long as he proposed to sit still rather than take action, it didn't much matter. All she needed was time, time to set up the peace that was now the only possible solution. A message to the deputies—since Kaanos didn't know about the flik-flik line, it would takes weeks at least— would give her some of the delay she required.

"If by some chance he forgets to invite me, make sure I know when and where this council will be held," Raesinia said. "It wouldn't do to seem entirely impotent."

Sothe nodded. "That won't be difficult."

"Nothing from the Borelgai, I assume?"

"Unfortunately, no. It may be that Whaler finds it too difficult to reach us, with the white riders on the prowl."

"Or he may be dead and Dorsay wondering why he doesn't return," Raesinia said, trying to suppress her own nerves. The silence from that direction was worrying. "In either case, once we're over the river, we'll make contact officially."

Sothe gave another nod. Raesinia waved a hand.

"There's nothing more for tonight. Go rest."

"Yes, Your Majesty." The assassin bowed and withdrew.

It was at times like this that Raesinia wished she *could* sleep. It would be so pleasant to pass a few hours in blissful unconsciousness, to rise refreshed with the morning sun. About the only way she'd be able to manage that would be if she blew her own head off, the results of which were generally not refreshing. She couldn't even read all night, since a lamp burning in the queen's quarters from dusk till morning might raise some suspicions. She lay on her bedroll, staring at the darkened cloth of the tent roof, and tried not to think about Marcus. It didn't work well.

If you have to think about him, think about something more pleasant. She went through their invasion of the Exchange Central Office, the way they'd laughed after their narrow escape. The times she'd caught his eyes lingering on her. She wasn't entirely sure there was anything to that, that it wasn't more than a figment of wishful memory.

He must care for me. "Don't give up," he'd written in a message he couldn't have known whether she'd receive. *But is it just his proper care for his queen? Or is it for me as a . . . a woman?*

She could barely form the thought, it felt so bizarre. She had simply never thought of herself that way. She wasn't *ignorant*—a princess' education was not quite so rarefied as most people believed, and in any event she'd spent her nights in with University students for years. But such affairs had always seemed like the customs of a distant land, mostly inexplicable and nothing really to do with her. Poor Ben, one of her revolutionary band who'd died in her arms, had been in love with her, but she'd never felt more for him than the friendship she had for all her comrades.

Even now she was far from certain what she wanted, except that she badly wanted to know what *Marcus* wanted. And that she wanted him back safe, telling the story of yet another thrilling escape, laughing reluctantly when her gentle prodding broke through his shell of proper behavior.

We're almost there. Raesinia took a deep breath and let it out. *Come on, Marcus. Make it back, just one more time.*

The news, when it came, was so incomprehensibly bad that Raesinia took a moment to fit the jagged fact of it into her mind. The young cavalryman waited on bent knee, trembling slightly. Beside him, Alek Giforte's face was blank and unreadable.

All around them the Grand Army continued marching, trudging up the last ridge before the valley of the Syzria. Raesinia fancied she could *see* the information spreading, running through the army like an unstoppable virus, jumping from mind to mind without even needing lips to speak it.

"You're certain?" she said stupidly.

"Yes, Your Majesty." The trooper swallowed. "The Borelgai flag flies over Polkhaiz. Infantry in white uniforms guard the approaches. I saw them with my own eyes. I'm sorry."

"We had troops there," Raesinia said. "Three divisions. What happened to them?"

"I don't know," the trooper said. "But my sergeant estimated the size of the Borelgai camp at forty thousand men. It may be that our forces were compelled to withdraw in the face of such strength."

"That's damn near their whole army," Giforte said. "I thought Dorsay was supposed to be cautious."

It's Vansfeldt all over again. Marcus' lessons in strategy came back to her. *How to defeat a more powerful opponent: assume a strong position that he can be forced or goaded to attack.*

"Giforte. Send word to all the division-generals that I wish to speak to them at once." There was no putting it off any longer. "And find Sothe. I don't care how."

"Yes, Your Majesty."

Giforte hurried off, taking the trooper with him. Raesinia waited by the side of the road, watching the endless stream of ragged men flow past. Few of them looked up at their queen, though they could hardly fail to recognize her.

Joanna and Barely, her two bodyguards, stuck to her side like ever-present shadows.

Sothe arrived, materializing out of the snow so quickly that Raesinia guessed she'd heard the news on her own.

"Your Majesty," the assassin said.

"Go to Polkhaiz," Raesinia said. "Find Dorsay. Tell him I need to speak with him, *now*."

Sothe shifted uncomfortably. "I don't like leaving you here—"

"You know this is what I need the most," Raesinia said. "*Go*, please, and return as soon as you can."

"Understood." Sothe bowed. "Be careful."

To Raesinia's intense irritation, it took until that evening to gather the generals. Their excuses were, she had to admit, not unreasonable—once it became generally known that they were marching toward an enemy and not friendly depots, it took every officer's careful attention to keep the column from dissolving into a confused mess. As it was, they'd reached their planned camp-site, a few miles on the north side of the Syzria. Raesinia had hoped they'd have a feast, brought out by the troops they'd left behind in Polkhaiz. Instead, she sat at the head of her inadequate map table, waiting for the officers theoretically sworn to her service.

Cyte arrived first. If she hadn't known better, Raesinia would hardly have recognized her as the student radical who'd helped storm the Vendre. That girl had been pudgy faced with baby fat, eyes ringed with dramatic dark makeup and fashionably unfashionable tomboyish clothes. It had all spoken of insecurity, a desperate desire to prove that she deserved the place she occupied. The young woman who faced her now was gaunt from the rigors of the march, dark hair grown ragged, face unadorned, but utterly comfortable in her rumpled blue uniform. She bowed, not the least overawed by the presence of her queen.

"Captain Cytomandiclea." Raesinia had looked up the correct pronunciation.

"Cyte, if you like, Your Majesty," Cyte said with a very slight smile. "I know it's a mouthful."

"Cyte, then," Raesinia said, offering a tentative smile in return. "How are things with the Second Division? Have you had any trouble with the colonels?"

"Thank you, Your Majesty. Nothing I couldn't handle. Colonel Giforte has been helpful."

"Good." Raesinia hesitated. "I know there's been no word of General Ihernglass—"

Cyte opened her mouth, paused, then said, "*He* will make it back. I'm certain of it."

Raesinia nodded, taking the meaning. She knew about Winter's gender, and Cyte obviously did as well, but it was best to be cautious when expecting others. Sothe said that camp gossip claimed Winter and Cyte were lovers, and watching her face as she spoke, Raesinia could believe it. There was a deep heartsickness there, buried under an iron core of faith.

"I'm sure General d'Ivoire will return as well," Cyte added.

"Indeed," a new voice drawled. The tent flap opened, and General Kaanos came in. "So many wayward generals. Let's hope they all make it home safe."

Kaanos was a big man, though thinned like all of them by the light rations. His face was framed by wild hair, a bristly mustache, and thick muttonchops, with his actual features nearly lost among all the whiskers. He scratched the back of one big, hairy hand with the other and sketched a bow in Raesinia's direction. He acknowledged Cyte when she saluted, and folded himself into a chair on one side of the table.

"Division-General Kaanos," Raesinia said. "Thank you for joining us."

"Yer Majesty," Kaanos said, with an insolent slur. "Someone has to figure out how to get us out of this mess."

Raesinia kept her features calm, but frowned inwardly. Sothe had warned her that Kaanos would not be friendly, but he seemed downright hostile. Before she could probe him further, the flap opened again, admitting two more officers.

Division-General Valiant Solwen was a man who seemed designed for horse-back; on the ground, his short legs and broad shoulders made him look a bit like an ape in a tailored uniform. The remains of a fashionable pencil mustache were just about visible on his upper lip through a week's growth of stubble. Christopher de Manzet, in contrast, had managed to maintain his grooming. He was not out of his forties, but already bald as an egg, with a fringe of brown hair at the back of his skull and a neat goatee. Alone of those present, he didn't give the impression that he'd slept in his uniform.

Giforte was the last to arrive, muttering apologies. He looked even worse than he had the night before, dark circles under his eyes like spreading bruises in a pale, haggard face. He shuffled over beside Raesinia, clutching a sheaf of paper.

"Gentlemen," Raesinia said, after they'd settled themselves. "Thank you for joining me. I assume you all know the situation?"

"Dorsay's taken Polkhaiz and dug in across the river," Solwen said. "Which puts us in quite a pickle."

"A bit more than a pickle," de Manzet said, looking disapprovingly around the table. "We are in grave danger."

"I think we all understand that," Raesinia said. "The question is what we're going to do about it."

"Only one thing to do," Kaanos said. "We attack at daybreak."

There was a long pause.

"Attack?" Solwen said. "Over the bridge?"

"Forget the bridge. The river's still frozen solid." Kaanos leaned forward. "We'll fix Dorsay in place with a frontal attack and encircle the town on both sides. He'll have to pull out of his defenses or be cut off."

"I'm not sure that's wise," Cyte said. "Dorsay's had time to prepare, and he'll have anticipated something like this."

"Besides," Giforte said, "we don't have the strength."

"We have more men than he does," Kaanos said.

"In theory. I don't have accurate roll calls for the past week." Giforte shook his sheaf of paper. "Our cavalry is badly depleted and our artillery is a wreck. Our men are exhausted, and Dorsay's are fresh."

"Fortunately," Kaanos snapped, "I don't have to ask for opinions. I'm the one in command here. You'll all get your orders by dawn."

Damn. Raesinia took a breath. "I think we need to consider alternatives."

"All due respect, Your Majesty, but I don't need to ask for *your* opinion, either."

De Manzet looked aghast. "General Kaanos—"

"I don't work for you," Kaanos continued, looking at Raesinia. "I work for the people of Vordan. They appointed the Deputies-General, and the deputies tapped the First Consul to run the army. He set up the chain of command, and since he and General d'Ivoire are gone, that leaves me at the top of it. What you want doesn't come into it."

"I say," Solwen said weakly. "That's a bit . . . well, harsh, isn't it?"

"Do you disagree?" Kaanos said.

"Not as such. But . . ."

"But nothing. If she doesn't like it, she can take it up with the deputies."

"I'd like to open negotiations with the Borelgai," Raesinia said, looking away from Kaanos. "I have reason to think they will be receptive."

"Oh, I'm sure they'd listen," Kaanos said. "They'll keep talking for as long as you want. You know why?" He thumped his fist on the table. "Because we're starving, while they have plenty of *our* supplies to eat! Every day they can keep us jabbering is another day's food gone."

"I fear General Kaanos is right," de Manzet said, polite but patronizing. "They have little incentive to bargain."

"Better to try, at least," Giforte said. "I'm telling you we are not strong enough to attack."

"We're not going to get any stronger," Kaanos said. "And they're not going to get any weaker. As I see it, we have two choices. We can strike now, or we can give up and throw ourselves on the Duke of Brookspring's mercy. Anything else is just idiocy." He shoved his chair back. "I, for one, am not ready to give up. Thank you for your *advice*, Your Majesty. The rest of you, expect your orders in the morning."

A breath of cold air flooded in as he ducked through the tent flap, and the lanterns flickered. Slowly, de Manzet also stood up, and gave Raesinia an elegant bow.

"Your Majesty," he said. "General Kaanos could have put that more delicately, but I believe he is correct. An attack is risky, but we have no choice. If you'll excuse me, I need to prepare my men."

He departed, with another bow.

"An attack would be a disaster," Giforte said to Solwen. "You see that, don't you?"

"Dorsay's not a fool," Cyte said. "He'll be ready for a simple flanking maneuver."

Solwen sighed. "You're probably right. But what can we do? He's in command."

"*I* am Queen of Vordan," Raesinia said, not entirely without petulance.

Solwen flushed. "Of course, Your Majesty. But . . . military matters, you know. They can be very complicated. Best left to the experts." He got up. "Speaking of which. I have things to attend to. But it will all turn out for the best, you'll see." He bowed. "Good night."

"I've seen street beggars with more spine," Giforte said when he was gone.

"He's in a difficult position," Raesinia said.

"He's a coward."

"For wanting to attack?"

Giforte's face twisted. "There's more than one kind of cowardice. Some people would rather die gloriously than face a hard truth."

"Well, I for one would prefer not to die at all," said Cyte. "And I think I can speak for everyone in my division on that point. What are we going to do?"

"What would happen," Raesinia said thoughtfully, "if I ordered Kaanos arrested?"

Giforte sucked breath through his teeth. "Nothing good."

"You think he'd actually try to fight back?" Cyte said. "Against his own queen?"

"I think he's backed into a corner, and he can't see a way out," Giforte said. "That makes a man dangerous."

"What about de Manzet?" Raesinia said. "He was Royal Army."

"Hard to say," Giforte mused. "He strikes me as someone who looks after his own interests. Right now that seems to mean following orders, if only to avoid responsibility."

"And Solwen won't stand up for himself," Raesinia said. "So it all comes back to Kaanos." She indicated the papers in Giforte's hand. "Is the situation really that bad?"

He nodded. "We're down to the dregs. If we issue everything that's left tomorrow, it'll be maybe a half ration. After that, we're boiling our boots."

"Saints and martyrs," Raesinia swore, the profanity drawing an approving grin from Cyte. "Then it's tonight or nothing."

"Do you really think Dorsay will negotiate?" Cyte said. "I hate to say it, but Kaanos might be right. He's holding all the cards."

"Only here and now." Raesinia glared at the tent flap for a moment, willing Sothe to appear with an answer from the Borelgai. Nothing happened, and she let out a sigh. "But there may be a few more tricks left to play."

It was nearly midnight when the scratch at the flap came. Raesinia, who had been studying the maps for the hundredth time for lack of anything better to do, jumped out of her chair in her haste. She threw the tent open and found Sothe waiting beside a cloaked and hooded man.

"I hope we didn't wake you, Your Majesty," the man said. The voice was Whaler's. He stepped inside, limping badly, and pulled back his hood. A fresh, livid cut marred his scalp, held closed with gut stitches.

"I don't think I'll sleep tonight," Raesinia said, completely truthfully. "Are you all right?"

He grinned. "Souvenirs of my last attempt to reach you, thanks to our northern friends. I tried to explain to them that we're supposed to be allies, but they didn't seem inclined to listen."

Sothe, kicking snow off her boots, let the tent flap fall closed behind her. "I took the liberty of bringing him here at once," she said. "Under the circumstances, I thought it best not to delay."

"Of course," Raesinia said, then hesitated. Whaler was technically an enemy. "My generals are . . . making plans."

"They will attack at first light," Whaler said, limping a few more paces and collapsing into a chair. "Forgive me, Your Majesty. The ride was not kind to my hip."

"Why do you say they will attack?"

"Because it is the obvious thing to do." He raised an eyebrow. "Is it true that the First Consul was lost at the Kovria?"

"Yes. Which you obviously already know."

"I apologize for my bluntness, Your Majesty, but I must be clear on this point. Is he dead?"

Raesinia paused. "He was wounded by a Murnskai assassin. Later, he and Column-General d'Ivoire were with a division that was cut off by the tribesmen. We hope they'll be able to win free and join up with us, but as to whether Janus will recover, I don't know."

"That's certainly a delicate state of affairs."

"Now you must forgive *me* for being blunt," Raesinia said. "Does Dorsay's offer still stand?"

"The situation has grown *delicate* on our side as well," Whaler said. "Orlanko's faction has gained strength as Vordanai fortunes have turned. There is some sentiment that we should . . . ah . . . kick you while you're down."

"The Grand Army is not Vordan," Raesinia said. "Even if we all die here, the war will go on. Indeed, at that point, it may be impossible to stop."

"His Grace agrees," Whaler said. "Given time, I think the difficulties can be overcome."

"We haven't *got* time. Kaanos will attack in the morning, and I can't stop him. I don't even know if I should try. The men are starving." *There has to be something.* What they needed to do was preserve the status quo—not forcing the issue with an assault, but still avoiding an outright surrender. Raesinia blinked as an audacious idea occurred to her. "We left depots full to bursting in Polkhaiz. Is the food still there?"

"We are well supplied, yes," Whaler said.

"Tell Dorsay I need a gesture of good faith to give to *my* people before we can negotiate."

"If you're going to suggest we withdraw from Polkhaiz—"

"No, of course not. But if you were to ship food to our side of the river—not much, say enough to supply the army for a day . . ."

"Then that would buy us a day." Whaler frowned. "We'd be in the same position tomorrow."

"And you'd provide another shipment. And so on. Until we either strike a deal or decide to fight it out after all."

"Hmm." He tipped his head. "It's unorthodox, I'll say that much. But it may work. Orlanko will scream bloody murder, but he doesn't actually have command over military operations. You realize, of course, that this won't hold for long."

"It doesn't need to." *Just long enough.* "But I need your assurance tonight."

"Damn." Whaler levered himself to his feet, wincing. "And here I thought I was done with riding for a while."

"Stay here," Raesinia told Barely.

"Your Majesty . . ." The woman hesitated. "Are you sure?"

"I think I'll be safe visiting one of my own generals."

Joanna raised an eyebrow eloquently, but as always said nothing. Barely scratched the side of her head and nodded. Racsinia left them at the intersection and followed the aisle down the row of Third Division tents. The rest of the camp was a good deal more ragged than it had once been, but here, within sight of their commanders, standards were still kept up.

Two sentries waited in front of General Kaanos' tent. They looked down at her curiously, and then she saw recognition in their eyes. Both bowed deep.

"I need to see the general," Raesinia said.

"He's sleeping, Your Majesty." One guard looked at the other.

"It's important."

If Kaanos had given them specific orders, they still might keep her out. *Then we'll have to wait until morning and toss the dice.* But she wanted to talk to him, at least, and see if there was a way to avoid a confrontation.

"One moment, Your Majesty." The guard turned and rapped, hesitantly, at the tent pole. After a moment a sleepy voice answered.

"What?"

"The . . . ah . . . queen is here to see you, sir. She says it's important."

Silence for a long moment. Then, "Let her in."

The guards stepped aside. Raesinia pushed through the tent flap, blinking as a lantern flared. Kaanos sat at a folding table, shaking out a match. He wore his underclothes, with a thick blanket wrapped around his shoulders. With his hairy face, it made him look even more like a bear.

"Forgive me if I'm not properly dressed, Your Majesty," he said. "But you didn't give me much warning."

"I don't stand on ceremony." Raesinia crossed the tent and stood in front of the table. "You have to call off the attack."

"This again?" Kaanos shook his head. "You said it was important."

"I've exchanged messengers with Dorsay. We can come to an agreement—"

"I told you," Kaanos said wearily. "He'll string you along until we're so weak we'll have to surrender. Didn't they teach you politics at Ohnlei?" He cocked his head. "Or was it all just dancing and smiling?"

Raesinia returned his gaze levelly. After a moment of silence, she said, "May I ask a question?"

"You're the queen," Kaanos said. "You can ask whatever you like."

"What have I done to so offend you?"

There was another pause. Kaanos shifted the blanket around his shoulders and ran his fingers through his bristly beard.

"You know I served in Khandar," he said.

"With Column-General d'Ivoire," Raesinia said. "I know."

"Do you know why?"

She shook her head.

"Sometimes it's hard for me to even remember," he said. "There was a fight. Some noble brat who said some things he shouldn't have in a tavern. That sort of thing happens every night, but shiny spurs went out a window and landed badly. Broke his leg, and the cutters said he'd need a cane to walk. He went to his father, and his father talked to his friends . . ." He spread his hands. "And there I was, eating sand for the rest of my career."

Raesinia nodded. Marcus had told her that Khandar was used as a dumping ground, a hardship post for officers who'd ruined their careers.

"It was just as well, I told myself," Kaanos went on. "In the old Royal Army, captain was as high as someone like me could ever make it. We were just about worthy to keep a battalion pointed in the right direction, as long as some-

one with the right blood was actually in *charge*. At least in Khandar I only had
to put up with old Colonel Warus.

"Then everything went to shit there. You have no idea what that was like.
One minute we owned the city, and the next minute mobs of grayskins were
killing anyone in a blue uniform."

"I might know more than you think," Raesinia said quietly. "I was at the
fall of the Vendre."

Kaanos inclined his head, conceding the point. "It was Marcus who got us
out of that. We all would have ended up roasted if not for him. He kept the
Colonials together long enough to get clear of the city and send for help."

"And my father sent you Janus," Raesinia said.

"Another goddamned noble with a brilliant plan," Kaanos said. "I told
Marcus we ought to have stuffed him into a dune and taken ship for home."

"But Janus *won*. He beat the Redeemers."

"And what good did that do anybody? I lost friends all through that fight,
and in the end we left everything behind and scuttled back to Vordan to save *you*."

He didn't know about the Thousand Names, of course, or the secret war
against the Priests of the Black. Raesinia felt an unexpected surge of sympathy.

"He's mad," Kaanos said. "You know that, don't you? Vhalnich's crazy.
He'd have to be crazy to bring us to a place like this. Snow in June!"

"So what are you doing here?" Raesinia said. "You could have left the
army after the revolution. Why stay?"

"Because Marcus asked me to," Kaanos said softly. "Vhalnich had his hooks
in deep by then. I couldn't say anything to Marcus, so the only thing left was to
go along for the ride. I owed him that much." He shook his head. "Now they're
both dead."

"We don't know that."

"We didn't leave them any supplies. If they'd broken through, we'd have
heard by now. They're dead, *Your Majesty*. Marcus left me in charge of this army,
and I'll be damned if I let it starve in the snow. Tomorrow we'll break Dorsay's
line, and then we'll get the *hell* out of this godforsaken country."

There was grief in his voice, under the anger. Raesinia considered. *If I tell
him the plan, I might be able to bring him around.* But that would sacrifice the ele-
ment of surprise if he *didn't* agree. *And he won't.* He'd fixed the idea of an attack
in his head, one more charge to avenge Marcus and show everyone. She felt
sorry for him.

"Division-General," she said. "I believe that Marcus will make it back alive. But more important, if he were here, you know he'd do whatever he could to keep the soldiers safe—"

"Bullshit," Kaanos said. "If that were true, we'd never have come this far. Marcus would do whatever Janus told him to, because Janus hypnotized him along with the rest of you." He sighed. "First chance Vordan's ever had to be rid of the whole batch of noble parasites and the revolution turns things over to Janus bet fucking Vhalnich first chance they get."

"All I'm trying to do is make peace," Raesinia said.

"Then you shouldn't have chosen that mad bastard for First Consul. Now Dorsay has us where he wants us, and all we can do is try to fight our way out." He fixed her with an angry glare. "Now, if you'll excuse me, *Your Majesty*, I'd like to get a little more sleep. God only knows what's going to happen in the morning."

He gave a stiff, shallow bow, and turned away. Raesinia watched him for a moment longer, then left the tent, nodding her thanks at the guards. They'd most likely heard every word, but they stared straight ahead and said nothing.

Sothe and Cyte were waiting for her back at her own tent, with Barely and Joanna.

"No luck?" Cyte said.

"He's in mourning for Marcus," Raesinia said. "I don't think he heard a word I said."

"Dorsay's people are waiting for the signal," Sothe said.

Raesinia turned to look south, across the frozen river. The lights of Polkhaiz were just visible.

"Do it," she said.

The Grand Army was thrown into chaos at first light by the smell of frying bacon.

It came from the Second Division camp, where the Girls' Own had taken down some tents to make a clear space and set up makeshift tables. Bonfires had been lit, with big cauldrons set to boiling above them. When cooking equipment was lacking, the soldiers had improvised; bacon sizzled on upside-down kettles, on the backs of shovels, and even carefully laid out on bayonets.

When soldiers from the other divisions came to investigate, they were welcomed. Parked beyond the frying bacon and the cauldrons of army soup were wagons full of bread and vegetables, a bounty that seemed to the hungry men to have been shipped in from a different world. It had been easy to forget, over the past few weeks, that there was a land beyond this endless, unnatural snowscape with its dark forests and frozen rivers. Now they were forcibly reminded.

Rumor spread beyond the ability of the officers to control it. Girls' Own soldiers drove smaller wagons into the other camps and tossed loaves of fresh-baked bread into grateful hands, unloaded box after box of hardtack, and even brought fresh meat for the pots. All across the Grand Army, men piled up anything that would burn, shoveled snow into cauldrons, and watched the flames grow with desperate hunger.

The queen, the women told the other soldiers. The queen had negotiated with the Borelgai, and this was the result.

Raesinia sat in her tent, cutting slices from a ham that the Duke of Brook-spring had sent to her in particular, with his compliments. One by one, the generals arrived, and Sothe led them aside and spoke to them in low tones. Then they waited by the side of the tent; Raesinia was amused, though not surprised, to hear stomachs growling.

Kaanos was the last to appear. His face was bright red with fury under his vast spray of whiskers.

"What the *hell* do you think you're doing?" he said, stalking past Barely and Joanna to stand in front of Raesinia. "We ought to be getting into formation *right now*. Do you have any idea how much danger this puts us in? If the Borelgai were to attack at this moment, they could roll up the whole army before we could fire a shot!"

"They must know that," Raesinia said. "And yet they don't attack. Odd, no?"

What it meant, she knew, was that Dorsay's faction still held sway over Orlanko's. *But no need to tell* him *that*.

"This is treason," Kaanos said. "You've sold us out."

"I've negotiated for food when we were starving," Raesinia said. "That's a strange definition of 'selling us out.'"

"You've undermined my authority!" Kaanos shouted.

"Ah. As to that." Raesinia pushed back from the table and stood up. The top of her skull barely came up to Kaanos' chin, and she had to tilt her head back to look him in the eye. "Division-General Morwen Kaanos, you are under arrest for refusing to obey orders from your queen."

"You can't be serious." Kaanos looked up at the other generals. "You're not going to stand for this, are you?"

"The queen has my support," said Cyte.

"And mine," Giforte added.

"The thing is," Solwen said wretchedly, "the thing *is*, Mor, I'm not sure what I can *actually* do about it." He scratched the side of his head, looking embarrassed. "I mean, she *is* the queen, when all is said and done."

"She doesn't have any right to give orders here!" Kaanos shouted.

"She disagrees," Solwen said. "And what should I do, order my men to shoot her?"

"Put *her* under arrest for treason!" Kaanos looked from Solwen to de Manzet. "You both know I'm right. If you bring your men here—"

"My men are mostly enjoying their first hot breakfast for weeks," de Manzet said quietly. "What do you think they'd say if I told them to put it down and come arrest the queen?"

"That's about the shape of it," Solwen said.

"*My* men won't stand for it," Kaanos said, whirling back to Raesinia. "Unlike these fucking cowards."

"As Division-General de Manzet said," Raesinia murmured, "your men are . . . busy. And we will explain things to them."

"You highborn are all the same," Kaanos hissed. "Traitors, all of you."

Raesinia gave a tired shrug and nodded to Barely and Joanna. They had a half dozen hard-eyed women behind them, handpicked by Colonel Giforte for reliability. Joanna took Kaanos by the arm, and all the fight went out of the general. He seemed to deflate.

"Hell," he said. "It's your party, then."

He left, the soldiers falling in around him. Raesinia turned back to the other generals.

"Legally," she said, "since the Deputies-General have yet to approve a full constitution, the procedure may be a bit unclear. But I think we can speak in broad terms. The Crown and the deputies designated the First Consul, Janus bet Vhalnich, to command the armed forces of Vordan. He is now missing, however, and in his absence that authority descends back to where it has traditionally rested—that is, with the sovereign." She let her eyes roam down the short row of officers. "Are we in agreement on this?"

Cyte was grinning. Even Giforte smiled, though his face was still haggard. Solwen's face was pinched, and de Manzet's calculating. But they both nodded, and all four of them chorused, "Yes, Your Majesty."

"Good." Raesinia turned to Sothe. "Please fetch General Solwen's second in command, so we can inform him of the situation."

That commander, a young colonel named Sebatish, turned out to be very understanding. Raesinia put him in charge of the Third Division and made sure that he publicly acknowledged her authority. The others were doing the same. It wasn't a guarantee against mutiny, but if the common soldiers knew who was supposed to be in command, their officers would be less likely to take their loyalty for granted.

"Neatly done," Sothe said, when they were finally alone again.

"Never underestimate what can be accomplished by a little bacon at the right moment," Raesinia said. "Kaanos didn't *want* to turn the army against itself, but he would have if that were the only way out I'd left him. I had to take it away before putting pressure on him."

"Will you execute him?"

"Oh God, no. We'll find a diplomatic place to put him, assuming we get out of this at all." Raesinia leaned back in her chair. "Speaking of which. Any word from Dorsay?"

"He's agreed to a meeting. We're working on a mutually agreeable venue."

"Don't nitpick too hard. Kaanos was right that he's got us where he wants us. Our only advantage is that he doesn't *want* us destroyed, but if Orlanko gets control, that won't last—"

There was a frantic rap at the tent post. Sothe shot to her feet, one hand dropping to the hilt of a knife.

"Come in," Raesinia said, sitting straighter.

"Your Majesty." A ranker poked his head through the tent flap. "It's Division-General Stokes."

Give-Em-Hell? But he was with Marcus— "He's here?"

"Yes, Your Majesty. He's wounded, but he said he had to see you immediately."

Raesinia met Sothe's gaze for a moment. "Bring him in."

They pulled the sheets off the bedroll while two rankers carried the general in. Give-Em-Hell's uniform was filthy, crusted with blood on one side and stained with dust and sweat. His breathing came fast, and he looked around for a moment as though he didn't understand what he was seeing. Then his eyes found Raesinia.

"Your Majesty," he gasped out. "Thank God Almighty."

"Lie down, General," Raesinia said. "Someone get him some water."

Give-Em-Hell allowed himself to be lowered onto the bedroll, coughing. He took a greedy gulp from a proffered canteen, then handed it back.

"Been riding for days," he said, mustache quivering. "Left the others behind. Very important."

"What's important?" Raesinia said. "Where you with Marcus? What happened?"

"Marcus! Yes!" He shook his head. "Mind's not working straight. Marcus. At a ford upriver from Isket, a few days' march."

"That's where you left him?" Raesinia said eagerly. "Was he all right?"

"Pinned down," Give-Em-Hell muttered. "Too many. White riders, bone men. Still fighting, I hope to God. Don't know for how long." He took a deep breath. "Help him. Please."

Then, with a sigh, the cavalry general sank down on the bedroll and closed his eyes. A few moments later his mustache began to vibrate with a colossal snoring.

"Fetch a cutter," Raesinia told one of the rankers. "And bring me whoever is in command of the cavalry at once."

"Your Majesty," Sothe said, as the two young men hurried to obey. "General Stokes didn't mention Janus."

"You think that means he's dead?" Raesinia said.

"I think that means we don't know," Sothe said. "And if he's *not*, and we manage to win through to them, matters might become . . . complicated."

There was a long silence.

"We are hard-pressed as it is," Sothe went on. "A rescue mission would be extremely risky." She looked down, avoiding Raesinia's eyes. "This is the nature of command, Your Majesty. Difficult decisions sometimes need to be made."

Difficult decisions. Raesinia glanced from the sleeping Give-Em-Hell to Sothe and back again. *Is that what this is? Sacrifice thousands of men, or let things get complicated?*

She closed her eyes, and saw Marcus holding out his hand.

CHAPTER SIXTEEN

WINTER

Winter awoke from a dream of an endless, freezing hell and found herself lying in a comfortable bed, covered by a warm, scratchy wool blanket.

She struggled to keep her breathing even. *Calm.* She tried to think, eyes closed. *We found . . . someplace warm. And then . . .* She remembered helping the rest of her diminished party through the crack in the rock, into the pleasant air of the strange valley. Alex had been saying something, something urgent, but Winter hadn't been able to focus. Days of exhaustion and terror, too long deferred, had come to claim their due.

So where am I? Carefully, she cracked one eye. Her bed was at one end of a long row of beds. The room was carved from stone, with rock walls and a rough, low ceiling. Thick wool carpets covered the floor, dyed in colorful, abstract patterns. A narrow window—more like an arrow slit—gave Winter an abbreviated view of the green valley she remembered, hemmed in on all sides by massive snowcapped peaks.

Her uniform was gone, she realized. Peeking under the blanket revealed that someone had dressed her in a loose woolen shift. There were also bandages she didn't remember, one around her leg and another on her arm. The wrappings on her hand were fresh, too. She tried to flex her fingers, automatically, and a wave of pain crashed over her, so powerful that she bit her lip to keep from crying out.

There was the scrape of a chair, and footsteps. Winter hurriedly closed her eyes again and feigned sleep. Whoever had taken them might not intend immediate harm, but until she knew what was going on it was best to be cautious.

"Well?" The voice was Alex's, speaking Hamveltai. "Are they going to kill me?"

"The Eldest is very angry with you." This was a young man's voice, grave and solemn.

"That's nothing new," Alex said. "And?"

"Maxwell argued very passionately on your behalf. The Eldest has agreed to postpone judgment until we know what sort of trouble you have brought with you this time."

"I told him—"

"The Eldest would prefer to hear from the strangers themselves."

"Fine." Alex sounded frustrated. "Can I at least go back to my room?"

"Or to Maxwell's?" There was a faint teasing note in the young man's tone.

"That's my business," Alex sniffed.

The young man sighed. "The Eldest says you have freedom of the temple, provided you swear not to leave before the matter has been decided."

"Fine," Alex said. "Let me know when he's made up his damn mind. I won't hold my breath."

"He's only trying to keep everyone safe," the young man said. "Honestly, Alex, what the hell were you thinking?"

"I was thinking that everyone in this damn place would rather *talk* about a problem than actually *do* something about it. I was thinking that we might miss a chance that would never come again, because the Eldest would rather spend years discussing it than take the slightest risk."

"The Eldest's first duty is to the Mountain."

"I know," Alex snarled, in the tones of someone who'd had the argument many times. "That's why I left."

"But you came back. You brought *them* here."

"What was I supposed to do? They all would have died."

"Some would say, so much the better."

"Fuck that." Alex took a deep breath. "They helped me when they didn't have any reason to trust me. *She* helped me."

"What's her name?"

"Winter."

"That's appropriate," the young man said, with subtle humor. "Her demon is very powerful. Do you know what it does?"

"I've never seen her use it," Alex said.

"Has she woken up at all?"

"She thrashed a little bit, but no."

"Her hand needs tending." The young man sighed. "Go and see Maxwell before he explodes."

A pause, and then more footsteps.

"Alex?"

She stopped. "What?"

"I'm glad you're all right."

Alex snorted. "Maybe wait until the Eldest has decided not to cut my head off to say that."

The young man crossed the room, soft slippers hissing on the carpet, to stand beside Winter's bed.

"Winter?" he said. "Winter, wake up."

Winter opened her eyes. He was waiting a few steps away, with his hands crossed behind his back. He looked about twenty years old, with a serious face and short, dark hair. He wore a long, flowing outfit, something like a priest's robes, but made of rough-spun wool and patterned with intricate, twisting spirals and chains.

"Do you understand me?" he said, then switched to Murnskai. "Is this easier?"

"Hamveltai, please," Winter said, trying to coax her memory to offer up that language.

"Alex has tried to teach me Vordanai, but she didn't have the patience for my slow progress," he said.

"This is fine," Winter said. "Where am I?"

"We call it the Mountain. It's not far from Elysium."

"My soldiers. Bobby and the others. Are they all right?"

"Yes. You and Bobby are being kept separately, because of your powers. The rest are with the acolytes below."

Winter let out a sigh of relief. Then, as what he'd said sank in, she stiffened. Infernivore was pressing at the edges of her mind, as it always did when she was around Alex, but now that the girl had gone she realized it wasn't only Alex who had provoked the reaction.

"You have a demon, too," she said. "Who are you?"

"I do." The young man inclined his head. "My name is Abraham."

"What are you going to do with us?"

"Right now I would like to heal your hand. It is badly frostbitten, and the flesh is infected. If we leave it be, you will lose several fingers at least, and possibly the whole thing."

Winter looked at the wrappings and grimaced. "You want to take the fingers off to save the rest?"

"That won't be necessary. My demon can repair it, if you give me permission to do so."

She blinked. "Your demon needs permission?"

"*I* need permission." Abraham gave a sad smile. "It's a rule I have made for myself."

"Well, if you can do something, please go ahead. It hurts like hell already."

"One moment." Abraham positioned her hand palm-up on the bed, every movement sending shooting pain down her arm. He put his own hand on top of hers.

"Wait," Winter said. She remembered Bobby, lying wounded in a tent in Khandar, and Feor's offer. "This isn't going to . . . change me, is it?"

"No. Don't worry. Just relax."

Winter closed her eyes. Infernivore was thrashing, eager to surge through the connection and devour Abraham's demon, but her will held it back. She could feel a cold prickling in her skin, spreading under the bandages, like silver threads slipping painlessly through the inflamed flesh. Almost at once the agony began to fade, replaced by a *crawling* sensation, as though ants were marching under her skin. She gritted her teeth, fighting the urge to yank her hand away. After a long interval, the feeling faded, along with the last traces of pain. Abraham let out a sigh and lifted his hand.

"That's better," he said. "Wash it well when you take the bandage off. You'll need to eat something, too. Do you think you can get out of bed?"

Winter nodded, feeling light-headed. She flexed her fingers and felt them respond without the stabs of agony. *Saints and martyrs.* "Your demon can . . . heal people? Can it heal *anything*?"

"It is limited by my knowledge of the body," Abraham said. "Some wounds are easier than others. And I can do nothing for those who have already passed on."

That's still a hell of a gift. Winter sat up, fighting a wave of dizziness, and slipped her legs over the edge of the bed. She waited a moment, then tottered to her feet. Abraham came over, holding out a long, loose garment like a fuzzy bathrobe, which Winter gratefully shrugged into. There was a pair of slippers at the foot of the bed, and she shuffled into these as well.

"Thank you," she said. "For everything, I mean."

"You may wish to wait to thank me until the Eldest has made his decision,"

Abraham said. "You and your soldiers represent a serious problem. Alex should not have brought you here."

"She saved our lives," Winter said. "I won't tell her she was wrong."

Abraham sighed. "I know. She is . . . impulsive."

"So what is this Eldest likely to do with us?"

"I will let him explain. For now, come with me."

Abraham led the way out of the long room and into a narrow corridor, floored with the same colorful carpets. At a junction, water flowed out of a carved stone pipe into a basin. There was a wooden cup, and at Abraham's nod Winter filled it and gulped down delicious, bitterly cold water. After she guzzled another few cups, he helped her untangle the bandage on her injured hand. It came away stubbornly at first, the bottom layers crusty with pus and dried blood, and the stench made Winter gag. When they had it off, the skin underneath was a ruin of cracked black and red, and she needed no urging to plunge it into the basin. The cold made her gasp, but she rubbed frantically with her other hand, dead, rotten flesh and dried skin sloughing away to reveal fresh, healthy pink underneath. At last she lifted her hand, as uncalloused as a newborn's, numb from the chilly water but completely whole.

"That's . . . wow." Winter made a fist and blinked back tears. "I didn't realize it had gotten so bad."

"We are familiar with such injuries in the mountains. The cold numbs pain and hides fever. A man can walk for days with his feet rotting in his boots." He gave a very slight smile. "You are fortunate I was here to help you."

"You've seen the others, too? Some of them had injuries."

"Of course. Although there was one—Bobby?" When Winter nodded, he went on. "Apologies, we didn't have much language in common. Her body has been changed by another demon, in a way I've never seen, and I didn't dare interfere with it. She didn't seem to need my assistance, however."

"She'll be fine," Winter said. "Where is she? I need to tell the others I'm all right."

"You must see the Eldest first," Abraham said firmly. "Follow me."

Winter started to protest, but she bit her tongue. She badly wanted to know what was going on, and this Eldest might have answers. She fell in behind Abraham as he walked down the twisting rock corridors, never hesitating in spite of the mazelike sameness of the halls. They passed several larger rooms with curtain doorways, but no people. Eventually they came to a long spiral stair, each step worn nearly round by the passage of endless feet. Winter climbed carefully, ascending at least two stories, and found herself in a much larger space.

It looked like a natural cavern that had been widened and straightened, forming an irregular room with one edge open to the outside. They were a considerable height above the valley floor, and from here Winter could see almost the entirety of it. The near end was farmland, neat plots of vegetables and grain divided by fieldstone fences. The rest was given over to pasture, with several flocks of sheep grazing peacefully, watched by men and dogs.

The view was so arresting it was a moment before Winter took in the rest of the room. A large fire, tended by a robed boy, burned like a beacon on the lip of the cliff. More carpets covered the floor, strewn with broad, flat pillows. On one of these sat an old man, with a bald skull and a wispy white beard. Off to his left, Alex sat cross-legged on another pillow, with a boy about her age beside her. She radiated frustration, while his expression was one of stolid, serious determination.

"I have brought the leader of the strangers, Eldest," Abraham said in Murnskai, bowing low. "Her name is Winter."

"Thank you," the old man said. His eyes, deeply set in his wrinkled face, were lively and bright. "She will be hungry. Antov, something to eat for our guest."

A boy who'd been sitting by the stairs scrambled away. Abraham led Winter to another pair of pillows, and Winter sat, uneasily trying to imitate the others.

"My Murnskai is poor," Winter said in that language, as best she could. "You will need to speak slowly—"

"We can speak Vordanai if you prefer," the old man said, with a heavy accent. "Or Hamveltai. That ought to include everyone, I think."

"Thank you," Winter said. "And thank you for helping us. I am sorry if we've caused you any trouble."

"I know you do not wish us harm," the Eldest said. "But I want you to understand the danger you represent. You bear a demon. You know of the Priests of the Black?"

"Of course she does," Alex cut in. "I told you—"

"I would remind you, young Alex, that *your* punishment is still being considered." The old man's friendly tone hid a hint of steel. "Please be silent."

"Yes," Winter said. "I've fought the Black Priests many times. They want me dead."

"Then without engaging in tedious explanation, it is enough to say that they are just as eager to destroy us. We live in their very shadow, and our only defense is remaining hidden. Only a very few are permitted to find the Mountain, and of those only a handful can be trusted to leave again. An offhand comment in a tavern, a reference in a journal discovered in a hundred years— any of these things could destroy us like a snowflake in a bonfire. You understand this?"

"I think so." She couldn't sense a demon from the old man, though it was hard to tell with both Alex and Abraham so close. "My soldiers and I will swear any oath of secrecy you care to name. But we have to get to Elysium."

"Why?"

Alex opened her mouth, and the Eldest shot her a warning glance. Winter said, "Our leader, Janus bet Vhalnich, has been trying to destroy the Priests of the Black. One of their assassins wounded him, with a magical poison that we believe will only be cured by her death. We have followed her this far."

"You risk your lives with a small chance of success. Vhalnich is so important?"

Winter nodded. "He is . . . a great man who has done a great deal for me. And I have seen the cruelty of the Priests of the Black. I have to save him, if I can."

"I see."

The boy Antov reappeared, with a tray of fresh-baked, steaming bread and a bowl of thick red soup. Winter hadn't realized how hungry she was until that moment; she practically grabbed the food out of his hands, scooping up the red stuff with the bread and wolfing it down. It was thick, with beans and tomatoes, and at that moment it was the best food she'd ever tasted.

"The healing," Abraham said apologetically. "It leaves her needing energy."

"Sorry," Winter mumbled, mouth full.

"It's nothing," the Eldest said, a faint smile bringing out the lines in his face. "You truly intend to go to Elysium?"

Winter nodded as she ripped into the bread. "It's our only chance to save him."

"You're certain he still lives?"

"No." She swallowed and took a deep breath. "I can only hope."

"We can do it," Alex said. "There's a way—"

This time it was the boy sitting beside her who elbowed Alex in the ribs. Winter cleared her throat.

"Alex has been very helpful to us," she said. "And she only volunteered to bring us here when there was no other way. Please don't be hard on her."

"Alex has some learning to do on the nature of hospitality and responsibility," the Eldest said. "But that is not your affair. Tell me this. If Vhalnich is saved, do you believe he can win this war against the Priests of the Black?"

"Yes," Winter said without hesitation.

"A great many people have sought to bring them down. Even your Farus the Fourth failed."

"Farus the Fourth didn't know what he was up against," Winter said. "Janus does. He's been working toward this from the beginning."

Winter was increasingly certain that was the case. It all made sense, when you looked at it from that angle. The expedition to Khandar had given Janus the Thousand Names and popular standing as a war hero. His return to Vordan and the Velt campaign had built up his support to the point where he was named First Consul. Every step of the larger campaign, the supernatural preparations and the military ones, had been planned for this.

"It has been many years since we dared to dream the Black Priests might be defeated," the Eldest said. "Many, many years."

"It's dangerous," the young man said. "If she fails, she might end up in a torture chamber, and she won't keep our secret for long."

"I am aware of that, Maxwell," the Eldest said. "But as Alex is so fond of telling us, there is a time when one must stop considering and take action."

"Finally," Alex burst out. "I—"

"This *may* be that time," the Eldest cut in. "I wish to hear more of Vhalnich and his fight. Winter, are you willing to tell the story?"

"Some of it is secret," Winter said.

"Naturally. Here is an offer, then. A secret for a secret. You must have questions for me?"

"Yes," Winter said. "But—"

"Eldest!" Maxwell said. "What are you going to tell her?"

"Whatever she wants to know," the Eldest said firmly. "Our greatest secret is our very existence, and she already knows that. Anything else is small by comparison. And I suspect we may discover some areas of mutual understanding."

"All right," Winter said. "If that's what you need to let us go."

"That remains to be seen." The Eldest got to his feet, surprisingly spry considering his frail appearance. "Let me show you the archive."

Another stair, at the back of the room, led down into the mountain again. There were no windows here, and the Eldest carried a smoky lantern to light the way. The others remained behind, a furious argument between Alex and Maxwell beginning almost immediately.

"You have questions," the Eldest said.

"I hardly know where to start," Winter said. "What *is* this place? Who are you? Why—"

"It is best to begin at the beginning," the old man said, chuckling a little. "Do you know anything about the founding of the Karisai Church?"

"Only what's in the *Wisdoms*," Winter admitted. "Karis obtained the Grace from the Lord and then founded the Church to teach people the right way to live, so that the Beast wouldn't return."

"The Beast of Judgment," the Eldest intoned. "When you think about it, what do you picture?"

Winter frowned. At Mrs. Wilmore's, there had been a painting of Karis banishing the Beast. The monster had been mostly hidden in shadow, but it had looked vaguely like an enormous black wolf, with long fangs and glowing red eyes. But that had always felt allegorical to her, not *really* real. "I can't say that I've thought much about it."

"Never? It is the most important story in the *Wisdoms*. Surely you learned it practically in the cradle."

"Of course. I guess . . ." She groped for words. "I never thought of the Beast as a *thing*, like a monster. I figured it was more of a concept. Like a representation of God's wrath."

"You are not far from the truth, though not for the reason you think." The Eldest raised his lantern to illuminate an intersection, then turned left. The tunnels here were dusty and unadorned, with no rooms leading off of them. "The reality is that the Beast of Judgment is a demon, not entirely unlike the one you bear."

"A *demon*? But . . ." Winter trailed off.

"But?"

"The Beast was going to destroy the *world*. Some of the demons I've seen have been terrifying, but none of them even come close to that."

"It's not clear that the Beast would have destroyed the world itself. But humanity? Oh, yes. It is the most powerful demon ever to appear, and it differs from the others in two key respects. First, it is not restricted to a single host. It *spreads*. This is the essence of its power. If it had been left unchecked, every human being would have eventually been brought into its dominion. God chose His tool of destruction well."

"How do you know all of this?" Winter said. "I've never heard anyone speak of the Beast that way."

"I am coming to that." The Eldest looked over his shoulder and smiled. "The second difference between the Beast and a common demon is that the Beast is intelligent in its own right. Most demons have no more reason than a cat or a wolf, but the Beast is to them as humans are to animals. It *remembers*, down through the centuries. It learns."

Winter nodded slowly. She'd always thought of Infernivore as a kind of animal, with its own moods and hungers, but no smarter than, say, a dog. A lot like a dog, in fact—eager to attack, but still waiting for its master's command. She tried to imagine sharing her soul with something that could *think*, and shivered.

"The Church has done its best to suppress the truth," the Eldest went on. "But *we* remember, though they try to destroy us. Karis was a sorcerer, a man who had studied the art of summoning demons. In an age of great minds, he was one of the greatest. When the Beast first arose, sent by God to destroy mankind, he alone saw what would come. He prayed, and God, impressed by his piety and will, granted him the knowledge and strength to confront the monster. Karis sacrificed himself to the Beast, even as his followers eradicated all the other hosts, leaving it confined to his body alone. His acolytes learned the Beast's name, the greatest and most powerful of the demon names. You understand the nature of demons and their names?"

"Not really," Winter confessed, feeling like she was barely treading water. "Janus has explained a little."

"A demon can be summoned from the hells by the incantation of its name. Each name refers to only a single creature, and if it is already in this world, reciting the name is useless. But the demons work ceaselessly to reach our world if they are left to their own devices, and now and again they succeed. Sometimes a child is born with a demon, without any summoning." He cocked his head. "Is that how it was with you? Or did you speak a name?"

"I spoke . . . something." Feor had called it a *naath*, but Winter guessed it amounted to the same thing. "It hurt so much I thought I would die."

"You very well might have. The more powerful the demon, the harder it is for a human soul to bear its weight. An unworthy host dies at once. This also means the more powerful the demon, the more difficult it is for it to be born into the world.

"What Karis realized was that the Beast, being intelligent, would learn from its failure. If it was loosed again, it would never be so foolish as to allow all its hosts to be hunted down. And if it arose in a corner of the world where there was no one to oppose it, then it would grow out of control before it could be stopped. He understood the nature of the task God had set him, and those who came after him." The Eldest halted, looking at Winter. "For thirteen hundred years, the Church has held the Beast captive. When one host dies, a search is made for another who can bear the weight of it. As long as it is in this world, it can be kept under lock and key. If it is allowed to return to the hells, it could arise anywhere, and if it finds itself beyond the reach of the Church, then humanity is doomed. *This* is the nature of the Grace. Only as long as the Church maintains its vigil is God's instrument of vengeance kept from the world."

"Wait. This is *still* going on?" Winter said. "You're not serious." Even after everything she'd seen, things like this—Karis, the Beast, sorcery—felt like they belonged only in ancient history.

"I am. The Beast of Judgment is interred in a cell under Elysium."

"Brass fucking Balls of the—" Winter stopped. "I mean. Damn."

"Indeed."

"So where do *you* come in?"

The Eldest turned and continued walking. "Three hundred years after Karis' sacrifice, there came to the Church the greatest leader since the Savior's death."

"Saint Elleusis Ligamenti," Winter said, eager to show she wasn't entirely ignorant. "He founded Elysium and split the Church into the three orders, and launched the holy wars."

"Correct," the Eldest said. "He also took it upon himself to codify Church doctrine and eliminate sects whose beliefs had been branded as heresy."

"People were sacrificing animals and so on, right? Pagan rituals they'd held on to." There had been a paragraph or so to that effect in one of Winter's history books. It made her think of Khandar and the endless ranks of their animal-headed gods.

"There was some of that," the Eldest agreed. "But the largest split was a philosophical disagreement over the nature of demon-summoning. In the early days of the Church, priests—following in Karis' footsteps—gathered the names of demons and used them for their own ends. Sorcery was more common then. But as the Church's power grew, one group, headed by Ligamenti, held that *anyone* who hosted a demon was condemned to eternal torment, no matter for what purposes the demon was used. That the goal of the Church should be to imprison all demons as they'd imprisoned the Beast, and banish sorcery from the world forever.

"We called them the Purifiers. At the time my ancestors called themselves the Pragmatists, and they believed that demons were tools to be used for good or evil. Where they refer to us at all, however, the Church now calls us the Mages, and our belief the Mages' Heresy. It is a useful enough name for our purposes.

"So there was war between the Church and the Mages. Sorcery had never been popular with the common people, no matter the purpose, and Ligamenti raised them against us. Some of us tried to fight back, taking shelter with the tyrants and kings who ruled much of the continent, but they were eventually destroyed as the domain of the Church expanded. Others fled beyond Ligamenti's reach. And my own ancestors chose to hide, here on the Mountain, and hope that Ligamenti and his Purifiers would destroy themselves."

The Eldest stopped in front of an iron-banded wooden door. He fished under his robe and removed an ancient brass key, which he fitted into a keyhole worked into the banding. The door swung inward on noiseless, well-oiled hinges, and the old man raised his lantern high.

"Here we are," he said. "Unless I miss my guess, you've seen something like this before?"

Winter stepped around him into the doorway. The room beyond was small and nearly empty, with only a small fire pit at the other end with a couple of pillows beside it. Lining the walls were huge tablets, taller than she was, that reflected the lantern with the dull gleam of burnished steel. Standing out like dark ink on the surface were row after row of strange characters, deeply incised into the metal, spelling out what Winter now knew to be the names of demons.

The Eldest kindled the fire pit, and he and Winter sat down between the ancient slabs. In the most detached way she could manage, she told him the story of what had happened in Khandar—Feor, the meeting with Mother and her cult, and the discovery of the Thousand Names—and the conflicts they'd had with the Priests of the Black since her return to Vordan. The old man listened without changing his expression, stirring the fire from time to time with an iron poker and sending sparks whirling toward the ceiling.

"I had guessed . . . some of this," he said when she was done. "We are isolated here, but not so completely as it might appear. There had always been a rumor—more of a legend now—that one of the greatest of the Mages fled to

Khandar with her archives after the fall of the Demon King. The Priests of the Black have tried several times to reach it without success."

"The Thousand Names," Winter said, looking at the tablets all around them.

"This is another archive," the old man said. "A smaller one, though it contains the names of several powerful creatures. The ancient Mages wanted their records to last and to be difficult to steal."

"So some of these Mages made it to Khandar, and then the archive fell into the hands of the cultists?"

"From your story, I would guess that it was more of a transformation of the one into the other. Traditions change as they are passed down, unless you live apart from the world as we do here." He shook his head. "I would love to meet this Feor."

"That can probably be arranged." The thought snapped Winter back to reality. "If you're willing to let us go, that is."

"I think I have no choice. If Vhalnich has the Thousand Names, he—or his allies, if he dies—might be able to challenge the Church." He sighed. "My ancestors may have burned for revenge against Ligamenti and his Purifiers, but all I want is to keep my people safe. We have built a home here. But . . ."

"But?"

"The Beast." He poked the fire. "The vigil *must* be maintained. One reason my ancestors felt the Purifiers were misguided was that if knowledge of sorcery faded from the world, as Ligamenti claimed it must, then the understanding of the need to keep up the watch might fade as well. The Priests of the Black have banished demons to history and children's stories, but the Beast of Judgment is *real*. If they fall, if their order is destroyed, then it will return. Not immediately—the Beast is powerful, and it can enter our world on its own only with great difficulty. But it *will* come, one year or another, and we will not be able to stop it again."

"I don't know if Janus knows all this," Winter said. "But I'm certain that he wouldn't want to release the Beast of Judgment. He doesn't want to annihilate humanity."

"If I offer you our help, this is my price. You must convince him to take on this responsibility. Will you swear to that?"

"I will," Winter said. She was surprised at how easily the words came. The Eldest's sincerity was apparent, and she couldn't see how lying to her would help him. *Besides, if we take Elysium, we'll get the truth either way.* If there *was* something there that could destroy mankind, she was sure Janus would agree that keeping it locked up was only common sense.

"Then you will have our aid, such as it is," the old man said. He stood and stretched, back popping audibly. "There are ways into Elysium that have been forgotten for a thousand years. And I'm sure Alex will wish to come with you."

"Is she one of yours?" Winter said. "Did she get her demon from here?"

"Oh, no." The Eldest gave a sad smile. "From time to time we take in strays. Wild demon-hosts, those who have fled the Priests of the Black and their Penitent Damned. Alex and Abraham both came to us that way, together."

"The Penitent Damned." That had been bothering Winter. "You said Ligamenti and the Purifiers rejected the use of demons. Why do the Black Priests use them now?"

"Hypocrisy and hairsplitting." The old man rolled his eyes. "Ligamenti at least had the courage to reject sorcery outright, in spite of its advantages. Later generations were not so stalwart. They rationalized that while hosting a demon results in unalterable damnation, that sacrifice could be justified—a few souls condemned to eternal torment in exchange for many saved from the endless fires. The Penitent Damned are those who have willingly given up their chance at a reward in the next life in order to help the Church in this one." He shook his head. "I don't know whether to laugh at them or take pity on those whose self-loathing rises to such a pitch."

"The Mages don't believe carrying a demon means damnation?"

"Of course not," the Eldest said gently. "Some children are *born* with demons, remember? Can you look at a sleeping infant and honestly tell me that God would condemn that babe to hell for such an accident? No. God judges us for our *actions*, however we carry them out. A demon can be used for evil, just as a sword can. But it can be used for good, too."

Winter, never particularly religious, had always been uncertain whether she really believed in heaven and hell. But with Infernivore wrapped around her soul, it was nice to know that there was more than one opinion on the subject.

The Eldest led the way back, following a different path. He brought her to a curtained doorway, which led into a large hall on the ground level, open to the outside with more arrow-slit windows. A number of Mountain people were gathered, in their colorful wool robes, surrounding a small knot of Vordanai. Winter's chest relaxed slightly at the sight of Bobby, Red, and the rest of the Girls' Own soldiers, who were trying to converse with a number of young Mountain men in a fractured pidgin of three or four different languages.

"Winter!" Bobby jumped to her feet as they entered, pushing through the crowd. She didn't bother with a salute, but wrapped Winter in a hug so powerful Winter felt her ribs creak. "Are you all right?"

"I will be, if you let go of me," Winter said.

"I told them I wanted to see you, but none of them seemed to understand," Bobby said, stepping back. "They haven't treated us badly, though. There's food, and . . ." She lowered her voice. "One of them can heal wounds. He brought down Ivers' fever and closed the arrow cut on Varner's leg."

"I know. He saw to my hand, too." She held up her fresh pink fingers.

"Alex keeps telling us to wait. Do you even know where we *are*? Why is it so warm?"

Winter glanced at the Eldest. "He hasn't explained that, actually. But I told him what we're here to do, and they're going to help us get into Elysium."

Bobby gave a relieved sigh. "Glad to hear it, sir. I was hoping we wouldn't have to fight our way out. There are a lot of kids here." She whispered again. "A few other demons, too, I think."

"It'll be all right," Winter said. "We're all on the same side. I think."

"I was surprised when they told me about your followers," the Eldest said in Hamveltai, coming up beside Winter. "Are all soldiers in Vordan women?"

"Not *all*," Winter said. "But some. A few."

"Among some of the northern tribes, the women fight alongside the men," the Eldest mused. "And of course the Tyrant's Legions infamously took anyone willing to serve." He smiled at Winter. "One advantage of standing apart from the world is that you can see how the wheel of history turns and turns again."

"Who's he?" Bobby said. Her Hamveltai was as weak as her Murnskai. For a moment Winter wished Cyte were here, with her gift for languages. *And how she would have loved talking to the Eldest about his wheel of history.* She pushed the thought aside. Cyte was—hopefully—safe, back in the Grand Army's camp. *I wouldn't wish what we went through to get here on anybody.*

"He's in charge here," Winter said in Vordanai. "Sort of a head priest, I think."

"Oh!" Bobby offered the Eldest an awkward bow, which he returned. "Tell him thanks for the food."

"It's nothing," the old man said, when Winter translated. "The Mountain is generous with us."

The other soldiers had drifted over by now, and Winter found herself pressed into service as a makeshift translator for the next hour, rendering Vordanai into an ugly mix of Murnskai and Hamveltai. These seemed to be the primary and secondary languages of the Mountain, respectively, though their pronunciation of the latter was a little odd compared to the Velt dialect Winter had learned. The Mountain people were eager for news of the world, though Winter was surprised to find they were remarkably up to date in their knowledge of the outside.

"Eldest!" The curtained door flew open, and a girl in her midteens came in. She wore a long shirt and leather pants instead of the usual robes, and her dark hair was tied in two long pigtails. "Eldest, I have news—" She stopped, eyes widening as she saw the outsiders.

"As do I," the Eldest said. "Welcome back, Snowfox."

"Who are these people?" The girl's eyes narrowed as she looked at Winter. Winter concentrated hard in return, but Infernivore showed no interest. *She doesn't have a demon. So why is she picking me out?*

"Let me explain," the Eldest said, putting a hand on her shoulder. "Winter, I will send for you in perhaps an hour. It has been a long day, I realize, but from what you have told me time is of the essence."

"Thank you, Eldest," Winter said.

With a final suspicious look from the girl, the two of them left the room.

"What was that about?" Bobby asked.

"Damned if I know," Winter said.

The boy was about five years old, his hair a white blond almost as light as Winter's. He hid behind his mother, peeking around the edge of her skirts. The woman had the pale skin, dark hair, and dark eyes of most Murnskai, which made the boy's features all the more arresting; in addition to his mop of golden hair, his eyes were a bright, shining yellow, like the eyes of a cat caught in a lantern's glare.

"He read the name of a demon?" Winter said. The woman spoke only Murnskai, so the conversation was a slow and inexact affair. "Really?"

"Yes. The Eldest said that of all the young ones, he was the best—" And then a word Winter didn't understand. *Candidate? Sacrifice?* "The Sunbringer prefers children as its hosts."

"You weren't afraid that it would hurt him?" Winter said.

"Of course I was." She pulled the boy close with one arm and gave him a squeeze. "But someone must bear the burden if we are to survive. Besides, the

Sunbringer is one of the gentlest of demons. And Rimi has always been a bright child. It took him barely a month to learn its name."

"Ivn-fa-toth!" the boy said. His mother grinned and ruffled his hair.

"That kid keeps the whole valley warm?" Bobby said.

When Winter translated, the Mountain woman nodded. "Rimi visits the wards spread around the edges of the valley once a year and renews their power. He and Snowfox keep us safe and happy here."

"Happy," the boy agreed solemnly.

There was a rustle in the curtained doorway, and Alex appeared. Rimi gave a happy cry and rushed over to her.

"Hello, Rimi," Alex said.

"Alex! Can we swing?"

At Winter's questioning glance, Alex blushed slightly. "The kids like it when I use my power to swing them along the cliffs." She glared at Winter as though daring her to comment.

"That sounds like fun," Winter said, a little awkwardly.

"Not now, Rimi," Alex said. "I need to take Winter and Bobby to see the Eldest. Stay here with your mother, and we can swing later, okay?"

After detaching the child, which took some effort, Alex led Winter and Bobby through the maze of corridors the Mountain people had carved into the rock. They followed the same staircase Winter had taken the last time, to the room where she'd been introduced to the Eldest, which she gathered was some kind of inner sanctuary.

"I think I understand a little better what it might have cost you to bring us here," Winter said as they climbed. "I wanted to thank you."

"Yes," Alex said. "Well. I couldn't just leave you to die, could I?"

"You could have."

"I'm just glad you managed to come to an accommodation with the Eldest," she said.

"How long have you been living here?"

"Half a year or so. They saved us from the Priests of the Black." Alex shuddered slightly. "Abraham seemed happy to just settle down, but I couldn't stand it. When I heard about Janus, I went to find him." She frowned. "I'm sorry I couldn't tell you all this before."

"I understand." Winter grinned. "Given how it turned out, I can hardly complain, can I?"

They reached the big room, where they found the Eldest waiting. Beside him was the girl Winter had seen earlier and the young priest they'd called Maxwell. The six of them sat on pillows in a rough circle. Alex, beside Bobby, kept up a running translation for her benefit.

"Snowfox," the Eldest said, "I want you to tell Winter and the others what you saw."

The girl still looked suspicious, but she nodded. "I was on one of my regular routes, swinging around the south end of Elysium. When I saw there was a lot of activity, I stayed to watch. People were leaving, a *lot* of people. They had wagons, horses, mules, everything."

"Which way were they going?" Maxwell said.

"Southeast," Snowfox said.

"That's the Mohkba road," Alex said for Winter and Bobby's benefit. "It goes south to the pass, then east to the capital."

"How many people, exactly?" Maxwell pressed. "Dozens? A hundred?"

"A lot more than that," Snowfox said. "Thousands."

"It can't have been *thousands*," Maxwell said. "There aren't that many people *in* Elysium. The Priests of the White and Red can't be more than ten thousand altogether."

"I didn't *count* them," the girl said. "But I know what I saw."

"I believe her," the Eldest said. "And I can think of only one explanation. The Church thinks Vhalnich's army will reach Elysium, and they are fleeing beyond his reach."

"But the army isn't here," Winter said. "It's still camped at the Kovria."

"They can't track an army in this weather," Snowfox said. "But they can track *you*. The have sensitives who can feel a demon-host miles away. For all they know, you're at the head of a division."

"But the Priests of the Black would never abandon their citadel," Maxwell said. "They would lose too much."

The Eldest nodded. "They will remain, to protect the Beast and their archives."

"Which means the poisonous Penitent is probably still there," Winter said. "We still need to get inside."

"There are a great many ways into Elysium," the Eldest said. "Some are more dangerous than others. Snowfox can show you one of them and guide you as far as the walls."

Winter looked at the girl. "Are you certain? I don't want to put her in danger."

"I can look after myself," Snowfox snapped.

"And you will need her," the Eldest said. "Her power is our greatest asset."

"Her power?" Winter frowned. "She's a demon-host?"

"Weird, isn't it?" Alex said. Snowfox rolled her eyes at her.

"Her demon grants protection from other demons' senses," the Eldest said. "That power, imbued into the wards around the valley, is what keeps us hidden. If she goes with you, the Black Priest's sensitives will not be able to find you until you leave her side."

"In that case, we'd be very grateful for your help, Snowfox," Winter said, inclining her head.

The girl's cheeks pinked and she sat up a little straighter. "If the Eldest thinks it's a good idea."

"Alex," the Eldest said. "You wish to go with the Vordanai?"

"I do," she said. "If I have a chance to strike back at the Black Priests, I want to take it."

"Maxwell will also accompany you," the Eldest said, nodding. "He has studied our maps of Elysium and knows a good deal about the Penitent Damned."

Maxwell nodded at the old man, and Winter sensed there had been a long conversation on this particular topic. She cleared her throat.

"How long will it take to get there?" she said. "We should leave as soon as we can."

"If we start at dawn, we'll get to Elysium by dusk," Snowfox said. "There's no point trying to move over the mountains in the dark."

"Tomorrow morning, then," the Eldest said. "I will pray for all of you."

CHAPTER SEVENTEEN

MARCUS

"Fire!" Viera screamed.

The cannons belched flaming death. Canister rounds sprayed balls over the ford, turning the icy water to froth in a thousand tiny waterspouts. The ragged line of bone women dissolved into chaos, figures punched off their feet, struggling to stay upright, or slumping into the water. Marcus felt a moment of crawling horror as he watched them—any who were wounded and couldn't walk would drown or freeze in the bone-chilling torrent.

The volley was the signal for the bone women to break formation, casting aside their big hide shields and sprinting across the river at the Vordanai line. They shouted as they ran, waving spears in the air, heedless of the danger. The rest of the bone men came on behind them, archers holding their bows over their heads to keep them out of the water, horsemen pounding past on wings of spray. In the forest on the north side of the river, Marcus could see shadows moving through the trees—white riders, moving in like vultures to pick at a dying animal.

He and Fitz stood in the center of the camp, on a wagon they'd made into an improvised command post. The slope gave him a clear view of the river and the oncoming mass of bone people. Every day since Give-Em-Hell had departed, the tribesmen had assaulted their defenses, but so far the Vordanai had held them off. *So far.*

"Give them one more!" Viera shouted. "One more, then fall back! Move, move!"

The artillerymen, bone-weary and working with numbed fingers, loaded and repositioned their pieces faster than Marcus would have thought possible. It wasn't fast enough; some of the archers paused in midstream to loose, and shafts were falling among the cannoneers before the second volley was ready. Men were hit and staggered away, or kept working grimly with arrows jutting from an arm or a leg, stepping over the thrashing bodies of their companions.

"Ready!" Viera said, as her crews withdrew from their guns. Two arrows whistled past her, but her face was alive with anticipation. *"Fire!"*

Double canister this time, at barely a hundred yards, slamming out into the bone women like God's own scythe. A few unlucky souls in the lead were struck by a half dozen balls at once and simply disintegrated, stray limbs pinwheeling over the river trailing arterial sprays of blood. The swath of destruction extended for hundreds of yards, cutting down some and sparing others. An archer dropped his bow and clutched his throat, hot blood pulsing between his fingers and staining the front of his leather jerkin. Another woman in the act of helping a comrade collapsed atop her body, hands slapping feebly at the water.

"Back!" Viera shouted. "Back to the walls!"

The cannoneers scrambled backward, swearing and stumbling in the snow. One man fell on his face, and no one could spare a moment to help him; he was already dead, in spite of his screaming. Viera led the way, running up the sloping wall of packed, mounded snow. It was coated in ice, and she began to slip backward, but before she could fall Andy leaned over and grabbed her arm, pulling her over the parapet. All along the rampart, First Division soldiers did the same, hoisting the cannoneers up and out of the way before bringing their muskets back in line.

The walls had been Marcus' concept, but Fitz had made them work. At the War College, the younger boys had built snow forts in the winter, practicing attack and defense with arsenals of packed snowballs and down-stuffed coats for armor. Digging into the frozen earth of the north bank of the Kovria was out of the question, and so Marcus had proposed using the only construction material available.

He'd been thinking of a low wall that might slow down a charge or trip up a horse, but Fitz, as usual, had seen further. That first night, while the rankers packed snow into chest-high ramparts and wondered if their commanders had gone mad, Fitz had melted cauldron after cauldron of snow over the bonfire. He'd had them pour the still-cold water over the top, and the night's chill had frozen it solid, leaving a layer of hard, slippery ice. More snow and more ice had followed, the men setting to the work with a will once they understood the purpose of it.

By the time the bone men attacked the next morning, there was a low, broad fortress overlooking the ford, and the soldiers spent every spare moment further strengthening their position. The walls were built up, and fire steps constructed on the inside, while wooden stakes were hammered into the ice to deter charging horses. Tents were cannibalized for cloth, which the men stretched across wooden frames over their firing positions to block descending arrows.

Only the cannons had to remain outside the protective cordon. No wall made of snow, however reinforced with ice, could handle the shock and recoil of a twelve-pounder firing. Every time the bone men charged, the cannoneers stood to their pieces as long as they could, then vaulted the wall just ahead of the maddened horde of tribesmen. Every time there were fewer of them to go back out. Viera picked men from the infantry and gave them a crash course in gunnery, but the firing was still slower and less accurate.

A few moments longer and the bone women were among the guns, screaming and whooping. The artilleryman who'd fallen struggled back to his feet, only to be transfixed by a thrown spear. He slumped down again, propped at an angle on the weapon that had punched through his belly. Arrows began to fall on the ice fortress, ripping down with soft *zip, zip, zip* noises. The tent canvas, two or three layers thick, caught and tangled many of the shafts, but some punched through with enough force to kill, or found the gaps between the makeshift sheets. A soldier at Marcus' side stumbled back from the wall, swearing, as an arrow drew a long, ugly gash up his arm. More arrows came from behind, the white riders venturing close enough to fire at the undermanned defenses there.

Lieutenants and sergeants shouted the order to fire, and the wall of the fortress was suddenly billowing with gray powder smoke. Balls ripped into the bone women, sending them stumbling rubber-legged to fall in a heap or staggering back toward the dubious safety of the river. Many of those who were hit simply came on, driven by madness or faith or both. Marcus saw a young woman holding her guts in with one hand while casting a spear with the other. Blood slicked another's face from where a ball had creased her scalp, but she grinned and kept running, teeth shockingly white against the crimson stain.

Behind the rampart some men loaded and handed readied muskets up to others, who stood on the fire step to loose into the oncoming mob. Arrows were coming in flat now, a harder shot but with no protection from the improvised defenses, and a man went down screaming with a shaft in his eye. The fastest of the bone women had reached the base of the wall, threading their way between the icy wooden stakes. The first few charges had stalled here, the spearwomen unable to get purchase on the iced-over surface of the wall, but they had learned from those attacks. Now the bone women stowed their spears and took small axes or long knives in each hand, stabbing these weapons into the ice to make hand- and footholds. It was slow work, and the defenders leaned out to fire down into them as they came, deadly at point-blank range. But more bone women waited a few steps back, spears at the ready, hurling them whenever a man showed himself over the parapet. Marcus saw more than one soldier scream and vanish over the edge, to be slaughtered in the milling mass below.

When they'd built their ladders of axes and knives high enough, the bone women swarmed up it, jumping from the highest point to catch the lip of the wall. The first to try it, a fierce-eyed girl who couldn't have been more than sixteen, threw her arms over the rampart, only to get a bayonet through the throat from the Colonial on the other side. She slid down the wall, leaving a long, red slick on the ice, but two more spearwomen ascended in her place. The Colonial thrust at one of them, but she slipped aside, grabbing the front of his uniform and pulling him over the edge. His scream mingled with shouts of triumph from below. The second bone woman lifted herself over the rampart and got her spear up in time to block a thrust from a desperate Vordanai soldier, wielding her weapon with deadly efficiency as she knocked his bayonet aside and slashed his belly open. Then a sergeant raised a pistol and shot her in the chest, and she reeled backward and vanished over the wall.

"It's not going to hold," Fitz said conversationally.

"Balls of the Beast," Marcus swore. He looked around—all four sides of the makeshift fort were engulfed in powder smoke, where the bone men cavalry and the white riders were trading arrows for musket balls, but it was here facing the ford that they were coming over the wall. He and Fitz stood in the center, under another improvised shelter. Beneath it were their practically nonexistent stores, the ever-growing ranks of the wounded, and the reserve—eight companies from the First and Second Battalions, shrunken to perhaps five hundred men under the relentless assaults.

"I'll lead the attack," Fitz said, hand dropping to his sword.

"No!" Marcus surprised himself with his vehemence. "Not this time."

"You're in command," Fitz said.

"And the men need to see me sharing the danger," Marcus said in low tones. "Besides, you know as well as I do that we can't afford to lose you, either."

"As you wish, sir." Fitz straightened and saluted. "Good luck."

"Thanks." Marcus drew his sword, the battered cavalry saber he'd carried all the way from Khandar. "Reserve! With me! To the wall!"

A roar came from behind him, answered by scattered cheers from the troops on the rampart. They'd built three large ramps of snow leading up to the fire step, and Marcus ran for the middle one, right where the bone women were on the verge of breaking through. His men came on behind him. With friends and enemies thoroughly mixed, there was no room for musket-fire, so they met spears with bayonets.

Spears, Marcus thought, had definite advantages. He cut the first bone woman down from behind while she was administering the coup de grace to a fallen Colonial, then leapt over her corpse to engage two more. They backed off, keeping him at a distance, and for a moment it was all he could do to fend off their thrusts with frantic parries. The one on the left shifted to engage a soldier coming up behind him, and Marcus took the opportunity to dodge the other's spear, reaching out with his free hand to grab it just behind the head. He yanked, and she stumbled forward, off-balance. His other hand came up, the heavy guard of his saber crushing her nose with a spurt of blood. Her legs went out from under her, and his sword shot forward, almost automatically, and punched into her chest as smooth as a knife into butter. Her eyes went wide, and she died with a shiver.

Girls. Five days of constant attacks had given him a thorough education in how deadly the bone women were. But every so often, in the middle of the fight, his perspective would slip, and they'd go from being *the enemy* to *young women*, people he'd always been taught he had to protect. It was stupid, he was well aware, but—

But nothing, he snarled at himself. *It's stupid and it'll get you killed.* He turned away from the girl's corpse and pushed his way to the wall, hacking through the press of struggling bodies. A woman was pushed against him by someone else's shove, bone fetishes clattering on her leathers, and Marcus slammed a knee into her midriff and smashed her on the top of her skull with his pommel as she went down. When he got to the rampart, another bone woman was just climbing over, and he kicked her in the chin and watched her fall into the press. More hands appeared on the edge, and he hacked down at them, sending fingers flying. An arrow brushed his arm, opening a long cut, but he was too keyed up to feel more than a dull sting.

The reserve turned the fight, driving the bone women back over the wall. The defenders' muskets once again began to sound, cutting down spearwomen at the base of the wall by the score and taking a toll on the archers. At some unheard signal, the attack broke off, cavalry wheeling away from the walls and spearwomen running for the ford and the shelter of the other side of the river. The white riders retreated into the woods, leaving a few of their number dead on the frozen plain.

A ragged cheer rose from the defenders. *It's hard to muster much excitement when you know they'll be back tomorrow.* But for now, at least, they were still alive.

"I want them stripped for anything we can use," Marcus said. "Horses butchered. Bodies dragged to the pit."

"Yes, sir," Fitz said. He was wrapping a bandage around Marcus' arm himself; Marcus refused to burden the overworked cutters with such a minor injury. "What about the wounded?"

"The usual," Marcus muttered, not meeting his subordinate's eye.

That meant that any who could walk would be turned loose outside the walls, to make their way to their own camp as best they could. Any who couldn't got a slit throat. It went against all the rules of civilized war, but as Marcus had to keep reminding himself, they were well away from civilization here. The simple fact was that they couldn't feed their own men, let alone the enemy.

"Understood, sir." Fitz tied off the bandage. "That should hold you. I'll check it in the morning."

"Thanks." Marcus felt a little embarrassed by his earlier outburst. "Sorry for running off like that. I just needed to . . . *do* something."

"I understand, sir. And it *is* good for the men to see you fighting alongside them. Just be careful."

"Has anyone taken Janus his dinner?"

"Not yet."

"I'll do it, then." Janus' tent was the one quiet—or nearly quiet—place in a camp overrun with the moans of the wounded and dying.

"Make sure to eat something yourself, sir," Fitz said.

There was little enough to eat, even for high-ranking officers. A few crackers of hardtack and strips of boiled horsemeat, with a few tiny wrinkled fruits that looked like pickled plums. The latter came from the enemy, looted from the pockets and pouches of dead bone women. The horses came from the enemy, too; the last of theirs had been killed and eaten days before.

The Colonial guards on Janus' tent stepped aside as Marcus came in. Janus was sitting up in bed, which wasn't unusual these days. Since the fighting had started, he'd shown more animation, talking to whoever was present. Unfortunately, not a lot of what he said made any *sense*, and his fever was still practically hot enough to fry an egg. Marcus wasn't sure if this represented an improvement. Breakfast that morning, for example, had been accompanied by a lecture on the mating habits of scorpions and how this represented an adaptation to their various environments.

Janus looked over as Marcus entered. His skin was alarmingly pale, and his already thin face had turned cadaverous. His gray eyes were huge and fever-bright.

"Marcus!" he said. That was a positive sign; Janus didn't always seem to know whom he was talking to.

"Good evening, sir," Marcus said. "I've brought—"

"Marcus, do you think I'm a genius?" Janus said.

That was less positive. Marcus made his way to the bed, holding the tray with its pathetic meal in front of him. "I—" he began.

"Of course you do," Janus said, speaking just slightly too fast. "It's obvious from your behavior, faith and hero worship, common enough traits. Why shouldn't you? I encourage the notion, taking advantage of preexisting embedded cultural tropes—genius as eccentric means less likely to be questioned, greater trust required, highly advantageous. Can hardly place blame for deliberately inspired ideation. And yet. And *yet*, Marcus!"

"Sir?" Marcus held out a cracker of hardtack. "You should eat something."

Janus snatched the hardtack, bit down triumphantly, and chewed the sandpapery stuff with every evidence of enjoyment.

"The question is whether you understand the *nature* of genius," he said, spraying crumbs. "If not, how can you—as a proxy for the common man, Ligamenti's *hitsujikai*—be expected to recognize it when you encounter it? Is genius merely above-average performance, or is it, must it be something more than that, something *qualitative*, or are we merely splitting syntactical hairs, or is there a sliding scale, Quartier's distribution but along which axis? Which axis, Marcus?"

"I'm not sure I follow, sir," Marcus said, offering some of the boiled meat.

"I have seen the real thing." Janus' tone suddenly darkened, all the energy draining out of him. He accepted the meat and chewed mechanically, shoulders sagging.

"Genius?" Marcus said, hoping to keep up his end of the conversation.

Janus swallowed. "You think I'm out of the ordinary." His voice was a whisper. "*She* could do everything I can do, and yet she outshone me, the sun against a candle. Looking at her was staring destiny in the face. I knew she was going to reshape the world, overturn kingdoms and empires, change the course of history. I *knew* it. And then . . ."

He let out a long breath and settled back to the pillows.

"Sir?" Marcus said, eager to keep him talking. "Are we talking about Mya?"

"Mya." Janus' eyes slowly closed. "We have to help her, Marcus. Lost in shadow. All that strength, lost. We're so close. Just a little farther." His voice fell to a whisper. "It's there, under Elysium. My demon . . ." He lay still and quiet.

"Sir?"

Marcus checked Janus' breathing, which was shallow but steady. His forehead was frighteningly warm to the touch. Marcus sighed and left the rest of food beside the bed, in case he woke up.

Outside the tent, Andy was waiting for him. Her uniform was filthy with sweat and blood.

"You all right?" Marcus said. "You look like you've been butchering hogs."

The comment, under other circumstances, might have been in bad taste, but Abby only gave a morbid chuckle.

"One of them tried to grab me after I stabbed her. Ended up well covered in it. What about you? Your arm okay?"

He raised the bandaged limb for her inspection. It was starting to hurt, but he kept the pain out of his face. "Just a scratch. I'll be fine."

"How's *he* doing?"

"Not well," Marcus said. "He's not getting *worse*, but he can't stay like this forever. He's losing weight. And he . . . babbles."

Mya. Janus talked about her incessantly in his delirium. Marcus still didn't know if she'd been a friend, family, or a lover, or even if she was real, but her name was one of the few things that could get a reaction when Janus was in his worst states. *He thinks she's waiting for him under Elysium.* An odd thought struck him. *Maybe she's the demon he's looking for?*

"Damn." Andy shook her head. "You think Give-Em-Hell made it?"

"No way to know. We just have to hold on as long as we can." *It's Weltae all over again.* For a moment he was back in Khandar, trapped in an ancient temple surrounded by Redeemers, with only a faith in Janus to hold on to. *But this time Janus is unconscious, and it's Raesinia I have to have faith in.*

"Yeah." Andy looked uncomfortable. "Look. I've been on the walls for the past few days—"

"I know. You've been amazing."

"Thanks." She let out a deep breath. "They're not going to hold, Marcus. Not for much longer. I don't know if it'll be tomorrow or the next day, but they'll break, and when they do it'll be bad. All that's keeping them here is knowing there's nowhere else to go."

"I know."

There was only so much he could ask of the same few battalions of tired, ragged men. The bone women and their archers had been roughly handled every time they'd crossed the river, but they had a large enough force to send fresh troops into every assault, to be met by the same exhausted defenders. To make matters worse, those same defenders had to care for their own wounded, add fresh ice to the walls, and drag hundreds of bloody corpses out of the line of fire.

"We have to do something different," Andy said. "I've been talking with Viera. She had an idea, but it's a bit . . ." She shrugged. "Well. You know Viera."

Which meant that the idea involved something exploding spectacularly. "At this point, I'm not going to rule anything out," he said. "Let's hear it."

"I don't like it," Colonel Morag said. He was Royal Army, square jawed and stout, though some of his portliness had wasted away as the siege went on. "I can't ask my men to fight in such dangerous conditions."

"Which is exactly why we're not going to tell them," Andy said. "If anyone asks, we're just reinforcing the wall."

"That's even worse," said the colonel. He looked to Fitz. "Sir, you can't expect us to go along with this. Too much could go wrong."

The other senior officers gathered in the tent muttered agreement. Viera, who'd explained her plan in clipped, precise tones, now sat and regarded them with undisguised scorn. Fitz sat beside Marcus and Andy, his expression bland as always.

"The column-general thinks it will work," he said.

"With respect," Morag said, "the column-general got us into this in the first place. If we'd stayed in place, we might have been able to rebuild the bridge by now. As it is—"

"Do you have a better plan, Colonel?" Andy snapped. "Because as it stands they're going to be boiling us for our bones before long."

"We should attack," Morag said immediately. "Break through their line and then break up. If we spread out into the forest, most of us can get away."

"Get away so that we can starve in the woods, you mean," Andy said.

"Better than getting killed here," Morag said. "Or getting blown sky-high—"

"I've gone over the plan with Janus," Marcus said quietly. "He think it will work."

That silenced the gathering. The colonels looked at one another.

"You didn't mention that the First Consul was awake," Morag said accusingly.

"He's very weak," Marcus said. "But he has . . . moments of lucidity. I showed it to him after Andy came to me this afternoon."

"Well." Morag swallowed. "If the First Consul approves, I suppose it's not my place to argue."

It's not your place to argue anyway, Marcus wanted to say, but he held his tongue. Morag and the others were clearly hanging on to military discipline by their fingertips. "Viera will show you the work that needs to be done. We want to keep it quiet, understand?" *If word gets out, no telling what* that *will do to morale.* "If I hear any rumors, the people sitting in this tent are going to be very unhappy."

"Understood, sir," Morag said. There was a matching chorus from the others.

"Viera, show them what they need to do."

"Yes, sir," Viera said with a sly grin. She escorted the senior officers out, herding them like a sheepdog.

"Did Janus really—" Fitz said quietly.

"Of course not," Marcus said. "He has no idea where we are. But if they need to believe it . . ." He shrugged, exhaustion settling over him like a coat.

"You think it will work?"

Marcus looked at Andy. "I think it'll buy us at least one more day."

"I suppose that's nothing to scoff at." Fitz got to his feet. "If you'll excuse me, sir."

"Go. Get some rest."

Fitz nodded and left the command tent, if the tiny space they sat in could be dignified with the name. Marcus was left alone with Andy. She'd changed her shirt to one a bit less bloodstained, though brown patches still discolored her coat. It hung loose around her shoulders; like Morag, she'd lost weight, though she hadn't had as much to lose.

"They'll come again in the morning," Andy said.

"Probably."

"Even if this works, it won't hold them long," Andy said. "Maybe until the next day."

"Probably."

"So we're all going to die."

Marcus sighed. "Probably."

"Okay." Andy took a deep breath, let it out, and rolled her shoulders. "Why doesn't that scare me like it used to?"

"Because you're tired," Marcus said. He'd been to that strange place beyond fear more than once. "When you're tired enough, dying just seems like a chance to rest."

"Saints and goddamned martyrs." Andy shook her head. "You're still sleeping in Janus' tent?"

"Someone has to look after him," Marcus said.

She nodded. "I've got my own tent now. Some lieutenant caught an arrow and nobody objected when I took it over." She cocked her head. "You're welcome to join me."

Marcus blinked. "I'm not pressed for space, if that's what you mean—"

Andy sighed and shuffled across the tent on her knees, sitting down again immediately opposite him.

"Marcus," she said. "Please listen carefully."

"All right."

She cleared her throat. "Would *you*"—she pointed at him—"like to come to my tent with *me* and . . . " She turned the finger on herself, then brought both fingers together in an obscene gesture.

"Oh." He swallowed. "Look, Andy, I don't . . . I mean . . ."

"I know, I know. I'm half your age, you don't see me that way, you're my commander, blah, blah, blah." She shrugged. "That might seem more important if we weren't all going to die tomorrow or the day after. As it is, I don't mind admitting I developed a bit of a crush on you back in Vordan. If this is going to be our last chance, I thought I would ask."

"It's not that," Marcus said. "Well, I mean, I guess it *is* that. I just . . ." He raised his hands helplessly. "I don't know. But I can't."

"It's all right," she said. "I'm sure I can find someone. Viera and I are the only two women in camp, after all, and not everyone has Fitz's preferences." She ran a hand through her hair. "I just thought I'd put the offer on the table."

"Thank you. I'm . . . flattered, I guess." Frankly, Marcus would have expected to find himself more scandalized. *I'm too tired for that, too.*

Andy smiled. "Just don't come crying to me after we're dead."

She got to her feet, bent over in the low-ceilinged tent, and went to the flap.

"I'll see you in the morning," Marcus said.

"Good night, Marcus." Andy paused and looked back. "Do you really not know why you can't, or are you just saying that?"

"Andy . . ." Marcus shook her head. "It just feels . . . wrong. I—"

"I only ask," she interrupted, "because it seems pretty obvious from where I'm sitting. You're in love with the queen, aren't you?"

Janus was still asleep when Marcus returned to their tent, shaking out his bed-roll in the far corner and pulling off his boots.

You're in love with the queen, aren't you?

I can't be, can I? In the abstract, he supposed, he could see how it might look that way. Raesinia was smart, funny, pretty. *And sometimes, when she looks at me, I almost think . . .*

But she was the *Queen of Vordan.* It was like saying you were in love with the moon.

He tested himself, carefully, as he might probe uncertain footing in the dark. *Can I imagine holding her? Kissing her? Touching her? Is that really what I want?*

It didn't work. Not even in the wildest reaches of fantasies could he make "the Queen of Vordan" and "Marcus d'Ivoire" fit together. It was just too absurd.

But . . .

If he forgot, just for a moment, that she was the queen, everything changed. The woman who'd raided Exchange Central at his side, in a red courier's uniform, breaking in and hiding from the guards and laughing madly when it was all over. The woman who'd stood with a Black Priest's blade to her throat on the *Rosnik* and demanded he leave her behind. The woman who'd listened so earnestly while he explained strategy and tactics, learning everything she could to help her do her duty.

The woman who'd come to him in the middle of the night with a knife and shared a secret hardly anyone else knew.

He could hold *her*, kiss *her*. Raesinia. Not the Queen of Vordan, but a human being.

Maybe Andy's right.

". . . swear," Janus mumbled. Marcus' heart jumped in his chest. The First Consul lay twisted on his bed, breathing hard, sweat standing out on his skin. *Isn't that supposed to be good, with a fever?* When the problem was a magical poison, though, who knew anything?

"I swear," Janus said. "I will find you. If I have to fight the Beast itself, I will get you back. You will have the life you ought to have had. I should be the one down in the dark. I should . . ."

He rolled over, eyes still closed.

". . . not there," he mumbled. "Not among the Mages, not in Khandar. *Must* be there. Only place. Elysium . . ."

He snorted, and was silent again. Marcus lay down on his own bedroll, listening to Janus' shallow breath, and closed his eyes.

If I see Raesinia again, he told himself, *I'll tell her.*

Under the circumstances, it seemed like a safe enough promise.

"Brass Balls of the *fucking* Beast," Marcus said, peering south over the river. "Where the hell did they all come from?"

"That's got to be close to their whole force," Fitz said, watching the ranks of spearwomen and archers form up on the opposite bank. "They're not holding anything back."

"What changed?" It was disquieting to realize that the previous week of attacks had been relatively small affairs, a few thousand strong. That was not true now—Marcus guessed there were at least fifteen thousand men and women getting ready to come over the river, with more lurking in the woods or on horseback at the flanks.

"Maybe they're just tired of waiting," Fitz said.

"I was hoping they'd get tired of dying first." Marcus shook his head. "It won't help them *that* much. The ford isn't wide enough for that whole mess to come at us at once."

"My guess is they're not going to back off when they get their nose bloodied," Fitz said. "Whoever's in charge over there wants us dead, and they don't care how many of their people they have to spend to get it."

"Saints and bloody martyrs." Marcus sighed. "Right. Here we go, then." He peered over the rampart, down to where Viera and her cannoneers were getting their guns ready. "Captain Galiel!"

"What?" she said, shading her eyes to look up at him.

"Everything's ready?"

She nodded. "And Lieutenant Cosk knows what to do if anything happens to me. I left him with the reserve."

Good idea. Marcus hadn't thought of that, but of course Viera's position with the artillery, outside the wall, was a dangerous one. He turned around to find Andy climbing up to the wall.

"They're coming," he said. "A hell of a lot of them."

"You're not kidding," Andy said with a low whistle.

"Try to hang back a little," Marcus said. "And if things look like they're going bad . . ." He shot a significant look at the ice under his feet.

"Believe me, I'm trying not to think about it," Andy said.

"Assuming we live," Marcus said, "remind me that I need to thank you."

"What for?"

"Something you said last night," Marcus said. "It . . . clarified things."

"You know me," Andy said cheerfully. "Always clarifying things."

"They're moving," Fitz said. "We'd better get to the reserve."

Marcus clapped Andy on the shoulder and moved off. The center of the camp was on higher ground than the wall near the river, so their command position was just an old wagon bed resting on a couple of hardtack boxes. It was tall enough to see over the wall and give a good view of the ford beyond, where the bone people were already wading into the freezing water. The spearwomen had split into a number of bands, each a thousand or two strong, stretched into a long, thin formation covering the width of the ford. There were considerable gaps between them, so they would reach the Vordanai line in successive waves. Bands of archers prowled the spaces between.

"Smart," Fitz said. "If one unit breaks, it can flee without sweeping away the ones behind it, like it would if they were packed tight."

"And it doesn't make such a nice target for our cannon." Marcus frowned. "This is going to be bad." *Not that there was much chance it would ever be any other way.*

Viera started firing solid shot at long range, cannonballs plowing into the shallow river and throwing up giant waterspouts. It didn't do much damage to the loose formations, but as she'd remarked to Marcus the night before, there wasn't much point in conserving ammunition. Once the leading formation of spearwomen advanced to within five hundred yards, the guns switched to canister and the firing became more serious. Once again mangled bodies thrashed in the water or floated limply with the current.

Viera's gunners kept firing until the very last moment, slamming double canister into the enemy lines until the charging spearwomen were practically on top of them. More than one man was cut down in turn, hit by an arrow or simply a little bit too slow getting back over the wall. Perhaps because of their bravery, however, the first line of bone women was wavering before it even reached the wall, newly coated in ice to repair the cracks from yesterday's assault. Arrows stuck in the canvas overhead until it sagged under their weight, and some broke through or found gaps and hit the defenders, but the ragged volleys of musketry from behind the ramparts quickly broke up the wave of attackers. Before long they were fleeing back into the ford, passing through the loosely ordered ranks of the next wave. Marcus hoped these new attackers would be discouraged, but they only shouted jeeringly at the broken troops as they ran.

"White riders making a nuisance of themselves, as usual." Fitz pointed to the north, where pale-coated men on ponies had emerged to challenge the rear defenses of the fortress. They didn't have the numbers to mount a close-in assault, but their constant harrying kept the defenders from pulling men from the other walls to reinforce the troops facing the ford.

"Bastards just wait for the guns to start up," Marcus spat. "They know we don't have any cavalry to go after them."

Fitz nodded. "We haven't seen much of the Murnskai cuirassiers, either. I wonder if they're still out there."

"Not if they have any sense," Marcus muttered. "They'd be wasted here." He sent up a silent prayer of thanks that the bone people's Murnskai allies apparently didn't have any cannon. Even the smallest field-gun would have smashed his snow-and-ice fortification like it was made of matchsticks.

The second wave of bone women charged, flowing around the stationary clumps of archers who were now exchanging fire with the muskets on the wall. As usual, the enemy were getting the worst of it, with no cover and inferior weapons, but they had more than enough lives to spend to even the scales. Marcus saw Andy shouting and waving her sword, and the troops shifted fire to the advancing spearwomen as they reached the bank. There hadn't been enough time for Viera and her cannoneers to return to their pieces, so the second wave didn't have to run the deadly gamut of canister to reach the wall. Smoke rolled down and across them when they got to the bottom, once again hammering axes, knives, or wooden spikes into the icy surface to make it climbable.

Fighting with desperate fury, the defenders pushed the bone women back over the rampart wherever they found purchase. The second wave was still milling about the base of the wall when the third wave arrived, and the combination of increased pressure and mounting losses from the arrows drove the Vordanai back. Fitz, without a word, led the reserve forward at a trot, charging up the snow-ramps and slamming into the enemy in a wave of flashing bayonets. Once again the spearwomen were thrown from the wall. But this time, secure in the knowledge that fresh troops were coming up behind them, they didn't break, only tried again, a dense-packed mass of screaming warriors held at bay only by a dozen feet of ice and packed snow. The fight turned and turned again, fallen bodies trampled into the churned mix of mud and snow at the base of the wall or unceremoniously rolled aside to make room for fresh defenders.

One more card to play before we throw the dice. The mixed metaphor made Marcus smile for a moment. He nodded to Fossard, the regimental cutter, and the man and his assistants fanned out through the infirmary, pushing and prodding and pleading. Marcus drew his sword and held it in the air, to serve as a rallying point. In a few moments they started to trickle in, men who were pale with fever or mottled with bruises, men wrapped in bandages or with sleeves freshly pinned up. Every man who could still walk, Marcus had said, and the cutters had taken him at his word. A few collapsed in the snow, and others lacked even the strength to pick up a weapon. The rest collected bayoneted muskets and captured spears from a pile near Marcus' feet and gathered into some semblance of a formation. It was more of a rough blob than anything with ranks, but Marcus saluted them with his sword anyway, and got a ragged cheer.

It was probably time for a rousing speech, but he'd never been good at those, and in any case the rattle and bang of musketry all along the walls and the scream of combat would have drowned out his words. Marcus swept his sword down, pointing at the wall, and hopped down from his vantage point. *No use staying at the command post when there's nothing left to command.*

He ran, aiming for where he could see the blue line bulging. The men behind him, a couple of hundred cripples and sick, raised a shout that would have done credit to twice their number. The bone women turned to receive them in a horrible clash of spears and bayonets, blades tearing flesh on all sides. Marcus ducked low, slipping beneath the initial shock, then popped up inside the reach of the first rank of bone women, laying about him for all he was worth. Blood flew, and where the spears fell away his men pressed into the gap, shoving and punching when the press got too close for weapons.

Time disappeared into a red haze. There was only an ocean of bodies, men and women, Vordanai and bone people, sometimes pressed together so tight he could hardly breathe, sometimes receding enough that he could dodge and fence with his enemies. At first they'd been fighting on the ramps, but step by step they pushed the enemy back toward the rampart. Some bone women were jumping off, risking the spikes and bodies below to get away. *They're breaking—*

Then, with a hoarse scream, a fresh tide of spearwomen surged up and over the defenses. Glancing over the rampart, Marcus could see that the fourth wave had paused, waiting for the fifth, and the two units had hit the wall together. The defenders were exhausted, and these new attackers hadn't suffered any musketry on their approach; they were fresh and screaming for blood, and they shattered the Vordanai line like glass.

The fact that there was nowhere to run was forgotten in the heat of the moment, overwhelmed by the desperate need to get *away*. Men ran in ones and twos, then whole groups together, backing away in a fighting retreat or simply throwing their weapons down and fleeing for their lives. Some officers tried to hold them, calling them cowards and hurling threats, while others simply joined in with the tide. Those who held firm were quickly surrounded and cut down by the bone women, who pressed on as fast as they could get over the wall.

Marcus, sword still in hand, slashed a woman across the belly and jumped down from the wall before her companion could get around her. He saw Viera nearby, two of her cannoneers fighting at her side, wielding long sponge-staffs as though they were spears. She held a lit torch, and as their eyes locked Marcus jerked his head toward the base of the wall. *Do it.*

"Andy!" Marcus shouted, his voice nearly inaudible over the din. "Get clear! Everyone *run!*"

Viera bent, running the torch along a length of line, then tossed it aside as the fuse took fire. She turned on her heel and sprinted, long-legged strides catching up with the fleeing soldiers. Marcus lagged close to the back of the pack, looking for Andy. Fitz shouted something at him from the middle of a group of soldiers executing a slower, more controlled retreat, but Marcus couldn't understand and waved him on.

Finally, he saw Andy, jumping down from the wall with the last half dozen Vordanai. A cut on her cheek had coated her face in blood, but her sword still flashed, fending off the spears that stabbed down at her. The men around her started to run, but she paused, looking for something. Marcus saw her mouth go wide as she shouted an unheard oath. He followed her gaze and realized that the sparking, hissing fuse had gone dark.

"Andy!" Marcus skidded to a halt in a spray of snow. "Viera, Fitz—it's gone out. We have to—"

But there was no time, no time for anything. The bone people were over the wall, victorious spearwomen spreading out through the makeshift fortress, attacking the other walls from behind. There was nothing left to stop them. *We're all going to die.*

Andy dove, rolled, came up with Viera's torch in her hand. It flared to life, embers reignited by the rush of wind. Andy ran along the fuse, looking for the place where it had gone out. She barely saw the bone woman in front of her, fierce-looking with her blood-stiffened hair and rattling fetishes, until it was much too late. The steel-headed spear went into Andy's belly and came out through her back, trailing blood. The bone woman yanked it free with another crimson spray and spun away, looking for another victim as Andy collapsed to her knees.

"Andy!" Marcus' shout rose to a scream. He saw her turn her head, eyes meeting his, and she gave him a broad smile. Then she turned away, eyes following the fuse to where it disappeared into a dark cavity in the snow. As she fell forward, she hurled the torch, fire describing a circle in the air as it spun end over end into the hole and out of sight.

There was a moment of silence, and then the world went white.

Gunpowder had been the one resource the Grand Army had had more than enough of, and much of it had been left behind with the First Division. Viera had hoarded as much as she could, and her cannoneers had buried barrels of the stuff underneath the south wall, scooping out the snow and replacing it with hard wooden kegs. They'd packed the space around them with spare musket balls from canister rounds, but this turned out to be an unnecessary addition. The layers of ice on the wall shattered in the colossal blast, transformed instantly into a million flying, deadly fragments. They scythed through the tight-packed mass of bone women at the base of the wall, the cheering spearwomen and archers atop it, and the wounded Vordanai who'd been unable to get clear in time. The explosion lofted snow hundreds of feet into the air, a white spray that was followed almost at once by a rising cloud of black smoke. Viera's precious guns were tossed like toys, splintered wreckage landing in the river. Beyond, the masses of bone people waiting to cross broke up, fleeing for their lives.

Marcus sat on the wagon bed, looking out at the crater where the southern wall of his fortress had been. The survivors of the First Division mostly seemed stunned, unprepared for their good fortune; they sat in small groups, staring, or talked in low, reverent tones. The white riders had retreated, too, spooked by the blast.

But they'll be back. It wouldn't be enough. The explosion, and the subsequent counterattack against the shattered remnants who'd survived, had slaughtered most of the bone people who'd made it into the fortress. *Call it five or six thousand.* But there were still tens of thousands of enemy left, and Marcus hardly had enough bodies to man the walls, even if he'd still *had* walls. *Which I don't.* There was no way the dazed, shocked survivors could repair the damage overnight, and in the morning the bone people would resume their assault.

Andy and Viera were right. It bought us a day. He looked at the sun, which was just touching the horizon. The light was slowly turning golden. *For however much good that does us.*

Andy . . .

"Sir?" It was Fitz. "Do you want me to get the men started rebuilding the wall?"

"We don't have time."

"The enemy may hesitate. If they give us another day—"

"They won't." Marcus sighed. "Let them rest, Fitz. They've earned it, don't you think?"

"Yes, sir." He paused. "I'm sorry, sir. She was a good soldier."

"She might have disagreed with you," Marcus said with a slight smile. "But you're right. In the end it's not all about crisp salutes and shiny boots."

Fitz, who had both, kept a diplomatic silence.

As always, Marcus felt guilty in his grief. Thousands had died today, men whom he had ordered into battle, men whose names he hadn't even known. But he hadn't lived beside those men, hadn't watched while they bore up after losing friends, hadn't *known* them. One familiar face seemed more precious than a thousand anonymous graves, for all that he knew that was wrong.

The sun slipped slowly below the horizon, and the sky went from orange to red to black. The men began to feel the cold, and it roused them from their stupor. Even if they would die in the morning, there was still the night to make it through: fires to light, meals to cook, long-hoarded liquor to drink for a lucky few. *I wonder if the blast woke Janus up and what he thought of it.* If he'd been in charge, Marcus was certain, he'd have come up with something better. *But he's lost in dreams of Mya, whoever she is.*

"Marcus!" At first he thought the voice was part of his reverie. "Marcus, is that you?"

"Sir?" Marcus turned to find Janus standing in the snow, wearing boots, his dressing gown, and a coat wrapped around his shoulders. "Sir! You shouldn't be out here! You're not well."

"Marcus!" Janus took a careful step up onto the wagon bed. "Under ordinary circumstances I'd agree with you, but I seem to be recovered—" He lost his balance and wobbled, and Marcus hurriedly caught him by the arm. "At least somewhat," he added a little sheepishly. "And since no one had come to see me, I thought I'd venture forth and see what all the commotion was." He waved a hand. "It's a nice fortress, but it seems to be missing a wall."

"We were forced to blow it up," Marcus mumbled, grief and astonishment at war in his face. "Sir, are you really all right?"

"I suspect it will take some time to regain my good health," Janus said. "But yes, for the moment."

Ihernglass must have succeeded. Marcus had long since written Winter and her company off for dead. *God Almighty, they could have gotten all the way to Elysium and back by now!*

If Janus is awake, then maybe . . . But no. Even Janus couldn't perform miracles. With what they had left, there was no way to resist the bone people's next attack, no matter who was in command. Marcus slumped.

"I'm . . . glad, sir," he said finally. "I wish I had better news for you. About all I can offer is that we can die together, on our feet."

Janus smiled his summer-lightning smile. "A noble sentiment, Marcus. But in this case a touch premature. That is what I came to tell you." He pointed out into the darkness. "You see?"

Marcus struggled to follow his finger. Then, from the darkening tree line to the south, there was a bright flash and then another. Two long, one short, one long—

"That's a flik-flik," Marcus whispered.

"Indeed." Janus peered at it intently. "I only caught part of the message, but it seems—"

But Marcus didn't need a translation. Deep in his chest a tight knot let go.

"It's Raesinia."

Part Four

SHADE

"I don't believe it," Duke Orlanko said. "There must be some mistake."

"No mistake," Ionkovo said. *You sniveling coward,* he added to himself. "We've had several reports, all saying the same thing. Vhalnich and d'Ivoire are alive and coming south."

"Again." The Last Duke's plump face was going purple with rage, matching the color of his robe. His spectacles were askew. "Will *nothing* rid us of these heretics?" He rounded on Ionkovo. *"You* told me they were going to be dealt with!"

"So the pontifex informed me," Ionkovo said. "But Vhalnich has proven most resourceful in the past."

He was not about to tell Orlanko that he now received no answer at all from Elysium. Something had gone badly wrong.

For the last month he'd been stuck here, playing nursemaid to the ex-spymaster. In Ionkovo's opinion, the Last Duke's grip on sanity had been shattered by the revolution, and he'd been sliding steadily further into delusion ever since. Unfortunately, the Pontifex of the Black wanted him for a puppet king of Vordan, so Ionkovo's orders were to stay by his side.

"If Dorsay hadn't been so eager to cut a deal, Vhalnich wouldn't have an army to come back to," Orlanko fumed. "He's a damned traitor."

"Do you want him removed?" Ionkovo said. He yawned ostentatiously.

"Not yet," the Last Duke said. "Let me think."

He sat down behind the cheap wooden desk. Dorsay's army had taken over Polkhaiz, but the miserable little town didn't have much to offer in the way of accommodations. The only truly nice building was the mayor's house, and Dorsay had taken that for his headquarters. Orlanko was stuck with what had been a general store on the edge of town; the front room still smelled of pickles and fish paste.

"Removing Dorsay by itself wouldn't be good enough," Orlanko muttered, chair squeaking as he shifted his weight. "He's only a cat's-paw for those in Borel who want peace at any price. If we kill him and Vhalnich returns to Vordan, we're no closer to getting what we want."

"If Vhalnich makes peace and returns to Vordan, we're even farther," Ionkovo pointed out. *Though perhaps then the pontifex would agree that you've outlived your usefulness.*

"Indeed. We need to rid ourselves of the whole lot of them all at once. Dorsay, Vhalnich, d'Ivoire, the queen. All of them." Orlanko looked up, eyes suddenly huge through his spectacles. "When will they return to their camp?"

"Tomorrow, I'm told," Ionkovo said.

"Good. My men will be ready."

Ionkovo stifled a smirk. Orlanko had been making noises about rebuilding his precious Concordat, but all he'd actually done was sweep together a few hundred thugs and mercenaries from the ports along the Split Coast. They looked fierce enough in their dark coats, but they had none of the skill or discipline of the old Ministry of Information. *I suppose they'll serve as cannon fodder.*

"We'll take them all together," Orlanko said, half to himself, then looked back at Ionkovo. "Organize the teams. I want Vhalnich, d'Ivoire, and Dorsay dead by dawn of the day after tomorrow, and Raesinia in a bag at my feet."

Finally. Ionkovo gave a lazy grin. "As you say, Your Grace. Will there be anything else?"

That evening Ionkovo slipped through the vague shapes of the twilight world, emerging in a small copse of trees just outside of Polkhaiz. A small campfire threw long, flickering shadows, and he pulled himself out of one of them and into the light.

The man sitting beside the campfire was not surprised by this. The light gleamed across his face in a thousand tiny pinpricks, reflected from the shards of black glass that made up his obsidian mask.

"Shade," he said. He spoke Murnskai with a Hamveltai accent, upper-class and cultured.

"Mirror," Ionkovo said. "Anything to report?"

"The woods are just as empty as they were yesterday and the day before," Mirror said, his tone an echo of Ionkovo's own impatience.

"Orlanko's ready to move at last," Ionkovo said. "Tomorrow night, when Vhalnich returns. We're to take him, the queen, d'Ivoire, and Dorsay."

"That should certainly stir the pot," Mirror said.

"It will serve our purposes. At the very least it will provoke a battle between the Borelgai and Vordanai armies. Even with Vhalnich gone, we will need to carry the war forward to reclaim the Thousand Names and ensure Vordan is cleansed of heresy."

Mirror nodded. "So where do you want me?"

"They'll see Orlanko's men coming," Ionkovo said. "If Vhalnich doesn't have spies in our camp, he's not the strategist they say he is. But they can't know *you're* here." He pursed his lips. "D'Ivoire doesn't matter. I'll take the queen, and you make certain of Dorsay. Once that's done, I'll meet up with you, and we can tackle Vhalnich. Ihernglass is still missing, and I've seen no sign of the Khandarai. If Vhalnich has any demons left, he'll be keeping them close, I'm sure."

"Understood. And afterward?"

"Collect our communicator, then back to Elysium. Orlanko can handle the rest." *Or make a mess of it, for all I care. I need to know what the hell is going on.*

"Another ride across the frozen wastes of Murnsk," Mirror said dolefully. "Just what I was looking forward to."

CHAPTER EIGHTEEN

RAESINIA

"Marcus!"

Raesinia wanted to jump out of her chair and hug him. Considered doing it, even, but in the end decided not to. This was partly because it looked like, small though she was, she would bowl him over. Marcus was thinner that she remembered, his face sagging and gray, his normally neat beard shaggy and overgrown.

"Your Majesty," he said. His eyes fell on a nearby chair with such obvious longing that Raesinia winced and hurriedly gestured for him to sit. He lowered himself into it with the characteristic hesitation of someone who had just spent an extended time in the saddle.

They were in one of the upper rooms of a two-story stone inn on the north bank of Syzria, just over the bridge from Polkhaiz. The main body of the Grand Army was camped a little bit to the north, but since beginning her negotiations with Dorsay Raesinia had moved her quarters here. There was a pleasing symmetry to the symbolism, and in any case, the inn, mean as it was, was considerably more comfortable than her tent. *And it takes me out of the direct reach of any of the generals who might be tempted to try something foolish.* The upper floor had a large bedroom and several small ones that all let onto a common room, intended for a wealthy traveler and his servants.

Marcus' uniform was nearly as gray as his face, dusty from the road and stained by sweat. Here and there faint dark patches marked where bloodstains had been scrubbed away, and a bulky bandage still circled one arm. Raesinia gestured to a servant, who ghosted over with a pitcher of wine and a glass. Marcus stared at these as though he'd forgotten what they were for, but once the deep, thick red was poured, he gulped it down convulsively.

"It's good," he said. He took a deep breath and looked up at her. "I'm sorry for my poor state, Your Majesty. It's been a long ride, and before that—"

"It's nothing," Raesinia said, accepting a glass of her own. The wine *was* good, another gift from Dorsay. "I'm just glad you're safe."

"It was a close thing," Marcus said. "Closer even than I knew at the time. Colonel Reinhardt had to fight through half a regiment of Murnskai cuirassiers before he could take the bone people from behind. He's a very gallant man." Marcus shook his head. "Is Give-Em-Hell all right? They told me he made it here, but that he wasn't in good shape."

"He was lightly wounded, but it was mostly exhaustion. He'll be fine. A few more of his men have trickled in over the past several days, too. That was a hell of a thing you asked them to do."

"I know. I thought it was about the only chance we had."

"It worked." Raesinia smiled. "You saved the First Division."

"Not all of it," Marcus said flatly. "We lost . . . too many." He poured himself another glass of wine. "Andy's dead."

"Andy?" A hand tightened around Raesinia's heart. Andy had been with them all through the fighting in Vordan, including that awful skirmish aboard the *Rosnik* where Ionkovo had taken Raesinia prisoner. "God. I'm sorry, Marcus."

"She probably saved us all." He took a swallow, eyes closed. "Viera—Captain Galiel—was also amazing. We'll have to promote her. And Fitz . . ." He shrugged. "Not much more room to promote Fitz, I suppose."

"I'm sure everyone performed wonders," Raesinia said. She hated herself the moment the sentiment left her lips; it was an ingratiating, *political* thing to say, reminding her of the reason Marcus was here instead of enjoying a well-deserved rest. *Because I need him, and I want to make sure I get to him before anyone else does.* She cleared her throat. "What about Janus?"

"He's still alive. I assume the couriers have told you that much," Marcus said. "We've been keeping the details from the men."

"And?"

"I . . . don't quite know. Up until just before the force you sent arrived, he wasn't doing well. Sometimes he'd sleep, sometimes he'd talk, but . . . it didn't make a lot of sense. I thought he was dying. After Reinhardt arrived with the cavalry, things changed. They put him in the back of a cart, and he still sleeps most of the day, but he looks better and the fever is gone."

"Do you think that Winter tracked down the Penitent?"

"I don't know what else *to* think. But it's been much too long. Even wounded, the assassin could have made it back to Elysium twice over."

"Maybe she just died of the knife Sothe stuck in her. Even Penitent Damned aren't immune to a festering wound."

"It's possible. I find it hard to believe we'd get *that* lucky." He shrugged. "Regardless, I think he'll recover soon. It won't be long before he's fit to take command."

So. There it is. She'd rehearsed a dozen different versions of this conversation, varying based on Janus' health and other factors. This was going to be one of the hardest, but at least she knew where she stood. "Have you spoken with anyone since you returned?"

"No. They told me you wanted to see me as soon as possible." He swallowed. "And there's something I need to talk to you about—"

She held up a hand, and he paused. Raesinia nodded at the servant—one of the few remaining from the entourage that had followed her all this way—and he left the room with a bow. Barely and Joanna were outside, making sure no one eavesdropped through the inn's thin interior walls.

"Things have been difficult in the army," Raesinia said. "With you, Janus, and Fitz all cut off, and Winter still away, it was a bit . . . confusing."

"That leaves . . ." Marcus paused to run down the seniority list. "Mor in command. General Kaanos, of the Third Division." He grimaced. "I can't imagine he got along well with you."

"He's under arrest."

"Oh, saints and martyrs. What did he do this time?"

"It's a long story."

"I'll bet," Marcus said dryly. "So who *is* in charge?"

"I am," Raesinia said. "With the First Consul gone, I argued that command reverts to the Crown. The others were . . . persuaded by my analysis."

"You're not serious," Marcus said. "But . . ." Raesinia arched an eyebrow, and he hesitated. "Forgive me, Your Majesty, but you don't have any military training. The little bit I explained to you was just theory. The basics."

"I know. Don't worry, I haven't decided that a few lessons make me Farus the Fourth come again." Raesinia grinned. "Your Colonel Giforte and Winter's Captain Cyte have been doing most of what needs to be done. My main contribution has been preventing the others from doing anything foolish."

Marcus relaxed a little. "Giforte knows what he's doing. I'm glad he's been helpful." He shrugged. "Now that Janus is back, we can straighten things out. Give it a few more days—" He frowned, looking at her. "What's wrong?"

And here we cross the line. "You know we're facing a Borelgai army across the river."

"I gathered something of the sort. Dorsay?"

She nodded. "He has our depots in Polkhaiz. Our own supplies are all but gone. We had to open negotiations."

"Open—" Marcus' eyes narrowed. "You've *surrendered* to Dorsay?"

"No. So far we've just . . . talked. And he's agreed to keep us supplied while negotiations continue."

"But he'll hardly settle for anything less than capitulation," Marcus said. "He's got us trapped here, with no supply line, and the fact that we're willing to talk shows how weak we are."

"General Kaanos wanted to attack across the river the first day we got here."

Marcus snorted. "That sounds more like a Give-Em-Hell plan. Dorsay will be dug in, and even if we pushed through him, he could destroy the depots when he fell back. Mor ought to have more sense."

"Don't be too hard on him," Raesinia said. "He thought you were dead. He has a lot of respect for you, you know."

"Mor? Really?" Marcus looked taken aback, then shook his head. "Regardless. If things are so bad, why is Dorsay still negotiating?"

"Because the situation is more complicated than just one army against another. Dorsay wants peace, and he's got the ear of the King of Borel. He knows that if he presses us to destruction, or outright surrender, Vordan won't give up the war."

"Hell. This really *is* your territory and not mine. Can we bluff him, somehow? All we need is to get south of Syzria and back to Tsivny. There should be supplies there, fresh troops from the divisions we left behind—"

"Marcus," Raesinia said. "Dorsay and I agree on this. The war has gone on long enough. If we have a chance for peace, we ought to take it."

There was a long pause.

"If Borel wants to withdraw from the war . . ." Marcus said tentatively.

"It won't be just that. It may take a while for Murnsk to come to the table, but I believe they'll have no choice in the end. In the meantime, if we try to advance on Elysium, it'll ruin any chance of peace. Even if the king wanted it, his people wouldn't let him." She shook her head. "It has to end. Status quo ante."

"Janus will never agree," Marcus said. "And you know why. Nothing Dorsay can do will bind the Black Priests." He looked at her carefully. "You're not still thinking about sacrificing yourself for the good of Vordan? Janus is recovering and the weather is getting warmer. If we can just get out of here and regroup, there's nothing to stop us from getting there the next time."

"And then what?" Raesinia said, harsher than she might have liked. "Dorsay says it'll be the Wars of Religion all over again, and he's not wrong. Nobody is worth putting the country through that, not even the queen." Her fists clenched. "And I don't need to sacrifice myself, not really. If I abdicate I could just . . . leave." *We could just leave.* She banished the thought.

"It's not just you. Winter has her own demon. Feor, too."

"I'll take them with me," Raesinia said. "Go back to Khandar if we have to. Somewhere they won't find us."

"You're talking about surrender," Marcus said. "Not to Dorsay but to the Black Priests."

"Yes!" She could see Marcus set his jaw, and something in her despaired. "Marcus, think about what you're fighting for. You and I wanted to save Vordan from Orlanko, and it's *saved*. I'm not going to drag millions of people into war for the sake of a handful, or to keep some ancient tablets out of the hands of a bunch of crazy priests—"

Marcus barked a laugh, and Raesinia stopped, surprised. He shook his head.

"There's the sticking point," he said. "I'm talking about this like I get to make the decision. The Black Priests wants the Thousand Names, and Janus will never give those up, even if you *do* abdicate. So why bother . . . ?"

He trailed off, seeing something in her eyes. Raesinia looked away.

"One of Dorsay's conditions is that Janus be removed from his post," she said quietly. "It makes sense. It presents their public with a victory and takes away a sword that would otherwise be hanging over their heads."

"You want to sell him out," Marcus said.

"He'll be given all honors," Raesinia said. "He'll just retire to his own estate and be simple Count Mieran again. It's not a bad life."

"After everything he's done for you. *We've* done for you." Marcus' face reddened. "Orlanko would have had his regency without Janus. You'd be in a cell under Elysium by now."

"You think I don't know that?" Raesinia said. "You think this is easy for me? But I'm the *queen*, Marcus. I need to think about what's best for the country. And despite everything he's done for me, I no longer think that Vordan is Janus' primary concern." She waved a hand, trying to encompass their present situation. "Do you?"

"I . . ." All at once the fire seemed to go out of Marcus. He slumped in his chair.

"What's wrong?"

Marcus looked down at his knees and was silent for a while. Eventually, he said, "While Janus was ill, he would . . . talk. Sometimes to me, sometimes as though I wasn't there. I don't think he really knew what he was saying."

"What did he say?"

"There was someone named Mya. I think she died. Do you have any idea who that could be?"

Raesinia shook her head wordlessly. Marcus went on, his anger replaced with a deepening melancholy.

"He talked about her a lot. He loved her, I think, though what their relationship was I have no idea. Assuming she was real at all. This could all be fever dreams and nonsense."

"What does she have to do with all this?"

"I don't know. I shouldn't be telling you this." Marcus shook his head. "Janus is my friend."

"Please, Marcus."

Another pause. "I think," Marcus said, "that Janus is *looking* for something. He kept saying he wanted to help her, and he mentioned . . . a fishing line? It's hard to remember exactly. But whatever it was, he said we were close, just the way he talked to me about Elysium."

"To help her?" Raesinia felt her skin prickle. She became aware of the binding, slumbering and quiescent, wrapped around her soul and keeping her dead body going. "I thought you said she was dead."

"I could be wrong. Or . . . I don't know. It could be the raving of a man just this side of the grave." Marcus shivered. "It wasn't easy to listen to. Janus is always so controlled. Hearing him like that was like seeing him without his skin."

"But you think this *thing* that he wants is in Elysium?" Raesinia pressed. "*That's* why he pushed so hard to get there?"

"I don't *know*." Marcus gripped the arm of the chair. "Why does it matter what I think, anyway? If you've made a deal with Dorsay—"

"The deal relies on me being able to command the army," Raesinia said. "If Janus countermands my orders . . ."

"He wouldn't do that," Marcus said. "You're the queen."

"I'm not so certain." She leaned forward. "I *need* you, Marcus. The army loves you. The generals respect you. If you're at my side, we can avoid any confusion."

Marcus looked up at her with hollow eyes. "I wonder if this is what Adrecht Roston said to his men before they turned on me."

"I don't—"

"It doesn't matter." Marcus got to his feet. "If Janus is such a danger, why did you bother to rescue him?"

"Because there were thousands of other soldiers with him." *Because* you *were there.* "I'm not heartless. I'm just trying to do what's best."

"By asking me to turn on the one man I've trusted all this time. Who has saved my life more often than I can count, not to mention yours."

"Yes," Raesinia said, fighting to keep a quaver out of her voice. "Because that *is* what's best."

There was a cold silence.

"What have you done with him?" Marcus said.

"He's in the old storage shed." It was just about the only other building on this side of the river. "Sothe has got people from the Girls' Own guarding him. The story is that he's still too sick to move." She took a long breath. "All we need to do is send him home, under a nice, discreet guard, and keep him out of the way for a few months."

"You have a lot of faith in Dorsay."

"I do," Raesinia said. "I think he's a good man."

Another silence. Marcus turned to the door.

"Where are you going?" Raesinia said.

"Where do you think?" Marcus snapped.

"What is he going to do?" Sothe said once Marcus had left.

"I don't know," Raesinia said. She was slumped in her chair, drinking what was left of the wine for the look of the thing.

"I could stop him." Sothe sounded hesitant, and Raesinia looked at her sharply.

"Don't even suggest that we should kill Marcus."

"No," the assassin said. "It has become clear to me that he is . . ." She shook her head. "It doesn't matter. But I could detain him temporarily, I think."

"Are you certain? Even the Girls' Own might not be willing to hold him."

"You may be right." Sothe frowned. "Then what do you propose to do?"

Raesinia shrugged, exhausted. "Wait."

MARCUS

Stupid, stupid, stupid.

He'd almost said it. All through the exhausting ride south, after the cavalry's surprise attack had broken through the bone people's line, he'd thought about his promise to himself. That it had been made when he'd expected to die didn't make it any less binding, he decided. He tried to plan the conversation, but never got further than his own halting explanation of his feelings. He couldn't imagine what Raesinia would do—laugh? Sneer? Be offended at his temerity? *Or say* . . .

But he hadn't even gotten the chance. She'd made it very clear what she thought of him. *I need you, Marcus.* As a general, as a tool, because he had the loyalty of the soldiers and the respect of the officers. *Fine. That's what she wants from me. I just have to accept it.*

Now, standing in the snow in front of the door to an innyard shed, he had to decide what to do about it.

Two guards, both women, saluted as he approached. He recognized them, vaguely, from the group Winter had taken to rescue Raesinia from the Directory. Marcus gave them an austere nod, but softened a little as the smaller one grinned broadly.

"It's good to see you safe, sir," she said. Her larger companion nodded vigorously.

"Thanks," Marcus said. "Though I don't feel safe quite yet."

"I understand," she said, then hesitated. "Sir—can I ask—"

"What is it?"

"Has there been any word of General Ihernglass?"

"No word, as such," Marcus said. "But we have . . . some reason to believe that he's alive. Or was a few days ago, at least." *Assuming that our theory about the Penitent is true, and a dozen other things besides.*

"That's something, sir," the guard said. "Thank you."

Marcus nodded at the door. "Is he awake?"

"I think so, sir. He hasn't asked for anything, but I've heard him moving about."

"I'll speak to him, then."

The larger guard dragged the door open. It was a heavy thing, hinges squealing with neglect. The storehouse was a squat, windowless building, thickly built from the same stone as the inn, with a high, peaked roof. Inside, only a few broken barrels and empty sacks remained from its original purpose. A bed had been dragged over from the inn, with a portable writing desk beside it. The only lantern stood on the desk, throwing long shadows.

Janus sat on a cushion in front of the desk, pen laid neatly in front of him across a blank page. He looked up as the door opened, letting in the cloud-shrouded rays of the late-afternoon sun. After Marcus stepped inside, the guard dragged the door closed again, leaving them alone in the lantern-light. Janus' gray eyes gleamed, but they were sunk in deep, shadowed sockets, like gemstones in the eyes of a skull.

"Sir," Marcus said. "How are you feeling?"

"Considerably better now that I'm not spending my days in the back of a cart," Janus said. "I've been trying to put together a picture of the tactical situation, but everyone is so damned solicitous of my health that it's taken me longer than it should. I believe I have the basics, however. I must say, Raesinia has managed well in a difficult period, though she's waited too long to take a few basic steps." He turned to the writing desk. "We have five divisions at Tsivny, though three of them were rather roughly handled by Dorsay when he took Polkhaiz. But they've had time to recover, and they're ideally positioned to advance against the Borelgai flank. If we can keep the bluff of negotiations going long enough for them to begin to move—"

"Sir—"

"Which reminds me. Rationing ought to begin immediately. Whatever food Dorsay sends us should be collected and as much as possible stockpiled to build up a reserve. Once he's maneuvered out of his position, we should be able to cover him with a small force and slip by to the south. Then we'll have a secure line to our base and a chance to regroup, and with any luck the weather will continue to improve."

"Sir. Can I ask a few questions?"

Janus blinked. The fever-brightness was gone from his eyes, but there was still something *off* about his expression. It was a little too eager, a little too *forced*.

"Certainly, Marcus."

"You intend to resume command?"

"Of course." He patted his chest. "As you can see, my health has returned, more or less. I'll need some time to recover physically from the effects of being bedridden so long, but I should be able to at least sit a horse. Just don't schedule me for any sword fights in the near future, eh?"

Marcus forced a smile. "And you're planning to resume the drive on Elysium?"

Janus' expression grew more serious, and he nodded. "That remains the objective, as it always has. We've suffered a setback, obviously, but we're far from beaten. The Pontifex of the Black must be scraping the bottom of his bag of tricks if he's willing to inflict such harm on his own people. Once we've extracted ourselves from our current predicament and spent some time resting the soldiers, Dorsay won't have the strength to block us, and the emperor won't be able to assemble a new army before the end of the year. There'll be nothing to stand in our way, and we'll have two or three months of good weather left. I anticipate a satisfactory result."

"At the peace conference, you said you wanted to occupy Elysium to ensure the Church's good behavior. We won't be able to stay there long before winter comes."

Janus shrugged. "You know that was only for public consumption. If we can stomp out the nest of vipers that is the Priests of the Black, I will consider the campaign a success."

Marcus felt his mind turning, involuntarily, to follow Janus' path. This had been his power, ever since Marcus had first met him, in a miserable little fortress on the edge of the desert in Khandar. When he was talking, everything he said sounded so right, so *reasonable*. It was a bit like the power Danton Aurenne had displayed over the crowds in Vordan, except that in Janus' case there was nothing supernatural about it. Something about the force of his mind bent the course of everyone around him, like a mighty river carving out a valley that lesser streams couldn't help but flow into. *But . . .*

They'd been together a long time. Not much more than a year, in truth, but it felt like an eternity. Marcus thought he knew Janus as well as anyone could. *I ought to know his tricks by now.* While he swept you up in his vision, he was a master at *leaving out* inconvenient details and implications. *And he doesn't like too many questions.*

"And then what?" Marcus said.

Janus cocked his head. "What do you mean?"

"Assume it all works. The Black Priests are destroyed, and we make it back to Vordan. What happens next?"

"Ah." Janus shrugged. "The next project would be freeing Raesinia from her demon. It's possible that Ihernglass' Infernivore would be able to do it, but the question is whether it will leave Raesinia alive or dead afterward. I hope to find some knowledge in Elysium to assist with that."

Marcus' chest tightened. "You started this when the king asked you to help Raesinia, didn't you? So what's next for *you*, when that's accomplished? Will you stay on as First Consul?"

The smile was entirely gone from Janus' face. His eyes bored into Marcus like steel-headed drills. "You've been talking to her, I see."

"Will you?"

"If needed," Janus said coldly. "As long as Vordan is threatened by its enemies, I will continue to defend it."

"And when will *that* stop?" Marcus said. "If we destroy Elysium, the Sworn Church nations will never make peace."

"Unless we force them to." Janus' eyes gleamed. "Is that what you're worried about? I have plans, Marcus—depend on it. A rebuilt Vordanai fleet, to sweep the Borels from the seas. We will march into Viadre and dictate peace at sword point. And the emperor's position isn't as secure as it appears—weaken him enough, and with the right inducements the whole Murnskai house of cards will come crashing down. We only need play one petty lord against another until they never threaten Vordan again."

"War, in other words." *On and on, forever.*

"Until we finally win." Janus' smile returned just for a moment. "Don't tell me the prospect upsets you. When we came back from Khandar, you were practically itching to get into the field. War is your profession, Marcus, and you have a talent for it."

The hell of it was, Janus was right. He *had* been eager to take his troops against the enemy after so long wasting away in the backwaters of Khandar.

"I may have lost my taste for it," Marcus said.

"Ah." Janus shrugged. "You have done well in my service, and you will be rewarded, never fear. If field command is no longer what you want, then there are any number of other posts. Minister of war, perhaps. I'm sure the queen can be persuaded to part with a title and an estate, as well."

"It's not that," Marcus said. "It's not about me." *Andy. Hayver. Adrecht. God knows how many others.* "It's too much, Janus. The cost is too high. It's not *worth* it." He shook his head, throat getting thick. "If we beat them, in another generation they'll get back up and start the next round. Again and again, forever. My children's children will still be at war."

"They'll be at war anyway," Janus said. "In the last century, no decade has passed without a major war somewhere or other. War will always be with us. The question is whether you want to *win*."

"Is that really what this is about? Winning the war?"

"Of course. What else is there?"

"Who was Mya?"

Marcus was watching closely. Janus' self-control was awesome, except for the rare moments when his temper broke through, but it wasn't perfect. There was a flicker in his eyes, a tension at the corner of his lips, just for an instant. No one who didn't know him well would have noticed, but Marcus saw it, and he could see in Janus' eyes that his commander *knew* he had seen it. There was a long moment of silence.

"Where did you hear that name?" Janus said.

"From you," Marcus said quietly. "When you were ill. She seemed to be on your mind."

"Fever dreams," Janus said, and blew out a long breath. "I see."

"She's not real?"

"She was real," Janus said. He looked away, eyes hooded. "We all have our scars, Marcus. You of all people should understand that."

"And Elysium? Is it for her sake?"

Another pause, just for an instant. "Don't be silly. That's the distant past, and we have the present to worry about."

He's lying. The sudden certainty was like a weight on Marcus' heart, dragging him into despair. Once again Janus could read his expressions like a book. His lip tightened.

"What are you really doing here?" Janus said after a moment.

"Raesinia is negotiating with Dorsay," Marcus said.

"I know that. But she can't seriously believe he'll keep faith longer than he needs to. You have to help her. She's naive—"

"She's the farthest thing from naive, and you know it. She thinks Dorsay means it."

"It's not her decision to make."

"She's the *queen*."

"And this is an army in the field, and *I* am the First Consul." Janus' voice dropped toward a snarl. "Dorsay must know that. Any deal he makes with her will be purely for show."

"One of his conditions is that you leave your position," Marcus said.

Janus blinked, then stared at him in silence.

"You'll resign," Marcus said, feeling increasingly uncomfortable. "You'll return to Mieran County a hero. Whatever you need from the Crown—"

"You support her in this?"

"I . . ." Marcus shook his head. "I think she's right. We've beaten every army they've sent against us. Now is the time to make a peace that will *last*. If we push on, if we sack Elysium . . ."

"The Black Priests won't give up."

"She knows that," Marcus said with a fresh spike of pain.

"And if I walked out this door right now and ordered the generals to attack?"

Marcus closed his eyes. "Please don't."

Another pause.

"I truly never thought it would come to this." Janus' voice was small, almost lost. "Raesinia was clearly an alliance of convenience. But you, Marcus. I thought . . ."

"I'm sorry," Marcus said. "I really am. If there were another way . . ."

"You know where you would be without me?" Janus looked up again, his eyes wild. "Decorating some Redeemer's spit in Khandar! You'd have *nothing* without my help. You've been tagging along behind me like a tail on a kite, and now you have the gall to tell *me* you know what's right?" Janus' lip curled. "As though you could get the tenth part of my plan into your tiny mind. You could have been a great man, Marcus d'Ivoire, if only you were smart enough to shut up and do as you were told!"

"Please—"

"Don't bother. I haven't come this far to fail now." Janus slashed a hand through the air. "If you and the queen are against me, *so be it*. You have no idea what you're up against."

"Janus." Marcus felt tears building at the corners of his eyes. "Please don't do this."

"If you're going to stab me in the back, at least be honest about it, you pompous, ungrateful—"

There was a knock at the door.

"Sir?" The guard's voice was heavily muffled. "Sorry to bother you, Column-General, but there's a message here for the First Consul. Says it's extremely urgent."

Marcus looked at Janus. The mad anger had vanished from his face, replaced by his usual pleasant mask. Only the narrow set of his eyes betrayed a hint of his feelings.

"Bring it in," Marcus said, wiping his face on his sleeve. The door creaked open, and the guard came in with a single folded slip of paper. Marcus took it, thanked her, and waited until she had left again.

"You may as well read it," Janus muttered. "If you're to be my jailer, you have the right to censor my correspondence."

"You know I can't." The note was meaningless to Marcus, a mass of random letters. He handed it to Janus, who scanned it briefly and grunted. "What does it say?"

Janus stared at him for a moment, the mask back in place, gray eyes inscrutable.

"Some time ago," he said, "I placed several spies with Duke Orlanko. I thought he might eventually make a move, and apparently I was right." Janus waved the paper. "His little cadre of hired killers will be busy tonight. Dorsay, Raesinia, you, and myself. Quite the catch." He shook his head. "The Last Duke is not even *original* in his treasons."

"We need to warn—"

"You have a choice," Janus said. "This is exactly what we need. If Dorsay dies, the Borelgai army will fall into confusion and our task is much simplified. You know Raesinia can't be killed. You and I have merely to protect ourselves, and everything will fall into our hands." He paused, and Marcus was astonished to see his hands were trembling. "Please, Marcus. Trust me, just one more time. We're so close."

Marcus turned away, and it felt like tearing a part of himself loose.

"I'm going to warn the queen," he said. "We'll make sure you're well protected here."

Without looking back, he went to the door and rapped. The guard outside began the laborious process of dragging it open.

"Ionkovo," Janus said.

"What?"

"Ionkovo is with Orlanko. Be careful."

Marcus blinked rapidly. "Thank you."

CHAPTER NINETEEN

WINTER

The path that Snowfox, Alex, and Maxwell led them on didn't even qualify as a trail. It was more like a series of markers—a boulder here, a narrow gap there, a rocky shelf that *looked* impassable but, on close inspection, had a crack in it *just* wide enough to descend. For a time they trekked across a glacier; underneath the recent snowfall, Maxwell told them, was a river of ice, which ran all the way to the sharp-edged tip of the mountain.

They went on foot, since no mount, however sure-footed, could have managed. In addition to the trio from the Mountain, there was Winter, Bobby, Sergeant Red, and a ranker named Millie Varner. Winter had asked for volunteers, and predictably all the soldiers had been ready to come with her, in spite of the dangers. Red had picked Millie for her off-battlefield skills. She'd been one of Jane's Leatherbacks, and before that she'd been a street thief. She was small and dark haired, with a knack for blending easily into shadows. She and Red had left their muskets behind, borrowing short, straight-bladed swords of ancient manufacture from the armory at the Mountain. Winter wished they had more pistols, but the Eldest had had none to offer.

They'd departed just after dawn, under a clear blue sky that promised none of the vicious snow and wind of the past week. Snowfox mostly led the way, more comfortable on the rocks and snow than any of the adults. She scampered up cliff faces and across drifts of ice with all the casual indestructibility of youth, looking back when she got to the other side to see what was keeping everyone. She still hadn't spoken more than a few words to Winter, though Winter caught the girl staring in her direction when she thought no one was looking.

When they paused at midday to eat a lunch of flatbread, boiled eggs, and dried meat, Winter sat down on a rock next to Snowfox. The girl froze for a moment, as though fighting the urge to flee, then went back to eating with a studied nonchalance.

"I wanted to ask about how we'll be getting in," Winter said, "and what we can expect once we're inside."

"It's an old tunnel," Snowfox said, looking down at her food. "Elysium is kept warm by hot springs from under the mountain. Where they come up, there's a lot of very old pipes and passageways, and some of them the priests haven't looked at in centuries. There's a grate at the end, but it's rusted through, and it leads into the basements."

"Then what?"

The girl shrugged. "It depends where you want to go. Maxwell knows more about the interior than I do, but it's a maze. And with most of the priests leaving, I'm sure everything is in chaos."

Winter pursed her lips, but she'd expected that. Her tentative plan was to take the first person they met prisoner and demand information. Priests of the Black might rather die than give anything up, but no organization of that size could operate without menials to clean, cook, and so on. Those, Winter hoped, would not be quite so dedicated. The only flaw was that they probably wouldn't know exactly where to find the poisonous Penitent, either.

Snowfox shuffled sideways, turning away from Winter. When Winter tried to catch her eye, the girl flinched.

"What's wrong?" Winter said. "The Eldest said you could trust me, didn't he?"

"It's not that," Snowfox said. "There's something wrong with my demon. It feels . . . frightened, I think? More and more as we get closer to Elysium. And every time I look at you, it jumps a little."

"You can sense other demons, even though they can't sense you?"

She nodded. "Better than most people, the Eldest says. It's part of what my demon does. Yours is stronger than anything I've ever seen, much stronger than mine or Alex's. Abraham's might come close. That might be why mine is so frightened."

Winter reached out to Infernivore. She'd trained herself not to pay much attention to the thing's sudden moods, since with Alex around it was generally just reacting to her presence. Now, with Snowfox's power hiding Alex and even the tiny trace of power Bobby gave off, she expected to find the demon quiescent. Instead, it was fully awake, attention focused on the south. *Toward Elysium.* They were still too far to feel another demon's presence, but there was definitely *something* there, like the glow of the sun when it was just below the horizon.

Maybe there are so many demons they all run together. That was a pleasant thought. Winter shook her head and turned back to Snowfox, who had apparently conquered her demon's fear and was watching Winter carefully again.

"Where did you find your demon?" the girl said. "The Priests of the Black don't have anything like it."

"In Khandar," Winter said. "On an archive a lot like the one your Eldest keeps, actually."

"It must have been dangerous to read the name of something so strong."

Winter remembered the feeling of being ripped apart as Infernivore had wrapped around her soul. "I suppose it was. I didn't know at the time. There was a Penitent Damned trying to kill us." Winter cocked her head. "What about you? How old were you when you read the name?"

"Ten. Too young, the Eldest said, but I had the best chance, and I said I wanted to do it. The last Snowfox had died of a fever, and it's too important to the Mountain to take chances." A shadow crossed her face. "My sister was supposed to be the new Snowfox. She tried to read the name when she was fourteen, but she . . . didn't succeed."

There was only one way to fail to read the name of a demon. Winter swallowed. "You're very brave," she said, and meant it. She couldn't imagine how hard it would be to begin the incantation, knowing the likely outcome.

"It needed to be done," Snowfox said simply. She stuck the last strip of meat in her mouth and got to her feet. "We should keep moving."

The last few hours of the trek took them along a cleft in the mountain so narrow they were nearly underground. A great rock had split, leaving a jagged crevice a few feet wide and hundreds of feet deep. It was *warm* at the bottom, as though the rocks had been soaking in the sun of the Great Desol, and endless drips from melting snow pattered all around them. Farther up, snow and ice jammed in the crevice formed irregular crisscrossing bridges and archways, like a boulevard designed by a mad architect.

The entrance, when they finally found it, was so innocuous that Winter might have walked right by. A small pile of rubble marked a gap in the wall of the crevice, with a dark, warm space beyond. Red lit a lantern, and its light revealed a tunnel—narrow and close roofed, but definitely worked stone.

"That way goes to some of the sulfur pools," Snowfox said. "The other way joins up with a larger passage and goes back to Elysium. Just keep going forward and you'll find your way to the basement. You shouldn't see anyone before the grate."

"Thank you," Winter said.

The girl put on a fierce expression, but there was a slight flush in her cheeks. "I'll stay here for another day. If you can get back to me by then, I can shield you on your way out. If not, I'll go back, and you're on your own." She paused. "I'm sorry I can't come with you."

"We understand," Maxwell said, laying a hand on her shoulder. "You're too valuable, and your duty is to the Mountain. We're grateful to you for bringing us this far."

"You know your way around in there?" Winter said to the priest.

"Not very well," he said. "All we have are maps, but I've studied them. I'll do what I can."

"Okay." Winter turned to the others. "Alex and Millie, you're in front." The two thieves would almost certainly be the quietest of the group. "Red, Bobby, make sure nobody sneaks up on us. Maxwell, stay with me."

Maxwell raised no objections to her taking command, for which Winter was grateful. When he nodded, she went on. "If you see anyone, try to take them alive, but remember that if the alarm goes up we're already probably dead. So whatever you do, we can't have any screams or shots."

Millie gulped and nodded. Alex looked grim. At Winter's gesture, the two of them slipped into the tunnel. Winter gave them a count of five, then entered herself, with Maxwell on her heels. Bobby and Red brought up the rear.

It was certainly claustrophobic. Maxwell carried the lantern, sending twisting shadows racing ahead of them. Even Winter had to walk slightly hunched, and Red and Maxwell were bent nearly double. There was a pipe bracketed to one wall, its brass fittings turning green with age, and the water it carried was hot enough to make it painful to the touch. Inside her multiple layers of thick cloth, Winter was sweating freely, and when the corridor joined up with another, larger tunnel at an angle, she called a halt so they could all shed their outer garments.

This new tunnel was wider but just as low ceilinged. More pipes fed in at various angles, running along the walls in thick bundles. They were of varying vintages, some empty and riddled with rusty holes, others comparatively new. After what seemed like an age, they reached the grate Snowfox had mentioned, mounted on hinges that had long ago rusted solid. It hung open just wide enough to admit one person at a time. Alex, dressed now in tight-fitting thief's blacks, slipped through first, and Millie followed. Red, the largest of the group, got stuck on a protruding bar; Bobby bent it out of the way with a quiet squeal of protesting metal, which apparently surprised no one.

"We should be out of Snowfox's range by now, right?" Winter whispered to Maxwell. When he nodded, she again turned her attention to Infernivore, and frowned. "Alex, can you feel anything?"

"Not . . . exactly." Alex's brow creased. "There's *something* there, but it's like I can't quite find it. It's sort of . . . diffuse?"

"Maybe the Black Priests have someone like Snowfox in their collection," Maxwell said.

"That makes sense," Winter said. Infernivore *did* feel eager, but its attention wasn't aimed in any particular direction, as though the power it was sensing suffused the air all around her. "It's going to make this harder, though. Alex, Millie, get a little farther out. We're hoping to run into a lamp-lighter or a laundress or something."

"Do the Priests of the Black do laundry?" Bobby said.

"Somebody's got to wash all those sinister robes," Millie said. "Otherwise they'd end up as the Priests of the Grayish Brown."

There was a round of smiles. Winter was grateful for the levity, which helped keep her thoughts off the reality of her situation. Even if some of its inhabitants had fled, this was still *Elysium*, the heart of the Sworn Church. Ever since Khandar, she'd thought of it more as a malevolent force than a real place, but here she was walking its halls, hoping to kill one of the Penitent Damned right under the noses of the Priests of the Black. *The only good thing is that it's such a dumb plan I doubt they'll expect us to try it.*

For the headquarters of a sinister order, it was surprisingly ordinary-looking. Once they moved into the basement proper and out of the tunnels, the ceiling was higher and braziers at regular intervals lit the way. Some of the stonework was ancient and crumbling, while other parts looked freshly repaired; a brazier that had been tarnished nearly black with age stood beside one that might have been forged yesterday. All of Elysium was like that, Winter guessed—constructed, rebuilt, and added to incrementally over the centuries, with the most recent innovations sitting beside things that had been unchanged for a thousand years.

There were, in fact, laundries, great copper vats that were the terminus of some of the pipes they'd followed. Nobody seemed to be minding them at the moment, however, and they moved on. Other open doorways revealed storerooms full of soap and candles, stacks of tin plates in bins waiting to be washed, even toilets. It was a bit odd, Winter thought, to imagine the Pontifex of the Black sitting down for a long shit, and she grinned to herself as they moved past.

Up ahead there was a brief scuffle and then a sharp intake of breath. Winter hurried forward and found Alex with her arms around a young man in a dark gray robe, one of her hands over his mouth while the other held a knife to his throat. Another young man, similarly dressed, was slumped against the wall, feet kicking weakly as a slick of crimson poured from his slashed throat. Millie, gory knife in hand, was breathing hard.

"He was going to shout for the guards," Millie said.

"It's all right," Winter said. "Bobby, help her stash him in one of the rooms, and we'll use his robe to mop up the blood. If we blow out the brazier, nobody will notice for a while." She turned to the living prisoner and switched to Murnskai. "You understand me? Nod carefully."

The boy—it was a boy, not more than sixteen—nodded very slightly, exquisitely aware of the knife at his throat.

"If you scream, you'll end up like him. Do you understand?"

Another nod. Winter caught Alex's eye, and the thief removed her hand, keeping the knife in place.

"You didn't have to kill him," the boy said. "He wasn't going to shout. There's no guards here anyway. He was just trying to warn me."

"Quiet," Winter said. "Whisper. What do you mean there's no guards?"

"Everyone's in the cathedral. The pontifex's orders. We were just sent out to fetch more food from the stores."

"Who's 'everyone'?" Winter said. "The Black Priests?"

"*Everyone*," the boy said miserably. "The Priests, the servants, even the prisoners from the deep cells. The pontifex has us all praying nonstop while he administers a personal blessing. I haven't had my turn yet, but it won't be long."

"Why?" Winter said.

"I don't know. It has something to do with Vhalnich. Brian says"—he swallowed, skin pressing against the knife—"*said* that Vhalnich was coming to destroy the Church, and the pontifex was preparing some sort of great magic that would get rid of him."

"Wait." Maxwell pushed his way forward. "You said the pontifex brought the prisoners *out* of the deep cells?"

The boy nodded. "A lot of them are in pretty bad shape, too. As pale as dead fish."

Maxwell beckoned to Winter. Winter said in Vordanai, "Alex, get him to tell you how to get to the cathedral by a route where we won't be seen."

"Got it," Alex said. "Then . . ." She glanced at the knife.

Winter's throat went tight. "Just . . . gag him and tie him up. We'll ditch him somewhere and be out of here before he's found."

There was, she thought, a little relief on Alex's face. "Right."

Winter took a few steps back down the corridor, with Maxwell behind her. "What's going on?"

"Something's very wrong," Maxwell said. "The Eldest explained to you the purpose of the Black Priests, didn't he?"

Winter nodded. "To keep the Beast imprisoned."

"And as many other demons as they can catch. That's what the deep cells are for. Only a few people are faithful enough to be trusted in the field as the Penitent Damned, and they get the most useful demons. The rest are kept in the dungeons until they die, when another host is found to keep that demon from arising in the wild. Most of them are *never* let out of their cells, much less brought together and taken somewhere to pray."

"If the Church really thinks that Janus is coming to destroy them any day, maybe they're just pulling out whatever they have left."

"But those prisoners aren't like the Penitents. They're the ones who *aren't* loyal to the Church, who can't be trusted with their powers. Putting them all together is more likely to cause a riot than anything helpful."

"Desperate people do stupid things," Winter said, but her gut told her that he was right. Something *was* strange here. "What do you suggest we do? If everyone is in the cathedral, presumably that includes our Penitent."

"It's going to be hard to get to her if she's in the middle of a mob."

"If we can get a reasonable vantage point, Alex is as good as a rifle," Winter said, glancing over her shoulder. Alex and Millie had hog-tied the young servant, with a strip torn from his robe forced into his mouth. "If the cathedral here is like the one in Vordan, there'll be a gallery. That might be what we need."

"Getting away afterward is going to be the hard part," the priest said. His eyes lingered on Alex, Winter noted. "I hope you've got a plan."

"One step at a time," Winter said.

"The cathedral is aboveground," Alex said. "Our friend gave me the route, but it comes up at the edge of the central square. If anyone's watching, they'll see us if we try to approach that way."

"Let's go as far as we can," Winter said, "and see if we can find another way

in." She looked from Alex to Bobby and smiled. "We may have a few uncon-
ventional options."

As Alex had said, the boy's route led to a long stairway, upper steps coated with
snow, that surfaced in a broad, flat square. Winter left the rest of the group
behind and wormed her way to the top on her belly, letting as little show over
the lip of the stairs as possible.

The square was big, maybe as big as Farus' Triumph back in Vordan. Directly in front of her was a long, low building faced with white marble, its facade
encrusted with statues and columns. A similar building mirrored it on the other
side of the square, faced in red. Across from the steps was what had to be the
cathedral, a monstrous stone construction that towered over its surroundings. A
huge circular stained-glass window looked out like an eye from just below the
peaked roof, at least three stories above the ground. Two asymmetrical towers,
one fat and square and the other slender and round, rose from the two front
corners. Like the rest of Elysium, its stone was a patchwork of fresh and weath-
ered, which might explain the mishmash of architectural styles.

More interestingly for Winter's purpose, there were more stained-glass
windows along the sides of the cathedral, where it ran parallel to the white-
faced building. She shuffled back down the steps and gathered her team.

"Okay," she said. "There's a building over *there*, all in white."

"That's the Priests of the White administrative headquarters," Maxwell
said. "A pretty new addition."

"Where we want to be is on its roof," Winter said. "That should get us onto
the cathedral on one of its blind sides. We'll need to watch the towers, though."

"How far is it to the white building?" Bobby said.

"Maybe sixty feet," Winter said. "I don't think we could all run for it without being spotted. But there was a corridor in that direction a little ways back.
Come on."

She led them back the way they'd come, then turned right, down a side
corridor. It led to a doorway, with another storeroom beyond stacked with
small votive candles and boxes of worn copies of the *Wisdoms*. There were no
other exits.

"This is almost underneath the white building," Winter said. "It has its
own basements, I assume?"

"It should," Maxwell said.

"Bobby?" Winter said. "See if you can make us a door."

Bobby grinned. "It might be a little loud."

"If that kid was right, there shouldn't be anyone to hear."

"Here goes, then."

Bobby took a deep breath, pivoted on the ball of her foot, and delivered a roundhouse punch to the stone wall at the back of the storeroom. There was a *crunch* and an explosion of small stones and dust, which left everyone coughing.

"Sorry," Bobby said, as the air slowly cleared. "I wasn't expecting that."

The blow had had the desired effect, Winter was gratified to see. As she'd expected, the wall separating this tunnel from the basements of the white building wasn't very thick. Bobby's punch had shattered the stone, fracturing it in a bull's-eye pattern like a rock thrown through a window. A little light filtered through the center, where bits of stone had fallen away, and Bobby was able to clear a respectable-sized hole in a few more moments.

"You okay?" Winter said, as the others came forward to help move the rubble.

Bobby made a face. "Think I broke a bone in my hand or something," she said. "It'll be all right in a few minutes. Next time I'll use a pickax."

Winter shot her a grin. When the hole was wide enough, Alex and Millie slipped through, with the others following when the two thieves waved them forward.

"Maxwell," Winter said, "do you know the layout here?"

The priest shook his head. "It's too new. We don't have maps this recent."

"Then we'll just have to look for the stairs. Keep an eye out."

Even more than the deeper tunnels, the basements of the Priests of the White were shockingly banal. Here the theme was paper—every room they passed was lined with shelves, which until recently had been stacked higher with bound volumes, wrapped scrolls, and loose sheets. Some of them were still untouched, but most appeared to have been emptied in a hurry, stray books and torn pages lying on the floor under mud tracks from many boots.

At the end of the hall, marble-faced stairs led up to the main floor, which presented a similar prospect. Large, open rooms with many desks alternated with more storage, with a side corridor leading to a well-equipped kitchen and canteen. Paper was everywhere, carpeting the floors as though the building had been hit by a blizzard of the stuff. It rustled around their feet as they walked, but nothing else moved in the vast space. On impulse, Winter reached down and picked up a page, parsing the unfamiliar Murnskai script with difficulty:

Fitness Report for Father Muren Nasidov, assigned to Saint Vilek's of West Ristev

Overall: Good. Some concerns Nasidov may be becoming too close to his congregation. Recommend transfer after no more than one year.

Detail—

"Saints and martyrs," Winter muttered, letting the sheet fall. "This is worse than Orlanko's Cobweb."

"I think that's the stairs," Alex called.

A narrow, seldom-used staircase led upward past a ring of overhanging galleries, ending in a locked trapdoor. Winter looked back to Bobby, but before they could rearrange the group to shuffle her to the front, Alex had popped the lock with a pair of thin metal picks. Millie raised her eyebrows, impressed.

"I told you I was the greatest thief in the world," Alex said with a shrug. "Besides, this is kid stuff."

"Open it carefully," Winter said. "Someone may be watching from the tower."

Alex nodded and pushed the trapdoor open a few inches. She put her eye to the crack for a full minute, then looked over her shoulder.

"If they're there, I can't see them."

Winter gestured her forward. One by one, they climbed the last few steps and emerged onto the roof of the white building. It was made of overlapping slate shingles, sharply peaked to keep the snow off, which made the footing somewhat treacherous. The sun was nearly down in the west, the yellow-orange of sunset already fading to purple and black overhead. Just ahead of them, the side of the cathedral rose like a mountain, twice the height of the white building even without its towers. The thinner tower loomed far overhead, but as best Winter could tell there were no windows on its slim sides. It widened at the very top to support a covered platform, but that seemed to be empty except for an enormous bronze bell. A spiderweb of ropes and lines connected it to the larger tower on the other side of the cathedral, supporting long strings of double-circle flags in alternating red and white, along with representative emblems of Murnsk, Borel, and the other Sworn Church nations.

Of more direct interest were the stained-glass windows, each about ten feet high and three feet across, that pierced the thick stone wall of the cathedral at regular intervals. The gap from the edge of the white building's roof to the cathedral's side was perhaps ten feet, longer than Winter had guessed from the ground.

"Bobby, we're going to need something to use as a bridge," Winter said. "Can you go back downstairs and grab one of those long benches?"

Bobby nodded and disappeared back down the trapdoor. Winter turned to Alex.

"Try to keep the hole as small as possible," she said. "We don't want anyone down below noticing."

"Got it."

Alex flexed her fingers, like a pianist preparing for a performance, and extended a hand. A black sphere formed around it, then sent a lance of pure darkness into the stone beside the window. It stuck there, quivering as though anchored to the rock, and Alex nonchalantly stepped into space. She swung across the gap on her line of shadow, coming to rest boots-first against the wall in what was obviously a well-practiced maneuver.

From there she walked herself sideways until she was right beside the window and fired another line into the rock from her other hand. Putting her weight on this new anchor, she let the first one vanish like a wisp of smoke, leaning over to examine the glass. Darkness gathered around her hand again, and thin, quick spears of black punched out like a swarm of snakes, tracing a rotating circular pattern. A moment later they twined around a section of the stained-glass mosaic and pulled it away, leaving a hole big enough to crawl through. A few bits of glass dropped from the cut edge, but the rest stayed together, held in place by the leaded frame.

Bobby returned, carrying one of the long benches with the legs broken off. With some difficulty, Maxwell helped her work it up through the trapdoor and along the roof until they were opposite the window. Bobby stood it on end and let it tilt across the gap until it came to rest against the cathedral wall, and Alex guided it down and into the hole, making a narrow but sturdy-looking bridge.

"Not bad," Alex said. "Maybe not *quite* worthy of Metzing, but not bad at all."

All that remained was for them to crawl across, one by one. Alex went first, dropping lightly off the wall and onto the plank, then shimmying through the hole. Millie and Maxwell followed. Red looked down at the narrow alley between the buildings, thirty feet below, and swallowed.

"Something wrong?" Winter said.

"I'm not good with heights," the big sergeant admitted. "Give me a moment."

Eyes closed, she edged out onto the bench, crawling on hands and knees. Millie, waiting on the other side, took her arm as soon as she was close enough and guided her the rest of the way. When she was through, Winter looked at Bobby.

"No problems with heights?"

"Not that I've noticed," Bobby said. "You?"

"Maybe a few . . . twinges." Winter took a deep breath, dropped to her knees, and shuffled out onto the board. She kept her eyes locked on Millie's encouraging face and tried her best to ignore the tingling, hollow feeling in the pit of her stomach. When she was across, she squeezed through the hole in the stained glass with a sigh of relief, and found Millie and Red squatting in a narrow, darkened alcove. Alex and Maxwell were pressed against each other, leaning against the wall, and it took Winter a moment to realize they were kissing enthusiastically. Alex broke away after a moment, blushing only a little.

"Sorry," she muttered. "It's been a long time since I did any thievery. It gets me excited."

Winter raised an eyebrow but said nothing. Bobby emerged from the hole and got to her feet, dusting herself off.

"Maxwell?" Winter said. The priest still had one hand in Alex's, their fingers entwined. "Am I right in thinking this place is going to look a lot like most cathedrals?"

He nodded, keeping his voice to a whisper. "This is the Widow's Gallery. The main hall is down below. The speaker's balcony is over there"—he gestured to the right—"with the priest's quarters and so on behind it. Stairway down is the other way."

"Right. We need to find a spot where we can get a good look at the main hall without being seen. Alex, you make sure the gallery is clear. The rest of you, stay down."

Alex nodded and padded forward. They were standing in a nook, a notch in the thick stone wall designed to admit light from the stained-glass window. Now that it was nearly full dark, they didn't have to worry about presenting a silhouette against the lit glass, and no lights were visible on the gallery level, with only a weak radiance shining up from below.

"Looks like we're alone up here," Alex hissed. "I can see down below, but . . . you'd better come take a look."

Winter hunched over and shuffled forward. The gallery was a horseshoe-shaped balcony, stretching out fifteen feet from the wall on three sides of the great hall. Unlike the gallery of the cathedral in Vordan, where she'd nearly been trapped by Orlanko's black-coats, this one was in fairly good repair, with its wooden boards solid underfoot and covered by dusty wool carpets. A waist-high railing at the edge provided at least a token effort to prevent people from falling to their deaths among the pews thirty feet below. Alex, lying on her stomach, had shuffled to the very edge and peeked over, and Winter followed her example.

The great hall of the cathedral was packed with people. Pews, braziers, and other furniture had been dragged aside, leaving the enormous oval of floor entirely full of neat ranks of kneeling figures. Many wore robes, either the black of priests or the gray of servants, but others were dressed in ragged shirts and trousers, and some were entirely naked. The precision of their arrangement was unnerving, reminding Winter of a battalion arranged for attack. At a glance, she guessed there were at least a thousand of them, maybe more; they extended beyond her line of sight beneath the gallery in all directions.

"Balls of the Beast," she swore. "I know the boy said 'everyone,' but I didn't think they'd all be *here*."

"They don't even look like they're praying," Alex whispered. It was nearly silent in the vast space, so quiet they could hear the occasional cough from the congregation gathered below. "They're just . . . waiting."

"Some of them aren't in good shape, either." A few of the naked figures were so emaciated it was hard to tell if they were men or women. Others were missing arms, or just hands, and many had weeping sores at their wrists, as though they'd spent a great deal of time shackled.

"Can you see your Penitent?"

Winter shook her head. "Too many black robes. She could be down there and I'd never know it. Damn. We may have to rethink this."

"I've got an idea, but let me run it by Maxwell," Alex said. She backed away from the edge on hands and knees, then sat up. *"Shit!"*

There was a sharp, wet sound. Winter bounced to her feet, hand falling to her sword. A young man in a black robe stood in front of Alex, with one of her black spears extending from her outstretched hand right through his breastbone. A moment later, it faded away, and he swayed slightly and coughed. Blood flecked his mouth.

"What's wrong—" Bobby said, coming out of the alcove. Her sword slid free with a rasp, leveled at the throat of the stranger. "Don't make a sound!"

"The pontifex sends me to greet you," the young man said in Vordanai. His voice had an unhealthy gurgle to it, and he coughed again. "He wishes you to join him in the west tower. He sends his . . . his kind . . ." The young man's knees gave way, and he toppled to the floor with a *thump*. Blood gushed from his mouth as he strained to mouth one more word. ". . . regards."

Winter stared as the young man convulsed once, then died. *What the* hell *was that?*

"We have to get out of here," Alex said, hands tightening. "They're onto us."

"That may be problematic," Bobby said. She pointed to the left, in the direction of the main staircase. A group of robed figures at least a dozen strong had just come up, walking unhurriedly in their direction.

"Over here, too!" Millie said, voice high with fear. Another dozen black robes were closing in from the other end of the gallery.

"Back over the bridge," Winter said, but Maxwell was already peering out the hole.

"There's at least four of them waiting on the other side," he said.

"Saints and fucking martyrs," Winter said. She turned back to the group coming from the stairs.

"Charge 'em," Red suggested. "We can break through, make a run for the main doors."

"There's another thousand downstairs," Alex said.

"They're not even armed," Winter said. "What the hell is going on?"

"The pontifex sends me to greet you," the closest black-robed figure said, coming to a halt. "He wishes you to join him in the west tower. He sends his kind regards, and assures you that you will be perfectly safe."

Winter looked down at the corpse, then back at the second messenger. If he'd noticed his dead comrade, his pleasant expression betrayed nothing.

"Well?" Red said, her sword half-drawn. "Winter?"

"I think we go to the west tower," Winter said.

"Are you kidding?" Millie squeaked. "That has to be a trap!"

"I don't think it could be any *more* of a trap than what we're in now," Maxwell said calmly.

"What the hell would the Pontifex of the Black want to *talk* to us for?" Millie said.

As far as Winter could see, there was only one reason. "He wants to negotiate," she said. *I hope.* "With Janus' army so close, maybe he's ready to talk terms."

"You don't sound very sure of that," Alex said.

"I'm not. But it's the only scenario where we have half a chance of getting out of here alive." She straightened up, taking her hand off her sword, and raised her voice. "All right. Take us to the pontifex."

One of the strangely calm men led them around the gallery, to where a stone staircase twisted upward into the larger of the cathedral's two towers. The other robed figures, to Winter's surprise, stayed behind. They didn't even ask the intruders to relinquish their weapons. *Either they're very confident or very stupid.* Either way, she'd find out soon enough.

The staircase spiraled around the outside wall of the tower, giving views through arched doorways into broad rooms. What furniture there was had been pushed aside, and the chambers were packed with more people, kneeling in rows with their heads bowed. The calm and quiet of the priests and their servants were beginning to feel almost unnatural. *Are they* drugged? *Or is this some ritual they've all trained for?* The Priests of the Black managed to convince people who thought bearing a demon meant an eternity in hell to do it *anyway* for the good of the Church; they obviously had a considerable influence over their followers.

Four floors up, one of the rooms was different. There were more people, but instead of waiting in neat rows, they were huddled together in the center of the room. Most of them were servants in gray robes, with a few of the half-clothed figures Winter guessed were prisoners. They watched the group of intruders go past with a mixture of curiosity and fear that she hadn't seen on any other faces. *What the* fuck *is going on here?*

The fifth floor was the top of the tower, a bit wider than the others. It was set up as a sumptuous office, with a vast desk of polished oak so ancient it was nearly black. Winter couldn't imagine how they'd gotten it up the stairs, and the same was true of the heavy glass-paneled shelves, which bore rows of tattered, ancient books. Thick carpet was soft underfoot, and a row of elaborately carved chairs cushioned in red and white velvet sat in front of the desk. The whole setup rang a distant bell in Winter's mind, but it took her a moment to place it—it was almost identical to the way Mrs. Wilmore had arranged her office back at the Prison, with her on one side of a massive, intimidating desk and rows of disappointing students sitting on the other. *Is this where the pontifex brings his priests for a scolding?*

There were three robed figures behind the desk, all wearing the glittering obsidian masks of the Priests of the Black. One, tall and broad shouldered, sat in a cushioned armchair, while the other two, probably women by their builds, stood off to his left. None of them were obviously armed, but they didn't need to be. *Any one of them could be a Penitent.*

"Winter Ihernglass," the man behind the desk said in Vordanai. His voice was a liquid rasp, as though something had damaged his throat. "And her side-kick Bobby Forester. I'm afraid I don't know the rest of you. I am the Pontifex of the Black."

There was a long silence. Winter's eyes flicked to the corners of the room, but there were no guards waiting there, only the young man who'd been their guide standing beside her. *He must either be a Penitent himself or have these two women here to protect him.* Infernivore was no help; the demon was straining at her will, but in no particular direction, as though there were demons all around. *He's very confident in his power, to invite us in here. But if he doesn't know what Infernivore does, or what Bobby and Alex can do, maybe we can cut the head off the Black Priests here and now.* That, of course, would probably mean none of them would get out alive, with the possible exception of Bobby.

"I know why you're here, of course," the pontifex said. "You want Viper, the Penitent Damned who poisoned your precious Vhalnich. As a gesture of good faith, you may have her."

The two women stepped around the desk, and the one in back, taller, reached forward and pulled the mask off of the other. The face underneath was unfamiliar to Winter, plain and spotted with scars. She looked at Winter impassively, and Winter strained toward her with Infernivore. She still felt nothing useful.

"Alex?" Winter said quietly. "Is she the one we were following?"

"I can't tell." There was a lot of tension in Alex's voice, carefully disguised. "I can't even sense *you*."

The taller woman drew a long, curved dagger from a pocket of her dark robe, and Winter took a reflexive step back, hand dropping to her sword. Before she could say anything, the masked woman drew the knife in a smooth motion across the Penitent's throat, leaving a gush of crimson in its wake. The shorter woman dropped to the floor like a sack of potatoes, without even a gurgle. Waves of red pulsed into the plush carpet. The masked woman tossed the dagger beside her victim and stepped back.

"There," the pontifex said. "Your goal is accomplished."

Winter's mind whirled, discarding one conversational gambit after another. Her brow furrowed, and finally she could only give vent to her frustration.

"What the *fuck* is going on?" she said. "Why would you want to *help* us? And what's to stop us from killing you right now?"

"The answer to all of your questions is the same," the pontifex said. "Because I am not in charge here anymore."

"What?" Maxwell said. "That's not possible."

"If you're not in charge," Winter said, "who is?"

The remaining woman pulled off her mask. The face underneath had thinned, and the glorious red hair was once again hacked short into an unruly mop a few inches long, but the green eyes were still the same brilliant green. Winter's eyes went wide.

"I am," said Jane, with a smile like a shark.

CHAPTER TWENTY

MARCUS

"I don't like this plan," Sothe said. "I should have stayed with Raesinia."

"Raesinia's got Barely and Joanna and half a company of the Girls' Own watching her," Marcus said quietly. "Not to mention she can't be killed."

"Ionkovo's come for her before. He's too clever by half. The last time I left her alone, *you* let him grab her."

"This time she'll be ready for him," Marcus said. "I'm more worried about him turning up *here*. We could already be too late."

"If they'd started shooting, there'd be more commotion." Sothe stood by the rail that lined the edge of the wooden bridge and peered into the darkness. Lanterns and cook fires lit up the small town of Polkhaiz, but there was no obvious sign of an alarm. "I could go in on my own."

"There might be too many guards even for you," Marcus said.

Sothe opened her mouth to object, then said nothing. Her attitude toward him was different than he remembered. He was used to the assassin treating him as a sort of semi-competent junior officer, and while she still snapped at him in unguarded moments, she would periodically go quiet and thoughtful. He wasn't sure which state he found more unnerving.

She nodded at a point of light moving on the far end of the bridge. "Here he comes."

After a moment Marcus could make out the outline of three men. Two carried muskets with fixed bayonets and wore tall shakos, leaving the third looking short by comparison. It took them a few minutes to cross the bridge over the frozen river, and Marcus resisted the impulse to shout at them to hurry or double-check his own weapons. Two pistols were strapped to his side, along with the sword at his belt, and Sothe carried a long blade in a scabbard in addition to her usual complement of smaller weapons.

"Sothe," the man said with a nod.

"Whaler," Sothe said. "Thank you for responding so quickly."

"Who's that with you?"

"Column-General Marcus d'Ivoire," Sothe said. "We need to see the duke at once."

"His Grace will be in bed," Whaler said. "It can't wait till morning?"

"I'm afraid not," Marcus cut in. "Please. It's important."

Whaler raised the lantern to examine Marcus, then shrugged cheerfully.

"God help you if it isn't, column-general or no," he said. "I've seen His Grace shout at the *king* for waking him up before breakfast. Come along."

He turned and started back across the bridge. The two guards fell in alongside Marcus and Sothe when they followed. They *were* big men, Marcus noted, both six-footers and broad shouldered. Their shakos were lined with white fur, which marked them as Life Guards, the personal regiment of the King of Borel, from which he assigned companies to accompany his favored commanders and friends. They were supposedly elite, although Marcus had seen too many "elite" palace troops who failed to stand up to the test of actual battle. *For Dorsay's sake, I hope they're as good as their reputation.*

"Whaler's putting on a show," Sothe whispered. "Dorsay will have heard by now that you and Janus are back. He needs to know how this affects his deal with Raesinia."

"Whatever gets us in there quickly." The back of Marcus' neck felt itchy, expecting an attack at any moment. He'd argued for simply sending Dorsay a warning, but Sothe had pointed out that here on the Borelgai side of the line they had no idea whom they could trust. *Anyone could be working for Orlanko.*

A dozen more guards, ordinary Borelgai soldiers in their mud-red uniforms, stood at stiff attention and saluted as their party came down from the southern end of the bridge. Beyond was Polkhaiz, ablaze with lamps and campfires. Marcus couldn't help looking around, out of professional curiosity, and assessing the state of the Borels' defenses. They were formidable, he decided. The buildings closest to the bridge had clearly been reinforced and loopholed to turn them into blockhouses, and a line of four cannon sat across the main street like a particularly forbidding barricade. To the left and right, where the land sloped to meet the river, shallow trenches had been dug in the frozen soil at what must have been enormous effort, with heavy logs laid across their fronts to make breastworks. More cannon sat in pits up to their muzzles, and the cold, hard earth would make those positions almost as tough as a fortress' embrasures.

Some of the work looked very recent; the Borelgai army clearly wasn't slacking while the duke negotiated with the Vordanai. *No wonder he's happy to feed us. It keeps us from attacking, and his position gets stronger every day.* He felt desperately grateful that Raesinia had stopped Mor from launching his assault. *Across the ice, under all those guns, with this nightmare of a town at the end?* Not to mention the Borelgai cavalry, who no doubt waited on the plains beyond. *No army in the world could storm this place.*

Beyond the first row of houses and their defenses, most of Polkhaiz seemed to be given over to housing for Dorsay's officers. Sentries stood in the streets and by the doorways of even the commonest houses, and most buildings had at least a dozen horses harnessed outside. More men saluted as Whaler led them off the main street, down a lane between the Sworn Church and one of the bigger houses. Farther on, a tall fence obscured the ground of a large manor, with the peaked roofs of the upper stories and a few tall pines showing above it. Another pair of Life Guards sentries watched the main gate.

At Whaler's wave, the two soldiers swung the iron gate open. Beyond was a short lane, leading across a snow-covered field to the house's front door. The two men from the front kept pace behind them, and two more stood beside the tall columns that flanked the entrance. They were considerably shorter and less impressive than the two who accompanied Whaler, and something prickled Marcus' memory.

"Send someone to wake the duke," Whaler was saying. "And bring something warm to drink for our guests—"

Looking casually over his shoulder, Marcus saw that the two men behind them were also short and not particularly well turned out, shakos cocked and uniforms sloppy. The cuffs were folded over—*as though they didn't quite fit*—

"Trap," he muttered to Sothe. He saw her eyes go wide, then cold and hard. When she moved, he was ready.

Marcus threw himself down and sideways, getting clear of the line of fire between the two pairs of converging guards. Sothe did something similar, but far more graceful, rolling into a crouch and coming up with steel in her hand. A knife flashed across the distance between her and one of the door guards, catching him in the throat. His companion brought his musket up, aimed at

Sothe, while the pair behind them each took a step forward and rammed their bayonets into the backs of Whaler's companions.

The first guard fired, the sound of the weapon shatteringly loud in the stillness, but Sothe was no longer where he was aiming. She'd slipped sideways, lithe as a shadow, and drawn her sword. Powder smoke billowed around her as she came forward, and the guard brought up his musket in a clumsy parry, far too late. She slipped under his guard, ran him through the belly, and smashed the side of his head with her pommel as he went down for good measure.

Meanwhile, Whaler was scrambling under his coat for a weapon. One of the two real Life Guards was down, but the other had managed to half turn, tearing a chunk of bloody meat out of his back but getting a gloved hand on his opponent's weapon. The false guard jerked the musket back and fired, catching his wounded assailant in the chest, and this time the Life Guard went down. By then Marcus had one of his pistols drawn, however, and he aimed carefully and pulled the trigger. The false guard flopped backward into the snow.

Another report made him look around. The second gate guard staggered back, missing a good chunk of the back of his skull, and collapsed. Whaler, a pistol in one hand, glared down at him in contempt, then winced and slapped a hand to his leg. There was a long cut there, quickly staining his trousers crimson.

As though the shots had been a signal, there was a furious round of firing from inside the house, muzzle flashes lighting up the windows as if there were a thunderstorm within.

"What—" Whaler looked from Marcus, still holding his spent pistol, to the dead guards. "This isn't your Vordanai, is it." It wasn't a question.

"It's Orlanko," Marcus said. "We were hoping to get here before he moved. Can you walk?"

Whaler straightened up, putting weight on his injured leg. His face went white, but he nodded. "At least back to the road."

"Get help," Marcus said. "Anyone you're sure you can trust. We'll try to get to the duke. Go!"

Whaler nodded without argument and hobbled back toward the gate. Marcus tossed his pistol aside and walked to Sothe, who was staring at the house intently. As Marcus opened his mouth to speak, she grabbed his arm and dragged him to the side, and the big double doors at the front of the manor swung open. Six musket barrels emerged, firing a salvo that raised sprays of snow from where they'd just been standing.

"This way!" Sothe let go of his arm and ran, somehow skipping lightly over the snow that lay several feet deep around the side of the house. Marcus slogged after her, sinking in with every step. She stopped in the shadow of a pair of pine trees, and he crashed to the ground beside her, panting.

"Do you know where you're going?" he said.

"No," Sothe said shortly. "But we're not getting in that way." She cocked her head, not taking her eyes from the building. "What tipped you off?"

"They weren't tall enough," Marcus muttered. "I had friends in the War College who met Borelgai delegations, and they said there was a height requirement for the Life Guards. The king likes his soldiers big and strapping."

"Orlanko must have taken the real guards by surprise and swapped uniforms," Sothe said. "But *someone* is still fighting in there, so we've still got a chance. You really want to go in after Dorsay?"

Marcus let out a deep breath. "Raesinia seems to think he's important. And Orlanko wanting him dead is a big mark in his favor in my book."

"Fair enough. Stay behind me, and be as quiet as you can."

As quiet as Marcus could be was not very quiet compared to Sothe, who moved like a zephyr through the snow and low bushes. Marcus could see flickering lanterns at the front door, but the men didn't seem to be making any move to come after them. He and Sothe crept slowly around the corner of the house, and once the lanterns were out of view, Sothe straightened up and hurried to the wall.

"They'll be watching the front and back doors," she said. "And the main staircase, if Orlanko's got them following the old Concordat procedure. We could try to find a servants' stair, but that's risky. Can you climb a rope?"

Marcus nodded. "Have you got a—"

"Hold this."

Sothe had produced a coil of rope—black, of course, and as thin as a ramrod—from a back pocket. She handed one end to Marcus, looped the other over her shoulder, and began to climb the wall. It was mortared stone, with cracks between the rocks for finger- and toeholds, but even so Marcus gaped at the fluid ease with which the assassin gained the second story. There were windows there, the shutters closed and locked, but that also seemed to present no obstacle. Holding on with one hand, Sothe slipped a thin-bladed tool through to flip the catch, pulled the shutter open, and shattered the pane with her elbow. She reached through the resulting gap, turned the lock, and raised the sash. The whole ascent had taken perhaps sixty seconds.

Karis Almighty. Marcus wondered, not for the first time, where Raesinia had found this terrifying woman. Sothe had told him once that she used to work for Orlanko, which explained her knowledge of Concordat procedure, but she remained closemouthed about the circumstances. He shook his head weakly as the rope twitched in his hand, and he felt two solid tugs.

Thankfully, the thin rope was knotted every couple of feet, though Marcus' thick boots still made the climb harder than it ought to have been. He grabbed the windowsill, watching for broken glass, and hauled himself in. Sothe was already at the door of what turned out to be a small guest bedroom, neat and well furnished.

"I can hear them moving around, but nobody's shooting," Sothe said. "Stay here for a minute."

Marcus crouched obediently and waited while she opened the door a fraction and ghosted out into the darkened corridor. A shot split the quiet, making him jump, but on reflection it sounded as though it had come from the other end of the house. A few moments later Sothe's hand appeared, beckoning him forward, and he stepped carefully into the corridor. She led him forward to a corner, then pressed herself against the wall.

"There's more of them than I thought," she said. "But they don't know we're here. I think Dorsay's got some guards left, barricaded in the master suite." She nodded at the corner. "That's down here, past the main stairs. There's at least six of them trying to figure out what to do next, plus the group downstairs."

"Hell," Marcus said. "Maybe we ought to wait for Whaler."

"No telling if he got away or if Orlanko's people picked him up. They may have reinforcements on the way for all we know."

She reached into the lining of her coat and withdrew a stack of half a dozen thin throwing knives, little steel arrowheads weighted at one end. Then she shrugged out of the garment, leaving her in only her tight-fitting blacks. More blackened steel was visible in sheaths on her hips and thighs.

"I'll take the ones facing Dorsay's room," she said. "I need you to handle anyone who comes up the stairs. Think you can manage?"

"Shit. Not much choice." Marcus drew his sword in his right hand and his pistol in his left. "I'm right behind you."

Sothe nodded, fanning the knives in her left hand. She peeked around the corner, paused, then backed up a step and started to run. Marcus followed, feeling clumsy as usual in her wake. It was about thirty feet to the end of the corridor, where a pair of double doors leading to the master suite had been broken open and hung splintered and useless. Six men in rough wool and leather had taken cover behind a sofa and a sideboard they'd dragged into the line of fire. Opposite them, another door was already holed by musket balls. Each man had a short sword, and most of them had pistols, which they were frantically trying to reload.

The first knife left Sothe's hand when she was halfway down the corridor, carrying with it her own considerable momentum. It buried itself in a man's skull, so deep that only the weighted end showed, and he slumped forward without a murmur. The man next to him half turned and got the second blade in the throat; he got out a gurgling shriek that alerted the others they were under attack. By then Sothe was at the doorway, and a third blade flashed out and missed a man by a hairbreadth when he threw himself to the ground. The closest of Orlanko's killers raised his sword to cut her down, and Sothe flipped the three remaining knives in her left hand in his direction. They didn't have the power or accuracy of her previous throws, but they were enough to make him flinch, and Sothe used the same spinning motion to draw her sword and slash him across the chest.

She'll handle them. Right. Marcus had reached the stairs, which extended to the first floor at right angles to the corridor. A brief glance showed him two men on the stairs themselves and four more by the front door. The scream and the clomping of his boots had alerted them, and the first two were already moving, pounding up the steps with weapons drawn. Marcus skidded to a halt at the corner of the steps, where the upstairs wall hid him from view, and clicked back the hammer on his pistol.

He had only a moment to wait. When he heard the footsteps approach, he swung his sword around the corner at waist height, wrist jolting as it sliced through flesh and found bone. The wounded man shouted, stumbling back, and Marcus jerked his sword free and stepped around the corner. As he'd hoped, the second attacker had been forced to sidestep the first, leaving him wrong-footed. Marcus raised his pistol and shot him in the chest at point-blank range, so close that even left-handed he couldn't miss. The man staggered and fell bonelessly down the stairs. Marcus dropped the pistol and slid back behind the wall, just ahead of a pair of shots from below that knocked plaster from the opposite wall. He heard a shot from behind him as well, but when he looked around, Sothe was fighting the last of Orlanko's men, driving him back with neat, efficient swordplay before killing him with a thrust to the heart.

He risked a look down the stairs. The four men at the door, along with the one he'd cut, seemed to be conferring. Marcus retreated to the anteroom, where Sothe was finishing a groaning survivor with her sword and retrieving her throwing knives.

"That was . . ." Marcus looked around at the splayed corpses. Sothe herself bore a shallow cut on her arm and another on her hip, but seemed otherwise unharmed. "Impressive."

"Too slow." She shrugged. "I'm getting old. How many left down there?"

"Four or five. They don't seem to be in a hurry."

"See if you can talk to Dorsay."

Marcus crouched behind the sofa, in case his voice drew a gunshot, and shouted, "Duke Dorsay? Are you all right?"

A young, gruff male voice answered. "Who the hell is that? What's going on out there?"

"Orlanko's people are trying to kill the duke," Marcus said. "Is he hurt?"

"I'm all right," came an older man's voice. "Who's out there?"

"Marcus d'Ivoire," Marcus said. "Queen Raesinia sent me when we got warning of Orlanko's attack."

"That goddamned snake," Dorsay fumed. "Jeffery, get the door open."

"Your Grace, this could be a trick—" said the young man, who had to be one of the Life Guards.

"Can you get out the window?" Sothe interrupted.

"My wall-climbing days are a long way behind me," Dorsay said. "But we might be able to knot together some bedsheets. Why?"

"They're coming." She picked out a throwing knife, wiped it on her sleeve, and waited.

Marcus heard the footsteps a moment later. It sounded like at least a half dozen men, maybe more. As the first one came into view at the top of the stairs, Sothe let the blade fly, a perfect throw that sank into the attacker's throat just above his collarbone. He fell, and it was only a moment later that Marcus registered he'd been dressed in tight-fitting black, like Sothe, and had worn a multifaceted mask that glittered in the light of the lanterns.

Two more men, in similar costumes, leapt over the corpse without a pause and kept coming. They had long, curved swords, blades blackened to dull the sheen. Sothe hurled another knife, which caught one of them in the eye, and he tumbled to a halt, while Marcus stepped in to block the other one. Their swords met with a shivering scream of steel, and as his opponent bulled forward, Marcus lashed out with a kick to the other man's kneecap. The masked figure stumbled, and Marcus danced away from his clumsy counterstroke and planted his saber in the man's chest.

"Penitents?" he said to Sothe.

Her eyes narrowed. "Something's wrong. What happened to the first one?"

Marcus looked up. The first attacker was gone, Sothe's knife lying bloody on the carpet where his corpse had been. Then, as he watched, the second body faded away, turning translucent as mist and then vanishing entirely. The third corpse, with Marcus' sword still in its chest, vanished in the same fashion a moment later.

Another man came around the corner, armed and dressed like all the others. He gave them a brief look, followed by an exaggerated shrug, his mask clicking. The air around him went *strange*, overlapping images that didn't quite line up, like looking into a mirror spiderwebbed with cracks. For a moment there were four identical copies of the man, all staring back at Marcus, and then—

—the odd effect was gone, and there were four identical copies of the man standing in the corridor.

"Penitent," Sothe said grimly.

"Your Grace," Marcus said, raising his sword again, "I'd hurry with those bedsheets."

RAESINIA

"Joanna and I should stay with you, at least," Barely said. Joanna nodded emphatically.

"We've been over this. I want you to stay in the room with Janus," Raesinia said.

The two women looked at each other helplessly. "But—" Barely began.

"Winter told you to obey my orders, didn't she?" Raesinia said.

"She told us to protect you," Barely said, and her companion gave another nod.

Raesinia sighed. "Well, I'm the Queen of Vordan, and *I'm* telling you to obey orders. Go watch Janus, and make sure none of the others stay in the building. I want everyone at the sentry line."

Barely looked like she'd just sucked on a lemon, but she nodded. "Yes, Your Majesty."

Joanna looked at Raesinia, shook her head, and then glared down at Barely. The smaller woman shrugged.

"She's the queen, Jo. What am I supposed to do?"

"I'll be fine," Raesinia said. *The two of you saved me once already. I don't want you to get killed trying it again.*

She didn't want anyone to get killed if she could help it. The Girls' Own and Grenadier Guards who protected her were all outside the inn, watching every approach for the arrival of Orlanko's hired killers. Raesinia hoped that surprise and numbers would make any fight out there a short one. *And anyone in here with me is only going to end up with a slit throat.* Muskets and vigilance were no match for a man who could walk through walls.

As Barely and Joanna went reluctantly downstairs, Raesinia moved from the suite's dining room into the small servant's bedroom. Viera was there, wiping her gray hands carefully with a damp cloth.

"It's ready?" Raesinia said.

The artillerywoman nodded. "It's not as good as the milled stuff," she said in her Hamveltai accent, "but I think it will serve."

"Good. You should get out of here before things get started."

"You know what will happen here?" Viera gestured around. "If you're too close—"

"Believe me," Raesinia said tightly, "I understand."

"Be careful." Viera picked up her mortar and pestle. "Good luck."

"Thanks."

When she was gone, too, Raesinia shut the door to the suite. She lit lanterns in the dining room and the larger bedroom, but not in the servant's bedroom; one of the inn's lamps hung just outside the window, though, and the furniture cast long shadows. When she was satisfied, she picked up a loaded pistol from the dining room table, took it to the large bedroom, and sat down on the bed to wait.

It would be a laugh if, after all this, he didn't come. It was just possible that Ionkovo would try for Janus first. Raesinia had tried to make that as difficult as possible by packing the First Consul's rooms with soldiers, hopefully too many for even a Penitent Damned to handle. But she thought he would come for her, instead. *He had me once before and let me get away.* Ionkovo had seemed like a proud man, and she was sure it galled him. *Plus, he probably thinks I'm the easier target.*

Her heart was beating fast in spite of everything. She could face the worst threats with equanimity, provided she could see them coming; her rational mind knew she had nothing to fear from knives, pistols, or falls from the wall of a castle. But a lurking, unseen danger still managed to raise a primal response.

Her mouth was very dry, and she wondered if she had time to get up for some water—

"Hello, Raesinia." Ionkovo's cultured, Murnskai-accented voice was unmistakable.

Raesinia turned and fired. Ionkovo had emerged from the shadow of a wardrobe, and at the sound of the shot he jerked back into it, darkness rippling behind him like black water. *Balls of the Beast, but he's fast.* Her shot had been wide, smashing a hole in the wood paneling a good foot clear of the wardrobe. She dropped the pistol, turned, and jerked backward as a hand shot out from under the bed and closed around her wrist.

"That's a rude way to greet an old friend," Ionkovo said, yanking her sideways off the bed.

Raesinia let herself fall, trying to twist free of his grip. She got herself turned over and planted a foot in his chest, but his other hand came out from behind his back holding a long, thin knife. He brought it down with expert precision, angling it just left of her breastbone to slip between her ribs and slice clean through her heart. Raesinia felt the tip emerge from her back and bite into the wooden floor.

"That ought to slow even you down, I think," Ionkovo said. "Pinned like a butterfly in a case. You may not be able to die, but I imagine it's hard to accomplish much with a spike in your heart."

Raesinia blinked, fighting the distant signals from her body, which wanted to tell her she was in unimaginable agony. She could feel the binding tingling all over, fighting to keep her flesh repaired as her blood went thick and stale. A spreading pool of red coated the floor underneath her, seeping down in between the floorboards.

"It somehow feels like we've been here before, don't you think?" Ionkovo was in full Penitent Damned uniform, black mask gleaming. "Last time I made the mistake of handing you over to that incompetent Maurisk. I ought to have known it wouldn't work."

The best Raesinia could manage was a raspy whisper. "Your Penitents didn't do any better."

"An old fool, a dullard, and a novice," Ionkovo said dismissively. "The pontifex has always placed too much emphasis on the abilities of the demon and not enough on those of the man, in my opinion. A power like mine, while not as formidable as a brute like Twist's might seem, is considerably more . . . subtle." He cocked his head, reflections shifting on his mask. "Also, I guarantee no one is coming to save you this time. Ihernglass is dead by now, General d'Ivoire is walking into a trap, and I don't sense your friend the sandstorm."

Marcus! Raesinia's heart would have jumped if it hadn't been slashed in half. She blinked slowly and managed to raise her head a few inches.

"I don't . . . need help . . . to deal with you." Her vision went spotty for a moment with the effort of speech.

"Bold words." Ionkovo leaned forward. "We'll see how brave you feel after a trip through the shadows."

Chapter Twenty-One

WINTER

Bobby recovered her tongue before Winter did. "Jane. I thought you were . . ." She hesitated, looking over at Winter. "Gone."

Jane looked between the two of them. "I imagine you did. Guard dead, prisoner missing. What else were you supposed to think?"

"What happened?" Winter said. Her voice was a trembling croak. "What are you doing *here*?"

"Simple enough. I didn't escape. Ionkovo kidnapped me. He brought me here to ask questions about *you*. When he was done . . ." She shrugged. "They found another use for me."

"Winter," Maxwell said, a note of warning in his voice, but Winter spoke over him.

"And now you're in charge?" Winter said. "What the hell does that mean? You've become one of *them*?"

"It's a little more complicated than that," Jane said. "It's more accurate to say *they* have become one of *me*, if that makes any sense." She looked over Winter's shoulder, and her eyes widened. "Red? Is that you? I didn't recognize you with your hair down."

"Jane?" Red said, stepping tentatively forward. "That's really you?"

"Come here and let me have a look at you." Jane took a step forward, smiling, and looked up into Red's eyes. There was a flash of strange, crimson light, and then Red was laughing. The big sergeant stepped away, an odd grin on her freckled face.

"*Winter*," Maxwell said. "Whoever you think that is, it isn't her."

"How would you know?" Jane said. "Do you want me to tell you some secrets, Winter? Do you remember the time we stole Mistress Gormenthal's lunch?" Her smile widened. "Or where we were the first time I got my hand under your shirt?"

She pulled the trigger. "In Janus' office." Winter's throat was very dry. "You tried to shoot me. Why?"

"To be honest, I don't really know," Jane said. "It was the only way out I could think of. Maybe I thought, if we both died there, we'd be together afterward. Or maybe I was so angry and scared I just twitched." She shrugged. "It doesn't matter, does it? You're alive. I'm alive. And there's nothing to stop us anymore."

"You're not Jane, are you?" Winter said. She had been watching her old lover's eyes. They were still green, but where they had once been bright, sparkling with her sarcastic humor, now they were as dead as cold stones. Her expression was *wrong*, with all of the old Jane's swagger but none of the vulnerability underneath. "Maxwell, what have they done to her?"

"I'm hurt," Jane said, before the priest could speak. "I'm *more* than Jane, that's all. Everything she was is still here. But now there's also . . . something else."

"The Beast of Judgment," Maxwell hissed.

"If you say so," Jane said. She jerked her head at the pontifex. "This oaf thought he could use me against Vhalnich. I may have encouraged him a little, I must admit."

"I am an arrogant, blustering idiot," the pontifex said in a singsong voice. "I deserved everything I got."

"Max," Alex hissed. "What now?"

"Get out," Maxwell said. "Don't let them get close, any of them. If you can't escape, slit your own throat."

"That's a little harsh," Jane said. "But I suppose I shouldn't criticize."

Red suddenly moved, slipping behind Winter and grabbing both her arms at the elbows. Jane stepped forward, inches from Winter's face.

"No chance of a kiss?" she murmured. "I suppose not. But give it a moment."

"Winter!"

Bobby's shout seemed distant. Time felt like it was slowing down. Winter started to struggle, fighting Red's overwhelmingly strong grip, but Jane's eyes already seemed to fill the world. Deep down, in the center of her pupils, there was a tiny red spark. It grew outward, spreading like flame across paper, devouring the black and then the green and then *on* and through the tiny gap between them and into Winter's body. She felt herself drawing breath for a scream, far too late—

And one of her hands brushed Jane's arm.

Infernivore leapt across the gap between souls, a mad dog whose leash had finally snapped. Even as crimson light filled her eyes, she could feel her own demon surging into Jane. Through the link, she could *see* the Beast of Judgment, a vast, branching mass of vermillion threads, like a tangle of spiderwebs dripping fresh blood. Infernivore threw itself at the alien thing, wrapping over and around it, converting the substance of the Beast into more of itself. At the same time, the red filaments were reaching into Winter, drawing her soul into the sticky cocoon of the Beast's embrace, ready to consume everything that she was and vomit up a piece of themselves that would live behind her eyes forever.

For a long moment the two were locked together, a pair of snakes with their jaws on each other's tails, trying to eat faster than they were eaten. Winter realized she could feel the mind of the Beast, down at the center of that mass of twisting, pulsing red. It was ancient and young, both at once, with thousands of sets of memories stretching back a dozen centuries. The pontifex was in there, and the Penitent Viper, and hundreds of others, clamoring fragments shouting in dead languages. And down at the very bottom—

Jane? She *was* there; Winter could feel it. The sense of her slipped from her mental grip, like silky red hair sliding through her fingers. *Jane, please!*

Winter? The Beast shifted. Jane was a part of it, but *it* was a part of *her*, more than any of the others; she had spoken the name that had called it into the world, and the ancient consciousness of the Beast had used her mind as a template for this incarnation of itself.

I'm going to help you, Winter told her, at the center of the whirling maelstrom of demonic power. *I'm going to get you out.*

No, Jane thought. There was none of the mockery that had dripped like venom from the Beast/Jane hybrid. Winter wasn't sure deception was possible here, with mind joined directly to mind. *You don't understand. I did this for you. Everything that came between us—Mrs. Wilmore, Ganhide, Abby, Janus—they don't matter anymore. Fate wants us to be apart, but not even fate can stand against the power of the Beast.* Winter saw Jane's familiar half smile, felt phantom arms wrapping around her. *Come back to me. Please.*

I can't. Infernivore and the Beast thrashed against each other, and Winter felt as though she were trying to scream above a thunderstorm. *I won't!*

Jane's voice shifted into the dark tone that was always lurking just beneath the surface. *You will.*

Then, crashing down over everything, there was a wave of *fear*. Not from

Jane, or any of the other fragmented personalities trapped in the Beast's web, but from the creature itself. Its power was flowing into Infernivore, even as it wrapped itself around Winter's mind. Winter had a sudden vision of the Beast taking her into itself, just as it was itself consumed, the two snakes consuming each other entirely until nothing was left. It would mean utter destruction for the Beast, the end of its thousand-year life. Infernivore and the Beast were too evenly matched, and their fight was spiraling toward mutual annihilation.

This the Beast would not risk. In the real world, only a fraction of a second had passed. Red abruptly let go and shoved herself between Winter and Jane, pushing them apart and breaking the connection between the demons. In the instant before they were separated, Winter heard a thought/command ripple out from the demon to all its myriad selves—

Keep Winter alive. Destroy the others.

"Winter!" someone screamed.

Winter blinked. She felt as though she were waking from a deep sleep, her mind cold and slow. Someone stood above her—*Maxwell?*—but her vision was blurred.

"Don't get close to her!" the priest said. "The Beast has her now!"

"No!" Bobby, eyes tightly closed, lifted Red off the ground and threw her across the room. The big sergeant slammed into one of the bookcases, glass shattering, and fell in a heap. "We have to help her!"

The pontifex stood from behind the desk, moving nimbly for an old man. As he reached up to pull off his black mask, twin spears of darkness flashed out, punching through his chest one below the other. They held him in place for a moment and then withdrew. The leader of the Priests of the Black took a single, wobbling step forward, then collapsed at the foot of his desk, blood gushing from two neat holes. At the same time there was a pistol shot, and Winter saw the young priest who'd been their guide tumble backward down the stairs like a broken toy. Millie tossed her smoking weapon aside, eyes wide.

Jane. Winter blinked and sat up. Jane lay by the desk, near the pontifex, not obviously hurt but not moving either. Maxwell, at Winter's side, took a step back and fumbled for a weapon.

"I'm okay," Winter said, slurring her words a little. "It's . . . my demon . . . fought it off. I'm . . . still me."

"You can't trust—"

Bobby stepped over, grabbed Winter's arm, and hauled her to her feet. For a moment they were eye to eye, inches apart, and then Bobby turned away.

"She's fine," Bobby said. "But we're not going to be in a minute. They're coming."

"Coming," Winter mumbled. "They . . ." She felt herself return to full consciousness, as though she'd suddenly plunged into an ice-water bath. "Oh, *fuck*. We have to get out of here."

"Agreed," Alex said, her hands still wrapped in black globes.

"Focus on *how*," Bobby said. She put her hands under the desk and, with a grunt, lifted the half-ton mass of ancient wood into the air. Winter hastily cleared out of her way as she took a few shaking steps to the doorway and shoved it through. The desk was nearly as wide as the stairs, and though it didn't block the way completely, it made a formidable barricade. "We're not going that way. Listen."

The admonition was unnecessary. There were footsteps on the stairs, hundreds of them, a dense crowd pressing toward the top of the tower in eerie, determined silence.

"Windows, then," Alex said.

She ran to the window, with Winter right behind her. Here on the top floor of the tower, they were wide, many-paned things that looked as old as the cathedral itself. They weren't designed to open, but Alex's lines of shadow slashed through them, and lead and glass sprayed outward into the night. A gust of cold wind slammed into Winter like a hammer, and the room was suddenly noisy with creaking ropes and snapping flags. The rat's nest of lines between the tower and its neighbor seemed to fill the world, with the peaked roof of the cathedral itself far, far below.

"I could get clear," Alex said. "But my lines aren't strong enough to carry everybody. We'll have to use the ropes."

"They're not strong enough, either," Millie said, poking her head out. "Those are barely more than clotheslines."

"I've got an idea," Alex said. She leaned out and fired a beam of darkness upward. "Give me a minute."

"You may not have that long!" Bobby shouted as Alex swung out the window.

She had her sword drawn. The first of the attackers had reached the jammed desk, and he scrambled up on it and came forward on all fours without a pause, his eyes glowing a gory crimson. Bobby shut her eyes as he came close and swung, blade catching him just above the ear. A normal person's swing might have glanced off the skull, but with Bobby's strength, the man's head exploded in a shower of bone and brain.

Two more men in black robes were right behind him, climbing over his body as it twitched in its final convulsions, hands reaching for Bobby. Her wild swing took off an arm at the elbow, but then they were on top of her, grabbing her sword, fingers closing over the blade even as it cut them to the bone.

Winter glanced across the room to make sure Jane and Red hadn't moved, then stepped up beside Bobby, drawing her own sword. She slashed down, severing another hand, but by then more black-robed figures were crawling through the doorway, pulling themselves along the maimed, still-struggling bodies below them. One, a heavyset man who might have looked friendly if not for the red light in his eyes, pushed off the one-armed man beneath him and came down on top of Bobby, arms around her shoulders, pressing her down with his bulk. Another man reached for Winter, and she backpedaled and stabbed him through the eye, his body jerking spastically. She spun to help Bobby, but the younger woman was already pushing back to her feet, throwing the heavy man into the ceiling so hard Winter heard the *crunch* of breaking bone.

With a *creak* of straining wood, the pile of attackers pushed forward, even the dead ones. There were more of them behind, Winter realized, shoving on the bodies and the desk together. At the same time, another man slithered through the narrowing gap at the top and threw himself at Bobby, slamming a fist into her stomach. Bobby grunted and brought her hand down on his back, breaking his spine with an audible *snap*, but his hands still scrabbled at her. She was fighting blind, not daring to open her eyes in the red glare of the Beast's gaze, and it was a few moments before her groping fingers found his head and tore him away.

We can't hold this. Ordinarily, Winter would have considered this an excellent defensive position, with one narrow, half-barricaded doorway. But ordinary defense relied on an enemy who was reluctant to die, and the Beast had a thousand bodies to throw away. Bobby's strength would keep them back for a while, but even she would tire soon.

"Alex!" Winter said. "Whatever you're doing, hurry—"

The pile of bodies that blocked most of the doorway toppled forward, shoved from behind. Bobby, unable to see it coming, flailed wildly as she was borne down by dead priests, gore spraying wildly. More attackers jumped down from the desk, two burly priests in the lead and then a wild press of flesh—

priests, servants, and prisoners, all crammed together in the curving stair leading up to the top floor.

"Bobby!" Winter hacked and slashed at the mob in front of her but made
no progress—for every person she cut down, others circled around, forcing her
to give ground or be grabbed from behind. Bobby was invisible, thrashing
under a mound of enemies, living and dead.

Millie, at the window, had her own sword out, but her first cut was tentative, and one of the priests grabbed the blade from her hands and wrenched it
away. He reached for her with slashed, bleeding fingers, and she screamed and
took a step back, onto the windowsill. She kicked her attacker in the face,
looked over her shoulder, and jumped.

"Millie, wait—" Alex's voice came from outside.

Maxwell slashed back and forth with his own sword until it was wrenched
from his hands. The Beast's bodies grabbed him, slamming him against the
tower wall, arms and legs pinioned. He squeezed his eyes shut, but more hands
pawed at his face, prying his eyelids apart as a black-robed figure leaned in close.

"Help!" The young priest's voice rose to a terrified squeak. "Winter! *Alex!*
Help, *please*—"

His scream died in a strangled gurgle as the red light washed over him. A
moment later Alex appeared in the window, trailing a knotted mass of cords
wrapped over and around one another. When she saw the swarming, grappling
things in the tower, lit by the hellish crimson glow of their own eyes, her face went
slack for a moment, and then a wild look came over her. She raised her hands, and
the globes of blackness expanded, growing to the size of twin cannonballs.

Some instinct made Winter throw herself flat. Ropes of darkness burst out
from both of Alex's hands, spearing outward in every direction like the thorns
of a cactus. They punched through cloth, flesh, and bone, and wherever they
struck they multiplied into smaller bursts of darkness, little balls of black filaments that ripped apart whatever they hit from the inside out. The room was
suddenly full of intersecting lines of black, blooming like hideous flowers
among sprays of blood and shredded flesh.

When the lines of darkness vanished an instant later, there was a moment
of shocked stillness. Alex took a deep breath, swaying, and Winter forced herself to her feet. She sprinted to the window, boots slipping on flesh and blood,
and grabbed Alex just before she toppled backward off the tower. The girl
blinked quickly, taking several rapid breaths, and then her eyes regained their
focus.

"Max," she said. "Where is he?"

"Right here." Maxwell stood up, shrugging off the limp bodies of the men who'd been holding him. His eyes glowed red. "Come over here, Alex. I had everything wrong. Let me explain."

"Oh. Oh, Karis, *fucking* God, no." Alex was whimpering. "Please . . ."

Other figures were rising from the carnage. Winter saw Red, her back studded with bits of broken glass, helping Jane to her feet. All around were dozens of priests and servants, some of them missing limbs or bleeding from long gashes, eyes still glowing maliciously.

"It's not so bad," Maxwell said. "Honestly. I love you, Alex—would I lie to you—"

Alex surged out of Winter's grasp, and a line of pure darkness connected her for a moment to the man who'd been her lover. It punched into his skull and out the other side, cracking the stone of the tower wall behind him. The glow in his eyes died, and he fell without another sound.

The pile of bodies heaved, and Bobby forced her way up, clutching her side. She was covered in blood, as though she'd bathed in the stuff, but her eyes were still firmly closed. She turned in a circle, and Winter screamed her name.

"Bobby! Over here!"

Bobby started to run, slipping and stumbling on the bodies. One of the mutilated priests grabbed her, but she shrugged him off and made it to the edge of the room. Winter took her hand, and nearly got her arm ripped off for her trouble before she gasped out a warning.

"Sorry." Bobby opened one eye a crack. "You okay?"

Winter nodded. "We're getting out of here. Just jump, if you have to."

"Use this," Alex said, handing Winter the knotted cord. "It should take your weight."

"And then what?" said Jane, from across the room. "This is *Elysium*. Where are you going to run?"

"Go," Winter told Alex and Bobby.

Alex swung out the window, hanging from her own line of darkness. Bobby took hold of the knotted cord, hesitated, then stepped out the window. The line creaked under her weight, but held. She gripped it in one hand and stood on the face of the tower, holding out her hand for Winter.

"You can't leave me," Jane said. "Not this time."

Winter jumped on the windowsill and took Bobby's hand. Just as she stepped clear, an arm shot out from the piled bodies at her feet, fastening around her ankle. For a single, teetering moment, she was balanced, pulled into the room by the grip at her feet and away by her grip on Bobby. Then her fingers, coated with blood, slipped from Bobby's hand. More of the Beast's bodies were closing in, running frantically to grab her. Winter took a deep breath, closed her eyes, and let herself tumble forward.

There was a moment of free fall.

Then something hit her around the waist, hard enough to bruise. It was Bobby's arm—she'd jumped off the tower, one hand extended to catch Winter. Her other hand reached out for one of the spiderweb of thin cords that connected the two towers, which snapped instantly under their combined weight. There was another below it, and another, each supporting them for only a fraction of a second before giving way. Then they were through the web, hurtling toward the slate roof of the cathedral. Bobby curled up, rolling so her body was beneath Winter's, and then—

—*impact*. Winter's head slammed hard into Bobby's chest, slate crunching underneath them. The breath was knocked from her body, and for a moment she couldn't take another. She sat up, gasping, and felt a flaring pain in her arm that turned her vision gray. Her left hand hung at an odd angle, as though an extra joint had been added to the limb, and when she tried to move it, pain and nausea welled up until she vomited.

When her stomach was empty, she wiped her mouth with her good hand and looked down at Bobby. It was impossible to tell how badly she was injured, since she was absolutely covered in blood, but she wasn't moving. The worse she was hurt, the longer it usually took her to heal. *She saved my life. Jumped off the tower and grabbed me.* She looked up at the web of fluttering flags and broken lines, and shuddered.

Alex landed beside her in a crouch, a line of darkness fading away above her. "Winter? Saints and martyrs, are you *alive?*"

"Bobby got underneath me." Winter clambered unsteadily to her feet, fighting another vision-blurring spike of pain. "She's not in good shape, and my arm is broken, I think. Help me lift her."

"But—"

"She'll survive," Winter said fiercely. "We just need to find somewhere to hide before they catch up."

Alex nodded, her eyes wide and face pale. She and Winter hoisted Bobby to her feet, trying to ignore the way her head lolled, and with her limp body hanging between them they started walking. Winter let Alex set the course, concentrating on keeping her footing on the slippery slate and trying not to think about the sick tearing sensations in her left arm every time it moved.

Another body lay on the slate ahead of them. *Millie.*

"She tried to grab one of the lines," Alex whispered. "But it wouldn't hold her weight." There was no need to ask if they should try to help her. Her head was the wrong *shape,* like a half-deflated balloon.

Winter lurched under Bobby's weight when Alex slipped out to open a trapdoor with a muffled *snap* as one of her shadow lances smashed the lock. Below it was a ladder, leading to a dark, dusty corridor. Alex went down first, and Winter had little choice but to push Bobby over the opening and let her fall through. She herself tried to climb down one-handed, but one of the rungs brushed against her dangling left arm and her vision went gray and spotty again. When it cleared, she found herself on the floor, with Alex underneath her.

"Sorry," Winter said. Her head was spinning, and she would have vomited again if there had been anything in her stomach. She swallowed acid and struggled to her feet. "Help me with Bobby."

They were in the upper story of the cathedral, a maze of passages and tiny rooms like its counterpart in Vordan. Winter and Alex stumbled through them at random, dragging Bobby's limp body. Winter's only thought was to get away from the trapdoor—it would take the Beast some time to get anyone up to these attics, but it had undoubtedly watched where they'd fallen. After a half dozen identical-looking corridors and random turnings, she picked a room with a particularly dusty door and opened it, careful not to leave obvious streaks in the coating. Inside were stacks of moldering wall hangings, moth-eaten and forgotten. *Perfect.*

Winter pushed inside and kicked the door closed behind her. What light filtered beneath it showed only shadowy outlines. She and Alex dragged Bobby to one of the stacks and let her down gently, and then Winter sagged against another.

A light flared. Alex held a match up to Winter's face.

"Don't," Winter said. "The light. They'll see it from the hall."

"I just need to do something about your arm," Alex said. She bit her lip, examining the break. "It looks . . . not *too* bad. I can get it straightened and tied down." She shook the match out, lit another, and started rummaging around the room.

"You know what you're doing?"

"Only a little. I learned from Abraham." Alex shook her head. "Where the hell is he when you need him?"

"I . . ." Winter swallowed again. "I'm sorry. About Maxwell."

"Me too." Alex's voice was tight. She lit a third match and knelt by Winter. "Okay. This is probably going to hurt."

"If I'm lucky, I'll pass out." Winter closed her eyes. "Give me something to bite."

Alex put a leather sheath in Winter's mouth. It tasted of dust and blood. Winter sucked in a breath through her nose, trying to get ready—

Her left arm exploded, sending glowing lances of pain shooting through her body. She bit down hard on the sheath, but even so, a moan forced its way past before, mercifully, she passed out.

When she woke, she had no idea how much time had passed, only that her mouth was dry and tasted of blood. She reached for the canteen strapped to her side and felt a moment of panic when her left arm wouldn't move. It was tied to a splintery length of wood wrapped in threadbare cloth, with more strips of cloth binding it tight against her chest. That brought everything crashing back, and for a moment it was all she could do to fight back bile.

Eventually, she managed to sit up and get the canteen out, awkwardly opening it with one hand and gulping the contents. Water splashed on her chin. Across the room, she heard someone stirring, though it was too dark to see anything.

"Winter?" Alex said groggily.

"Mmm." Winter emptied the canteen and set it aside. "Yeah."

"How are you feeling?"

"A little better." Her arm hurt, but it was a dull, red-hot throb instead of a white-hot burn. "You did a good job."

"Thanks," Alex said. "I wanted to do something for Bobby, but I wasn't sure where to start."

"Bobby's demon will do more for her than we can." Winter abruptly lowered her voice. "Have you heard anything?"

"People moving around in the distance, a couple of times. They must be searching, but they haven't come close yet."

"Do you have any idea where we are?"

"I . . . *think* I do," Alex said. "I know which direction the main stairs are, at least."

"That's more than I've got," Winter said. "So that's good."

She paused, glancing in the direction where Bobby's motionless, shadowed form lay. *How long will it take her to heal?* When the Desoltai had cut her down, it had been most of a night before she recovered, and this injury was probably worse. *But she said the healing was getting faster.*

"Have you got any matches left?"

"Yeah." Alex shuffled closer. "Why?"

"I want to take a look at Bobby."

A moment later a light bloomed in the darkness. Winter shaded her eyes briefly, then pushed herself over to where Bobby lay. She was liberally coated with blood, now drying into a flaking brown crust, and Winter brushed it off her face with her filthy sleeve. Her breath hissed. The skin of Bobby's cheeks was shot through with white, like veins of marble embedded in the ordinary flesh. They spiderwebbed across her wherever Winter looked, crisscrossing her forehead and forming circles around her eyes. Part of her hair had changed, too, the brown streaked with stony white.

"Karis Almighty," Alex said. "What's happening to her?"

"It's part of the healing," Winter said. "Other than that, I have no idea."

Bobby shifted slightly, and she gave a faint moan. Alex shook out the match.

"It won't be long, I think," Winter said. "Once she can walk, we'll try to find a way out of here." *Assuming the Beast doesn't find us first.*

"Yeah." Alex's shadow shuffled in place, folding in on herself. Her voice was very small. "Fuck. Why did it end up like this? Why did he . . . ?"

"We didn't know," Winter said. *That the pontifex had let the Beast loose. And Jane . . .*

"I should have . . . I don't know." Alex swallowed a sob, turning it into something more like a hiccup. "*Fuck.* After last time, after the old man, I swore that no one was going to be able to do this to me again. Then I get all sobby over the first pretty face that comes along. What the hell is wrong with me?"

"Alex, please," Winter said. "Don't. He deserves better."

"I know." Alex paused. "Who was that woman? The one who tried to . . . you know."

"Jane Verity," Winter said. "My . . . lover." *And best friend, and savior, and the person I hurt more deeply than anyone, and lost and found and lost again . . .* "She *was* my lover. And then she tried to kill me. I thought she ran away after that."

"But they brought her here and made her into the Beast?"

"Apparently."

There was a long silence. "I'm sorry," Alex said after a while. "I'm just . . . not sure what to say."

"Neither am I."

Alex's voice went quiet again. "I just want to go home."

"Me too."

"Home" was a strange concept, Winter thought. There wasn't a *place* she could call home in all the world. What she wanted to go back to was Cyte, and her old tent, and the comfortable routine of marches and drill and camp. *Maybe home is just a matter of habits.*

"Alex," Winter said. "If you were alone, could you get out of here?"

"What?" Alex said. "Why does it matter? I'm not—"

"Please. Just answer."

"I mean, probably," Alex said reluctantly. "I can climb the walls and move a lot faster than the Beast's people can. Unless it has any Penitents left."

"It doesn't," Winter said absently. "The Beast will extinguish any other demon it comes across. There isn't room for two of them in one soul."

The poison demon had been banished as soon as the Penitent that carried it was taken by the Beast. *Which means that Janus at least has a chance.*

"But why do you ask?" Alex said. "Please."

"If they catch us," Winter said slowly, "and there's no way for me and Bobby to get out, I want you to run."

"I won't," Alex said grimly. "I'm not just going to save myself while you—"

"It's not about you," Winter said. "Listen. You wanted to help us, and now I'm giving you an assignment. We have to warn people about this—do you understand? The Beast is not going to stay here in Elysium. If nobody stops it, it will keep spreading, on and on, until there's nothing left. Right now we may be the only people who know that it's gotten loose."

"Oh," Alex said. She sounded stunned. "I hadn't . . . thought about that."

"So here's your mission. First, go to the Mountain and warn the Eldest. He may know something important, and some of my people are still waiting there. Take them with you and go south. Find Janus." She swallowed. "If he's dead, find Marcus d'Ivoire, or Raesinia, or whoever's in charge. But you have to warn them. We're going to have to warn everybody."

"I understand," Alex said. "But it won't matter, because we're all getting out of here."

Bobby gave another moan, and shifted.

"Bobby?" Winter said.

"Winter?" She sat up.

"How do you feel?" Winter said.

"Like I fell off a fucking cathedral tower," Bobby said. "Are you okay?"

"More or less. Can you walk? We need to move as soon as we can."

"I think I can walk, but I can't see worth a damn. Where are we?"

"Still in the cathedral," Alex put in. "In the attics."

Bobby groaned. "If I never see another cathedral as long as I live, it'll be too soon. What happened to the others?"

"Dead," Winter said simply.

"Fuck," Bobby said very quietly. Then, "Okay. What now?"

CHAPTER TWENTY-TWO

MARCUS

Three of the identical masked copies rushed the doorway where Marcus and Sothe stood side by side. Sothe whipped a knife at them as they charged, sending one tumbling to the floor, and then she and Marcus met the other two with swords in hand. The strange duplicates were competent swordsmen, and Marcus fended off his opponent with a clumsy parry and watched him dance away from the return strike. As he closed in again, though, Sothe came at him from the side, having neatly disposed of her own enemy, and slashed him across the gut with her long blade.

The bodies faded, just as they had before. The last remaining duplicate, standing at the end of the corridor, gave an exaggerated shrug.

"I can keep this up all day," he said, the air blurring and fracturing around him. "Can you?"

Then there were four of him again, and three were charging. This time Sothe's knife blurred over the shoulders of the charging duplicates and sank deep in the chest of the one in the rear. He fell with a clatter, but this didn't seem to discomfit the others. Two of them pressed the charge home, while the third pulled up short. Marcus surprised one of them with a low sweep that cracked his knee and sent him sprawling, while Sothe drove the other's blade from his hands and skewered him. She stepped forward, another throwing knife already in hand, and whipped it down the corridor just as the air cracked and sparkled. The Penitent ducked, but not quite fast enough, and the blade slashed a line of blood along his shoulder. An instant later, there were four men in the corridor, all with identical wounds. The other duplicates, even the one Marcus had deliberately crippled but left alive, had vanished.

"Ahhh," Sothe murmured. "Marcus. You see?"

"I think so," Marcus said, "but—"

The Penitent charged, and it was clear at once that he'd been toying with them. Duplicates engaged, slashed, took wounds, and reappeared almost instantly, the air a continuous sparkle of mirror cracks and flashing light. Even with the defensive advantage of holding the doorway, Marcus would have been overwhelmed at once if it hadn't been for Sothe. As usual, she fought with an elegance and poise he couldn't hope to match, cutting down one foe after another with barely a pause for breath.

One of the duplicates threw himself at Marcus, arms spread wide, not even using his sword. Startled, Marcus instinctively thrust, and the black-masked figure impaled himself, hands reaching for Marcus' wrist. The Penitent dragged Marcus' sword down, and another duplicate bulled past, slipping to Marcus' right until he was inside the suite. Sothe spun, slashing the duplicate in front of her and throwing a blade at the one that had slipped by, but it was too late. The air cracked and sparkled, and there were three Penitents in the room with them, spreading out to draw them apart while one still waited in the corridor.

"Back to back," Sothe said, turning to keep the figures in view. Marcus retreated from the doorway, snatching up a loaded pistol from one of the fallen mercenaries in his left hand. He set his back against Sothe's and waited, as the four identical Penitents took up equally spaced positions around them.

They all cocked their heads, mirrored gestures creepily synchronous. Then, again as one, they began to laugh.

"What," Marcus growled, "is so funny?"

"I just realized who I'm fighting," one of the Penitents said. "Our mutual friend the Last Duke has generously shared his files with us, you see. You're Marcus d'Ivoire, aren't you? And *you* we know very well, of course. The elusive Gray Rose. Orlanko is quite effusive about you, did you know that? Your betrayal hurt him deeply."

Gray Rose. Marcus blinked. *I've heard that before.*

"Orlanko betrayed *me*," Sothe said. "And every other loyal member of the Ministry. He betrayed Vordan and the king."

"Whereas *you* served them so well?" The Penitent laughed again. "Marcus, do you have any idea what this woman has done? How many hundreds she's killed at Orlanko's orders?"

"I don't deny what I am," Sothe said.

Ages ago, it seemed, Janus had sent him a file, decrypted from the Concordat archives. It had described the murder of Marcus' family in numbing, clinical detail, another routine operation during the Ministry of Information's reign of terror. At the time what had stood out to him was the fact that his younger sister, Ellie, had escaped their net. But the Concordat agent whose name was at the bottom, who'd executed the plan—

"The Gray Rose," Marcus whispered. "It was you. You killed them."

"Marcus—" Sothe began.

"All this time," Marcus said. "I've been fighting next to you, and *you* killed them."

"I can never make up for that, but—"

"I think you can." Marcus spun, turning his back on the Penitent, and raised the pistol. "You fucking monster. Balls of the Beast. Were you laughing at me when I said I wanted revenge?"

"No," Sothe said. She turned around, keeping her hands at her sides. "After I . . . left the Concordat, and I devoted myself to Raesinia's service, I had a great deal of time to think. When you returned, at first I was frightened."

"Frightened? You?"

"The only thing that matters to me is Raesinia," Sothe said. "She got close to you, and I worried you might hurt her. I worried . . ." She took a deep breath. "I thought it might not matter. When we thought you were lost at Isket, I felt a moment of relief. It was a terrible thing to feel, a *monstrous* thing, but I did.

"But then you came back. And something became clear to me. You are my punishment, Marcus. You were always meant to be."

That was possibly the most Marcus had heard Sothe say at any given time. He realized with a start that her eyes were gleaming with tears. He fixed her with his gaze, keeping his expression fierce.

"You were right," he said. "I *am* your punishment."

He pulled the trigger. At the same time, he spun, shifting his aim to the Penitent visible over Sothe's left shoulder. The pistol went off with a wrist-deadening blast, and Marcus let it fall, already pushing off for a thrust at the Penitent by his own right shoulder. The man had stepped closer, fascinated by the confrontation, and Marcus' sword slipped in smoothly under his rib cage. As he moved, he saw Sothe turning, glittering steel leaving both her hands at once.

For an instant everything froze. Then four black-masked bodies collapsed simultaneously. This time none of them faded away.

Marcus let out a breath. "Idiot. If he'd had any sense he'd have stabbed me as soon as I turned away."

"Indeed," Sothe said. "I got the feeling he liked hearing himself talk—"

She stopped as Marcus turned around, having retrieved a second pistol from the ground. He pulled the hammer back with a dull *click*, aiming it at her chest.

"If he was lying," Marcus said, "now would be a very good time to say so."

Marcus wasn't sure what he expected. A blur of steel possibly, as Sothe easily dodged his clumsy shot and sank her knives in his throat. His hands were slick with sweat, and his finger trembled on the trigger.

"He wasn't lying," Sothe said. "I was . . . I am . . . the Gray Rose, Orlanko's greatest assassin."

"You killed my parents."

"I did."

"You would have killed me, if I'd stayed in Vordan."

"That wouldn't have been my decision," Sothe said. "But I would have done it, if I'd been ordered to."

"Why?" Marcus' vision blurred, and he blinked away tears, keeping the pistol trained. "For . . . some financial *bullshit*? A controlling interest in some company?"

Sothe shrugged. "Because I was directed to do so."

"By Orlanko?"

She nodded.

"You never questioned him? Never thought that killing totally innocent people—"

"Innocence or guilt was *his* decision. I carried out my tasks."

The barrel of the pistol fell a fraction of an inch. "What changed?"

"Raesinia." Sothe smiled, very slightly. "After she nearly died and Orlanko's allies saved her, he gave me the task of watching over her. That was when he began to lay his plans for the regency. I had . . ." She gave a tiny shrug. "I had always imagined I was doing the king's work, as communicated by his faithful servant. I realize now that I thought of the king as a sort of . . . god, a perfect being removed from the realm of mere mortals. But the king was dying, and Raesinia was going to be queen. And I *knew* her. She was human, just a scared girl who'd been forced into something she barely understood. I could no longer deceive myself that Orlanko wanted the best for her."

"So you switched sides."

"In practice it was more complicated. I laid a false trail that kept the Concordat from realizing where I had gone. But essentially, yes."

"And I suppose," Marcus said acidly, "you'll tell me that everything you've done since has been trying to repent for what you did in Orlanko's service."

"No. There is no question of repentance." Sothe stood a little straighter. "I am a blade that opens throats in the dark. For a long time I was wielded for an unworthy purpose. Now I believe my wielder is worthy, but that is all that has changed."

"And if I shoot you?"

"Then it will be what I deserve. And what you deserve, perhaps." She closed her eyes.

He wasn't going to do it. Marcus had known that, at some level, from the very start. He couldn't imagine facing Raesinia afterward, explaining to her what he'd done. Couldn't imagine cutting down the ally who'd fought so skillfully and tenaciously at his side. But, more than any of that, shooting a person—a woman—in cold blood, when they posed no threat, was simply not something he was capable of. *More fool me.* He let the pistol fall to his side.

"You can't stay here," he said. From now on, whenever he saw her face, he would imagine the flames. "Go. I don't care where. I don't ever want to see you again."

Sothe opened her eyes and nodded.

"Take care of Raesinia," she said. "She isn't as tough as she pretends to be."

"I will," Marcus said. "She's my queen."

He closed his eyes just for a moment. When he opened them again, Sothe was gone.

RAESINIA

Raesinia did not, strictly speaking, need a heart.

She sometimes fancied that the binding, and the sense it gave her of the functioning of her own body, meant that she knew more about how people worked than even the doctor-professors of the University. She could move, for a while, without blood pumping through her veins. It damaged the muscles, but the binding could repair that almost as quickly as it happened. *The question is whether I can move fast enough.*

Her gummy eyes blinked and tried to focus. Ionkovo stood over her, face invisible behind his glittering mask. The door was a few feet away. Beyond that, the dining room, with doors to the small bedroom and the stairwell.

Outside, she heard a popping sound. *Muskets.* Ionkovo cocked his head.

"Orlanko's people," he said. "No doubt they'll be slaughtered." He lowered his voice in the manner of someone imparting a secret. "I'm afraid the Last Duke is a bit past his prime. He seems inclined to solve every problem by slitting throats, and the quality of his throat slitters has fallen off considerably." He straightened up. "Speaking of which, where *is* your private killer? If she fought Wren to a standstill, I would have liked a chance at her."

"With Marcus," Raesinia grated. "Whatever trap you've laid, they've fought their way out of it by now."

"I doubt that. Mirror is a vain man, but an effective one."

Raesinia said nothing. She lay perfectly still, not even breathing. Ionkovo regarded her a moment, then bent to one knee and leaned closer.

"Here's the question I want answered," he said. "I know the Mages, the servants of the Beast, are protecting you. Are you one of them? Or are you merely a dupe? I must say, I suspect the latter. One could almost pity you. Your whole life, you've been nothing but a pawn, shuffled from side to side without knowing—"

Raesinia moved. Her hand came up, grabbing the long knife that pinned her and ripping it out with a spray of blood. At the same time, she kicked out, her foot catching Ionkovo on the shin. He fell sideways, swearing in Murnskai, and Raesinia scrambled to her hands and knees, blood drooling from the gash on her chest and splattering on the floor. The binding was already at work, stitching together the shredded scraps of tough muscle, though it was hampered somewhat by the need to keep her limbs moving as well.

She reached the doorway and felt another impact, a short-bladed throwing knife that sank into her stomach. Ionkovo stood up from the shadow of the sideboard, another blade in his hand. He tossed it in the air, idly, pinching the descending point between two fingers.

"Honestly, Your Majesty, what do you expect to achieve?" he said. "You don't think you can *run* from me, do you? The shadow road is faster than any horse or carriage." He whipped the other knife across the room, and it appeared like magic in Raesinia's shoulder. Metal grated against bone as she moved.

"Then again," Ionkovo said, "still trying when you ought to have given up the ghost is more or less your specialty, isn't it?"

Raesinia felt her heart start again with a lurch, and she took a gasping breath. She pulled the knife from her gut with another gush of blood and threw it left-handed at Ionkovo. Her aim was way off, and the weapon clattered handle-first against the wall. The Penitent laughed.

"Points for effort," he said. "But not much else."

The binding sparkled throughout her body, repairing her muscles, leaving the shredded skin and intestine for later. Raesinia pulled the other knife from her shoulder, threw it as well, and ran, keeping the dining room table between herself and Ionkovo. She feinted toward the door to the stairwell, then turned back, running for the small bedroom. She'd nearly made it when an arm reached out from a shadow near the floor and slashed a blade across the back of her foot. The leg gave way, and she toppled to the floor, just inside the doorway.

Raesinia crawled forward determinedly until she'd made it to the servant's bed. She used it to pull herself to a sitting position, the long blade that had skewered her still in her right hand. Her left dug frantically in her pocket. The light from the window cast long, deep shadows, and Ionkovo pulled himself out of one of them like a man emerging from a swim.

"And now what?" he said. "Back the other way? I must say, I'm having fun."

"Do you know what your problem is?" Raesinia said with a savage grin. Blood trickled from the corners of her mouth.

Ionkovo leaned forward. "Enlighten me."

Raesinia threw the long blade in her right hand. It still wasn't accurate, but it was better than she'd been left-handed, and Ionkovo reacted reflexively by stepping back into the safety of the darkness. As he did, Raesinia dragged the match in her left hand across the wood of the bed, sparking it to life.

Flash powder, spread over the bed, caught instantly. Viera had spent all afternoon grinding a few handfuls of coarse gunpowder to a fine dust. It burned *fast*, flame crossing the room too quickly for the eye to follow with an explosive *whoomph*. They'd spread it across the floor as well, and all the furniture. It was so fine it had suffused the air, drifting and waiting for the slightest spark.

There hadn't been time to make very much of the stuff. Raesinia felt her skin heat and her eyebrows frizzle, but it wasn't much more than you'd get peering into the mouth of a bakery oven. But it burned *bright*, and it was everywhere. For a moment there were no shadows in the room.

She heard a strangled gurgle and a thump. After a few seconds, when the dazzling light had faded from her eyes and the tendon in her foot had reknotted itself, she got to her feet.

Ionkovo had been stepping backward into the shadow when the flash had gone off. Its sudden vanishing had sliced him apart more neatly than any cutter could have managed, along a diagonal line roughly halfway up his torso. The half body had fallen on its side, and Raesinia could see heart, lungs, and other viscera, all neatly cross-sectioned, as though a master butcher had prepared a demonstration for his apprentices. Blood had splattered in torrents across the floor.

"Your problem," Raesinia said wearily, "is that you expect the same trick to work every time."

Muffled musketry continued to filter in from outside. Raesinia waited for a while, until the binding had closed her more obvious wounds and burns, then wrapped herself in a coat and went to see what was happening.

WINTER

When Bobby could walk without wobbling, Alex eased open the door to their hiding spot, revealing a darkened corridor that to all appearances hadn't been disturbed in years. The thief took the lead once again, moving in almost total silence, while Bobby and Winter shuffled along far enough behind her that their footsteps wouldn't alert any watchers.

The relatively short rest appeared to have refreshed Alex's strength, and Bobby's supernatural healing was as effective as usual, so Winter felt like she was the one holding the group back. In spite of Alex's work, her arm shifted slightly in its sling as she walked, and each time it did it brought a surge of pain. She felt drained, as though someone had knocked out a cork and let all the strength leak out of her.

Alex led the way through the maze of attic corridors, more by intuition and guesswork than actual knowledge. She kept them moving in the right direction, though, toward the back of the cathedral, where several stairways would lead down to the main floors and the streets outside. Footprints in the dust showed that some of the corridors had been searched, but they encountered no one.

The first staircase they came to was a narrow, rickety thing, leading down at least four switchbacking flights. Winter gritted her teeth as they descended, moving as smoothly as possible to spare her arm any jouncing. They passed through a floor full of small stone cells that might have belonged to servants or apprentice priests, and down into the vast kitchens. Everything was dark, the braziers on the walls burned out and the great ovens extinguished. Alex slipped through the shadows to a back door, flipped the latch, and pulled it open.

A naked woman, skeletally thin and turning blue from cold, stood on the other side, just inches away. Her gaunt face twisted into a rictus of a smile.

"There—" she began, and one of Alex's lances of shadow punched through her head. She collapsed, but another voice outside took up the sentence without a break.

"—you are," it said. "Searching the whole cathedral seemed impractical, so I decided to wait by the doors. I guessed—"

Winter couldn't see the speaker, but Alex raised her hand, and the voice cut off abruptly. Another picked up, a little farther away.

"—you wouldn't want to stay here indefinitely." The Beast paused. "You know killing these bodies is pointless, don't you? Do it all day if you like—I have plenty—but honestly, why bother?"

"Alex, *move*," Winter said. "We can't fight them."

Alex stumbled out the door, with Winter and Bobby behind her. A narrow alley ran along the back of the cathedral, with a high wall on the other side. One end was blocked by an iron grating, but the other led out into a larger street, and Winter pointed that way. Several people, all near-naked, unhealthy-looking prisoners, stood along the rear wall of the cathedral and watched with interested but unconcerned expressions. When the Beast spoke, its voice moved smoothly from one to the next as Winter and the others ran past.

"Winter always was—"

"—the smart one. But I'm—"

"—not sure what your plan is, here. Do—"

"—you have any idea how big Elysium is?"

"Bobby, grab her," Winter said as they neared the street and passed by another thin woman. "Don't let her look at us."

Bobby nodded and took the woman by the arm. She made no attempt to resist, but her eyes began to glow red, the Beast's light shining forth and looking for a soul for grab on to. Bobby kept her own eyes shut until she'd gotten hold of the woman's shoulders, forcing her to face away.

I have to try. The prospect of engaging the Beast with Infernivore again made Winter cringe, but it was the only thing that had made the demon show any sign of fear. *If I can destroy it . . .*

She laid her hand against the back of the woman's neck and extended her will. Infernivore leapt forward with a mental snarl, but the shocking collision of demon against demon never came. Instead, the strand of the Beast that was inside the woman simply snapped as soon as Infernivore grabbed it, leaving her entirely empty. Infernivore retreated, unsatisfied. When Bobby let go, the woman collapsed, twitching weakly.

"See?" a man's voice said, farther down the alley. "Smart. But that's not going to work."

I can't get hold of them. When she'd used Infernivore on Jane, the two demons had clashed so fiercely the struggle had nearly ripped them both apart. *But Jane is the center of the Beast, the nexus. These are just . . . limbs.*

"Shit." Winter looked at Alex. "Can we get back to the tunnels?"

"The white building ought to be that way." Alex pointed to the right, down a street lined on both sides by low timber houses with peaked slate roofs. They looked cozy and well kept up; Winter guessed this was a part of the fortress-city where priests or senior servants had lived. Many of the doors stood open, and inside she could see the same signs of hasty evacuation that had been so obvious in the archives of the Priests of the White. *So the White and the Red ran from Janus, and the Black unleashed the Beast . . .*

Four or five people had collected behind them in the alley. In the direction Alex had pointed, there were two more, but they were jogging away.

"It knows it needs more bodies to have a chance against you and Bobby," Winter said.

"That's right!" a voice called from behind them. "Straight out of your tactics manual. Never engage recklessly."

"We have to get clear before it collects itself," Winter said. "Time to run."

Every step across the uneven, snow-covered cobblestones was an agony. Bobby and Alex pulled ahead, then slowed, waiting for Winter to catch up. *Damn, damn, damn.* The Beast was keeping pace easily behind them, though one of the unhealthy-looking prisoners had simply collapsed in the middle of the road. None of the others made any attempt to help him.

Another street junction loomed. Alex pointed left, then slowed as at least two dozen people appeared from that side, rounding the corner in a loose group. Unlike the Beast's bodies thus far, they carried impromptu weapons, lengths of wood, pokers, and chunks of stone. Behind them, Winter could see more priests and half-dressed prisoners filing out of houses.

"This way!" Bobby shouted, turning in the opposite direction. Alex and Winter followed, now running nowhere but *away.* The streets were a neat grid spreading out behind the cathedral, so every hundred feet they came to an intersection. Packs of armed men blocked one way after another, though none of them made any attempt to attack.

"They're . . . herding . . . us," Winter managed, through teeth gritted against her pain.

Alex nodded. "We can try to break through them."

"It'll have reserve lines," Winter said.

That was in the tactics manual, too. *It's too fast, damn it.* Against a human opponent, speed and confusion always offered a chance for a small force against a large one, especially in a crowded city like Elysium. But the Beast had no need to send messengers with reports and orders. Its soldiers moved like the limbs of a single body, responding fluidly and instantly. *God Almighty. If it was in command of a real army, it would be unstoppable.*

Her mind was wandering. *Pain and exhaustion.* Now her lungs burned, and her skin felt ice-cold. Her legs were wobbly, as though her bones had turned to noodles. Her arm was the center of her world, a reservoir of pain that sloshed over with every step.

Bobby turned a corner and practically ran into a black-robed man, who reached out to grab her arm. His eyes glowed red, but she averted her gaze in time. She gripped his arm in turn and twisted, audibly snapping the bone with a casual motion before shoving him away. Alex raised her hands, and shadow lines cut down two people beyond him. But there were more, at least twenty. Winter turned to look in the other direction, ready to run, and found another group blocking them. The gang that followed them had grown with every turn, a hundred people or more, most of them holding clubs and stones.

"Brass Balls of the *fucking*—" Winter stopped, mid-profanity. One of the Beast's bodies laughed, and Alex cut the man down with a beam of darkness, but another picked it up, and then another. The three women backed against the facade of one of the houses, now surrounded by a vast semicircle of cackling pursuers.

"Inside!" Alex said.

She shattered the door handle with a flick of shadow, pushed the door open, and slipped in. Winter and Bobby followed. The bottom floor of the house was a single room, with a table and chairs, a fireplace in one wall, a wooden staircase, and another door leading to a small storeroom. *Nothing we can use and no way out.*

Alex jammed the door shut, and almost at once it began to shudder with impacts from the outside. There was a window, tightly shuttered, and that began to vibrate, too.

"Upstairs?" Alex said. But there was a slight quaver in her voice.

"Go upstairs, get to the roof, and get out of here," Winter said.

"But—"

"Remember what I told you?"

"She's right," Bobby said. "If you can get away, do it."

Winter drew her sword in her good hand as fingers pried the shutters apart. "Just promise me you'll bring everyone back here and kill this thing."

Alex ran to the stairs. Halfway up, she stopped at the sound of splintering wood; the attackers had torn one of the shutters away, ripping through the oiled cloth that served in place of glass. Winter slashed down at the groping hands, sending fingers spinning.

"Just *go*!" Winter screamed. Alex gave a frustrated shout and ran.

Now what? For a moment, a strange peace seemed to descend. *Would it be better to die or to let the Beast take me?* Her sword slashed instinctively, leaving long cuts on hands and arms. A big man grabbed the sill with both hands and tried to pull himself through, and Winter brought her blade down on his skull. A mistake, she realized immediately. The weapon bit several inches into the tough bone and stuck, and even as the man slumped forward, half in and half out of the window, two smaller women in prisoner's rags climbed over his back. Winter gave ground, looking for anything else she could use as a weapon.

Bobby slammed into one of the women shoulder-first, sending her flying across the room to hit the plaster with a wet smack. The other attacker brought a length of wood down on Bobby's shoulder, but it seemed to have no effect at all, and Bobby's return punch sent her spinning to the floor. Grabbing the solid board she'd wielded, Bobby turned back to the door, which was now jammed open by a flood of attackers. Winter backed up against the fireplace and picked up the poker as Bobby laid out two boys in servants' robes with fast blows of her club.

Sergeant Red was the next one through the door. Half her freckled face was purpling into a huge bruise, but she grinned at Bobby and spread her hands.

"Going to kill me, too, Bobby?" Red said. "Go ahead."

No, no, no, no—Winter opened her mouth to scream a warning, but it was too late. Bobby checked her swing just for an instant, showing the slightest hesitation to smash in that friendly, familiar face. That was enough. Red bulled in close, putting one arm around Bobby's waist, as though they were dancing. Her other hand took hold of a big clay jug hanging by a strap on her back, which she jerked free and brought down on Bobby's skull. It shattered, the contents gushing all over the two of them. Bobby, her hair plastered flat, looked more surprised than hurt.

Another of the Beast's bodies, a heavily scarred prisoner with only one arm, pushed through the door with a flaming brand. Winter tried to reach him, but more attackers got in her way, threatening to grab her as she clubbed them wildly with the poker. The scarred man lurched forward, flailing with his torch, and scored a glancing blow on Bobby's shoulder. The stuff from the clay jug ignited at once, flames engulfing Bobby and Red as they spun together in the center of the room. Drops spattered to the floor and on the table, and small fires started there, too, but Winter only had eyes for Bobby. She was screaming, inaudible over the roar of the flames, beating wildly at Red with both hands. Winter's throat was a mass of pain, and it was only then she realized she was screaming, too.

She felt herself being lifted by several people at once, careless of her broken arm, and *that* pain was strong enough that it took all the breath out of her. The Beast carried her up the stairs, into a small, plain bedroom, and four of its bodies laid her on the bed. Her poker was gone, dropped somewhere, and they all carried heavy clubs. From downstairs, flames crackled and spit.

One of the priests, a tall, thin man whose black robe had been badly singed, said, "Time to choose, Winter. You must know by now that I can't take you if you don't want me to. But if you hold that demon back, you can still join me. You've seen it, haven't you? What's waiting for you?"

An endless, crimson sea, everything that makes me me *ripped away from my soul and mixed with a million other half ghosts, not quite alive and not quite dead, eternity in the mind of the Beast—*

Bobby. Oh God, Bobby. Winter had no idea if she would die or not. Thus far Bobby had healed from every injury she'd suffered. *But burning alive?* She didn't know which would be worse. *What if she's alive, somehow, even as her body blackens and chars and oh God oh God—*

"Or," the Beast went on, "you just have to wait a few minutes, and this building will be consumed, and you along with it. Enough of me is Jane that I don't want that, but you haven't given me much of a choice."

I don't want to die. Please. Someone help. Images flashed through her mind. *Cyte, Janus, Abby.* The terror that welled up was from the deepest part of her mind, so old she barely remembered it. *Marcus, please. I don't want to burn.*

"Okay, I lied," said the Beast. Hands grabbed her. "You're going out the window. This may hurt—"

There was a wet *crunch.* Winter opened her eyes.

At the bedroom door was a figure made of living flames. *Bobby.* She had reached out a hand and grabbed the skull of the man holding Winter's feet, then tightened that hand into a fist. The bone had presented no more resistance than a rotten fruit, blood and gore spattering everywhere. The woman beside him brought her club around, and it bounced away as though it had struck solid stone. Bobby slammed a casual backhand into her chest with a crunch of breaking ribs. Her other hand shot out and grabbed the third of the Beast's bodies by the throat, fingers digging in and tearing away a meaty chunk, leaving arterial sprays spurting from the ruin that remained.

"Well," said the priest in the scorched robe. "That's . . . unexpected."

Bobby, flames guttering out now, slammed a fist into his face, reducing it to a pulp.

Oh God Almighty. Winter pulled her legs away from the fire, huddling at the back of the bed. The last few flames flickered and died. Bobby stepped forward, and ash flaked off her, revealing something gleaming and white underneath.

"Bobby?" Winter whispered. "Can you hear me?"

Very slowly the figure nodded. It brought one hand up to its face and brushed the ash from its cheek. Underneath was the face of a statue, polished white marble shot through with dark veins.

"Are you . . . ?" Winter faltered. *What the hell am I supposed to say?*

Bobby looked over her shoulder at the doorway. Smoke was pouring up toward the roof, and flames were already licking at the top of the stairs. She bent, very carefully, and held out her arms.

"You want me to . . . ?" Winter said.

Bobby nodded again.

Winter crawled forward, and Bobby slipped an arm behind her back and another under her legs and lifted her as an adult might lift a child. More of the ash was flaking away, revealing a marble statue perfect in every detail, a perfect human figure framed in brilliant white stone. When Winter touched her skin, it was smooth and hard, unyielding, but warmer than blood.

But how are we going to get out *of here?* Even if Bobby could survive another trip through the raging inferno downstairs, Winter certainly couldn't. *And there's still hundreds of those things waiting outside.* Bobby couldn't fight them *all. Could she?*

Bobby straightened up. There was a crackling, tearing sound, followed by a delicate hum, like a finger dragged around a wineglass. Winter's eyes went wide. Something emerged from Bobby's back, a crystalline structure of tiny, delicate pieces, unfolding outward and upward—

Wings. She has wings.

They were made of hundreds of tiny crystals in place of feathers, breaking the light of the fire into a thousand rainbows sprayed against the wall. Bobby looked down at Winter, then up at the ceiling. Winter, understanding, tucked her head against Bobby's marble breast and covered her face with her good arm.

Bobby took off with a single wingbeat, crystals chiming in a glorious chorus. There was a moment of chaotic impact, splintering wood and fracturing slate, and then they were free, rising into the cold, clear air above Elysium, the sun just peeking over the eastern horizon. Winter got a momentary glimpse of the fortress-city, with its cathedral spires and huge, looming walls, and then Bobby's wings beat again and it became a blur. Clouds whipped around them in tattered streamers of white, and the mountains began to fall away.

It was *cold*, so high up, cold enough that Winter's fingers felt numb. She pressed herself against Bobby, drinking in the heat of her marble skin, and Bobby shifted her grip slightly to hold her passenger closer. In that warmth, listening to the steady beat of Bobby's wings, Winter fell asleep.

CHAPTER TWENTY-THREE

MARCUS

Marcus only narrowly avoided being shot on his way out of the smoky wreck of Dorsay's headquarters. Orlanko's remaining men had fled, only to be cut down or captured by a converging ring of furious Life Guards and other Borelgai soldiers summoned by Whaler. Shouting from the doorway, Marcus had difficulty convincing them he wasn't another of the hired killers, until Whaler intervened personally. Even then he was disarmed and watched while Life Guards in their fox-fur shakos searched the building.

Eventually Whaler appeared, walking with the aid of a cane, a bulky bandage wrapped around his leg. Marcus was sitting on the ground by the gate, with several Life Guards standing over him. Whaler waved them away and, painfully, lowered himself to sit opposite.

"Sorry about that," he said. "Things have obviously been a little confused, and Captain Hezro is on edge. Your friend Sothe isn't hiding around here anywhere, is she?"

"I don't think so," Marcus said. *And if she is, you won't find her.* "Is Dorsay all right?"

"I believe His Grace rolled his ankle, but the main injury seems to be to his pride. As he put it, 'When I got married thirty years ago, I swore to Hennie that my days of climbing out bedroom windows on knotted-up bedsheets were over.'" Whaler smiled. "He's secure, and sends his thanks."

"What about Orlanko?"

"He appears to have fled. My men will track him down, of course."

"And our camp? There was supposed to be an attack there, as well."

"Our sentries observed some firing across the river, but it didn't last long. If your people were warned, I imagine Orlanko's men ran into stiff resistance."

"I need to get back." Marcus pushed himself to his feet. The weariness that adrenaline had temporarily banished had returned in full force, making him sway on his feet. "I have to see Raesinia."

"Understandable." Whaler held out a hand, and Marcus pulled him up. "Thank you. Would you like me to get you a carriage?"

"Please," Marcus said. He didn't think he could walk more than a few steps, much less all the way across the bridge.

Whaler gestured to one of the Life Guards, who hurried off. "Please convey to the queen, when you see her, that His Grace is eager to resume negotiations as soon as possible. Now that Duke Orlanko has revealed his true colors, the faction at court that supported him will be temporarily discredited, so we have a rare chance to strike a deal."

"She'll be happy to hear it." *If she's all right. She'll be all right. How can she not?*

"For what it's worth, you have my personal thanks as well." Whaler put out his hand. "You saved my life and the life of my master. I am in your debt, Column-General d'Ivoire."

Marcus shook hesitantly. The clatter of horses announced the arrival of the carriage, and Whaler stepped away, supporting himself on his cane.

"I hope we'll meet again," he said.

"So do I," Marcus said automatically.

The truth was, he thought as he climbed aboard, was that he didn't know *what* he hoped for. He'd turned his back on Janus, the man who'd been his closest ally since the Redeemers had overturned his quiet life in Khandar. He'd had his parents' murderer in his grasp, offering him the revenge he'd long sought, and he'd let her go. All he wanted now was to assure himself that Raesinia was safe and then collapse into a bed, preferably for at least a week.

It was only a quarter of an hour's ride back to the inn, but he fell asleep anyway, head resting against the chilly window. The Borelgai driver touched his shoulder when they arrived, and Marcus thanked the man groggily and climbed down. Grenadier Guards and Girls' Own soldiers were everywhere, in the process of cleaning up after a firefight. There seemed to be quite a few bodies in the non-descript laborer's clothes of Orlanko's killers. The soldiers saluted when they saw him, and he waved them back to work, motioning a Girls' Own sergeant to his side.

"What happened?" he said.

"Assassination attempt, sir," the young woman said. "Just as you predicted. We were ready for them, and they didn't even get close. A few of ours injured, none killed."

"The queen's all right?"

She frowned slightly. "I think so, sir. She called for us to fetch Barely and Joanna, and they went inside with a few others. Nobody else has been allowed in."

Damn. Something *happened.* But Raesinia was still here and still alive. Marcus thanked the sergeant and went to the inn's door, which opened slightly at his knock. Joanna, Raesinia's tall, mute bodyguard, stood in the doorway and beckoned Marcus inside.

"Where is she?" he said.

Joanna pointed to the stairs. Marcus took them two at a time, in spite of his exhaustion. When he got to the doorway at the top he froze, mouth open. The suite was a disaster, with blood staining the carpets and slicked on the floor-boards, as though someone had just finished slaughtering a steer. The door to the small bedroom looked *charred,* and there were dark smoke stains on the plaster ceiling. Several knives, still crusted with blood, lay on the floor.

"Raesinia!" Marcus said, heart beating fast. "Where are you?"

"Marcus?" Raesinia emerged from the large bedroom, wearing a silk dressing gown. It was clean, but her skin was still smeared with soot and blood, with more caked into her hair. She ran to him in bare feet, heedless of the mess on the floor, and wrapped her arms around him. "Marcus! Oh, thank God."

For a moment Marcus tried to remember if there was a protocol for what to do when you were suddenly hugged by the Queen of Vordan. Then he gave up and put his arms gently around her shoulders.

"You're okay?" Marcus said. "When I saw all this—"

Raesinia turned her head to look at Joanna, who'd come up behind Marcus. "You just brought him right up here? You might have said something."

Joanna rolled her eyes, shrugged, and went back downstairs.

Raesinia turned back to Marcus. "Of course I'm okay," she said. "How many times do I have to tell you I can't die? But Ionkovo said he'd set a trap for you, and I was . . . concerned."

"Ionkovo was here?"

Raesinia nodded. "He's dead."

Thank God. No more looking sidelong at shadows. "Good."

"What about Dorsay?"

"We got there just in time. There was another Penitent waiting for us, but Sothe and I dealt with him. Sothe . . ." He hesitated.

"I got a message from her just a few minutes ago," Raesinia said. "Don't worry."

A message? He shook his head. *Later.* "What about Janus?"

"Another skirmish. He's fine."

"And . . ."

"He doesn't seem to have tried to do anything . . . rash," Raesinia said. "He wants to see you."

"Balls of the Beast," Marcus groaned. "I'd better go."

"In the morning, he said." Raesinia smiled. "You must be exhausted."

"Thank God." Marcus could feel his eyelids closing already.

"I've got something I want to talk to you about, too," Raesinia said. "But it can wait until you're more than half-conscious."

Marcus slept downstairs, on a pile of bedding laid out on the floor, while soldiers and messengers came and talked and went out again. It was the best sleep he'd ever gotten, darkness closing in as soon as he put down his head, like slipping into deep, lightless water. When he awoke, only a few Grenadier Guards remained on watch, and the sun was well up. He ate breakfast—the best food he'd had in weeks, real bread, bacon, and eggs, courtesy of the Duke of Brookspring's generosity—and then went to the storage shed where the First Consul of the Kingdom of Vordan was confined.

The guards admitted him without question. Janus, always an early riser, had found someone to launder and fold his uniform, and now looked as clean as if he'd just stepped off the parade ground. Marcus, still sweat-stained and stinking, felt shabby by comparison, and ancient War College instincts made him expect a dressing-down and extra punishment duties. Janus merely nodded at his salute, however, sitting in the ratty chair in front of the tiny writing desk. Marcus was not surprised to see pen and paper in front of him. Once before, in the dungeons of the Vendre awaiting news of his fate, Janus had occupied his time writing letters.

"Good morning, Marcus," he said, with no trace of last night's bitterness.

"Good morning, sir," Marcus said. "You're feeling better?"

"Almost completely recovered, I think. Good food is a remarkable restorative, though I am lacking exercise." He flashed a brief, brilliant smile. "I believe I heard a little disturbance last night?"

"Your information was correct," Marcus said. "Orlanko's men tried to move on you and Raesinia, but we stopped them cold. Ionkovo is dead."

"And the Duke of Brookspring?"

"Alive. I went to warn him myself."

"Very noble of you." If there was a sarcastic tone to these words, it was well hidden.

"I wanted to thank you," Marcus said. "That message from your agent was in code. You didn't have to tell me what it said."

Janus raised an eyebrow. "If I hadn't, I might be dead right now."

"You didn't have to mention the attack on Dorsay, then."

"I suppose not." Janus leaned back in his chair. "Did General Ihernglass ever tell you about what happened when I was arrested by Directory agents, back when I was commanding the Army of the East?"

"No, sir," Marcus said cautiously. He still half expected a sudden explosion—Janus was capable of going from affable to infuriated with shocking speed, on the rare occasions when he showed his temper.

"To make a long story short, I went along quietly, but I made sure Ihernglass knew what was happening. He led a group of loyal men to rescue me, and everything else—the march on Vordan, the First Consul's post—followed."

"I see," Marcus said noncommittally.

"Afterward, Ihernglass asked me why I hadn't simply given him instructions to rescue me, if I'd known what was going to happen. I told him . . ." Janus paused. "I said that sometimes I see the way forward so clearly that I don't realize it isn't obvious to everyone. He was my proxy, you see. I let him make the decision, to turn the army against the Directory, because he understood the men and women of the Army of the East in a way I never could.

"Fate has, at times, a shocking sense of irony. Last night I realized that it had placed you, against my wishes, into a similar position. I know . . . I *knew* the way forward, but I didn't know . . ." He shook his head. "It doesn't matter. You made your decision."

"I betrayed you," Marcus said. His throat was thick. "Sir—"

Janus raised a finger. "I prefer to think of it like this. If *you*, one of the most loyal men I have ever known, would not follow me, what chance would I have had of persuading the rest of the army? The country? You were my proxy for all those men and women outside, Marcus, however little I might have liked the answer. So, in the end, it's for the best."

Marcus blinked. "I . . . wasn't expecting to hear that."

"I spoke to you harshly," Janus said. "You didn't deserve it, and I apologize. As you said, you have always done what you believe to be right."

"Not always. Sometimes I'm not sure what *is* right." Marcus walked over to the bed and sat down. "I found the woman who killed my parents. One of Orlanko's people."

"Oh?" Janus dragged the chair around to face him. "And?"

"She told me it was my right to shoot her, if I wanted."

"And you let her go." At Marcus' surprised expression, Janus laughed. "Honestly, Marcus, sometimes you can be extremely predictable."

"Was that the right thing to do?" Marcus said. "If I'd shot her—"

"Then she'd be dead. Would you feel better?"

"I don't know. Probably not." Marcus shook his head. "My sister's still out there, somewhere."

"I'm sure the queen will help you find her. I'd offer you my assistance as well, of course, but I doubt I'm going to be in a position to accomplish much."

Marcus looked up. "Sir. You should talk to the queen. Whatever happened between you, you can come to some kind of compromise. The army needs you."

"No, Marcus. The Borelgai and the others would never accept that. Dorsay is right; there can never be peace while I sit in the First Consul's chair." He spread his hands. "I'm sure Mieran County has missed my guiding hand. The servants have no doubt let the vegetable garden go to ruin in my absence. There will be plenty for me to do."

"And you're all right with that?" Marcus said. "What about Elysium?"

There was a long silence. Janus stared, gray eyes focused on something far beyond the wall of the shed. He smiled, ever so slightly.

"Do you believe in God, Marcus?"

"Excuse me?" Marcus said.

"God. From the *Wisdoms* and so on. Heaven and the hells."

"I suppose so." Marcus hesitated. "He never seems as *direct* as He was in the *Wisdoms*, though. I've never believed in trusting in faith alone to get me out of a tight spot."

"Very wise," Janus said. "Would it surprise you if I said there was a time when I believed in God?"

"I think nothing about you would surprise me, sir."

"It was the notion that there was a plan for the world. I could see it so clearly, see my part in it. You have no idea how wonderful that is, to know your exact position in the grand design, to have the course of your life spread out in front of you like a map." Janus looked into Marcus' eyes for a moment, then turned away. "Then it all went wrong, and I was off the map. Everything I've done since then has been trying to find a way back."

Marcus scratched his beard. "Maybe you're better off. Having someone else plan out your life for you doesn't sound so appealing to me."

Janus laughed again.

Marcus shot him a suspicious look. "What's so funny?"

"Nothing," Janus said. "Sometimes you're smarter than you give yourself credit for."

"Thank you, sir. I think."

"Go and find Raesinia. She's waiting for you."

"Yes, sir." Marcus stood up.

"And come visit me in Mieran County," Janus said. "Especially in the fall. The fresh apples are extraordinary."

"I will, sir." Marcus paused in the doorway. "Thank you."

Janus smiled, just for a moment, and turned back to his letter.

RAESINIA

The Grand Army of Vordan was going home.

The legal wrangling would take years, of course, or possibly longer, depending on how things went in the Deputies-General. But the basic requirements of the peace were not far from what Dorsay had first proposed at the conference, back at the beginning of summer. Borel and its allies would recognize Raesinia as the legitimate Queen of Vordan, the Deputies-General as the ruling body, with territorial boundaries the same as they'd been before the war. Duke Orlanko would be treated as a criminal and handed over to Vordanai authorities, if he was ever captured. And Count Janus bet Vhalnich Mieran would retire as a hero, returning home to Mieran County for a well-deserved rest.

Some among the deputies would be grateful for the war's end. Others would no doubt want to push for more—changes to the treaty that had ended the War of the Princes, for example, which had forbidden Vordan from constructing a deepwater navy. Murnsk's status was uncertain, and there was talk of a revolution brewing in Mohkba. There would also be the matter of compensation from Hamvelt, and the settlement of the scrip and bonds the Directory had issued so freely. Some promises would have to be kept, and others broken. That, Raesinia thought, was statecraft in a nutshell.

But for the moment what mattered was that the army was marching south. A vast blue column, reunited south of Polkhaiz, and once again well supplied and well fed. As it moved by easy stages, the weather changed, the unnatural cold giving way to the pleasant days of late spring. The land would take longer to recover, however—everywhere they went, they passed fields full of dead, rotting crops, smothered under the blanket of unseasonable snow. One of Raesinia's first tasks when they reached Talbonn was going to be arranging shipments of staples to the devastated areas, which would both buy some goodwill with the people there and give Vordanai diplomats extra ammunition at the negotiating table.

Until then, however, she once again found herself with very little to do. She'd happily pardoned Morwen Kaanos, who'd written her a gruff but sincere apology. Giforte came up with lists, units to visit and awards to distribute. Letters to sign to widowed wives and bereaved husbands, mourning parents and orphaned children. There would be more of that, a great deal more, when they reached Vordan. Raesinia felt Sothe's absence constantly, like an amputated limb. *Come back soon. Please.*

Marcus, of course, was always busy, coordinating the march and the reorganization of the more battered parts of the army. She saw him most nights for dinner, though, in the new tent her entourage had put together by cannibalizing several smaller ones. It lacked the beauty of the pavilion she'd left behind north of Isket, but there was a certain earnestness to its neatly stitched improvisations that made Raesinia smile.

Janus was already gone. They'd spoken only briefly.

"When you're finished," he'd said, after she'd explained her plan, "come and see me."

She still wasn't sure what to think about that. He'd departed in a carriage, with a mounted escort from the Girls' Own. It was a long drive to Mieran County, even now that the roads had dried.

We can cross that bridge when we come to it. Right now, another bridge was before her, and she was determined to deal with it, however much it made her heart thump and her stomach burn with acid.

Marcus came in, hanging his coat—brand-new, the buttons still gleaming—on the rack by the door. Servants ghosted over, pulling out his chair and offering him wine when he sat. Raesinia was on the other side of the table, going through another stack of Giforte's letters to those who'd lost family.

"A good day?" she said without looking up.

"More or less." Marcus yawned. "Two or three more days to Tsivny. Another few weeks to Talbonn. We'll be back in Vordan well before the end of summer."

"Good." Raesinia signed her name and pushed the letters aside. "Still no word from Ihernglass?"

"No," Marcus said. "Our communication with the Murnskai is still sketchy, though. Whaler says he's trying all the channels he knows. Nobody seems to be able to get any messengers to Elysium, but there's still a lot of northern tribes wandering around in that area. It may be a while before we hear anything."

"He could be alive," Raesinia said.

"He could be," Marcus agreed. "I had to stop Captain Cyte from taking a company to go and look for him. I told her it might not help the peace process."

Raesinia sighed. "Poor girl."

"I'm going to make her a colonel," Marcus said. "That might keep her busy enough to take her mind off it."

"I doubt it," Raesinia said.

There was an uncomfortable silence. *Damn, damn, damn.* This was not how she'd envisioned things going.

"What's for dinner?" Marcus said, unsubtle as always. "I don't think I'm ever going to take decent food for granted again."

Do it, Raesinia told herself. *Just do it. Or it'll never get done.*

"B-before that," she managed, "I need to talk to you about something." At her discreet signal, the waiting servants filed out through the tent flap. *The last thing I need is an audience.*

"Oh?" Marcus said. "Is something wrong?"

"When we get back to Vordan . . ." She paused, feeling for a moment as she had standing on the lip of the Prince's Tower, about to step off into empty space. The soles of her feet tingled.

"When we get back to Vordan," Marcus prompted.

"When we get back to Vordan," Raesinia said, in a rush, "I think that you and I should get married."

There was another, even more uncomfortable silence. The wineglass, nearly empty, dropped from Marcus' fingers and rolled across the table, leaving a purple trail on the tablecloth. His eyes had gone as wide as if Raesinia had just shot him in the chest.

"Married?" he said after a long while. His voice was tiny.

Raesinia nodded eagerly. "I've been thinking about what happens now. We talked a little bit about it, remember? I can't stay queen for too long, or it'll become obvious that I'm not getting older. Before that happens, I want to get everything well established, so there's as little uncertainty as possible. That means

Vordan needs a king whom everyone already knows and respects. And the succession—"

"The *succession*," Marcus said, eyes blank.

"I don't think it's possible for me to have children," Raesinia said. "In my current state, I mean. So we'll have to discreetly acquire one and present it as ours, but that shouldn't be too difficult. The important thing is that there will be *continuity*. The country needs a stable monarchy more than ever, to balance the hot-heads in the Deputies-General."

"You want me," Marcus said, "to be *King of Vordan*."

"Yes." Raesinia grinned. *This is going better than I expected.* She'd spent a great deal of time thinking about his possible reactions. "I know you worry that you're not a noble, but honestly, it isn't going to make a difference. You're a *hero*. Even if I weren't marrying you, I'd have to make you at least a count for what you've done, and maybe a duke." She put on a wicked smile. "There's a thought. Now that the Last Duke is officially a traitor, his land is forfeit to the Crown. How would you like to be Duke Orlanko?"

"No," Marcus said.

"I don't blame you," Raesinia said. "I'm sure we can find something more—"

"I mean no to all of it," Marcus said. "I won't do it."

Raesinia blinked. She stared at Marcus, and to her astonishment found that there were tears in his eyes.

"Why?" she said, all the nervousness she'd tried to banish returning in a rush.

"It's—" Marcus gritted his teeth. "I don't . . ."

"Is it me?" Raesinia took a deep breath. "If the thought of being married to me is objectionable, it doesn't have to be for long. And we don't actually have to . . . you know." Raesinia found her own tears threatening, and angrily wiped them away. "I need your help, Marcus."

"No!" Marcus said, shooting to his feet. "It's not that. I mean, that's the whole problem."

"What is?"

"You need my *help*. You want me to do this because I fit into your plan to do what's best for Vordan, right?"

"I'm the queen," Raesinia said. "I have to think of what's best for Vordan."

"Could you please stop being the queen for one damned minute?" Marcus roared.

Raesinia looked up at him, temporarily at a loss for words. A blush rapidly spread across his cheeks, and he scratched his beard.

"Sorry," he said. "But every time I feel like I've gotten a little closer to you, you treat me like a . . . a *tool*. Just another piece for you to move on the game board. Is that really the only way you can think?" He shook his head. "When we were hiding from the Directory, and you were incognito—"

"I was happy," Raesinia said quietly.

"I thought . . ." Marcus looked away. "I don't know. Maybe I'm being foolish."

"You're not foolish." Raesinia swallowed. "Suppose I weren't the queen. What would you say?"

"Am I still Column-General of the Grand Army?"

"Only if you want to be."

Marcus closed his eyes. "Then I'd say I think I fell in love with you somewhere along the way. With Raesinia Orboan, not the Queen of Vordan. And I'd very much like to know . . ." He broke off, blush deepening. "How you feel, I suppose."

"I . . ." Raesinia's tongue felt as thick and dry as leather, and her heart hammered in her chest. It was one thing to say you wanted to marry someone for perfectly logical and defensible reasons, but *this* was quite another. "I think," she said very carefully, "that I may have fallen in love with you, too."

"Oh." Marcus' eyes had gone wide again. "Really?"

"Really." Raesinia took a deep breath. "But you know that I *can't* just stop being the queen. I can't stop thinking about politics forever."

"It doesn't have to be forever," Marcus said, smiling a little. "Just every once in a while."

The breath went out of her in a whoosh. "Then you *will* do it?"

He nodded, very slowly, as though worried the world might shatter if he moved too fast. "But not because the queen is asking me to."

"No." Raesinia closed her eyes. "Thank you."

When she opened them again, he was standing there, waiting. Raesinia's heart was still beating fast, but it was a different kind of feeling, a not entirely unpleasant one. She got to her feet and straightened up, the top of her head coming up just past his chin.

"Column-General," she said, "would it irretrievably compromise the gravity of your office if I were to kiss you?"

"No," Marcus said. "But would it be an offense against the dignity of the queen?"

"Probably," Raesinia said. "But the hell with it."

They kissed. At one point Raesinia was pretty sure her heart stopped, but she didn't think Marcus noticed.

WINTER

Winter felt crushed grass against her cheek.

She opened her eyes. She was lying on her side with something hard pressed against her back. Around her was a grassy field, dead and brown but free of snow, with a white-covered pine forest beyond it and a clear blue sky overhead.

Bobby. She wasn't sure how much of what she remembered had actually happened. *The mountains unrolling in front of me, like a map. Clouds. And* . . . She didn't know what had happened next.

She sat up, and both her head and her arm began throbbing at once. Winter closed her eyes for a moment and put her good hand to her forehead until the waves of pain subsided. When blood stopped pounding in her ears, she looked around again, and her breath caught in her throat.

"Bobby!"

It was Bobby that Winter had been propped against. She sat with her knees drawn up to her chest, arms wrapped around her legs and her head lowered. Her glorious crystal wings were curled in, too, encircling her in an interlocking web of transparent feathers. She was naked, her skin the perfect, smooth white of marble, shot through with twisting veins of gray. Her many wounds, captured like scars as her body healed in this strange new way, were now erased, subsumed into the whole.

A wind whipped across the clearing, and the grass rustled. There was no other sound.

"Bobby, can you hear me?" Winter said.

Hesitantly, she reached out and touched the crystal, and found it as hard and unyielding as rock. Shifting around behind Bobby, she could see the knobs of her spine standing out from her bent back, rendered in stone as though by a master sculptor. The skin, when Winter touched it, felt like marble in truth, cold and solid.

No. Winter put a hand on Bobby's shoulder and shook her, or tried to. It was like trying to shake a mountain. *No, no, no. She'll be okay. She's always been okay.*

The space she stood in was perfectly circular. For a radius of five or six yards around Bobby, the thin snow had melted entirely, leaving the clearing of dead grass. Beyond the forest, she could see the blued shapes of mountains, but they looked a long way off. *Where the hell are we? How long were we flying?*

"Bobby, *please*," Winter said. "Get up. You have to get up."

The statue made no response. Winter reached out with Infernivore, trying to feel for Bobby's demon, though she'd never managed that before. She reached *in* to the statue, searching for something her demon could get ahold of, and found only the emptiness of lifeless stone.

"No, no, *no*," Winter said. She slammed her good hand against Bobby's shoulder, hard enough to bruise. "Not you, too. *Get up!* You have to . . . to . . ." Her eyes were filling with tears, and her hand throbbed. "Please. One more time? I promise, I'll never let you hurt yourself to save me again. Just . . ." Her knees trembled, and she sank against Bobby's cold, hard back. "Don't leave me here. Please."

Infernivore shifted inside her. For a wild moment Winter thought it had picked up some trace of Bobby, but the demon's attention was elsewhere. The cold wind shifted against her cheek, turning hot and dry, and for a moment Winter smelled the baking sand of a desert more than three thousand miles away. Flying grit stung her eyes, and she had to put an arm up to shield them.

After a few moments the wind died, and Winter looked up. A tornado of sand fell away, revealing a man in the loose, dark robes of the Desoltai. His face was covered by a metal mask, crude and plain, with two rectangular gashes for the eyes and another for the mouth.

"You," Winter whispered. *Malik-dan-Belial. The Steel Ghost.* Marcus had told her of his encounters with the Khandarai in Vordan. "What are you doing here?"

"It has required some effort to find you, Winter Ihernglass," the Ghost said, in accented Vordanai. "I apologize it took me so long. Even dust on the wind can only travel so quickly."

"You—" Winter shook her head and looked back at Bobby. "You were part of Mother's cult, weren't you? Just like Feor. Please, help her. You must know *something*. I'll do whatever you want—"

"She is gone," the Steel Ghost said. His voice held surprising gentleness. "I am sorry."

"No! Her demon—Feor's demon, whatever it is—it brings her back!"

"Not this time." The Ghost sat on his haunches, bringing himself to Winter's level. "Feor carried *obv-scar-iot*, but Mother never truly taught her its nature. In our language, it might be called 'Sacred Guardian.' The Church here calls it Caryatid. In ancient days, in times of great need, a young woman would be chosen to be imbued with the *naath*'s power. After the ritual, the guardian would step into the sacred flame and be transformed from her mortal flesh into a creature of the divine. She would gain the strength to defend her kin." He looked at the statue. "But only for a short time. A mortal spirit cannot ride the divine for long."

"That's not fair." Winter turned, putting her back to Bobby's, and sank to the ground. "No one told her that."

"No. But Feor is not to blame. She knew only that her power could save your friend's life."

"If I hadn't let her burn—"

"*Obv-scar-iot* would have claimed her anyway, in time," the Ghost said. "You must have observed its progress."

The marble patches, slowly spreading. Bobby's increasing strength and ever-faster healing. Winter lowered her head. *If I'd kept her safe, she still would have lived longer.*

"It is the will of the gods," the Ghost said. "Some lives burn out."

"Fuck your gods," Winter said. She rubbed her eyes again, cursing the tears. "What the hell do you want? Are you here just to taunt me?"

"I have been to the Mountain," the Ghost said. "Alex told me she saw the two of you fly from Elysium."

"You saw Alex?" Winter said. "She made it?"

The Ghost nodded. "And I have spoken with the Eldest. He told me what it is you carry."

"Infernivore." Winter spat the name like a curse. "You want it, don't you?"

"Infernivore"—the Ghost pronounced the name carefully—"is the great treasure of my order. The Eldest told you of the Mages' Heresy?"

Winter nodded.

"His people have preserved more history than ours, but there are things they never knew. It was not only the need to preserve their own lives that sent the ancient Mages fleeing to Khandar. They had discovered Infernivore, and for that the Priests of the Black wanted them destroyed."

Winter gave a long sigh. "Did you really come here to give me a lesson in theological history?"

"The ancient Mages sought Infernivore because they wanted to destroy the Beast of Judgment once and for all," the Steel Ghost said. "To the Priests of the Black, this was the darkest of heresy, bound to unleash the vengeance of their god against the world. They believed that holding the Beast in check was a sacred task, by which they proved humanity's worthiness to survive.

"But now the Beast is free of its prison, and even as we speak it spreads like a plague across the world. It has learned, in its captivity, and it will not allow itself to be wiped out again. The *naath* you bear, the weapon of the ancient Mages, is the only thing in the world that can stop it."

The Ghost bowed his head and extended his hands, prostrating himself against the grass. Winter looked down at him uncomfortably.

"You asked me why I am here, Winter Ihernglass," he said. "It is because I have come to beg for your help."

EPILOGUE

ORLANKO

"What's wrong?" the Last Duke said. "Why can't you tell me what's happening?"

"I d-don't *know*, Your Grace!"

He leaned close to the terrified girl, though he was aware this did little good. Her blindfold had gotten lost somewhere along the way, and he could see the empty sockets where her eyes had long ago been removed. She was sweating, breathing hard, though whether her terror was of him or something else he had no idea.

"I can't feel her," she said. "I can't feel my sister."

"Is she dead? Is that it?"

"If she had d-died, I would be dead, too," the pathetic creature wept. "She's *gone*. I d-don't understand."

"I need to speak to the Pontifex of the Black," Orlanko grated. "You *will* contact him, or I will have you stripped naked and whipped."

"I c-can't." She doubled over, sobbing. "You don't understand. I can't feel her at all . . ."

Disgusted, the Last Duke got to his feet. He gestured, and one of his black-coats came over.

"Lock her in a storeroom," he said. "No food or water. We'll see if she's more motivated in the morning."

"Yes, Your Grace," the man said. He took the weeping girl by the shoulders and frog-marched her out of the room.

They were in the coastal city of Vorsk, in what had once been a Concordat safehouse. In its heyday, the Ministry of Information had had them scattered all over Vordan and its neighbors, quiet buildings owned under untraceable names, waiting until an agent had need of them. Duke Orlanko had never expected to use one *himself*, of course. But he'd never expected to be here, either, far from home, reduced to an escort of barely two dozen half-reliable men, with both Vordanai and Borelgai forces hunting for him. All he had left was *her*, his last connection to the Priests of the Black and their Penitent Damned, and even this seemed to have finally failed.

No, he thought angrily. *It hasn't failed. She's just playing dumb.* Possibly on orders from the pontifex, he thought. No doubt his allies were displeased after the recent setbacks. *Once she's sufficiently cowed to let me speak with him, I can explain the circumstances.* There was still room to negotiate.

The safehouse's bedroom was a modest but comfortable one, with a large bed, a fireplace, and a private washroom. There were also—and he knew this because he'd checked for himself—discreet metal bars lining all the windows, two bolts on the door, and a kennel full of guard dogs downstairs. He'd put two men on the roof, and two men on the *neighboring* roof, watching the first two. More at the front door, the back door, and on the main stairs.

He would sleep, he decided. *There's nothing more to be done tonight.* In the morning he would have another try with the girl and personally investigate the ships in the harbor. *I need a captain I can trust.* If Orlanko had learned anything from the last few months, it was the importance of seeing to things himself. *Too much has been trusted to too many incompetents.* The *new* Concordat, when it rose from the ashes, would not tolerate such weakness.

Once he'd changed into his dressing gown, he blew out all the lamps but one. He never slept in darkness, not anymore. He checked, one final time, that the primed and loaded pistol was secure in its place beneath his pillow and then set his spectacles aside and put his head down. Sleep came easily; it had been a long day on the road, trying to make good time while not being so obvious someone would report his presence to Dorsay or Vhalnich.

"Your Grace."

He awoke with a start, then pretended he'd merely turned over in his sleep, mumbling something incoherent.

"Don't bother," the voice said. A woman's voice. "I can hear your breathing."

Orlanko opened his eyes a fraction. A dark silhouette stood in front of the lantern, throwing a shadow across the bed.

"If I shout," he said, "a dozen men will be in here in less than a minute."

"Go ahead," the woman said. "If you think any of your pathetic sellswords will be a match for me."

"You," Orlanko said very quietly. He reached out and fumbled for his spectacles.

"Me," said the Gray Rose.

"I never believed you were dead," he said. "Not really. Andreas was always so certain. But I made him leave you alone."

"Out of the goodness of your heart, I suppose?"

"Because I always respected you," Orlanko said, heart pounding. His hand moved, a fraction of an inch at a time, under his pillow. "You were my greatest creation."

"I was," the Gray Rose said. "I was the only one who frightened you."

"Are you here to kill me?" Orlanko said.

"I'm here to tie up loose ends."

He felt his throat tighten and he shoved his hand all the way under the pillow, searching for the pistol. *Not there.* Where had the damn thing gone? *Maybe it slipped down—*

"Looking for this?" the Gray Rose said, raising the weapon in one hand.

"Wait," Orlanko forced out. He pushed his spectacles up his nose with one trembling finger. "Just wait a minute. We can come to an agreement."

"I doubt that."

"There must be something you want!"

"I've already gotten it," she said. "I confronted my fate, and I was given a . . . reprieve." She pulled back the pistol's hammer with a dull *click*. "When I face it again, I want to be sure to do so with no regrets."

The Last Duke screamed as she pulled the trigger.

JANUS

The carriage rattled along a lonely, winding road, through a forest tinted gold by the setting sun.

Janus sat in the neatly appointed interior, his chin in his hands, swaying gently with the motion of the vehicle. A young woman in a neat blue uniform sat across from him, a pistol in her lap and a musket resting on the seat beside her. She kept her eye on the window. The six Girls' Own soldiers changed positions in shifts, one driving, two riding alongside the carriage, two sitting on the roof, and one resting inside. Janus was impressed with their professionalism.

Ihernglass did a good job training them. One of his better ideas, cultivating her.

It was not in his nature to dwell overmuch on failure. Once launched, a cannonball in flight was in the hands of implacable, impersonal forces. If it missed the target, no amount of wishing or self-flagellation would make it change course. He'd come close, but the machine he'd built to support him hadn't quite been up to the task.

Still. It wasn't completely useless. The Thousand Names were much more conveniently located in Vordan than Khandar, and he ought to be able to reacquire them in due course. *Access to them, at least.* Physical possession of the archive was not a requirement, after all.

More important was the knowledge that the Mages still existed. The Steel Ghost's interventions in Vordan City had to be on their behalf. *I can use them.*

The trouble, he reflected, was that Elysium was as much a symbol as it was an actual place. It was that, as much as anything, that he'd overlooked. Janus' logical mind had little use for symbols, but they were important to the masses. *Perhaps trying to get there at the head of an army was always doomed to failure. Too much history to get in the way.* Next time he'd be more circumspect. *A small force, equipped with demons to counter the Penitent Damned, perhaps armed with the knowledge of the Mages.* It would, in many ways, be a relief. War and the affairs of state always reminded him of his inadequacies.

For her, the Grand Army would have stormed Elysium. They would have stormed all the hells. A little snow would not have stopped her.

He closed his eyes. *I'm still coming,* he told her. *It will just take a little longer.*

The young woman pulled the window ajar. "Beth?" she shouted. "Do you see—"

There was a *crack* from outside, a pistol shot at close range, and the high, humanlike screaming of a stricken horse. Almost immediately, more shots came from directly overhead.

"Beth!" the young woman said. "God *damn* it. Jenny, what the hell is going on?"

"Came out of nowhere!" someone shouted back. "I don't—"

Another pair of shots, and the voice cut off abruptly. The guard in the carriage picked up her pistol and glanced at him, eyes narrowed suspiciously.

"Stay put," she said.

Janus gave her an innocuous smile. Behind it, his mind was already working, considering the identity of the attackers, discarding one possibility after another. There was another exchange of fire, and another scream, this one high and human. Something flashed past the window and landed on the road.

The guard opened the door, revealing two horses running alongside at a gallop. She steadied her aim and shot the first rider, a young man in a brown woodsman's outfit. A return shot splintered the roof of the carriage, and the guard yanked the door closed, then feverishly began reloading her pistol. Before she finished, another shot blasted the latch of the opposite door to splinters, and it flapped open. An older man in a torn coat swung off his horse and through the doorway, a long knife in his hand. The guard dove for her musket with its fixed bayonet, but he was quicker, grabbing her by the arm and shoving her back against the wall. Her fist connected with his jaw, but he plunged the knife into her chest, three times in quick succession, and she sank against the seat with a gurgle.

Loyalists from the army, come to rescue me? Unlikely. The attack spoke of careful coordination between multiple forces, and he didn't think any officer with sufficient skill to plan it would be so foolish. *Assassins, then? But why?* Orlanko might want to kill him out of sheer rage, but Janus doubted he could muster this much of an effort anymore. *Borel? Dorsay might want to make certain of his peace.* But he still rated it a distant possibility. *To the people of Vordan, I am a hero. If I die under mysterious circumstances, then that would threaten the peace, not ensure it.* The same went for Hamvelt and Murnsk. *And if the Priests of the Black had the resources left to try such a thing, you'd think they would have done it earlier.*

He looked up at the man with the bloody knife and shrugged, one hand slipping to the hilt of his rapier.

"I must say, sir," Janus said, "you have me at a disadvantage."

"I thought I might," the man said. "Janus bet Vhalnich."

"Are you going to try to kill me?"

The man looked down at the knife, then tossed it aside. "Oh, no. You're much too useful for that."

"Excellent." Janus smiled. "Then I'm certain we can come to some arrangement."

"I'm sure we can," the man said. He leaned in closer. In the depths of his eyes, something glowed red.